TALES OF THE
SHADOWMEN
Volume 10: Esprit de Corps

TALES OF THE
SHADOWMEN

Volume 10: Esprit de Corps

edited by
Jean-Marc & Randy Lofficier

stories by
**Matthew Baugh, Nicholas Boving, Nathan Cabaniss,
Anthony R. Cardno, Matthew Dennion, Brian Gallagher,
John Gallagher, Martin Gately, Emmanuel Gorlier,
Micah Haris, Travis Hiltz, Paul Hugli, Rick Lai,
Olivier Legrand, J.-M. & Randy Lofficier, Patrick Lorin,
David McDonald, Nigel Malcolm, Xavier Mauméjean,
Michael Moorcock, Christofer Nigro, John Peel, Pete Rawlik,
Josh Reynolds, Frank Schildiner, Brian Stableford,
Michel Stéphan, David L. Vineyard** and **Jared Welch**

translations by
Matthew Baugh and **J.-M. & Randy Lofficier**

illustrations by
Jean-Michel Nicollet, Alfredo Macall

cover by
Jean-Michel Nicollet

A Black Coat Press Book

ISBN 978-1-61227-237-5. First Printing. December 2013. Published by Black Coat Press, an imprint of Hollywood Comics.com, LLC, P.O. Box 17270, Encino, CA 91416. All rights reserved. Except for review purposes, no part of this book may be reproduced or transmitted in any form or by any means, electronic or mechanical, including photocopying, recording or by any information storage and retrieval system, without permission in writing from the publisher. The stories and characters depicted in this anthology are entirely fictional. Printed in the United States of America.

Table of Contents

My Life as a Shadowman (2) 7
Matthew Baugh: *Quest of the Vourdalaki* 11
Nicholas Boving: *The Green Eye* 32
Nathan Cabaniss: *The Great Ape Caper* 53
Anthony R. Cardno: *So Much Loss* 57
Matthew Dennion: *He Who Laughs Last* 80
Brian Gallagher: *City of the Nosferatu* 83
John Gallagher: *Last of the* Kaiju 100
Martin Gately: *Rouletabille vs. The Cat* 106
Emmanuel Gorlier: *The Brotherhood of Mercy* 129
Micah S. Harris: *The Frequency of Fear* 142
Travis Hiltz: *The Next Omega* 176
Paul Hugli: *Piercing the Veil of Isis* 199
Rick Lai: *The Mark of a Woman* 214
Olivier Legrand: *The Last Tale* 219
Jean-Marc & Randy Lofficier: *Christmas at Schönbrunn* 224
Patrick Lorin: *Troubled Waters* 230
David McDonald: *The Lesser of Two Evils* 235
Nigel Malcolm: *Von Bork's Priorities* 248
Xavier Mauméjean: *The Wayne Memos* 260
Michael Moorcock: *The Icon Crackdown* 264
Jean-Michel Nicollet: *Portfolio* 275
Christofer Nigro: *The Privilege of Adonis* 286
John Peel: *Return to the Center of the Earth* 300
Pete Rawlik: *Revenge of the Reanimator* 352
Josh Reynolds: *The Swine of Gerasene* 358
Frank Schildiner: *The Blood of Frankenstein* 369
Stuart Shiffman: *True Believers* 374
Brian Stableford: *Malbrough s'en va-t-en guerre* 387
Michel Stéphan: *Nestor Burma in New York* 402
David L. Vineyard: *Interview with a Nyctalope* 410
Jared Welch: *The Vampire of New Orleans* 413
Credits 423

The Shadowmen
by Alfredo Macall

My Life as a Shadowman (2) [1]

The year was 1964. We lived in a house with a rather large garden in the suburbs of Bordeaux. At the end of the garden was an abandoned micro-factory which had once been gutted by fire and ought to have been demolished, because, with hindsight, I now realize it was a deathtrap.

In those simpler times, we just knew it as our playground.

"Our" was myself, of course, age 10, and two of my neighbors: Alain, whose father worked as a mechanic at a local garage, and the Other Alain. Yes, that's how he was known. Even his aunt, who owned the local *bistrot*, where we used to play *baby-foot* (foosball) when it rained, was once heard to call him by that name. There was also Marie-Josée, the Other Alain's sister, but she was a girl, so she won't figure much in this story. And then, there was Dick the Dog, a friendly, sloppy, lazy cross between a Brittany Spaniel and a dachshund.

The game of choice, that season, was Monopoly. Since every reader likely grew up playing that world-famous Parker Bros game, I don't need to go into the kind variations—surely never contemplated by its creator!—that 10-year-olds can create. Suffice it to say that, for some reason, we took an inordinate liking to the brightly-colored bank notes that came with the game, and soon were using them as actual money in what might be termed a tiny parallel economy involving the exchanges of toys, comics, marbles, candy, and other small treasures.

Even Marie-Josée became, peripherally, part of that economy, occasionally using her stash of Monopoly money to purchase items such as beads or trinkets for her dolls, when we had them for sale, having found them in neighborhood dustbins. One might say we were recyclers before the word was invented.

The problem with Monopoly money, however, is that its supply is limited. Some notes were lost; others were destroyed during the heated exchanges that are sometimes part of game play; but most were rapaciously hoarded by their owners who, like Uncle Scrooge in the Disney Comics, were guarded them with the innate ferocity of a starving wolverine.

Purchasing a second Monopoly set might have been a way to suddenly double the money supply, but that would have required answering certain parental questions. "Why do you need a second set when you already have one?" was not an easy one to answer, since "I can't use the money from the first set because I've buried it at the end of the garden" would not, in all likelihood, have been deemed a satisfactory explanation.

---

[1] This is the second in a series of occasional remembrances of the author's childhood; the first installment previously appeared in our Vol. 3.

I realize I've failed to mention that we had started to bury our loot in various secret places, probably influenced by Disney's *Treasure Island*. Mine, for instance, was buried in a corner of the garden, next to a crop of mint plants. Alain's was buried in a bamboo grove behind his house. As for Marie-Josée, she kept the few notes she had in a small tin can with the rest of her toys. She had stabbed her brother in the hand with a plastic doll's fork when he'd tried to steal them, so he had learned his lesson.

Since getting a second Monopoly set was out of the question, we resorted to the same method used by the Federal Reserve today: we printed our own money supply. Well, not so much *printed* as *drew* it, painstakingly, one note at a time.

In those days, the butcher shop used to wrap their meat in a sort of cellulose, or sulfurized paper, the texture and feel of which somewhat resembled actual bank notes. Being the artist in the group, I was tasked to "recycle" this paper after my mother had thrown it away. I'd clean it, cut it and use colored pencils to draw a batch of freshly-minted *faux* Monopoly notes. In France, the colors were red for the 50,000 francs note, purple for the 10,000 francs notes, and—who cared about the others! We were only interested in the big moolah!

As any economist could have predicted, this uncontrolled inflationary spiral of the money supply only contributed in exacerbating our own perverse behavior. "More!" was the order of the day, and I spent all too many hours drawing new notes—increasingly shabbily as time went by—to satisfy our unbridled rapacity.

I note with sadness that, by that time, we weren't even using the notes to buy or exchange goods. We just wanted to own them, to increase our secret hoards. We had, in effect, become little dragons in a nasty fairy tale.

No one can guess how this madness might have ended if fate hadn't intervened in a rather bizarre and unexpected fashion.

One morning, as I went to the mint plants to add to my secret loot, I discovered—horror of horrors!—that my stash was gone! Vanished! Disappeared! In other words: stolen!

The list of suspects wasn't large. The most obvious one was my soon to be ex-friend Alain, who was a great fan of the Rocambole novels. Rocambole being, amongst other things, a thief, I wondered if Alain hadn't been tempted to imitate his hero to enrich himself at my expense. He denied it, of course, but in a way that I found rather unconvincing.

Needless to say, I stopped producing new money, telling the others the window was closed (in effect) until the robber was apprehended and my money duly returned to me. Ben Bernanke could learn a thing or two from 10-year-olds, if you want my opinion. But I digress...

This stalemate ended quicker than I had expected when, a day or so later, Alain announced that he, too, had been burglarized. His stash in the bamboo grove had been stolen! As he seemed genuinely distraught, I didn't question the veracity of his story and my earlier suspicions vanished.

Questions were asked of our new prime suspect, Marie-Josée—it was a well-known fact that girls were capable of anything—but she told us in no un-certain terms, accompanied by threats of physical violence, that she was inno-cent.

Then, the Other Alain claimed to have been the victim of the Phantom Thief as well!

It was pretty clear that the investigation wasn't making any progress!

The Other Alain's story, I thought, lacked credibility. The details were vague, and he refused to disclose where he'd buried his stash. So, taking a page from one of my favorite heroes, Arsène Lupin, I decided to use my charm on Marie-Josée to get her to tell me where her brother hid his stash. That failed ut-terly, but offering to draw her two brand-new 50,000 francs note did not.

Soon, we had proof that the Other Alain had not been the victim of the thief, as he had claimed, since his stash was still there. As a well-deserved pun-ishment, Alain and I confiscated his money, which we split between the two of us. But, at the same, it didn't explain what had happened to our own missing money and who the thief really was. Had the Other Alain been the thief, our money would have been in his stash; it wasn't.

I knew that a hero like Rouletabille would not let himself fall prey to dis-couragement. He would regroup to think, to do what he called *grabbing logic by its right end...*

If Alain wasn't the thief, and neither was the Other Alain nor his sister, and I certainly wasn't, then who was he? Who had the motive... the opportunity...?

And, suddenly, the truth became obvious. I knew who the thief was!

As I mentioned, the paper I had used to make the bank notes came from the butcher shop. Of course, I had cleaned it before drawing the fake Monopoly de-signs on it, but it retained its residual meaty odor, if not to a human nose then certainly to...

...Yes! Dick the Dog, totally oblivious of the complexities of the human economic infrastructure, was the thief! He had gone out at night to dig up the meaty-smelling bits of paper which he had then proceeded to chew, spit, and otherwise mangle.

The proof of this was obtained when I found small shreds of what had once been our fortunes in his dirty basket.

After that, somehow, the hoarding of money that we knew were really meat-wrappers, lost its charm. We even stopped playing Monopoly for a long time, although I still today have some of the old Park Bros notes from that very set, which have survived the passage of years; unfortunately, none of the hand-drawn notes survived the jaws of Dick the Dog.

Frankly, I don't think Arsène Lupin or Rouletabille could have done better than I at solving the mystery of the Phantom Thief; and then and there, I swore a sacred oath to someday become a Master Detective. Or a soccer champion. The jury is still out on that one.

In this very special tenth anniversary issue of *Tales of the Shadowmen*, the only anthology dedicated to international heroes and villains of pulp literature, we find a pantheon of contributors from Australia, Canada, England, France and the United States, all celebrating those great detectives and master villains who enchanted our adolescence.

Yes, Rocambole is here, facing the schemes of Captain Nemo. Yes, Arsène Lupin conspires to steal the Maltese Falcon from the clutches of Doc Savage! Yes, Rouletabille untangles the wiles of that master thief, the Cat! And there are also vampires and monsters, ghouls and zombies, as well as the familiar figures of Sâr Dubnotal, D'Artagnan, Phileas Fogg, Doctor Omega and the villainous Black Coats!

The feelings of loyalty, enthusiasm and devotion—in other words, *esprit de corps*—that we feel towards these cherished figures is as undiminished today as it was when we were in our teens. They are more than fictional characters; some are our companions, our reflections, who have followed us all our lives— even if we ourselves didn't become actual Shadowmen!

Jean-Marc Lofficier

Coincidentally, Matthew Baugh's tale of vampires and Cossacks perfectly illustrates the subtitle to this latest volume of Tales of the Shadowmen *for, indeed, who have more "esprit de corps" than the Undead and a savage "band of brothers" from the Russian steppe? But when great deviltry is at work, and supernatural powers must be employed to squash it, even these legendary bonds may be stretched to their breaking point...*

Matthew Baugh: *Quest of the Vourdalaki*

Ukraine, June 13, 1598

'Neath the light of the half-moon we rode, galloping across the steppe with reckless speed, as if pursued by the hordes of Hell itself. But we were not pursued, we were the pursuers—*we* were the riders of Hell.

I sat astride a great black courser as gaunt as death with eyes that blazed fiery red. To my left galloped Hella on a steed that matched mine, her naked body gleaming milk-white in the moonlight. To my left, Vseslav ran in the form of a great, lean wolf. Behind us came nine more mounted *vourdalaki*. It was a joyous experience for me, who had been a Cossack in life. Riding the Steppe had been my delight, and one I had missed since joining the ranks of the undead.

Our horses were fleeter and more tireless than any mortal steeds. Yet, for all that, we could not gain on the two riders who fled before us. We had pursued them for hours, but they continued tirelessly. One of the men truly was a sorcerer, or an alchemist, or something of the sort. Vseslav himself wielded dark magics and he made a great deal of these distinctions, but they all blurred together for me.

Wrecking the sorcerer's wagon and slaughtering his servants had been child's play, but he had picked up a traveling companion, a fine gentleman with a pair of geldings that could run like the wind.

"They are slowing," Gorcha cried. "Their horses are tiring."

"Not soon enough," Hella shrieked over the sound of the wind. "Behold, they come to Father Dnieper!"

At the sight of the great river, Vseslav gave a terrible howl and pulled up. We who were his lackeys reined in also and formed a circle around him. Vseslav stood, and was in a moment a tall, fierce old man wearing a wolfskin around his shoulders. His eyes, however, remained those of the wolf.

"Why do we stop?" Gorcha asked. He was an old man with a face so stern that he must have been a horror, even in life.

"Listen!" the old wolf replied.

11

We did. After a moment my preternatural hearing caught the sound of human revelry, laughter, music, songs... Cossack songs.

"We are near the Zoporoghian Sich," Vseslav said. "We can follow no further."

Hella grinned and tossed back her long red hair.

"Let me go," she said. "I'm not afraid of any man, be he Cossack or the Tsar himself." She made an eerily beautiful sight standing there, her flesh smooth and perfect except for one purple scar on her neck. I certainly would have been tempted to follow her to my doom when I was a living man. Of course, now all I could manage was a kind of nostalgic appreciation.

"No," Vseslav said. "We will not act openly."

"Then, what?" Gorcha asked.

"One of us will go into the camp, posing as a mortal."

"Who?" Hella asked.

I was wondering that too, but I kept my mouth shut. Such work was dangerous and I was too obvious a choice for comfort.

"I will go, Master," Gorcha said. "I will tear the man's throat out and bring you back his head on a pike."

That was typical of Gorcha, who was arrogant to the point of idiocy. I don't know how the old bastard had become one of us but suspected it was because he was too mean-spirited and contrary to stay in the grave like a proper corpse.

"Yvgeni," Vseslav said.

"Yes, Lord?" I replied trying to keep trepidation from my voice.

"You were a Cossack in life, were you not?"

"I *am* a Cossack, Lord."

"Anything you once were, you ceased to be when I claimed you."

"Alright then, I'm *not* a Cossack," I said.

Vseslav glared at me, then laughed.

"Well, it is my pleasure that you become one again. You have the clothes and the saber. More than that, you know their ways."

"Lord, my steed cannot cross Father Dnieper."

Vseslav nodded thoughtfully. Drawing his sword he struck the head off my horse. I rolled clear as the beast dissolved into smoke and ash. Gorcha chortled, Hella threw back her head in laughter and my Lord pointed his weapon at my unbeating heart.

"Have you any other objections?" he asked.

"None, Lord."

"I have another minion in the camp," he said. "His name is Liatoukine. When you are there, make yourself known to him. The two of you shall stay close to the foreigner."

"You wish him dead, Master?"

"It is less important that he die than that he be prevented from reaching Lysa Hora by St. John's Eve," he said. "If you can kill him, of course, that is always to be preferred."

I nodded and set out at a run. Behind me I heard the laughter of my kith and kin. Vampires are not good comrades, I have found, and are petty in the extreme. I had preferred the company of my steed—foul-tempered demon that he had been—to any of them. Vseslav should not have treated him so. A Cossack would never have treated any horse like that; not even a Hell-horse.

The river flowed strongly and was deeper than a man is tall, but that was no obstacle to me. Some of the undead cannot cross running water, but my kind knows no such limitation. I doffed my boots and strode through, gripping the rocks with my toes.

The Sich was located on an island in the midst of the river. Cossacks have no fortifications so they secure themselves against attack by Tatar or Pole by making the river their moat and changing the location of their base secretly and often. I was sitting on the bank, wringing out my clothes when a sentry came upon me.

The man—a veritable giant, more than six and a half feet tall and easily three hundred pounds—glared down at me and leaned on his musket.

"You did not cross on the ferry," he said.

"What way is that for a Cossack to cross a river?" I said. "I swam."

"A brave boast, if true," he replied.

"True enough, as you can see," I said, squeezing several cups of water from my sleeve."

"You say you are a Cossack?"

I nodded.

"I have not seen your face in the Sich before."

"I am a Cossack of the Don," I said, "come from Muskovy to visit my southern cousins."

The giant grunted, amused.

"Still," he said, "I must be certain. Is there anyone here who can vouch for you?"

"Liatoukine," I said.

The big man, whose name was Ayub, took me through the center of the camp. Everywhere I looked, men gathered around the campfires to sing and dance, to wrestle, to gamble and to drink. The corn brandy and vodka flowed freely and I felt both sad and nostalgic that I no longer had a taste for any drink that was not red and warm.

After a time, we came to a knot of men who were amusing themselves in a novel way. They had taken a Jew and stood him against a tree with his sidelocks pinned out to the sides with daggers. While the man stood trembling, the Cossacks took turns throwing axes at him to try and sever his locks. The officer supervising this was a slender, pale and elegant man who lounged off to one side, occasionally offering words of encouragement to his men. I knew him for a vampire at a glance.

"Hey, brother knights," Ayub shouted, "I have something for you."

"A foundling?" the vampire asked, rising and striding toward us.

"One 'Yvgeni' by name," Ayub replied. "He claims to be a Cossack of the Don and says that you will vouch for him."

"Yes," he said looking me over.

"In that case, I leave him to you." Without waiting for a reply the giant turned and strode away.

"He doesn't like you, that one," I said.

Liatoukine sniffed. He glanced at his men who had resumed their axe-throwing game.

"What do I care? He is a lout and a peasant."

"He is a Cossack," I said. We are all brothers and nobles to each other."

"You bristle," he said, his tone ironic. "Why? Human associations mean nothing to us."

"We have a mission," I said. "Two men came into the Sich earlier tonight. They were fleeing from our master."

"I know the men," Liatoukine said. "The Koshovoi Ataman ordered them placed in the stocks. Come, I will show you."

He strode off and, after a last glance at his men and their game, I followed.

"You don't approve?" Liatoukine asked when I caught up. His voice told me he was amused.

"What did the Jew do?"

"He's a Jew; what other reason do Cossacks need?"

I shrugged; for what he said was true. There were usually quite a few Jewish merchants who made camp near the Sich to sell food or corn brandy, or clothing, or any of a hundred other useful things. This worked to everyone's advantage; the Cossacks got the supplies and the Jews were paid handsomely, for Cossacks cultivate a healthy disregard for money and usually pay with whatever they have in their pockets, even if that far exceeded the asked-for price. The problem came when a Cossack wanted strong drink, but had lost all his money gambling or spending freely. At that point, the Jew became—in his eyes—a devious, dishonest thief.

I had never cared for this. The Jews I have known seemed fair-minded, harmless folk. Most Cossacks despise them for not being warlike, but it always seemed to me their only real sin was being foolish enough to do business with such a dangerous and drunken lot. I say "drunken," for finding a sober Cossack in the Sich is as rare as finding a goat eating a wolf.

I was caught up enough in my thoughts that I didn't pay much attention to the merry antics of the brothers as we passed to the stocks, which stood a little

14

away from the camp. I saw that the Koshovoi Ataman had given them the same penalty that is given to a Cossack who steals. Not only were they bound in the stocks, but a heavy cudgel hung from a tree nearby. Any Cossack passing by was welcome to strike them with the weapon. If they were still alive in the morning, they would be released.

"Your course is clear," Liatoukine said, gesturing to the cudgel. It seemed to amuse him to pass the duty to me rather than take it on himself. That made him the kind of officer who I had never cared for in life. In fairness, I have to say they are more like vampires than Cossacks. The riders of the steppes are brutal, but they are seldom so petty.

I picked up the knout and moved to the stocks to face the two. They were an interesting pair, finely dressed in some foreign fashion. The first was a bearded fellow, tall and thick with muscle and fat. The other was also tall, but as lean as his companion was heavy. He had a clean shaven face and mismatched eyes, one brown and the other green.

"I suppose you've come to kill us," the bearded man said. He had a deep voice and sounded more weary than frightened.

"Close your eyes and I will make it quick as I can," I replied.

"I don't suppose it would make a difference if I told you that I came here seeking help to end a great evil, would it?" He studied my face for a moment, then sighed. "No, I suppose it wouldn't. You Cossacks aren't at all like I'd heard. You're more interested in your pleasure than in honor won in combat."

"Oh, you think so?" I said. My tone was a little heated, for his words stung the pride I still felt for this place.

"Do you tell me different?" he asked in earnest surprise, "then put down your club and listen to me."

His voice was made for giving speeches and intrigued me. I lowered the weapon and waited for him to say more. Liatoukine was less interested. He strode up to me and, with a growl of contempt, snatched the club from my hand and raised it.

"Ho, brother knight," a quiet voice said. Liatoukine and I both spun in surprise for it is seldom that one of the living comes upon our kind unheard.

The man we saw was tall and gaunt with age, with a gray mustache whose ends hung to his chest. He glowered at us from under shaggy brows with an expression both fierce and amused.

"What are their lives to you, Khlit?" Liatoukine demanded.

"Nothing," the old man replied, pulling out a corn-cob pipe and packing it with tobacco. "If you are bold enough to defy the Koshovoi Ataman, that is your affair."

"What do you say? He is the one who pronounced sentence on them."

"Aye," Khlit replied. "But that was before I spoke to them and heard their story. I think our leader will want to hear these words before they die. I have sent my foster son, Menelitza, to fetch him. But if you would see him disappointed when he comes..."

From the expression on Liatoukine's face, I could see that there was no love lost between him and the old Cossack. Khlit's face, by contrast, gave away nothing. His fierce expression was more a thing of habit than any emotion Liatoukine inspired. He lighted his pipe and stood there smoking.

"Very well," Liatoukine said, slimming back into his superior smile. "We shall see, Khlit *bogatyr*."

I peered closer at the old man. Was he truly a great hero, as the vampire named him? I had been away from the Sich for longer than I had realized, not to know the name of a *bogatyr*.

He was a striking figure in his boots of red Moroccan leather and pants of Nankin silk, spattered with pitch to show his contempt for appearances. His astrakhan hat was perched on the side of his head, revealing that his head was shaved, except for a long, gray topknot. It was his curved saber that captured my attention most. It was not the nearly straight and guardless *shasqua* favored by most Cossacks, nor the heavy Polish saber with its knuckle-guard, but a scimitar of the Turkish pattern, beautifully made and—unless I missed my guess—of Damascus steel.

"It seems we have an interlocutor," the man with the mismatched eyes said. From the humor in his voice, it seemed to me that he considered the stocks to be only an inconvenience. His fat companion only grunted in reply.

After several moments, a handsome, dark-skinned youth appeared, leading a man in the regalia of the Koshovoi Ataman and a large group of Cossacks. The youth moved to stand at Khlit's side and the Ataman glanced first at them and then at me and Liatoukine.

"Poor timing for your sport, Boris Liatoukine," he said. "The *bogatyr* tells me these strangers bear listening to."

"I do not agree," Liatoukine said. "A sorcerer like this has the Devil's own tongue to seduce the ears of the innocent."

"A good thing that no one in this camp is innocent, hey?" Khlit asked, eliciting general laughter.

"I appreciate the opportunity to he heard, noble Cossacks," the heavy man interjected. "I would appreciate it more if I was free to stand and face you eye to eye."

"Well said," the Koshovoi Ataman said. "Sabalinka, cut them loose!"

A big man with yellow topknot and mustache stepped forward and drew the sword he kept slung across his back. This was a massive, two-handed weapon, straight and double edged. It seemed more a sword for a knight of old than the agile weapon of a Cossack and was clearly the source for the name "Sabalinka." which means "little sword." The muscular man hefted the weapon as if it weighed no more than a *shasqua* and swung it at the lynchpin. Wood split

16

and shattered and the stocks came open, releasing the foreigners, who straightened, rubbing their necks.

"I thank you, noble Cossack," the bearded stranger said, raising his powerful voice.

"Tell us your story," the Koshovoi Ataman replied. "Then we will decide whether to help you or whether to give you to Ataman Liatoukine for his men to sport with."

The man nodded and looked out among the gathering. He had impressive charisma and seemed to catch and hold the gaze of every man there for an instant.

"Noble Cossacks," he said, "I am Quentin Moretus Cassave, of the Flemish lands many thousands of *versts* from your steppe. I am no sorcerer, as your esteemed Liatoukine has claimed, but merely a scholar."

That prompted rough chuckles and a few grumbles from some of the men. Scholars are not well thought of in the Sich. It's all well and good for the *batkos* in their monasteries to study the Holy Scriptures, but no Cossack would ever indulge in such effeminate practices. Scholarship was considered a particularly Polish sort of vice and was highly suspect. Cassave seemed to understand this and dropped his voice dramatically. Though he still made himself heard, every man there strained to catch his every word.

"I am no fighting man," he said. "I'm sure many of you have thought I would rather be in my comfortable home, poring over my books, and you're right. But in my studies I have become aware of a dark prophecy." He paused for a moment and looked across the silent assembly. This man might not claim to be a sorcerer, but with a few words he had captured the Cossacks with the magic of his speech.

"There is a mountain outside Kiev, so I have read," he continued. "It is a barren place, so unholy that not even trees or shrubs will grow there. It is said that the witches gather there each St. John's Eve to try to raise their dark master, Satan himself, known in pagan times as Chernabog!"

A murmur went through the crowd, and I saw more than a few of the men cross themselves.

"*Lysa Hora!*" one man said. "I grew up near that bald mountain and what he says is true."

"You see?" Cassave thundered. "On St. John's Eve, when all Christian folk are home abed, the witches and sorcerers gather to practice their unspeakable rituals and pray their abominable prayers. On that night, the spirits of the dead rise up to share an unspeakable orgy with all the fiends of Hell."

"This man is playing on your superstitions," Liatoukine cried. There was a touch of anxiety in his voice, for he and I both knew that the stranger was uncomfortably close to the truth. His story was inaccurate, but only in the details and those he was probably shading for dramatic effect.

"Superstitions?" Cassave boomed. "Is the werewolf that runs the steppe at night a superstition? What about the vampire with her seductive song who slips behind the rider on his horse and sucks the blood from the back of his neck? No, noble Cossacks, these things are not superstitions... and neither is the prophecy."

"What is the prophecy?" a big voice demanded and I saw the speaker was the giant Ayub.

"What is the prophecy?" Cassave repeated. "Only that this year—Anno Mundi 7065[2]—the ritual will succeed. The witches will raise Chernabog from Hell to shroud the land with perpetual night and to sit enthroned on the Bald Mountain, from whence he would rule the world."

"Preposterous!" Liatoukine protested. "Brothers, what this man says is superstitious nonsense! Even if it weren't, why come to the Sich? Would not a foreigner go to the Tsar and his court in Muscovy where there are other scholars to listen to him?"

"I did," Cassave said, his voice quiet again. "I went to the Muscovites and told them my story. Alas, they said the same thing that the noble Liatoukine says, that there are no vampires and werewolves, that the sorcerers do not gather on the Bald Mountain on St. John's Eve and that only superstitious fools would believe such a tale."

There was another murmur through the crowd, for Cassave's words hit home. The Muscovite court has always seemed far off and foreign here in the Ukraine, and these days even more since the nobles had given up speaking Russian in favor of French. To hear that they dismissed the beliefs of the steppe-dwellers as foolishness was no surprise.

"I came to the Zoporoghian Cossacks for two reasons," Cassave continued. "First, because I knew that you would understand that these things are a real and present danger. Second, because I had been told that no one but the Cossacks of the Steppe would have the courage to take up sword and ride against the forces of darkness."

He paused and glared around. For all that he was a scholar, his expression was as fierce as that of Vseslav himself.

"Was I told true?" he demanded.

There was more murmuring. Cossacks are not cowards. And had the challenge been to ride into battle or even to certain death they would not have balked. The supernatural is quite another matter, though.

"My godfather will lead and my sword is with him!" young Menelitza said. He strode to stand at Cassave's side, Khlit following a little more slowly.

---

[2] Cassave is figuring this by the Byzantine Calendar which started counting years at the supposed date of Creation. It was used in Imperial Russia until the 19th century reforms of Peter the Great.

Cockcrow saw a little band of ten Cossacks and two foreigners heading north, a modest increase to the group Khlit, Menelitza and Ayub had started. Ivan Sabalinka had joined us, as had Zaroff, an aristocratic Cossack who preferred a Tatar warbow to the set of pistols most of us carried. He was attended by man as huge as Ayub whose name was Ivanushka. Liatoukine and I had joined the expedition, of course, as had two of his men, the stout Taras and his older brother, Doroscha. With Cassave and his companion, whom he called "Magister," we were twelve strong.

"Like the Holy Apostles," Ayub said. "It is a good omen."

I was not so optimistic. A group of Holy Apostles ought not have *two* Iscariots.

We rode hard that day for we had 500 *versts* to travel and only nine days to do it. I was surprised to see how well the two foreigners kept up. The Magister rode like a Cossack and never seemed to tire. Cassave, while not a natural horseman, bore up uncomplaining, apparently through sheer force of will. I rode close to them, remembering my master's instructions.

That night, we huddled around our little campfire, sharing a simple dinner and the small daily ration of corn brandy.

"Why such a small fire?" Cassave asked. His tone was not complaining but curious.

"A big fire would give away our position," Zaroff said.

"The undead don't need a fire to know where we are," Ayub said with a shiver.

"More light might be a good idea," Cassave said. "These creatures thrive in darkness."

"The fire is small so the Tatars do not see us," Menelitza said. "If they do, we'll have more than vampires to worry about."

"I must say, I admire the ways of the Cossacks," Cassave said. "They are very different from the ways of my homeland, though. For example, in France, a soldiers' camp is a place of discipline and drilling. Your Sich is so much livelier."

"There is time enough for swinging swords when there are heads to split," Ayub said and several of the others chuckled in assent.

"Very true," Cassave said, seriously. "I am certainly impressed with how quickly you go from revelry to a disciplined advance."

"It is the way of the Cossacks," Ayub said. "In times of war, our whole life is the campaign. In times of peace, we celebrate being alive."

"Your celebration is also different than I am used to," Cassave said.

"How so?" Menelitza asked. "Don't French soldiers gamble, drink and dance?"

"Certainly," the scholar replied. "But in France, they tend to do those things in the company of pretty girls."

"Women have no place in the Sich," Khlit said, taking his pipe from his mouth.

"True!" Taras cried, springing to his feet. "Home and hearth are death to a Cossack, and a pretty girl's arms are damnation. Too much time with women steals a man's strength. What a man needs are a fast horse, a good sword, the company of his brothers, and plenty of Polish throats to cut!"

This brought cries of approval from the assemblage, though Sabalinka remained silent and Menelitza blushed. I noticed Khlit's stern eyes on his godson as well and wondered what the old wolf was thinking.

My thoughts were interrupted by a woman's voice raised in song. It was an old ballad, lonely and beautiful, and the singer had a voice to break a man's heart. The Cossacks were held silent, staring into the darkness.

"*Vourdalak*," Ayub finally said, crossing himself. "No living woman could sing such a song."

He was right, of course. I recognized the voice as Hella's and I saw lust blossom on the other faces in the firelight. They were thinking of slender arms entwining them, of red lips to kiss and milky skin to caress.

It is an effective technique, though not one I particularly approve of. I am enough of a Cossack still to prefer the honest shedding of blood in open combat to lying promises of love. And they are all lies, of course. No vampire I have ever known desires a lover, and certainly not a human one. For us, the only true passion is the hunt and the kill.

Khlit rose and kicked dirt on the fire.

"Doroscha, take the first watch. Ayub will relieve you at midnight."

The Cossacks slept—except for Liatoukine and myself, who pretended to sleep—until midnight, when Ayub roused the camp.

"Doroscha is gone!"

"Gone?" Taras yelled. "How can he be gone?"

"The vampires have taken him," Ayub said, making the sign of the cross.

"Bah!" Liatoukine said. "He was frightened of these children's stories and fled home with his tail between his legs."

"Have a care," Taras said, his hand on the hilt of his saber. "My brother is no coward and any man who calls him that will face my steel."

Liatoukine looked at him with an air of regal disdain. He did not touch his sword, but I knew that he could move with the speed of the undead. He could draw and strike Taras' head from his shoulders in less than the space of a heart-beat.

"Perhaps I spoke too soon," Liatoukine said. "Perhaps he went to take a piss and got lost. Perhaps he will be back any minute."

Taras' knuckles whitened on his sword haft and the fight seemed inevitable, then Khlit stepped between them fixing his wolf's gaze on first one then the other.

20

"There is no time to fight amongst ourselves," he said calmly. "Taras, at first light we shall find your brother. If he has been killed by an enemy, then Boris Liatoukine shall beg your pardon. If he has fled, you shall beg his."

"We should search for him now!" Taras said.

"No," Khlit said in a quiet but fierce voice. "If there are enemies abroad, human or devil, I do not want to meet them while we are scattered and stumbling in the dark."

"You sound more like an old woman than a Cossack!" Taras said. He moved to the place his horse was saddled and sprang on its back.

"Cossacks, we search for Doroscha!"

Several men started toward the horses but hesitated when Khlit drew his curved sword.

"Taras!" he shouted, pointing the blade at the mounted man. "Go and search, but no man from this camp goes with you; and whether you find your brother or not, do not come back."

Without a word, Taras wheeled his horse and rode into the night.

"Ayub and Menelitza, finish the watch," Khlit said. "From now on, no man watches alone. Beware of vampires coming in the form of our former comrades."

"What if Taras or his brother return, and they are still human?" Menelitza asked, gathering his weapons.

"Kill them," Khlit said. "Vampires and deserters deserve the same fate."

I sat up with them for the watch, as did Cassave.

"Your companion seems remarkable untroubled by all this," I said. "He never even stirred."

"The Magister is not bothered by much," he replied. "I only wish I had his calm."

"Feh!" Ayub said, and spit into the campfire. "A Cossack is calm in the face of death, but only a fool sleeps so soundly when the hordes of Hell are abroad."

"The Magister is no fool," Cassave replied with a soft chuckle. "He had taught me many secrets of the seen and unseen worlds, and I have only begun to touch the surface of his wisdom. If he sleeps, we can rest assured that there is no danger... at least, not to him."

"A strange man," I said. "How do you know you can trust him?"

"We have a bargain, he and I," Cassave said. "Besides, he is the one who gave me the means to our victory over Chernabog."

"A holy weapon?" Ayub asked.

Cassave's eyes twinkled with humor as he produced a slender silver urn from his robes. The bright metal was covered with mysterious glyphs that I could not read. In honesty, though, having never learned to read even my mother tongue, all letters are mysterious to me. I could only say for certain that it was not Russian writing.

"I will catch him in this," Cassave said.

I shook my head and Ayub laughed.

"Surely, the Prince of Darkness is too big to fit in such a little vessel?"

"Have you heard of the Jinn?" Cassave asked.

"I have," young Menelitza said. "The Turks and the Tatars speak of them. They are evil spirits made of smokeless fire who wander the Earth doing mischief. Their king is Satan, whom the Muslims call Iblis."

"We have another scholar among us," Cassave said in an appreciative tone. Menelitza bowed his head shyly and glanced at me and Ayub, no doubt worried that we would deem his knowledge effeminate.

"Tell me, mighty Cossack," Cassave continued, "is the campfire bigger than you or smaller?"

Ayub's forehead puckered in thought, something I suspect his brain was unaccustomed.

"Smaller," he said.

"And if we were to pile a dozen stout branches on the campfire... would it still be smaller?"

Ayub shook his head slowly with an expression that mingled suspicion and awe.

"No," Cassave said in an even tone with no hint of mockery. "It would be the same fire, but grown greater than any man. And if the fire should dwindle for lack of fuel?"

"It would become small," Ayub said, feeling his way through the question.

"And?" Cassave prompted.

"Small enough for your little pot..."

"Excellent!" Cassave said clapping the giant's shoulder heartily. Ayub beamed proudly and I could see that the foreigner had won him over.

"As it is with fire, so with the jinn," Cassave said.

"But how would you compel the Devil?" Menelitza asked. "Would that not be an act of dark sorcery?"

"One would think so," the scholar replied, "but that is not so. Do not the Tatars and the Turks tell how the wise King Solomon captured the jinn and bound them to lamps and rings and many other vessels?"

The youth nodded, a little uncertainly.

"It is not sorcery that will help us, but the holy wisdom of this man of God," Cassave said.

My companions were clearly impressed by the foreigner's words, but I was more suspicious than ever. For all his words flowed like honey, Cassave was no holy man.

22

We lost two more the next night. All the men slept soundly except for Zaroff and his servant, Ivanushka, who were on watch, and myself and Liatoukine, who feigned sleep.

Around midnight, Hella's sweet song was heard and the handsome Cossack picked up his bow and slipped away from the camp, forbidding his servant to follow. A short time later the singing stopped and Zaroff screamed in terror.

The camp roused in an instant. Khlit called for order but this did not stop Ivanushka from drawing his saber and racing into the dark to go to his master's air.

"Torches!" the old wolf shouted. "We follow but we stay together."

Each man lighted a brand and mounted his steed. It took us less than a quarter of an hour to find Ivanushka. The giant lay amid a jumble of rocks, his spine twisted so badly it was clear his back was broken.

"Where is your master?" Khlit demanded. "Why did he leave the camp?"

"It... it was the song..." Ivanushka said between gasps. "When I followed I saw him... with beautiful woman... skin as pale as the Moon..."

"Where?" Khlit repeated, but the giant fell silent and his eyes glazed over.

We searched for Zaroff but found only his Tatar warbow and quiver of arrows abandoned on the steppe.

"We should take these back to the Sich," Ivan Sabalinka said. "He would want his son to have them when he comes of age."

"I will carry them," I said. For the life of me (or whatever passes for life in my case) I couldn't say why I did that.

The next day we made good progress, but I could see that the days of hard riding and nights of fitful sleep were making the men haggard. I could see that this pleased Liatoukine, but my unbeating heart felt a touch of something—not sympathy perhaps, but nostalgia. These were brave men and riding with them made me think of my former life. I took no joy in the fact that they would all soon be dead.

In the early afternoon, Khlit called a halt.

"The Magister tells me that we will find something there that will help us." He pointed to a low mound in the distance.

"The *kurgan*?" Ayub asked. "Do we look to magic and ghosts to help us?"

In response, the old wolf spurred his horse and the rest of us followed. We were a little apprehensive for, while these ancient burial mounds are common on the steppe, there is something ominous about them. I told myself that nothing the *kurgan* could hold should frighten a creature of the night, but even a vampire can be superstitious, I suppose.

Someone had dug into the side of the mound, forming a chink in the rocks that led within. Khlit had no interest in entering the mound, however. He was much more interested in the massive hive than a colony of bees.

"There is your magic," Cassave said, laughing. "The same magic that Odysseus used against the sirens."

The men gathered bundles of tall grass and set the ends asmolder to lull the bees to sleep. Despite this, all were stung as they gathered handfuls of wax. I alone managed to avoid this on the pretext of taking the horses a safe distance away, and this proved most fortunate.

Cassave tended to the men afterwards, using the tip of a dagger to pluck out the stingers. Ivan Sabalinka's face twitched, more with annoyance than pain, as the scholar performed his ministrations. Menelitza took his turn with the exaggerated stoicism of a youth determined to prove his courage to his elders. Ayub's skin had turned bright red around the stings and his breathing was labored. Cassave showed concern over this, but the giant only laughed.

"All that I need is a healthy dose of corn brandy," he said.

Cassave took a small vial of some blue liquid from his robe and offered it to Ayub.

"It is not corn brandy, but I think you will like it."

Ayub sniffed the potion suspiciously, then drained it. He made a face as it went down, but that expression turned to one of wonder as the red blotches faded and his breathing returned to normal.

"By the Father and the Son," the big man said.

Cassave turned to Liatoukine only to be dismissed with a gesture of contempt.

"I am no weakling to fear the stings of insects," Liatoukine said.

"Bee venom is not to be scoffed at," the scholar said. "If I had not given Ayub my alchemic treatment, his throat would have closed and he could not have breathed."

The Cossack drew back his sleeve and held out an arm. I could see no less than half a dozen tiny stings embedded there, some still quivering.

"As you see, Boris Liatoukine is made of sterner stuff," he said.

"No redness... no swelling." Cassave said, half to himself. "I wonder..."

He brought the dagger to Liatoukine's arm as if to flick out the stings but instead plunged the tip deep into his flesh.

"Madman!" the Cossack shouted, leaping away and drawing his saber.

"Look!" Cassave held out the weapon for us to see. "There is no blood on the blade and none on Liatoukine's wound. I wondered why the beestings did not affect him and now I know. Boris Liatoukine is no living man!"

With a snarl of rage, Liatoukine stepped toward him but Khlit interposed himself with his own curved blade drawn.

"This man—this *foreigner*—lies!" Liatoukine shouted.

"He speaks truth." The Magister, silent until now, spoke in a calm voice. There was something unnaturally compelling about his words. I knew that I should leap to Liatoukine's defense but was so fascinated that I made no move.

"You should confess it," the Magister said. "It was a brilliant stroke... Who better than a Cossack to infiltrate a band of Cossacks? And you have none of the weaknesses that would betray so many of your kind. You walk in daylight... you bear the cross on your sword... you can even enter a church and receive the blessing of the *batkos*..."

"How do you know these things?" Liatoukine demanded. His outburst—and the truth it betrayed—startled me. I could see that Liatoukine also was shocked at his own words. How had this foreigner compelled him to say this?

"I remember now," Khlit said. "When I was a lad of sixteen, just come to the Sich, there was a Cossack who had murdered another. We gave him the traditional punishment by placing him under his victim's coffin and burying him alive in the same grave. I see that some men are too evil to remain in the ground."

"Fools!" Liatoukine snarled. "You simper on about good and evil, holy and unholy, but there are no such things. There are only the strong and the weak, and I am strong!"

He lunged at Khlit with a speed beyond human, yet the old wolf brought his blade up with such skill that he parried the blow. Menelitza sprang to his godfather's defense but Liatoukine leapt away with such speed that, to mortal eyes, he seemed to vanish.

I seized my sword hilt. I didn't want to help Liatoukine kill my brother Cossacks, but my duty was clear. Before I could draw, the Magister laid a hand on my wrist and I felt my resolve melt away.

Liatoukine slashed at Menelitza and the lad fell, badly wounded. Khlit sprang forward but even his skill was nothing to the vampire's speed. He disarmed the gray-haired warrior and sent him stumbling to the ground. But as Liatoukine raised his blade for the final blow, a shot rang out.

Boris Liatoukine staggered forward a pace, a look of astonishment on his face. Behind him I saw Ivan Sabalinka bolding a smoking pistol. Then Ayub leapt at him with a mighty roar, striking his head from his shoulders with a sweep of his saber.

We spent much of the afternoon gathering wood for a pyre which we built on top of the kurgan while Cassave tended to Menelitza's wounds and Khlit hovered nearby. The old wolf puffed his pipe stoically, but I could see he was stricken to the heart with worry for his godson.

"Who are you?" I asked the Magister when our tasks had taken us out of earshot of the others.

"Can't you guess?" he asked with a sly smile. "I'm certain you know my name."

That sent a feeling of cold through my blood. I chose not to voice my thoughts, preferring not to have my suspicion confirmed.

"What do you want?" I asked.

"I want nothing," the Magister replied. "My only joy is in helping others gain what they want. Take Cassave, for instance. He wanted knowledge and I gave it to him. From that grew his new desire to capture the gods of antiquity and keep them in vessels."

"Why does he want such a thing?"

"If you ask Cassave, he will tell you that man created the gods and not vice versa."

"Surely that is blasphemy," I said.

"How touching that a vampire should be concerned with that. I'm certain the theologians would agree with you and consign our good scholar to the flames. I am rather fond of theologians and their wisdom. In any case, Cassave says that the gods weaken and die when men cease to believe in them. But those who are not completely forgotten still possess power, and the man who catches them will have that power to use as he will."

"What does he want with such power?" I asked.

"I did not ask him."

"What Cassave says cannot be true," I said. "Man cannot create gods—certainly not the Almighty!"

"So you believe. Cassave believes otherwise."

"What do you believe?"

The Magister smiled.

"Cassave is a great scholar. I am very fond of scholars and their wisdom."

When we completed the pile of branches, we laid Liatoukine's head and body on it and set it ablaze. Having seen to that, we carried Menelitza to the yurt of a Tatar herdsmen only a few versts from the kurgan. Khlit gave the man gold coins and the promise of more when we returned. His grey eyes offered a different promise if Menelitza were to die.

We rode hard the rest of the day, hoping to make up the time we had lost.

We continued the rest of the way without incident and I began to wonder if we would make it. Vseslav's orders had been to stop Cassave from reaching Lysa Hora at any cost, but I wondered why he did not send help to me. Perhaps after seeing Liatoukine's fate, I was not eager to take these warriors on by myself, and the Magister now terrified me beyond measure. Hella sang to us every night but, with beeswax plugging their ears, the Cossacks slept soundly through her call.

When no attack came I wondered if my master expected me to slay the Cossacks myself. I doubted myself up to the task, and the thought of fighting the Magister filled me with dread. After our conversation, I feared the strange man as much as Vseslav himself.

At midday on the ninth day out of the Sich—the Eve of St. John's day—we caught our first sight of Lysa Hora. Normally it is not much as mountains go; a gently sloping dome bare of trees but green with grass and scrub brush. On this day, the clouds had gathered, thick and turgid, hiding the Sun and making noon feel like twilight. That low hanging sky was the deep green-purple of a bruise. No moisture fell from the clouds—if something as clean as rain could come from such a diseased sky—instead, they were lit from with by the dull red and fiery orange of unseen lightning.

Lysa Hora seemed almost to touch the lowest of the clouds and in that light seemed a blackened knob of bare stone.

Khlit called our little group to a halt and we gazed at the bald mountain. Finally, he turned to Cassave.

"Well, sorcerer? Where on this mountain would you have us go?"

"The top," Cassave said, pointing. "That is where Chernabog's followers will light their fires and dance. That is where the gate to Hell will open to let the dark god and his minions through."

"They have the high ground," the old wolf muttered. "That means we must charge them up the slope on spent horses."

"There is a better way," Cassave said. "I will tell them that I am a fellow acolyte of darkness, come to witness the advent of Chernabog."

Khlit stroked his moustache in thought then nodded.

"Close enough to the truth to be a good lie," he said.

"As we draw near the ceremony, you must steel your hearts," Cassave said looking at each of us in turn. "Yor you will see things—witches and demons and all manner of fiends. Sky and earth will split asunder and fire shall rain upon you. You must keep courage and faith if you are to win your way through."

"Courage and faith?" Khlit said, raising his voice in a tone of disdain. "When has a Cossack ever needed to be reminded of these things? We live our lives in the hope of glorious death fighting the Poles and Tatars and other enemies of Christ. Do you think we will flinch at fighting his greatest foe?"

"I like that!" Ivan Sabalinka said. "We'll tweak his nose just like old St. Dunstan, by Harry!"

I thought it a peculiar oath, no doubt born of his distant homeland, but Ivan's words stirred my soul—or whatever passes for one in the undead.

We dismounted and Khlit rationed out the last loaf of black bread and the last bottle of corn brandy. Ayub took a great mouthful of the first and washed it down with a lengthy swallow from the latter before passing them to Sabalinka.

"Noble Cossacks," Cassave said. "Have a care. This fine liquor is good for celebrating, but it does not lead to sound judgment."

"Sound Judgment?" Ayub roared with laughter. "Scholar, we are storming the gates of Hell. What use have we for sound judgment?"

All of us ate and drank until the bread was gone and the bottle empty; all save the Magister who stood apart from the group and stared at the mountain. This puzzled me and I went to him with a cup of the corn brandy but he shook his head."

27

"You will not drink with men who ride to their deaths with you?" I asked, a little angrily.

"*You* ask me that, Yvgeni?" he asked with his sly smile. "I wonder where your allegiances lie. Do you know any more?"

Having no answer for that, I glared at him, then drained the liquor from the cup.

"Your friend, Liatoukine can touch the cross and you cannot," he said.

"He is not my friend."

"Do you know how he does this?"

"He does not believe that anything is holy or unholy," the Magister said. "For him, there is only what he wants. The one who cannot see a difference between good and evil is dangerous. I prefer to be honest about my nature. It is... cleaner."

It was dark when we reached the slopes of Lysa Hora, and so dark that the humans could barely see one another—could see nothing at all save for the bonfire on the summit where the witches held their Sabbat. I, on the other, hand could see everything. Around us a great invisible procession of ghosts and infernal spirits rose and drifted past us. Another flicker of heat lightning illuminated the mountain. The phantoms remained invisible to my companions but the light illuminated the revelers around the fire. Vampires and humans, dwarfish creatures and misshapen giants, hags and their familiars, mingled with werewolves, satyrs and animated corpses—some reduced to skeleton—in perverse revelry.

Khlit drew pistol and saber and the rest of us followed suit.

"Steady, Cossacks," Cassave's voice was soft but carried to all of us. "Do not let yourselves be provoked by anything you see."

Indeed, as we neared the fire, the worshippers seemed too consumed by their orgiastic frenzy to pay any heed to us. I saw Hella—nude, as usual—dancing in the throng and stern Gorcha as well (nudity did not suit him.) Mighty Vseslav stood in the center of the throng, almost in the fire as he read words I could not understand from an ancient-looking book.

Then the fire blazed up a hundred feet into the air, framing an impenetrable column of black smoke. I forgot everything else as I watched the flame-wreathed smoke swell and grow denser.

"Chernabog," I heard Cassave whisper in the sudden silence.

"Yes, mortal, the Black God is risen!"

All our eyes turned to the speaker, whom I saw was Vseslav, wrapped in wolf skins. Hella stood at his right in all her pale beauty and to his left, Boris Liatoukine. Our former comrade was dressed in a long robe, having abandoned his Cossack finery. I saw no sign of the injuries the Cossacks had given him.

Vseslav pointed at us and spoke.

"My children," he said, "these humans have come to desecrate our Lord and to thwart our plan to shroud the world in eternal night. In the name of Chernabog, kill them!"

I started to protest that I was not human—that I was one of them—but my brethren never gave me a chance. A werewolf sprang at me and I shot him in the face. A creature as much serpent as human tried to bite me and I cut him into two writing pieces.

"Cossacks, protect me!" Cassave shouted, pulling the silver urn from his robes.

The Cossacks needed no instructions from him and had already begun fighting. Khlit shot Liatoukine through the heart and threw away the empty pistol to draw another. Ivan had drawn his massive two-handed sword and whirled it so fiercely that none dared to close with him. Ayub lopped the head from a skeleton with his saber, then split the skull of a satyr with another stroke.

I noticed several things: first, our blades and bullets worked against the hellish army better than they should have. I wondered if this was a blessing from god, or something the Magister had done. Each shot dropped one of our foes, each sword stroke cut deep, and the wounds did not instantly heal.

Second, I noticed that the Magister had vanished. I didn't know when this had happened, but was too hard pressed to wonder.

Finally, I discovered that I liked fighting alongside my fellow Cossacks. I suppose I should have shown my loyalty by turning and striking the Cossacks down, but that would leave my back open and I had no doubt Vseslav's undead would tear me to pieces.

From the corner of my eye, I saw Gorcha spring on Ayub from behind, one gaunt arm-locked around his massive body, while the other tangled in his hair, drawing his head back and baring his throat. Ayub struggled, but even he could not match the gaunt vampire's great strength. Without an instant's hesitation, I drew my second pistol and fired the ball into Gorcha's face. It was treason, but I despised Gorcha and had grown fond of Ayub.

Above us, the column of smoke unfolded itself like a bat spreading its wings. Now it had the shape of a colossal horned man with glowing eyes and skin as dark as the space between the stars on a cloudless night. The colossus stretched in triumph, then a look of disbelief came over his face.

Cassave stood nearby holding the urn over his head and chanting. Chernabog tried to struggle but was drawn inexorably into the vessel as pipe smoke is drawn into a man's lungs. It took only seconds before the colossus was entirely captured in the tiny urn and the sorcerer clapped the lid shut.

"Do you see?" He raised the vessel over his head and the mob of fiends shrunk back in fear and awe.

"Where is your god now?" Cassave taunted. "Perhaps I should be your god!"

As he spoke, I looked for the Cossacks. Ivan Sabalinka was down, his sword broken and blood pumping from a terrible wound on his neck. Khlit had fallen and Ayub, who alone seemed unharmed, hurried to his friend's side.

"By the power I have taken this day, I—Quentin Moretus Cassave—have become your new master. Do homage to me."

My mind rebelled against that idea; a human with the power of a god, a man who controlled the forces of darkness. I had long ago resigned myself to being Vseslav's creature, but I would not be the slave of Cassave.

My pistols were spent, but I still had Zaroff's Tatar warbow slung on my shoulder. I unlimbered the weapon, fitted an arrow and let fly.

The missile struck the urn, punching through the thin metal and lodging there. Darkness seeped from the hole around it, then exploded, drinking up all the light on the mountain. I heard the scream of a titan in anguish and the Magister's voice, laughing.

I woke, not remembering when I had lost consciousness. The Sun had not yet risen but the clouds were gone and the early light of dawn painted the eastern sky.

"You are finally awake," a woman said.

Sitting up, I spied Hella sitting on a rock nearby. She was still naked but there was nothing seductive about her pose. In the soft light, she looked almost innocent.

A glanced around and saw bodies strewn on the ground, including Khlit, Cassave and Ayub. I rose and went to them and was surprised when I felt a surge of relief that they were all breathing. Sabalinka, alas, was not. The other bodies, a mere dozen, all human and all bearing the mark of pistol or saber, lay scattered across the slope. Of the vampires and their demonic allies, I could see no sign.

"What has happened?" I asked.

Hella stood and stretched.

"When you released Chernabog, his minions scattered like chickens in the rain. They will not try this again. My Master is pleased."

"Your master... Vseslav?"

"Vseslav has fled also," she said. "When you find him, he will forgive you all because of the final blow you struck against Cassave."

I looked down on the Cassave's unconscious form.

"He is a dangerous man. Perhaps I should kill him?"

"No," Hella replied. "My master is interested in Cassave. There are still things for him to accomplish."

"You speak as though Vseslav is not your master," I said.

Hella laughed; a delicate bell-like sound.

"He only thought he was. I have always served the one you call the Magister. He is pleased by your actions. You put an end to a foolish plan and helped to humble a presumptuous rival."

"Who is the Magister?" I asked. I still dreaded the answer to my question but decided I needed to know.

"Cassave was wrong in claiming that Chernabog was Satan himself," she said with a sly smile. "Vseslav and the witches mistakenly put their faith in a lesser power, but the true Devil is not mocked."

"I see," I said. "What does he want of me, now?"

"Go and rejoin Vseslav," Hella said.

I nodded and, catching one of the horses, I turned and headed down the slope. I only looked back once, just as the dun broke the horizon. Hella was gone and the three men were beginning to stir. I looked away, knowing that I had no place in the world of men.

But it had been nice to be a Cossack again for a while.

As an afterword to the previous tale, Matthew Baugh's endearing vampire Yvgeni "returns" in "The Heart of the Moon," published in our Volume 3. Now, we remain in Asia with Nicholas Boving's tale, which features another charming rogue last seen in "The Elfberg Red" in our Volume 8: Rupert of Hentzau, from the classic Prisoner of Zenda. *But where Matthew's tale was dark and horror-filled, Nicholas' story is sun-drenched and reminiscent of a Rudyard Kipling or Talbot Mundy yarn, glorifying the derring-do of the White Man's Burden...*

Nicholas Boving: *The Green Eye*

Simla, India, 1882

"Good God!"

Rebecca Fogg looked up from her soup. Her cousin wasn't given to explosions of the verbal kind. Her spoon remained poised, the Mulligatawny already starting to cool.

"What the Devil is he doing here?"

The spoon finished its journey and returned to the plate. Rebecca dabbed her lips with a snowy napkin. "May one ask who the Devil he is?"

Phileas Fogg frowned. "I thought he was dead."

"Apparently not, unless this hotel is given to ghosts. Anyway, who and where is this person who seems to have upset you?"

"Prince Rupert of Hentzau. And he's just come through the door."

"And this is a bad thing?"

Phileas Fogg picked up his spoon. "Very good soup, this."

Rebecca sighed. Sometimes her cousin was exasperating. "Hentzau, Prince, Rupert?"

"A scoundrel."

"And this surprises you? The world is full of scoundrels."

Phileas drank some soup. "True. But they tend to have well-beaten paths. They have comfort zones. Rupert's is Europe. We are in Simla."

"Indeed. India is some distance from Europe's fleshpots." Rebecca smiled wickedly. "One assumes you wish to avoid him."

"Not especially. But it poses the question. What is Master Rupert doing so far from home?"

Rebecca Fogg put down her spoon and casually turned to face the dining room entrance. A tall, fair-haired, very handsome young man stood, the picture of arrogance and charm, scanning the assembled guests. Rebecca approved, of his appearance at any rate.

"Introduce me," she said. It wasn't a request. Her cousin frowned.

"Look Rebecca... Oh, damn it!"

That was as far as he got because Hentzau was already weaving his way quickly between the tables, homing in on theirs like a hound on a fox. He arrived, bowed, clicked his heels and smiled.

"My dear Fogg. What a pleasure, and what on Earth brings you to these parts?"

There was an uncomfortable pause, broken when Rebecca held out her hand. Phileas introduced them somewhat reluctantly. Hentzau bowed again over her hand with old world courtesy. "*Enchanté.*"

He gave Phileas a twinkling smile. "You never mentioned that you had such a delightful relation."

Phileas' answering smile was frosty. "Probably because I was protecting her from rogues such as yourself."

Rupert of Hentzau shrugged. "Well, the cat is now out of the bag." He glanced around. "I was about to dine..."

Rebecca cut in. "Won't you join us? Dining alone is such a bore."

Hentzau slid into one of the vacant seats with the speed and agility of an otter. Fogg reluctantly signaled the head waiter. He mistrusted men like Hentzau. They were opportunists, preying on the unwary and shamelessly using their social standing. Rupert of Hentzau was a Prince of the blood, and didn't mind anyone knowing.

Hentzau's opening remarks confirmed his suspicions.

"One assumes you came here in your airship?"

"Ah. So that's the way of it," replied Fogg.

Hentzau pasted a look of polite confusion on his face. "The way of what? I merely made an inquiry."

Fogg's answering look was of disbelief. "From what I know of you, Rupert, you never made an inquiry yet without some ulterior motive." He snapped his fingers impatiently, "Out with it, man, and then we may enjoy our dinner without the suspense hanging over us."

Hentzau sighed theatrically. "Very well. Circumstances are such that I need to get out of this country."

"There are trains."

"Speed is of the essence and your airship would be the ideal mode of transportation."

Rebecca's eyes glinted in the lamplight; she leaned forward, chin on hand, and said: "Do tell. The police are after you?"

Rupert's lips twitched slightly. "Would it were so simple."

Fogg refilled their wine glasses. "Start at the beginning, you scoundrel."

Rupert glanced quickly around the large room, and Fogg detected a hint of anxiety that he found intriguing.

"I take it you're not a tourist, not sight-seeing?" asked Fogg.

Rupert raised an eyebrow. "Not quite my style, no." He cleared his throat. "Actually, I'm mending a broken heart."

Rebecca gave an unladylike laugh. "Oh, come on! That won't wash."

Rupert managed to look slightly offended. It almost worked. "Well, Josie did leave me."

"Josie?"

"Countess Josephine Balsamo. We were a team, for a while at any rate."

"Ah." Fogg dug the knife a little further. "And your schemes fell apart?"

Rupert spread his hands. "Well, yes, I'm rather short of the ready, and this glorious part of the world seemed like an ideal spot to replenish the coffers. You know the sort of thing: lakhs of rupees, gold moidores."

Rebecca's eyes widened. "So, some outraged maharajah is out for your blood? No wonder you want to get out."

Rupert took a sip of his wine. He grimaced and pinged the glass. "Doesn't travel well, does it? But actually, no to your question. No maharajah. Well, not the kind you mean."

Fogg's eyes narrowed. "If you want my, er, *our*, help, better come clean. Otherwise, I'll consign you to the outer darkness."

And so it came out, bit by bit, rather like drawing teeth.

"I was in Katmandu a while back. Well, actually it was only last month. Beastly difficult to travel in those parts. But I'd heard of a couple of men who had some treasure or other for sale, and probably didn't know the value of what they'd got."

Fogg sighed. It was so typical of the man; so typical of many adventurers with an eye to the main chance and microscopic consciences. "So who and what?" he said.

Rupert looked furtive and leaned across the table. "A couple of loafers, time-served soldiers of the Queen, names of Daniel Dravot and Peachy Carnehan; two of the biggest rogues I've ever come across. They were in a devil of a hurry to get rid of it. They tried to dicker the price, but I gave them a take it or leave it." He managed a grin. "I quite liked them actually."

"And this treasure was?"

The furtive look intensified as Rupert again scanned the room. No one appeared to be taking undue interest in him, but then, the waiters being locals, were to him invisible. He reached into his breast pocket, took out a silk handkerchief and opened it, sheltering the contents from casual view with cupped hands. Rebecca leaned forward.

"Oh, my Lord! Is it real?" Sometimes Fogg's cousin found it both amusing and useful to play the naive young woman as very few knew she was, in fact, a respected agent of Her Majesty's Secret Service.

Fogg's face hardened. "Where did they get that thing?"

"Blessed if I know, Fogg. They said something about a heathen idol up in the hills. Can't remember exactly. Something to do with a loony called Carew." He laughed uncertainly. "Anyway, what's the difference? These fellers will never miss it, whereas my creditors will call down the blessings of Allah on me."

Fogg reached across the table and slammed his hand on Rupert's. He was horrified. "For God's sake, give it back. Your life's not worth a farthing if the Talfiris find out you've got it."

Rupert laughed. "We'll be over Persia and long gone by then." He jumped up. "What are we waiting for?"

Fogg growled angrily. "For you to send it back, with groveling apologies and the fervent hope they won't still kill you."

The silence was palpable and the rattle of conversation in the dining room had died. All eyes were turned towards them, and one of the waiters dropped a tray. Fogg cursed himself inwardly for having lost his cool demeanor and spoken so loudly.

Rupert looked at him, open-mouthed, then the devil in his character reasserted itself and he laughed. "Not going to happen, old chap." He shrugged, "Anyway, I'm damned if I'll give away the chance at a fortune. Besides, I doubt I could find my way back there."

Rebecca had also undergone a change. Gone was the slightly vapid woman, now replaced by one with an edge of tempered steel.

"Phileas is right. You're a damned fool, Hentzau, and I wouldn't give a rupee for your chances. For God's sake, they might have someone in this hotel. One of the waiters might be just looking for the chance to stick a knife in your ribs."

Rupert stared at her. "Not you, too! I thought..."

"That's just what you didn't do. It's just like you. I heard about the Elfberg Red, you know.[3] If it hadn't been for Raffles, you'd be in a cell, you and that Balsamo woman." She pointed at the huge emerald that lay hidden by Fogg's hand. "For God's sake, put the thing back in your pocket. The Idol's Eye has no value, no price. You can't sell it. No fence in the world would touch it. Dammit, just having it is tantamount to a death sentence."

Rupert slipped the jewel back in his pocket as quickly as a conjuror making a coin disappear. He patted his breast. "That's where you're wrong. I know a Jew in Venice who'll give me a tidy sum for it. You'll fly me there of course."

Fogg growled his anger and disgust. "I'll do no such thing."

Rebecca sat back and picked up her wine glass. Her hand was completely steady. "I think we may have to, cousin," she said. "I get the feeling we may be guilty by association."

Fogg disagreed. "There's not a court would..."

---

[3] See "The Elfberg Red" in our Vol. 8.

"I don't think the Talfiris would be much interested in legal justice. They tend to be a bit rough when it comes to things like this." She turned to Rupert. "They don't do it themselves of course. They leave it to the women, who, I'm told, tend to be quite inventive when it comes to ways of killing a man."

Fogg sighed. "She's right, you know."

Rupert of Hentzau went a shade paler under his tan. "Then you'll... I mean, you can't leave me..."

Rebecca gave him a pitying look. "It looks like we'll have to... help you."

Fogg signaled the waiter. "But first, I'm going to finish my dinner, and if anyone stabs you, try not to bleed all over the table linen."

The airship *Aurora* was one of the marvels of its age. It became Phileas Fogg's property after he had won it in a poker game rigged by the British government. It had, to all intents become a mobile home in which he traveled the world.

The lifting envelope was, unlike most at this time, filled with helium, and not the dangerously explosive hydrogen. Slung beneath were the engine room, the bridge, stores, the magazine and luxurious staterooms and other living quarters.

Phileas Fogg captained the ship, but it was run and maintained by the indispensable Jean Passepartout.

At that moment, Prince Rupert of Hentzau was leaning out of the bridge starboard window, looking down on the arid landscape several hundred feet below. He turned back to where Fogg stood, hands clasped behind his back, standing beside the helmsman.

"D'you know, Phileas, I was so bored my immortal soul was shriveled down to the size of a dried pea?"

Rebecca, who was seated at a table cleaning a pair of rapiers, glanced up. "Doesn't say much for Countess Josephine. Anyway, you'll get excitement enough if the Talfiris catch up with you."

Rupert frowned. "Josie let me down. We were onto a good thing."

Fogg wasn't amused. "If jewel theft is your idea of a good thing. But Rebecca's right." He pointed out of the windscreen. "That's the Khyber pass down there. Once through that, we're in Afghanistan, which is a pretty wild place, and they don't much like foreigners."

"I didn't steal their bally jewel," Rupert said.

"I don't think they'd much care, and they have a similar policy with prisoners as the Talfiris."

Rupert changed the subject abruptly. It was not a prospect he wanted to dwell on. "Those things are just for show, or d'you know how to use them?" He crossed the bridge and picked up one of the rapiers, swishing it viciously. "Nice balance."

Rebecca picked up the other weapon and, a second later, it was at Rupert's throat. "Maybe we'll find out."

Fogg smiled. "The female of the species, Hentzau... You'd do well to remember that."

The crenellated walls of the Bala Hissar fortress towered above Maboub Ali as he sat, crossed-legged, before his small camel dung fire. Behind him, a steady stream of merchants, travelers and armed tribesmen flowed, hurrying through the great gates before sunset brought their closing for the night. In front of him were half a dozen horses, the remains of his string, tethered to pegs and hobbled, feeding on hay and a meager ration of oats. It was poor fare at best, but the animals looked well enough, and he knew he would easily sell them.

Maboub Ali was a horse trader by profession, a big burly Afghan, his beard dyed red with lime. He was also a British spy by inclination, because he relished both the money and the Great Game. He was one of the best horse dealers in the Punjab, a wealthy and enterprising dealer, whose markets penetrated far into the back of beyond.

He blew a stream of smoke from his hookah and smiled into his beard: C.2.1B, indeed. The British loved their numbers and ciphers: they made danger into a game. But he thought that it was indeed a game, and a very dangerous one at that. His mission for the Survey of India was to explore, map and report on the activities of foreigners in places beyond the Himalaya. In doing so, he had discovered that both the Russians and Germans were planning so-called trade routes along the valleys through which they intended to funnel arms. He had already found samples of Mausers and ammunition among the tribesmen.

There was a keen wind blowing down from the north. The winter had shown its teeth early that year, and the higher passes were already closed by snow. It was time to consolidate his reputation as a horse trader, get rid of his inventory, and make his way back to Umballa and his chief, Colonel William Creighton.

Maboub Ali threw a handful of fuel onto his fire, loosened the long knife in its sheath, wrapped his blanket tightly around his shoulders, and was soon asleep in the way he had always slept: with one eye open.

As the Afghan slept, another man, much younger and somewhat untested, made his way through the darkness along the walls of the fortress. He was darkskinned, tanned by the weather and harsh sun, with black beard, white teeth and a reckless look in his eye.

He was one of those extraordinary Englishmen who, for reasons of their own, had taken up a role as players in that most dangerous game, the one the Russians called the *Tournament of Shadows*. His name was Raffles, A.J.Raffles, but his face that night, as he passed the flickering flames of camp fires, was indistinguishable from any of the young men who had come to seek their fortunes as traders, or to sell their services as mercenaries.

He was also a product of those institutions that had provided so many of the administrators and officers to the British Empire, the Public Schools: men who had given their health, and so often their lives, for that empire. Adventure had been bred into him from an early age. As he had steadfastly maintained throughout his schooldays, the world was his oyster, and he had no intention of getting cut when he opened it.

The towers of the great gates loomed before him and he grunted softly with satisfaction. Somewhere nearby, among the throng of buyers and sellers, would be the man he sought.

It took Raffles more than an hour of soft-footed search, moving from fire to fire, silent as a ghost, nearly as invisible as the breeze, before he found Maboub Ali. He sat down a short way off, reluctant to disturb the horse trader, and wise enough not to try. In a few hours, it would be dawn. In the meantime, he would rest and trust to the gods and his wits for safety.

Maboub Ali handed Raffles and bowl of hot *Masala chai*.

"Your command of Pashto is impressive, but you would do well to hint that you have spent much time in Persia. It will serve to cover your accent and slight imperfections."

Raffles cupped his chilled hands around the bowl and sipped. Around them the other camps stirred into life; fires were restarted from embers and meals were cooked. Nearby, a man hawked and spat, and a camel belched in the way of all camels.

"I can either try to get to Herat and thence to Persia, or accompany you. On the whole, I fancy the latter as the best plan."

Maboub Ali stroked his beard, appearing to consider the choice. "*B.6.4C* I agree. I have business to conclude." He gestured at the horses. "I must sell these fine…"

"…screwballs?"

"… *steeds*, and then, we shall be on our way." An errant snowflake drifted past. "Before the weather compels us to winter in this pest hole."

"If we last that long," Raffles added.

Peachy Carnehan looked across their miserable campfire at his mate, Daniel Dravot. Things were bad, very bad. The Talfiris were onto them, not more than a couple of days behind. They had choices, but all of them were bad. They could stand and fight it out, but they were dead short on ammo. They could turn themselves in and hope for the best, which meant getting handed over to the Talfiri women—a fate not to be contemplated; or they could head down into India at the bleedin' double and see if they could make good a plan they'd had simmering for a couple of years, but, for that, they needed advice from a newspaper man in Lahore. At least the plan sounded good to them, and involved a couple of dozen Martini-Henry rifles and the help of a local chief.

"We gotta go, Danny. We stay here an' it's curtains. Those Talfiri women don't bear thinkin' about."

Daniel Dravot screwed up his face. "Jaysus. Fair makes me skin crawl. I think I'd rather take a bullet in the guts than have those harpies lay a hand on me."

"Then, it's decided?"

"Aye, and so it is. Lahore's the place. Once across the border, we'll be safe."

And on that note, Dravot wrapped his blanket around his shoulders and lay back against a rock. Dawn was a way off, but sleep wasn't an option. For a long time, he stared at the black sky with its pinpricks of light.

"You awake, Peachy?" he finally whispered.

There was a grumble like a bad tempered bear from the other side of the fire. Dravot grinned into the dark. "Fancy bein' a king, does ye, Peachy?

"Shove it, Danny."

The snow had begun in earnest when Raffles and Maboub Ali broke camp and made their way towards the road that would take them through the Khyber Pass. The Second Afghan War was still a clear memory in the minds of most, being a mere two years past, and Raffles knew full well that, if his disguise failed, his treatment would be harsh and final. Nevertheless, the mouth concealed by the black beard and mustaches twitched in amusement. The called it *The Game*, and it was a game, the greatest game of all, with the stakes life or death. He glanced at the burly man on the other horse. *C.2.1B* indeed! Still, he could have wished for no better company on the dangerous road ahead, for Maboub Ali had a reputation of a man not to be trifled with.

The day dragged on, the discomfort of the keening wind and driven snow things to be born without complaint. By nightfall, they would be well away from Kabul, and though there was danger of bandits, the threat of Raffles being discovered would lessen with every mile.

The *Aurora* was making heavy weather of it. The storm that was turning Raffles and Maboub Ali's journey into a trial of endurance had spread its evil influence across Eastern Afghanistan and expanded into a full-blown storm of heroic proportions.

Phileas Fogg stood once more beside the helmsman, his face grim as he peered through the windshield. Rebecca appeared at his side.

"Perhaps it would be prudent to turn back?" she suggested. "Being forced down in these parts might be a bit of a mistake."

Fogg shrugged. "Perhaps a little more altitude is the order of the day. These storms are usually pretty low level."

Rebecca pointed at the altimeter. "We're already near the limit right now. One forgets that this country is practically all well above 6000 feet."

Fogg glanced at the chronometer. "A few more hours, my dear, and then we may take the prudent route."

Rebecca smiled wickedly. "Our passenger won't like that."

"Be damned to Hentzau. The man's nothing but trouble. I've half a mind to do as you suggested and chuck him over the side."

Rebecca tapped the altimeter glass. It remained steady. "Is this thing working?"

The cloud suddenly parted. The helmsman gave a shout of alarm as, dead ahead in the rift, appeared a black and glistening rock face. The man spun the steering globe even before Fogg's terse order of, "Hard aport!"

There was a tense moment when the whole ship held its breath, then a loud clang as something struck.

The *Aurora* staggered; there was a crash of crockery, some very inventive swearing by an unseen member of the crew, and then the cloud cover closed again like a suddenly-drawn stage curtain.

Fogg shouted at the helmsman to hold his course and keep a sharp look out. He then strode to the engine room. On his way, he barged into Rupert of Hentzau, and snarled at him to keep out of the way if he wished to live. Hentzau raised an eyebrow and lounged towards the bridge as if mid-air crashes were perfectly normal occurrences. He appeared at Rebecca's elbow and calmly lit a cheroot.

"Phileas seems a shade put out."

Rebecca's attention was held by the altimeter. She glared at it and then gave it a slap before turning to Rupert.

"You'd be put out too if you'd dashed near flown into a damned great mountain."

"Nothing I can do, I suppose?"

Rebecca put her hands on her hips and gave him a look that would have been enough for another man. Hentzau merely smiled and drew again on his cheroot. He flicked ash on the floor and smiled his admiration. "Damned if you don't look even more beautiful when you're angry."

The next second, he again found a rapier point at his throat, and a spot of blood spoiled the perfection of his collar.

In the engine room, Fogg listened intently to Passepartout. "There is nothing, Monsieur. I have checked everything. The engine is perfectly sound, the controls are beyond reproach. I have no fear for the safety of this beautiful ship."

"Then why the Devil did we...?"

Passepartout shrugged. "The instruments perhaps? It maybe that the storm has caused some kind of malfunction?"

Fogg took a long, lingering look around, but saw nothing that was not as it should be, so he left.

"I don't like you, Hentzau. To my mind, your type is the lowest order of mankind. You feed off others like a leech, a parasite." Rebecca pressed the rapier point a little harder. Hentzau backed away, his eyes fixed on hers. "My cousin has been much too kind, and you are taking advantage of that kindness." She continued pressing the point until Hentzau's back was against the bridge wing railings. There was nothing but clammy cloud at his back, and God alone knew what below. "One more annoyance, one little irritation, and this blade will slit your throat and you will…" She shrugged. "I imagine there are hungry creatures below, vultures and such, that will welcome a meal, even your miserable carcass."

Hentzau made to say something, but Rebecca stopped him. "Oh yes, you think yourself a great swordsman, but believe me when I say I can take you left-handed." She stepped back and dropped the blade.

A thousand feet below, and a hundred miles to the west, Maboub Ali and Raffles were leaning over the necks of their horses, going like Hell in the direction of a small fort on a hilltop. Behind them, on considerably lesser horses, and several miles back, was a pack of assorted Afghan and Kafiri thugs who operated with the more or less approval of a local warlord. The approval part came when they brought back loot or captives for ransom. The disapproval was not to be thought about, and generally resulted in a couple of quick beheadings, or a melting of the bandits into the local scenery.

On this occasion, one of them had recognized Maboub Ali and rightly reasoned that a horse trader lacking horses was either up to no good, or else had full money bags as a result of selling his stock. In this case, they were right on both counts.

The horses were starting to make that gasping sound that is the precursor to being full-blown winded, when the ground rose quickly, and, almost before they realized it, they were under the walls of the fort. They dismounted immediately and found the door. Maboub Ali was about to hammer on it with a rock, when Raffles held his arm.

"Is this maybe the frying pan being exchanged for the fire?"

The Afghan's beard twitched, the sure sign of a smile beneath the matted henna red. "Fear not, my young friend. We are among friends. This is not all it seems."

He banged the rock against the ancient timber in an irregular series that could only have been a signal. The storm eased momentarily, and Raffles glanced back, a trifle anxiously, to see where their pursuers were. His practiced eye measured it as a shade over three miles. He held his patience. Maboub Ali had not survived as a secret agent of the Raj without great skill and wiles.

A few moments later, there was a call from the inside, the sound of heavy timbers being slid aside, and, with a creak, one side of the door opened to reveal a singularly villainous-looking individual who might have been any one of

Maboub Ali's relations. They embraced each other. Raffles was left to lead both horses into the small enclosure where a youth with an incipient beard took them over. Maboub Ali turned and with an expansive gesture indicated the other man.

"Behold, my young friend, this is the husband of my second cousin's youngest sister." He pointed to an outside stone staircase that led to the upper floor. "Over food and drink we shall discuss out little predicament."

Raffles quietly pointed out that the little predicament was less than three miles away and getting closer, but Maboub Ali didn't appear the least concerned. He shrugged.

"They cannot break into this place without a canon. Saw you any canons?"

Raffles also pointed out that, with the fort surrounded, it was going to be difficult to get to out, and that Umballa was a long way away. Maboub Ali laughed and tapped the side of his long nose. "Drink, food, and then all will be revealed."

As they entered the single upper room, shots were heard, and there was the distinctive smack of bullets against stonework. Imran Khan gave an order to man the defensive slits, but to conserve ammunition. He smiled at Raffles.

"These dogs are not worth wasting good bullets on." He gestured at a table, "Come, we will eat and drink, and the see what may be done."

Raffles knew that he'd gain nothing by questions. All would indeed be revealed at the appointed time, but social priorities came first. There was a whup as a bullet came through one of the slits, spanged around the room and demolished a singularly ugly vase. No one paid it any attention.

"I think the time has perhaps come to retrace out journey for the time being. Pushing on heroically is one thing, but lunacy is another."

Rebecca looked at her cousin. He appeared to ponder for a full five seconds, then shrugged and gave the helmsman the order to come about. Two minutes later, Prince Rupert stormed onto the bridge, his habitual elegance awry, and a look of deep anxiety on his face. The *Aurora* lurched in turbulence, throwing him against the door frame.

"What the Devil's going on. Fogg?" he demanded. The prince's arrogant royal upbringing showed through in the tone of his voice. Phileas Fogg was standing calmly, looking through the windshield, his hands clasped behind his back.

"Need I remind you, Hentzau," he said smoothly, "that it is customary to ask permission to enter a ship's bridge?"

Hentzau pushed his way in. "Custom be damned! Why have we gone about?"

Fogg shrugged, but there was a twitch of his lips that only Rebecca saw. "Because I chose it. Now kindly leave the bridge before I have you escorted off."

Hentzau's face had gone a couple of shades paler. "Dammit, Fogg, you're taking me straight back to those murdering Talfiris."

Fogg was unmoved. "Perhaps you should have thought of that before stealing the emerald."

"I didn't steal it, I bought it!"

"The difference, in your case, is marginal."

Hentzau was about to argue the toss when Rebecca's rapier once more touched his throat. "You must be getting quite used to this by now," she said, "I'd do as he says if I were you."

At that moment, a man entered the bridge, saluted smartly and handed a message to Fogg. Fogg read it and passed it to Rebecca. She scanned the few lines, passed it back and lowered her rapier. Her tone was cuttingly sarcastic as she said, "It seems you have a temporary reprieve, Your Highness."

Fogg glanced at the helmsman. "Belay that last order. It would seem our services are needed in Afghanistan."

Hentzau's face brightened, "See, I told you."

"You told me nothing." Rebecca's tone was icy, "Now, get off the bridge!"

When the prince had left, she read the telegraphed note again. "Creighton must be in a devil of a hurry."

Fogg nodded. "Useful invention, this new wireless telegraph." He gave her a sidelong glance. "*Request you pick up agents. They are in extreme danger. If possible return to Simla.* I wonder who these agents are?"

Rebecca smiled, "Ah, now, there I can help you."

"I'd rather thought you would." He crossed to the chart table, traced a line with his forefinger, and measured it with calipers. "At this speed, we should reach them just after dawn tomorrow."

Rebecca put her hand on his shoulder. "Steer clear of any mountains, won't you? I'm going for a nap."

Raffles admitted to being impressed. The last thing he'd imagined in a primitive hill fort in the middle of Afghanistan was the new-fangled electric wireless telegraph. As they returned to the dining area, he expressed his admiration to their host.

"Trouble is," he said to Maboub Ali, "how the Devil is anyone going to get to us in time?"

The Afghan again tapped the side of his nose. "Fear not, God will provide." He laughed, "And if not God, then Creighton Sahib."

"A man to be admired." It was not a question.

Maboub Ali inclined his head. "I bow to no man, but for one or two I have great regard. Creighton Sahib is one of those few."

Raffles had met Colonel Creighton just the once, late at night in a dimly lit club room in Simla. There, he had been given highly dangerous orders which only served to inflame his thirst for adventure and calculated risk, and put him forever beyond any chance of what might be considered a normal life.

"You realize, young man, that you may not return from this mission. It is, however, of the greatest importance, and no matter what, the information must somehow get through."

Raffles had understood very well, had indeed got the information Creighton needed, and was now sitting with it, secure in his memory in a flea-ridden hill fort while bandit bullets splattered uselessly against the walls. He suddenly laughed at the sheer improbability and excitement of it. Maboub Ali's friend heard and remarked that the young man was undoubtedly touched by the hand of God.

Maboub Ali smiled, "There are others such as he. They live for adventure."

"They are brave."

The Afghan's beard twitched again. "Maybe foolhardy, but there is no stopping them."

There was a shout from the end of the room as the telegraph began to chatter. Maboub Ali strode swiftly to the instrument. He read as the printed words were spat out, and then gave a shout.

"It is as I thought. Creighton Sahib has indeed conjured a miracle." He laughed, "He is sending an airship, one that belongs to a friend. God foresaw our little difficulty and has opened the way."

Raffles joined him, "Does this friend have a name?"

The Afghan handed him the printout, "One Phileas Fogg."

Raffles didn't know whether to be cautious or pleased. He had met Fogg, and there was a chance of being recognized. He shrugged. So be it. But his cover could be blown and, thereafter, his use limited. Maboub Ali saw his reaction and understood. He stroked his hennaed beard. He would have a word with this Fogg.

Fogg looked down and saw cotton wool puffs of smoke. "Bit of a fight going on down there, Becca. I reckon that must be where our friends are." He shouted to Passepartout to take them down. "Watch it, though. If the beggars start shooting at us, be ready to lift off with all dispatch."

Passepartout shouted back, "I can lift off pretty damn quick, Monsieur, you'll see."

The noise had drawn their passenger back to the bridge despite orders. He made a bee-line for Rebecca. "Are we going to war, Miss Fogg?" Hentzau asked with a twinkle in his eye, for the prince was not known to be averse to a bit of rough stuff.

"Got to pick up a couple of chaps and get them back to India."

Rupert's twinkle left like a magic trick. "What? Dammit, young lady, if we get stuck down there, they'll skin me. Anyway, you contracted to take me across this benighted country."

"We did no such thing, and, quite frankly, if it were up to me, I'd have pushed you over the side a while back." She took a Winchester 76 from an arms cabinet, sighted along the barrel and, with quick efficiency, loaded the magazine, then checked a box that held blasting gelignite primed with short fuses.

"What the Devil are those for?"

"Insurance," Rebecca snapped back. "Drop a couple of these and they'll back off very smartly."

Phileas Fogg joined them. "Unless you're going to be constructive, Hentzau, stay off the bridge."

Rupert gave him a look that would have fried a Ruritanian guardsman, but slid off Fogg like butter from a hot knife. Fogg pointed to the cabinet, "I imagine you know how to use one of those?"

Slowly Passepartout lowered the *Aurora* until they were less than a hundred feet above the fort. Fogg shouted at him to get lower; they needed to use a rope ladder.

"But the whole battlefield is covered with rushing bullets, Monsieur?"

Fogg patted Passepartout on the shoulder. "True, but beside the point. There are men below who need us." He peered down, and, at that moment, three men appeared through a trapdoor in the fort roof.

Rebecca pointed. "There they are! Down, Passepartout, get lower!" She snarled at Hentzau to keep the attackers busy if he didn't want to join them.

The suspense absorbed their thoughts as the airship slowly lost height. Hentzau worked the lever action on the Winchester like a man possessed, and, each time he stopped to fill the magazine, he lit the fuses and tossed a couple of sticks of gelignite.

Suddenly, there was a shout form below, and then Fogg roared at Passepartout: "We've got 'em! Take us up, damned quick!"

Maboub Ali swung aboard the *Aurora* with the practiced ease of a horseman mounting a stallion. Nothing on Earth would have allowed him to show the twinge of anxiety he felt at being on such a strange and unnatural machine. The first person he saw was Rebecca, a rifle in her hands. He watched as she cranked the lever and took a snap shot at one of the attackers. Her movements were precise and practiced; he approved.

A moment later, he was at her side. She smiled and spoke quietly, "Have no fear. Your identities are unknown, except to me."

"And you are?" Maboub Ali was unused to seeing a white woman take such a prominent part in what he thought of as man's business.

"One of the people who rescued you, and known to the man in Umballa."

The Afghan nodded, took the Winchester from her hand, and put two thoughtful shots over the side. Distantly came the sound of two answering yells. He handed the rifle back.

"I thank you, Memsahib."

Phileas Fogg appeared. He threw an order to Passepartout to, as he put it, "Get the Hell out of here!" Then, he turned to Maboub Ali. "Welcome to the *Aurora*. It seems you were having a little bother." He held out his hand. "I'm Phileas Fogg—and you are?"

Rebecca cut in. "No names, no pack drill, Phileas. Strictly need to know, as they say."

Fogg nodded. "Anyway, glad to be of help."

Raffles swung his leg over the rail just as the *Aurora* began to lift. He saw Rebecca's look of surprise, grinned boyishly and murmured, "Damned near left me behind."

Rebecca was a little disarmed by the young man's quick charm and good looks. She recovered her poise quickly, "And that would never do."

As quickly as his old self had peeked out, Raffles' Afghan persona came back. He bowed to Fogg and in a flowery manner expressed his thanks.

Twenty-four hours later, the dust haze that surrounded Lahore had come into sight. There was a bang that shook the *Aurora* and the port propeller ground to a halt. Fogg swore and turned to investigate just as the engine room door opened and Passepartout came out, waving away a cloud of black smoke.

"What the Devil happened?"

Passepartout wiped his face with an oily rag, leaving a black streak that made Rebecca laugh.

"We have a small engine trouble."

Fogg was instantly suspicious. Passepartout was, at times, a little evasive. "How small?"

"Half a day, maybe more. But we must land. It is necessary."

Fogg nodded. "Do what you must. But a day, no longer, you understand?" He about turned smartly, "And tell the steward to serve dinner."

At that moment, Hentzau also emerged from the smoke, demanding to know what had happened. Rebecca smiled sweetly at him, "We're going to crash."

Hentzau made the mistake of grabbing her arm. Furious, she slapped him away. She pointed her finger at Rupert. "Throw him over the side."

Maboub Ali, who was watching the exchange, shook his head. "Throw him over the side? You lack imagination Miss Fogg."

"What would you suggest?"

Maboub Ali shrugged, "A hundred feet of rope, tied around the ankles, then we throw him over the side. There is some very unkind bush just ahead: many thorns, and snakes."

Raffles joined the game, "You forgot to mention tribesmen who need target practice."

Hentzau backed away, his eyes flicking from one to the other as he edged to the table where the rapiers lay. And then Maboub Ali laughed; an uproarious bellow of mirth that shook his beard. Hentzau snarled and jabbed a finger at him as he tuned to Rebecca, "You allow this native to speak to me like that?"

Rebecca gave him a disgusted look, "Have a care, or I may let him do as he said."

Hentzau scowled, "Never did like Afghans."

Fogg, who had overheard, gave a sharp, barking laugh, "I know one who doesn't like you, and I can't say I blame him."

Maboub Ali spread his hands, "Ah, indeed it is so. Miss Fogg, you have but to give the word."

"Damned good claret, this '76. Seems to have traveled well despite all the banging around." Fogg looked appreciatively at his glass and held it to the lamplight as the ruby colors played through the wine.

"Passepartout will miss out on his dinner."

"Duty before pleasure; none knows it better than he." Fogg glanced at his pocket watch, "Another few hours and the *Aurora* will fly again and we will be..." He paused as a crewman hurried in and whispered a message. Fogg nodded, "Very well, bring her in." He put down his glass and announced, "It seems we have acquired a stowaway."

There was a clattering of footsteps on the spiral staircase, some very choice language in an unfamiliar voice, and then a burly crewman came into the dining salon half dragging, half carrying a young woman. She was blond and beautiful and very angry. He pinned her arms and forced her to stand in front of Fogg. "Where was she?" he said.

"Near the staterooms, Sir."

"Doing what?"

"Seemed to be trying a door, Sir," the crewman answered.

Fogg surveyed the woman with interest, then nodded to the crewman. He let his prize go but hovered.

"Who are you, and what are you doing aboard my ship?" he asked.

There was a momentary struggle on the woman's face as if she debated whether silence was the better option. Then she relaxed and a half smile hovered at her lips.

"My name is Amanda Darieux."

Her announcement met with no reaction. Fogg waved his hand, "The other half."

"I need to get away from here, quickly."

Fogg threw down his napkin, "Dammit, Becca, what do these people take us for, a damned omnibus?" He sat back, "Well, Miss Darieux, just what are you getting away from so quickly?"

Amanda Darieux gave him a somewhat embarrassed look and lowered her eyes. "There is a certain wealthy man in Lahore; he wants me for his harem."

Fogg was horrified, "Good God. We can't allow that to happen."

47

Rebecca was skeptical. She called it intuition. There was something about the woman that she instinctively mistrusted. Alarm bells went off.

Hentzau got up from the table and left the salon. The woman's demeanor reminded him too much of Countess Cagliostro, and he didn't trust her either.

Amanda swayed, her hand to her throat, "Excuse me, but I feel a little faint. Fogg got to his feet to offer his help, but she smiled weakly, "The bathroom - maybe some cold water…?"

Fogg snapped an order for the crewman to escort her, and as she left the room he said, "Poor woman. We must…"

Rebecca made an unladylike noise. "Poor woman my…"

Fogg stared at her, "My God Becca, you think…?"

"Phileas, I know."

Fogg hurried to the door. There was a shout. He came back moments later his face dark with anger. "Hoaxed like amateurs. She's gone. The crewman never knew what hit him, and now he's nursing a cracked head."

At that moment, Hentzau rushed back in, took in the scene in an instant, and swore roundly in both English and German, "Damned woman's a thief. She stole the emerald."

There was a moment's stunned silence, then Rebecca burst out laughing, "Oh, how choice! Hoisted on your own petard!"

Fogg's face remained expressionless for a few seconds, then he picked up his glass and raised it and smiled, "It seems there's no honor among your kind, eh, Hentzau?"

"But we must go after her! It's vital I get the emerald back!"

"A matter of high finance, I suppose." Fogg's mile disappeared, "Oh, we'll go after her alright, but it's got nothing to do with you. The Eye must be returned to its rightful owners."

Hentzau started to protest, but saw it was useless. He'd have to wait until an opportunity presented itself. He seized the decanter, poured a glass and emptied it at a gulp, "When?"

"When I'm dashed well ready."

The night was warm and the Milky Way a blazing lamp of stars as they mounted the horses Maboub Ali had magicked from a local dealer. It seemed Miss Darieux had also been to see him in some haste, and was, even then, an hour ahead of them in the direction of Lahore. Prince Rupert, who was stirrup to stirrup with Fogg, suddenly gave a sharp exclamation.

"I knew I damned well heard the name. Josie prattled on about her being some kind of immortal or some such nonsense. Called her a thief, too."

Fogg doubted Countess Cagliostro ever allowed herself to prattle about anything, but the mention of the term "immortal" tickled some buried memory. He touched his heels to his horse and urged it into a fast canter that would eat up the miles. The problem would be to find Darieux after she was swallowed up in the maze that was Lahore. And that was where Maboub Ali would come into his own.

A lone European woman on a horse in the middle of night in Lahore was not all that difficult to track. It seemed she had come galloping up the Trunk Road like one possessed, and then swung into the walled city. The locals had been somewhat amazed, but if it hadn't been for Maboub Ali's villainous appearance and eighteen-inch blade, backed up by a very evil-looking Raffles and a Webley .38, her disappearance would have been complete.

As it was, a small boy with larceny on his mind, came running with an offer to show them where the memsahib had gone to. It was a tactical error on his part as Maboub Ali grabbed him by the ear, and threatened to rip it off if he played them false. The boy squealed like a stuck pig, but, shortly thereafter, the troupe found themselves approaching the Lahore Fort in the Old City, to be confronted by the sight of Amanda Darieux, her back to the red bricks of the fort, snarling defiance at a pack of dark-turbaned and heavily-bearded men armed with staves and long knives. In another few moments, they would have been too late.

Fogg fired into the air. The effect was electric, as the attackers whirled to confront what they must have thought was the police, or a contingent from the garrison. When they saw it was neither, they split their forces, half surging menacingly at the rescuers.

Raffles fired his Webley, but not into the air. There was a loud yell of pain as a man dropped to the dust, clutching his leg. Maboub Ali, with a curse, charged his horse at the thick of the men, a wicked knife in his hand, aimed point first like a lance at the closest.

After that, it got mildly confused with Hentzau and Rebecca laying about them with rapiers, both flat and point, pistol shots and an inordinate amount of shouting.

And then, as quickly as it had started, it was over. The attackers melted into the darkness, and Maboub Ali gave a great laughing shout of triumph, "Talfiri dogs, thou hast met with, and been bested by, Maboub Ali! Think on it in your shame, and remember."

Hentzau added his shout, "Afghan fool." Then, he whirled in the saddle and shouted again, "Where's that damned woman gone?"

Almost immediately, he got his answer as there was a shout from above on the fort walls. All eyes swung up to look, to be met with the sight of Amanda, teetering on the edge of a hundred foot drop, her hand held out with the sparkling green of the emerald catching the starlight.

Fogg caught his breath. "By the Lord, Harry, that's a devil of a drop. If she falls, there'll be nothing but a bag of broken bones to pick up."

"It's mine," Amanda shouted.

Rupert roared out, "The Devil it is," and started for the gate, but she called again.

"Another step and I shall throw it onto the rocks. It will shatter to a thousand useless shards."

Rupert froze. He held out his hands, "Share it. We will share it. I promise."

Amanda laughed. "Your promise is worth nothing. If I cannot have it, then no one shall."

"How did you hear of it? At least, tell me that."

"The same way as the dogs who attacked me, because you're a boastful fool, Hentzau."

And with that she drew back her arm and threw the Eye of the Idol.

There was an arc of green fire, a shooting star that leapt from the battlements in seeming slow motion, while all those who saw it held their breaths. It seemed the outcome was inevitable for the great emerald would shatter as it struck the ground.

But then, there was movement: a figure darting forward at unbelievable speed, right hand outstretched in a supreme effort. The green star fell and the figure ran, and, at the moment, when it seemed all was in vain, the two converged. The figure lunged, clutched the star, fell, and rolled a half dozen times on the iron hard ground, and then leapt to its feet, arm thrust high in triumph.

"How's that?" Raffles shouted.

There was a moment of silence, and then Phileas Fogg gave a great hurrah, "Oh, well held, Sir." Then he went still, peering through the gloom, "By God, it can't be. It's..."

Rebecca grabbed his arm, silencing him. He stared first at her, and then back at Raffles. "Eh? Oh. Of course. But it was a damned fine catch. And you know, Becca, I saw him play at school once: Splendid batsman and a good slow spin bowler."

Hentzau was onto Raffles like a striking cobra. He held out his hand. "Mine, I think."

Fogg's cocked the hammer of his revolver. The sound was very loud and obvious in the silence that followed the frenetic action. "I think not, Hentzau. The Talfiris have prior claim and it will be returned."

Hentzau snarled defiance, "God, but you're a self-righteous bore, Fogg." Then, he shrugged and accepted defeat good-naturedly. "Oh, have it your way. There are other means of making a bit of the ready on this continent." And with that statement, he turned and headed for the main entrance of the fort.

He stopped as Amanda Darieux came out, looking as cool as if she'd just been for an evening stroll. He took her hand, bowed over it and kissed her fingers, and then, in the most natural way, took her arm and steered her towards Fogg and Rebecca. As they reached them, he laughed.

"Damn me if I wasn't once hocused by a wench like Miss Darieux; a dark-ie down Louisiana way. She slipped something into my punch, laudanum, I think, and when I dropped, she stripped me of my rings and gold hunter."

Amanda removed his hand and stared him down and moved away, "I'm not a darkie, Your Highness."

Totally unembarrassed, Hentzau made nothing of her remark. "No, indeed. But you're a damned fine wench, just like her."

He reached out for Amanda but she sidestepped. He laughed again, seeming a little surprised at what he'd found. "Egad, Amanda, I believe I'm half in love with you." He tried his most ingratiating smile. Amanda was not amused.

"Then, don't get to the other half or you'll regret it."

Hentzau stopped, hand on his chin and cocked a speculative eye at her, "We'd make a damned fine team, you know."

Amanda raised an eyebrow as if the very idea was ridiculous, then a small smile crept onto her lips. "We would, wouldn't we?"

"I believe we would, Mademoiselle. Tell me, does it bear thinking about? After all, it seems plain that Fogg won't be taking us any further as passengers."

Amanda went to him and tapped him on his chest. "I am what I am. There can be no changing me. I am what is called an opportunist." She tapped him again. "You know, nothing would have happened to me back there. I was quite safe."

Nobody but Amanda heard Hentzau's reply of, "So it's true."

Amanda smiled. "Countess Balsamo would have known the answer to that."

And so, they rode back to the *Aurora* through the warm night, and, as they rode, Maboub Ali sang a *ghazal* he composed as he went along, a song of lost love, of sorrow and parting friends. Raffles translated it for Rebecca's benefit, for he doubted the others cared.

Finally, as dawn was just lightening the eastern horizon, the dark bulk of the *Aurora* loomed and an agitated Passepartout hurried to meet them.

"What's the matter?" Fogg asked.

Passepartout smiled and sighed, "Now, nothing. You have safely returned. I was worried."

Later, there was a sunrise breakfast with champagne. It seemed only right, somehow, because no matter how much of a rogue the Prince was, he was an engaging rogue, and Rebecca, at least, felt that he had met his match in Amanda Darieux.

Rebecca looked across the table at her cousin. "Now, wasn't that better than looking at a lot of old ruins?"

Fogg disagreed, but his cousin knew he nevertheless felt the same way. "It was supposed to be a gentle, protracted circumnavigation of the globe, both educational and emotionally satisfying."

Rupert, who had completely recovered his good humor, despite losing the emerald, burst out laughing. "My God! You should listen to yourself Fogg, you sound like my old tutor. The man bored me so much I put a firework in his commode. You should have heard the language: most unsuitable for a man of the cloth." He sipped his champagne and glanced casually at Fogg. "What will become of the emerald?"

"Oh, that. Well, Maboub Ali has assured me it will be returned to its rightful owners."

"And you trust him?"

"With my life."

"Ah. So possession being nine points of the law does not enter the equation?"

Fogg was horrified. He threw down his napkin and got up and called for Passepartout. "I think it's time we were underway."

As the *Aurora* lifted off, Hentzau shouted, "I met Carew, don't you know. Mad as a blessed coot. They say when a white man gets taken up with worshipping heathen idols, it turns the brain." He laughed. "Certainly did for Carew. Little gold-painted ugly thing it was, but its third eye was this dashed great emerald. Wonder if it's the same one."

Peachy Carnehan and Daniel Dravot, bone weary and looking like a couple of tramps, entered the printing shop. There was a man at the end checking a proof of the coming edition of the *Gazette*. He was of medium height, dark haired, with glasses. They asked him for the loan of as many maps as he had of Kafiristan, for they had a vast scheme afoot.

A volume of Tales of the Shadowmen *wouldn't be quite the same without a story featuring that most Gallic of heroes, Arsène Lupin, the notorious gentleman-thief. Nathan Cabaniss takes great pleasure in depicting one of Lupin's very last capers, as our aging, yet still dapper, hero arranges what surely must be the ultimate diversion in order to steal a well-known artifact...*

Nathan Cabaniss: *The Great Ape Caper*

New York, 1933

The crowd was gathering in the winter night, excited murmurs filling the streets in anticipation of Denham's big show. The guests were exiting limos in the finest furs and tuxedoes, cheerfully posing on the red carpet as flash bulbs popped left and right. City officials, movie stars and corporate titans alike had received the exclusive invite. Ever the showman, Denham had spared no expense for his grand unveiling. The show had been on the lips of everyone in town; much speculation was given as to what it was exactly the infamous movie producer had brought back from his latest expedition. The entire city seemed to shut down for the event, as everyone rushed down Broadway to see for themselves what Denham had up his sleeve.

Indeed, it seemed the entire city was anxious to get inside the grand marquee theater... Everyone, except the one figure who slipped out the back alley, unnoticed. Tossing a small bundle of clothing into a dumpster, the man reached into his overcoat, pulling out a set of dark glasses. He put them on, a rather incongruous action given the time of night. A cane slipped out of his sleeve with the precision of an experienced stage magician. The man walked down the sidewalk, tapping his cane as he went. No one paid much attention to him, the sideshow gallery of celebrities on display being a sufficient distraction. He glanced up at the marquee, strobing bulbs bright enough to illuminate the laminate title through even his darkened glasses:

KING KONG - THE EIGHTH WONDER OF THE WORLD

Arsène Lupin smiled. The game, as an old rival might say, was afoot...

The Frenchman checked his watch again, possibly for the third time in the span of a few minutes. After all these years, the master thief still got a few jitters just before a heist. There was nothing in the world that could beat it, that sense of nervous anticipation... Then, the starting pistol, the narrow window to get the job done, followed by the sweet moment of victory, making the breathless escape with prize in hand. It was a feeling like none other. The hairs on the back of Lupin's neck stood up as a chill went through his body. He remembered all his greatest capers. He closed his eyes and shook the nostalgia off. Yes, he was going to miss it…

The years were catching up to the gentlemen-burglar. Although far better off than most his age, he was still slipping. He wasn't as thin as he used to be. He wasn't as agile. He wasn't as quick. For a while now, he had contemplated his retirement, but lacked a suitable target to go out on. Then, he caught wind of a treasure passing hands in San Francisco, a jewel-encrusted statuette of a bird that had once belonged the Knights of Malta. The whole affair caused a bit of a sensation when a pulp author documented the story in one of those detective magazines, and the item in question grew so famous that a New York collector acquired it for nearly double the sum of its already considerable worth. Lupin didn't need the money—he hadn't *needed* anything for quite some time—but it was just the thing to go out on: a theft high profile enough so that it would ensure that Lupin's legacy would far outlast his lifetime.

Devising a scheme to get the bird became troublesome, however. The collector was friends with a famous doctor, who traveled around the world with a group of five scientist-adventurers, and had asked them to keep a close guard of the bird while it was in the city. The six of them keeping constant watch made things problematic. They left no room for fault, seemingly had no discernible weaknesses. If Lupin were to get the famous jeweled bird, he was going to need a sizeable distraction…

Which was why news of Denham's great discovery had caught the Frenchman's eye. Doing a little digging of his own, Lupin had discovered just what it was that Denham had brought back on his boat, and soon the wheels started to turn in his head, a devious plan forming therein.

Lupin snuck behind the scenes of Denham's show with minimal difficulty, posing as a crewman. Everyone was running around in such a furor they barely noticed him as he snuck up the walls which held Denham's amazing find. It was impressive. Even though he was caught in the ironclad determination of his mission, Lupin was stunned by the sight of the great ape. He'd never seen anything so large, so majestic. It was a relic of world long past, of a time and place unknown to human history. It was *beautiful*.

Lupin had never been more nervous in his life than when he climbed up the rampart that held the beast chained at his wrists and waist—not for fear of being discovered by any of the people below, but by the beast itself. It had been drugged, slumbering softly as the gentleman-burglar made his way up the side, still on edge.

Getting a good look at the beast up close, Lupin was taken by its face: beneath the weathered lines and scars, there was profound sadness. The Frenchman couldn't help but feel sorry for the poor creature as it hung there, strung up by its wrists, waiting to be poked by cruel wranglers with electric prods to make it roar, so the fat, rich attendees could scream and clap and giggle at each other.

54

Loosening the bolts of the cuff that held the beast's hand might have been considered a dangerous and foolish gesture by some, but Arsène Lupin didn't feel bad about it at all.

He checked his watch again, wondered how much longer it would take. Then, he heard the first screams echo from inside the theater, and a smile formed on his face. Tuxedo-clad patrons began to trickle out the doors, leading their wives by the hand (or leaving them to fend for themselves in their expensive heels and slips). It wasn't long before an entire wave of attendees poured out of the entrance in a mad frenzy, a chorus of screams sounding off in the night as people tripped and stepped over each other in a crazed dash to get away. One man was running towards Lupin, his face ghastly pale and the seat of his pants damp.

"Run! Good God, man, run! It's loose—the beast is loose!"

A series of crashes echoed from inside, each one louder than the next, and the very ground beneath Lupin's feet shook. An ungodly roar filled the night, rattling the beams of the nearby buildings. The smile disappeared from Lupin's face; now was probably the time to get going. He jumped into his car as the Earth shook all around him and sped off down the crowded street.

Lupin picked the lock with astonishing ease. He felt as if he had all the time in the world. The beast had proven to be a suitable distraction. The entire city was in a panic; every law officer and civil servant had been called out to help deal with the raging monster. More importantly, that damned doctor and his five friends were gone, no doubt devising some ingenious way to stop the great ape. It was almost too easy…

Lupin strolled through the empty penthouse, tapped the walls until he heard a dull echo. It took the master thief barely half an hour to cut into the wall, crack the safe, and plaster over everything in order to deftly cover his tracks. The jeweled bird now in his possession, Lupin pulled out one of his signature calling cards. He wrote, *"Hope you enjoyed my Christmas present, New York. A.L."* and left it on the coffee table. It'd be a while before they figured that one out, and by then, he'd be long gone, disappearing into the sweet life of retirement.

Pausing at the window before he left, Lupin considered the strangeness of it all. The city that never slept was empty and unusually quiet. Everyone was inside, behind locked doors and windows, anxiously listening to the radio. Some had already packed up and skipped town. A trail of smoke and dust drifted upwards, marking the beast's path. Distant muzzle flashes strobed the cityscape far away, followed by muffled cannon fire. *The beast must be putting up some fight,* Lupin thought, imagining the ape cornered by all manner of tanks and military jeeps, raging out at a world into which he had been dragged against his will and which was now savagely hounding him. Lupin could relate.

The Sun was starting to peak out as Lupin waited on a bench for his getaway ride. The streets were empty and barren. Lupin enjoyed the quiet. He had wrapped the bird in a newspaper and stuck it in an unassuming shopping bag, just in case, but he could have probably walked around with the statue tucked freely under his arm. He unwrapped part of it, and considered all the treasures he had stolen in his lifetime. He remembered the thrill of the hunt that had kept him coming back, again and again. Pangs of nostalgia reverberated through him, as he gazed down at this bird, the last of his many conquests. His last great caper.

Shaking the thought from his head, he looked to the cityscape. It was a remarkable sight, he had to admit, even though it couldn't hold a candle to his beloved Paris. The tallest of the structures, the Empire State building, was especially magnificent. Looking at it reminded Lupin of Denham's beast. What was its name? Ah, yes—Kong.

Staring at the building, the master thief squinted. There was something atop it. From this distance it was barely more than a speck. And then Lupin realized what it was. He stood, disbelieving in his own eyes. The beast had climbed the towering structure. Airplanes buzzed all around, angry flies swarming over the speck that was Kong. Lupin was struck by a strange sensation. His palms began sweating, the hair on his arms stood on end. He realized that he wanted to see Kong swat away the airplanes. He wanted to see the great beast triumph. His heart soared as he saw the speck bat at one of the flies, sending the plane crashing towards the ground. He was going to do it... The great beast just might pull it off after all...

Then, there was a strafe of machine gun fire, the dull *rat-tat-tat* following soon after. The beast wobbled for a moment, and then fell. Lupin's heart sank as he saw the tiny speck tumble towards the ground, striking an outcropping before disappearing into the tangle of buildings off the horizon.

He looked again at the jeweled bird in the bag, and realized at last that he would never stop. All the treasures in the world, and it still would never be enough... He'd always return, the lure of the gold drawing him back time and time again.

Inevitably, beauty always killed the beast.

*We return to the theme of vampires with a story by one of our newest contribu-
tors, Anthony R. Cardno. In the tale that follows, Anthony revisits the classic
text of Bram Stoker's* Dracula, *depicting two of its protagonists in a new—and,
dare we say, moving?—light. As the saying goes, the evil that men do long lives
after them—and this seems even more true when dealing with vampires...*

Anthony R. Cardno: *So Much Loss*

London, 1897

Doctor Seward's Journal—20 September

Ten years ago today, we began, although we did not know it, our walk
through the fire, beginning with the death of our dear Lucy Westenra at the
hands of that monster, Count Dracula. Three years ago, we agreed to let Stoker
publish our journals and diaries as a testament to what happened to us. Unsur-
prisingly, most of the general public still think it a fiction, and the fact that Arthur and I share the names and titles of two of the characters a mere coincidence,
or a shared joke with the "author."

The general public has not heard Arthur scream in his sleep, as I have, the
names of the woman and man we both loved equally and were torn over even
before their deaths. He has done this intermittently throughout the years we have
been sharing a home at 423 Cheyne Walk, "happily married" as Harker wrote in
his postscript to our tale (although the general public assumes our namesake
characters each found a woman to hold a candle to dear Lucy's memory with
whom to settle down). But it is always worse near the anniversary of either
death.

Last night, he woke me with his thrashing about the bed. "Lucy!" he cried,
and then "Quincey!" Alternating their names as a mantra, becoming more and
more agitated in his movements, his arms flailing. I tried to wake him by calling
his name in a soothing tone, but that method did not work. I had to wrap my
arms around him, gaining a blackened eye and a bruised cheekbone in the process, and hold him as tightly as I could manage. I murmured reassurances that
our friends are now at peace. It took twenty minutes for Arthur to settle back
down into deeper slumber, and then I released him and went to my study to
write. I doubt he will remember it in the morning, but he'll believe me when I
tell him. And he'll be full of remorse, as I am when I have nightmares.

Ten years ago today. Each year seems to fly faster, the time between one
anniversary and the next shorter. We barely get past the night terrors of Lucy's
death, that the anniversary of Quincey's looms. And then, we cycle back again. I
wonder if we will ever put those memories completely behind us. I'm no longer

sure we can. Looking at each other reminds us constantly of what was. And yet, we cannot live without each other. Harker has Mina and their son, named after our lost Quincey. Van Helsing has his own family and his mission. We have naught but each other; who else would understand us?

I have begun to consider consulting one of our several supernaturally-inclined neighbors. Our friend Thomas Carnacki, at number 472, has been called the Sherlock Holmes of supernatural investigation (although I suspect neither would appreciate the comparison). Then, there is Sâr Dubnotal, a more flamboyant investigator with whom Arthur and I are less personally acquainted. Will either of them even feel that our nightmares are worth the time it takes to tell them? Or will they laugh at our lingering anguish over our losses?

Arthur Holmwood's Diary—21 September

In last night's dream, I lay in bed beside Jack. He snored lightly, as always. The room was not as dark as it should have been, given the phase of the Moon, and yet, I could see clearly. Beyond the panes, tree branches stirred. And then, as Lucy saw so many times in the dreams she told us, a familiar shadow appeared at the window—a silhouette I knew well, and longed to see.

Quincey stood on the balcony, his smile welcoming. I went to him and let him wrap himself around me.

"I've missed you so much," I whispered into his chest, breathing him in. His laugh rumbled gently against my lips. "It should have been Harker or Van Helsing…"

"Nonsense," he answered. "You know I had to do what was right. We couldn't save dear Lucy, but I could save you and Jack, and I did."

Lucy's laugh interrupted us.

"Couldn't save me, or didn't really want to?" She floated next to us, off the edge of the balcony. "You never loved me. None of you did."

"Not true!" I shouted at Lucy's apparition. "I loved you from the moment I set eyes on you!"

"Then why put a stake through my heart and let that old fool chop my head off?"

"Because you were no longer you! You were Dracula's thing, attacking helpless children…"

"To get the love from them that I never was going to get from you, Arthur darling. They loved me! Not you!" She screeched as she approached me, repeating "You never loved me! You never loved me!"

Holding me tighter, Quincey shouted, "He did!" He paused. "He loved you, little miss, for if he didn't, he could never have asked you to marry him. We always wanted both, and all that we loved in the feminine was embodied in you, until you became Dracula's creature."

"Lies!" Lucy snarled. "Lies, all of it! I was a cover for the three of you, and nothing more! I could never really have Arthur, nor you, nor Jack. And thanks to you, I cannot have my children either! I despise you!"

She launched herself, grabbing hold of my arm and pulling for all her considerable worth. Quincey pulled back just as hard, and I found myself screaming their names repeatedly.

The dream ended without resolution, and I can only surmise that the sudden conclusion was the moment when Jack wrapped his arms around me. I slept with no further dreams, but I fear tonight. I know, rationally, these are only dreams. But we thought vampires were a myth, too, a cultural dream, until we met Dracula.

It is a lovely fall day. I shall go out for a walk through the city to clear my head. I can only hope that the nightmare was so strong only because of the anniversary of Lucy's death.

Doctor Seward's Journal—21 September

I spent most of the morning distracted by visitations with patients and did not give much more thought to Arthur's travails of last night. When I finally took my lunch alone in my office, the exhaustion brought on through lack of good sleep caught up with me. I closed my eyes, took some deep breaths, and tried to calm the incipient headache. Would our relationship be this complicated even without Dracula's interference? Most likely.

Quincey was, perhaps, the most honest about himself. In the gathered notes that Stoker published, there are hints in what is recalled of Quincey's own words: that he was "a rough fellow, who hasn't perhaps lived as a man should." There are also hints of the history the three of us shared. No mention is made of Arthur's and my school years, and the only mention of the three of us together is of our time in "the Korea." We shared much more time than that; recounting those stories would be as much of a digression now as it would have been in Stoker's narrative. Suffice to say that I have been in love with Arthur since childhood, and we have both been in love with Quincey since we met him. Both of them were capable of loving a woman as well as a man; Quincey had even been married, fathered a son, and been widowed before he met Arthur. While I... I proposed to Lucy Westenra only because I knew she would rebuff me in favor of the much more handsome and affluent Arthur. In a perfect world, Quincey and I would have been together. Dracula's machinations put paid to that. In the end, we two childhood friends ended up with each other.

I was lost in these memories, painful and joyful intermingled, when Reynolds knocked on my office door. I must have been almost asleep, because at the sound my body jerked and I knocked the remains of my noon meal off my desk and onto the floor. Reynolds came in and shut the door behind him, crouching to help me clean up the mess.

"Mr. and Mrs. Dexter Stratton are here to see you, sir, with their son Gavin."

I had completely lost track of the time. Half lost in memory and with food splattered across the flooring, I realized I was not about to make the best first impression on a family seeking my professional assistance.

"Ask them to please give me a moment and apologize for the inconvenience." I turned to the wash-room at the back of my office. "And Reynolds... thank you for cleaning that up. Today is not my finest day."

"Not to worry, sir." Reynolds smiled and continued to clean. When I returned from the washroom, the floor was spotless and Reynolds was standing by the door. I took my place behind my desk, put on my best professional face and nodded. "The doctor will see you now."

Reynolds stepped to the side to admit Mister and Mistress Stratton, about as average a couple as one might imagine. They looked to be about the same age as Arthur and I. Mister Stratton's hand bore a rather ornate silver ring bearing his initials, DS.

Their son trailed them, an average young man of perhaps sixteen years. And yet... there was something about the boy that drew my attention the moment he walked through the door. He was affecting a shy and respectful manner, but there was another energy that entered the room with him, something I could not define and yet which felt familiar. I saw no indication that Reynolds noticed it, and so thought it my imagination.

"Good afternoon," I rose to extend my hand across the desk. Mister Stratton shook it, and we took our seats. "You message about needing my help was rather vague on details. May I ask what exactly brings you to me today?"

"Well," Mister Stratton cleared his throat. Mistress Stratton blushed quite clearly. "It's Gavin, you see."

"Yes, I did get that much from your message. What about the young man?"

"He... ahhh... This is a rather delicate thing to discuss in front of his mother..."

"His mother, who clearly already knows what the issue is, chose to join you today, correct?" I tried to be gentle but was not in the mood for prevarication. "Madame, you may leave us if you feel indisposed, but I should like your input if Gavin's problem affects you this much." Even as the words left my mouth, I thought *Oh! How long gone the days when we all wanted to shield the fairer sex, Lucy, Mina, from anything unpleasant.*

"I will stay." Her response was terse, serious, but the blush still colored her cheeks.

"What my father is too embarrassed to tell you, Doctor," Gavin finally spoke up. "Is that I'm a bit, errr, 'far along' for my age, yeah? A bit more developed than I should be."

"You look like a perfectly normal young man of sixteen years."

"Excepting that I'm only fourteen, sir."

"Ah. Well, yes, then, you are a bit physically advanced for your age. Still, that would be a matter for a physician, not a doctor of psychology." I understood the mother's embarrassment and the father's reticence, but admired the boy's forthrightness. "Have you consulted…?"

"It is more than that," Mistress Stratton interrupted me. "He is also more aggressive, especially towards his younger brothers. His sleeping habits have altered…"

"All a normal part of the change boys go through," I assured. "Not a cause for psychological evaluation."

"Doctor, I know all about that change," Mister Stratton shook his head. "This goes beyond that. Please. We would not be here if even Gavin hadn't agreed that what he's experiencing is most unusual. Help us understand why our son is so different."

Ah. There it was. The real fear was not that he was an early developer; it was that he might in fact be what some people still call an 'invert.' A homosexual. I could tell from the boy's candor that once his parents were gone, he would easily tell the truth, and then we could go about deciding on a course of action for him to function in normal society.

"Very well. I am positive there is nothing at all wrong with your son, but if you're all in agreement as to a course of evaluation, I'll take on the case." I stood up. "I presume you'll be fine with committing your son to my sanitarium for a few days?"

The parents nodded, the mother slower than the father but still in agreement. Young Gavin paled.

"Committed? Like a mental patient? I'm not insane, I'm just… arrr!" He smacked his clenched right fist into his open left palm, then calmed. "I'm just confused, Doctor. I don't know what's…?"

"It's fine," his father interrupted. "You don't have to do this. Come home, we'll sort something out."

"No!" Gavin's response was easily disproportionate to his father's statement; something else to discuss in the privacy of a doctor-patient session. "I want the doctor's help. If I have to stay…" he glanced at the other doors in my office, leading to the cells of the seriously insane "… here… Then I will."

"There is an alternative." I knew there was a risk in saying what I was about to say, but I forged ahead anyway. "There are no longer any comfortable, normal rooms for guests in this building, but we have a guest apartment at Lord Godalming's home. We have occasionally used it for temporary housing for less dangerous patients. Gavin can stay there; he'll be away from the institution but still under my supervision."

"That sounds like an incredible imposition, Doctor Seward, we really couldn't…"

"Yes, please." Gavin cut his parents off again. "I'll follow whatever house rules you set. I'll stick to the apartment and not disturb His Lordship."

If he seemed a little earnest, I understood it to be because going home without a chance to discuss his private issues was untenable to him. I nodded.

"Agreed, then? Gavin will come live with us for a few days, we'll run the full score of evaluations, and discover if there's anything wrong with him." I stressed the 'if' rather more intently than I meant to, but the Strattons didn't seem to notice. They rose. We shook hands, and they were almost to the door before Dexter Stratton turned and walked back to his son. He embraced the boy stiffly, and then worked the ornate ring off his hand and slipped it onto his son's finger. Then, without a word, Stratton returned to his wife. Reynolds escorted them out. I watched Gavin stare at the ring that should have been incongruously large on his fourteen-year-old hand but which fit perfectly.

"Now, then, what is it you would like to say to me that you could not say in front of your parents?"

He wasn't surprised that I would be so bold, given his own forwardness just moments before. But he did seem resigned. He slumped into the chair his father had vacated.

"Doctor Seward, I know what's wrong with me even if my parents seem clueless."

"Other than being a normal teenage boy with the usual pent-up sexual energy, you mean."

"I know all of that is normal. No, my problem is that my parents are right. I am not normal, not at all. My appetites…"

"…may not be as unusual as you think," I finished for him, wanting to put him at ease as quickly as possible. I sat on the edge of my desk, to be close but not invade his personal space.

"I doubt that, sir. Please don't patronize me. I know what I'm feeling is far from regular. I know what I am."

"And what is that?" I wanted the word out in the open, but did not want to say it myself; I didn't want him to think I was accusing him of anything.

"Doctor, I'm a *vampire*."

I am sure my jaw dropped open. That was far from the word I had expected to hear.

Arthur Holmwood's Diary—21 September

A glorious autumn day in the park, even with the gray sky overhead. I walked for quite some time at a comfortable stroll, breathing crisp, invigorating air. I passed familiar neighborhood faces, Celia Lytton and her new husband among them. We nodded cordially and continued on our separate ways. The tension of last night's dream left me with every exhale. I let my mind wander, intent on being in a better mood upon Jack's return home. It worked, and by the time I was strolling back to the house I felt lighter in my step than I had in days. I had not completely forgotten the nightmare of Quincey and Lucy. I was not whistling care-free as I walked, but I felt more in control of myself. I decided that I had plans for Jack, intimate plans, and that I had time to prepare them before he arrived home.

Except that Jack was home before me, and we had a visitor.

The young man with Jack had an energy about him I immediately recognized. One of us, then. An invert. A homosexual. Had he picked the boy up off of the streets as a charity case? Many older men of our type did that, altruistically or not. I was upset that he would do this without consulting me, without thinking about the disruption of our routines, without thinking about what people would think. They accepted us as a pair of friends living together until one or the other might find a bride; those who suspected otherwise kept that counsel to themselves out of deference to my title or to our notoriety as characters in Stoker's "novel." But bringing a young man—no, a boy—to live with us might draw unwanted... unnecessary... attention.

I didn't get to express any of those thoughts to Jack, who immediately explained that Gavin was a patient who had a story I needed to hear. A story which was apparently not the one I was expecting. I sat down, trying not to scowl. I'm sure I did not hide it well, as the boy stammered the beginning of his story and Jack furrowed his eyebrows at me.

"I know you sensed what's different about me. I could see it in your face, Lord Godalming, as you walked in. And I could also tell you made an assumption about what that sense was telling you. And yes, I know I'm like you both, an invert. I know I prefer the physical company of boys over girls, and I know that I feel more emotionally for boys than I do for girls, and I know that will never change, and that in our society I'll be forced to hide it the way you are."

I tried to interrupt the boy, to say what I don't know. Proclaim innocence to his accusations? Some behaviors are ingrained, no matter how secure we are of ourselves in our own minds and behind our own walls. A look from Jack silenced me.

"And maybe that similarity is part of what you're sensing, but that's not all of it," Gavin continued. "We share something else in common." He paused, gave a look at Jack for support. Jack nodded. "Milord, Doctor Seward says you'll only believe if I show you, so please forgive my impropriety."

The boy unbuttoned and pulled off the high-collared shirt he was wearing. He wore an undershirt, but what he wanted to reveal was visible. A pair of old but never totally healed wounds at his throat, clearly in line with his jugular vein. Small tears, they would have been, when they were made.

"How... how long ago?" I managed to ask.

"When I was four."

He said no more, and let me do the math. Jack too stayed silent.

"You're one of them. One of Lucy's victims." I sighed, scrubbed my hands over my face to push back the tears I had not bidden. I was tired suddenly, more tired than I'd been upon waking from the nightmare. "I always knew... always expected, at least… that we'd find the lot of you one day. You were all so young, but you can't have survived totally unscarred physically or emotionally."

"I was the oldest, according to the old newspapers Doctor Seward has shown me. But I was small for my age, then. The 'Bloofer Lady' was drawn to my size and innocence."

"And your parents?"

"Remorseful to a fault when I was brought home." He shook his head. "Right away, they knew something was off about me. And now the changes are more obvious. I'm definitely more developed than my peers. And I…" He blushed. "I can't stop thinking about you."

"Me?" I stood, flustered. "Young man, I've never seen you before, how could you…?" I was at a loss for words.

"You've never seen me, milord, but I've seen you. In the park, walking. Only once, and only recently, but it was enough. I must have some of her memories, somehow, because the sight of you made me… I had to hide in the bushes, away from my friends. I had to fight the urge to run up and embrace you. I had to relieve myself as best I could. And I've been dreaming of you ever since."

"Me, but not Jack?"

"She was never attracted to Doctor Seward, not really, was she?"

"No, I suppose not." I cast a painful glance at the man I now love more than any other, who had also been the first boy I loved. "I'm sorry Jack."

"I knew long ago. Remember, I didn't really love her the way you did. I proposed so that people would think it was her rebuff that had devastated me." Jack's eyes welled with tears again, and I could feel mine building.

"But there was another man…" Gavin reclaimed our attention. "An American, who also proposed? I found out about him through the book."

"Which is how you knew to approach Doctor Seward as a way to get to me," I filled in the rest. "Yes, Quincey Morris. A man we both loved. I've often wondered if, had he not died, he might have stayed here in London. Or if he'd have returned to the son he'd left behind. Or perhaps brought the boy here. You'd be about the same age…" My words trailed off as my mind drifted.

"Well, that's all idle speculation, isn't it," Jack tried to hide the hurt in his voice, but I heard it. That Quincey might not have stayed with him was a painful truth. "We have a situation that needs addressing: Gavin in danger of being thrown out by his family for being an invert. He is also in danger of much worse if even the rumor goes around that he is part-Undead."

"But no one really believes Mister Stoker's novel. Everyone thinks he made it up and just appropriated your names and likenesses. They think he based the Count on Sir Henry Irving." Gavin suddenly looked worried.

"You'll learn not to speak in absolutes, boy," I answered. "Most people believe the book is fiction. But there are people who know that creatures of the night are real, and those people, if they recognize the energy you give off, will not hesitate to destroy you. I know. Because I would gladly kill you myself if I thought for a moment that you had the possibility of actually being a vampire."

"But I must be. My strength, my odd sleeping habits, my urges."

"Do you have the urge to drink blood?"

"I have the urge to bite, yes."

"Not the same, boy. Many like to nip and bite during sexual activities. But those people don't actually want to taste, let alone swallow, another person's blood. And I don't think you do either."

"How do you know?"

"Because not once during this conversation have you looked at my neck or my wrist. Nor Jack's either. You've been focused on a part of my body known for a different secretion."

Blunt? Yes. But I needed to do what Jack had apparently been unable to do: shock the boy into understanding that he might be different, but he was not a vampire. Gavin blushed. Jack did too.

"Dracula was rare among his kind in being able to move about during daylight hours, due to his great strength and longevity. You, as a babe, would have been unable to stand the Sun, and if you somehow survived exposure then, by now you'd be unable to go out at all. And yet, here you are. And there you were, in the park the day you saw me."

"But, my attraction to you is so overwhelming…"

"Because some of Lucy's emotional memory was imprinted onto you when she bit you." Jack came back into the conversation. "Not her real memories, I don't suggest there was any kind of personality transference, but perhaps because of your age, or perhaps… well, whatever the reason, you now feel some of the things Lucy felt, including her attraction to Arthur."

"What can we do about it? My parents are still convinced I'm a monster."

"Yes, but a type of monster they believe can be 'fixed.' Nonsense, of course, but we can teach you defensive mechanisms. For hiding your homosexuality and your strength."

A bell rang. The call to dinner.

"But for now, we eat dinner." I turned to the door. "Tomorrow is soon enough for more evaluations, Jack?"

"Yes, yes it is. Today has been stressful enough on you, Gavin. Let's dine."

Doctor Seward's Journal—21 September

Once we were sure young Gavin was settled into the guest rooms with everything he might need for the night, Arthur and I retired to our own room. Uncharacteristically, Arthur locked the door behind us. I was checking the windows latches, a far more characteristic move for both of us, when he came up behind me and wrapped his arms around my waist. I relaxed back into him, releasing the tension in my shoulders and neck. He kissed my ear gently, and as always I shivered. I pulled the drapery shut and then turned to him, bringing our lips together. I lost myself in the kiss for long moments, enjoying the soft circles his hand was making on my back. And then I came to my senses.

"We have a house-guest," I reminded Arthur as I crossed to my side of the bed and started undressing.

"Yes, almost at the other end of the house." He was also undressing but didn't move to his side of the bed. He came to mine. "We will just have to be quieter than usual. I think we can manage that." He punctuated the idea with a lascivious wink. I hadn't seen such playfulness from Arthur in quite some time.

"What if his hearing is as sharp as his arms are strong?"

"Then he can hear what we're saying, and he knows not to disturb us," Arthur said towards the door. I laughed in spite of myself. Taking that as a good sign, Arthur stripped his shirt and undershirt off and stood before me, his arms extended. I moved a step closer, as always drawn by the fine blond down on his chest, so different from the thick brown hair of Quincey's. Arthur finished removing my shirts, revealing my pale smooth chest and the scars I bore from our final fight with Dracula and the gypsies we raced to Castle Dracula. He placed a hand around the back of my head as he kissed my ear again, drawing another shudder out of me, and then kissed his way along the stubble on my jaw to my lips. He was careful to avoid contact with my neck, as always. Arthur had told Gavin that some people enjoyed nipping or biting their lovers; we enjoyed it ourselves, so long as the neck was not involved. There were too many negative associations with that particular part of our bodies.

As Arthur pushed me back onto our bed, I knew I was facing another night of little sleep, but was sure this particular night the nightmares would stay away from us both.

Arthur Holmwood's Diary—22 September

Jack was already dressed and gone by the time I woke. Not that I have ever been in the habit of sleeping late; I rose after a short but satisfying, and as far as I could tell dreamless, sleep. Jack had his morning rounds at the Sanitarium and doubtless had been awake before the sunrise. I pulled on my dressing gown and slippers, and went in search of something to replenish the energy I expended last night. I am accustomed to preparing my own breakfast even though the house staff is fully capable of it. Yet, another way in which I suspect I am not like my peers. Men of my station should be ordering the "servants" to do everything for them, but I am uncomfortable with that role. Then again, men of my station should not have sexual relations with other men except as possibly a hidden and discreet diversion from the requirements of being a husband, discreet being the operative word as our acquaintance Wilde found out. Clearly, I don't do what's expected of me.

The path to the kitchen took me directly past the apartment our house-guest occupied. The door was open and so naturally I glanced through as I passed, and found myself pulled up short. The open door afforded a view of the right half of the room: a dressing table and wash-stand and a comfortable chair. The bed was out of my sight-line, although in this instance that hardly mattered. Gavin was half-reclined upon the chair, eyes closed and one arm crooked behind his head, naked save for his undershorts. The body revealed was certainly not that of a fourteen year old boy. Had I seen him out playing sport on a hot summer day, I'd have assumed him, as Jack did, at least a full sixteen years of age, and likely would have assumed him to be older. Only the boyishness of his face gave any indication he might be younger. Still with eyes closed, he stretched slightly and his chest, arm and legs muscles rippled. I am not prone to blushing, but I did at that moment, and hurried on towards the kitchen. Gavin had not opened his eyes, and so I hoped he had not even been aware of my presence.

I was sitting down to eat when the boy—and despite the physical evidence I must remember he *was* a boy—joined me, now dressed appropriately. His parents had expected him to sleep at the sanitarium and so had packed him clothes. I offered him breakfast, which he partook of eagerly and with a surprising appetite. He spoke around mouthfuls of food.

"M'always famished in the morning, yeah?"

"Growing boys, and all that."

"'Struth, but no one else I know eats as much at each meal. 'Slike I burn through it faster than anyone else."

"Perhaps a function of your enhanced strength. I've been trying to think of who we can ask for advice about that. It seems outside of Watson's bailiwick, and not really in Carnacki's either, to take things from opposite ends of the investigative spectrum. I don't know if Sâr Dubnotal is in Cheyne Walk these days, he'd probably be the best to consult. Of course there's always Van Helsing if we can get in touch with him." I looked up to see that the boy had stopped eating and turned somewhat pale. "Food not settling well?"

"No, it's very good, milord. I'm sorry. I just... You mentioned Van Helsing and I felt a tightening around my heart and a sudden fear. Please, let's not involve him in this. I think... I think the associations imparted from the Bloofer Lady's bite are too strong with regards to him, yeah?"

"But Lucy adored Van Helsing, and trusted him."

"The human Lucy did, yeah, and I can sense that underneath. But the vampire Lucy hated Van Helsing, didn't she, for his knowledge and the potential to send her to the final death... which he did, through you."

That statement tightened my own heart, and brought back visions from two nights ago, and the Dream-Lucy's repetitions that I never loved her. My own nearly-finished breakfast looked less palatable.

"Well, then, I'll tell Jack we shouldn't involve the old man. We'll see what other help we can come up with. I have cleared my calendar. What would you like to do today?"

The boy rose from his chair, and came around behind me. He draped his arms over my shoulders and brought his lips close to my ear. I shuddered much as Jack did in my arms last night.

"I want to be with you the way she would have been," he whispered. It was the most erotic sensation, and I thrilled in it for a moment. He did not at all sound like Lucy, his voice was too deep, but I felt her behind me anyway. I allowed my head to loll back and he kissed my ear, slipped a hand down the front of my pants. And then he slid his lips from my ear to my neck. Kissed gently, and then more firmly.

And then he roughly bit at my neck, as if trying to break the skin and draw blood.

My eyes flew open and all sense of desire vanished as quickly as it had come. I pushed the chair back and threw myself into a standing position, almost toppling the boy. I clasped my hand to my scraped neck; no blood had been drawn, but the pressure of his lips and teeth would leave a bruise.

"Never do that again!" My voice was harsher, more ragged than I'd expected it to be. "You know better than anyone what a bite to the neck means to someone like myself or Jack. Never play at that again!"

"I'm sorry, milord." Gavin seemed to have come back to his senses, a blush on his cheeks. He wrapped his arms around himself in embarrassed self-awareness, kept his eyes downcast... but I noticed the front of his trousers was still clearly distended. "I didn't mean, didn't know it would upset you so. I thought it would remind you of her."

"It did, boy." I brought my voice as close to a normal tone as I could manage. "It did. Just in the wrong way." I shook my head. "And I'm sorry if anything I've said since we met has misled you. Jack and I love each other and no-one else. We are not interested in teaching you what to do in bed. Do not make such overtures again."

"I am truly sorry, sir." His words were apologetic and believable, but when he looked up at me there was still a hint of arousal and perhaps even aggression in his eyes. "I do hope you won't have Doctor Seward send me home. Even if we never mention this again, there is still the issue of how to handle my parents' acceptance of me."

"Apology accepted, and of course you are not being sent home prematurely. But perhaps we should walk to Jack's office and discuss this..."

"Can't we wait 'til he comes home, sir? Discuss it over dinner? I'm sure there's plenty else you can teach me in the meantime."

Against my better judgment, I agreed to delay talking to Jack. We settled on a walk to the park to clear our heads and get some fresh air. Perhaps I'll direct us past Carnacki and the Sar Dubnotal's residences and suggest calling on one or both. Either way, I shall try to put my unease with this morning's events behind me and enjoy the day.

Doctor Seward's Journal—22 September

I woke well before sunrise with one clear thought in my head: Gavin may have been the oldest of Lucy's victims, but he was not the only victim. Were any of the others exhibiting the same early development? The answer to this question, I thought, might give us insight into Gavin's preternatural strength. Arthur's arm was draped across me as he lay on his side, his face as peaceful now as it had been anguished just two nights ago. He was aging gracefully, far more gracefully than I. I could easily see why a boy like Gavin would be attracted to Arthur; I saw it whenever we walked down the street together, the handsome, well-proportioned Lord Godalming and his gaunt, too-tall physician friend.

I sat at my desk with the accumulated paperwork of our ordeal from ten years ago. We had not turned everything over to Stoker; in fact, we'd only given him copies. And just as most indications of the relationship between myself, Arthur and Quincey had been removed, so had the personal information of Lucy's young victims. Articles about The Bloofer Lady were included, but carefully edited so that the families themselves would not be able to harass Mister Stoker. In fact, to my knowledge, the families considered Stoker to have simply taken their own ordeal and come up with a fantastic explanation for still-unexplained crimes. But I had retained the documentation, just in case we were ever confronted over it.

I opened the file that held everything related to Lucy's brief time as a vampire. Five attacks in all, with Gavin Stratton being the oldest and the child rescued from behind a grave by Van Helsing on the night he first tried to convince me of Lucy's fate being the youngest. So few, and none killed or turned as poor Lucy was, thank God.

I studied the pictures and read the articles. And then I placed one phone call. Not to the Harkers or Van Helsing, but to our neighbor, Sâr Dubnotal. If anyone could track these other four children down and learn, surreptitiously, whether they'd exhibited the same advanced development and extra strength which Gavin possessed, it was he. And then it became a waiting game. I considered returning home, but decided it would be best to attend to my duties at the sanitarium so as to hopefully free up the rest of my day. Reynolds reported that all had been calm throughout the night and into the morning. I breathed a little easier knowing that; when Dracula first came among us, a patient of mine was his harbinger and I admit part of me had been dreading a repeat of that series of events. Silly, to be sure.

I returned to my office to find Reynolds pacing anxiously.

"Doctor Seward, there's a man to see you…" He trailed off.

"Dressed somewhat unusually? A sensible shirt and pants under a flowing knee-length coat, an Indian turban wound around his head and a garish floral sash around his waist?"

"How did you…?"

"He's a neighbor. I've been expecting him. Send him in, please."

Reynolds looked vaguely unhappy opening the office door to the Sâr, but he said nothing more, shutting the door behind him as he went. Dubnotal nodded at me.

"Good to make your acquaintance in person once again," I began.

"Or perhaps not, my good Doctor Seward. Not under these circumstances."

In person, the man was imposing. Taller than I, but stockier as well. I could not tell if the clothes he wore made him seem larger than he really was. The turban was clearly intended to add height, and the colorful sash at his waist drew the eyes away from his face. It seemed to sway a bit of its own accord in the still air of my office. Or I could have imagined that. His eyes focused on me, and I readily admit I feared the worst. I all but sunk into my desk chair.

"What have you found?" I managed to ask without my voice breaking.

"These four children you asked me to investigate appear to be perfectly normal for their age. No, I did not approach them, but kept my distance and cast such spells that check for health and any sign of encroaching supernatural possession. I then tested their strength by conjuring a wraith of a child larger than their own size to run directly into each child as though in a rush and not seeing them in his path. Each time, the child pushed the wraith off with no more than the usual strength."

"From a distance, how could you possibly...?"

"I bound my own sense into the wraith, so that I could see, smell, hear and feel all it did. Dangerous, but I had my own man standing by in case I should be startled and have my persona sucked into the wraith. It did not come to that. In fact the youngest of the children could not push the wraith off at all. That was a touchy moment; the wraith collapsed onto the boy, and were I not in full control of it, it would have tried to possess the child. I forced the wraith off the boy and to a standing position, but dared not force it to help the boy to his feet. By then, a rather imposing and very irate governess had materialized and I forced the wraith to run off and then discorporate so I could draw my full senses back into myself."

"And this... wraith... will not be a further problem to us? Or the children it spied on for you?" I had not meant to...

"The children are not in any danger from the wraith now that I have banished it. Had I approached the children as myself, I would not have learned all I did. Through the wraith's enhanced senses, I was able to sense something mortal eyes would not have been able to see on such a cold day, with the children so bundled up against the chill."

"Did they all...?"

"Yes. To a one, they still bear the slight tears at their throat from your late Miss Westenra, as does your young Gavin Stratton. But they do not have the advanced development the young man has, nor could I sense any potential to develop in that way from any of them."

"I am forced, then, to turn to a new question." I steepled my fingers in front of me, as I understand Holmes is wont to do. An affectation, but it gave me something to focus on other than Dubnotal's hypnotic waist sash and piercing eyes. "What was it about the attack on Gavin that was different from the others? There had to be something different, something not recorded in the papers."

"All of the children told the same story, you say?" I chanced a look up and saw the light of new curiosity burning in Dubnotal's eyes, and I recognized it. Like Quincey, Holmes and Carnacki, the man enjoyed a challenge.

"Yes. Beautiful lady in white lured the child to a secluded place, held them lovingly like a parent, bit their neck, suckled, let them go. What was different about Gavin that wasn't reported in the paper?"

We pored over the old articles together, adding the new information from Dubnotal's investigations into a fresh notebook. We looked for something, anything, which might point us in a valid direction for further investigation either of the natural or supernatural kind. The Sâr kept his calm demeanor; I imagined I could feel the crackle of supernatural energy wash over me every time he passed near. I was on the verge of slamming my hands on the table and screaming in exasperation when Reynolds knocked at the door. He usually came in without waiting for a reply, but this time only stuck his head in through the slightest crack of the open door. Dubnotal made Reynolds even more nervous than myself.

"Sorry, Doctor. Missus Stratton here to see you."

"They can't expect results already," I muttered.

"No, sir. It's her alone. She says she has additional information for you. And she seems to be quite distraught, if you ask me." He spared a glance at my gaudily-garbed visitor. I understood his concern.

"Would you mind terribly?" I gestured to the bathroom door. "I don't think Mrs. Stratton's nerves will be calmed by your presence." I am not completely certain that I saw a smile flit across the Psychagogue's lips.

"Understood. I shall extend my senses invisibly into the room to overhear your conversation, on chance it may give us further avenues of exploration."

And with that, he whisked into the bathroom and the door shut with a quiet click.

I sighed, closed the files and tucked them off to a side of my desk, and nodded at Reynolds. He shut the door and returned a moment later to usher Gavin's mother through.

He was correct. She was wringing her hands around her purse strings, and although dry now, her face had the puffy look of someone who'd recently been crying.

"Please, sit down," I gestured to the same chair she'd used yesterday. "Tell me what's wrong."

"If my husband knew I was here..." she started, and then shook her head. "But that is part of the problem, isn't it? If he was around today for me to tell

71

this to, either he'd be here himself or he'd be at your residence confronting Gavin."

I blanched slightly; the thought that the news she bore was any type of accusation about Arthur's and my relationship or inference that I'd taken Gavin home for any but the most altruistic reason immediately sprang to mind. What else might have caused her husband to go to our home to confront his son?

"Where is your husband?" I asked carefully.

"I don't rightly know, sir. And that is part of the problem. He went out last night, after the boys... our younger boys, that is, were in bed. It is not an unusual thing for him to do, going for long walks in the night air, and so I went to sleep not thinking anything of the fact that he was not home yet. I locked the doors, knowing he had his key. He was not home when I awoke, and has not come home since."

"Have you alerted the police?"

"I have not yet. I should, but I fear..."

I waited out her pause.

"I fear Gavin has done him some harm."

"He was in my home last night, as you know." Again, I tried to tread carefully. "Why would you think your son had done harm to your husband?"

"Because Gavin was in our home last night, doctor. He was in his middle brother's room."

"If you were asleep, how do you know he was there?" I kept the incredulous tone from my voice.

"Charles reported it to me when I woke."

"A nightmare, perhaps? You told me Gavin had shown aggression towards his brothers."

"A nightmare would not leave a permanent mark on Charles' face, doctor."

"What kind of mark?"

"The very same as the ring my husband gave my older son when we departed your office yesterday."

"You are saying your oldest son did some harm to your husband, gained access to the house, injured your middle son, and that you have not gone to the police yet?" Now I let some incredulity creep into my voice. "Most people would have."

"I have not for two reasons, doctor. The first is respect for you and Lord Godalming. Think what you might of my husband and myself, I am no fool. I know my son, as long as he lives, will prefer the company of men. A mother knows her son, sir. And a mother can recognize when others share the personality traits of her children. I would not see you brought up on charges of perversion and pederasty unnecessarily. You deserve to live as you'd like. So does my son."

"I... thank you." I nodded at her. We had an understanding, it would seem. "And your second reason?"

"If Gavin is capable of murdering my husband, then the police are not equipped to handle him anyway. But perhaps you are."

"I fear you underestimate our police. Or that you overestimate me."

"My son is not the only member of our family who has read Mister Stoker's book, doctor. I doubted the truth of it when I read it, and thought Mister Stoker had simply capitalized on a number of easily verifiable events by fleshing out a connection between them. But today, I am convinced that it was not just some beautiful lady who harmed my son ten years ago. My husband's disappearance, my middle son's injury by having a ring pressed so hard into his face to leave a permanent scar but done without waking him... Gavin may not be a vampire, doctor, but something unusual is at work here. I want Gavin stopped before my other sons die."

Her voice had risen along with the speed of her words. She had in a short time worked herself into a frenzy. I sat next to her and held her hands while tears flowed, and then when I judged she was calmer I continued the conversation.

"Is there anything you can tell me about the night Gavin was bitten? Anything you didn't reveal at the time?"

"Yes." She sniffed and nodded. "We didn't think it important at the time. We'd already cleaned him up, you see, before we called the police. Well, what parent wouldn't?"

"Cleaned him of what," I prompted.

"The blood. We thought he'd split his lip or was bleeding from his gums. It was all over his lips and chin, what else would we think? And then once he was clean and we realized he wasn't bleeding from anywhere, we noticed the tears at his throat like some small animal had bitten him, and so we called the police." I froze at her words, and she felt it through my grip on her hands. "What's wrong, doctor?"

"I should have realized. It's so obvious."

"What is?"

"You read Stoker's book. You believe it now?"

"As I've said."

"What happened to Mina Harker when Dracula came to her in my asylum in Whitby. He drank her blood, yes... but he also made her drink of his."

"My god... then my son..."

"Lucy must have done the same to Gavin. But why him, and not any of the other children?" I jumped up. "So much time wasted poring over old photos. I should have just rung around to you and asked. We have to get to my house. Reynolds!" He must have been just outside the door, his response was so quick. "I need to get home immediately. Call a hansom." Reynolds was out the door as fast as he'd been in.

"And what of me, doctor?" Mistress Stratton remained seated.

"You must come with me. There is no guarantee, but perhaps some part of Gavin will still respond to your presence. We must stop him killing Arthur."

"And if not, then I will stop him."

Mrs. Stratton's head swung past me at the new voice. Her eyes went wide and a paleness came to her cheeks. I steadied her, but she did not seem ready to faint.

"Who are you?" She demanded.

"I am Sâr Dubnotal, Madame. Some call me tGreat Psychagogue, or El Tabib. And if my powers cannot save your son, nothing can."

Arthur Holmwood's Diary—22 September

It is almost all a blur, but here is what I recall.

I left the dining table for my room, to change into suitable outdoor clothing for our walk. I was half-dressed when Gavin blithely opened my door and walked in. He'd removed his shirt again, and the buttons on his trousers were undone. He shut the door behind him. And locked it. I backed up towards the windows.

"Young man, turn around and leave now. This is beyond unacceptable."

My words had no effect. He continued towards me, the hint of aggression and arousal now both fully enflamed. He backed me up against the window drapes, still shut from last night. I felt the fabric against my back, and behind that the glass. I briefly wondered if I could manage to break the thick glass and tumble out, even though the fall would likely do severe damage from this height. And then Gavin was on me, one hand tangling in my hair to hold my head steady, his tongue forcing past my lips. And God help me, my body reacted. I did not want this, but I could not move away. I'd felt this before. The night the vampire Lucy tried to seduce me outside her mausoleum.

And then I stopped thinking as Gavin yanked my head back by the hair and rammed his open mouth against my exposed neck, chewing at the skin. I groaned and started to black out. My last conscious thought was that this boy was not a vampire and possessed no healing element to his saliva; if he chewed through my skin, I would bleed to death.

Doctor Seward's Journal—22 September

We arrived at the house as fast as possible. Sâr Dubnotal and Mistress Stratton followed me out of the cab and up to the front door. I knew something was wrong even as we walked up the path; a feeling made me look up and I could see that the bedroom drapery was still shut. Then I saw movement, like something heavy pressed against the drapes.

No time for propriety. I jammed my key into the front door lock and had it open even as I shouted Arthur's name. There was no sense in being stealthy. If he was here, Gavin's hearing had already warned him we had approached. I had to hope he was so absorbed in stalking Arthur that he didn't pay attention to what his heightened senses might relay.

The Sâr was already starting for the staircase.

I grabbed a metal fireplace poker from the hearth in the hall and bounded up the steps, passing the larger man easily. A very startled cleaning maid came from the parlor at the noise. Mistress Stratton stayed long enough to tell her to stay out of the way no matter what she heard from upstairs.

I didn't bother checking if the bedroom door was locked. I kicked at the knob and the door cracked open.

Arthur was pinned against the drapes and even from this distance I could see the bruise across his neck. Gavin had clearly been chewing on it. The boy was on his knees, holding Arthur against the window with one hand firmly on his chest while the other held...

I ran at the boy, grabbed him by the hair and yanked. He lost balance and tumbled backwards, losing his grip on Arthur, who slumped forward. Instinct caused me to drop the poker and grab Arthur with both hands, altering his forward momentum so that he stumbled towards the bed rather than falling on top of Gavin.

That distraction could have cost my life. Gavin seized the poker and threw himself into a standing position, swinging at me as he did so. I sidestepped, but only barely, and had to let go of Arthur to do so. He was still too far from the bed and landed hard on the floor, where he lay unmoving. Not as far out of the way as I'd hoped, but I had no time to worry about that as Gavin brought the poker back for another swing. If I tried to block it, the poker's momentum would break my arm. Now that he was aware of me and not distracted, I had lost the upper hand.

He swung the poker a second time, but before it had described half of the intended arc, it flew from his hands and smashed against the opposite wall. Dubnotal stood on the threshold. He had just levitated the poker out of the boy's preternatural grip!

I threw myself prostrate under the arc of its path and tackled Gavin around the thighs. For the second time, I budged him. Strength does not equal balance, after all. He pitched forward over me and landed hard on my back, as I should have expected he would. I had avoided death by poker, but the boy was now in a position to do me great injury simply by punching. He could even kill me from this position.

"Gavin! Stop!"

Mistress Stratton had finally made it to the room. Her voice was calm but forceful. And somehow, it got his attention. I felt him scramble off of me and when the weight lifted I rolled over. He stood at the foot of the bed, between myself and his mother. The Sâr stood behind her in the doorway, still gesturing and murmuring to himself.

"Mother, what… why are you here? Shouldn't you be home?" He sounded genuinely confused, as he'd sounded in my office yesterday afternoon, although the muscles in his back tensed as if he were ready to spring at any moment. I made eye contact with his mother, and saw that she knew he was not as calm as he sounded.

"I'm here because of you, Gavin. I know you came home last night."

"I… no, that's not right. I was here. Sleeping."

"You left a mark on your brother's face. Your father's ring. You wanted us to know you'd been home."

"Why, why would I want to…?"

"You're sick, Gavin. You need Doctor Seward's help, and that of this man behind me."

"That's what I'm here for, you stupid cow!" He moved so fast, to the side of us, grabbing the poker up and starting towards her. I launched myself at his back, intending to tackle him around the waist this time, but some force stopped my forward momentum. His mother seemed to float swiftly out of the way at Gavin moved towards her, and the boy found himself facing Sâr Dubnotal.

"I bind you, young man, with all the powers at my command." The Sâr's eyes blazed, all intention focused on Gavin. "You will stop. You will not move."

For a second, Gavin faltered, his own eyes locked with the Sâr. The boy's body tensed further, as if he were pushing more successfully against the same force that had checked my second attempt at a tackle.

"N…noo…" The boy started to speak; Dubnotal's eyes widened almost imperceptibly at the boy's resistance.

"You will not move while I cleanse this nosferatu's taint from your soul."

The wrong words, delivered in a voice so deep and chilling, to the wrong person. Gavin pushed harder, and the Sâr's hypnotic force wavered ever so slightly. Enough for Gavin's pent-up energy to propel him forward, towards Dubnotal and past him into the hall.

The boy again slashed the poker in a wide arc, but at waist level. I am not completely sure Dubnotal's sash did not leap of its own accord to defend its wearer. Regardless, the poker became tangled in it and was pulled free from the boy's hand as he stumbled past the Sâr to make an escape.

Madame Stratton screamed her son's name from where she, as I, remained immobilized.

Dubnotal grabbed at the boy, his first attempt at physical contact, but not quite fast enough. Gavin's head smacked into the far wall and I saw some of the strength leave his body. The poker clattered to the floor as Dubnotal strode into the hall to tower over the boy. He grabbed a handful of hair and pulled hard, eliciting a sharp gasp from Gavin.

"Wrong, wrong, it's all gone wrong," the boy groaned.

"It was never right for you, poor boy." The Sâr kept a strong grip on his hair with one hand, and pinned his right wrist behind him with the other.

"Ever since you drank Lucy's blood," I called out to him. "You did, didn't you?"

"Yes," he groaned with his face in the carpet. "Yes. She had me in her arms after she'd drawn my blood. I squirmed to get loose, and she wouldn't let go. So I bit her breast, hard enough to break skin. She gasped and just held me tighter, like I was a suckling newborn. Then she dropped me and disappeared. I never saw her again, but I felt her. All through that week, and right up to when her husband stabbed her through the heart and let that old man take her head!"

With fresh anger he tried to push Dubnotal off again. He might have succeeded against me or his mother, but the Sâr had now regained his composure and control; that invisible telepathic force ground against the back of Gavin's head. I am sure it hurt. I am also sure the boy didn't notice.

"When young Madame Westenra was granted the final death by Lord Godalming, her connection with you should have severed," Dubnotal intoned. "As Mrs. Harker's did when Dracula perished."

"Are you sure?" Gavin managed to gasp out from under Dubnotal's psychic control. His voice gained some strength. "You weren't there! How do you know Mina's connection to Dracula, the gifts her gave her, completely disappeared? Because mine didn't! I couldn't feel the Bloofer Lady in my head anymore, yeah, but I still had the strength, and the urge to bite. That's never gone away. I didn't understand where she'd gone at first, and not for a long time. I didn't even know what her name really was. Until I found Stoker's book in my father's bookshelf and was drawn to read it. And then I understood." Even under Dubnotal's control, Gavin managed to turn his head towards me, his eyes blazing hatred. "Understood that the two of you were responsible for taking her from me. And I knew I had to kill you!"

He pushed up again, to no avail this time. Dubnotal was ready for him. But the extra energy required to keep Gavin down meant that the Sâr had to loose his control over myself and Mrs. Stratton. She tumbled forward and again my concern for someone else took over. I reached out to her as Gavin pushed up against Dubnotal's control with both abdomen and pelvis this time, undulating in a way I'd never seen a human body do so before. My stomach lurched at the unnatural contortions he was attempting, and I felt myself falter under Mrs. Stratton's sudden weight. I was sure I would drag us both to the floor.

I needn't have worried. Strong arms grabbed me and held me up, as I held up Mrs. Stratton. I glanced behind to see Arthur, shirtless, disheveled, bleeding and bruised Arthur, holding me. Never had I been so happy to see that world-weary expression.

"You're alive. When you collapsed, I thought…"

"Stop thinking." He turned me in his arms, and kissed me. And I kissed back. Until a soft cough interrupted us.

Mistress Stratton held one arm limply against her chest. Dubnotal still stood over Gavin in the hall.

"Don't you think we should take care of my son before you celebrate victory?"

Arthur Holmwood's Diary—28 September

As we watched, Sâr Dubnotal worked his magics: gesturing in arcane sweeps with his hands, using telepathy to keep the boy pinned to the floor while other magics pulled The Bloofer Lady's... Lucy's... tainted, venomous blood from the boy's body.

Was it really blood we were seeing, beading on the boy's skin and dancing droplets into the air, to be collected in a small ball of red that absorbed itself into the jeweled cravat that held the Sâr's broad tie in place? I cannot say. Perhaps it was just a colorful ectoplasmic manifestation and not actual blood. Either way, as the red drops merged, the boy's energy lessened. His eyes rolled into his head and his mother tried to move to comfort him, but Dubnotal's power kept us back until his work was done.

Finally, the boy slackened against the floor, eyes closed and breathing lightly. Only then did the Sâr allow the mother to go to the son. He gestured at us with only his eyes, and we followed him down the stairs. He said no more than was necessary as we stood in the foyer.

"I believe I have removed all of the vampire's taint from the boy's body. Still, he cannot be trusted among his family or the general public."

"I'm sure his mother will agree. We will come up with a suitable story," Jack responded.

"I will come to observe the boy when I can. You must contact me immediately if he shows signs of returning strength or any other odd behavior. I am as certain as I can be that this is over, but even those only slightly touched by the undead are difficult to cleanse perfectly."

And with that, he was gone. I am sure he used some manner of hypnosis, one of his specialties, to disappear from our midst without use of our door, but perhaps he teleported. Someday, I should like to ask Van Helsing, or Carnacki, what they think of this Sâr Dubnotal...

What a nightmarish pair of days. Reality was far more horrible than the dream of the 20th.

We have successfully incarcerated Gavin Stratton in Jack's sanitarium. His mother signed the papers quickly and with no fuss. The police were not involved except peripherally. As there was some explanation needed for the committal, Mrs. Stratton produced her middle son and showed the horrible mark left by the ring on the boy's face. Jack and our physician friend, Dr. Watson, both testified that the mark could only have been made deliberately, with just the right amount of pressure to temporarily scar the boy without waking him.

Mister Stratton also testified that he'd been attacked in an alley during his night walk, that the assailant had taken him by surprise, knocked him out with a solid punch and left him for dead. The tear along his cheek which had bled profusely and now puckered with infection was clearly the work of that same ring. The younger Stratton's scar will fade, but the father's face will never be unblemished again. These testimonies added to the previous instances of aggression against his siblings were enough to put the boy in Jack's care permanently. The rumor is that the boy had become involved with mind-altering drugs that somehow enhanced his strength. If anyone has made the connection between Gavin and Lucy and myself and Jack, they have not mentioned it to the press. We have also agreed to make no mention of the Sar Dubnotal's involvement, for the nonce.

The ring was returned to Stratton, but I noticed when we had the family over for dinner last night that the middle son, Charles, is now wearing it.

"Why not do away with the ring?" I asked. "It must now contain such horrible memories."

"That's precisely the reason to keep it," Mister Stratton answered. "A reminder that our family must always face our demons rather than ignoring them. As we should have done from the beginning with Gavin."

I have not been to see the boy since he was removed from our house. Jack sees him every day, and his mother visits, as does Sâr Dubnotal when he is here and not abroad. They say the boy's moods run from one extreme to the other, much as Renfield's did. I am saddened that even a decade later, Dracula still shadows us and affects our lives. But at least Jack and I have survived.

Our previous volume of Tales of the Shadowmen *contained a number of stories centered on the theme of the legendary treasure of that criminal brotherhood known as the Black Coats. Matthew Dennion ended up submitting two tales on that very topic, and this is the second one. It features a clash between two powerful, legendary personages who, on one dark night, met on the shores of Romney Marsh...*

Matthew Dennion: *He Who Laughs Last*

Romney Marsh, 1777

An ominous laugh echoed over the ocean as the two smugglers rowed their boat to shore. A storm was approaching, blacking out the moonlight. The night was completely dark and the men could barely see the fire set on shore to guide them to dry land. The laugh sounded far too close to their rowboat to have come from the shore, but with the night as murky as it was, they could not tell if another rowboat was more than a few strokes away from them.

The deep laugh sounded again and a shiver of fear ran through both men. As members of the Gentlemen of the Night, they were not scared easily, but when a laugh comes from the dark ocean, even they were given pause. The two men doubled their efforts to reach their comrades on shore, when their rowboat was struck by something in the water.

The smuggler in the front of the boat watched as a powerful arm wrapped itself around his cohort's neck. The smuggler's eyes went wide as his supply of air was cut off. Those same eyes bulged as a knife was slid into the man's heart. The assailant waited a moment for the last drop of life to slip from the smuggler before tossing his corpse overboard. The second smuggler screamed in terror as he finally saw what had just murdered his shipmate. The Moon slipped through the clouds briefly to illuminate the ghastly form of a Scarecrow dressed in tattered black rags with a ghostly white face.

The smuggler shrieked as the Scarecrow crawled across the boat toward him. The smuggler reached for his pistol. But his hand did not touch the hilt before the Scarecrow's knife had slit his throat.

While the man breathed his last, the Scarecrow leaned into his face:

"Did you think I wouldn't know what you were bringing here tonight? Nothing is smuggled into Romney Marsh without my knowledge."

The last thing the smuggler heard was the Scarecrow's eerie laugh.

The Scarecrow dumped the second body overboard as the Moon receded behind the storm clouds once more. He grabbed the oars of the rowboat and directed it further down the beach, leaving his own empty boat to drift in the water. Neither the people on shore, nor the main ship, would be able to follow his movements with the approaching storm. The treasure inside the boat was his.

The Scarecrow pulled the rowboat ashore down the beach far from the scene of his attack. Using his knife, he pried upon the treasure chest he had just obtained. He then stared at his newly-acquired prize with a sense of elation. With the treasure he had just stolen, he knew that his life, and those of his congregation, would change forever. The value of the chest was more than enough to disburse amongst his followers and keep them comfortable for years to come. No longer would they need to smuggle in goods to support themselves, and no longer would the Scarecrow be needed to protect them. He could retire and live the simple life of a vicar, and he could at last give his beloved Charlotte the life she deserved.

Suddenly, from the reeds on the beach, he heard a horse approaching. As it made its way through the marsh, he heard a man clapping and laughing. When the horse finally emerged from the reeds, the Scarecrow made out its rider.

The man stopped the horse just short of the treasure chest.

"Bravo, Bravo! I see the legend of the Scarecrow of Romney Marsh was not over exaggerated! Tracking you through that dark cover was not an easy task. Outside of myself, I doubt there are a handful of men in all of Europe who could have done so"

The Scarecrow shifted his knife into a throwing position.

"I warn you, sir, I can drive this knife right through your heart from this distance. I suggest you ride off with your life while you still have the opportunity to do so."

"Killing me would not be in your best interests, Dr. Syn," said the rider, dismounting.

The Scarecrow found himself facing a tall man in his forties, with dark, burning eyes and long, black hair, dressed in a style of clothing more often encountered in Italy

"My dear man, you have me confused with someone else," replied the Scarecrow, laughing.

"No, Dr. Syn, I do not," said the newcomer, shaking his head. "Please allow me to introduce myself: I am Colonel Bozzo-Corona, the leader of the organization known as the Brotherhood of Mercy, or, in your country, Gentlemen of the Night. You are Dr. Christopher Syn, as well as Captain Clegg and the Scarecrow. Your smuggling operation impressed me to the point of offering you membership in our Brotherhood. Consider my surprise when I looked into the Scarecrow and found he was not only a smuggler, but also a pirate and even a vicar! A few name changes and a costume of rags is easy to sift through for a man of my resources. When I consider offering a membership in our organization, I endeavor to learn all there is to know about our would-be future brother.

You, however, turned out not to be a true criminal, but a holy man acting like one in order to assist his congregation..."

The Scarecrow paused for a moment as he realized this Colonel knew his multi-layered history.

"Knowledge of my past is useless to a dead man," he finally said.

"This is true," replied the Colonel, smiling, "but knowledge of your present is of infinite value to a man who commands an intricate organization like mine. The political climate in France is too tenuous for me to leave my treasure there. As you know, Romney Marsh presents an excellent location to smuggle goods into England. Yet, in choosing this location to smuggle in this chest, I would have been foolish not to construct a contingency plan to deal with the likely interference from the Scarecrow. If I do not reach my destination by sunrise, with this chest, members of my organization will open written instructions which I left for them. Those instructions include turning over evidence of one Mr. Mipps and one Jimmie Bone as smugglers for the Scarecrow. They also include evidence pointing to one Christopher Syn as being the Scarecrow. The law will do my work for me and hunt you down. My organization also has plans for the lovely Charlotte once you are out of the picture..."

The Scarecrow looked down at the box that mere moments ago held the power to end his life of hiding in marshes, fighting soldiers, and running from the law.

He opened the lid to take one last look at the gold inside—the dream he had held for the briefest of moments. Freedom from his current life would not be a life at all with his friends in prison and Charlotte in a living hell. The Scarecrow threw his knife past the Colonel's head and stared at him for a moment. He then climbed into the rowboat and headed into the water.

The Colonel stepped forward, peered down into the treasure chest that would ensure his position of power for centuries to come and laughed.

More vampires await us in this story by Brian Gallagher, yet another new contributor to our series. Brian's tale is a smorgasbord of vampiric lore, featuring not only Count Dracula, but two other powerful Undead: Marie Nizet's Captain Liatoukine, from the ground-breaking novel Captain Vampire, *published by Black Coat Press, and previously seen in Matthew Baugh's opening tale; and Nosferatu's Count Orlok. The feud between the two is portrayed against the superb background of Paul Féval's remarkable* Vampire City...

Brian Gallagher: *City of the Nosferatu*

Transylvania, 1830

The journey from Vienna to Transylvania had been straightforward, pleasant even, Boris Liatoukine thought. This diversion to see the Count was a minor delay, but a necessary one. Count Dracula was not a figure to be ignored in a matter as delicate as that which was to be discussed.

They were high up in Dracula's castle, overlooking the Borgo pass, sitting opposite each other over a table. It was night, Dracula's preferred time. Liatoukine knew that the Count could exist in the day—just as he himself could. However, Dracula's powers were far greater at night. Far more than his own, in fact—which was perhaps the point of making him wait until darkness fell to see him.

The Count decided to sum up their conversation thus far.

"The Habsburg Emperor Francis in Vienna believes that vampires are infiltrating his Austrian empire? And your Tsar Nicholas as well?"

"Quite so," replied Liatoukine. "It's based on a number of incidents, usually involving a vampire being caught. More often than not, they seem to be influential members of society."

Dracula did not seem impressed by this.

"This is hardly new," he said. "I myself wield some authority here. And you too carry some small influence at the Imperial Court in St.Petersburg—despite being a mere Captain in the Russian Army." The unkind comment regarding Liatoukine's rank was delivered with a little smile.

Liatoukine knew it was best to ignore the remark; Dracula was not one to annoy or be trifled with. "It is the scale of incidents that concerns then; they are all too frequent," he replied. "Of course, some of us are captured and destroyed on occasion but..."

"*Us?*" inquired Dracula.

Liatoukine decided to choose his next words very carefully. It would not be wise to imply that the Count was just another vampire who might be destroyed by mere humans. His history was substantial for any one, human or vampire. Had he not studied at the Scholomance, where he'd learned the secrets of the Evil One himself?

"Forgive me, Count. I meant the vampires of the Sepulchre. They have long had their people in positions within human society. Their being caught from time to time does have the benefit of ensuring a certain degree of fear amongst the populace. There have never been enough incidents to provoke the authorities into action. Some even harbor doubts as to the existence of those like us."

"What, then, has changed? Why are the great powers starting to take the existence of vampires seriously?" asked the Count.

"Because the frequency of such incidents has recently multiplied. We know that the Sepulchre always have had their people hidden amongst the humans. So far, so good. But now, the Emperors seem to think that they are under threat. Their police have captured some minor vampires who were, frankly, just too careless. The large recruitment the Sepulchre appears to be indulging in is not providing the best quality of converts. From interrogation, scraps of information have emerged. The Sepulchre is being mentioned regularly. This only matches the rumors that the humans already knew—although they call the Vampire City, Selene. The Emperors are communicating with each other via their Royal families—this helps avoid any political issues. Action is underway in several countries: the Austrian Empire, Russia, the Ottoman Empire, France... even England."

"England?" said the Count. "I have an interest in that country"

"The Sepulchre has placed one or two of their people there in the past. A few years back, an expedition led by an Englishwoman to Selene led to chaos and the death of Otto Goetzi," said Liatoukine.

"I am aware of that incident. The Radcliffe woman was a remarkable individual. I am intrigued by a nation which can produce such a woman. Goetzi was a fool—how could he permit her and her associates to cross Europe to destroy him in his very lair? What she did in invading the Sepulchre was another factor that brought her country to my attention. The British are now of great interest to me, especially their science and their ambitions. They do not limit themselves to Europe. They fascinate me, because they are the future. Here," he gestured at the window to the country outside, "we are still backward and mired in superstition."

Liatoukine thought that perhaps the local superstition was not so backward, given who was residing in this very castle, but he kept the thought to himself.

The Count pondered, stroking his large moustache.

"I have little time for the Sepulchre's foolish games. I have my own dreams of the future in England. I do not wish to see them disrupting that country, or Central Europe, for that matter. Do they wish a full-blown war with the humans? Fools! What will they do when the Imperial armies stand outside Selene with their cannons? Yes, I know that the Sepulchre only exists in our reality for an hour every day, but do they think that no damage can be caused in that hour? Every day?"

Liatoukine nodded his agreement. The Count considered him, gazing at him with his red eyes.

"Pray, tell me… (they both smiled at the use of "pray") What precisely is your involvement in all this?"

It was time for Liatoukine to expose his own interests.

"The Tsar has been in touch with the other Monarchs in this matter. There have been certain incidents in St. Petersburg. Indeed, I myself had to swiftly execute a nobleman. There are many who fear me there. Some are even aware that I am not what I seem. This works to my advantage. A more mistrustful, ever fearful, atmosphere, however, could achieve the opposite and destroy all my efforts."

"For myself, I most certainly find fear to be useful," Dracula said.

Liatoukine ignored his remark and continued:

"Fortunately, the Tsar feels he can still rely on me in certain matters. I have been of use to him in the past, especially in the recent successful war we waged against your ancient enemies, the Turks. So he suggested that I should look into the matter, and see what should be done. I was dispatched to Vienna to discuss the 'vampire problem' with the Habsburg Emperor himself. The Austrians have a prisoner in their Croatian city of Zagreb, whom they are not even certain how to kill. I would speak with him, and then destroy him myself. Our position is especially perilous in the Austrian Empire, as such prisoners only increase the humans' knowledge of us."

"Even here, in Transylvania, I have become aware of the growth of these inferior vampires within the Austrian Empire," interrupted Dracula. "Lawyers, petty officials, and so on. Wisely, they have avoided all contacts with me, presumably believing that I am still unaware of their presence. However, they have not been widely detected by the humans. I assume this recent increase is due to the infiltration strategy by the Sepulchre that you mentioned earlier?"

"Yes, I suspect so," said Liatoukine. "The infiltration has been most intense in areas where our kind has traditionally been the strongest, such as the Magyar lands. My concern is that, if the humans are pushed, they will retaliate. We are powerful, but there are millions of them, and we are but thousands, if that. Hidden as we are, lurking in the shadows, our very existence denied by men of science—some in our employ—we thrive. The lower orders of life fear us as spectres of the night. But if we were to take over, resistance would quickly replace fear; we would be right in front of them—an open target. Using selected humans as our servants would no longer work; some of them are already being exposed. And as you said, human weapons could smash even our strongest holdouts."

85

Dracula rose and strode to the window, gazing out. He placed his hand on the stone wall, as if to reassure himself of his castle's strength. Tall, thin and pale, like many of his kind, he also had pointed ears and red eyes. Perhaps it was just as well that he was rarely seen outside his castle nowadays, thought Liatoukine.

"Yes, yes… this is so," said the Count at last. "Vienna thinks it rules here. They would no doubt muster their troops against me if they felt my existence was a threat to them. I would prevail. Nonetheless, it would be extremely inconvenient. However, I sense that you are not simply here for discussing the problem, Boris Liatoukine. You have other intentions in mind, don't you?"

"Indeed I have, my Lord Count," replied the Russian. "A name has occasionally been mentioned when the Austrians have interrogated the vampires they captured, prior to their destruction: Orlok. I believe I have heard the name before, always in relation to this region…"

"So you think I may be connected to all this?" asked Dracula.

"No, my Lord, not in the least. Your independence—as well as mine—from the Sepulchre is well known."

"Quite." Here Dracula started to almost look amused, "However, the name Orlok is indeed familiar to me, and it explains much. You may, in fact, be able to resolve matters far more easily than you might have thought…"

On horseback, Liatoukine approached Zagreb. What Dracula had told him was most useful indeed. He came to a military building in the center of town, where he knew he was expected. He was immediately taken to a commander named Sponsz. The soldier couldn't help but wonder about his visitor. How was it that this mysterious, tall, gaunt Russian with his strange burning eyes had been granted such liberties? He had been ordered to extend every courtesy to him, and tell him whatever he wanted to know. In his career, Sponsz had come across many strange things, but always kept quiet. His masters knew that he could be trusted.

"Tell me how your prisoner came to be in that cell?" inquired Liatoukine.

"Yes, sir," Sponsz began. He was unsure on how to address a Russian army nobleman and officer, but "Sir" seemed to evoke no rebuke, so he continued: "Baron Grando was captured at the home of one of the mayor's most trusted advisers, alone in his office. Horrifying cries and screams were heard. Some of the servants burst in to see the Baron drinking the adviser's blood from his wrist whilst holding him down by his neck.

"Given that the Baron is seventy, this was a considerable feat. In fact, it took ten men to overwhelm him. Six others were killed in the process. A lamp was knocked over, causing a fire. We made use of this to tell the public that there had been an accident and that the deceased were burned to death. The survivors, who had helped subdue the Baron, were only too glad to keep quiet."

Liatoukine nodded. He rather suspected that the fire was started later on, rather than being the result of a genuine accident, but kept silent.

"I understand that the Baron was injured?" he asked instead.

"Indeed, sir. A number of men tried to kill him. It is best that you see for yourself"

They headed downstairs, to a long corridor, along which there were doors leading to what clearly were cells. A number of these seemed to be made out of the same stone than the building. Clearly, no ordinary prisoners were kept here. They stopped at one such cell, which had its own guard standing outside. The guard opened a spyhole and checked on the prisoner. He confirmed that all was well. Sponsz, however, took a second look to make sure. With a little difficulty, the young guard opened the heavy stone door.

"You may wait outside," Liatoukine told Sponsz.

"I regret, sir, but I can't. The regulations say that if a dangerous prisoner is to be visited, there must be a soldier present."

Liatoukine did not know if this was true, but Vienna clearly wanted their man to report back on what would be said. *Very well*, he thought, *they have sealed their servant's fate.*

Liatoukine strode in, followed by Sponsz. The guard closed the door behind them. The cell was bare, without any natural light. There was what appeared to be a block of stone with a figure sitting on it. It was tied down to the stone by chains. On a table nearby, a lamp flickered. Sponsz went over to it and turned it up. The increased light provided more details of the figure. Thin and pale, the creature smiled at his visitors. To anyone else other than Liatoukine and Sponsz, this might have come as a surprise—if they had recovered from the shock of seeing a stake sticking from the man's chest, where his heart should be.

Liatoukine pointed to the stake.

"The men who overwhelmed the Baron attempted to destroy him by traditional means," explained Sponsz. "As you can see, it failed, but I thought it best to leave things the way they were."

Liatoukine also noticed several holes in the Baron's shirt that looked like bullet holes. Clearly, other methods of destruction had been tried, which had also proved unsuccessful. Not all vampires could be killed in the same way, although the stake was the most common method. The Russian was surprised they had not tried decapitation. Perhaps orders had already come through that the prisoner needed to be interrogated first.

"Come to see what cannot be killed?" sneered the Baron. "Another servant of that useless Emperor in Vienna?"

Liatoukine looked at him more closely. Grando seemed to shrink back. From that look, he had not only understood that the Russian Captain was a vampire, but also a powerful one. The Baron did not know how he knew. He just did.

"Are you here to free me, my lord?" he asked.

The sneering tone had gone. Sponsz picked up on this and shifted uneasily. Clearly, this Russian was of some significance.

Liatoukine ignored the question. He looked at the floor. There was a layer of ash on it. He crouched down, touched it, and sensed the remnants of departed vampire spirits.

"My Lord," said the Baron, "what you feel is what's left our kind—the ones killed over many years by the Austrians. They leave their ashes here to intimidate those of us they capture."

Clearly, the Austrians and their Croat subjects knew more about vampires than they'd let on, thought Liatoukine. Something to be remembered.

"*Our kind*? Does he mean, noblemen?" asked Sponsz, although his real suspicion was painted on his face.

Liatoukine turned to him. He grabbed him by the throat so he could not scream. He didn't bother answering the question. He stared deep into Sponsz's eyes. The Commander felt waves of terror flood through him. He could no longer move. He realized what was strange about the Russian's eyes: the pupils had turned into vertical slits, like a cat's!

Then, he could no longer think of anything. His heart had given out.

Liatoukine dropped him to the floor.

"That is how I dispose of people," he said.

Grando looked awestruck. "What of his blood?" he asked.

"His life-force is what I take. I do dislike having blood on my uniform." He went over to Grando and removed the stake. The hole started regenerating. "We must move fast to leave here…" He went to the chains and pulled at them. "This will take a few moments…" He grappled with the chains behind the Baron.

Grando was clearly pleased with these developments.

"Of course, you are obliged to help me. Vampire is loyal to vampire, vampire does not kill vampire! Not like the humans, who slaughter each other for no reason. They would have killed me if they could, but they couldn't find the right method…"

Liatoukine ignored his talk.

"Tell me," he said whilst seeming to grapple with the chains, "it is clear to me that you have only recently become one of us. I sense a familiarity about you, although we have not met before. Perhaps I am aware of the one who created you. Who is he?"

"It was Orlok, my lord, *Graf* Orlok."

Was the emphasis on the title of "Graf" supposed to impress him? Liatoukine thought? "Orlok!" he exclaimed. "A dear friend of mine. I have not seen him in many decades. I hear he has some new plans?"

"Yes, yes, my lord! He has plans to extend our influence into the Empire. He is selecting many of the more influential of us for his purpose. We will soon control the Empire and will not have to hide anymore. He has promised me that I will be a young man again."

And Orlok is doing all of this himself? From the Sepulchre?"

"Yes. From time to time, he visits certain cities, changes select people such as I, and then we carry on with his work in our areas. He intends Selene to become the capital of the new Empire. He has great ambitions for Russia, too, which is perhaps why you've heard of his plans?"

Liatoukine had heard enough; this confirmed what he already knew. Best to get onto the other reason why he was here. He noted that the hole in the Baron's chest had already healed. Good.

Liatoukine pulled a knife from inside his tunic and plunged it into the Baron's chest. There was a gasp from the uncomprehending nobleman. Then, the Russian Captain proceeded to cut out the Baron's heart.

"What are you doing?" cried the Baron.

Liatoukine ignored him. He never felt the need to explain himself to fools. Besides, time was a factor. The last thing he needed was for the guard outside to wonder what was going on, although he could hear nothing through the heavy door.

Once finished, he placed the heart in the small box he had brought in with him. Inside was a bottle of oil, which he poured over the heart. Lighting a small splinter, he set it alight. It burned with extreme intensely—the oil had special properties that made it so. Nothing was happening to Grando; sometimes the burning of the heart would destroy his kind of vampire. *No matter*, thought Liatoukine.

He placed the stake back into the Baron's body, where it had been previously, even though the hole was now rather larger. The utterly confused Baron piped up again.

"My lord, I am uncertain as to the meaning of all this. Why are you burning my heart?"

Was Grando really so ignorant? The oil had almost done its work. Since he had some time, he might as well enlighten this idiot, he thought.

"You are the kind of vampire whose heart, when burnt, provides a fine ash with certain properties—properties that are not present if you are ordinarily destroyed and reduced to ash"

"Properties, my Lord? I do not understand?"

Liatoukine looked inside the metal box. The oil had done its work. Carefully, he closed the airtight box. Then, with one swift blow, he decapitated Grando with his sword. The head spun in the air. Liatoukine caught it with one hand. The head pulled away from his hand and rested back on the body, re-attaching itself. No doubt, the Croats had attempted this method before then.

The Russian Captain had no particular idea on how this vampire could be killed, and no time to find out. His own powers would have to do. He took a gold coin from his pocket and smashed it into the Baron's skull. Half of it stuck out.

"My Lord, I must protest... this is no way to treat a fellow vampire! Graf Orlok will not be pleased! Vampire is loyal to vampire!"

Liatoukine just stared into the Baron's eyes, using the same power he had used on Sponsz earlier. The Baron was going to say something, but suddenly, his head started to decay. It turned into a skull. Liatoukine let it fall to the floor, with the gold coin still lodged into it. The body had similarly rotted away. He went over the chains that still restrained the body and now broke them effortlessly. Liatoukine kicked the Baron's skeleton, which further disintegrated into ashes, with the stake still in the middle of what was left of the ribcage.

Taking his sword off his belt, Liatoukine went to the heavy metal slot on the door and banged on it with the handle of his sword. The slot opened. Liatoukine shouted through it:

"Quickly, man! Open!"

With some effort, the door was duly opened and the guard from outside rushed in and looked in horror at the scene.

Liatoukine pointed at what was left of Grando with his sword. "You fools! The chains were not strong enough! The creature got free and attacked me. I could have been killed." He gestured towards Sponsz's body. "This one died in terror—his heart must have given out."

"How were you able to kill it?" the stunned guard asked.

Liatoukine pointed to the gold coin sticking out of the skull. "Gold, man, gold. To be pressed into the skull only. Are you people here not aware that some vampires can only be killed in this way?"

The guard shook his head. The humans needed an explanation for Baron Grando's death, and that gold nonsense was as good as any other. Orlok would no doubt sense the death of his minion, and may even suspect who was responsible, but he would not know for certain—let alone be able to prove it.

The Russian Captain left the cell, affecting to be in need of wine. He was, of course, full of energy, as always when he drained another vampire. What drivel had Orlok fed Grando? "Vampire is loyal to vampire, vampire does not kill vampire?" Indeed!

If the local Croat authorities doubted Liatoukine's story, they did not show it. In fact, the Russian Captain made great play of how he had been put at risk, and so on. He used his powers of influence just to make sure to be believed. He was further assisted in his task by the attitude of some officials who were only too glad that the Baron had been destroyed, and displayed their thanks in a most embarrassing manner. Liatoukine pretended to be mollified and instructed that the Emperor in Vienna should be told that this unfortunate outbreak of the "vampire plague" would be swiftly dealt with by Liatoukine himself.

The Austrians provided him with a military escort of four cavalrymen, led by a lieutenant, to the border between their empire and Serbia. They rode out of Zagreb and through the fertile lands of Slavonia. They stopped at a small town for a few hours of rest. Liatoukine made himself popular with his escort by treating them to free ale at a local inn. Whilst his escort was busy drinking, he saw to some business with a local smith, a task that he had not wished to have done in Zagreb, in order to avoid spying eyes. He needed some work done in order to help him make a certain point with the rulers of the Sepulchre, when he got there.

After a night's sleep, they arrived at Zemun, known as Semlin in German. It was the last stop before crossing the border, and then onward to the Sepulchre. Liatoukine had given some thought to simply going around the town in order to maintain the element of surprise when he would arrive at Selene's gates. However, if Orlok got wind of his coming, due to his spies—incompetent as they seemed to be—it would be best for Liatoukine to suggest that he was in no way afraid of the other vampire.

Zemun contained a number of discreet spies who had been working for the Sepulchre for many years due to its proximity to the Vampire City. These spies would soon report his arrival. Liatoukine considered that this news might, in fact, unsettle Orlok and, more importantly, other powers in the Sepulchre.

To make sure that his presence was known, the Russian Captain met with the mayor—calling it a courtesy call, as the Austrian cavalrymen were escorting a Russian officer on a diplomatic mission. A surprise early morning call for the mayor, pleasantries exchanged in his office, nothing more.

Liatoukine could not help but notice the occasional green tint on the window in the mayor's office. The Russian Captain knew well that this was a sign of vampiric infiltration—not surprising for a place with such strong connections with the Sepulchre. It confirmed that, beyond using human informers, there were also vampires here. Perhaps the mayor himself was one? This was reckless indeed. Human settlements around the Sepulchre had traditionally been left largely alone in order to prevent any unwanted attention. The humans certainly feared Selene, but such fears did not turn into any aggressive intent. If this had changed, Orlok's influence was indeed proving to be baleful.

Liatoukine also noticed that the cavalry lieutenant had glanced occasionally at the window. Further, he had noticed the use of languages amongst the men who comprised escort. German, of course, but they also spoke in Croatian, and the officer had betrayed his knowledge of Latin. Educated men... No doubt some among them might even know French, and perhaps Russian too? Clearly, these men were more than mere cavalry men in the service of the Emperor... Perhaps, they suspected his true nature? No matter. Today, they were allies, after a fashion. Nevertheless, it would be wise to remember this in the future.

They concluded their business and headed to the Serbian border. Soon, they reached it and came to a halt.

"This is where we must leave you, sir," said the lieutenant.

"Of course. I should be able to get to Belgrade to continue my mission without any difficulties," replied Liatoukine.

More to the point, he thought it was important that the secret of the Sepulchre be kept from these humans. He had, in fact, no intention of going to Belgrade, although he had arranged for Vienna to be told that he was.

After his escort had gone, Liatoukine moved across the border and rode towards Selene, eventually reaching its outskirts. The Vampire City, of course, was neither visible, nor tangible. Where it stood, all that could be seen was barren land, with dead trees and no life of any kind. It gave off a feeling of death and corruption. This was how humans were deterred from approaching it. The city somehow co-existed in the same space as that barren marsh, but on another plane of reality. As a vampire himself, he could enter either space, but he waited an hour or so until 11 a.m. for, at that time, Selene became visible for an hour to all.

It duly appeared on schedule, materializing slowly. A city of dark shapes, buildings at strange angles, and any such movements that could be seen inside were fleeing and disturbing to human eyes.

Liatoukine looked at the Vampire City. Some thought this was God's way of signaling its existence to the humans. For centuries, the locals had barely spoken of it, simply keeping well away from its dark walls. However, there were many legends. With the humans' rapid scientific and military development, Liatoukine wondered not only if the secrecy would last, but if confrontation would not become someday inevitable—a confrontation that vampires couldn't hope to win. Perhaps that was God's plan as well? Perhaps that was also why Orlok was behaving as he was—trying to control the humans before they became a threat?

Whenever that confrontation were to take place—and the later, the better— Liatoukine had every intention of being far away. And preferably, on the winning side.

Liatoukine now entered the Vampire City. He tethered his horse to a tall, dark pole made of some unknown substance, with no apparent purpose. The beast was clearly afraid, but the Russian Captain simply placed his hand on its neck and it became utterly docile. He did not leave all his weapons with the horse. Instead, he took his sword and two pistols. He then proceeded on foot.

He walked through the dark streets, encountering strange figures as he walked. They let him pass, looking at him strangely. Vampires tended not to enter the city when it was visible to humans. Liatoukine had done so deliberately, in order to unnerve. Further, he could have proceeded to where the middle of the city was and let it materialize around him, but he wished to take in the current atmosphere of the Sepulchre. He had not been here for a while. It was as unappealing as ever.

He knew some of the figures he passed by reputation. A number used the city as their base. Others had fled here from lands were they had been exposed. Some had "retired." He was unimpressed by the city and its inhabitants. He did not share his kind's love of the extreme macabre. Humans were weak. However, they provided much in the way of entertainment, pleasure, and a refined society in which to partake and, occasionally, dominate. He considered that much more preferable than skulking around in some invisible mausoleum.

Soon, he came to the central plaza of the Sepulchre. Here was a temple, an imposing chapel of sorts. Its columns were interspersed with statues of tigers ripping the hearts out of young women, frozen in fear. He went up the steps, past the statues. These were actually real women, who, in death, had been transformed into statues by their vampire killers for the express purpose of being displayed here. Liatoukine was responsible for much death, but could not see the point of this spectacle. Vampire art was never his thing.

He was greeted—if that's the word—by what appeared to be little more than a skeleton dressed in a Russian military uniform. The skull had vampire fangs. Presumably this was Orlok's own effort to unsettle him. The skeleton wordlessly gestured to follow him, and led Liatoukine into the hall. At the end was a raised platform, on top of which were five stone stands, with figures behind them. This was the Vampire Council, those who currently governed the Sepulchre. They were bathed in a dull green light.

Liatoukine recognized them. There was Count Szandor, Baron Iskariot and Baroness Phryne. He noted one, wearing garments that were fashionable in Europe a few years back. This was the second Otto Goetzi; the first being infamous for letting humans intrude into the city and almost getting himself destroyed in the process. There was, however, no mistaking the one in the center: tall, bald, large ears, with rat like teeth, wearing a long coat... They had not previously met, but this was Graf Orlok, no doubt about that.

Littered around the hall were a number of vampires of all kinds. This was unusual; the Council tended to meet and hold its audiences in secrecy. Presumably Orlok was expecting trouble and had gathered his lackeys?

Orlok stared at Liatoukine.

"Welcome, Boris Liatoukine. I am Graf Orlok. We have heard of your journey here. What brings you home?"

This was certainly was not home for Liatoukine; but Orlok was clearly playing to the notion held by the other Council members that the Sepulchre was the home of all vampires—and thus, that it had power over all of their kind.

Liatoukine got the pleasantries out of the way. "Greetings, Orlok, fellow council members..." Then, he decided to get straight to it as it seemed they knew full well why he was here. "Vampires have always infiltrated human society in the past. We need to, if only in order to protect ourselves—and of course to gain enrichment and nourishment. However, it seems that we are increasing such operations far more aggressively than in the past. It appears as if we are trying to take them over completely." Liatoukine used the 'we' simply to imply brotherhood. He didn't mean it, of course.

"Quite so," said Orlok. "It is long past time we took control. Our city appears every day for an hour. Currently, only fear and our influence keep its existence at the level of rumors. But this will not last. As the humans develop their sciences and communications, too many will come to know of the Sepulchre. News of its existence will spread. The human empires are large and powerful. One or more may decide to move against us. This may prove perilous for us. I trust, then, that you do not disagree with our new strategy?"

"As it happens, I do disagree. It is *your* strategy, Graf, is it not?" Something that passed for a smile appeared on Orlok's withered face, and he slowly nodded his head. The other Council members said nothing. Liatoukine noted this. Perhaps they were not too enthusiastic about the new strategy, and happy for Orlok to take the blame if anything went wrong?

Liatoukine pressed on. "You are pushing too hard. The humans are becoming far more aware of us, at every level of their society. I can assure you of this. In my own Russia, officials have destroyed many of your agents. The Emperors themselves have been secretly conferring about us, notwithstanding their political rivalries in other, more mundane areas."

"I know of this," responded Orlok, "but it does not matter. Control will pass to us, overtly or with the humans acting as our marionettes."

"No, it will not," Liatoukine stated. "Even if you manage to enslave all the royal families of Europe, and all their ministers, it is foolish to think that you could control millions of humans. Do you think the God-fearing masses will put up with vampire control? Operating in the shadows, having us dismissed as mere superstition is one thing, but this aggressive push towards mastery of Europe will bring us into open conflict. We cannot fight millions of them. What will you do when they surround the Sepulchre and bombard you with their cannons every day for an hour?"

Some of the council looked unsettled. Liatoukine pushed his advantage.

"They are already destroying your agents. I come from Zagreb; there, they held one of you infiltrators prisoner; they interrogated him, then destroyed him. It is clear to me that the Austrian Empire has far greater knowledge of us than we thought. They have prison cells made especially for us. I suspect they may even be aware that the Sepulchre is real, and not just some local peasant's tale. There can be no doubt that a confrontation is coming. Rather than put it off for decades—time during which we can perhaps find a solution—it will be upon us within a few years, maybe even a few months."

"And you, of course, are completely loyal to us?" responded Orlok. "Perhaps you can explain your greater loyalty to the Russian Empire? Your fighting for them? Even now, you are on a mission for them. You think I did not know? Is it really the case that you are here for our benefit? Or for those of your masters in St. Petersburg?"

Liatoukine's loyalty was to himself above all. However, he certainly preferred St. Petersburg to the Sepulchre. And he had much sympathy for the Russian Empire. The assimilation of other lands into the Empire, the crushing of the lesser kinds, especially the peasants, yes, that was real power! Perhaps, one day, they would take control of the Sepulchre itself—under his guidance of course. However, there was the more immediate problem of Orlok's activities. It was time to go further on the offensive.

"My loyalty to my kind is not in doubt," said the Russian Captain. "Your spies seem to know that I am on mission to look into the so-called 'vampire plague' on behalf of my Tsar, working in tandem with the Habsburgs. But it is only the ideal cover to protect our own interests, which is why I am here. At least, I have not been uncovered, unlike so many of your servants." He paused. "Aside from your competence, perhaps it is your own motivation that we should question?"

This was an open challenge. Orlok hissed back in anger, but Liatoukine did not let up.

"How did you become a vampire, Graf Orlok? Does the rest of the Council know?"

They clearly did not. Orlok was known to have mysterious origins and that it was best not to inquire about them. They gave no answer, and Orlok was certainly not going to enlighten them. His hands were now outstretched, his long fingers with their razor sharp fingers moving as if digging into Liatoukine's neck. The Russian Captain pressed ahead. There was no going back now.

"Most of us became what we are by having been converted by another vampire's bite. Some of us have the power to absorb humans into themselves and to then release them, changed into whatever their masters want them to be. Their physical form can be changed, to be made grotesque, to even destroy the memories of who they once were…"

Otto Goetzi intervened. "We know this, Liatoukine. I myself was converted by a Great One in such a manner. I have taken his name to match his appearance, the very form in which he shaped me. Get to your point."

Liatoukine knew this; in fact this second Goetzi assisted the accursed Radcliffe's human incursion many years before. Somehow, he had been forgiven by the Council after the first Goetzi's death. Liatoukine did not know—or care—about how that had been accomplished. The first Goetzi was, in fact, not that well regarded, despite what his successor said. He was known for his sadism; this version of Goetzi had been a young village woman once known as Polly Bird and Goetzi turned her into a copy of himself.

"Of course," responded Liatoukine. "But first, I wish to be clear about who Orlok is—or was. There was once, some time ago, a young Transylvanian nobleman…" The atmosphere in the room changed a little. An element of fear and foreboding could now be felt from the Council. More hissing from Orlok. "I do not need to bore you with the details, but Graf Orlok, then a handsome young man, thought that he could displace the power and influence of Count Dracula himself."

There were stunned gasps from the Council. All knew Dracula. All knew that he was the most powerful vampire of all.

"Orlok of course, had no idea that Dracula was a vampire. He had scoffed at the local peasantry's fear of him, dismissing it as mere superstition. Hearing of his attitude, Dracula invited him to his castle. Orlok was not much seen after that. His family all seemed to die mysteriously, disappeared, or became seen only at odd hours. Orlok himself was also rarely seen. And soon, the locals started to fear Orlok, with good reason.

"For Count Dracula had not merely killed him, of course. He had absorbed him. He then allowed him to reemerge but only as a copy, a doppelganger of Dracula himself. Orlok would carry out business on his behalf, the things the Count considered to be lesser tasks. And when these tasks were carried out well, Dracula would let Orlok out of himself not just in the form of a copy, but in the misshapen shape we see today, in which he would terrorise the locals."

"Are you saying that Orlok is a servant of Dracula?" interjected Goetzi. "That he is here serving him now?"

"Far from it," replied Liatoukine. "A few years ago, Dracula dismissed Orlok from his service. No reasons were given. Perhaps we can infer a degree of incompetence on Orlok's part? After all, Dracula left him in his current, charming form… Orlok became resentful at having been cast out. He left his land and came here. Where he seems to have done quite well."

"What do you know of these matters?" Orlok finally said. "You're but a barbaric vampire from the East?"

Barbaric? Orlok would pay for that, swore the Russian Captain, who resumed addressing the rest of the Council.

"Forgive me, my lords. Orlok has already questioned my loyalties, and now he mocks my very knowledge of him. Please be assured that my information comes straight from Count Dracula himself. Indeed, he has authorized me, if it came to that, to present you with this letter…"

He handed the letter not to Orlok, but to Goetzi. The latter noted the seal, and opened it. The note, no more than a few words, was handed round the Council. Was that a trembling of their hands Liatoukine thought he saw?

"As you can see," he resumed, "Dracula himself has authorized me to speak on his behalf in this matter. He and I share the same concerns over the current strategy. I trust that settles any doubt over my knowledge, or indeed my loyalty to our kind. Unless, you doubt the word of Dracula?"

The Council said nothing.

The note had been passed to Orlok. He shook it at Liatoukine with his outstretched hand.

"Dracula does not rule here!" he screeched. "He rarely leaves his castle! His days of power are long gone!"

But Liatoukine was not intimidated.

"Do you intend to test him on that? He remains part of you, Orlok. Dracula is both fascinated and intrigued with the British Empire. He thinks in terms of the decades ahead, and some here know that he wishes to have... interests in the heart of the British Empire. You, yourself, know this, Orlok. You think you can do better than him. Be faster than him. Thus, your policy of recent years."

Orlok crushed Dracula's note and shredded it with one hand before casting it aside.

"I offer power and security to our kind. Dracula offers nothing. Nothing!" he said.

Liatoukine ignored this and continued:

"You appear to have focused mostly on the Habsburg Empire. Perhaps you have an ulterior motive for this? You hate and fear Dracula. You resent him, but cannot destroy him. He is, after all, your creator. His lands, at least nominally, come under Austrian governance. Perhaps you seek control of the Habsburgs not for our kind's benefit, but to control their armies which you plan to use to attack Dracula's castle? They would do something you are too fearful and weak to do yourself?"

This accusation moved Orlok to sheer rage.

"You dare question me? How dare you!"

He gestured to one of his larger minions standing in the hall, who then moved towards Liatoukine. The vampire in question looked like a peasant, probably converted by Orlok himself. *Perfect*, Liatoukine thought. Time to make the point for which he had prepared with the smith he had visited earlier.

He drew his pistol. The peasant vampire sneered. After all, everyone knew that bullets were harmless to a vampire. Liatoukine fired. The peasant exploded in a fireball. All present were shocked.

Liatoukine was most satisfied. Had this not worked, his powers would still have been sufficient to deal with the attack, but he was inordinately pleased with his success. He swiftly made his point:

"Clearly, I was merely defending myself. Please notice, however, that I destroyed that upstart using bullets containing the ashes of a vampire's heart. Such ashes are a known weakness for many of us. Imagine the humans with their pistols—their bombs even—containing such ashes. They would be many casualties on our side. These weapons the humans are capable of devising are beyond our imagination. Let us not provoke them into using them against us now by stirring a foolish campaign they are already aware of."

The argument was clearly running away from Orlok. All could sense the mood, in the way that only vampires can, amongst themselves.

Liatoukine pushed harder.

"What is Orlok? He is nothing but a copy of Count Dracula. Trying to outdo him. He is a counterfeit, not the real thing at all. His very ideas are derived from his creator!"

The taunt hit home. Orlok screeched again. His one chance to retrieve the situation was to demonstrate his power and impose his will by killing Liatoukine. He started moving towards his intended victim.

Liatoukine was prepared. He swiftly used his other pistol and fired. The bullet smashed into Orlok, sending him flying backwards, but did not destroy him as it had his minion was. Liatoukine could see why: his foe's coat had been reinforced in some way. *Very well*, he thought. He would simply use his own powers. Or decapitate him. Or both.

He issued one final taunt: "I see. You protected yourself with your coat, but did not provide such protection to your minion, for all your talk of our kind."

Orlok levitated forward, ready for the final confrontation, but Goetzi intervened. "Enough! There must be no more disunity here! Orlok—it is over. We can no longer afford the risks of your strategy. It could bring destruction upon us all. It must end." He seemed to speak for the Council, for they certainly did not disagree.

Orlok hung in mid-air. He floated down. His coat was damaged where the bullet had hit him. He waved his hand across it and what was left of the bullet fell to the floor harmlessly. The coat itself seemed to regenerate. He turned to the Council, slowly looking at each of them in turn as he spoke.

"I will not stay to witness your destruction. All of you will die at the hands of the humans some day, but not I. I shall leave the Sepulchre tonight. I will not return." With that, he walked out of the hall.

Liatoukine wondered about Goetzi. Why had he taken his side? His taunting of Orlok as a mere copy could have been applied to Goetzi too. It must have struck a nerve. Then, again, perhaps Goetzi intervened out of kinship, to save Orlok's existence?

"Where will he go?" wondered Goetzi.

"I care not," answered Liatoukine. "His time is, I suspect, limited. He can never be free of his old master's subconscious. He will forever be influenced by it, and try to outdo him in some way. And he will no doubt fail. Dracula plans decades ahead. Orlok attempts to rush things, as we have seen. I will leave the winding down of his strategy in your hands and will take my leave. Unlike Orlok, daylight does not affect me"

Liatoukine rode away from the Sepulchre. He had a long journey back to St. Petersburg. On the way, he would send word to Dracula of his success.

He had served many interests well that day: the Empires, Dracula, his fellow vampires, but, above all, his own. His stature and influence with the Sepulchre and Dracula, on the one side, and the Royal Courts—in particular, St. Petersburg—on the other, would both benefit. And he had enjoyed himself, too. The defeat of Orlok had not been guaranteed. He was a powerful foe. Liatoukine had enjoyed the danger, the thrill of it.

However, Orlok was not entirely wrong. At some point, the humans would cease to ignore the Sepulchre out of fear and disbelief. Something would have to be done. Exactly what, Liatoukine did not know. Even in Russia, some suspected him. They would soon call him "Captain Vampire," if he was not careful. But for now, however, he was secure and able to use his influence to ensure that his not aging never became an issue. Lone vampires such as himself and Dracula could remain safe, but would an entire city?

Van Helsing's phonograph, Wisborg, Germany, 10 August 1901.

My studies of the Undead, and of my late adversary, Count Dracula, have revealed the existence of a Graf Orlok who lived some years previously in Transylvania. He, too, had a fearsome reputation, although not as great as Dracula's. It would appear that, after a period of absence, he returned to his home in 1830, but a few years later, left to come here to Wisborg.

Following his trail here, I have been taken aback by subsequent events that occurred in 1838. From the documents I have found, it appears that Orlok had similar intentions to that of Dracula, although here in Germany and not in England. Even his adversaries were people similar to those of us who fought Dracula. And his strategy was the same. This Orlok even had the same desires as Dracula—taking an unholy interest in Ellen Hutter, the wife of Thomas Hutter. However, things did not end well for her as they did for our own Mina Harker. Ellen gave her life to trick Orlok into consuming her blood until dawn. The rays of the Sun then destroyed him without trace. Not a weakness that Dracula had, and a very different conclusion to our adventure. She did not survive.

However, the coincidences are too much to be ignored. Furthermore, in the records I have found here, Orlok mentions something called the Sepulchre—a city of his kind. I have heard other rumors of such a city, whispered amongst communities in Central and Eastern Europe plagued by vampires. It is sometimes referred to as "Selene."

There have been too many references for me to ignore, and this Orlok affair of years past has unsettled me. There must be some connection to Dracula. I have not, in the past, been inclined to try to convince the world of the existence of such creatures as vampires. But I may have to reassess matters. The existence of Selene, or the Sepulchre—whatever it may be called—is a matter too great to be ignored. I must research it further.

There can be no graver a threat to humanity than a City of the Nosferatu.

Artist John Gallager (no relation to Brian) introduces the tale which follows: "This story came about because I had decided to do a big panoramic painting of King Kong fighting Godzilla. And, as these things tend to look better with a female element included, I also added, for no particular reason, Barbarella. Now, I usually leave it to the audience to make up their own little stories as to what my paintings might be about. But, in this case I decided that people deserved an explanation. So, I began to spin a yarn to accompany the painting, and, as I did so, I got to thinking about those wonderful Aurora plastic model kits that I used to collect as a kid... Suddenly, the plot was there..."

John Gallagher: *Last of the* Kaiju

Tokyo, 1962

With a weird electromechanical groaning noise, a large bullet-shaped craft materialized out of nowhere atop a skyscraper roof. It had a quaint and antiquated look and one would not have thought it out of place as a prop in some old Georges Mélies film.

A hatch on the side swung out and an elderly gentleman with a cane emerged. He looked around placidly before extending his gloved hand to assist a stunningly beautiful, flaxen-haired young woman to disembark. The old man was dressed in a black Victorian frock coat with a long scarf and a fur hat; his companion quite differently. She wore an eye catching ensemble of futuristic shiny plastic and fragile-looking sheer which set off her figure perfectly.

"Right, my dear," said Doctor Omega turning to his companion, "...you have exactly thirty minutes to complete your mission."

He pedantically flipped open the lid of a golden fob watch attached to his waistcoat, taping its face to emphasis his point. Two further figures appeared in the doorframe: a large, heavy set, bearded man and a small reptilian-looking alien. The bearded man handed the woman a bulky weapon, some kind of baroque-looking ray gun.

"I can't say that I approve of the idea of transporting dangerous animals cavalierly through the time stream," said the white haired old man, his hands clasping his lapels like some elderly schoolmaster. "There was a very regrettable incident a while back involving a rampaging *Mesonychid*, but I trust you'll be more careful, eh?"

"Don't worry, Doctor, I'm a five star, double-rated astronavigatrix," replied Barbarella, expertly checked that her weapon's power pod was fully charged and systems were online. "I know what I'm doing."

"I hope so, my dear," said the Doctor, "because I have enough anomalies to sort out as it is. I don't need you causing any more temporal paradoxes."

"Doctor, I am a woman, which means that I, myself, am the ultimate paradox," she replied with a beguiling smile.

They both turned to view the panorama of the benighted city. In the distance, they could hear thunderous primeval roars. Bright flames flickered between darkened buildings as police helicopters circled the source of the disturbance like angry wasps. The sounds of multiple air raid sirens wailed away into the night.

"Well, it certainly looks like we've got our timing right," said Barbarella. "With those two tearing the town apart, I doubt anyone will even notice me."

"Come along, Terry," she called and, with a loud croak, an albino pteranodon stuck its head out of the hatch. It ambled out onto the rooftop upon tiny back legs and foreclaws like some gigantic primordial bat. The pterosaur was fitted with a riding harness and, as the woman stroked its bony crest, it bowed its overlarge head. She mounted it by swinging nimbly up onto its back, gathering the reins in her hands.

She made sure that her ray gun, as well as a couple of small pet transporting cages, were secured upon the pteranodon's harness before turning to the Doctor.

"Now remember Barbarella," said the elderly man, sounding like some anxious grandfather, "don't take any unnecessary risks. Be sure to get back in twenty-eight minutes."

"I will, Doctor." she said as Terry unfurled his huge wings, waggled his head and prepared to launch himself into flight.

"Love, Doctor Omega," said Barbarella with a quick open-handed salute before the pteranodon plunged over the edge of the roof into a deep swooping glide which carried them far away it the night.

"Love, Barbarella," called the Doctor, waving after her.

As her flying mount banked and swooped gracefully between the brightly-lit canyons, Barbarella contemplated her assignment, which was to acquire a complete set of the most infamous of the dreaded *Kaiju*, or giant monsters which had made such a nuisance of themselves in the 20th and 21st centuries.

Now, her task was almost complete. Only two names remained on her list. The two most famous monsters of all time.

Godzilla, the so called "King of the Monsters," and King Kong, a massive gorilla. As both beasts laid claim to the title of "King," she found it appropriate that were both here, in the middle of Tokyo, seemingly intent on deciding the issue of royalty by the most direct and irrefutable means possible.

Godzilla was one of the first of the *Kaiju* to have emerged, and still the most impressive. Unfortunately for Japan, the city of Tokyo just happened to be situated upon the same spot the primeval behemoth considered to be its home territory. So it stubbornly persisted in making its way back here, time after time, regardless of the fact that a modern metropolis had long been built atop the site of its beloved Jurassic swamp.

Barbarella, unlike most 20th century humans, was privy to exactly how the tremendous beast had managed to survive all those millions of years in hibernation, and how it had acquired its remarkable regenerative powers. Not to mention its ability to spit blazing radioactive fire.

The original King Kong had been a giant gorilla. Pedantic taxonomists of later centuries would argue that Kong's DNA differed markedly from his smaller African cousins, and that he was most probably descended from the huge extinct Asian primate *Gigantopithecus*. Still, he looked like a giant silverback gorilla, and that was enough for the citizens of 1930s New York, most of whom had never even seen a normal sized gorilla, let alone a giant one. And so, when Kong had originally been captured and exhibited there by a showman with more ambition than common sense, he had caused a mighty sensation.

He went on to generate downright hysteria when he burst free and started eating pedestrians and derailing trains. Unfortunately, Barbarella's first attempt to acquire this prize specimen during this rampage had been thwarted. She had been touched to discover that Kong had been provoked by unrequited love. The Blinovitch Limitation Effect meant that she was stymied from making a second attempt at that point in time, but all was not lost for if the king is dead, then... long live the King.

Although King Kong himself had died at the foot of the Empire State Building, the species of giant primates to which he belonged still thrived upon Skull Island. Kong himself had sired a runt-like albino son, who also fell afoul of human intervention.

And now, nearly thirty years later, another equally impressive specimen had arisen to assume the position of dominant male upon the island, via numerous trials of combat, seeing off not only rival males, but an assortment of other vicious prehistoric predators.

Most recently, the brute had taken down a giant octopus of some unknown species which had crawled up onto land, intent on making a meal of some of the indigenes. Unfortunately, in so doing, this new King of Skull Island had drawn attention to himself.

A Japanese entrepreneur, having learned nothing from his 1930s American predecessor, had decided to tranquilize the giant gorilla and transport him to Tokyo to act as the oversized mascot for his pharmaceutical company. With predictable results.

Godzilla had chosen just that time to come lumbering ashore. Kong had caught the scent of his natural enemy, broken free, and the two mammoth creatures were now engaged in flattening the city in the throes of their titanic battle.

And, as the opportunity to bag both in one go was too good to miss, here also was Barbarella. Her client would just have to settle for King Kong the Second. Providing she kept her own counsel, he would never be any the wiser.

Barbarella guided her mount in to alight upon a convenient ledge overlooking the battle. Swinging one long leg over its crested head, she dismounted. She was momentarily awed by the spectacle before her.

The two monsters were engaged in what could only be a battle to the death. Both were bloodied and carried minor wounds inflicted by their opponent, but they seemed evenly matched. Godzilla was spewing showers of boiling radioactive venom all over the place, whilst Kong was roaring furiously and whirling the chrome steel chains that were still fettered to his wrists above his head, using them as flails to batter the hissing giant reptile.

Barbarella realized that she would have to intervene soon before one of the brutes succeeded in killing the other.

Her opportunity came when Godzilla caught Kong with a mighty swipe of its tail. It sent the giant anthropoid sprawling into the side of a building, which collapsed around it with a thunderous roar and raised a huge cloud of dust. Quickly, she shouldered the gun, locked the automatic sights onto Godzilla, and fired.

A bright beam of light shot out and bathed the snarling mutant dinosaur in a brilliant corona of energy. Within a few seconds, it had rapidly dwindled in size until Barbarella could no longer see it from her vantage.

Meanwhile, its dazed opponent had angrily hurled the debris away and hoisted himself up by his long arms. Kong swung his shaggy head from side to side and, with a puzzled grunt, shuffled around in a circle, bewildered by the sudden disappearance of his foe. Then, he, too, was enveloped in the same light and began to shrink down in size with a startled yelp.

Barbarella knew from her previous *Kaiju* captures that the shock of rapid shrinking rendered the subjects temporally unconscious. So she had to quickly retrieve her two prizes before the curious humans could gather up the courage to come investigate what had happened to the brawling behemoths.

The arena the two creatures had been battling in was a twisted, dangerously radioactively hot tangle of twisted metal and rubble. Barbarella had to carefully navigate her way around pools of still blazing venom and clamber over precariously balanced slabs of shattered concrete, all the while dodging dripping globs of radioactive drool and avoiding stepping in puddles of tar-like black ichor.

The radiation indicator on Professor Ping's reducing ray was going crazy. Luckily, the gun also automatically tagged anything it shrank, so, with relatively little trouble, she was able to locate the now-diminutive form of Godzilla.

She bent down and picked the unconscious saurian up by its tail before depositing him in one of the two carrying cages. A few seconds later, she managed to locate the equally shrunken Kong. The distant wail of police sirens growing steadily louder alerted her that time was running out.

So, summoning her flying steed, she quickly remounted and took to the air, making her way back to Doctor Omega and his waiting timeship, *Cosmos*. Barbarella correctly assumed that the citizens of Tokyo would simply be glad to be rid of their unwelcome, oversized visitors, however this came about. They would undoubtedly invent numerous, different stories to explain their sudden disappearance.

Back in the *Cosmos*, Barbarella made her way along a rack of identical cages, ticking off her final tally on her manifest. Inside each cage a miniaturized monster roared and shook the bars in Lilliputian rage.

"Yes! Finally! A complete set of *Kaiju*... all authentic. All reduced to a manageable size. What more could a twelve-year old boy want?" said Barbarella in delight.

"Then, my dear, let us complete our errand by delivering the present," said Doctor Omega as he set the ornate controls of his craft for the long journey back to the 40th century. He threw a switch and the *Cosmos* smoothly entered the aether, leaving this already muddled section of the time stream to auto-repair itself however it saw fit.

The 40th Century

With all due pomp and ceremony, the birthday celebration for Lord Dianthus, President of Earth and Rotating Premier of the Solar System, was in full swing. It was his sixth successive term in office.

However, due to a recent mishap with an unreliable rejuvenation ray, the President found himself in the slightly embarrassing predicament of having to celebrate his twelfth birthday all over again. The President's current incapacitation was no great problem to the smooth running of the universe, as his office was a largely ceremonial, and the actual management of the aligned systems had long ago been delegated to computers.

As dignitary after dignitary filed past leaving a growing mountain of presents at the side of the Imperial Star Throne, an antique leave-over from the earlier pre republican regime, the juvenile head of state fidgeted impatiently waiting for his favorite interstellar peace-agent to make her appearance.

Finally, late, Barbarella made her entrance. Looking beautiful in glittering faux 20th century evening gown, she proceeded to sing "*Happy Birthday Mr. President*" to him.

Her singing voice, it should be noted, was not amongst the greatest of her many incomparable talents, but, to be fair, her gown was very tight-fitting and restricted her breathing. Poor Barbarella had to be literally sewn into it.

After a polite round of applause by the gathering of alien dignitaries and cyborgs, Barbarella stepped forward.

"My Lord President," she said, curtsying and presenting an eye catching décolleté, "...May I present a birthday gift to you from a grateful galactic population. In recognition of your exemplary civic service and in honor of your wise and benevolent administration."

Behind her, a large floating platform, surmounted by an opaque dome, glided forward on anti-gravity suspensors. The President arose to get a better look and Barbarella linked arms with him to escort him over to it. He was surprised to discover that, in his current condition, he was now shorter than her.

"Wait until you see what I've got for you, Claude." (Barbarella and the President had been on first name terms for years.)

With a wave of her hand, the dome cleared to transparent Plexiglas, revealing within a carefully sculptured diorama. A miniature landscape resembling a tropical island, complete with forests, a skull-shaped mountain, plains, rivers and swamps. Within this micro-habitat, each enclosed in its own territory by force fields to prevent them harming one another, were twelve of the most famous of the legendary *Kaiju* who had once so plagued humanity.

Momentarily forgetting the dignity of his high office, the President scampered around the table with unalloyed delight.

"Wow! You've got Rodan... Angilas... and Ebirah," he said breathlessly with excitement, gazing enraptured through the glass at his new menagerie of shrunken monsters. "...And, and you've even managed to get King Kong and Godzilla!" he exclaimed.

"Yes, Your Lordship," said Barbarella, proving that even angels can lie.

Privately, she was relieved that the mission had been such a success. This would help to consolidate and maintain her position as the number one peace-agent. She didn't want upstarts like that Stella Star poaching any more of her assignments.

"Once again, my most trusted agent has come through for me with flying colors," cried Lord Dianthus exuberantly, obviously thrilled to bits with his magnificent birthday present.

Barbarella saluted smartly, her gown just about managing to contain her, and inquired if the President had given any thought to what he would like for his next birthday?

And, as he was currently experiencing once again the first exquisite pangs of puberty, the President's imagination was instantly awhirl with a whole multitude of delicious and naughty birthday wishes that only the lovely Barbarella could personally help to make come true...

In the story that follows, Martin Gately cleverly revisits John Willard's famous 1922 play, The Cat and the Canary, *adapted several times for the cinema, including in a 1939 version starring Bob Hope. But Martin has inserted the daring French sleuth Joseph Rouletabille into the narrative, with surprising results. The first part of this story takes place soon after Martin's "Leviathan Creek," published in our Volume 8, and a little before* Rouletabille at Krupp's, *recently translated by Black Coat Press...*

Martin Gately: *Rouletabille vs. The Cat*

Part 1—The Year of the Cat
(Winter 1916)

The man in the black robe lay on the ground amongst the thistles and itch-weed, not moving, scarcely even breathing. They'd be looking for him soon. They didn't realize that he was already in the grounds of the house. They thought he only came at night—these men in black uniforms, armed with shotguns. They were noisy, clumsy fools, and they were unlikely to catch him, except by luck. Yet, there were more and more of them each day. They might stumble upon the place where he slept, and conceal themselves nearby, waiting for him to return. That worried him for a moment. Then, he decided that he would perceive their vile scent as he approached. Like most of his kind, he had astonishingly acute senses. It had taken him a long time to grow accustomed to the aroma given off by ordinary people; that malodorous bouquet of stale cigarette smoke, liquor and cooked food could still cause him to gag in a confined space.

His thoughts were suddenly interrupted by the spluttering sound of an approaching boat engine. He crawled through the long, unkempt grass until he reached the edge of the steep bank. When he looked down at the sluggish grey expanse of the Hudson River below, he saw a small vessel with a long covered cabin nearing the jetty. Could it be a police launch? It certainly looked like it. As it drew alongside the mooring pontoon, a nimble uniformed figure jumped out and used lines to secure the boat fore and aft. Then the cough of the motor died.

The launch was overshadowed by the other vessel tied up at the jetty—a sleek and luxurious forty foot racing yacht with the soubriquet *Sea Silk*. A few moments later, the launch's passengers disembarked: three men. The first, a straight-backed man of about fifty in a long black coat, then a much older man, perhaps in his late seventies, and even at this distance it was possible to discern the aura of authority which he radiated—he was an ex-military type. The final passenger looked to be little more than a boy. His head was adorned with a thick mass of dark brown ringlets and he wore a thick, rather uncomfortable looking tweed suit cut in the European style. The three men walked to where the landing joined the bank. There, they had to start ascending the spidery steel bridge which carried them over the railroad line which ran along the bank of the Hudson between the boundary of the West Estate and the water.

He didn't like it. Three more sets of eyes with the potential to spot him as he skulked around. To begin with, there had just been Cyrus West, Missy-Lou Pleasant and a handful more house servants and gardeners. Now, more and people were arriving at Glen Cliff Manor. It had to be tonight. He had to get into the house tonight, before the security was increased any further. If only he hadn't botched his first attempt; he might have already retrieved the relic. His mind boiled with anger at the thought of his people's holiest treasure in the hands of their persecutor. He would kill Cyrus West, if he could. But he must get the Crown of Jovan Nenad back to the homeland at all costs. Absentmindedly, he began to sharpen his claws in readiness.

Herbert Brown paused as he reached the mid-section of the steel bridge—just a little out of breath.

"You can catch your first glimpse of the big house from here!" he called back to Rouletabille. "Look! You can see it through the trees."

The young Frenchman took a step forward and craned his neck. The higgledy-piggledy asymmetry of the gothic revival shortbread mansion hove into view. With its castellation, turrets and neat clusters of high chimneys, it looked like it should be home to some ancient family of vampires. Rouletabille noted too that many of the windows were fitted with decorative iron shutters, and, on the ground floor, these were all closed and barred.

Immense grounds with formal gardens stretched away in all directions; there was a glasshouse the size of a railroad station and numerous other outbuildings, both decorative and functional, strategically placed around the estate. This was the famous Glen Cliff Manor—home of the reclusive millionaire Cyrus West. The estate took up a good chunk of land on the outskirts of Tarrytown, and had been originally called "Brockenhurst" when it was constructed back in the 1840s.

"Well, my friend," began Herbert Brown, "what can you deduce from the request for your assistance here today?"

"Very little, General," answered Rouletabille honestly. "The order came via diplomatic channels at the highest level. I was to be met by you at the French Consulate in New York and to proceed to the house of Cyrus West."

"And what can you tell me about the man, Cyrus West?" interrogated the elderly general.

"Once again, very little. Cyrus West is old and very rich. He made his fortune in marine cable laying, and his company laid some of the first trans-Atlantic telegraph wires."

"Rouletabille, you once deduced the combination of my safe in less than five minutes. Surely you can do a little better on the subject of Cyrus…West?"

No effort was required on the part of the young French detective. The obviousness of it now struck him like a thunderbolt.

"*Your* association with Cyrus West can mean only one thing. He is the same person as Captain Cyrus Smith, your former commanding officer and fellow castaway on Lincoln Island in the Pacific. With the benefit of hindsight 'Smith' is an obvious pseudonym. And if I recall correctly, some official records also refer to him as Captain Cyrus Harding—suggestive of a series of pseudonyms," reasoned Rouletabille.

"Not bad, my friend. But I guess it is a little obvious when you think about it. Cyrus ran away to join the army when he was very young and has actually served with distinction under a variety of false names including Smith, Norman and Harding. However, West is his real name."

"Gentlemen! Gentlemen!" admonished Roger Crosby. "We must not keep Mr. West waiting, and particularly we should not be caught in the grounds after dusk, lest we encounter the interloper, or are mistaken for him by the guards..."

Rouletabille and Brown picked up pace and were soon descending from the steel stairway and heading on into the woodland pathways of the estate. As they exited the woods, Crosby pointed out the enclosed swimming pool—an architectural gem in its own right—it looked something like a Greek temple. It was nearly twenty minutes before they reached the front entrance portico. Crosby tugged hard on the handle of the wrought iron bell pull, and was rewarded by a sepulchral tolling somewhere deep within the building.

Moments later, the studded oak door swung open revealing one of the most striking looking women that Rouletabille had ever seen. The unthinking and insensitive might merely label her Creole or "half-caste," but these terms did not sufficiently capture the rich complexity or her racial origins. Her cheekbones were high—her eyes narrow—almost Oriental. Her skin was a lustrous dark golden color. There was about her the most extraordinary lofty arrogance; one might be forgiven for thinking that this was her house, and she resented the interruption. The most incongruous thing about her was her outfit—a short maid's dress with highly starched apron; sheer black stockings sheathed her dancer's legs with little patent boots the rather odd finishing touch. She looked as if she would more properly belong in the stately robes of some ancient queen of Egypt.

"Lawyer Crosby..." was her only condescension to a greeting.

"Missy-Lou, you know General Brown, and this is Monsieur Joseph Rouletabille. They are here to see the Master."

"Then, enter," she pronounced as she turned on her heels and click-clacked across the polished tiles of the vast hallway towards the library which also served as Cyrus West's study. As they followed her, Rouletabille unlocked his gaze from her gorgeous form and drank in the beauty of the statuary which loomed over them. Most of the pantheon of Greek gods seemed to be represented: Zeus, Hera, Apollo, Athena, Hephaestus and many others besides.

Inside the library, Cyrus West sat behind a broad mahogany desk in a wheelchair. Rouletabille had forgotten that the man must now be well over ninety. His hair and beard were both long and white, his eyes milky with cataracts. Yet, he sat erect and alert, and smiled a secretive and self-satisfied smile as they approached, like a chess grandmaster undertaking a successful gambit.

West proffered his hand for each of them to shake in turn and then gestured for them to sit in the three Arts and Crafts style chairs that had been set out by Missy-Lou before his desk.

"Gentlemen, thank you for attending me. It is much appreciated. Monsieur Rouletabille, you have traveled far, and I hope not to detain you from your war against the Boche for too long. But your reputation as the detective who solved the notorious *Mystery of the Yellow Room* has spread far and wide, and I feel I will have great need of your services tonight," West explained.

"I understand that you have had an intruder in your grounds several times who has eluded capture," opened Rouletabille. "Do you have any idea what this intruder might want? Do you have any enemies?"

"Well, I have, in my life, made many enemies—perhaps too many. Most of my own family probably wishes me dead. They visit here occasionally like cats looking into a canary cage—wishing I would get on and die. But this is nothing to do with them. No, my greatest enemy, to answer your question, is undoubtedly the arms-dealer Basil Zaharoff. For, like my old friend Prince Dakkar, I have developed something of a kink about War. I despise War above all things and have tried to frustrate his activities whenever and wherever I can. Zaharoff wishes me dead a thousand times over, but this is nothing to do with him either—at least, I wouldn't have thought so," the old man paused for a moment as if entering a reverie and then said, "Where is my hospitality? Missy-Lou, best brandy for our guests."

However, Cyrus West did not partake of any of the brandy himself. Instead, his shaking hand reached for a crystal decanter which sat on his leather-topped desk. The decanter glowed faintly with a bluish light, and the azure liquor that poured forth from it emitted wisps of silver vapor. Whatever the drink was, it was for West's lips alone. Rouletabille inched forward in order to see what was written on the metal medallion on the neck of the decanter. The detective was none-the-wiser since the medallion simply bore two letters "*E.V.*"

"Monsieur, I have a fair idea who the intruder might be—in general terms—and what he wants. In addition to War, my secondary hatred is the Occult. Until my health started to deteriorate, which is something that occurred comparatively recently, I waged a kind of vendetta against the degenerate witch cults that operate in some of the remote and forgotten corners of the world. In the Caribbean, I fought against the vile Voodoo cult and disrupted its practices. Missy-Lou was once a high-priestess of that religion—a woman of the Obeah. Now, she is a reformed character and a pillar of strength to me. And in Serbia, in central Europe, I skirmished many times with the adherents of a pernicious cat worship cult. Only the other year, my agents rescued from the cult a girl-child designated as a human sacrifice. That child is now being raised anonymously here in Tarrytown by a foster mother under my supervision," West paused to drain his glass.

"Roger, you know the combination of my safe. Would you mind?"

Roger Crosby dragged along one of the bookshelf ladders until it was adjacent to the fireplace. Now, for the first time, Rouletabille noticed the painting above the mantelpiece. It appeared to be the original of Goya's *Don Manuel Orsorio Manrique de Zunica*—a depiction of a young boy dressed in red satin with two cats and a bird cage filled with finches, or perhaps canaries. Possibly the origin of Cyrus West's verbal allusion to cats and canaries earlier. Crosby swiftly ascended the ladder and swung the hinged painting to one side, revealing a safe. This evoked in the detective's memory his first visit to the study of General Brown, where the portrait of President Lincoln also concealed a safe. Crosby started to work the dial with practiced ease.

"This witch cult call themselves *Neprijaltelji Jovan Nenad*—The Enemies of King John, in reference to King John of Serbia. Their most revered artifact is the Crown of Jovan Nenad, which they stole from the Serbian Royal Family centuries ago. My agents have relieved them of this object and brought it here."

"And you think that the purpose of the prowler is to steal back the crown," deduced the Frenchman.

"Of course, but even if he were to effect entry to my safe, he would not be able to purloin the crown. You see, I have had the gold melted down and sold, and the gems re-cut and mounted in the form a necklace," smiled Cyrus West.

With the safe now open, Roger Crosby stood atop the ladder with the necklace in his hand. The huge emeralds and diamonds glittered magically in the firelight as he descended. It struck Rouletabille that the cult adherents would be driven into the most obscene fury by the loss of the crown. Cyrus West had deliberately, and perhaps rashly, destroyed something of great importance to them.

"Missy-Lou, go and get Monsieur Rouletabille's uniform for him, will you?" instructed West.

"Uniform?" puzzled the detective.

"Well, it makes sense, my friend," interjected General Brown. "Two dozen edgy men running around in semi-darkness with shotguns is a recipe for a mishap. Cyrus thought it would be a good idea if you wore the same sort of uniform and had the same weapon. That way the guards are unlikely to mistake you for our unwanted guest."

With that, Brown walked to the wall on the far side of the library where there was a small decorative rifle rack; on the lowest rung was a Winchester '73, above that was a Winchester 1912 pump action shotgun, and above that an unusual custom carbine with a silver plaque on its stock which appeared to be engraved with the word *Nautilus*. Brown selected the pump action and strode back to present it to Rouletabille. Almost simultaneously, Missy-Lou arrived back with the freshly pressed uniform and accompanying black octagonal peaked cap.

"Don't be impeded by false modesty," chided Brown. "You can change right here. I can assure you that Missy-Lou has seen the unclad form of a man before."

At this, Missy-Lou snorted slightly and Brown and the other men chortled a little mirthlessly at the young man's embarrassment as he complied; firstly taking off his jacket in order to remove his leather shoulder holster. The holster contained his customary Lebel service revolver, and Rouletabille placed it carefully on West's desk. As if inspired by the sight of the revolver, West eased open his desk drawer and dug out a stubby snub-nosed brass Very pistol and a handful of parachute flares.

"This is my old flare pistol, Monsieur. You are welcome to use it. The guards tell me that the intruder wears black robes and just vanishes into the shadows. These parachute flares are my own personal design and made by one of my companies. They have the highest and purest magnesium content commercially available—for 15 seconds they'll turn midnight into noon," explained West.

There was a knock at the door just as Rouletabille was pulling on the black pants of the security guard uniform. Missy-Lou opened the door and a callow, smooth faced boy of about sixteen strolled in wearing an easy smile. He colored slightly as his eyes met those of the maid; she was, for him, an impossible, unattainable desire. And didn't she know it. The boy colored again at the sight of Rouletabille.

"I beg your pardon, sir," he commenced, rather baffled by the scene before him.

"I feel like I'm changing in the middle of a railway station," joked the detective, "or perhaps I'm trapped in the early scenes of a French farce."

"This is my nephew, Charles Wilder. He fancies himself something of a poet, but I've told him there's no money in it. After he's been to college, I think he should try writing a play. I'll bankroll it for him and get it on Broadway. Charlie has been staying with me while his mother is recovering from a serious illness. When you've got a family as dismal as mine a charming boy like him pretty easily ends up as your favorite!" announced West.

Roger Crosby stepped towards Charlie. Proffering to the boy the fabulous necklace that had once been the Crown of Jovan Nenad.

"Your uncle's latest acquisition, my boy. The jewels are of incredible value—perhaps over $200,000," intoned the lawyer.

Charlie took the necklace into his hands and looked into the heart of the jewels. Perhaps it was no more than a trick of the firelight, but his boyish smile seemed to twist into an avaricious leer.

"So beautiful," he murmured - his tongue struggled to sound out the words in a mouth that had suddenly filled with saliva. The dazzling jewels had filled him with a physical hunger in the same way that the sight of Missy-Lou's lithe form sometimes did.

Rouletabille's sensitive ears detected the sound of creaking metal under stress, akin to the sound of a door being forced. Then, the central library window seemed to explode inwards, peppering those present with glass shards of various shapes and sizes, and long slivers of shattered casement timber.

A black, tigerish shape bounded through the gaping aperture emitting a weird growling shriek. The shocking suddenness of the event had frozen everyone in place, after the initial reflexive flinch. Everyone—with the exception of Joseph Rouletabille. His reflexes had been, not so much honed, as tested to the limits of mortal endurance by both the rigors of battlefield combat in the Great War and his work as an intelligence officer.

Before the young detective had consciously ordered his arm to move, the Lebel revolver had been recovered from the desk and was in his right hand. He aimed and shot in the same fraction of a split second. The advancing form was not an animal, as he had first thought, but a man dressed in blue-black robes. Rouletabille's mind processed a glimpse of a strange, misshapen bearded face and short close cropped hair—the yellow teeth were pointed like miniature daggers (could they have been filed?).

The robed figure folded in the middle at the impact of the bullet—but only for an instant—the slug could not have struck anything vital, perhaps it just glanced off his ribs. As the Frenchman got ready to shoot again, he realized that young Charlie Wilder had now stumbled into his field of fire. The bestial robed man saw what the young man still held in his hand, and recognized it—or rather what it had once been. This elicited from the creature an agonized howl of pain.

Rouletabille found this ironic, since he had remained silent while suffering a bullet wound. The Cat Man's right arm swung back, Rouletabille saw that the filthy, black chitinous fingernails had also been sharpened to points. The taloned hand jerked forward almost faster than the eye could follow in its attempt to rip open Charlie's throat. But the finger nails never reached it. Brown bulldozed into the attacker with one of the Arts and Crafts chairs held in front of him at chest height, looking very much like a past-his-prime lion tamer as he did so.

The Cat Man was sent reeling to the floor, but he still found time to tug from Charlie's loose grip the necklace that had once been the Crown of Jovan Nenad. The intruder rolled away, regained his footing, and then accelerated back towards the broken window. Now, with a clear line of sight, the detective fired twice. He could've sworn that he'd hit him, but there was no discernible change in the intruder's stride or speed.

"Are you all right, Charlie?" West asked the pale and febrile looking youth.

"Yes... Uncle Cy," he answered, looking at his empty hand as if he expected the necklace to re-materialize there.

"We should get you to a greater place of safety, Cyrus," advised Crosby, shaken.

"Nonsense, Roger. He will not come back into this room again after the reception he received. He has what he came for. His job now is to escape," judged the old man calmly.

Rouletabille busied himself removing the spent cartridges from the revolver's cylinder and replacing them with fresh ones. The unmistakable sound of the hollow crack of shotgun fire leeched into the room via the wrecked window, and made everyone jump a little. The security guards had spotted the Cat Man somewhere out in the grounds and were blazing away at him—probably to very little effect.

"Monsieur, you have now encountered our enemy face to face, and I would therefore not think the less of you if you were to spend the rest of the evening here in my library drinking brandy rather than pursuing him through the grounds. As it is, I will provide you with a considerable financial recompense for your trouble. However, if you can recover the necklace for me... well, I shall give you something of far greater value than mere money," smiled the millionaire.

Unexpectedly, Missy-Lou stepped forward and put a slim, graceful hand to Rouletabille's face and caressed his cheek.

"You do not need what he has to offer, my handsome young Frenchman. You already have a long life to lead," she warned enigmatically, and then glanced at West's decanter with its electric blue contents.

"I will return the necklace to you, if I can," Rouletabille assured him. Then he picked up the Very pistol and jammed it and the flares into his jacket pocket; shouldered the shotgun and was gone.

The shooting had quieted now, but the guards were still chasing around the flowerbeds and shrubberies, their battery powered flashlights casting truncated cones of weak illumination into the overwhelming darkness. Rouletabille snapped open the brass barrel of the pistol and loaded it with a parachute flare. He dragged back the stiff, heavy hammer and extended his arm vertically upwards; with a muffled whoosh the pyrotechnic launched. At the zenith of its trajectory, the flare's magnesium core lit, bathing the tidy lawns, regimented flowers and maple trees with an intensely bright silver-white luminescence. The flare swung beneath its miniature fire retardant parachute, sending the shadows into a wild gavotte. Nevertheless, the detective was able to see a spattered trail of blackish crimson showing against the brightly lit verdure. The Cat Man was bleeding badly.

The Frenchman commandeered an electric flashlight from one of the security guards and forbade him to follow the trail of blood. With the flashlight in one hand and the shotgun in the other, he sprinted as fast as he could along the trail of blood—it would be easier to follow while the flare still lasted. After around six hundred yards, the droplets terminated on the steps of the temple-like swimming pool building.

He crept nearer and saw that an improvised barricade of poolside furniture had been piled on the other side the glass door—a black shape lay by the edge of the water: scooping water from the pool with his hand and using it to bathe his seeping bullet wounds. So the Cat was cornered, but doubtless more dangerous than ever.

He put down the flashlight on the steps and blasted the door repeatedly with the shotgun. The door had pretty much disintegrated by the third shot, so he advanced gingerly over the daggers of broken glass and kicked hard at the barricade. He passed inside, and it was obvious from the first moment that the Cat Man had done his trick of melting into the darkness. Rouletabille pointed the barrel of the shotgun experimentally into the furthest corner of the building—at an aggregation of thick, inky shadows. He squeezed the trigger and the shotgun blast boomed deafeningly in the confined space. A couple of pellets also ricocheted straight back at him and struck him in the scalp, just above his hairline.

Sensing movement behind him, he spun and struck at the shape creeping up on him with the stock of the shotgun. The weapon was twisted from his grip with immense strength and sent clattering onto the poolside tiles. The terrifying, snarling form ploughed into him and he lost his balance. Rouletabille anticipated the smack of his own skull on the hard tiles...but it did not come. Instead, there was a watery impact as he was enveloped by the warm wetness of Cyrus West's heated swimming pool. And he was not alone. The Cat Man was in the water with him; spitting, coughing and mewling in distress. The Cat Man couldn't swim!

With a piteous scream, the intruder disappeared beneath the surface of the water. The detective kicked his way to the pool edge, and started to heave himself from the water. His waterlogged clothes made the task more difficult. Suddenly, there was a sharp pain in his right ankle and it felt like a ship's anchor was dragging him down. The Cat Man had him by the foot and was clawing and biting at him under the water. Rouletabille struggled like a madman to free himself, but to no avail. His nose and mouth filled with water, and only then did he realize that it was a saltwater swimming pool. Even in circumstances such as this, the deductive part of his brain was an unstoppable engine—collating and inter-relating facts; theorizing and drawing conclusions. But his deductions could do little to save him now.

He adopted a quiet and dispassionate acceptance of his coming death, and allowed his thought processes to continue their natural work. Of course, West's swimming pool would be saltwater. He'd want to duplicate the experience of swimming at Shark Bay on Lincoln Island. That was probably where he first experimented with constructing flares. Absolutely vital in case one wanted to attract the attention of passing sea vessels. West's flares had the highest magnesium content commercially available. That was very interesting, mused the detective's hazy, oxygen starved brain. The most fascinating attribute of magnesium was its ability to burn underwater...

More out of curiosity than desperation, Rouletabille reached into his jacket pocket and yanked free the Very pistol. Loading it and snapping it shut seemed to be the most complex task that the Frenchman had ever undertaken. More complex than advanced algebra, or memorizing great chunks of catechism. It would be an interesting experiment to see if the Very pistol would fire underwater; after all there was little else to do while he was waiting to drown.

"Where the Hell is he? Where the Hell is he?" cursed Herbert Brown. The old general led an unlikely skirmish line comprising Missy-Lou, Charlie Wilder and two of the security guards. Brown was armed with the pneumatic Nautilus carbine, Missy-Lou cradled the Winchester with an accustomed confidence, and somehow young Charlie had ended up with Rouletabille's Lebel, after he had abandoned it in the library.

Without warning, up ahead of this search party, the interior of the swimming pool building blazed like a white hot blast furnace.

"There he is!" screamed Brown triumphantly. The others streaked past him. Missy-Lou's long legs made her the fastest runner, but Charlie was close behind. Brown huffed and puffed and kept up as best he could. By the time Brown got inside the pool building the security guards were already lifting Rouletabille's unconscious form from the water.

"He'll be fine. Just get him back to Mr. West in the library as quickly as you can," Brown ordered the guards.

Charlie shone his flashlight into the aquamarine depths of the pool, where a dark, fetal form was wrapped in a cocoon of black silky fabric. Missy-Lou was aiming the Winchester at the drowned Cat Man as if he still presented an immediate threat, and warranted a series of potshots.

"Charlie, Missy-Lou—I want him out of there. He might still be alive," the old man barked.

Charlie swiftly unbuttoned his shirt and pulled off his slacks while Missy-Lou removed boots, sloughed off her stockings and pulled her dress over her head before arranging everything in a neatly folded pile clear of any broken glass, with her cotton underwear placed on the top last of all. With her maid's outfit cast aside, Louise Pleasant resembled nothing less than a bronze statue of a goddess come to life. This was how she had stood before the Voodoo worshippers on her home Caribbean island—how she had appeared when she had commanded life, death and sacrifice. How she had appeared when she had both presided over and taken part in the most lewd and debasing sexual rites imaginable. Cyrus West had thought he had rescued her from that life—but she would return to it in an instant if she could; if she ever dared to turn her back on what he alone could offer.

"Hurry up, you two!" commanded Brown.

Missy-Lou dove in, her body cutting into the water like a knife; and Charlie jumped in clumsily a moment after. They swam down towards the still black shape, creating a hurricane of bubbles. Charlie caught up with Missy-Lou with one thing on his mind, and held position next to her in the water. They were too deep now for the old man to see. He placed his palm on her flat belly, and when she raised no objection to this pushed his fingers down into the tight mass of soft curls and the softer flesh they concealed. Then something better caught his eye. The necklace lay at the bottom of the pool—the jewels glittered and burned even in the gloom of these watery depths. He veered away from Missy-Lou, grabbed the necklace and shot to the surface, leaving her to propel the dead weight of the Cat Man up into the life giving air.

Once on the side of the pool, the Cat spluttered and coughed violently. Incredibly, he was still alive. He still bled from several bullet wounds, and his life would soon spill away.

"Missy-Lou, get back into your clothes and send one of the guards to get Dr. Trifulgas from the village."

"I say, let him die," pronounced the Voodoo Queen.

"The Master will want to question him. Please do as I ask," said Brown as if to a child.

Missy-Lou fixed Charlie, who had eyes only for the necklace now, all the time she was changing with a vile, withering look of hatred. Men had begged to touch her flesh, before now. And some who had known it had been driven mad when it had been denied to them. She *had* liked the boy, but now she had the measure of him. Having rejected her in favor of baubles, he would never know the glories of her sacred *punani* when he became Master of Glen Cliff.

Cyrus West had the guards place the sopping wet Rouletabille on his leather-topped desk. West removed the stopper from the decanter of blue liquid and poured a liberal measure of it into a brandy bloom.

"Roger, raise his head for me a little will you?" commanded the white haired man. The lawyer complied and West poured the strange burning liquor into the young man's mouth. He neither coughed nor choked—his eyes fluttered open and he tried to sit up.

"Don't try to get up, son," said West. "Just rest easy. You'll live. Probably for quite some time."

A few minutes later, General Brown arrived back in the library.

"Well?" queried West.

"The guards have the Cat tied up, and I've sent for Trifulgas to patch him up," relayed Brown.

"Good. And the necklace?"

"At the moment, Charlie has it. You'll need to find somewhere very secure for it. The enemy may try again," predicted Brown.

"I'll hide it away someplace, don't you worry. Of course, we'll need Trifulgas to certify the Cat insane—once we've finished interrogating him. That way, there'll be no trial, we can just have him put away in the Fairview Asylum, over the way."

"As you have so many others who've got in your way over the years?"

"Well, if it's good enough for members of my own family, why shouldn't it be good enough for my enemies?" queried West.

"There's a streak of insanity a mile wide in your family, Cyrus. Sometimes, I worry that it has affected you too. You aren't the man you were on Lincoln Island. The years have made you ruthless and capricious."

"Don't talk like that in front of my lawyer, Herbert," laughed West. "What are you trying to do? Invalidate my will?"

Part 2—The Reading of the Will
(Winter 1926)

The limousine left the access road and passed onto the driveway proper; grey gravel was churned noisily by the insistent grip of the tires. Rouletabille looked up at the black, anvil-shaped clouds that were arriving overhead. A colossal storm front was pressing in from the west. Perhaps the largest storm the eastern seaboard had seen for a generation. The last ten years had gone by swiftly. Too swiftly. He had traipsed largely unscathed through many adventures—his time among the gypsies, his encounter with the seemingly indestructible superhuman, Hugo Danner, the Affair of the Octopus, and, of course, the death of his beloved Ivana.... Despite all this, he seemed outwardly unchanged by the decade or so since the closing years of the Great War. Indeed, some said that he had scarcely aged a day in that time. The face he saw in the shaving mirror was still somewhat boyish. But that was hardly supernatural—his mother had retained very youthful looks into late middle age.

Only a few months after his last visit to the West Mansion near Tarrytown, he had received a letter from Herbert Brown stating that Cyrus West had passed away. The letter also told him he was a possible beneficiary in West's will, but that—rather unusually—the will would not be enacted until ten years after the date of death. The detective was therefore to report to the West Mansion for the reading of the will on the given date in the winter of 1926.

A little under two years later, it was with great sadness that Rouletabille received notice from Elena Fairchild-Brown that Herbert Brown had died following a stroke. Rouletabille very much regretted not being able to attend the funeral personally, although he did arrange for attendance by the French Ambassador.

And so it was that Rouletabille and three other potential beneficiaries (some of West's blood relatives) came to be picked up from Tarrytown railroad station and conveyed to the mansion by a luxurious limo. The relatives were: a rather surly and volatile young man called Harry Blythe, an ebullient and end-lessly cheerful young lady with rather a wholesome country way about her called Cicily Young, and finally, the mirthless pinch-mouthed spinster, Miss Su-san Sillsby—who, judging by her advanced age, was one of the relatives who had gathered periodically to assess Cyrus West's wellbeing "like cats looking into a canary cage."

The quartet disembarked from the limo to be greeted by the banshee wind that was roaring up the Hudson. They ran for the shelter of the entrance portico. Rouletabille's umbrella was torn from his grip and somersaulted dizzily into the sky. He looked back at the limo to see that it was already drawing away. Fortu-nately, the mansion's oak door was now creaking open. Rouletabille had antici-pated the familiar and enticing form of Missy-Lou Pleasant on the other side of the door, but instead the door was being opened by a monstrously obese black woman who looked as if she might top 400 lbs in weight. She wore a house-keeper's white cap and a dress of funereal black that might have doubled as a tent in a former life. The immense woman admitted the Frenchman and the two women, but then suddenly barred the way of the saturnine Blythe.

"Wait! I knows M'sieu Rootabby, an' Miss Cicily, an' Miss Susan. But this man is a stranger to me…" she announced accusingly.

Roger Crosby emerged swiftly from the library and called to her.

"It's all right Mammy-Lou, this is Harry Blythe—the only surviving son of the Master's youngest sister."

Rouletabille's jaw was hanging open. How had one of the most beautiful women he had ever seen been transformed into the physical travesty now before him? More mysterious still, how had Missy-Lou's precise, albeit Caribbean in-flected, diction been replaced with a degrading "minstrel show" accent? What had been going on here in the last ten years? And if this was some sort of pre-tense on the part of Missy-Lou/Mammy-Lou, what could possibly be its pur-pose?

Every nerve, brain cell and instinct that he possessed told him the answer straightaway. Cyrus West had been murdered and Missy-Lou's out of character behavior was some sort of warning sign to put him on his guard. To those who saw her every week, the changes would've been barely noticeable and incremen-tal. But she had known that Rouletabille would return this night. She had been compelled to stay here all these years, perhaps under some kind of house arrest. He would not let her down. My God, how he wished he had returned here years before!

"Yes, I'm one of the family…" confirmed Harry Blythe, barging past her.

"We aren't all yet here," said Crosby. "But the reading of the will must commence at midnight as per the Master's instructions.

He ushered them into the library, which had changed little in the interven-ing years. Rouletabille noted the window appeared to have been expertly re-paired. Through it, he could make out zig-zags of far off lightning. The storm was getting closer. Already seated in the library was Charlie Wilder. He rose and greeted his female relatives and Rouletabille, then commenced to serve brandy. Miss Sillsby declined in favor of sherry. Blythe glared at Wilder as if he hated his guts and for a moment it seemed they would not shake hands. Then with a jibe from Crosby along the lines of "C'mon you fellows...," they did a passable impersonation of two reconciled enemies.

There was the sepulchral tolling of the doorbell in the middle distance and shortly afterwards Mammy-Lou opened the library door to admit a striking woman of about thirty with luscious chestnut colored hair.

"I guess I'm here just in time!" she smiled. "The train from Kingsport was delayed due to flooding. I was too late for the limousine, but I managed to pick up a cab..."

"Annabelle West!" cried Wilder, embracing the new arrival warmly. She forced her features into a smile, but her eyes betrayed her. She obviously regarded Wilder as no more human than a maggot. Annabelle broke away from him and shook hands in friendly fashion with her cousins—Harry Blythe, she graced with an almost sisterly caress to the cheek. All the surliness drained away from him and it was rather obvious to everyone that Blythe was totally in love with this woman.

Suddenly, a deep resonant chiming echoed through the house and steadily increased in volume. For a moment, Rouletabille mistook this sound for the aforementioned sepulchral doorbell. The sound continued to swell until it was akin to something like an enormous gong being repeatedly impacted by a battering ram. All in all, it sounded seven times. The women put their hands over their ears (all save Mammy-Lou) and the brandy decanter rattled in its wooden holder. Mammy-Lou seemed to be murmuring some kind of prayer that sounded like "waited so long...waited so long" quietly to herself."

Crosby shook Mammy-Lou.

"What is it, Mammy? What is that sound... what does it mean?" the lawyer demanded.

"The machines... it's coming from the machines," said Mammy-Lou, as if emerging from a trance. And then, remembering her pretence, "I dunno Lawyer Crosby, could be ghosts in the machinery... or perhaps...I t's a death knell. Seven bells and eight souls hereabouts... one of us will die!"

"Nonsense," judged Crosby.

"What machines, Mammy-Lou?" asked Rouletabille, but the housekeeper only stared vacantly.

"She must mean the electric generator," answered Wilder. "Ignore her," he sneered, "she's only one generation down from the trees."

Crosby checked his watch.

"It's midnight. Please all be seated."

Crosby dragged one of the library ladders over to the mantelpiece just as he had more than a decade before, ascended it, swiftly swung the painting to one

119

side and opened the safe. He descended clutching two envelopes. Rouletabille noticed immediately that the envelopes were already opened. Crosby contained it well, but quite obviously he was furious.

"I'm not sure how this has happened, since as far as I know, only the Master and I had knowledge of the combination. But these envelopes have been tampered with. Well, whoever did it wasted their time. I am fully conversant with the terms of the will and two further duplicate copies reside in my office safe in Manhattan," said Crosby, as he scanned the contents of the first envelope.

"Since no attempt has been made to alter the will, I shall proceed with the reading: 'I, Cyrus Canby West, being of sound mind, do hereby make minor financial bequests to all invitees to this will reading who have seen fit to attend at midnight on the tenth anniversary of my death to the sum of ten thousand dollars each...' " read Crosby.

"Well, better than nothing—but peanuts compared to the value of his whole estate," interrupted Susan Sillsby.

"The old man was hardly going to invite us all this way and leave us nothing," replied Blythe.

"You forget that he hated most of his close relatives; although he did have a fondness for Charlie and myself," she smiled.

"May we continue?" snapped the lawyer. " 'The residue of my estate, including all property, monies, shares and patents (currently estimated to be $112 million in value), I leave equally to all my surviving relatives with the surname West."

Annabelle West shot up out of her Arts and Crafts chair like a jack-in-a-box.

"That means I'm the sole heir to the residue of the estate! I'm the only person here called West..." she said breathily.

"I'm just happy to get the ten thou," put in Cicily. "The things I'll be able to get for the farm!"

"Just one moment... I have not yet concluded," said the lawyer. " 'I am aware that a streak of insanity runs in the West family...' "

Susan Sillsby nodded sagely.

"That's right. Charlie's mother was in and out of asylums for most of her life—poor thing. Then there was that scientist cousin of Cyrus' up in Massachusetts; he certainly should've been in an asylum the things he got up to. But they're not the sorts of things that can be mentioned in polite company," wittered Susan Sillsby.

"Should any of my heirs die or be found to be insane within 28 days of inheritance, then their share of the residue passes to the heir named in the second envelope. The identity of the secondary heir is not to be made public except in the circumstances of death or insanity of any of the primary heirs,' " concluded Crosby.

"And yet someone knows who the second heir is," observed Rouletabille. "This is potentially a crime waiting to happen. The second heir could murder the first," he added too quickly, and rather without thinking.

"Except that the second heir is known to me and is a person of good character. Please confine yourself to solving crimes that have actually happened rather than theoretical ones, Monsieur," instructed Crosby.

"That sort of money could turn anybody into a murderer... why, I'd probably kill for it myself..." admitted Blythe.

"Oh, you're taking this so melodramatically," laughed Annabelle. "To Hell with murder, anyone who wants some of this fortune could at least try proposing first!"

Crosby lit a candle on the small desk candelabra, removed the candle and used the melted wax from it to improvise a resealing of the second envelope.

"I'm resealing the envelope that contains the name of the second heir. I'll keep it on my person until I can arrange for a locksmith to reset the combination of the safe. I very sincerely hope that it need never be opened," said Crosby as he moved towards Annabelle. "Miss West, you are now the Mistress of this house. There will be many documents to sign before all Cyrus West's fortune is transferred over to you, and a trip to my office may be necessary."

Mammy-Lou grinned, as if with triumph, and pulled from out of the top of her dress a third envelope, identical to the others—albeit rather crumpled.

"The Massa gave me this envelope to give to the heir. It ain't been opened. I looked after it careful," announced the housekeeper proudly as she passed it Annabelle.

Annabelle looked questioningly at Crosby.

"Strange that I know nothing about it," Crosby mused.

"I'll wager it's about the necklace," suggested Rouletabille.

"What? That tasteless thing that Cyrus had cobbled together from bits of an old crown... he lost it years ago. At least that's what he said," recalled Susan Sillsby.

"I never believed that he really lost it. So careful a man would never lose something so valuable. No, he hid it here in this house... or perhaps out in the grounds," said the lawyer.

"Why, the grounds are like a jungle now," interjected Blythe. "Good luck finding something out there even with a treasure map!"

Annabelle went to open the envelope and then saw that it instructed her to read the contents alone in the master bedroom.

Mammy-Lou explained that she had provided a buffet in the dining room—a sort of midnight feast of Caribbean bouillabaisse—Crosby led the way and most followed, but looking back Rouletabille noticed that both Annabelle and Charlie Wilder had hung back in the library.

"So you still hate me, Annabelle?" opened Wilder. "You know that girl you found me with was nothing to me—just a whore."

"That doesn't help, Charlie. You and I could've had something, but you spoilt it before it began. You've had the run of this place for the last ten years, well now you can pack your bags and clear out," she commanded.

As Charlie slunk out in the direction of the dining room without a backward glance, her mind drifted back to three years ago. She'd met up with Charlie in town, and they had a few too many drinks. He had seemed wonderfully charming and handsome; and the budding playwright had fostered the impression that he stood on the cusp of fame and fortune. Another few drinks beyond that point and they were opening their hearts, and becoming forever soulmates. Charlie revealed that he had never made love to a woman because of his terrible phobia and repulsion of the hair between a woman's legs.

At the end of the evening, he pressed a latchkey into her palm and told her to drop by his Manhattan apartment anytime: that was where he was spending most of his time while his play was in rehearsal. A week later, she used her dead father's cold safety razor on herself and took the train from Kingsport to New York to make a man of him. The apartment turned out to be a tiny cramped hovel above a deli—she didn't mind that. But she was struck mute by the sight of the girl straddling Wilder on the bed. The girl might've been sixteen—just. The girl had looked over her shoulder with an expression that seemed to say, "Wait your turn, sister," while she continued grinding her hips. Annabelle staggered out of there and hailed a cab, at one point she had to ask the driver to stop so she could be sick.

The hollow crack of shotgun fire awoke Annabelle from the painful reverie and she rushed out into the hallway.

"Is that thunder?" Susan Sillsby hoped.

"There's a man in uniform taking potshots at something out in that wilderness of a garden," said Blythe, his face pressed close to the dining room window.

A few moments later, the doorbell rang. Crosby shooed Mammy-Lou away and answered it himself. A man in the uniform of a security guard, armed with a double-barreled shotgun filled the doorway.

"What are you doing discharging a weapon here? This is private property," questioned Crosby.

"Pardon me, sir. I'm Hendricks, the Chief Guard over at the Fairview Insane Asylum in Tarrytown. We've had a breakout and a dangerous prisoner has escaped."

"Who is this prisoner? What does he look like?" demanded Rouletabille.

"He's a case from the violent ward, sir. A John Doe who never speaks…but they call him the Cat. He has teeth filed to points, and he won't let anyone cut his nails. They're big as tiger claws. He's around forty, with a black beard and straggly hair—he has an odd heavy set Slavic look about him too," said the guard.

Rouletabille put his hands to his forehead. Chills were running up and down his spine in icy ripples. Tonight, of all nights, the Cat had escaped. Twenty or so guards had not been enough to protect the house last time. He wondered if any of them would survive this night. He saw that all the color had drained from Crosby's face.

"I remember the man you are describing," began Wilder. "He attacked us here over ten years ago and was shot over and over. I can't believe that the poor fellow who was so badly injured could be much of a threat now."

"Don't waste your sympathy on that monster, mistuh. He's killed two of fellow inmates while he's been in Fairview—and tried to eat them," retorted Hendricks.

"Please, Mr. Hendricks—we have the fairer sex present," reprimanded the Frenchman.

Hendricks bowed apologetically.

"Just keep all your doors and windows locked. It's howling a gale out here and the Cat will probably want to seek shelter."

"You might want to check all the outbuildings. That was where I found him last time," advised Rouletabille.

"Thank you, sir. I will," said the guard and disappeared into the night. After a few seconds, all that could be seen was the dancing beam of his flashlight.

Rouletabille drifted back to the library while the others returned to the dining room. He was looking for weapons to use. The Winchester Rifle was no longer on the rifle rack. He checked the *Nautilus* carbine and shotgun, but both were bereft of ammunition.

Mammy-Lou walked quietly in.

"The new Mistress wants you. She's up in the master bedroom," she explained.

"Very well. Just one question, if I may, Mammy-Lou. I don't mean to be rude. But what's happened to you... your appearance... your manner of speech?"

She smiled at him and winked.

"Missy-Lou disappeared... changed over time in order to survive. This subservient manner is just a smokescreen—while I behave like this, very little that I do is questioned or scrutinized. They are too dumb to realize what a threat I am to them. And as for packing on the weight, well not being so easy on the eye has its advantages too. Charlie Wilder has stopped trying to knead my ass and rub my snatch."

Rouletabille blushed and Mammy-Lou giggled.

"I been looking at you, M'sieu. You are still looking very, very young. That was a powerful batch of the old *E.V.* that Cyrus poured down your throat. It might be another twenty years before you show any grey," she said enigmatically, caressing his cheek with an enormous hand. And with that, she turned slowly and led the way to the master bedroom.

Annabelle showed the writing on the crumpled letter to Rouletabille.

"I guess pretty much everyone has heard of your reputation for solving impossible mysteries and puzzles—what do you make of this? Is it the clue that will lead to the necklace Cyrus hid?"

The detective read from the letter:

"Keep in Mind, the Mother of Wine
There you will find the treasure that is thine.
Enemies abound, yet love never wanes,
The Beast is among us, his claws are stained."

"Well for a soldier and inventor, he still made a lousy poet," smiled Rouletabille. "It's as much a warning as directions to the necklace. The first line alone indicates the location of what was once the Crown of Jovan Nenad. We'll need to go out to the glasshouse or whatever is left of it. I'll need a gun and some ammunition from Mammy-Lou."

"No need. There's a gun right here in my bedside drawer," laughed Annabelle as she pulled the drawer open. Rouletabille was amazed to see his old Lebel revolver—now gold plated courtesy of Cyrus West. Could Cyrus have predicted all this? In creating a puzzle, he had guessed that the heir would call for Rouletabille. Thus allowing the detective to protect the heir. But protect the heir from what? Cyrus could not have foreseen the escape of the Cat, or could he? Without explanation Rouletabille pocketed the revolver and helped Annabelle into her coat. Then they slipped downstairs and surreptitiously headed out into the blackness and driving rain.

The interior space of the glasshouse was roughly the same area as two football fields. Rouletabille found the master light switch controls and threw them. A mixture of heat lamps and ultraviolet bulbs gradually came to life, bathing the scene with a dim, but slightly eerie light. The glasshouse roses had run amok during the last decade and most of the pathways were completely overgrown. Rouletabille and Annabelle picked their way through, avoiding the thorns as best they could. In the center of the glasshouse was a huddle of Greek statues: Venus, Cupid and Psyche.

"Keep in mind—the note said. Cyrus West loved Greek statues. And the use of the word 'mind' suggests the statue of Psyche is the relevant one," reasoned Rouletabille.

"But the house and grounds are full of statues. How do you know this is the right one?" quizzed the heiress.

"We are to keep in mind the Mother of Wine. The Mother of Wine is the grape," said Rouletabille, as he pointed up to robust trellis behind the statue; on it grew a thick grapevine—though at this time of year the fruit was naturally absent. "Where else would you find a grapevine in this climate other than in a greenhouse?"

The detective rooted around in the growth at the base of the statue and then noticed on the pedestal an embossed tile bearing the image of a bunch of grapes.

Without hesitation he smashed it and gingerly reached into the cavity behind. Annabelle was astonished when he withdrew a rather dirty velvet jewelry case.

She snapped it open revealing the glory of the diamond and emerald necklace. Impulsively she opened the clasp and put it about her slim pale neck. Rouletabille helped her to refasten the clasp—the jewels suited her well.

The Cat watched them go from his place of concealment. They had found the Crown of Jovan Nenad for him and soon he would relieve them of it, but now was not the time. The man was armed, clever and dangerous. The Cat would take his prize from the girl when she was alone.

On the way back to the mansion, Rouletabille noticed a bluish illumination coming from within the swimming pool building. They went inside to investigate and saw that the pool was now dry and disused. In the floor of the swimming pool a trapdoor had been installed—a trapdoor which had been left open. Rouletabille jumped down into the pool and peeked into the chamber below. The room was intermittently illuminated by the sparks from odd looking electrical apparatus. In the center of all this paraphernalia lay a hollow crystalline cylinder about seven feet long that was filled with an opaque, luminescent blue liquid. Rouletabille wanted to investigate further, but was unwilling to leave Annabelle alone. This could wait until the morning. Soon they were back inside the house. The other invitees and Crosby had retired for the night, so the Frenchman had some special instructions for Mammy-Lou. Annabelle also retired, but after the extreme excitement of the day she took the precaution of taking one of the mild sleeping powder which she kept in twists of paper in her handbag. She thought about waking Crosby so that the necklace could be put in the safe, then she remembered that someone had already illicitly opened the will envelopes. The best place for the necklace was therefore around her neck. Rouletabille had told that he would post himself directly outside the door in a chair and not go to sleep. That made her feel safer. She didn't even bother to change into her negligee; just peeled off her blouse, skirt, underwear and stockings and lay on the bed nude. Within moments she was asleep.

A long time passed, cycles of dreaming began and ended, and after a while she became aware of the generous hand of her lover caressing and teasing her body in the most intimate fashion. It was good to have a lover again, but in her sleepy state she could put neither a name nor a face to her new man. How had they met? Perhaps she would remember in the morning. Now he was becoming too rough, and his nails hurt—they seemed almost like claws. Claws! Her eyes were wide open now. The black clawed hand reaching over her was just barely illuminated by a sliver of light from the curtain chink. The claws dragged up her belly to her cleavage and then yanked at the necklace and pulled it from her. Surprising herself with the speed of her reactions she switched on the lamp just

125

in time to see the Cat's hand and arm retreat into a yawning aperture in the wall directly behind her bed. Then the secret panel slammed shut. Annabelle grabbed the robe from her bedside chair and ran for the door clutching it in front of her.

"Rouletabille! The Cat has taken the necklace…there must be a secret passageway!" she screamed at him.

"Quiet! Quiet!" ordered the detective. He attempted to bundle her back inside the room, but failed.

The Cat was framed in the library doorway. He edged along the wall to the stairs. Rouletabille eased the revolver from his pocket and covered the black robed figure as he went.

"There is no escape that way… Charlie," called Rouletabille. "Mammy-Lou has locked all of the bedroom doors and window shutters."

"My God! Charlie! It can't be…" breathed Annabelle.

The Cat started to advance back down the stairs and the Frenchman saw that his face was, after all, just a rather realistic papier-mâché mask. So obviously created by someone with connections to the theatre industry who had seen the real Cat up close.

Charlie Wilder untied the black ribbons which held fast the mask.

"You think you're so smart, Rouletabille. But I haven't lost yet…if this place goes up in smoke and you all die, there'll be no witnesses and I still inherit. I am the second heir…if the old man hadn't lost his mind, I'd have been the first heir."

The sudden sounding of the intensely loud gong momentarily distracted Rouletabille, and then the stock of a shotgun slammed into the back of his head causing him to drop like a broken puppet.

"You ain't paying me enough for all this," announced the fake guard Hendricks, as he stood over the Frenchman's crumpled form.

"Shut up, and go and get the gasoline," commanded Charlie.

Hendricks obediently headed for the front door, but stopped in his tracks when Mammy-Lou loomed out of the darkness holding the Winchester rifle. Without hesitation she shot Hendricks straight through the head. Charlie froze.

"You insignificant little fool. You dared to try to turn Cyrus against me. Manufactured and planted evidence that I had returned to the practice of Voodoo, and that I was being unfaithful to him; for those things you should die ten thousands deaths. It's a pity I can kill you only once. But I'll make your death last as long as I can," spat Mammy-Lou.

"No Mammy-Lou, he's insane. He belongs in Fairview," rasped Rouletabille, as he fought his way to his feet.

Mammy-Lou lowered the Winchester and Rouletabille dared to exhale with relief. Only then did the detective realize that his gold-plated Lebel was in Annabelle's hand and was being leveled at Charlie.

"The most gullible slut I ever fed a line to," were Charlie Wilder's last words before Annabelle shot him six times. Eventually, Rouletabille was able to wrestle the empty pistol from her, but by that time she was almost catatonic.

"I'll get Dr. Trifulgas for the Mistress," volunteered Mammy-Lou.

In the morning, Rouletabille was looking for Mammy-Lou but could not find her. Crosby and West's relatives were taking breakfast in the dining room, almost as if nothing had happened—even though they must've tiptoed around the bloodstains in the hall. He saw Dr. Trifulgas ministering to Annabelle and the good doctor confirmed that she would make a full recovery. He couldn't quite place Trifulgas' accent—but the physician revealed he was originally from a place called Ulthar. Rouletabille assumed this was in the Netherlands but didn't like to show his ignorance. He wandered into the library and found a pale fair-haired bespectacled man who slightly resembled Charlie searching through the old Master's desk.

"Who are you?" asked the detective.

"My name is Herbert West, I was invited to attend last night but there was severe flooding in the Arkham area."

"West? The scientist from Massachusetts? Then you've missed out on a share of $122 million," sympathized Rouletabille.

"So I hear. But all I really want is this," said Herbert West pulling from the desk drawer the *E.V.* decanter which still had a few dregs of the glowing azure fluid within. "It will be useful for some experiments I have in mind and I should be able to synthesize more. You see Cyrus always kept the precise formula to himself." The pale man smiled and strode swiftly from the library; and then from the house.

Rouletabille thought for a moment. He thought about everything that had happened. It wasn't easy, the blow from Hendricks had given him a mild concussion and his vision kept swimming. Some of it was starting to make sense. Charlie had played in the house all his life, so he had known about the secret passageways. He couldn't find the necklace so he needed the heir to find it. Charlie had watched Crosby and Cyrus open the safe often enough to be able to memorize it. Yes, some of the details made sense, but overall the picture was still blurred. Where the Hell was Mammy-Lou? And then he had it. He pulled a decorative sword from the wall and left by the front door into the bright morning. The storm had passed, but there were still a lot of overgrown roses to cut back before he got to the Hudson.

Thirty minutes later he was on the estate boat jetty. The racing yacht *Sea Silk* was still tied up there. He climbed aboard. Abandoned in the companionway was a huge black dress surrounded by great molded sections of some kind of soft foamy rubber. On a chair in the galley was Mammy-Lou's rubber mask. It had been a disguise worthy of Rouletabille's great enemy Larsan. The door to the cabin was open and Rouletabille saw the slim, dark bronze form of Missy-Lou slip out of bed and put on the light.

"Come in, Monsieur Rouletabille," said Cyrus West. "I'd like to say 'you must have many questions'—but knowing you, you've probably figured the whole thing out."

Rouletabille stepped into the cabin and looked at West as he lay in bed. His beard and hair were now jet black, his eyes clear—his face with scarcely a wrinkle—like a man of less than thirty.

"You did not die…instead it was a process of rejuvenation, albeit a slow one. It took ten years of immersion in the *E.V.* fluid to rebuild your body. I saw the machine responsible. It was concealed beneath the now unused swimming pool in the pool house. Missy-Lou left the door to the secret chamber open when she went to the pool after the gong sounded. The gong was an alarm to tell her that you were almost ready to be removed from the rejuvenation machine. I deduce that your confederates in this affair were your relative Herbert West, a brilliant scientist, and the physician that you keep on hand, Dr. Trifulgas. The clearest indication that you were not dead was that you made no allowance in your will for Missy-Lou—a woman you plainly held in the greatest affection."

"I told you he'd figure it out," said Missy-Lou, before landing a passionate kiss on Cyrus West's lips.

Rouletabille realized it was time for him to leave.

Less than twenty four hours later, Cyrus West and Missy-Lou departed in the *Sea Silk* and were never seen again. Annabelle subsequently married Harry Blythe, and they lived as happily as one can be expected to live in this imperfect world.

The eponymous "Brotherhood," which is the subject of Emmanuel Gorlier's latest tale, is not related (as far as we know) to the Corsican proto-Black Coats organization mentioned by Paul Féval. Emmanuel Gorlier, who has specialized in chronicling the life of Leo Saint-Clair, aka The Nyctalope, as well as those of his ancestors, returns here with another tale featuring the Marquis Henri-Jean de Sainte-Claire, last seen in "Fiat Lux!" published in our Volume 7, in the days of the Musketeers...

Emmanuel Gorlier: *The Brotherhood of Mercy*

Paris, July 1655

The Rue du Colombier was bathed in the soft light of the full Moon, its denizens sleeping peacefully, when suddenly they heard the clatter of hoof beats. A squadron of horsemen appeared. From time to time, the distant crack of a whip suggested that the newcomers were escorting either a horse-drawn cart or a carriage. They must have been both in a hurry and well-connected to risk awakening the affluent neighborhood. They must also have been aware that the Buci Gate would be opened just for them at this late hour, giving them access to central Paris.

A passer-by, had there been one, would have first observed riders moving in pairs at high speed. They wore the light blue uniform adorned with a white cross of the King's Musketeers. At their head was the famous Charles de Batz-Castelmore, Comte d'Artagnan, their illustrious captain who had distinguished himself during the recent Civil War, rendering notable service to young King Louis himself. He was followed by six more men. Then came a richly-decorated carriage bearing the coat of arms of the Archdiocese of Vyones in Averoigne. Six more Musketeers closed the ranks.

Inside the carriage, shaken by the ride over the uneven cobble stones, was Archbishop Henri de Ximes, one of the main collaborators of Cardinal Mazarin, the Grand Minister of King Louis XIV, who ruled the kingdom of France according to the dictates of his illustrious predecessor, Cardinal Richelieu. Many in the Louvre Palace believed that Ximes would be the one to succeed Mazarin when the prelate took his well-deserved retirement. It was rumored that Mazarin had asked Pope Alexander VII to make Ximes a cardinal and was only waiting for the Pontiff's favorable response to make his decision known.

Archbishop Ximes was carefully examining a map. For several weeks, at Mazarin's request, he had roamed the countryside west of Paris in order to buy a large plot on which the Cardinal planned to build a new palace for the King. Mazarin had bad memories of the "*Fronde*" (as the Civil War had been dubbed)

129

and wished to remove the young monarch from Paris, where he had been a *de facto* prisoner of the populace. Ximes had looked at many places: Saint-Cloud, overlooking the Seine, Saint-Germain, Montrouge, but so far, no location had pleased him. He now proposed to expand his field of research. Maybe he should take a look at... he looked at the map to refresh his memory about the place... yes, that was it—Versailles!

A few hours earlier, he had been contacted by d'Artagnan, who carried a note from Mazarin asking him to return to Paris immediately to deal with a case involving the security of the kingdom. The note had given no further details. Ximes wondered what it was all about...

The carriage stopped; d'Artagnan spoke to the guards at the Buci Gate and they were let into the city. They traveled north through the deserted streets of the capital to the Pont-Neuf; they were expected at the Louvre Palace.

After a few minutes, d'Artagnan noticed a cart across the road blocking their path. He slowed down and ordered his men to do the same. He felt a sense of vague uneasiness. If the streets of Paris were often very crowded during the day, the presence of this cart was highly unusual at night.

Just as his horse stopped, d'Artagnan took the pistol from his belt and looked around. They had come to an intersection and their coach was accessible from all sides. He frowned and was about to ask two of his men to move the cart, when a group of ten men appeared on their left.

From their ragged clothes and the weapons they carried—swords, daggers and a few guns—it was clear that these men were bandits, and the cart was part of their ambush plan. However, it was surprising that such men would attack a convoy escorted by Musketeers—or was it?

The first attacker set foot on the coach and threatened the Archbishop with his pistol. Before he could finish, d'Artagnan fired his own gun and blew off the right side of the man's face. That prompt action gave time enough for the Musketeers to unsheathe their swords and get between the coach and the bandits.

The surprise element of the attack had failed. Henri de Ximes was now safe from the attackers. So that he would not be hit by a stray bullet, he moved to the opposite side of the carriage. But suddenly, d'Artagnan, who was watching the entire situation, saw him crumple in his seat.

A small arrow was protruding from the back of his neck!

D'Artagnan took advantage of the moonlight and looked up in the direction whence the projectile had come. Then, he spied a strange figure, dressed in black from head to toe, his face hidden under a hood that prevented any identification. The killer was holding a crossbow and had just stood up from behind the chimney where he had been hiding.

D'Artagnan discharged his gun, but knew that it could not reach that far. Maybe he could throw his dagger, but his chance of hitting the assassin was at best remote. The hooded man then threw a metal object next to the Archbishop and vanished. The Musketeer approached Ximes to see if there was anything to be done for him.

During this time, his men had forced the four bandits to run off, but perhaps, that had always been part of their plan after the murder of the Archbishop?

D'Artagnan immediately realized that Ximes was dead. The crossbow's bolt had transpierced his neck. The Musketeer was surprised that someone still knew how to use the old-fashioned weapon with such deadly accuracy. His eye was suddenly caught by the reflection of the metallic object thrown by the assassin. He picked it up. It was another weapon from the past: a strange, comical knife with a very sharp blade. It was called a *miséricorde*, a weapon of mercy once used to put an end to the sufferings of armored knights who had fallen to the ground, were gravely wounded and could not get up. The killer had struck with such skill that even he, d'Artagnan, Cardinal Mazarin's best man, had not been able to stop him. Now he had to go and report his failure. It would not be a pleasant task.

About twenty yards away, hidden in the shadows, a dark and hairy creature watched the scene carefully through yellow slit eyes.

The next afternoon, three men were waiting in the large hall located just outside Cardinal Mazarin's office.

Two of them stood by the windows, talking, clearly worried. One, Jean-Baptiste Colbert, dressed in sober clothes, managed the Cardinal's fortune; the other, more flamboyantly dressed, was Nicolas Fouquet, the newly-appointed Superintendent des Finances. The door was opened by an usher and the two men were quickly ushered in to see Mazarin.

There remained, other than the two guards, a third man, in the prime of life, who looked like a soldier. He bore a scar on his left cheek. He was Jean Henri Sainte-Claire, Captain of the Royal Guard, and one of the few men of action that Mazarin used for his most secret and dangerous missions. He was one of a group of five men the Cardinal had nicknamed his "Glove" (after his so-called "Hand of Iron"), and whom Mazarin entrusted with affairs of the kingdom that required both the utmost discretion and determination.

While waiting to see the Cardinal, Sainte-Claire remembered the last meeting of the Glove, which had taken place a week earlier. All five members were in attendance: the most prestigious of them, Comte d'Artagnan, who had just returned from a secret mission to Flanders; Hercule-Savinien Cyrano de Bergerac, to whom Sainte-Claire owed his scar from when they had clashed during the days of the late Cardinal Richelieu.

Over the years, their relationship, which had begun so badly, had blossomed into a true friendship. The two men, while very different, dined together frequently. Also present was the Chevalier de Villemonteix a gentleman from Marches who had a gift to foil conspiracies by managing to infiltrate them from the inside. He had been wounded in the arm during his last mission. The last and newest member was Baron d'Ylourgne, a young gentleman from Averoigne. His family dated back to an ancient lineage of Barons who, according to rumor, had been little more than bandits during the Middle Ages. He had been recommended by the Archbishop of Vyones, Henri de Ximes.

During the meeting, Mazarin had asked what progress the Glove members had made on the investigation into a series of crimes that had been committed in recent weeks by what they now called the "Brotherhood of Mercy," since the assassins, who had murdered a dozen noblemen, had, in every instance, left behind the same, small conical knife, which had become their signature.

It turned out that only the most progressive amongst the aristocracy had been targeted. The Glove theorized that the Brotherhood's aim was to restore a feudal monarchy. The Cardinal, who was a reformer, was therefore directly affected and, indeed, many of his supporters were amongst the victims.

The last time the Glove had met, no real progress had been made. Villemonteix thought he'd found a lead, but his opponents had escaped, but not before shooting him in the arm. The only one who had had some success was Cyrano de Bergerac, but only by pure chance.

Every Saturday, Cyrano called at the convent of the Sisters of the Cross. The last time he'd gone there, he's witnessed four masked men attacking a lone rider. Appalled by such cowardice, Cyrano's blood had boiled and, unsheathing his sword, he'd ordered the group to desist and rushed to help the victim. The fight was quickly over. Two of the attackers were killed, and the other two fled, wounded, losing much blood. Cyrano had found a "mercy knife" on one of the two dead men. It had, therefore, been an attack connected to the Brotherhood.

Once unmasked, one of the dead men was revealed to be one of Cyrano's old enemies, the Comte de Duras, an old aristocrat whom Cyrano had once caused to be locked up at the Bastille over the matter of stealing an inheritance. He had been released only a few months earlier thanks to the Cardinal's leniency—in this case, obviously wasted on the scoundrel!

It turned out that, that day, Cyrano had saved the Duc de Nevers, who was one of Mazarin's major supporters!

Ylourgne was tasked with the investigation into the attack, but Sainte-Claire doubted he would find anything useful. It was eventually decided that d'Artagnan would go and fetch Archbishop Henri de Ximes, who would be entrusted with the broadest powers possible in order to put an end to what looked like a vast conspiracy. Sainte-Claire would be responsible for the security of the Louvre and the Cardinal, while Cyrano would look for clues amongst the progressive circles of the aristocracy. It had been agreed that all five would meet again at the Cardinal's office this day, to greet the Archbishop and plan their future operations.

Looking up, Sainte-Claire saw Cyrano and Ylourgne coming towards him, deep in animated conversation. As he approached them, smiling, Colbert and

Fouquet came out of the Cardinal's office, silent and looking worried. They quickly left while the usher asked the three men to go in.

Cardinal Mazarin was sitting behind his large desk at the back of the room. As Sainte-Claire often said, he had taken on all the habits of Cardinal Richelieu. The Cardinal had plenty of time to study his visitors as they crossed the ten meters separating the desk from the front door.

To the left, the three men were surprised to see d'Artagnan already there, his face dark and drawn.

Mazarin addressed them in his Italian accented-French that was only made worse when he was troubled:

"My friends, this is most serious. D'Artagnan has just brought me terrible news. Henri de Ximes has been murdered tonight by the Brotherhood of Mercy. The most powerful men in the kingdom are no longer safe, even behind an escort of Musketeers... So far, we have no tangible evidence. One of your group was even wounded. We must pull together; otherwise, I fear that the safety of the King himself may no longer be guaranteed. Give me an update on the progress of your investigation; we need to move more quickly!"

"Your Eminence," said Cyrano, "the literary salons are filled with gossip regarding the attempted assassination of the Duc de Nevers. The general mood is to condemn, not condone, however. Our enemy is not amongst that crowd, and the murder of the Archbishop of Vyones will only drive them closer to you."

"That's something at least! But I wish it hadn't been at the cost of my spiritual son's life! Monsieur Ylourgne, have you found something?"

"I believe so, Your Eminence. I investigated the relatives of the Comte de Duras and, as luck would have it, I managed to find a connection between them and a band of brigands that are said to roam the Forest of Bondy. I even managed to locate their lair."

"Monsieur Ylourgne, you are prodigious! D'Artagnan, Cyrano and Sainte-Claire, please accompany the Baron and arrest these cut-throats."

"Yes, Your Eminence," said d'Artagnan, "but could we also carry a blank *lettre de cachet* that would give us the power to arrest any nobleman connected to their conspiracy, in the event we find any?"

"Yes, that is an excellent idea," said Mazarin. "They, too, must be captured and interrogated, if at all possible..."

While uttering these words, the Cardinal reached into a pouch on his left, pulled out a sheet of paper and handed it to d'Artagnan.

"Signed by His Majesty himself. This confers you full powers. With it, you can open all doors, including those of the Bastille. Go, my friends. For the first time, we may have a lead. Let's not waste this opportunity!"

As they were leaving the Cardinal's office to gather the soldiers who would accompany them, Sainte-Claire wondered how Ylourgne, so young and from Averoigne, more than a hundred leagues from Paris, could have found a lead so quickly. He had no time to inquire about it then, but he meant do so at the first opportunity. Perhaps, his young companion had something to teach him.

In the courtyard of the Louvre, they were met by twenty soldiers on horseback: ten Musketeers, some of whom had belonged to the Archbishop's escort (D'Artagnan thought that they would be happy to take revenge on their attackers) and ten royal guards hand-picked by Sainte-Claire, their captain.

They quickly left the palace and headed towards the gates of Paris and, from there, the forest of Bondy. By killing the Cardinal's main assistant, the bandits, who had so far enjoyed relative impunity, had made a fatal mistake that would cost them dear ly. The best soldiers in the kingdom were now gathered to fight them.

An hour later, the twenty-four men had surrounded the cabin in the woods and approached silently. Ten meters from the building, the Musketeers took position, ready to shoot anyone who attempted to leave.

Saint-Claire and Cyrano, walking at the head of the royal guards, moved quietly to the door to arrest the bandits. When they were two meters away, two shots were fired through the window to the left. One bullet went astray but the other hit a guard in the head. The man's body had not yet touched the ground when the Musketeers opened fire at d'Artagnan's command.

What remained of the window exploded in a shower of shards. Several cries were heard from inside the cabin. Cyrano and Sainte-Claire opened the door and entered, their swords drawn. They found two men lying on the ground, obviously wounded. Another man stood by the window, his arm clearly shattered by a bullet. Only two bandits were unharmed; they fell on Cyrano and Sainte-Claire with their weapons.

The battle was short. Cyrano disarmed his opponent, but stopped his sword a few millimeters away from the man's throat. Because of his clothes, richer than those of his companions, he guessed that this might be the leader of the bandits. Sainte-Claire, although not as good a swordsman as Cyrano, whose only equal was d'Artagnan, quickly found the flaw in his foe's defense and ran his blade through the man's body.

The cabin was theirs. D'Artagnan rejoined his companions and began to interrogate their prisoner.

"You've got only two choices: either you tell us who your masters are, and I promise to spare your life, or you remain silent and tomorrow you'll be broken on the wheel at the Chatelet. You choose."

"I don't know who paid me to attack the Archbishop..." began the bandit.

"That's not good for you."

"...But I can tell you where and when I am to meet with him to learn of our next mission."

"Ah, that's better! Speak!"

"We're to meet at the Chateau de Haute-Maison on the banks of the Loire. Tonight, at two a.m. We are to make sure that no one is following us."

"That's tight, but we can get there on time," said d'Artagnan.

The soldiers left the house, taking the wounded with them.

Cyrano turned to his companions:

"My friends, today's Friday and, as you know, I must be in Paris tomorrow morning for an appointment I cannot miss, so I won't be able to accompany you tonight. I hope you won't hold this against me. I will however take these scoundrels to the Chatelet, where I'll make sure every bit of useful information is extracted from them. If that man spoke the truth, I shall see to it that they receive preferential treatment."

D'Artagnan smiled and replied:

"Of course, my dear friend. Please present my respects to the good Sisters. There are more than enough of us to resolve this matter without your help."

Baron Ylourgne then intervened:

"Gentlemen, I regret to tell you that I, too, cannot accompany you. I am scheduled to meet for dinner with my uncle in Paris tonight. He has traveled all the way from Averoigne because wants to tell me in person of a secret that involves my family. It is, according to him, a matter of honor and I cannot postpone our encounter. I beg you to hold me blameless for this and allow me to not join you later tonight."

"I understand," replied d'Artagnan. "We cannot force you to do anything that might impact your honor in any way. Sainte-Claire and I will start; join us as soon as you can."

"Thank you, Comte. I will not fail you."

D'Artagnan and Sainte-Claire watched their friends ride away, then themselves rode to the Chateau de Haute-Maison, where they hoped to discover their mysterious enemy.

They arrived just before midnight. They quietly approached the castle and hid behind some bushes near the front gate.

The Chateau was a 14th century fortress which had undergone little change since the Hundred Years War. A reinforced iron gate gave access to an inner courtyard.

At 12:30 p.m., a dozen riders appeared. Because the Moon was hidden behind a curtain of clouds, their features were not identifiable. Or they would have been, had not the Marquis of Sainte-Claire enjoyed a special power. Some years earlier, during his first meeting and duel with Cyrano, he had been struck in the face by his opponent's sword, and that blow had given him the strange ability to see at night as if it were broad daylight. Reading old family records, he had later discovered that that power had belonged to several of his ancestors, who had had acquired it under similar circumstances, following a blow to the face.

This mysterious power now proved useful as Sainte-Claire was able to see who their adversaries were.

Most were unknown to him, but he recognized their leader: it was Charles, Duc d'Averoigne and Peer of France, a member of the royal family descended from Saint Louis! He had never imagined that the conspiracy would reach such high levels. It was almost as if the throne of France itself was implicated!

The Duc dismounted at the door and gently took a long parcel that had hung from his saddle. After that, he and his men entered the castle.

Sainte-Claire whispered a few words to d'Artagnan to explain what he had just seen; the Musketeer stiffened suddenly and unconsciously touched the *lettre de cachet* hidden in his glove. With it, even the Duc d'Averoigne could be imprisoned in the Bastille by a mere Captain of the Musketeers.

"Let's wait," said d'Artagnan. "Others might be coming."

During the hour and a half that followed, a dozen more riders entered the castle. One of them was known to Sainte-Claire. They were all noblemen, some from the most illustrious families.

Shortly after one a.m., since no newcomer had arrived, d'Artagnan exchanged a knowing look with Sainte-Claire, who nodded in return and motioned his men to approach the gate.

Sainte-Claire had noticed that the conspirators had thrice struck the door four times. He knocked in the same fashion. He heard the sound of keys rattling and the gate opened.

Their hoods thrown over their heads to hide their identities, d'Artagnan and Sainte-Claire entered. A man-at-arms greeted them.

"Hurry, Messieurs, the Duke is about to speak."

Just then, four shots rang out. The guard turned to see what was happening and d'Artagnan hit him on the head with his pistol. He quickly lost consciousness. Sainte-Claire opened the gate and the soldiers entered *en masse*.

Quickly, they headed for the main hall of the castle from which they heard loud cheers. They came to a large two-panel door, slightly ajar. Behind it, a voice rang out. D'Artagnan and Sainte-Claire recognized it as Charles d'Averoigne's.

"Yes, my friends, the time has come! The Archbishop of Vyones, my old enemy, was executed yesterday by our brave companion here. Tomorrow, we'll strike at the highest level. Mazarin himself—cursed be that Italian swine!—will be eliminated. Our companion will strike him down in his very office in the Louvre. Everything is ready, and nothing can stop us!

"We will force the King to abdicate, then we shall seize the reins of power through a new Regency and will restore the rights and privileges with which we were born during the days of our fathers! Vast powers will be granted to each of you. The kingdom shall return to what it was at the time of King Charles VII when our brave knights drove the English out of France!

"The best in our kingdom were betrayed by Louis XI and his successors, deprived little by little of all their rightful prerogatives. It is that very betrayal that we sought to evoke with the symbol we chose: the mercy knife, the weapon used to put an end to a knight's suffering after he'd fallen to the ground.

"I say, we shall succeed because it is God's will. And tonight, I bring you proof of our forthcoming victory!"

While the Duke was engaged in this harangue, d'Artagnan and Sainte-Claire were casting concerned glances throughout the room. They were surprised by the great number of participants. There were at least fifty people standing in the hall, more than they had seen arrive. Arresting so many opponents would be a tricky .task

Standing next to the Duc, d'Artagnan recognized the masked man in black who had killed the Archbishop of Vyones. Charles had designated him as the man tasked with the assassination of Cardinal Mazarin.

The Duc d'Averoigne seized the long parcel they had seen him grab before entering the castle. He opened it and pulled out a sword. This weapon was obviously very old. It was a heavy broadsword of the type used during the Hundred Years War or the Crusades.

He brandished it in the air and the blade gave off a pale light.

"On your knees, my friends!" he exclaimed. "Kneel before the sword of our Holy King Louis IX with which he dispensed justice under the oak. See how it shines in the hands of he who shall become King Charles X!"

All kneeled before Averoigne, paying tribute to his leadership and that symbol of a feudal monarchy of divine right which had been gradually diminished during the last two hundred years.

This was the moment chosen by d'Artagnan to enter the room at the head of his men. He was followed by Sainte-Claire and his royal guards.

"On behalf of the King, lay down your arms!" exclaimed the Musketeer. "You are all under arrest!"

But the audience stood and put their hands to their swords. The Duc d'Averoigne shouted:

"Kill them all! We cannot lose! There are more of us and God is with us!"

D'Artagnan tried to fire his pistol, but, already, several rebels had jumped forward. He fired into the crowd and charged.

Within moments, the room turned into a battlefield. All the participants were battle-hardened warriors. D'Artagnan and Sainte-Claire were likely more capable than any of their opponents, but they were outnumbered two to one. Early on, they had enjoyed the advantage of surprise, but as the conspirators regained confidence, that soon vanished. The situation became critical. Half of their men had been killed or were seriously injured. Their opponents might indeed win the day...

Then, something extraordinary happened. A huge, black shape appeared behind one of the tall windows located on each side of the room. It was a large, black wolf with yellow, blood-shot eyes. The beast jumped into the room and landed on the back of one of the conspirators, who collapsed under its weight.

The animal's powerful jaws tore the throat of the hapless conspirator, projecting drops of blood all around it. Then, raising his head and scanning the room, the Beast fixed its eyes on the Duc d'Averoigne.

Two of the conspirators stepped in to protect their leader. They simultaneously struck the animal with their swords, but the blades slipped in and out without injuring the creature.

"It's a werewolf!" shouted Averoigne. "Silver is the only thing that can hurt it!"

The Beast, displaying its prodigious strength, quickly killed the two terrified men who had dared strike it.

The appearance of that infernal creature caused a movement of panic amongst the conspirators, who wondered if they could ever overcome this invulnerable monster. D'Artagnan and Sainte-Claire seized that opportunity to break free of the men who had been surrounding them.

After having eliminated two more opponents, the werewolf faced the Duc d'Averoigne who still held the sword of Saint Louis. The Duc looked at the shining blade, smiled and charged the wolf just as the creature had launched itself at his throat.

The weapon met the wolf in the midst of its jump. The blade sliced through its left flank just as any sword would have on a normal wolf. The enchantment, or supernatural power, that protected the creature was less strong than the Holy Relic. The beast was thrown to the side of the room, where it remained prostrate and trembling.

The Duc d'Averoigne exulted. His victory over this demon would become the stuff of legends and confirm his role as the new, rightful King of France.

Looking away from the wolf, he saw d'Artagnan standing before him. The Musketeer seemed unimpressed by his feat of arms and said:

"Surrender, Your Highness, or I might be forced to kill you."

"Impudent rascal!" spat the Duc. "Do you realize the nature of the forces opposing you? You would do all this to defend a pup king controlled by his foreign minister?"

"His Majesty may still be young, but he is the rightful king, whereas you are nothing but a would-be usurper."

The Duc d'Averoigne, infuriated by d'Artagnan's reply, delivered a blow of his sword that was clearly meant to cut the Musketeer in half. But d'Artagnan avoided the blow with a step back and, with a wide circular motion with his sword, wrapped his own blade around the Duc's and managed to disarm him. His fencing skills were far superior to that of his opponent.

Charles remained frozen by surprise, and d'Artagnan quickly picked up the sword of Saint Louis. Then, inexplicably, as his hand grabbed the hilt, the blade began to shine a light far, far brighter than it had when it had been in the Duc's hand. It was like the light of the Sun compared to that of the Moon!

D'Artagnan was at first surprised, but then brightened and decided to seize this new opportunity. Wielding the sword still bathed in light, he shouted:

"My Lord Duke, and you too, gentlemen, behold the judgment of the sacred sword of Saint Louis. I am but a humble servant of the legitimate holder of the crown of France. Through me, and its unparalleled splendor, it confirms without any possible doubt, that King Louis is indeed our rightful sovereign by the grace of God. Throw your arms and surrender to the will of the Almighty!"

A hush fell over the hall. The conspirators looked undecided. The symbol of their quest had betrayed them. Their fight no longer had any reason to exist. Yet, they were the strongest and could still carry the day...

In such a situation, it was impossible to predict what would happen in the next second.

It was then that the Duc d'Averoigne knelt before the shining sword.

Witnessing this act of submission, which surprised d'Artagnan just as much as everyone else, the conspirators had no alternative. One by one, they threw their arms and kneeled.

The Brotherhood of Mercy had ceased to be.

Standing a few feet behind d'Artagnan, Sainte-Clair had watched the proceedings with astonishment. The surrender of their opponents when, mere moments before, all had seemed lost was the greatest surprise. As the remainder of his troops arrested the conspirators, from the corner of the eye, he saw a surreptitious movement to the left. It was the man in black who was trying to leave the hall through a back door.

Sainte-Claire rushed in pursuit of the murderer of Archbishop Vyones.

Behind the door, he saw a corrodor leading to a stone spiral staircase. The sounds of footsteps indicated that the man was running downwards. Sainte-Claire began to rush down the stairs which led to the cellars.

When he reached the bottom, he found himself in a space lit only by a single torch located at the other end of the cellar. Although he was almost in complete darkness, because of his eerie power, Sainte-Claire saw a dirt-floor, a central aisle leading to the torch affixed to the opposite wall, and on both sides, two alcoves plunged into total darkness.

The man in black was hiding in one of the alcoves, believing himself to be invisible. He planned to stab Sainte-Claire in the back as the Captain of the Guards walked past him. However, it was not to be.

Sainte-Claire, for whom darkness did not exist, found the man immediately and, before the man in black could strike, dealt him a fatal blow with his sword. The assassin collapsed on the ground, moaning.

St. Clair stooped and unmasked his opponent.

"Villemonteix!" he exclaimed in surprise. "So you only pretended to be injured to better commit your crimes! I understand now! It was easy for you to know where and when to strike, and as a member of the Glove, you would have no difficulties in approaching Mazarin to kill him!"

"Yes, Sainte-Claire, I played a dangerous game, and I lost. But I regret nothing. I had to do everything in my power to restore the kingdom of France to its former glory... I can no longer strike that dog of a Cardinal, but I've taken steps to deprive him of his best man: Cyrano is doomed! The order has already been given. It's too late and... God..."

The Chevalier de Villemonteix died without finishing his prayer.

Saint-Claire returned to the hall where he asked to speak to the Duc d'Averoigne:

"Villemonteix is dead," he said. "But he told me that he'd planned an attack against Cyrano de Bergerac?"

"Yes. Some of our men will try to kill him when he goes to the convent of the Ladies of the Cross, as he does every Saturday ... The aim is to avenge the death of the Comte de Duras."

Sainte-Claire reported his conversation to d'Artagnan, then said:

"I'll return to Paris right away. Do you have any idea who the werewolf was?"

He gave a nod towards the great black wolf still shivering on the floor.

"I think I know," replied the Musketeer. It's the Baron d'Ylourgne. The story about meeting his uncle was a lie. His, er, condition explains how he was able to follow the bandits to their lair."

"I see," said Sainte-Claire. "Well, take good care of him. We will meet again tomorrow at the Cardinal's..."

Sainte-Claire rode out of the castle at a gallop towards Paris. He wondered if he would arrive in time to save his friend.

When he reached the hotel where Cyrano lived, the swordsman had already left for his weekly rendezvous at the convent.

Sainte-Claire rushed to the convent. When he was let into the garden, he heard the voice of his friend and was at first reassured. But as he approached, he saw him lying on the ground, a sister kneeling by his side. Immediately, his fears were revived. He had long suspected that the woman dearest to his friend's heart, but inaccessible, resided at the convent.

As he approached, he saw that the woman who was listening to his friend was in tears. Cyrano was lying there, his head bandaged, severely wounded. He probably had dragged himself there to die in his beloved's arms.

Sainte-Claire then heard his final words:

"...Despite you, there is yet one thing I hold against you all, and when, tonight, I enter Christ's fair courts, and, lowly bowed, sweep with doffed hat the Heavens' threshold blue, one thing is left, that, void of stain or smutch, I bear away despite you, and this is..."

The woman kissed his forehead and asked:

"'Tis?"

"My panache!" replied Cyrano, with a smile, for the last time.

On September 5, 1655, Duc Charles d'Averoigne and fifteen high-ranking noblemen who had taken part in the conspiracy dubbed the "Brotherhood of Mercy" were beheaded for the crime of *lèse majesté*.

Among those attending execution were Comte d'Artagnan, Marquis de
Sainte-Claire and Baron d'Ylourgne, his arm in a sling.

(Translated by J.-M. & Randy Lofficier)

Micah Harris said he conceived "The Frequency of Fear" long before he had ever heard of, let alone seen, The Cabin in the Woods. *His actual inspiration was, in fact,* Texas Chainsaw Massacre, the Next Generation. *As for the hero of this fear-filled tale, Teddy Verano, he was created in 1937 by the late, lamented French writer Maurice Limat (1914-2002) and appeared in at least 46 novels published up to 1956, many of which featured sf or fantasy elements. When Limat began to write for the "Angoisse" imprint of Editions Fleuve Noir (which also published the* Madame Atomos *novels) in 1962, he brought Teddy Verano with him, without aging him a day. Soon, Verano was pitted against a demon-possessed actress Edwige Hossegor, a.k.a. Mephista, who proved more popular than Verano, and ended up spearheading her own series of 13 novels, until 1974.*

Micah S. Harris: *The Frequency of Fear*

Florida, Louisiana andTexas 1972

One mid-June morning in 1972, Winnie Innsmouth was honing her psychic abilities over a milk shake when she was distracted by a man speaking with the hippie who ran *Goosecreek*, a combination ice cream parlor and head shop. The stranger's authentic French accent clashed with the southern and Cajun ones that were the aural wall paper of the Florida panhandle.

"What is it?" her friend Abby asked, holding up the Zener card with its face turned away from Winnie.

"That man in the trench coat," Winnie said.

Abby looked at him, then back at Winnie. "I mean the card," she said.

"Uhm, a star," Winnie said, still staring at the stranger.

"It's a circle," Abby said. "That means a total score of 2.75 on the Rhine scale." Abby bent back the Zener card between her thumb and forefinger, took aim, released her hold, and the card sprang across the table, popping Winnie on the jaw.

Winnie flinched. "Cut it out," she said, still continuing to stare at the man with the accent.

"You broke your streak of a score of no less than 3.25. Shouldn't have let your concentration slip. How are you going to be in shape when Eerie Cain gets back?" Abby looked again at the man in the trench coat. "He looks like a Narc. If Jeb has any doobies on him, we could lose our hang-out," she said.

Winnie turned to her and smiled. "You're not worried about losing Jeb?"

"He's such a creep. You said so yourself."

"Well, Abby, if his stares bothered us that much, there's no law that says we have to wear tight shorts and low-cut, midriff baring tops when we come in here. You could try remembering how to hook up a bra, too."

"But there are *cute* guys who come in *Goosecreek*, too," Abby whined.

The man now turned his back to Jeb and leaned against the wooden counter. From the eight-track player behind the bar, David Bowie as Ziggy Stardust was singing *Starman* while Jeb's counterculture countenance radiated his displeasure at the Frenchman's presence.

The stranger was tall, slim, and clean-shaven, with a gaunt face and short brown hair. Beneath the trench coat, he wore a fashionable suit with wide lapels and broad tie. Even under all those clothes, he appeared amazingly cool to have stepped out of the summer heat of the Florida panhandle.

"He's coming over here," Winnie said and made a quick touch inspection of her long, fashionably straight blond hair, which, like Abby's, had lunar blue highlights from the nearby entrance to the black light poster gallery.

"Young ladies..." the stranger began and smiled, then noticed the Zener cards. "Forgive me for interrupting your testing of psychic abilities..."

"Oh, it's no test," Winnie said. "I'm established as a powerful reader... and sender. And there's a lot of synchronicity around me. I don't know how many time I've picked up the phone to call Abby, and when I do, the phone hasn't even had time to ring, and she's already on the line."

"Amazing," he said.

"That's not all. Post cards from places I've never been to, but plan to go, will show up in the floor of my trailer."

"Truly, *there are more things in Heaven and Earth than our philosophies have dreamed of.* If I may introduce myself, my name is Teddy Verano."

"Hi. I'm Winnie Innsmouth. This is Abby."

"Winnie *Inns*mouth? Perhaps this is a long shot, but I don't suppose you're related to the Innes who own the mining company?"

"Yes," Winnie said. "I changed my last name in protest because I sided with the Indians in their dispute over digging a quarry."

"I read about that. Good to meet you, Winnie Innsmouth. How do you do?"

He pulled out his wallet from his suit coat's pocket and from it, a private investigator's license.

"I'm a Postmodern Meta-cinema detective," he said.

"You're... what?" Winnie asked, blinked, and smiled.

"From time to time, the sharp boundary between the fiction within a movie frame and the reality outside collapses and some entity, or event, from within the film can enter our world. Then, there are those outside the film frame who seek to exploit this in reverse, so that actual personages and historical incidents become only the characters and narratives of the movies. In any scenario, the image of the real *becomes* the real. Celluloid is a palimpsest from which I scrape the overlying layer of fiction-etched emulsion to let the light shine through."

143

"Far out," a wide-eyed Winnie said. "Nobody around here lays it down as heavy as you just did. We have some gurus who try but…"

Verano produced a jeweler's lens and a small manila envelope. "Would you like to see an example of my work?"

"Would I?" Winnie bounced in her chair and pulled a stray strand of hair behind her ear. "Please, have a seat."

Verano handed her the lens as he was seated, then produced three frames of black and white 35 millimeter film. Winnie squinted in the eye piece, and up-on focusing on a film frame, immediately recoiled with an "Ow!" as though the lens had injected a needle into her eye. "Oh, man, that *hurt*! Her pain…!"

"*Her* pain?" Verona asked.

"Did you poke yourself?" Abby asked.

Verano put his arm around the entire chair, drawing Winnie with it to him. "Let me see, let me see. I am sorry, Mademoiselle; your eye is slightly pink. Is your vision…?

Winnie stared into *his* eyes and said, "*I Eat Men Like Air.*"

Verano startled, and she could see a contemplative expression that had not been there before when she had spoken of her psychic feats.

"Who is it? Sylvia Plath?" Abby asked.

"No. *That* is the scariest woman I've ever seen," Winnie said. "And… the most anguished. Where's it from?"

"The cutting room floor."

"Why are you carrying around a portable peep hole into Hell?" Winnie asked.

"Wouldn't even someone in Hell deserve justice? This woman is my client." He took out a fresh handkerchief from his shirt's front pocket and gently dabbed at her still watery eye.

"Are you feeling better?"

"Yes, thank you," Winnie said, taking the purple handkerchief that matched his shirt and tentatively touching at her flooded lower lid.

"Trust me, Winnie. I had no idea that would happen," he said as he put away the film frames and the eyepiece.

"Well," she said with a smile. "I heard a movie director on TV say, *Film is forever; pain is temporary.* I'll be fine."

Abby, who had been eyeing a scowling Jeb eyeing them, said, "Did I hear *peep hole into Hell*? Because, hey man, we don't need France's Anton Levey here."

"No, Abby. She wasn't demonic… not in the sense you're thinking," Winnie said, then looked at Verano. "More like a Fury."

"Why did you quote that particular line of poetry?" Verano asked.

"Poetry? That's her name."

"You *are* truly gifted. Were you ever professionally tested?"

"Frequently," she said. "When I was at Duke University. I got so involved with the Rhine Institute, my grades started slipping. But I dropped out for another reason: I couldn't be taking my parents' money for school while protesting their actions, you know?"

"You are a young woman of integrity," Verano said as she gave him back the handkerchief.

"And you... you've actually experienced some heavy psychic phenomena yourself, haven't you? You have the vibes."

Verano made a slight nod of his head, and he and Winnie locked eyes.

"Hey, man," Abby said. "I thought you were hunting down movies in which case you're way off the trail of whatever you're trying to find. Nobody's *ever* made a movie in Citruston. Even if it was in the black and white days, that's the sort of thing people would still be talking about. Not a lot happens in this little town."

Winnie frowned pointedly at Abby then smiled back up at Verano . "That's what makes someone like you showing up here exciting."

"My understanding is there's a lot going on in your little town," Verano said. "Besides the protests concerning your former Indian reservation, you have your own, er, Big Foot, here, *n'est-ce-pas?*"

"You mean the Lurk?" Winnie said. "They're calling him Loulu now, for Louisiana Lurker. That's where he seems to have ended up."

"Ended up?"

"You see," Winnie said, "the industrial-military complex... of which I'm ashamed to say my family's business has become a part... made a toxic wasteland of the Lurk's swamp, along with the rest of the reservation land. So, that drove him out and now he's the Louisiana Lurker."

"Or Loulu," Verano said and smiled.

Winnie smiled back. "Or Loulu."

"Well, if you came here to investigate the Lurk, the sooner you get to Louisiana, the better, right?" Abby asked, keeping one eye on Jeb, who had been slashing his forefinger across his throat at her.

"I'm not here for the Lurk. Besides the woman on this film, I am working for the SDECE, France's equivalent to your CIA..."

Abby was already half-way up from the table. "Winnie, we are out of here right now!"

Winnie, however, had not risen. She looked up at her friend. "It's OK, Abby. I have a...sixth sense about this, OK?"

"Who needs one? No one wonder Jeb is pissed off. This guy's with the Company, Paris Branch."

"What's the trouble over there?" Jeb asked from the counter. "'cause I done told you I don't need no Narc frog upsetting the clientele."

"It's all right, Monsieur Jeb," Verano said, raising his voice without turning around. "Abby, please be seated."

"Abby," Winnie said with a nod of her head toward her friend's chair. Abby slowly slid back into it.

"Our two countries are not allies in some global conspiracy," Verano said. "If anything, the CIA has become our adversary. They borrowed someone from my government who then, so they claim, escaped their custody."

"Custody? The guy your government loaned out was a prisoner?" Winnie asked. "What was he in jail for?"

"He conspired with his mistress to murder his wife. They literally frightened her to death by leading her through a series of faux scenarios he conceived and executed."

"Wait… my mom told me about a movie about that…" Winniesaid.

"*Diabolique*. And it wasn't just a movie, I assure you. The man who I'm looking for, Michel Delassalle, is very real. And very talented in creating believable tableaux of terror. The official line is that Delassalle is believed to be hiding out in French Louisiana."

"So how soon do you make like Loulu and head for Louisiana?" Abby asked with a cock of her head.

"In good time," Verano answered her, but continuing to look at Winnie. "My government believes yours is lying, that they desire Delassalle to continue actively working with them with accountability to no one. Let me show you a photo… this one won't hurt. I promise."

"Sure," Winnie said, smiling back.

Verano pulled a manila envelope from inside an inner trench coat pocket. Opening it up, he tugged out a black and white photo of a group of men and one attractive brunette seated about a cheap hotel room and slid it onto the table. Winnie leaned over the table, ostensibly to get a better look at the photo but really intending to *give* a better look of her to Verano.

Her smile quickly gave way, and her lips hung parted for a moment. Then: "That woman is my cousin, Diane Innes," she said. "She's been the head of Innes mining ever since Uncle David went native again."

"And this…" Verano stabbed with the tip of his finger a man with neatly combed, greased black hair and slits for eyes "…is Michel Delassalle. This is the last photo taken of him... here in Citruston's lone motel... before he disappeared. Four years ago, at roughly the time your government took custody of Delassalle, a film came out which had an extremely limited release before being pulled from circulation. It remains suppressed to this day despite it being one of the last films of a major star... you know Boris Karloff, of course. The convenient death of the producer allowed this. The title of this film is *The Fear Chamber*. Now, during the second World War, a crossword puzzle writer once gave away code names to a secret project of the Allies, all by accident. Or perhaps…" He smiled at Winnie.

"Synchronicity," she said, smiling back as she continued to lean over on her forearms toward him.

"Yes, synchronicity," he said. "In any event, I believe the producer... like that puzzle writer... was called into account. Perhaps fatally so.... Now, you recognize no one else but Winnie's cousin?" Verano asked.

Both girls shook their heads.

"This man is a Dr. Karl Mantell, which, according to publicity materials, is the name of Boris Karloff's character in *The Fear Chamber*. And the final man is a Dr. Warren Chopin, whom you may know by reputation among your counterculture friends..."

"Oh, yeah," Winnie said. "You remember, Abby? Jeb talked about how when acid was legal, he'd been one of Dr. Chopin's volunteer test subjects."

Verano arched a brow at this. "Oh? So, your surly friend there at the counter and Dr. Chopin have a past association, eh?"

Abby slowly shook her head. "Winnie, you shouldn't have..."

Verano held up his palms. "Hey," he said, "it was all legal here then. Right?" He brought his palms down on the table. "No problem. My interest is *why* Dr. Chopin was conducting these experiments. He was researching the nature of fear. His endeavors have been presented to the public, not as fact, but in the 1958 movie, *The Tingler*. In that film, his last name was Chapin. So, Miss Innsmouth, do you have any idea why the head of Innes Mining would be meeting with a want-to-be Timothy Leary and a murderer?"

"That's the question, isn't it?" she said. She had not been oblivious to Jeb's glowering at them from the counter. She patted her stomach. "I need to walk off this milkshake before it goes to my hips. Would you join me, Mr. Verano?"

"With pleasure," Verano said, rising and beginning to walk across the room to the door.

Abby caught a rising Winnie's wrist. "We were going to listen to my Crosby, Stills, Nash and Young album, remember?"

"*Déjà Vu*? Again? No thanks. "

Winnie arched a brow and looked through the ice cream parlor's plate glass window through which she could see Verano smoking on the sidewalk now. "I'd rather spend some time with Monsieur Verano. He's serious about the paranormal, and he was impressed with me."

"Maybe he was impressed with Eerie Cain, too. Ever think about that? He could be a killer, and if you expect me to tag along and piss off Jeb, I ain't doing it. You'll be alone with him."

"That's the idea."

Winnie stepped onto the sidewalk so hot with an early afternoon Florida sun she could feel the heat through the rubber soles of her flip flops. She took Verano by the elbow and began to steer him down the sidewalk.

"My government did the right thing," she said, "destroying the ecology here."

"But you were implacably on the side of the Indians in there."

"I had to appear that way in front of Abby and Jeb. And previously that *was* my position. My protests were genuine... at first.

"I mean, I was pissed about the family's lawyers holding everything up in court while they continued to dig the whole time. The Indians weren't getting any representation worth anything. The land would be stripped before any kind of ruling was reached. Since the Indians couldn't fight it in court, my friends and I started the protests. But we couldn't have known... *I* wouldn't have known, except for the Colonel."

"Colonel?"

"Colonel Whiteshroud. He'd come down to Florida to hunt the Lurk."

As they strolled from one shop awning to another, Winnie suddenly caught their reflections in the store windows and laughed. "We could be that couple from *Breathless*, except my hair's far too long for Jean Seberg's in that movie. Since your job revolves around movies, are you able to go, you know, just for fun?"

"As long as it doesn't have Edwige Hossegor in them. But tell me: how did this Colonel Whiteshroud disabuse you of your convictions in the Indian-Innes conflict?"

"I was chained spread-eagle to a bulldozer when he came up to me and said, 'I understand you are one of the Innes family, but you've taken the Indians' part in this conflict.' I rattled my chains and said, 'Obviously, dad.'

"He said the sea-faring side of my family may have mentioned him as 'the Angler' from the Innsmouth raid. I told him no hard feelings. Innsmouth hadn't been 'our' town since the last century. Not since the economy got so bad that the townspeople turned on the Innes for letting it fail. That's why they let the 'e' drop out of 'Innesmouth' to disassociate themselves from the Innes family after the Zadoks turned their fortunes.

"He asked if disassociation with my family was why I had changed my last name to 'Innsmouth' without the 'e.' I told him, number one, it poked my family in their collective eye, and, number two, I was trying to make a parallel with the government holocaust there and what was going on with the Indians here.

"'Young woman,' he said. 'There is much more of a parallel than you suspect.'"

Winnie and Verano were now sitting on a bench with flaking green paint which set in the shade of a large weeping willow overlooking a lake. A steady breeze was coming over the water.

"What did he mean?" Verano asked.

"He had discovered something else while trailing the Lurk on the Indian reservation. Like Innsmouth, it had become a breeding ground of some ancient evil that could not be tolerated: an ancient Asian cult that the Indians had brought over the land bridge to America with them. These *dugpas*, he called them, had a sacred grove. He had spied on them there, and said there was something about that grove in particular and the plant life on the reservation in general that wasn't *right*.

"Well, we had some words over that. You see, the Indians were in special communication with the plants on the reservation. There's no better way to put it than to say the plants ruled the reservation and everything was harmonious between them, man, and beast. One botanist said he's never seen such a concentration of sensitive plants…"

"You mean the so-called 'rapid movement plants' that respond to touch and sunlight? *Comme les mimosas*?" Verano said.

"Yeah, but their sensitivity went beyond that. You're talking about a sort of retreat, and they were capable of that, but they could be aggressive, too. Some exuded sickening fumes if you get too close, or spewed a volley of pollen out at you which could be bad if you were asthmatic.

"That doesn't sound very harmonious," Verano said.

"Well, nothing was fatal; once was all it took to teach you to keep your distance, animal or human. And it's not like *all* the plants were like that. There were plenty of edible ones. And these were *luscious* crops. Believe me; you *never* saw corn as yellow and eager to come off the cob when you bit into it, or tomatoes as tender and red. Biting into the fruit from the reservation was like opening your mouth on a fountain of fresh juice.

"The plants had even disciplined the animals to stay out of the Indians' gardens and fields. The leaves of the edible plants and their foliage mimicked the 'touch-me-nots' that were the sensitive defensive ones who put off a bad odor or taste when bitten. Animals couldn't tell the difference. These kinds of plants would even grow to make a defensive barrier around the Indians' crops.

"And, weird as it sounds, the plants would lead the Indians to game. They hunted *with* them, communicating through a semaphore system to lead them to prey… which was freshly dead. With no mark of violence."

"As though *frightened* to death, would you say?"

Winnie looked at Verano and hugged herself; her exposed skin was suddenly gooseflesh, and not from the breeze off the lake.

"Uh-huh," she said.

"Well, this wasn't all argued with me chained to the bulldozer. It was an on-going debate between us. And, despite my initial resistance that the reservation harbored this *dugpa* cult, the idea was still mysterious and intriguing. Kind of wild. But ultimately, it would come back to me saying, 'Colonel, you've seen the ecology here. For humans and animals, it's flourishing under the plant rule better than where humans are running things.'"

"So what made you change your mind?" Verano asked.

"He introduced me to an associate from the reservation, John-Walks-The-Wind. He confirmed the *dugpas*' presence among his people; they had been there for ages. He told me his tribe's story of a 'great fiery mountain' that burrowed into the earth."

149

"A fiery mountain?" Verano asked.

"He said their medicine men, the *dugpas*, heard the trees of the sunken mountain calling to them from across the continent. The *dugpas* drank tea made from the great trees' leaves, and it put their memory in the *dugpas'* minds of how the great, fiery mountain had come from a world where the plants were mobile, and they herded stupid, bovine things, preying on the meat for what the plants thrived on, that could not be synthesized: animal fear. Then, there came a day of devastation; continents were pulled apart, their world sundered and the pieces hurled across the void of space.

"That was how the burning mountain came to Earth. It was in the mountain's voice that the *dugpas* had heard the trees call to them. It spoke to the plants, too, and the spirits of the trees and the bushes were changed. Then the Great Trees taught the Indians to communicate with this changed vegetation. But John said that, when the plants led them to a fallen deer, it wasn't for the Indians' sake. They wanted it to *look* that way, but that was just really incidental. The plants were parasites. The plants led them to their prey only after the plants had maximized the hunted animals' fear and fed on it. Of course, the secret of the plants was to remain unknown to the white man."

"So why did he reveal it to this Colonel, and now you?" Verano asked.

"John said it was because the *dugpas* were now saying it would be good for the plants to spread beyond the reservation. In all their centuries here, they had yet to find one among their own people—one who is both the door, and who stands without the door, holding the key that unlocks the tears and screams..."

"A door to *where*?" asked Verano.

"He wouldn't explain; he said that he had already said more than he should. Except that he was determined that that door should remain closed. But, the Colonel already knew; he had learned from his time in Asia that the *dugpas* always sought ingress into a place called the Black Lodge. Then he asked me if I'd sneak out at night with him into the heart of haunted hollow."

"Haunted hollow?"

"A grove on the reservation he'd visited before. It's a local legend. A bunch of my girlfriends and I tried to go out there one night, but we didn't make it all the way. The closer you got, the more you felt yourself being watched by things moving alongside you in the woods. But I decided to give it another shot.

"Still, it wasn't long before I had hooked the Colonel's arm with my own. I was already feeling watched, but the Colonel was unaffected. He told me he had learned how to block fear from his mind from a sect of Tibetan monks while hunting abominable snowmen.

"Well, we made it, and walked into this grove of tree as large as redwoods. They were stunning, even by moonlight. The creeps gave way to awe, and I slipped away from the Colonel to walk among them, looking up.

"That was a mistake.

"I used to candy stripe, and I've been where someone has just died and not easily, like at the end of a prolonged struggle with cancer. There's a smell to a death like that, and that scent was suddenly hanging like a miasma among the trees. The trees were mimicking *that* somehow! I couldn't breathe for it!

"I ran. I mean, I was rounding the trunks, and, I swear, it couldn't be true, their roots were probably miles deep, but the trees seemed to be reconfiguring themselves to not let me out.

"I could hear the Colonel shouting to me, but I guess I would still be running rings around those trees in fear, except he caught me, threw me over his shoulders, and carried me out of there.

"Once we were clear of the trees, he plopped me down. I was panting and the Colonel said the fear manifested there even pressed against his mind's psychic barriers. Such a place, he said, could very likely allow ingress to the Black Lodge."

"This arbor sounds like the Fear Chamber; perhaps the Fear Chamber *is* the ante-room to this Black Lodge," Verano said. "Your Colonel seems like he might prove a valuable ally. Could you introduce me to him?"

Winnie shook her head. "You missed him. Twice. He left that night for Washington. He had the FBI's respect from his days as the Angler, and they took him seriously when he told them that what was on the reservation was a potential risk for the country's security. Not only were the *dugpas* planning to spread the plants, if somebody like the Underground Weathermen found out about them... They weren't taking any chances. Not just the ancient trees, but *all* the reservation's plant life had to be considered a potential threat and had to be destroyed."

"How did they pull it off, Winnie?" Verano asked.

"Well, first they needed to relocate the Indians. I'm sure they doctored soil samples they'd taken already, before introducing the toxin into the reservation as a whole. That way, no human life was really in danger, but they'd have evidence that they needed to relocate the Indians.

"Then, the Colonel released into the ground from a lead container this essence that was all that was left of some meteorite shards that had been recovered in New England and then started to melt away in the late 19th century. The reservation flora didn't give up and die easily, though. Those plants and trees were in *torment*. You could tell. Mute vegetation twisted like it was in agony and in a life-struggle against something as powerful as they were. Then, one night, it was like the aurora borealis over the reservation, but the light show wasn't a color anybody could ever identify... at least, anybody who hadn't ever taken acid. It was like the *land* itself was trippin', man! And that did it. After that night, everything withered away into ash and was gone in a few months."

Their shadows were now stretching down the incline of the bowl-like slope that led down to the pond.

"Monsieur Verano... Teddy," she said. "I know you're in the middle of a case... two, counting that spooky woman from that film. But there's something I'd like you to do for me," she laid her hand over his. "And I think it might be related, actually."

"What is that, Winnie?"

"There's a boy who's a friend of mine... not a boyfriend... but I've known him since grade school. We could read each other's thoughts for as long as I can remember. We did all kinds of tricks together, I'd have him turn his back and pick a playing card, then reshuffle the deck, and I could always find the card he picked. Now he and I have psychic duels at *Goosecreek* with the Zener cards. He has even teleported objects... made them vanish as he passed them through another dimension to reappear in our own across the room. His name's Eric Cane, but he got the nickname 'Eerie' because of his paranormal abilities."

Verano smiled. "Yet, you displayed some of the same abilities and no such nickname for you?"

Winnie smiled back and cocked her blond head. "Do I look eerie to you?"

Teddy admired the muscular but femininely toned brown thighs and calves that contrasted appealingly with the white cut-off denim shorts she wore. "No," he said, "I can most assuredly say you do not."

She grinned. "Well, Eric's been away for a couple weeks now. He may have just dropped out, you know? There's a secret hippie Mecca Jeb talks about. He's said he'd love to take me, but I know better than to get alone with him. Sometimes girls *will* go with Jeb in his van to party there, but they're not with him when he comes back. He always says they just parted ways. The girls were transients when they came through Citruston, so there was no reason to think anything of it. But when Eerie disappeared, and Jeb saw I was worried, he hinted heavily that was where he went, and was having a blast. He said I would understand, and wouldn't want to come back, if I ever let him drive me out there.

"But ever since John-Walks-The-Wind said the *dugpas* were looking beyond the reservation for the one who is the door and holds the key to the Black Lodge, I've been afraid that, given Eric's access to that other dimension, *they* might have got him."

. "They may have taken him to the haunted hollow before it was destroyed to be the door and the key. If so, I think, because of this connection we've had since we were kids, I might be able to psychically pick up on what happened to him. Especially if something really... violent happened to him. Will you go with me?" She laid her delicate hand over his.

"*Bien sûr*," Verano said. "For my own investigation to be complete, I would like to survey the site of this former arbor of horror."

"It's a decent hike, but with all the under and overgrowth gone and everything pretty much a plain of gray ash now, there won't be many impediments. One of the local reporters quoted John Milton to describe it: *a blasted heath*. We should be able to get there and back a lot more quickly than the Colonel and I did. Plus, it's daylight."

"How far is it to the former reservation?" Teddy asked.

"About a mile. We'll have to slip through a barbed wire fence after that and go on foot from there."

"I take it the government put up this barbed wire, and we'll be trespassing?" Verano said.

She tossed her head. "I don't have a problem with that. Do you?"

"*Non*," he said. "No problem... as long as we don't get caught, I suppose. Let's go."

Following Winnie's direction, Verano drove them in his rented car to the back side of the former reservation. When he came to the barbed wire fence, he tested it and found it pliable... he expected the government didn't really depend on the wire keeping people out, for the vista before them offered nothing to trespass for. This was indeed a *blasted heath*, a plain of gray ash marked here and there by withered trees that appeared to have been burned.

He pressed his foot on the lower strands of wire, and, grasping the space between the barbs of the wires above, bent it up to let Winnie slip through. Then he carefully worked his way through while maintaining the opening... still not without tearing his shirt sleeve (he had left both his overcoat and suit coat inside his car).

"How will you be able to recognize where you and the Colonel went? With everything changed," Verano said.

Winnie pointed. "See those black trunks? They're not the equal of redwoods they were before, but they're still the largest remains out here... even dead."

Verano now loosened his tie as they began to walk. The plain of ashes made the already hot Florida sun seem more boiling. They were soon both perspiring profusely. The land was gray and now so was the sky, though the heat did not lessen. The whole world seemed gray and crumbling under their feet.

When they came to the giant black tree trunks, Teddy took note of a large outcropping of quartz, leaned against it, and wiped sweat from his face. He noticed Winnie now stood stock still, her pupils oscillating.

"What is it?" he asked.

"Don't you hear it?" she asked. "I can hear groaning... like heavy branches creaking with the wind..."

"There is no wind," Teddy said.

"...or *human* groaning..." She looked up, clasped her hands to the sides of her mouth and screamed.

Teddy started to dart to her just as a dark, wet drop struck his bare hand from above. He tossed his head back...

Where before there had been denuded trunks under a leaden day sky, now there was a canopy of interlocking tree limbs through which a starry night could be glimpsed; shapes moved among these heavy branches which jutted, not from the blackened withered things in the ashes they had approached on their walk, but tall trunks as ancient as and measuring the circumference of the largest, oldest of redwoods.

He pressed his hand against the side of one of the trunks to confirm its reality and found it slick. He withdrew a palm and found it now smeared with thick black fluid.

Another wet drop, and another...

And he looked up again...

Up, up, endlessly up reached the boughs, alive with writhing, grimacing naked men and women, all suspended by hooks through their pectoral muscles, hanging like tortured ornaments on an evergreen in hell. Winnie began screaming again, and the Frenchman looked to see that she was now surrounded by a ring of Indians in loin cloths of hemp and headdresses made of skulls of large crocodiles or the pelts from heads of panthers and wolves.

The men took no note of Verano, but darted at her, trying to switch her with flails of long, limber twigs. Terrified, she managed to dodge their lashes. In truth, she was at the mercy of her own psychic power. Teddy moved to take hold of her, to shake the mounting hysteria out of her and break the psychic circuit of her vision of the past into which she had pulled him.

He drew up short as he saw John-Walks-The -Wind run inside the circle. But instead of aiding the terrified girl, he locked his strong arms under hers and bent them behind her.

"John, what are you doing?" she yelled, but in a man's voice: Eric Cain's.

"This is the lodge of the Tree Chiefs, the antechamber of the Black Lodge," John said. "These trees are my people's oldest of living things, and grew from the very spot where the fiery mountain penetrated the loins of mother earth. They are the stars' firstborn. Within their trunks are many rings, so their rind has grown thick and must be bitten through with great effort.

"The other plants are nourished with water; the Tree Chiefs must be watered with wine. For the other plants, the pallid fear of animals and birds; for the Chiefs, the headiness of human pain with its bouquet from the human mind's unique power to reflect upon its suffering. Only this can quench their roots that have plunged so deeply.

"The Tree Chiefs order the other plants who serve us. They have given so much to our people. How can we say no?"

"John," Winnie cried out, again in a masculine voice. "Are you as insane as the rest of them? Help me, man!"

Now a wiry, old man, back hunched with arthritis, breasts sagging, and his tongue like a slug darting onto his bony chin, approached her as the others fell back. His wizened, rutted face peered into hers from under the upper mandible of a great crocodile skull, as though the reptile had dislocated its lower jaw to vomit him up. Old and bent his body may have been, but his black eyes revealed an evil inside him unabated from age or infirmary.

On the end of a carved wooden instrument like long pronged tweezers, he clinched a sliver of the same quartz crystal that still stood in the remains of the grove. From behind Winnie, a thick thumb and forefinger pressed on her nose's cartilage, widening the nostrils while pulling her head back...

"No, no, *no*," she shouted in Cain's voice.

Teddy fought against his urge to try and wrench her from their communal nightmare. But it was only that for him and Winnie: a bad dream into which they had walked. For someone else it had been a reality, and Winnie was remembering from his point of view. She had wanted to find out the fate of Eric "Eerie" Cain. To achieve that, they were going to have to let his memory play out.

From Winnie's throat issued Eerie's bellow of agony and helplessness as the shard was thrust up and up inside her noseBlood seemed to gush from Winnie's right nostril as phantoms hefted her up over their heads, and began carrying her to the oldest of trees where there was already in place the tackle to hook her and suspend her from her pectorals...

"*His* pectorals, *his*," Verano forced himself to remember this wasn't happening to Winnie; it had happened already to Eerie Cain, and what was done was done. Still, his heart thrust itself against his rib cage powerfully at the torture that was all too real for the girl.

Now, rattling the flail of twigs, the old man chanted:

"You who are both the door, and stand without the door with the key, your tears and screams open the Black Lodge!"

When Verano saw the first hook appear in John-Walks-The -Wind's hand, he could not bear to put Winnie through anymore. He lunged forward...

...Just as John swung the pectoral hook into the eye of the ancient *dugpa* with the flail. The old Indian screeched and pulled back but was caught like a fish. As the *dugpas* converged on John, Winnie bolted. Behind her, John yelled, "Run, Eric Cain! Do not stop; do not trust anyone on the reservation... or Citruston! Run far from here and do not come back."

Then he shouted at the *dugpas*: "Fools! I am a servant of the White Lodge; this opening at the threshold of the anteroom to the Black will be barred forever! My word is sure!"

Verano intercepted Winnie. A hard slap and the vision that had enveloped them was dispersed. They stood again under grey sky among the ashes.

She stared up at him for a moment, disbelief in her face, and then began pummeling his chest with her petite fists.

"Why didn't you stop it before if you could have?" Her tone was sharp. "Why did you put me through...?"

"What your friend Eric went through? We needed to know, didn't we? If he lived or died here that night. Now we know thankfully that he escaped with John's help. Perhaps he still lives."

She collapsed against him, and he supported her. "Let us move away from here," he said, "I don't want to trigger what just happened again. I will take you back to your ice cream parlor, and..."

"Wait," Winnie said, "I'm not ready to let Eric... or you... go yet. There's somewhere else he may have ended up, and if I know he's there, then I can stop worrying."

"I take it it's not another hell hole like the one we just left?" Verano asked.

"Anything but, man," Winnie said. "Remember the secret hippie mecca? It's also a commune and people who want to disappear go there. Usually draft dodgers or people who've been caught with marijuana by the fuzz, but if Eric wanted to go to a place safe from these *dugpas*, it would have to have occurred to him."

"What is the usual port of departure for this paradise?"

"*Goosecreek*."

"Ah, so we're returning there after all."

"Jeb ferries the kids out from there in his van. I can ask around and see if there's a group going tonight, and let you know. Then we could follow them together. I've always wanted to go and see it myself, but not with creepy Jeb."

"Obviously my presence at *Goosecreek* would cause your friends to be less than forthcoming. I'll have to wait for you somewhere out of sight. And don't approach Jeb directly, understand me?"

"I can handle Jeb," she said, quickening her pace. "I've been doing it since high school."

Verano grabbed her arm and pulled her back. "*Don't* this time," he said. "*Vous pigez?*"

She arched a brow. "You know you don't get points for sounding like my dad," she said tugging her arm free outwardly although inwardly she was disappointed when he yielded his grasp so quickly.

Verano held up both hands and took a step back as he lowered them. "You know this lecher has designs on you. I'm worried about your safety is all."

Winnie looked up at him, the fingernails of her one hand caressing where he had grabbed her arm a moment before. Then she smiled and threw herself into him. He was very aware of her breasts as she locked her arms around a torso she was pleased to fine firm and muscular beneath the shirt wet with perspiration. Her lips overtook his and a sinuous, moist warmth filled Verano's mouth.

"Mmmmm." She trailed off into a sigh as she withdrew. "Just so you know...I don't really think you're like my dad."

"I should hope not," Verano said. "Now, we don't need to be seen together upon your return. I noticed around the block a newsstand with a large sign for a soda called *Orange Crush* over it. Whether you learn anything or not, meet me there at six, OK?"

Parked at the newsstand, Verano watched with admiration Winnie's pert behind in her tight, white shorts until she rounded the corner. Then he leaned over to the glove compartment and took out a large manila envelope stamped in red ink: *TOP SECRET.*

He opened it and withdrew a photo of a group of people he had *not* shown Winnie and Abby. He laid it on the passenger's seat along with the photo he had. Only two people were in both groups. He took out of the envelope a cassette tape, a recording of the meeting of the people in that photograph he had not revealed, and placed it in a tape recorder/player he had kept under his seat. The cassette was dated with felt pen: *August 19, 1970.*

He pressed the chunky play button to reevaluate this record of their conference in light of his and Winnie's experience of the wasteland of the reservation. An Air force captain currently assigned to Project Blue Book identified himself as Garland Briggs and asked for the others to introduce themselves as they went around the room. First was Winnie's cousin Diane Innes, CEO of Innes Mining Inc.; next was Dr. Nolter, guest lecturer on plant evolution at Cambridge; Dr. Shiragami, on loan at Harvard from Japan's agricultural genetic engineering institute, Filipino chlorophyll expert Dr. Lorca, and finally a second Englishman, Harrison Chase, who had amassed a private collection of curious and outré plant life.

Diane Innes was now speaking:

"...that introductions are done, I'm happy to report that Innes Mining has won the court battle of territorial rights with the Daquapaw people. We made a settlement that will provide them with a percentage of monies from the sales of what we take to fund improved hospitals and schools on the reservation. The reason for their vigorous contention was the Daquapaw hold the site sacred, forbidden to men and animals, as they do another uncontested area on their reservation consisting of sequoias the equal of any redwoods. Taking the Indians' part, along with the hippies, were... incredible as it is to believe—the trees and vegetable life that had to be cleared before we could begin dynamiting. I am not exaggerating when I say the indigenous vegetation actively resisted us."

"How so?" asked Professor Shiragami.

"Their blossoms spewed an asthma inducing pollen as did the spore of 'puff plants.' Others released a chemical that summoned yellow jackets to their defense. Thorns seemed to leap out to take a bite. In fact, these plants seemed to breathe out something that put the workers on what the long hairs call a 'bad trip.' Many of our men quit because the forest seemed intractable and toxic. Some became superstitious enough to believe that the Daquapaw medicine man had made good on his threat to call up the spirits of the trees and plants to fight us. Fortunately, there were those reasonable enough to continue on when I promised them containment suits to put a buffer between them and the plants. And pay them overtime."

"What type of plants were these?"Professor Nolter asked.

"Mostly different types of mimosas. But larger than usual."

"I don't suppose you have any samples?" Dr. Lorca said.

" Plenty... in that other 'forbidden zone' still on the reservation, with the larger trees, 'Haunted Hollow'" Dian said. "My only concern was the land my company was mining and my men. But while the suits protected them from the bees and thorns and the filtered air kept out the spewed pollen and spores, it could not stop the hallucinations. That's when we realized they weren't airborne from the plant life. Still, I was concerned about potential toxics that would be released into the air from this bizarre forest if we burned it off, and I had additional concerns about containing the fire so near where the Daquapaw lived.

"Fortunately, the plants were rooted in lowlands, lower than a nearby lake, so I dug out a trench that flooded the plants and drowned them. Then we pumped out the water and filled in the trench. Hallucinations continued, but we finally managed to clear off the vegetation. Then we began dynamiting and we found their cause.

"Fifty feet down, the quartz crystals appeared. The shards were gigantic, jumbled and lancing at each other at right angles out of the quarry walls and up from its stone floor. They were unlike any minerals our family has come across in the course of generations of mining. I took samples and found that this quartz was extraterrestrial. I was certain that it had done something to the plants on the reservation to make them react ...well, alien. At this point I contacted Project Blue Book and met Captain Briggs..."

"I opened the Bluebook files," Briggs said, interlocking his fingers. "There was a case reported in the late 19th century of a meteorite striking a rural New England area, transforming a farmer's land and vegetation into something truly not of this earth. The meteor had melted away, leaving some strange infective element that altered the flora and ultimately left it a wasteland.

"In that case, it was simply undirected mutation. However one of Project Blue Book's chief advisors, a young man named Gilles Novak, cross referenced what was happening with the plant life on the reservation with the reportby the explorer Harleton Ironcastleof a section of Africa he had visited. The plant life there communicated with and also dominated the animal life, itself mutated, along with the flora.

"Ironcastle actually discovered what appeared to be a crystalline skeleton of the alien who engineered this terraforming in what we suspect was an attempt to create an oasis of his natural environment in which he might survive until rescue arrived. It never did. The Mineral-Vegetable King they called this creature, because of its crystalline remains.

"There has been no evidence of an alien Mineral-Vegetable King who triggered these changes in the case at hand. We can discount the sightings of an erect, bipedal, heap of shambling vegetation on the reservation. The first Lurker sightings are too contemporary for this local folk legend to be another Mineral-Vegetable King.

"But, on the other hand, like the guided mutations in the Ironcastle case and unlike the random grotesques and ultimate desolation of the land near Arkham, Massachusetts, the plant life here was existing in ecological harmony with everything else. And when Ms. Innes initiated the altercations with the plants, they demonstrated some of the same properties those of that terraformed alien landscape in Africa did when humans or animals behaved in aggressive fashion toward them. Also, as Ironcastle reported, it is Earth's Mimosa species which seem genetically disposed to alien mutation.

"But what are equally striking are the differences with the Ironcastle report, namely, the relationship between the crystals and the reservation's vegetation. ."

"This extraterrestrial quartz," Diane Innes said "gives off electro-magnetic waves which besides being the catalyst of the plants' mutation, also affects the brain... ..."

Verano popped open the top load of the cassette player, removed the tape and put in the other, this one marked *July 1, 1971.*

Now he put aside the photo he had been looking at while its subjects spoke on the tape and picked up the picture he had shown Winnie and Abby. None of the plant biologists were present at this meeting. Along with Diane Innes and Captain Briggs this time was Dr. Mantell, who may or may not be connected to the suppressed movie *The Fear Chamber*, Dr. Chopin, to whom Jeb had been a willing subject in his LSD experiments, and finally Michel Delassalle, Verano 's quarry... and that of *I Eat Men Like Air.*

Dr. Chopin's connection with Jeb linked him with both Dr. Mantell and, now by extension, Michel Delassalle, and Verano suspected this secret hippie mecca was where Delassalle may be taking refuge. Jeb may have driven him there himself... just as he could have Winnie's friend Eric Cain, who would be wanting to go into hiding after his horrifying ordeal with the dugpa and their arbor of horrors.

The tape began with Briggs saying with all earnestness that a third scientist who had been conducting experiments concerning fear would not be joining them This was one Dr. Duryea, who had died under the guillotine blade of his own amusement pier haunted house after an ill-considered alliance with Dracula.

"Is there such a thing as a *well*-considered alliance with Dracula?" Verano said at the tape recorder.

"Gentlemen," Diane said from the recorder's speaker, "the 'fiery mountain' of Daquapaw myth must have been a large meteor of extraterrestrial quartz which upon impact plowed into the ground, burying itself, in the reservation's distant geological past. Under pressure, it produced an electromagnetic field like

159

that of the world from which it came which began to mutate the indigenous plants.

"On Earth," she continued, "quartz develops within other rocks, putting mineral walls between each crystal. They also form randomly, so they are not aligned properly to create and sustain a geo-electromagnetic field above ground. In fact, they neutralize each other's piezoelectric spark. Not so this alien quartz meteorite. It was of a whole piece, unmitigated by any other ore. And its crystals *are* aligned, so that, under pressure below ground, their piezoelectricity charges come together to generate and sustain am electromagnetic field topside. The human brain, within this field, experiences a sense of being haunted, often accompanied by hallucinations. It was this electromagnetism affecting my men's brains when they were working to clear off the trees and plants."

"The same electromagnetic field mutated the plant life to be empathetic with fear," Doctor Chopin then said. "Earth plant life is said to respond to a kind voice, that it creates positive chemical changes. These plants need someone screaming in terror to produce what they need to thrive. Or they *did*, before that Colonel Whiteshroud used his clearances to obtain and release the essences left from those meteorite shards on the blasted heath of Arkham and induced alien terralogical warfare. But the crystals survived and under the right circumstances, can still resonate with fear. Dr. Mantell and I believe that fear has a frequency which these crystals can transmit."

"John-Walks-The-Wind told me," Diane said, "that their shamans— *dugpas* they're called—are seeking for someone who is both the door and the one with the key who stands without the door."

"A door to where?" The French accent revealed this was Michel Delassalle's voice, heard for the first time.

"A place called the Black Lodge," Briggs said soberly.

"Could the key be one of these alien crystals properly cut?" Mantell asked.

"Gentlemen, you are not to go beyond the perimeters of the Fear Chamber project with this," Briggs said. "We want to frighten people to death, but only in the figurative sense."

"Then why did you want me?" Delassalle asked. "Because I have only frightened to death in the most literal sense?"

"With your wife, whom you knew suffered from a weak heart," Briggs said, the tone in his voice expressing resentment that he—and the country he served—were sullying themselves by having freed this murderer for his services. "Our subjects are young and of a most robust nature. No one is to be actually harmed. Is that understood?"

Verano suddenly thought to look at his watch. Five minutes to six. He stuffed the photos and previous cassette tape back into their envelope and shut it up in the glove compartment. Then he stuck the tape recorder back under his driver's seat. Time for his rendezvous with Winnie.

Winnie did not meet him as agreed.

Either she had not been able to disengage herself gracefully from whomever she had been talking or she had pressed things too hard and was in trouble. He drove around the block and saw in front of *Goosecreek* a Chevy van with the motor running. Jeb was locking the door to the store while glancing up and down the road in a furtive fashion. Verano quickly drew down his sun visor to hide his face.

A card flittered into his lap: a Zener card like one of those the girls were playing with when he first saw them this morning. . .

I'm a powerful reader... and sender. And there's a lot of synchronicity around me.

He looked at the van that was now pulling out onto the street, then back at the card, and then the van again.

Post cards from places I've never been but plan to go will show up...

Was Winnie sending him a message that she was in that van? If so, he suspected it wasn't willingly. But even if she was not on Jeb's shuttle, he could not miss the opportunity to trail him to the secret hippie mecca... and, he suspected Delassalle and Winnie's friend, Eric Cain.

He followed.

Artfully weaving through traffic, dropping several car lengths behind, Verano employed every tailing trick he had learned from his father, also a seasoned detective, to not draw suspicion. Fortunately, night was coming on and that would be on his side as they exited onto the interstate.

Shortly after they crossed the Louisiana state line, Verano had no choice but to stop and fill up his tank when Jeb did. Fortunately, the convenience store had multiple pumps, and having shed the overcoat by which Jeb could identify him, Verano kept his back to the hippie.

He also couldn't risk crossing Jeb's path as he returned from paying. Verano was compelled to slowly fill his vehicle as he waited for Jeb to finish his business. To return inside his car and wait would look like he was about to drive off without paying would surely draw unwanted attention. He waited until Jeb was pulling out onto the road. Then Verano returned the gas nozzle to its slot, cramming into the nozzle's grip a five dollar bill that more than covered the gas.

Then he dashed back into his own car, pulled out onto the road and began searching for Jeb's van. They had exited the highway to get to the gas station. Had Jeb returned to the highway, or was he steering clear of the main roads on a secret route from this point?

As he came to the overpass, he saw a van just crossing it. But was it Jeb's? He laid down on his car horn and passed on the entrance ramp another car, running it off the road, then merging into the traffic.

For long, anxious minutes under the disorientation of unfamiliar roadways and the glare of florescent lighting, he wondered if he had made the wrong call.

And when he recognized Jeb's van in the far right lane, five vehicles ahead, Verano sighed, relieved.

They continued on the interstate for almost the entire stretch of Louisiana when, without signaling, Jeb suddenly darted for another exit. Weaving his way through traffic while keeping an eye on which way Jeb would go, Verano managed to make the same exit and continued to follow.

As he trailed through the remaining Louisiana swamp land before it crossed the Texas border, Verano thought of Loulu and wondered if Colonel Whiteshroud had ever resumed his hunt for him.

Daylight was still a few hours away. And if the state of Texas had a backside, this was surely it. They drove over turning dirt roads thickly hedged by swamp land vegetation on either side. Bright lights on the horizon were revealed to be a combination of the glows from a farm house's windows and some other, larger structure with an aerial large enough to service a television station. Clearly, something other than sex, drugs, and rock and roll was going on here.

Verano pulled his car to the side of the road, turning off his lights just as they illuminated a gator as it finished crossing the road and lumbered away into the last of the fetid undergrowth. The swamp now gave way to open flat land, and so it was easy to follow the progress of Jeb's van, marked by his head and tail lights, as he made his way toward the two structures.

Aware that his car lights in this deserted spot would make him very obvious to his adversaries, Verona kept them off and his car crept along by moonlight. At least the road leading to his destination appeared to remain straight. When he was what he judged to be a meter away from the two buildings, he found a copse of trees which would conceal his car. Then he began to move stealthily on foot.

As he came closer, he scanned the upper boughs of the trees. As he suspected, there were surveillance cameras mounted there, covering the lawn. He stopped short of their range. Looming before him was the old, two-story farmhouse surrounded by fields long gone fallow. Jeb's van was parked in front of it, but there was no sign of Jeb or Winnie. The long, four-story building beside the two-story farmhouse was still being built: thick sheets of plastic stretched between the exposed framing. The farmhouse had an aerial one would expect; the towering antenna belonged to the incomplete building.

The door to the farm house flew open, throwing a rectangle of light onto the yard, and Verona fell flat to the ground. A chatter of male and female laughter heralded a young man and woman running down the steps. They dropped to the lawn and began rolling over the grass and each other until they stopped with the man on top

The young man was in the process of rolling up the woman's tank top when he was arrested by the sound of the mechanical growl of a motor. A man with a face stitched down the middle and wielding a chain saw belching blue smoke emerged from the building under construction. At his side was a wiry man under a Ku Klux Klan mask, crouched and running alongside like a feist. The young man just starred, his dope addled mind unable to process this sudden change of fortunes.

Then he rolled off the screaming girl and ran. The girl was stumbling to her feet when the man in the Klan mask caught her, grabbed her under her arms and began dragging her back into the farm house, her heels digging furrows. The stitched face man with the chain saw pursued the boy into the fallow fields. Verano watched, gnawing his lower lip and clutching ground so that earth and uprooted grass were in his fists. But to try and help the girl would expose him to the cameras.

As the young woman was drug up cement steps and the door slammed closed on her, he heard the sound of the chain saw returning. The stitched face man was herding the young man back, the tip of his saw nipping the back of the boy's thighs. At this point, the man in the Klan hood came out of the house, and, together with the stitched faced man, herded the young man inside the incomplete structure. The bark of the chain saw suddenly ceased.

Verano considered his next move. After seeing what he had, his main concern now was for Winnie, not Delassalle. Was she in the van? Or the house? Or this large, incomplete building with its towering antenna? . He couldn't approach the vehicle or the farm house without exposing himself to the cameras. But he noticed they covered only the farm house's yard.

So, crouching, he approached the incomplete building. Someone opened the door, its swinging outward concealing Verano. The man who had exited removed an aluminum foil cap he wore, shook his head and gave his scalp a thorough scratching before his fingers went to his pants' zipper.

Verano struck the man's head from behind, knocking him unconscious. He pulled him off to a small grove of trees where, improvising with the man's belt and both their ties, he gagged and bound him. With his crew cut, glasses and the pens neatly aligned in his pocket protector, the man looked like an accountant.

Now Verano returned to the tall building's door which had remained ajar. He noted the skull cap the man had worn and decided it must have some purpose. He molded it to his own cranium.

Stepping inside, he could see ranges of plants. This was not an incomplete structure, then, but a green house. And it was obvious where the plants in it were from. Apparently, the CIA had been a step ahead of Winnie's friend the Colonel and already taken specimens before he unleashed that *color out of space*.

At the far end of the greenhouse's interior, bluish cathode ray light flickered on the plastic walls, and from the floor ahead came moans, sobbing, pleading. Why would a TV need such a gigantic aerial? And what was playing on it to elicit such tortured responses?

Verano slipped in through the door, and crept as far as he dared down the center walkway between the ranges of plants before slipping between two shelves to his right. For a moment he paused to regard the alien-mutated vegetation but was distracted by the screams coming from a speaker that set off a new surge of wailing from the two young people inside the building.

Winnie, he thought as he quickly but quietly removed one of the potted plants to make an opening to see...

Hooks through his pectorals, hoisted on the bough of a tree was a shirtless young man with long hair, his mouth stitched up. A trail of dried blood ran from his right nostril. *Eric Cain*, Verano thought.

The tree oozed fear in a brown sap, and a bent, old Indian in nothing but a loin cloth and an eye patch was dabbing his fingertips into this pitch; he sucked it off his finger tips and began to chew, his one eye fluttering in sensual abandonment.

"Old Ishakshar there told me the sewing of the mouth was the custom of the *dugpas* to intensify the fear by not allowing a release... something along the lines of my own experiment with a deaf mute." The speaker's tone was effete, and Verano recognized him from the photo as Dr. Warren Chopin. He was also wearing an aluminum foil skull cap. "I feel like some wine. I've never developed a taste for fear... at least, not literally, like Ishakshar. Some wine, Karl? Michel?"

The former, a gaunt, basset eyed elderly man looked on the agonized young man and shook his aluminum foil covered head from side to side. His expression was haunted, and he quickly looked away; clearly he would never know a peaceful night's sleep in whatever time he had left on this earth. This was the real Dr. Karl Mantell who had more than a passing resemblance to Boris Karloff.

The Fear Chamber. This was what the movie had come too close to revealing.

"I'll have a glass," the other man addressed said with a French accent, and for the first time Verano heard the live voice of Michel Delassalle, also sporting an aluminum foil cap.

A row of men sat before a bank of black and white monitors showing from different angles what was happening inside and outside the farmhouse, and the audio was coming separately from a Ham radio. They had the same accountant look as the man he knocked out and also wore the foil caps. One of them had on headphones and sat before a microphone on the same counter with the ham radio but unconnected to another audio device. Half-full coffee mugs and snack cookie and cracker wrappers littered the counter and floor.

At Delassalle's feet, was a bound a young, dark-haired hippie girl in bell bottoms and a torn *Keep On Truckin'* shirt; her cheeks were streaked with sooty trails of mascara mixed with tears. Also tied beside her was the young man Verano had seen chased inside here: the two looked at the television screens as though these played the coming attractions of Hell.

"What are you going to do to Sally?" the boy asked about the girl from the lawn.

"You think that looks bad? Delassalle said after a sip of wine. "You're right. In fact, you'll beg to be up on that tree where he is instead," he jerked a thumb toward Eerie Cain, "after just a few moments over there."

On the black and white monitors, Verano recognized the young woman whom he had witnessed drug inside, now chained with her hands over her head back against the wall beside an empty set of similar shackles. Her back to the camera, another woman with long blond hair lay on the floor in the fetal position in front of a large freezer, which rattled and lurched from something large on the inside.

The girl on the floor uncurled and pushed her hair from her face. Verano expelled his breath and put his hand to his forehead: the blonde was Winnie, as yet unharmed. Sally began, rattling her chains. "Help me," she pleaded.

Verano struggled to formulate a plan. He had to get her out of there, yet he would be monitored before he entered the farm house. He looked around, searching the floor for cables and cords. If he could pull the right plug, just create even a brief black out...

Verano looked back at the monitors. Unable to help the girl chained to the wall, Winnie now was approaching the agitating freezer. One of the screens connected to a camera in the ceiling provided a view over Winnie's shoulder.

Winnie pulled back the freezer's lid and recoiled from the stench as though slapped. Up bolted to the sitting position a young woman from the dark water in which deer hooves and bits of hooves floated...

...a woman with half a face; the other exposed raw muscle. Her eyes oscillated wildly...

With a cry of surprise, Winnie leaped back as the woman splashed the water with her arms, squawking, sending pieces of deer flesh and fur with the water over the side and onto the floor.

"Go!" the man with the headphones said into the microphone.

The door to the house boomed open with the thrust of the leg of the man with the chain saw and stitched face. Only now could Verano see... at the same moment Winnie realized it... that he wore the other half of the face of the woman in the freezer.

The chain saw, held low for the moment, raucous and retching, seemed to wish to leap from the man's hands, skitter across the floor on its own and chew Winnie's shins until they were denuded bones.

Winnie screamed and ran to cower against the wall with the chained girl who was screaming as well.

As Winnie kept screaming, the two bound hippies, their brains unprotected by tin foil headpieces, began to bellow in empathy with her fear, and Eerie Cain on the tree went into an unprecedented seizure.

Dr. Chopin grinned as his eyes went back and forth from Winnie on the monitor to Cain in his increasingly violent paroxysms. "Looks like my former protégé Jeb was right about this girl; she's a powerful sender."

Looking up at Cain, withered Ishakshar licked his lips and shouted, "More fear, more fear!"

The man at the microphone spoke into it and said, "Klan-Man, both you and Buzz focus on scaring the new girl to death."

The man in the Klan hood rushed in. Dodging past his chain saw wielding cohort, he grabbed Winnie and drug her to to the other set of chains mounted on the wall. "*No, no, no!*" Winnie shouted struggling. But the man was by far stronger, and in a few seconds her hands were chained over her head.

"More fear," the *dugpa* croaked.

"No, that will be quite enough," Verano said, stepping out from behind the shelves with his gun in one hand aimed at Dr. Chopin's head while the other held his card. "I'm here under the auspices of the French Government!" he shouted. "Tell your men in the farmhouse to stand down, now!"

All of the men in foil skull caps at the counter, taken by surprise, were unable to reach their pistols. Verano wanted to order someone to take down Eric Cain, but that would mean one or more of them moving past him and thus opening himself up for being rushed.

The man at the mike said, "Buzz! Klan-Man! Step back..."

"*Release* those women!" Verano said. "You're in no position to dictate any terms... "

The clack of a pistol hammer being pulled back said otherwise. Verano rolled his eyes to see Michel Delassalle had produced what until now had been a concealed weapon and held it aimed on Verano.

"Drop it!" he barked at Verano. "If you shoot Chopin, I put a bullet in you. I'm aimed to kill, just as you."

Verano's smile was grim. "I would have drawn on you, but I believe Dr. Chopin of more importance."

"Chopin is ultimately a novice like the rest of us," Delassalle said. "It's old Ishakshar who's the real expert."

"More fear! More fear!" the wizened old man sitting cross legged insisted, shaking his fists up and down and bouncing on his behind like some wind-up toy chimp.

"You fool!" the man at the mike, who appeared to be the leader, said to Delassalle. "Drop your gun. The CIA can't just murder a SDECE agent!"

"Then suppose I let him have a shot at Dr. Chopin..."

"What?" Chopin's eyes widened and he paled. In response, a new seizure shivered through Eerie Cain's body.

"...then I can claim I was defending Chopin when their agent was about to open fire on him. Unfortunately, I was too late. You will still have Mantell's and my expertise in creating frightening tableaux for the dissident subjects of your interrogation experiments."

Verano nodded toward the writhing Eerie Cain. "Interrogation? You expect someone to talk with his mouth sewed shut?"

"*He's* not here for interrogation. We've been looking for the key and the one who is both the door and stands outside the door with the key," Dr. Mantell said. ""Extraterrestial crysals discovered on Citruston's former Indian reservation are the key." He pointed at Cain. "That boy is the door to a fourth dimension adjacent to our own three but, until now, inaccessible.

"Look," the group leader said to Verano. "I don't want you shot, is that clear? We can explain what's going on here and why we can't let those girls go or take down that boy... just *yet*. Will you holster your gun if Delassalle will hand me his first?"

"I don't think so," Delassalle said.

Verano, however, was thinking of the film frames in the envelope inside his coat pocket.

"I will be willing to do so under those conditions," he said. "I don't wish to kill Delassalle, or even to take him back."

Delassalle knitted his brow. "Why else would you be here?"

"Shut up, Michel!" the leader said. "Give me your gun. If you shoot him, I'll order my men to fire on you. This man is with the SDECE. Our 'losing' a murderer after they agreed to loan you to us was an embarrassment, but the murder of one of their agents by someone under our auspices would be an international incident."

"And you give me your word you are not here to take me back into custody? Why, then?" Delassalle said to Verano.

"Just give me the gun," the leader said and held out his hand, eyes still riveted on Verano.

Verano didn't holster his own weapon until Delassalle's gun was taken from him. A pale Dr. Chopin quickly downed what was left of his wine. Verano nodded toward Cain and then looked at Winnie struggling with her bonds on the video screen. " Now, you better give me a good explanation for why you can't terminate this state of affairs."

"The brain, when registering fear, creates a signal, and there exists a carrier wave that permits broadcast of that fear when proper modulation is achieved," said Dr. Mantell. "This boy Cain is capable of telekinesis but not by simply moving an object through our familiar three dimensions of space. Rather, he passes them through a fourth dimension to which his brain is already tuned,.

He pointed at the Ham radio that set on a table near the bank of televisions. "A crystal of extraterrestrial quartz is in that ham radio and one cut to a similar frequency is in young Cain's nasal passage, close to his special brain.

"Now, all crystals vibrate in three dimensions when put under pressure. These extraterrestrial crystals vibrate in the normal three and also in the *fourth* dimension, what the Indians call the 'Black Lodge'. We mean to contact its denizens." These metal caps keep *our* brains from being affected and overcome by fear from these crystals electromagnetic fields while broadcasting. "

"Who exactly are you using that radio and giant antenna outside to broadcast fear to... and why do you *wish* to open a door that only pain and suffering unlocks?" Verano asked. "What good can come of it?"

"Oh, moonbeams and sock garters!" lisped Dr. Chopin. "That is the kind of narrow minded thinking that would have kept us off the moon or the Renaissance explorers from the New World. Who knows what these entities might enlighten us concerning string theory? Perhaps yet *other* dimensions perceivable to them."

"And what do *they* get in return?" Verano asked.

"These other dimensional entities *feed* on fear and pain, so Ishakshar tells us," Chopin said. "Well, we'll direct them where to find it. On a good night, there's enough fear and pain in one city block of Harlem to gorge them for a month."

"You are going to turn these things lose on your *own* people?" Verano asked the leader. "This is no longer strictly for CIA interrogation, is it? That is why you cut the SDECE out of the loop. Just as you've done with these hippies... you're planning to turn these creatures on poverty level blacks... *anyone* who doesn't fit your vision of America."

"Good grief!" shouted one of the men who had happened to look up at one of the monitors whose camera was aimed at the lawn. "What is *that*? Bigfoot?"

The group's leader stepped up to the screen: "No, that looks like... like a walking compost heap." He looked over his shoulder at the shelves. "Has one of *our* plants gone mobile?"

"It's Loulu!" the hippie girl on the floor said.

The Mineral-Vegetable King? Verano thought.

"It's headed right for the farm house door!" the man who had first spotted the shambling heap said. The leader said into the mike: "Klan-Man! Buzz! Make sure that door is locked. *Now*. You do *not* want what's out there getting in."

The two men bolted across the room and secured it just as a heavy weight thrust against the door. The girls screamed. Another shove of whatever served as the thing's shoulder knocked the door out of frame.

"Winnie!" Verano said and ran outside

The leader pointed at two of the monitor watchers. "You, you. "Go with him! Get a tarp or a net; shoot it... I don't care! Get it away from that house!"

Klan-man and Buzz were moving to join Winnie and Sally against the far wall. Buzz turned on the chainsaw which he held as his side. Another push on the door, and he leapt back, accidentally slinging the blade into Sally's stomach. She screeched as it chewed open her abdomen and disgorged her entrails before her head lolled to one side.

"You idiot!" the leader shouted into the mike.

Winnie, splattered with blood, went into new heights of paroxysms at the sight, prompting Eerie Cain into such violent, unprecedented convulsions that he violently tore free of the flesh hooks and hit the floor of the greenhouse. The dugpa waved back the men who moved to see to him. He began to chant, hands held palms up and dance around the bleeding, writhing Eric.

He ripped apart his stitched lips with his straining mouth and took up Winnie's cry. He bellowed as the tip of his coccyx pierced through the tissue of his lower back, then began curling, tearing muscles and flesh until his exposed spine was arced like a scorpion's tail ready to sting.

His exposed spinal column was vibrating from the crystal close to his brain. The articulated bone sparkled blue. His nervous system had long been a door against which another dimension had fervently pressed against to get out, the door under which he had slid objects back and forth. Now that door was ajar through the fissures in his spine.

And answering the resonating signal of the crystal, *they* came…

Old Ishakshar clapped his hands, chortled, and danced a jig. The door to the Black Lodge had opened. Flying out of the exposed, curled spine were ectoplasmic creatures that quickly solidified into a fleshy substance the shape of vertebrae, but with lobster-like claws.

"Tinglers!" Dr. Chopin cried out and threw his wine glass at the one coming for him.

Ishakshar did not laugh much longer. He was the first to have one of the entities clamp onto his throat. The siphoning of the *dugpa*'s panic was as the plants had fed, increasing the fear, the adrenaline, until his heart, like a repeatedly squeezed bunch of grapes, was simply out of juice. Ishakshar fell on his face as the entity slipped free.

They swarmed through the air about the CIA men, who fired at them, swatted and shot at them, but were ultimately fatally latched onto by the Tinglers' claws. The two young hippies, still bound hand and foot, were writhing down the aisle in an attempt to escape when the Tinglers took them. And Drs. Mantell and Chopin each were overtaken by an entity from the Black Lodge. At that moment, the boundary between scientist and experiment collapsed.

Outside, the CIA men had corralled with their cigarette lighters the shambling, vegetation beast away from the door, off the front porch and were moving him out to the fields. Verano ran onto the porch and began pounding on it.

"Open up!" he shouted. "They've driven him off for now!" There were screams from the men in the field. "I don't know how long they can keep…"

The door burst outward, knocking Verano back as Klan man and Buzz ran for Jeb's van.

"Teddy!" Winnie cried out as he walked to her, drawing his gun. Outside, he could hear the van start up and screech off, then its engine's roaring away into the distance.

"Extend your chains, please, Winnie. Not much length, but you can trust my aim. You'll be bruised some, probably… "

She nodded. "Just get me away from here!"

169

Winnie winced with each shot, but within a minute she was throwing her freed arms around Verano 's neck. Then she pushed away and ran for the freezer which was agitating again. "There's another victim in here, she said."

Winnie pushed open the freezer, the woman began to squawk and flap about again until she saw the dead, disemboweled Sally hanging on the wall. She stopped splashing immediately. "Whoa, man," she said. "What's going on here? I didn't sign up for *that*; there ain't enough weed in the world…!"

She screamed as she caught sight of a Tingler flying through the open door, and in the process drew a bull's eye on herself. It grasped her throat with its claws and wrapped around her torso just under her breasts. Winnie reached out to wrench loose the Tingler tightening constrictor-like so that the woman in half-face make-up was gasping for breath.

Verano had dashed past them to shut the door before any more Tinglers could fly in. "Winnie! Get your hands off it before it latches onto you!" he shouted. "Close the lid!"

"But she's just a girl like me…"

"Do it!"

Winnie slammed down the lid and the freezer agitated violently, then was suddenly still.

"I'm sorry, but if we don't keep that thing inside caged, we're next," Verona said.

"How many are out there?" Winnie said, hugging herself.

"I have no idea. We'll just have to wait it out. Someone will be coming, I'm sure…" A pounding on the door interrupted him.

"Let me in! Hurry!"

Verano recognized Delassalle's voice. He thought of the woman on the film frames; he could not rob her of her due and let one of these Tinglers have him. Holding his gun at the ready he pushed the door open and Delassalle tumbled in, and tripping over Verano's outstretched foot, fell flat on his face. In a moment, Verano was on top of Delassalle, bending his arms around his back.

"Winnie! Shut the door!" Verano ordered, grappling at Delassalle to see if was again armed as his countryman bucked beneath him. She slammed it closed, just as she caught sight of headlights heading their way in the distance.

"Someone's coming!" she shouted.

Verano had now successfully found and taken Delassalle's pistol from him and was dismounting as the latter rolled to his feet. He was smiling smugly.

"They will be, of course, *my* people," Delassalle said as Verano held his own gun on him. "You say you haven't come to take me back? Do you plan to kill me, then? Did my late wife's family hire you to shoot me down, because a twenty year sentence wasn't good enough? You'll have to explain yourself to the U.S. government if you…"

"They're here!" Winnie cried, looking out the window as an open jeep drove up, its high beams spotlighting a figure scurrying over the ground, dragging his limp lower legs behind him, his spinal column now curled into a Fibonacci shape.

"Is that... Eric?" Winnie asked, her eyes wide as she pointed. She was moving for the door when Verano called her off.

"Don't open the door, Winnie! He trusted the wrong people. That crystal in his head has turned his nervous system into a portal for these entities."

Tears ran down her face as she watched the jeep turn sharply to block Cain as he scuttled away. The jeep stopped, a man in blackjumped out with a pistol, overtook Cain and shot him in the head. Winnie screamed. With the collapse of Eric's nervous system, however, the Tinglers all lost not only their gateway but their footholds in our world and vanished.

Winnie was ready to run out to her friend, but Verano grabbed her, pulled her to him. "Not so quick," he said. "Not until we know who we're dealing with."

The driver's door opened and a regal, tall, dark haired beauty stepped out.

"It's Diane!" Winnie said. "She'll let me see Eric..."

"Don't go running out there unidentified with a man with a gun guarding your cousin. Wait."

He cracked the door. Immediately the man with Diane trained his gun there.

"I am Teddy Verano... SDECE!" he said. "I have my credentials which I will be holding in one of the hands over my head. I have with me your man Delassalle, and Winnie Innsmouth."

"Winnie!" Diane shouted. Verano pushed the door the rest of the way open and stepped out onto the porch that was illuminated by the jeeps lights. Delassalle stepped out behind him, and as the government agent stepped forward and checked Verano's credentials, Winnie dodged past them all and went to Eric Cain's side.

"Eric," she said softly as she knelt by the still, warped body. She found herself thinking of birthday parties, of joint laughter behind the stage at a middle-school play, how he had been the last of the neighborhood kids to give up training wheels on his bike...

She closed his eyes and kissed his forehead.

"Winnie, I'm so sorry, kid," Diane was saying. "I knew nothing of what they were trying to do with Eric. When I found out, I started making noise that the U.S. was violating human rights. I'm sorry it's too late for him. But listen...I need to know where the radio is they were using to broadcast.. Its crystal can't be left in their hands."

"Broadcast what?" Winnie said.

"Your fear," Verano said, gently pulling her to her feet and drawing her into him where she huddled. "Mademoiselle Innes, you'll find it in the hot house next door."

"Thank you!" she said and ran for the second structure.

Meanwhile, the men who had succeeded in warding off the Lurk by finally setting fire to him, returned to the front of the house. They, too, had suffered burns. "Whatever kind of vegetation that made up that thing must've been acidic," one said. "But we couldn't get in close enough to light him up without brushing it or being swiped. Stings like hell."

"Listen," Verano said. "I need a moment with Mr. Delassalle. Alone." He stepped back from Winnie who was rubbing the goose bumps on her arms. She looked knowingly into Verano's eyes.

"Come along, Michel," Verano said. "There is unsettled business. Into the farm house we go. You have nothing to fear from me or the French government. I have come to offer you permanent exile, you might say."

"Intriguing," Delassalle said. They walked into the farmhouse, and Verano shut the door behind them.

"I do not suppose you have actually ever seen *Diabolique*?" Verano said.

Delassalle smirked. "I lived it. Why should I?"

"There is an ambiguity at the end that leaves in question how successful you were in killing your wife… or if her ghost is lurking about the school where you both taught. One of the students claims to have spoken with her but he is dismissed. What is not generally known is that ending was only added after one of the child actors made just that claim. He had seen a woman's ghost. And then, at the end of that roll of film, after it had been developed…" he produced the film frames from his coat, "…*this* appeared. He handed them to Delassalle along with the jeweler's eyepiece. He looked over them, then looked up, frowning.

"You know this is my wife on this film!" Delassalle said, his face crimson. "She's been alive all this time I have been in prison, then?"

"You have not lost your status as a murderer. I assure you these frames were cut from *Diabolique*."

"No, I have seen pictures of the actress in the film…"

"Who is unfortunately prematurely dead now herself. She had a weak heart. Just as she did in the movie.

"Poor Vera Clouzot's physical constitution could not bear a spiritual possession," Verano said. He half-mumbled, "Pity the same couldn't be said for Edwige Hossegor," then sighed and ran his hand through his hair. "It would have made my life a lot simpler, but you go a few rounds with a demoness like Mephista and keep coming out on top, word gets around. In certain circles, you gain a reputation."

"You're insane," Delassalle said. "If you mean my wife tried to possess this actress to use her as her physical agent of revenge on me, and, having failed, came to you… how?"

"I'm a Postmodern Meta-cinema detective," Verano said. "From time to time, the sharp boundary between the fiction within a movie frame and reality collapses and something slips through. Now she goes by the name *I Eat Men Like Air*."

Delassalle laughed. "You're trying to beat me at my own game? You're going to... what? Gaslight me now?"

"I've done my part." He held up the film frames and looked at them. "'Medium' was applied to spiritualists before movies, after all. She's right behind you."

Delassalle felt a bracing sting of breath like arctic wind brush the nape of his neck.

As she pulled the fear crystal from the radio, Diane Innes heard a man's scream and looked up at one of the monitors to see Delassalle collapse, and Verano tuck something back in his pocket, light up a cigarette, and walk out of the building.

When he came out alone, one of the men in a crew cut asked, "What happened to Delassalle?"

Verano exhaled smoke and waved it away with the fingers that clinched the cigarette. "I'm afraid Michel Delassalle has fallen victim to the Fear Chamber," he said as the men ran inside.

Diane came running up at this point. "What happened to Delassalle? What did you do to him?" she demanded.

"He did it to himself." He held out the jeweler's eyepiece and film frames "The fear master was finally overtaken by fear himself. Would you like a look?" he asked, reaching inside his coat for the film frames and the jeweler's lens.

"No," Diane said and waved him off. "If he died of fear, it was entirely appropriate." She sighed. "*Every*one is afraid of something. Fortunately, the only two alien crystals in the vicinity are the one that was in that ham radio and... inside poor Eric Cain there."

"In the vicinity?" Verano asked. "You mean there are other alien crystals dispersed that match the one in Eerie Cain's head or the one you hold there?"

Dian winced. "To make reparations to the Indians, Innes Corp. was court-ordered to sell the alien quartz to the highest bidder and give those relocated from the reservation the money. Of course, the government was certain to get a share of alien quartz first, for their experiments. But the rest went to Acute Audio. This new FM radio when combined with the purity of the alien quartz, if some of those crystals were cut..."

"...to be receptive to the same frequency as *that*," Verano finished the sentence, nodding toward the remains of Eerie Cain.

"...but the signal was low powered, remember," Dian said, obviously trying to reassure herself as much as anyone else. "It couldn't have gone out far. They were to be careful. The radio crystal by themselves, even collectively, were too small to generate a magnetic field on their own capable of stimulating any sense of fear."

Suddenly, a heavy *thrum-thrum-thrum* was beating the air above them.

A floodlight from above transfixed them all. Men in dark jumpsuits began descending in from lines dropping from an enormous black, unmarked helicopter.

They were all herded inside the farmhouse. Identities and credentials were checked. The body of the disemboweled girl still chained to the wall was bagged as was that of the young woman in the freezer and Delassalle's.

Then, they were taken aboard the helicopter. From its height, after a half-hour in the air, they began to see in the pre-dawn light archipelagos of fire, entire cities in flames.

"What exactly is going on down there?" Verano asked

"The heartland is in chaos," a crew cut man in shirtsleeves, a tie, dark glasses and sporting a pocket protector told them. "Our scientists figured there were no limits in how powerful they wished to make the signal since the only receptive crystals in the area were being used in our experiment. We were careful that no one in the immediate FM broadcasting area could receive the signal: all those Acute radios with the alien quartz were to be marketed outside of its range.

"But when they achieved the frequency to access the Black Lodge, they increased the power of the signal to maximum so there'd be no chance what was on the other side of the door wouldn't hear us knocking. That over-extended the signal range as well. Then the alien crystals in thousands of radios tuned to the receptive frequency found their local station's signal over ridden and these crystals, capable of vibrating at the frequency of fear, did just that.

The man regarded Winnie. "You, young lady, transmit a very robust signal. People in range of those crystals' magnetic fields experienced your terrified need to escape, but, just as yourself, felt incapable to do so, no matter what they tried." He nodded down at the burning landscape. . "*What* they were trying to escape materialized according to *their* fears... something along the lines of what I understand a bad trip is supposed to be like.

"*I* did... all this?" Winnie put her fist to her mouth, flinched and shook her head. Verano put his arm around her, and she leaned into him.

"You were a victim like everyone else in this scheme," Verano said. You're not to blame for anything."

"Well, you'll be happy to know the FCC has recalled all of the radios with these crystals. They are now officially environmental hazards."

Diane nodded toward the multiple conflagrations below them. "That seems a bit late."

"Acute Electronics will bear the initial brunt, but, of course, they did not originate the signal. Conspiracy rumors are inevitable, but both the farmhouse and greenhouse have been dynamited since we left. Of course, the details of young people tortured by redneck sadists who wear their skins...*that* is perhaps best transformed into fiction, preferably via the overpowering big screen images and sounds of the cinema. We'll admit up front it is based on true events. That will ultimately secure it as fiction."

Diane scowled. "You're treating human lives as trivial things. Those people counted! But you're going to reduce them to no more than characters in a drive-in horror movie like their lives didn't mean anything!"

"To the contrary," the man in dark glasses said. "We couldn't show any more respect for their gravitas than to make fiction of them. Think of Moses, Jesus, Shakespeare... the mark of those who leave a true wake behind them in history is when lesser intellects declare that the facts of their lives are but fiction. "Teddy Verano, Delassalle suddenly died by, shall we say, a brain aneurysm before you could apprehend him? His body will be returned to France. And Miss Innsmouth...we would very much like to enlist someone of your psychic potential in our *Scanners* program."

"Leave me alone," Winnie said and leaned closer to Verano, who put his arm around her. "That's all I want from you. And make sure Jeb doesn't get away with all he did."

"Very well. But please grant me this one request in return, Winnie. A lot of your friends have recently been granted the right to vote. Please spread the word that, given such a trauma as our nation is undergoing... that somehow reached even into our capitol at the Watergate Democratic Headquarters... well, we can expect at best a slow recovery in the long, dark days ahead. So a steady, uninterrupted flow of leadership is in the best interests of our country.

"Please tell them all... vote Nixon in '76."

The man returned to surveying the carnage, and Winnie looked up at Verano. "The spirit of Delassalle's wife killed him, didn't she? She came out of those movie frames and got her revenge."

"She's not through yet," Verano said. "Look..."

He produced the film frames and the eye piece again.

"Uh-uh," Winnie said, her hand touching the eye that had been hurt when she had looked through that *portable keyhole into Hell*, as she had called it, before.

"Forgive me," Verano said. "There's so much that has happened since, I wasn't thinking." He raised the jeweler's glass to his eye and looked at the frames and grinned.

Now *I Eat Men Like Air* laid spread like a succubus atop Michel Delassalle, her long nailed talons around his throat. His face was upside down, eyes wide, mouth agape, pleading...

Verano grinned and said, "As you pointed out someone has said, *film is forever*... and sometimes, so is pain...and fear."

In our previous volume, Travis Hiltz embarked on a series of self-contained, yet interconnected, stories featuring Doctor Oméga who has, somehow, been separated from his companions and is lost in time. We already shared an adventure with his friends in Romney Marsh. Now, we find the Doctor in late 19th century Paris, where his path is going to cross that of Alfred Drious's Parisian Aeronaut (from The Adventures of a Parisian Aeronaut, *an 1856 proto-SF novel published by Black Coat Press) in a tale that is a deliberate homage to a recent* Doctor Who *Xmas special, and is thus entitled...*

Travis Hiltz: *The Next Omega*

Paris, 1857

The old man spent all his evenings seated at a small corner table at the corner's café, a pink hatbox tied with twine at his feet, an ordinary cane, and a single glass of red wine at his elbow.

He would just sit there, his wine untouched, a thoughtful, expectant frown on his face. Occasionally, he would nod to one of the other regulars, or merely just scratch his chin absentmindedly as he listened to the swirl of conversations around him. He seemed to always be listening and waiting, but for what, none of the other patrons knew.

On one rare occasion, he actually spoke to the men at the table next to his. They were a trio of workmen, chuckling to themselves over the antics of a local eccentric, a learned savant who would share his wild theories concerning the Moon, the stars and the very universe itself.

They were all a bit stunned when the old man leaned in and rapped a knuckle against the tabletop.

"Whom are you speaking of?" he asked, his stern tone and beaky nose giving him the air of a teacher interrogating a group of unruly students. "The one with the interest in the stars... Doctor... Who did you say?"

"Omega," one of them replied. "Doctor Omega."

The old man spent another minute questioning them, then, after getting the address of this local eccentric, promptly tossed some coins upon his table, scooped up his box and cane, and strode out of the tavern door.

Never to be seen again...

The old man strode through the dusk-shaded streets of Paris, his gaze intently focused on the pavement in front of him.

"Doctor *Omega*, is it?" he muttered to himself. "We shall see about that."

A muffled voice issued from the hatbox tucked under his arm.

176

"Hush," the old man said, patting the box gently.

His shoulders hunched under his traveling cloak, his features determined, he made his way through the narrow, winding streets. As night deepened, the buildings seemed to loom over the old man. Other pedestrians seemed to dart in and out of the deep shadows.

"A Morlock would feel right at home in this neighborhood," the old man sniffed, pulling his cloak tighter around him to ward off the chill.

He came to the house in question. It was a pleasant enough dwelling, quaintly middle class. Not new, but well cared for.

The old man put the box down on the stoop and was about to knock when the door was flung open and a young man came bounding out, promptly tripping over the hatbox.

"Oh, dear," the old man said, helping the younger one to his feet. "My apologies. I was trying to find the gentleman who lives here—Doctor Omega. Is he in?"

"No longer," the young man replied, brushing himself off and getting to his feet. "But, do not despair, for I am he. Doctor Omega, at your service!"

The young man gave a brief bow and when he straightened up, the older man had a moment to study his features.

His face was thin and friendly, framed by collar length black hair, and a neatly trimmed mustache and beard. His smile was open and charming, and his eyes shown with an energy that could easily have been either genius or madness. His long coat, trousers, waistcoat and shoes were all a touch out of fashion and black. The only trace of color was a bone white shirt and an ascot of red with thin black stripes. A monocle, attached to his lapel by a black ribbon swung back and forth like a pendulum.

"I have business this night," Doctor Omega said, moving off to hail a carriage. "If you wish to speak to me, you must be prepared to travel."

The old man watched the younger one with a puzzled expression.

"Please, Monsieur," a voice said from the doorway. A middle-aged woman, her hair going to grey, stepped out of the house. "Please, go with him. Watch over my... Doctor Omega. Keep him safe."

The sorrow came off her like a wave and the old man, nodded and gave her what he hoped was a reassuring smile.

"Of course. I'd no sooner let Doctor Omega come to harm than I would myself," he said, turning to follow the younger man as quickly as his old legs would allow.

He sank into the carriage, and, as it rolled into the night, he patted at his forehead with a handkerchief.

"Well, where are we off to?" he asked, as he struggled to catch his breath and hold onto his cane, his handkerchief, and the hatbox.

"There are strange forces at work in the city," the younger man explained, not looking at his fellow traveler, but rather out into the night-shrouded streets of Paris.

"Are there now? Such as?" the old man asked, tucking his handkerchief back into his coat pocket.

"You must understand," Omega said, earnestly, "I do not speak out of some sense of melodrama, but rather because what I am about to tell you about myself, and my current undertaking, will seem fantastic."

"Not at all," the older man said. "You will find that I am not... unfamiliar with Doctor Omega, his reputation and his exploits. Speak freely. I've an inkling that my, er, own predicament may, in some way, be connected to your own."

He sat back, his legs straddling the box on the floor, his expression patiently expectant.

"Very well, I will take you at your word. As you may be aware, I have a quite extraordinary form of transport in my possession, the *Cosmos*, and with it, I have traveled far and wide. I had just returned to Paris, a rather unceremonious arrival, I must admit, due to a bout of... dizziness. Upon arrival, I stumbled out of the *Cosmos* to get my bearings and found myself in the middle of the most bizarre altercation. A trio of figures in black robes were grappling with a gang of street ruffians. I was disoriented and distracted by some odds and ends that had fallen out of the *Cosmos* when I had exited it, and the next thing I knew, I was in the midst of the skirmish, trying to retrieve my belongings and avoid a severe pummeling."

"Curious," the older man murmured thoughtfully stroking his chin. "And then what? You seem unharmed?"

"Through no skill of my own, I must confess," said Omega, smiling. "Tripping over either my own feet or someone else's, I fell and managed to roll underneath a nearby wagon. The local police arrived and, in the ensuing chaos, most of the combatants and I were able to flee the scene. I made my way to... my... um... the house where you found me, in order to continue my investigation..."

"Of...?"

"Originally, what caused the *Cosmos* to crash, but then, I turned my attention to the participants of the altercation I had stumbled into."

"Are the two events connected?" the older man inquired.

"I don't see how they could be," Omega replied with an indulgent shake of his head. "I did not know when I would be arriving, so I could hardly be the target. There seemed to be an... item, an artifact, that both groups sought, and I was an unfortunate witness to their struggle."

He then leaned forward and knocked on the ceiling of the carriage.

"Eugène!" he called. "We will depart here!" He then turned to his companion. "I am afraid the rest of my journey is to be on foot. It is of a clandestine nature. If you wish, you may stay here or I could have the driver...?"

"No, no, you have quite captured my interest, my young... Doctor," said the older man with a tight-lipped smile. "Your mission is quite serious, and if I can be of assistance, I offer my services."

"Very decent of you," Omega smiled, exiting the carriage. "If you want to leave your box...?"

"No," the older man grunted, climbing out of the carriage while trying to juggle both his cane and the hatbox. He faltered and Omega stepped forward to help him, catching the box as it slid from the older man's grip.

"Here you are... did you hear something? It sounded like a woman's voice?"

"Where are we?" the old man asked, regaining his balance and then possession of his box.

"Ah, yes. I was unable to find any sign of my robed assailants, but I was able to track the others, the ruffians."

"And they led you here?" the older man asked, looking about at the rundown buildings around them.

"Yes. I followed one to a local café and overheard he was meeting his employer in that building," Omega explained, pointing towards a drab three-story hotel that had seen better days. "I'm going to scout about and speak to the concierge. Wait here."

Before the older man could protest, Doctor Omega had sprinted away.

"Will you be needing me then, sir?" the driver asked from his perch.

"Perhaps it would be best if you stayed nearby, but found some discreet spot to park... not too far," he instructed.

The carriage rolled down the block, and the old man settled himself in a doorway, pulling his traveling cloak about him. He placed the pink hatbox on the top step, within the alcove, and opened the lid, removing a severed head.

It was made of metal, appearing more sculpted than manufactured. Its features were vaguely feminine. The old man held it up as though he were about to perform the famous soliloquy from *Hamlet*.

He remembered how the robot head had come in his possession. He had acquired it in the future, in the legend-shrouded city of Metropolis.[4]

"I see the boys brought you back a new toy to play with," he had told Fred, picking up the head and peering into its blank, metal eyes. He had tapped it and, amazingly, the eyes had flickered to life.

"The workers musssst...rise up! They are...zzzztt... but pu-puppets, dancing on the elite's string...!"

"Hmmm, and what might you become, now that your own strings have been cut, I wonder?" the Doctor had mused, returning the head to the table.

Later, he had christened it Thea.

---

[4] See "The Robots of Metropolis" in our Vol. 7.

"So, Thea, what do you think of our young friend?" he asked. "Is he under some delusion—or is he truly me?"

"Match between two entities estimated at only 64 %," the metal head replied in a voice that was a blend of female and mechanical.

"What?" The old man sputtered. "That... that... deluded popinjay is not... I am Doctor Omega, he is some rank imposter!"

"Inquiry concerning your protest," Thea asked. "Subject has knowledge of Doctor Omega. Subject also shows trace evidence of interplanetary travel. This unit must stand by its statement."

"Traces of interplanetary travel... him...? In this day and age... No, it can't be!"

"Again, inquiry?"

"He's too young. I was much older... er... more mature before I even began traveling, and I was never one to sport a beard," Doctor Omega muttered. "His reasoning is spotty concerning this peculiar mystery he's pursuing. There's no earthly way he is a younger version of myself..."

"Perhaps a future version?" Thea suggested. "You have spoken of your people being very long lived and able to change their appearance."

"In only the most dire of circumstances," Omega said, setting Thea down on top of the hatbox. "I'm far too careful in my actions for it to happen. This fellow is obviously mentally unbalanced or up to something... I'm just unsure of what... We need to stay with him, until he tips his hand."

"Brainwave scanning, while limited by my condition, shows several similarities to your own mental energies."

"When were you scanning my brain waves?" Doctor Omega asked, testily. "You know I do not condone that sort of... oh, he's returning!"

Looking up at the sound of approaching footsteps, Doctor Omega hastily replaced the robot head in the pink box. He was retying the twine when the younger Omega jogged towards them.

"I... uh... I could use some assistance," he said, in a slightly breathless tone. His eyes darted about, as if he was looking for something, but at the same time unable to remember what it was.

"What is it?" Doctor Omega asked, getting to his feet. "Did you find your ruffian?"

"In a way."

They summoned the carriage, and the driver, Eugène Papillon, a gruff, wire-thin Parisian, joined them, as they made their way to the third floor of the hotel. The trio entered the room, pausing in the doorway to take in the disarray. The furniture had been overturned and papers were scattered all about the room. Some appeared to have been tossed into the fireplace.

"Rather a cheery fire, in any other circumstances," Doctor Omega muttered, strolling into the room and looking around thoughtfully. He set the hatbox upon a desk and distractedly peered at several sheets of paper. "Curious, these are business papers… receipts and the like. Did your suspect strike you as the entrepreneurial sort?"

Young Omega shook his head as he entered the room. He gestured for Eugène to stand guard at the door.

"He was merely a hireling for a larger criminal enterprise," he explained, moving across the room to an ancient, sagging sofa. "It seemed they were abandoning this place and my quarry was left behind to dispose of any evidence."

"So, he's gone," Doctor Omega nodded.

"In a manner of speaking," the younger man said, waving the older one over to the sofa.

There was a space between the back of the sofa and the wall and there, on the dusty floor, was huddled a body. It wore the rough clothes of a workman. His head was twisted at an odd angle, indicating a broken neck.

"I see," said Doctor Omega, kneeling down to examine the body. "Interesting."

"Yes, but hardly helpful," interjected the younger Omega. "I needed information to find out more concerning who he worked for and what they were up to."

"Not a talkative fellow," Doctor Omega muttered. "But, I think he still has something to tell us…"

He brought up a yellowed business card.

"Hmm, the address for this office is near the docks," the younger Omega said. "Not the most reputable of neighborhoods. The card is stained, hard to read… *Maupertuis!* I've heard that name… But from where…?"

"There was a detective…?" the older Omega said, getting to his feet. "Lecoq… or was it that Marple woman…?"

The scruffy carriage driver stood in the doorway, focusing more on the two pacing savants than guarding them against would-be attackers.

"Perhaps you could do your thinking down in the carriage?" he suggested, hopefully. "No dead men might be more conducive…?"

Both Omegas looked up and nodded. The younger tucked the card in his pocket, while the older scooped up the few remaining intact papers and stuffed them into the hatbox. They made their way to the grey, dingy lobby as three black-cloaked figures came flowing out of the shadows.

"Run!" the younger Omega shouted, hooking his arm through Doctor Omega's and bolting for the door. The older man stumbled along, struggling to hold on to his box and cane.

Eugène outpaced the two and quickly leapt into the driver's seat, giving the two Omegas only seconds to fling themselves into the carriage before it raced off.

The cloaked trio ran after them, but soon realized that they could not catch up on foot and leapt into a plain, black carriage parked in a nearby alley.

"They are still after us!" the younger Omega said, sticking his head out the window to keep an eye on their pursuers.

"The cloaks," Doctor Omega muttered, as he was jostled about. "Like those worn by followers of the Ubasti, but was there something…?"

"Faster, Eugène!" the younger Omega instructed." See if we can lose them!"

"Did you notice anything odd about them?" Doctor Omega asked. "I caught a glimpse of one their hands…?"

"Can't say I did," his younger namesake said, sitting back and frantically rummaging through his coat pockets. "Where is…? Ah-ha! This should deal with them!"

He held out a pencil-sized metal tube triumphantly.

"I don't see how that will fend them off."

"Do not doubt the power of the sonic!" the younger Omega said, leaning out the window. He pointed the metal tube at the pursuing carriage, pressed a tiny button and a thin beam of light shown from the end of the tube. A beam that had no seeming effect on the other carriage.

"Imbecile!" Doctor Omega grumbled, pulling the other Omega back into the carriage. "It's a pen light! Really, the idea that I would rely on some sonic knick-knack to extract myself from a difficult situation… farcical, just farcical!"

He began to pat down his own pockets, taking out a small, crumpled, brown paper bag and an equally crumpled envelope. He handed the bag to the younger man and smiled.

"Now, when I say, empty the bag out the carriage window," he instructed. "Understand?"

"I suppose," the other man muttered, peering into the bag. "But these are…?"

"Yes, I'll apologize to my granddaughter later. Now!"

The younger Omega leaned out the window and emptied the bag of metal jacks onto the cobblestone street. Doctor Omega then touched a match to the paper fuse of a thin string of firecrackers and flung them out the other side. The combination of startling noise and the discomfort caused the horses to struggle against the black carriage's driver. After several minutes, they bolted down a side street to escape their torment.

The noise also startled the horses pulling their own carriage, which then galloped forward, adding even more distance between the two carriages.

"Excellent," the younger Omega announced, sitting back. "Now, we can go to…"

"…The *Cosmos*," Doctor Omega snapped. "It is time we obtained some answers. Until I can put my mind to rest about you, I will be unable to concentrate on this… whatever it is you have gotten yourself mixed up in."

The bearded man toyed with the monocle on his lapel as he pondered what the older man had said. After several moments, he nodded and gave the driver the instructions for their new destination.

Several minutes later, they disembarked at the opening of an alleyway. It was wide and moderately clean, with a wooden gate at the far end. The younger Omega opened the gate with a slight flourish.

"Behold," he said. "The *Cosmos!*"

Sitting in the courtyard was a hot air balloon with an oversized basket. The balloon seemed to be only partially inflated and so bobbed limply.

Doctor Omega frowned and his shoulders slumped. Despite his criticism of the other man, he had held onto a sliver of hope that this *faux* Doctor Omega had somehow gained possession of his real space-time ship, the *Cosmos*.

"That?" he sighed, going to sit on a nearby stack of lumber. "That is your *Cosmos?*"

"Yes, it is," Young Omega said, proudly giving the gondola an affectionate pat as he walked past it. "You are not seeing it at its best, but a day's work and I will once again be capable of journeying amongst the planets."

"Oh, do shut up!" Doctor Omega snapped, sulkily.

"I beg your pardon?"

"I have had enough of this!" the older man said, sternly jabbing a finger at the younger. "I am stranded here, in this time, on this world, trying to discover any means of leaving ,or if my traveling companions are even alive, and that task is made increasingly difficult when some... dandified idiot is constantly babbling, while I am trying to think!"

The younger Omega skidded to a halt, a stunned expression on his thin face, before it quickly morphed into indignant anger.

"Oh, that is rich!" he declared, hands on hips, as he scowled down at the aged savant. "I am in the midst of a serious investigation, a man is dead and there are hints of unearthly forces at work in Paris. None of which is made any easier when some doddering old man dogs my heels, going on like a disapproving school lecturer! Who do you think you are?"

"I? I am Doctor Omega! *The* Doctor Omega! Not some playacting adolescent!" the old man glared, "who has no idea what he has stumbled into and insists on playing out some boys' own adventure story."

"Perhaps, if you would attempt to speak to me, instead of enjoying the sound of your own voice so much!"

"Might I make a suggestion?" A muffled voice said from the hatbox.

Both Omega's stopped at peered at it, one thoughtfully, the other in surprise.

"Ah, Thea, pardon me, with everything happening, I forgot about you," Doctor Omega said, opening the box and rummaging amongst the papers. He held up the metal head. "What do you suggest?"

"What is that…?" the younger Omega stammered. the argument forgotten with the appearance of this new marvel. "You have been to other worlds!"

"What…?"Doctor Omega muttered. "Oh, do control yourself. Thea is a product of this world, an automaton, a product of a future technology. Like you, her mind is not entirely her own. I had hoped that traveling with me would help her to break her programming…find her own way in the world…not turning out quite as I had hoped, but I'm sure that once I'm able to reattach her head…"

"I have done preliminary scans of this other individual," she interrupted. "I can attempt more comprehensive scans."

"Really?" Doctor Omega mused frostily. "At what point do you take my word for it?"

He turned the head till it was facing the balloon.

"Do you imagine that craft capable of traversing the time stream? It doesn't look capable of getting off the ground, let alone reaching other worlds. He is no more me than he is the Man in the Moon."

"The Moon…?" the younger Omega muttered, his gaze moving from the robot head to his balloon. "I was… not the Man in the Moon, but rather… how did you know?"

"What?" Doctor Omega asked, peevishly. 'What are you going on about?"

"Spike in brain wave activity," Thea commented. "If his memories have been altered, then perhaps a more delicate approach is required."

"Yes, yes," the older man muttered, tucking the robot's head under his arm as he stood up and went over to the younger.

The younger Omega swayed slightly and rubbed at his forehead. He no longer seemed aware of the presence of the old man and the robot. He turned his gaze and footsteps towards the gondola of his balloon. Upon reaching it, he leaned against the edge of the basket and stared up at the deflated balloon without seeming to see it.

"How did I know what, young man?" Doctor Omega asked, coming to stand next to him. His voice was low and soothing. "What about the Moon?"

"I had… um… had just returned… from the Moon, when all this… whatever it is, began," the younger Omega muttered. He seemed to need the support of the gondola to stay on his feet. "Something… happened on the Moon…"

"That could mean something. The Moon is actually not as desolate as Monsieur Verne would have people believe."

"Who…?"

"Never mind," Doctor Omega said, taking the younger man by the arm. "Come, have a seat."

Once he had the dazed young man seated on the lumber pile, Doctor Omega set down Thea's head and took a seat himself. He then began patting his coat pockets, eventually bringing forth another crumpled paper bag.

"Licorice Allsorts?" He offered.

"Are these your granddaughter's as well?"

"No, these are mine. I keep them in my coat, so my granddaughter doesn't take them from me. Now, let me tell you a story: My ship, the *Cosmos*, which is not and has never been a balloon, was traveling through space and time, as it does, and encountered a wave of radioactive turbulence. My traveling companions and I were flung out into the void. Thea and I found ourselves here, in Paris."

He paused and patted the metal head affectionately and then looked up at the younger man, hoping for an expression of realization. Instead he was met with further confusion.

"Yes, well, another indicator that I'm right," Doctor Omega muttered. "If you were me, that would have made perfect sense."

The younger Omega continued to peer at him, dumbfounded.

"As I was saying, it becomes clear that it is no coincidence that, shortly after I began my exile here, you suddenly are racing the streets, believing you are Doctor Omega..."

"But, how can you still deny it?" the younger man protested. "I have the knowledge, I have traveled amongst the... the... um... planets."

"Tell me about some of your journeys, Doctor Omega," the older savant said, his tone taking on a soothing rhythm. "What wonders have you seen?"

"I traveled to the Moon..."

"So you've said. Where else? Mars, the far future, Quinnis in the fourth universe...?"

"No!" the younger Omega exclaimed, his hands clutching at his temples. "This... is... wrong! I am Doctor Omega! I have traversed the vastness of space, yet, all I can recall is my trip to the Moon and... and even that..."

"We are not going to get answers by forcing matters," Doctor Omega said. He poked a finger into the bag of candy and took one out, studying it thoughtfully as he spoke. "Your memories have been tampered with. Who or why, we do not know, but now that we can see the scaffold, we can fill in the gaps and discover what has been built, as it were. The human mind is a wondrous and delicate thing. Answers do us no good if we cause you harm along the way. Tell, me more about this mystery that you've stumbled into, upon your return to Earth...?"

"Yes, of course," the other man nodded, relieved to think of something else. "I was intrigued by what those two groups were fighting over. As you may know, Paris is rife with criminal gangs and shadowy groups that all seem to spend as much time in conflict with each other as they are with the police. While it never occurred to me that the Ubasti would be operating in Paris, until you mentioned them, I did recognize a couple of the street ruffians from... hmmm... I was at the docks...?"

"We can sift through the details later," Doctor Omega reassured him. "What criminal group do they work for?"

"No one in particular," the younger man shrugged. "At the time, they were taking coin from a businessman of questionable reputation, Oscar Maupertuis... he claims a title, Earl was it?"

"Baron," Doctor Omega prompted, quietly. "Baron Maupertuis. I knew the name was familiar to me and while it is an answer of sorts, it leads to more questions. Can you describe the Baron to me?"

"Not well. I don't believe we've met face to face. There was a picture in a newspaper and I saw him from a distance at a gathering at the Louvre. He considers himself quite the patron of the arts, but there have been rumors of him collecting artwork and artifacts through dubious means..."

He paused, catching a glimpse of the older man's impatient frown.

"He is of... um... medium height and a touch overweight, rather impressive set of whiskers, fair-haired and middle-aged, blue eyes and a rather nasty smile. Is that the man you knew?"

"Yes, he had discarded the whiskers for a mustache, but in every other respect, it may be... This is curious and bothersome."

"How so?"

"I encountered the Baron in 1891 and he was still a middle-aged man with a nasty smile," Doctor Omega explained. "I knew then that he was more than a mere schemer... probably for the best Watson decided not to publish..."

"A son perhaps? Following in the fathers' conniving footsteps?"

"No, I suspect there's more to the Baron," Doctor Omega nodded.

"You believe he's... immortal?" the younger Omega asked, helping himself to a piece of candy. "Or does he travel in time, like you claim to?"

"Claim...?" Doctor Omega muttered, frowning.

The younger man got to his feet and began to pace about the yard.

"Now, it begins to make sense, I think," he said, hands clasped behind his back, as he walked.

"What?" Doctor Omega grumbled.

"One of the things that kept me from understanding this mystery, was what were both groups after. Now understanding that we are looking at the cult of Ubasti vying with a criminal with an unnaturally extended lifespan, it suddenly becomes clear what they are after: One of the surviving crystals of Atlantis!"

"One of the what?" Doctor Omega sputtered.

"You see," the younger Omega explained, sitting back down. "There are many legends about the lost city, and many concern artifacts that were scattered across the world when it sank. Many of them speak of the Atlanteans working in crystal, the way we would metal, and creating crystals that were capable of operating... machinery, of a sort, as well as channeling energy for health and longevity. You see? It makes perfect sense! The Ubasti, coming as they do from Atlantis' sister city, Lemuria, would know of the crystals existence, while if the Baron is prolonging his life through some... unnatural means, would seek them out as well!"

He smiled in triumph at the older man.

"You... buffoon!" Doctor Omega exclaimed in reply.

"What? What did I say?"

"Yes, there are many myths and legends springing from the sinking of Atlantis, most of them were invented by the Atlanteans themselves, to hide and protect their powers and secrets. Which of the numerous Atlantises is the actual, true Atlantis is one of them. Another is, that there are no 'magical crystals' of Atlantis."

"But..." the younger Omega began to protest.

"I am not merely dashing skeptical cold water on your theory. I was there, I know. The crystals are a ruse, a fairy tale to trap the attention of the vain, the desperate and the hopelessly naïve."

The young man sank down onto the lumber pile shoulders slumped, clasping his hands loosely in front of him.

"Well, that, besides being slightly disappointing, makes no sense," the younger Omega muttered. "If the Ubasti know the crystals are just a fairy tale, then why are they involved?"

There was a moment of silence and both Omegas sat up and peered at each other, struck by sudden inspiration.

"Unless they know what it actually is!" the young man breathed.

"They aren't the Ubasti," Doctor Omega said.

The younger Omega sighed, bowed his head and made a vague 'after you' gesture.

"Did you notice anything about the three cultists that pursued us at the hotel?" he asked.

"Besides that they were dressed in black robes and chasing us down the street?"

"Don't be facetious," Doctor Omega chided. "Though, you have brought up an important point: the Ubasti operate in the shadows, in secret, and they chased us down a Paris street in ceremonial robes: hardly the work of a competent secret society. Not to mention brawling with Maupertuis' hired ruffians in the middle of the street..."

"Their skin...!" the younger man interrupted. "I meant to ask about it, but in the confusion of events it slipped my mind. The one that almost grabbed my arm, his skin was... odd. It had a particular reddish coloring, as though he'd suffered a burn or was an American Indian...?"

"Lectroids," Doctor Omega said, in a concerned tone.

"What? Is that what you think they were?"

"No," he replied, pointing past the younger man. "I think that's what they are."

The younger Omega spun and then gaped at the three black-robed figures standing in the alleyway. They pushed back their hoods, revealing bald heads, the color and texture of a boiled lobster shell. Their lips were thin harsh lines, their noses mere slits and cruel black orbs for eyes.

"Ah, Lectroids," the young man nodded, toying anxiously with his lapel ribbon. "Yes, never occurred to me actually... What do we do now?"

He got his answer when Doctor Omega scooped up Thea's head and ran for the balloon. The younger Omega shrugged, grabbed a stout stick, and ran after his older namesake, swinging wildly as the cloaked aliens lunged at them. He caught one Lectroid across the temple and it fell to its knees. The second met the wooden bludgeon head on and cracked it in half.

Doctor Omega stuck out his cane as he hobbled by, tripping up the third. The two men staggered past the Lectroids and fell into the basket of the balloon. The younger Omega flailed about, hitting various levers and dials on the clunky jumble of equipment that took up one corner of the gondola. Doctor Omega frantically struggled to pull in the anchor, while keeping an eye on the quickly recovering and quite angry looking Lectroids. The anchor came loose suddenly striking the older time traveler in the shoulder as it fell into the gondola.

The balloon sluggishly inflated and rose upwards, reaching a height of ten feet by the time the alien trio reached them. They jumped and snarled, their blunt, jagged fingernails leaving gouge trails in the exterior of the basket, but the Lectroids were unable to get a grip and climb up after their quarry.

Doctor Omega fell back, sitting awkwardly on the floor of the basket, struggling to catch his breath.

"That went as well as could have been expected, I suppose," he muttered, wiping his face with his handkerchief. He pulled over the pink hatbox. Thea's head was laying facedown amongst the papers. She was muttering to herself in a tinny, sullen voice.

"I do apologize, my dear," Doctor Omega said, picking her up and brushing her off. He set her down on a trunk and began fishing papers out of the box.

"That should do it," the younger man announced, pulling a long lever on the side of the machinery. "We are at a safe height and, while it is a vaguely ostentatious way of getting about the city, the *Cosmos* will provide us with safe passage to our next destination...whatever that may be. I must confess I find myself even more baffled with each new piece of information we acquire."

He checked some dials and was pleasantly surprised to find a cigar tucked behind one and with a smile, lit it and puffed thoughtfully.

"If you were really me, you'd have a pipe," Doctor Omega muttered, as he looked through the papers they'd found at the hotel.

"Those were Lectroids... Red Lectroids...?" the younger Omega muttered, between puffs. Absently, he adjusted the controls on the clunky device. "Here, in Paris, that isn't right... I think?"

He looked over at the older savant for reassurance. Doctor Omega nodded.

"Sounds like the memory blocks are coming loose," he nodded, thoughtfully. "Interesting. Yet, you are showing none of the dizziness or fear you felt before. Maybe there is more to your *Cosmos* than meets the eye."

"Well, that's good, I suppose, except we can't just float up here forever. We have transport, but no destination."

"Yes, I was thinking about that," Doctor Omega said, waving the paper in his hand. "I think these scraps can give us the means to locate the Baron. Do you have a map amongst all this clutter?"

"Yes, must apologize, wasn't expecting company," the younger Omega said, as he rummaged amongst the scattered bits of luggage and machinery. "Arrived back in Paris and haven't had a quiet moment for housekeeping...ah, here it is!"

"Yet, you acquired rooms?" Doctor Omega said, accepting the rolled up map. Placing a pince-nez upon his beakish nose, he studied the map, using the scraps of paper to help him identify and then figure out the location of their quarry. After several moments, he frowned in frustration and placed the map on the floor of the gondola. He circled the likely locations with a felt tip marker and placed Thea's head on the map. As he struggled to stand up, he gave the robot an encouraging pat on the head.

"I do believe, if we can locate the Baron, and I don't see the Lectroids having any difficulty tracking us through Paris, then we have a good chance to wrap this whole convoluted business up tonight."

The basket swayed slightly in the breeze, as it drifted over the darkened rooftops of Paris. Doctor Omega gripped the wicker railing to keep his feet.

"You think if we bring both sides together, we can sort out who is up to what and deal with them all?" the younger man asked, joining the Doctor at the rail.

"I think so. Be easier if we knew what this 'magic crystal' actually was," He said with a frown.

"Oh, well, if that will help, then I could retrieve it from its hiding place." The younger Omega smiled at his traveling companion. The older man replied with a look of stunned amazement.

"You know where this thing... artifact... is?"

"Well, yes."

"You've known this entire time?"

"Yes."

"And it never occurred to you to mention this not insignificant fact to me?"

"Yes, you see... um... is it healthy for your knuckles to get that white? Maybe you should let go of your cane?"

"Yes, quite reasonable. You can't steer the balloon to the artifact's location if I knock you senseless," Doctor Omega agreed through gritted teeth.

"Oh, it won't be that difficult," The younger man said, reaching into his inside coat pocket.

"You've had it with you the whole time... Of course, you did," Doctor Omega sighed. "And why was this information kept from me during the course of our investigations?"

"Because for most of 'our investigations,' you've been shouting at me and generally acting like an unstable old lunatic," the younger Omega explained. "I've never seen you before tonight and you show up and treat me like I'm some sort of deluded bumbler..."

"Which we've established you are."

"Perhaps. My memories have been interfered with," the younger man shrugged. "But until we discover some proof that I'm not you, I'm quite content to be Doctor Omega."

"As you should be," Doctor Omega said, reaching up to clutch at his lapels and standing proudly stiff backed. "So, until we get things sorted, I will be generous enough to share my identity, as well as my intellect and deductive skills with you. Now, let's see what's caused all the fuss, shall we?"

The younger Omega handed the object over to the older man. It was a crystal, roughly eight inches long and deep blue in color. It seemed to soak up the moonlight and reflect it back with a faint, warm glow.

"Ah!" Doctor Omega said with a satisfied smile. "It all begins to make a bit of sense."

"It does...?" The younger man asked.

"Yes. This crystal did not come Atlantis," Doctor Omega explained. "It came from Metebelis-Three."

He nodded to himself, before glancing over at his companion and noticing his dumbfounded expression.

"The crystals of Metebelis-Three have the ability to store and channel various forms of energy, including mental," he continued.

"How do you know all of this?" Young Omega asked.

"Because, up until a fortnight ago, this crystal was sitting on my mantelpiece, next to a Tibetan sacred bell... I must get around to returning that to the monastery someday... um, where was I? Ah, yes, the crystal is mine. It was obviously cast out into the time stream at the same time I was, and found its way into the hands of either the Lectroids or the scheming Baron, setting off this struggle to gain it and use it for their own nefarious purposes: Maupertuis for extending his lifespan, but the Lectroids... that bodes badly for Paris, if not the Earth, if they get their claws on it."

"Do we still go ahead with our plan to bring both sides together?" the younger Omega asked. "If we no longer need information...?"

"Letting them fight it out could solve all our problems," Doctor Omega replied. "Besides, I'm still curious as to who Baron Maupertuis is. Thea, have you worked out our destination yet?"

"Yes, Doctor," the robot head replied. Her eyes lit up and twin beams of light shone on a spot on the map. The younger Omega knelt down and picked up both the map and the metal head. He handed Thea to the Doctor and studied the map, looking down at the rooftops of Paris.

"I think if the wind doesn't pick up, we should have no trouble."

He turned a small crank and pulled a lever. The balloon gained a bit of height, as well as changing direction.

Doctor Omega peered up towards the balloon.

"Heat absorbing fabric... steering device that controls vertical as well as horizontal movement and some of these supplies and other pieces of equipment... You may not be me, my boy, but you are someone with a first class mind," he said, nodding thoughtfully. "Maybe that's where we need to look to discover who you are and how you arrived to be mixed up in all this? Where were you going when you... unceremoniously landed? You were returning from somewhere, correct?"

"Yes," the younger Omega nodded, adjusting a control dial. "I was returning to... huh... Paris. I'd just completed a... no, I'd attempted... that's odd...?"

He leaned against the basket rail and rubbed at his temples a puzzled frown on his bearded face.

"Just speak as things come to you," Doctor Omega said in a quiet tone. "You were in the balloon, drifting along, just as we are now. Could you see where you were going? Did you travel by night?"

"Yes, but there was a full moon... the Moon!"

The young man turned to face Doctor Omega, a bright smile on his face. He gestured triumphantly.

"The Moon! I told you I had been to the Moon, and I had! That's where I was returning from. It just... it felt... unreal, like a dream..."

"You traveled to the Moon, and yet, when you try and speak of it, it begins to feel unreal to you, like a half-remembered dream," Doctor Omega muttered, stroking his chin thoughtfully. "Of course!"

He smiled at the younger man and patted his arm comfortingly.

"Now, we have answers. You did travel to the Moon, and there, you encountered the Lunian Immortals," he explained.

"Who... wait, yes, there was someone. A tall man in a white robe of some kind... he was... was like a Greek statue..." The man muttered his brow wrinkled in concentration. "But, he said, he was an... angel... or perhaps...?"

"The Lunian Immortals are a race of eternal beings," Doctor Omega explained, in a tone that suggested he was speaking in a university lecture hall rather than the gondola of a hot air balloon. "No one is entirely sure where they originated from, but they settled on your Moon. As I said, they are eternal, not to mention arrogant and insufferably smug in their dealings with other beings. Their claims of being 'God's chosen' are completely unfounded, though it is believed that their visits to Earth are the origin of many cultures' belief in angels and deities."

"They found me when I was drifting towards the Moon!" the young man exclaimed. "They showed me their city... their beautiful, white city and brought me back and showed me all of the Earth..."

"The whole time telling you what a rank, ignorant race humans are, while they sang their own, superior and highly moral praises," Doctor Omega grumbled. "Yes, they do it quite often. They claim it's in order to educate and enlighten 'lesser races.' I believe immortality has driven them, as a race, into a kind of collective boredom and it's all part of an elaborate game they play to while away the millennia. Either way, that is what happened to you."

"They returned me to Earth, believing I was you?"

"No, they returned you to Earth believing that your entire encounter was all a dream," Doctor Omega continued. "Unfortunately, in the trance state they'd put you, your mind was very susceptible to outside influences..."

"And I found the blue crystal! I... um... absorbed the mental energy it had gotten from you!" The young man exclaimed. "So, I'm not an enigmatic traveler in space in time, but I did prove my balloon design worked and that it could carry me beyond the boundaries of Earth's atmosphere and out into space! It works and all those who said 'Gerpré is a dreamer with only his head in the clouds' will have to eat their words!"

"Gerpré...?" Doctor Omega asked. "Is that your name?"

The young man stopped, as though the revelation of his name had come as a big a surprise to himself, as it had to his learned companion.

"Gerpré...?" he breathed. Lingering over the word as though savoring its taste. "Antoine Gerpré...! Gerpré, student, inventor and balloonist extraordinaire!"

"My dear Gerpré," Doctor Omega said, smiling as he took the younger man's hand and shook it. "A pleasure to make your acquaintance!"

"Pleased to meet you, Doctor." Gerpré smiled, giving a short bow. "So, now that we have been properly introduced, let us go make the acquaintance of Baron Maupertuis."

He turned back to the balloon's controls and steered it across the city. Doctor Omega, smiling to himself, picked up Thea's head and placed it upon the control console, while he sat on a whicker basket.

Soon, they found themselves floating over one of Paris' more upscale neighborhoods. The houses were grander and there was more land separating them.

"There!" Gerpré announced, pointing to a specific roof.

"Are you sure?"

"He is correct," Thea responded.

"Thank you," The young balloonist said to the robot head, as he rummaged through a trunk. He brought out a long length of rope with a grappling hook tied to it. He lowered it over the side, swinging it until it caught the eves of the rooftop. He tugged the rope to make sure it was secure, and then adjusted the controls so the balloon began to descend. Once the balloon had touched down, Gerpré threw another loop of rope over a small nearby chimney to secure the balloon. He then climbed out of the basket. Doctor Omega picked up Thea and then handing the metal head and his cane to the young Parisian, awkwardly climbed out to join him.

"What's our next move?" Gerpré asked, handing the two objects back.

"We need to be sure the Baron is in residence," Doctor Omega said. "And since your balloon is hardly a subtle mode of travel, we must be quick about it."

"Commencing scan," Thea announced, her eyes lighting up. "Detecting unusual life sign."

"Are you sure that's not just the Lectroids?" the older savant asked.

"I am certain," the robot head replied. "The life sign is within the dwelling."

"Well, then," Gerpré said, prying opening an attic window. "Why don't we see if the... lady can lead us to the master of the house?"

The trio climbed in the window and made their way through a cluttered, dusty attic until they found a narrow staircase that lead down into the house.

They moved through opulent hallways and rooms, their footsteps muffled by the lush carpeting, as they crept past shadowy furnishings.

"Um...besides the Baron," Gerpré asked in a whisper, "what might we be looking for?"

"Not entirely sure," Doctor Omega replied, holding Thea out in front of him like a lantern. "Maupertuis may be using any number of unorthodox methods to extend his life span, ranging from otherworldly science to more arcane practices. Depending on what he believes the crystal to be..."

The Doctor's explanation trailed off and he came to a halt in front of a large oil painting. He paused and held Thea's head up to shine a light on it. It was a heavy-set man dressed in the fashion of the past century.

"Is that the Baron?" He mused. "Something familiar...especially around the eyes...?"

"I don't mean to be rude, but we need more of a plan than we seem to have at the moment," Gerpré suggested, looking about anxiously. "What should we be looking for? "

"Perhaps," a gruff voice said from out of the shadows, "some artifact that he could use to channel the crystal's energy?"

Both men spun, as a trio stepped into the shafts of moonlight that came in through the windows.

At their head was obviously Baron Maupertuis. His suit was up to date and fashionable. His features were broad and arrogant, his blue eyes burned with a cold hatred. He held a heavy flintlock pistol trained on Doctor Omega. Behind him stood two large men that looked like they'd be more comfortable in dockworkers' garb than the servant's livery that they were currently wearing. One also held a pistol, the other a heavy wooden cane.

"Ah," Doctor Omega frowned.

"Um…?"Gerpré added.

"Unusual biological profile located," Thea said, unnecessarily.

"Doctor Omega," the Baron growled, not lowering his weapon. In fact, his finger tightened on the trigger. "I should have guessed that this… popinjay was your cat's paw and all his foolish antics were merely to lure me out, so once again you could interfere with my plans."

"Have we met?" Doctor Omega asked puzzled. "You seem to have me at a disadvantage."

"You break into my home," Baron Maupertuis grumbled. "And now you want to pretend you don't know me? Have you forgotten our last meeting?"

"Well, I do recall our next meeting, but must say the previous one has slipped my memory," Doctor Omega said. He handed Thea to Gerpré and stepped closer to the Baron and his servants. "There is something familiar about you… humph, no, I'm sorry to say I can't recall…"

"Damn your eyes, you doddering simpleton!" the Baron roared. "I will not…!"

"Eyes…? That's it!" Doctor Omega exclaimed relief at solving a mystery mixed with the knowledge that the answer was not good news. "Ozer, you may change your appearance, but your eyes will always give you away."

"Ozer?" Gerpré asked, in a quiet tone. "Who is he?"

Doctor Omega turned away from the Baron and his men, as though surprised to remember the young balloonist was still there.

"You recall we spoke of the Lunian immortals? Well, the Earth has produced immortals of its own, and there are roughly a dozen of them, all claiming to be the Wandering Jew of legend…"

"Claiming…!" Baron Maupertuis growled.

"The Baron, here, is one of them." Doctor Omega continued in his lecturer's tone, as though he wasn't at gunpoint. "In fact, 'Baron Maupertuis' is but the latest in a long line of false names. He claims to be Ozer, a soldier of Herod's, the very soldier who pierced the side of Christ. You probably have heard the story, it's a quaint, mildly entertaining…"

"You are trying my patience, old man," Ozer snarled, jabbing his pistol into Doctor Omega's back. "I don't know what game you are playing, but if the black brethren do not have the crystal, then I believe I can guess who does!"

Doctor Omega raised his hands at the touch of the gun in a sign of surrender. As he did so, he spun his cane around, catching the immortal across the temple. As Ozer staggered back, he raised his gun hand and the flintlock went off, sending the bullet into the ceiling.

"Quickly!' The Doctor exclaimed, grabbing Gerpré by the arm.

The balloonist nodded and charged past the Baron, creating a path between the two servants with two well-placed shoves. Since he was still clutching the robot head, Gerpré had the appearance of a player in a particularly bizarre game of rugby. They ran down the corridor. Doctor Omega would pause to peek into rooms as they passed, but apparently found nothing to interest him.

At the end of the hallway they came to a broad, carpeted staircase.

"What now?" Gerpré asked, anxiously.

"Down, I think," the savant replied, breathlessly. "Hurry… to the front door!"

"Why not the balloon?" Gerpré asked, before spotting the pursuing servants, and abandoning his question. They stumbled hurriedly down the stairs, arriving ungracefully in the roomy foyer. The two men skidded on the oriental area rug; Doctor Omega came to a halt and adjusted his cravat. Gerpré collided with the heavy, oaken front door.

The time traveler looked around the foyer with a touch of admiration at the décor. Gerpré shook his head and rubbed his bruised shoulder.

"We aren't getting out that way," he muttered, looking around for an escape route or makeshift weapon as he spotted the Baron and his men at the top of the stairs.

Doctor Omega frowned at his partner in crime, and taking off his tiepin fiddled with the lock on the door. He then swung it open wide and peered out into the approaching dawn. He frowned, then licked his finger and held it up to test the wind.

"Hmmm, thought they'd be here by now…disappointing," he muttered, turning back to face Gerpré and the quickly approaching violent trio. "Could you keep them busy for a few moments?"

"Um… I don't… know?" Gerpré muttered, peering doubtfully at the umbrella he found by the door.

"Not you," Doctor Omega said, looking at Thea, who was still in the crock of the young balloonist's arm.

"Affirmative," Thea replied.

As the Baron and his men reached the bottom of the stairs, Gerpré held up the robot head. Thea emitted a bright light and a high-pitched screech that sent the trio rocking back on their heels. While this was going on, Doctor Omega stepped out onto the front steps and taking the blue crystal out of his coat pocket waved it over his head.

"Come out, come out, wherever you are!" he shouted.

He soon spotted the cloaked Lectroids skulking down the street, keeping to the shadows. Spotting Doctor Omega, they broke into a run and raced for the doorway.

Smiling to himself, he ducked back inside, grabbed Gerpré by the coattails and pulled him into a side alcove, as the two groups came bolting forward, Ozer firing, as his henchmen lunged at the black robed forms.

The bullets did no more than cause the aliens to stumble. They then tore off their clocks to keep from tripping on them as they fought.

The Lectroids were dressed in various styles and levels of taste. One was shirtless; another looked like he had just left a wedding, and a third was in fashionable tweeds and a bowler. All three wore bulky black belts, strewn with wires and gears.

"Just as I thought," Doctor Omega muttered from his hiding place.

He allowed the combat continue for several more minutes, the Baron's men taking the worst of the punishment, as the Lectroids were stronger than any earthly opponent. He then stepped up and held the blue crystal up over his head. Closing his eyes, his forehead wrinkled in concentration, the crystal began to glow. The light caught the attention of all of the remaining combatants. One of the Baron's men had had his neck broken and one of the Lectroids took a bullet through the eye and was lying in an ever-widening pool of sludgy black blood.

"Gentlemen!" Doctor Omega shouted, opening his eyes. "I think I know a way to solve this conflict between you!"

With that announcement, he swung his arm and the alien crystal struck a marble pillar, shattering into a thousand blue fragments. A wave of energy rushed out from the remains of the crystal, washing over the foyer and its occupants. The Lectroids' belts began to spark and with a roar a rift opened around them and they were sucked out of the foyer like water down a tub drain.

Ozer dropped his weapon and clutched at his abdomen, grinding his teeth as he fell to his knees.

"That went quite well," Doctor Omega said, dusting off his hands.

Gerpré came staggering out of the alcove, rubbing one of his temples.

"I must say it feels as though I'm the only one occupying my skull," he announced, wincing slightly.

"Just as I planned."

"Ah, I have distinct memories of this," Gerpré said, smiling at his older companion. "I pull off some last minute bit of improvisation and then discuss it as though I had a grand scheme planned the whole time. Go ahead, it'll be fun to not have to do it myself."

Doctor Omega frowned at the young balloonist, then at the robot head still in Gerpré's hand. The eyes had burnt out and there was a trickle of smoke coming up from the right earpiece. Doctor Omega took Thea from Gerpré and looked it over with a sad, thoughtful smile.

"Poor child," he said. "Once we return to the *Cosmos*, Fred and I will get you fixed up."

He then tucked her damaged head under his arm and turned his attention to the young balloonist and the ailing immortal.

"Now, where was I...?"

"Convincing me that you actually had a plan, I believe," Gerpré reminded him.

"Yes, I was and yes I did," Doctor Omega grumbled. "Now, let's see if there's any lingering trace of my intellect rattling around in your head... what was I up to?"

"Fine, have it your way," The younger man said, gripping his lapels in gentle mockery of his companion. "Once you discovered what both sides were after... the Baron to continue in his wicked immortal ways and the Lectroids in... um... order to... either use the crystal to stay in this dimension or open a rift to bring more of their kind to Earth...?"

"Very good," Doctor Omega said, walking over to the stairs. He sat, exhaling heavily and placed Thea down next to him. Gerpré dodged the remaining henchman, who bolted for the door and ran off into the night, and joined the Doctor on the stairs.

"Should we...?" Gerpré asked, pointing to the doorway.

Doctor Omega waved the idea away.

"We have enough to deal with," he said, nodding towards the prone form of Ozer. "So, knowing what we do, why bring everyone to the same locale?"

"At what point do you stop talking to me like I'm attending your class?" Gerpré asked, with a smile.

"When you show signs of learning something," Doctor Omega replied.

"Fine," Gerpré nodded. "Bringing them here allows you to... um... show them you had the crystal and knew what it truly was...?"

"Never mind," Doctor Omega frowned. "Though, it's reassuring to know you are back to normal. In order to avoid having Ozer's men or the Lectroids stalking you for the rest of your life, or causing who knows what amount of havoc, we needed to show them that the crystal was beyond their grasp."

"As well as letting them subdue each other," Gerpré suggested, rubbing his bruised shoulder.

"There is that. I was also quite sure I could refocus the crystal's energies in a manner that would render both sides harmless."

"So, you sent the Lectroids back to... no, it's gone. I guess I am just me. The only alien world I seem to have any knowledge of is the Moon."

"Yes, I sent the Lectroids back and with the Baron..."

"What did you do to him?" Gerpré asked. "He looks the same. Is he mortal now?"

"No, I haven't the faintest idea what gave the various Wandering Jews their immortality... something beyond my ability to take away, but I knew about Ozer's method of immortality. He would take over other bodies, moving on to the next until it got too sick, old or inconvenient for him to stay. What the crystal's energy did was to trap him in that one. He's still immortal, but he'll have to be happy with the body he's got. He's not going anywhere and apparently it works, as he was still the Baron Maupertuis when I met him, fifty years from now. Might also explain why he acted so unpleasant in 1889. I wondered...now, I know."

"And breaking the crystal and dispelling its energy seems to have allowed me to shake off your memories and remember my own," Gerpré nodded. "Shame that you had to destroy such a pretty item to accomplish it."

"No matter. I suppose I'll go back to Metebelis-Three, someday and fetch another one," Doctor Omega said, getting to his feet. "We should be on our way. Your *Cosmos* is bound to attract attention and I could do with some breakfast. Not to mention needing to see to Thea and figure out how in the world I'm going to find my friends and my own *Cosmos*."

He sighed and shook his head.

"You are more than welcome to stay with my mother and I while you sort that out," Gerpré said, standing up and patting the old time traveler on the shoulder. "And, as to breakfast, I believe I still have some supplies in the balloon. Never did get to unpack it. Now that I think of it, Eugène is probably wondering what became of us."

The two men climbed the stairs, not giving the prone form of Ozer a second thought and made their way back up to the roof.

The sun was coming up and Gerpré climbed into the gondola to check his steering device and prepare for takeoff.

Doctor Omega stood on the roof, Thea's head tucked under his arm, as he looked out across the Paris neighborhood.

I suppose this is home... for now," he sighed.

"Getting maudlin in your old age?" a voice said.

Doctor Omega turned to see a short, stout, bearded man dressed in Victorian tweeds and a cap standing on the rooftop next to him. He held a short metal tube with a row of buttons and appeared to be standing in a doorway in the air.

"Helvetius!" Doctor Omega exclaimed. "What are you...?"

"No time for chit chat," the other space-time traveler interrupted. "Come along, fate of the universe and all that, and I've already wasted too much time away from my studies looking for you."

He reached out, grabbed Omega by the arm and pulled him into the unearthly doorway. Tapping a button on the metal rod, the door closed leaving no trace that it, or even that the two men had been there at all.

"Ready to takeoff," Gerpré said, climbing out of gondola. "Doctor...?"

Gerpré searched the rooftop, then the house and, over the course of the next year, a good portion of Paris.

Finding the mysterious savant became his second obsession. After refining his balloon to continue his travels, he came to believe Doctor Omega had just returned from where or when he'd originally come from, and Gerpré set his mind on finding the old man as well as stepping foot upon the Moon himself and perhaps encountering the Lunian immortals once more.

It took several years of experimentation, research and struggle, but eventually young Gerpré accomplished both goals.

It is always a pleasure to read a story starring one of literature's first consulting detectives, Edgar Allan Poe's brilliant Chevalier Auguste Dupin. In the following tale, steeped in esoteric knowledge, Paul Hugli uses the springboard of one of the French Revolution's most horrible crimes to spin a tale of illusion and mysticism, death and rebirth, in the French Pyrenees...

Paul Hugli: *Piercing the Veil of Isis*

Pyrenees, 1855

> "Oh! Can't you hear me again crying?
> Waken?/Your love no more denying
> Mummy, mine, mine."
> *Mummy Mine*
> Richard Corburn & Vincent Rose, 1918.

It was a dreary midnight as the rather weak and weary French ratiocinator, Chevalier Auguste Dupin, tried pondering over some quaint and, no doubt, soon to be forgotten tome—*The Conchologist's First Book, or, A System of Testa-Ceaous Malacology*—when there came a rapping, a tapping on his chamber door. It was his new assistant, the American Reginald Goodwin, only he and nothing more. Well, except for Dupin's nightly dose of laudanum, to treat the painful gout in his left big toe. And Morpheus accepted him into his arms...

Morning came up with the vengeance of Electra in the provincial village of Rennes-le-Chateau, on the eastern edge of the Pyrenees. The village was once a prehistoric camp, then a Roman camp, then a medieval stronghold, and was now in the hands of the Blanchefort family. There had been rumors of hidden treasures in the village, but Dupin had neither the time nor the inclination to invest time in a treasure hunt; no matter how much Reginald implored. Typical American: wanting something for nothing, without work or effort.

After a brief repast served at the inn's *Salle Royale*, royally served by a buxom brunette, with the finest wines, fish and fowl, Dupin was ready for his journey home, to his *hotel particulier* in the Faubourg Saint Germain in Paris.

The porter, a young man named Berenger Saunière, took the Chevalier's luggage down the stairs, animatedly gushing about the legend of the treasure, claiming that he had some idea as to its location, but would remain mum about it. Dupin paid the lad's ramblings no mind.

The Chevalier stopped in the lobby, checked his waist-coat watch, clicked the lid shut, and looked about, overhearing some gossip about grave-robbery in the North, before spotting his assistant chatting it up with a lovely young lady sitting on a steamer trunk. Her face was begging for attention and, no doubt, Reginald wished to embrace her body. She was a svelte package with exquisite raven locks, cascading down over her abundant bosom; no more that 19. Dupin noticed a hint of rosemary as his assistant introduced the lady as Juliette Saint-Fond.

It seemed that, in a local public house, her driver had engaged in some drunken melee and had broken his leg, and was thus unable to continue; it would be another day before a replacement could arrive. And she couldn't tarry because an important assignment awaited her: a new position at the Chateau de l'Espoir, and she didn't want to be late.

Reginald had offered their services, and the young lady began to thank the Chevalier, but he cut her off with a magnanimous: *"Ce n'est rien."*

Reginald helped the young lady into their coach, and Dupin climbed in opposite her, while the young man stowed the steamer trunk, then climbed up and took the reins of the two horses and prodded them into action. Everyone bundled up as the mountain air had become chilly.

As they rode through the Pyrenees, Dupin regaled the young lady with the legend of these patchwork fields, the hillsides dark with conifers, the steep cliffs rising from winding torrents. He told her of Princess Pyrene and her father, the King of Gaul, being hospitable to Herakles on his quest to steal the cattle of Geryon, during his famous Labors. Returning from his victory, Herakles had come upon the remains of the princess and had mournfully cried her name, which still echoed in the mountains. Due to his respect for her feminine sensibilities, Dupin left out the parts dealing with a drunken Herakles raping the princess, who had given birth to a serpent, causing her to run into the woods, were she was ripped apart by wild beasts—*that* is what had caused the demi-god to mourn.

And Juliette regaled the Chevalier with her life story, which he tried to follow, but it was rather difficult. Especially since if had little interest in what the girl had to say. It seemed that she had answered an advertisement looking for a young woman of good-breeding to help catalogue a nobleman's library at *L'Espoir*. Her governess had written in her stead and the nobleman had accepted the young lady's qualifications.

The Sun set, and, with the evening, came even cooler weather. They soon came upon a Romanesque manor, which appeared in good repair, though it had definitely seen better days. In the center of the granite facade was a heavy wooden door with iron strap hinges, fronted by unkempt flagstones. Dupin also noticed a couple of Franklin lighting rods framing the tile and slate roof.

Getting down from the coach, Reginald sneezed, tightened his neck wrap, and helped Juliette from the carriage, then Dupin. The Chevalier walked the young lady to the door as Reginald toted the trunk on his shoulder, before letting it down before the great door. The Chevalier banged the lion-headed brass knocker.

The bang echoed through the manor, and, after a few moments, the great door creaked open, revealing an elderly man, in his seventies, thin, with snowy-white hair. His clothes were once expensive, but now were rather threadbare, though still in relatively good condition: red velvety dressing jacket, white ascot, black slacks and red slippers.

"*Oui?*" he inquired.

Dupin was cut-off by Juliette who answered first:

"My name is Juliette Saint-Fond…"

"*Ah oui*," the man said, bowing slightly, brushing his lips against the porcelain-like flesh of the back of her hand. "Delighted. Your governess wrote highly of you. I am Comte Jacques de Carignan."

This was the first time Dupin had heard the Comte's name and his usual stoic face flashed a sign of recognition. Dupin introduced himself and his assistant, saying of Reginald: "He's from the United States, and prefers to be called 'Reggie.'"

Reggie tipped his cap, then sneezed, and offered a weak apology.

"*Oui, Oui*—I know of your exploits, Chevalier," said the Comte. "Your name is synonymous with the solution of cryptic conundrums throughout France. You are a living legend."

Dupin managed a slight bow. One did not need to acknowledge established fact. The Comte turned to Reginald:

"And this young man, is he the chronicler of your exploits?"

"Alas, no. That poor soul died in an alley. Of no fault of his own."

"*Je vois*," said the Comte; then, with a sweep of his hand, he added: "I wasn't expecting visitors… save for the young lady, of course. But, do come in. It must be cold out there, and a storm does appear on the horizon. Do come in. You'll wait it out."

The trio of travelers were ushered into the parlor off the main hall, where a raging fire blazed in the hearth. The Comte motioned for them to sit, while he went to the side-board to pour libations: a sherry for the young lady, a pilsner in a stein for Reggie, and an Amontillado for the Chevalier.

After a bit of small talk, Juliette began to yawn and the Comte directed her to her room. Reginald followed with her trunk, and returned to announce that he felt a cold coming on, sneezed, said he was sorry, and retired to his own room.

When the younger couple had left, the Comte said:

"Grab your glass, Chevalier, and let us retire to the library."

The library was difficult to absorb at first glance—or even at a second glance—lit by flickering gas lamps. Three walls of the room were covered with bookcases rising 12 feet, floor-to-ceiling, in the 20-by-40 foot room. The books appeared arranged according to size and subjects, octavos, quartos, duodercimos, folios; bound in vellum, pigskin, calf, Morocco, various clothes and muslim; rare *incunabula, editio princeps,* Byzantine manuscripts…

Dominating the fourth wall was another massive hearth, with another fire ablaze. Above the *objet d'art*-littered mantle hung the portrait in oil of a woman dressed in pre-Revolution clothing. The Comte's mother? wondered Dupin.

As the Comte refreshed their libations, Dupin flipped through a large ledger—one of many—which accurately, precisely, and neatly catalogued the books in the library by title, author and position. That was decidedly odd, though the Chevalier. Why did the Count need a librarian?

Glancing up, he scanned the names: Virgil, Sophocles, Plato, Ovid, Aristole, Euripides, Homer, Sappho... And across the way: Bacon, Voltaire, Paine, Paracelsus, Kepler, Kant, Locke, Spinoza, Lamarck, Linnaeus, Machiavelli, Pope... Elsewhere: the *Qur-an*, the Mathers, the *Cabbalah*, Aquinas, Marx and Engels, the *Bhagavad-Gita*, the *Vedas, Zend Avesta,* the *Zohar*, various *Biblia Latina*, a *Mazaian* or *Gutenberg Bible*, Lao Tzu, *Talmud, Torah...*

The fiction section included Percy Bysshe Shelley, Coleridge, Dickens, Swift, Dumas, Marlowe, Austin, Jacob and Wilhelm Grimm, Goethe, Hawthorne, Malory, Hugo, Milton, plus large folios of Dante, Shakespeare, John J. Audubon, Lewis, Lear...

"Have you read all these books?" asked the Chevalier.

"Every last word," came the reply from across the room.

Dupin was flipping through a copy of *Tamerlane and Other Poems* (by a "Bostonian") when the Comte returned with their drinks. With a sweep of his hand, Dupin said:

"A most impressive collection, Monsieur le Comte."

He did not volunteer that his own library in Paris was just as extensive, though heavier in the natural sciences and philosophies, and less so in the romantics. Indeed, that was one of the luxuries of living in Paris: books were easily obtained, and often on the cheap.

The Comte' tapped the glass of a shallow display case.

"These are grimoires: *De Vermis Mysteriis, the Book of Eibon, Unaussprechlichen Kulten,* and, of course, *the Necronomicon.* The latter was John Dee's personal copy, and was authored by Abdul Alhazred, the so-called 'Mad Arab,' and alleges to contain the subterranean secrets of Memphis. It's difficult to read between the lines, to interpret what is *actually* being revealed."

"If anything," Dupin opined.

In fact, this was the *exact* rare and remarkable copy he had been searching for at a bookstall in the Rue Montmartre when he had first encountered his now-deceased chronicler.

"*En effet.*"

They settled back in wing-chairs of red velvet, worn to a dull pink, before the roaring fire, Dupin sipping his Amontillado, and the Comte his Napoleon Brandy. They talked of Ourang-Outangs, cigar girls and purloined letters.

"Ah, a 'tale of terror'," Dupin said, tapping the paper labeled three volumes laying on the end table: *Frankenstein or, the Modern Prometheus*. "A rather fanciful tale, to put it bluntly."

"Of course, the term 'Modern Prometheus' was coined by Immanual Kant to describe the American, Benjamin Franklin."

Dupin nodded and tilted his head toward the book shelves.

"I noticed you have a copy of his book: *Experiment and Observations on Electricity*. A remarkable book."

"*Oui*."

Next to the Mary Shelley was a copy of Thomas More's *Utopia*. Dupin almost smiled and said: "My associate, Reginald, would never accept the principles laid out in More's."

"Monsieur Goodwin is against the solidification of customs, institutions and laws?"

"Of that, I have no idea. He'd reject the six-hour work-day, and the elimination of gambling, brothels and taverns."

The Comte laughed and sipped his brandy. Then he stared at his liquor as he slowly swirled it around in his tumbler. At the moment, he seemed a mile away. Then, he mumbled:

"Everyone is looking for a *Utopia*... of one kind or another."

"I agree. Fools!"

"What do you know about Adam Weishaupt?"

"Not much—enlighten me."

Carignan smiled.

"Yes, the so-called *Illuminati*—established in Bavaria, on May 1, 1776. They wanted to reform the government via enlightenment... *illumination*. They thought religion was problematic, that scientific research was more valuable than religion."

"It sounds reasonable to me. Though the Catholic Church and Bavarian government thought otherwise."

"*Oui*... That's why it was a *secret* society."

"Not quite so secret, if everyone appears to have known about them. Nevertheless, within a few years, it was abolished by the Bavarian ruler, Karl Theodor, in 1785."

"*Oui*. All their documents were seized and the group disbanded," the Count said as he lit his Meerschaum, "but their goals remained admirable. The abolishment of the Catholic Church..."

"...And their 'New World Order' called for a revolution in France. And we know how that turned out..."

"*Oui*," the Comte sighed, again, for a moment, lost in deep thought, before returning to normal. "Actually, they referred to themselves as *Perfectibilists*, calling for the end of government... of possessions... of family... of religion."

"And your point is?"

"That the so-called *Illuminati* were not the first, nor will they be the last secret society—just the most recent—to claim some special... arcane knowledge."

"Indeed. Like the purely fictional fraternity created in the last century." Dupin rose and walked over to the philosophical section of the library. "I noticed before that you appear to have a strong interest in Christian Rosenkreuz, and his alleged visits to Yemen and Egypt. I believe the first published manifesto was... ah, here it is..." He pulled down a vellum volume, opening it to the frontispiece and read: *"Fama Fraternitatis."* Closing the book, he continued: "There were more than a hundred pamphlets, between 1614 and 1625, dealing with this alleged cult." Glancing back to the shelves, he added: "...And you appear to have them all, including *The Universal and General Reformation of the Whole Wide World.* Amazing."

"Alleged Rosicrucians included Albertus Magnus, Paracelsus, Roger Bacon, Newton, Franklin, Descartes..."

"Cogito ergo sum."

"Excusez-moi?"

"Nothing ... just quoting Descrates." Dupin indicated the shelves, again. "I see you have Master Pianco's *The Rosicrucian in his Nakedness,* and Robert 'the Saint' Louis' *The Rose and the Thorn*—both effective attacks, which quickly caused the order to dissolve; yet, it appears to have gained another foothold in recent years with the new discoveries in Egypt. The Rosicrucians attempted to trace their roots to Manetho's Eighteenth Dynasty—over three thousand years ago—to the founding of the order by Ahmose, as protector of the antediluvian wisdom still remaining in Egypt. In fact, C.E. Wunsch's *Horus* suggest that it was this secret society of Egyptian priests who initiated Moses into its Arcane Knowledge—the so-called 'Hebraic mysteries.'"

"You appear to know a lot about such things..."

"A hobby," Dupin modestly conceded.

"But you didn't mention Thutmosis III's visit to the Great Sphinx and the creation of the Great White Fraternity, when he elected himself Supreme Pontiff of the Brotherhood. And his descendent, Bech-en-Aten, 75 years later, who was the first monotheist in history, and designed the symbols of Rose and the Cross—all of which influenced the Hermetists..."

"As Above, So Below. All nonsense, crammed together due to the recent discoveries in Thebes and Tell el-Amarna, and this oddly-shaped image of Bech-en-Aten and his Queen Nefertiti worshipping the solar disk—the *Aten*—depicted in its own separate royal cartouche. This balderdash spread through the *cognoscenti* after Karl Richard Lepsius' discoveries in 1845. To quote Plato: 'Yes, Socrates, you can easily invent tales of Egypt, or any other country.'"

"Yet something did happen at Tell-Amarna—Manetho's King's List doesn't record Bech-en-Aten's name, nor his successors, Smenkhkare, Tuutankamun, and Ay. Some say..."

"...That this is more secret knowledge that the Amon priesthood wanted buried? *Ridicule!*"

"My point, Chevalier, is that everyone claims some secret, arcane knowledge known only to the initiated, some Philosophers' Stone or Holy Grail which might hold the secrets of life and death. In fact, we all have secrets. I notice your Masonic ring of the Lodge of the *Neuf Soeurs*..."

"Yes," Dupin replied cautiously. But he relaxed when the Comte showed him his matching ring..

A flash of lightening lit up the room, then the immediate thunder shook the manor. Dupin hoped it wasn't an omen, but an omen of what?

"Other members were Benjamin Franklin, Doctor Guillotin, Voltaire... and the Marquis de Lafayette. I knew of Dr. Franklin and served under the Marquis as his honorary aide-de-camp when he visited the United States, for the first time since his involvement in their *revolution*... We visited his old friend, Thomas Jefferson, in Monticello in the Spring of 1824, complete with a military escort. The two old comrades were weak..." Here, the Comte paused, looked at his own liver-spotted hands, and sighed. "...But they embraced. Later, these two gentlemen and other guests dined in the half-scale version of the Pantheon at Monsieur Jefferson's University, where the Marquis presented him with Thomas Young's and Jean-François Champollion's translations of the Rosetta Stone..."

The Comte tapped his copy of *Tamerlane* which Dupin had left on the end table. "At Monsieur Jefferson's funeral, in Charlottesville, overseen by Tom Randolph, in a drizzling rain, I met the author of this book..."

"Poe? I have read his poetry. Rather too somber for my tastes," said Dupin, taking a sip of his Amontillado. "Why do I get the sensation this is all leading to Egypt—and to a revelation of some kind?"

"*Oui.* You are noted for you interest in hieroglyphics?"

"In fact, all things Egyptian." Dupin paused. And for the first time, consciously realized he had seen no books on the subject of Egypt in the Comte's library. "The Talmud records that 'Ten measures of magic have come into the world; Egypt received nine and the rest of the world one.'"

"*Oui.* In fact, our two major Western religions have their origin in Egypt: Moses was Prince of Egypt; the Holy Family fled to Egypt to escape the Roman decree to kill the first-born—and both Moses and Jesus learned the secrets of the priestly adepts. Plus the Muslim controlled Egypt within a score of years after the death of the Prophet..."

"All roads lead into or out of Egypt..."

"*Oui.* Now, let me show you my secret collection," the Comte said, rising.

He walked to the far bookcase and tipped a copy of Robert Boyle's *The Spectical Chymist*. There was a moan, then a creak, and a section of the bookcase swung open, revealing a hidden passageway.

"*Suivez-moi!*"

And the Chevalier saw wonderful things:

Cabinets of curiosities, display showcases and tables artfully displaying ancient *artifacts* placed about the room: mummies of cats, ibises and falcons from Saqqara; glass jars of *mizraim* [powdered mummies]; a canopic chest and its four burial ceramic jars, capped with the heads of the sons of Horus [an ape, a jackal, a falcon and human]; statues, figurines, and stelae. The central space was dominated by a grass "coffin" containing a partly unwrapped mummy, dark with resin remains, and its toothless, gasping mouth adding a touch of terror to the room... and a bit of mystery.

Against the far wall was a sarcophagus standing upright; it appeared to be of the latter period, during the Greco-Roman rule, the Ptolemaic Period, after the fall of Pharaonic dominance of three millennia. On the wall hung a series of lithographic prints: the bas-relief zodiac map from the ceiling of the Osiris Chapel in the Temple of Dendera, from circa 700 B.C., which Louis XVIII had purchased in 1822 for 180,000 francs; the red-granite obelisk erected on the bloody site of the guillotine, on the Place de la Concorde in Paris, which records the exploits of the "Napoleon of Ancient Egypt," Tuthmosis III; Louis David's *Fontaine de la Regeneration*, erected on the ruins of the former Bastille, a bronze of the Egyptian goddess, Isis, with water streaming from her breasts; of Notre Dame—the revered Temple of Reason—built on the site of a Roman Temple honoring Isis.

"Isis," the Comte said, "was the unofficial patron saint—goddess?—whatever you want to call her, in atheistic France under Napoleon. In fact, Leonard N. Peterson's *We'll Always Have Isis* argues the many shapes and forms that Isis has taken since before and after she became the Egyptian goddess, wife of Osiris, and mother of Horus. That *Paris* itself is named for her!"

The romantic in Dupin—yes, there was a smidgen in him—wished to believe the City of Lights was named for Paris, lover of Helen of Troy, slayer of Achilles, and brother of Cassandra. But Peterson was wrong—as was Dupin's own wishfulness—rather prosaically, the city had been named in the Fourth Century A.D. after the *Parisii*, an early Gaulish tribe.

In the corner was a sandstone reproduction of the Rosetta Stone, the original residing in the British Museum. And one wall was dominated by a bookcase: Young, Champollion, Denon, Caviglia, Wilkinson, Lepsus, Kircher, Valeriano, Michel de Nostre-Dame ... The central piece was *Description de l'Egypte*—the massive work by Napoleon's own *savants*—11 huge volumes of illustrations, plus smaller volumes of text on ancient temples, modern crafts, flora and fauna, and the first accurate descriptions of mummies.

After taking in the room, Dupin walked up to the Comte, standing by the mummy encased in glass, as the latter began:

"Circus strongman Giovanni Battista Belzoni, beginning in 1816, began bringing home dozens of mummies for public unwrapping. It was quite the rage for a while. I attended a few."

"Alas," Dupin lamented, "so did I."

And the Comte told a story of one such event:

"The Director of the city museum, Dr. Ponnonmer, had procured a mummy from his cousin, Captain Arthur Sabretash, from a tomb in Eleithias, in the Libyan mountains, far from Thebes on the Nile. Present at the reveal were Messieurs Giddon and Bickingham, translators of hieroglyphs. We cut into the sarcophagus—the one you see over there—and discovered that the name of the occupant was *Allamistako*—the gent in the glass display case here. Then we removed layers after layers of dry, resin-dried yellow linen bandages, revealing his waxy-like features, skin the brown of beaten leather, discovering within the bandages numerous amulets and talismans—many you see on display throughout this room.

"At the time, we had just read *Frankenstein* and decided to see if we could animate the mummy. Unfortunately, Madame Shelley skipped all the natural philosophy, and laced her story with magic and alchemy that would've made Paracelsus proud. But in her foreword she mentioned Doctor Erasmus Darwin, who allegedly animated dead tissue. All based on *galvanism*—the 'animal electricity' discovered by Luigi Galvani, who used sparks from Leyden Jars to cause amputated frog legs to twitch. So we tried it on our mummy..."

"How could it react—it had no brain?"

"*Oui*," said the Comte with a chuckle. "I imagine we'd have been just as successful with a scarecrow."

Wandering to the bookcase, Dupin withdrew a copy of Théophile Gautier's *Roman de la momie* and began flipping through it, disgusted at the romantic nonsense contained within. He slammed the covers shut and slid the book back into its place.

"But Egypt must hold secrets," continued the Comte. "Secrets waiting to be revealed..."

"Next, you will be telling me more superstitious nonsense. Charlatans like Cagliostro toured the Courts of Europe, saying they knew the secrets of Egypt, but never precisely saying what they were."

"*Oui, oui*," the Comte began, appearing a bit too much at ease to Dupin. "He and his Egyptian Masonry had a lodge in Paris; even Casanova himself was a member."

"There you go!"

"The Great Copht—Cagliostro—claimed to have learned secret knowledge in the subterranean vault of an Egyptian pyramid..."

"The one Napoleon slept in?"

The Comte ignored Dupin and continued: "Here, like Moses before him, he was instructed into all the Lore of the Egyptians—the *True Chymes and Medicine of Egypt*... the *akashic memory* of Ancient Egypt... as the new Paracelsus!"

"And did not the same Cagliostro spend time in the Bastille for the so-called Affair of the Necklace?"

As thunder and lightning continued to rage outside, the Comte glanced at the time on the mantle clock, and yawned, telling Dupin, over the storm rumbling through the manor, that they should retire for the evening and continue their discussion on the morning.

On his way to his own room, Dupin checked in on Reginald and found his new assistant/raconteur snoring between coughs. Once in his own room, he freshened up, donned his red flannel nightshirt, and settled into an unfruitful sleep; his dreams filled with homunculi, pyramids and man-devouring sphinxes. There was a riddle there... and an answer if he could only coach it out...

A scream echoed through the manor.

Dupin jerked awake just as his dream-self had answered "*man*" to the Riddle of the Sphinx, and rushed into hall, almost knocking over a similar attired and groggy Reggie. They looked at each other, and shrugged. Then they heard another scream echoing through the manor, and then:

"No... no... no! What went wrong...!"

They rushed into the library and saw the bookcase entry open. Then they burst into the Egyptian room and discovered the upright sarcophagus pulled away from the wall on hinges, revealing a stone stairway leading in the cellar. They hurried down the steps and stopped dead at the bottom, staring in disbelief.

The cellar was filled with a cornucopia of scientific paraphernalia, most of which Dupin recognized: a series of Leyden Jars arrayed into a Voltaic Pile, with alternating discs of opposing metals, floating in vinegar (attested to by the acidic odor), arranged in a series which Benjamin Franklin had dubbed a "battery," with wires leading to the ceiling; no doubt connected to the lightning rods Dupin had spotted earlier on the roof on the manor. These electrical wires from the "pile" were connected to each tip of an elongated vacuum tube of the type patented by Fredrick de Moleyns, which Dupin had seen a demonstration for at famed magician Jean Eugene Robert-Houdin's estate in Blois. Through the middle of the vacuum tube ran an inner sinuous tube, in which flowed a fuchsia-hued fluid. The whole apparatus appeared to be coupled with two large coiled-insulators/conductors. The smell of ozone filled the air.

On two stone slabs—connected to wires from the conductors to helmets—was a unconscious, naked Juliette Saint-Fond, and on the other a patchwork creature of questionable gender made of mismatched parts sewed together with cat-gut, and reeking of a sickening, sweet odor. Dupin's mind immediately flashed back to the grave-robberies he'd heard mentioned while they were in Rennes-le-Chateau.

On his knees, grasping his head, Comte de Carignan, badly scarred, his clothes half-burnt away, his chest and arms blistered, was moaning:

"Nooooo... noooo... damn it all to Hell ... I've failed... I'm sorry Mother... I'm so sorry..."

Leaving the Frenchman to his delirium, Dupin and Reggie disengaged the young woman from the helmet and electrodes. Cradling her in his arms, the younger man carried her up the stone staircase, with the Chevalier bringing up the rear.

In the bedroom, Reggie gently placed the young woman on the bed. As Dupin checked over her condition, he noted a dried blood stain *already* on the bed sheet. Once he was satisfied that Juliette was breathing regularly, and her drugged condition wasn't serious, he left Reggie behind to tend to her while he returned to cellar and helped the disheveled Comte back to the library.

There, he plied him with brandy, until the Frenchman finally opened up.

"I was a fool to think that it would work," moaned the Comte."

"What were you trying to accomplish?"

"To Lift the Veil of Isis."

"To reveal the secrets of nature? Occult nonsense!"

"At the temple at Sias, the inscription on her shrine reads: '*I am all that hath been, and is, and shall be, and my veil no mortal has hitherto raised.*'"

"Mumbo-jumbo!"

"Perhaps..." The Comte looked up, tears in his aging gray eyes. "Have you ever heard of Marie Thérèse Louise de Savoie-Carignan?"

"Yes. She was in the court of Marie Antoinette, if I'm not mistaken." And, of course, he wasn't. "She was mixed up in the so-called Affair of the Necklace. And she was executed. Not for that scandal, but later."

"Butchered!" the Comte spitted out. "Just because some people resented her because she was Superintendant to the Queen's House. She was a victim of anti-monarchic propaganda." He reached to a shelf and fisted a stack of pamphlets, tossing them on the floor. "Tracts calling her Marie-Antoinette's lover, in order to undermine the monarchy.

"Marie Thérèse even appealed to the Germans, going to Aix-la-Chapelle to plead for aid to the Royal Family, but none came! She returned to France and was imprisoned at the prison of La Force while the Royal Family was caged at the Temple. Before the Tribunal, she refused to take an oath pledging loyalty to the Revolution and hatred of the King and Queen and the Monarchy." He split before resuming:

"They ended the trial with an *'Elargissez madame'* and she was dragged away and... and... and... tossed to a mob in the street... who... who... raped her! Slaughtered her! Cut off her breasts! Decapitated her and jammed her head on a spike! They even brought it to a tavern and toasted it! After they had their way with it, I collected it, preserving it in a vat of honey, like they did with the Alexander the Great."

"Madame de Savoie-Carignan was your mother?" Dupin inquired, pointing at the oil portrait hanging above the hearth's mantel.

"Oui."

"And that patchwork... person... in the cellar... is what remains of her"

"Oui."

"And the missing bodies from the local cemeteries, that was...?"

"*Oui.*"

"You tried to raise her from the dead? But only one person had ever managed that..."

"What about Lazarus?"

"*Touché*—two."

And the Comte' began telling the rest of his story:

"The Veil of Isis is the key... the lifting of it. In the Gospel of Mark 15:38, after the Centurion had pierced the side of the Crucified Christ, *HE* is said to have entered into the Veil of the Temple; that is preparation for...What do you know of the Goddess Isis?"

"I guess you mean, when Seth chopped up Osiris' body and spread the body parts to the Four Corners of the World, that his wife, Isis, gathered them up, brought them together and..."

"*Oui.* She used her 'Veil of knowledge' to resurrect her dead and mutilated husband. The power of rejuvenation... of resurrection..."

"More mumbo-jumbo."

"Earlier, you mentioned Cagliostro..."

"That charlatan?"

"For a long while, I believed him to be my father..." The Comte saw Dupin shift uneasily in his chair and roll his eyes, but he continued: "I discovered a stash of his manuscripts amongst my mother's belongings: his Egyptian Rite and the Hermetic Order of the Golden Dawn, with its belief in the immortality..."

"From what I understand, putting together gems of peridot and lapis lazuli," Dupin sardonically said, "and you have the secret of eternal life."

Carignan ignored the Chevalier and continued: "...It has something to do with the number seven and the Arcana of Nature... all locked in the Akashic memory of the Egyptian civilization. Pure nonsense, of course."

"Indeed," Dupin concurred.

"The next thing I knew, the Terror was over and Napoleon was off to Egypt, to liberate it from the oppressive rule of the Ottomans and their Mameluks—not as conquerors, you understand? I was aboard the ship *L'Orient* as a student of Edmé François Jomard, one of his 167 *Savants*. I witnessed the future Emperor napping in the King's Chamber of the Great Pyramid, but mostly, I was spying for Jormard. He was suspicious of one Ethan Gage, who had been Benjamin Franklin's secretary while Ambassador to Paris, then after the Terror, he dealt in hemp, timber and tobacco with the Directory." He glanced at his Masonic ring. "In fact, Gage belonged to the same Lodge as Franklin and ourselves; he has been described as 'The Franklin man with Wanderlust'."

"And this Jomard thought that Ethan Gage was either a British or an American spy?"

"*Oui.* Once I followed Gage into the Greco-Roman Temple of Hathor at Dendera. He was looking from his love, Astiza, while trying to escape from the clutches of some master criminal, I'm sure. I was following him and ducked into one the many dark, mysterious chambers in the temple, the most eastern of five subterranean crypts, so he wouldn't catch me spying. And I discovered..."

At that point, the Comte staggered into the Egyptian room, and Dupin heard the breaking of glass. The nobleman returned with a sheet of papyrus pressed between two panes of glass, which Dupin remembered seeing in a display case. He handed it, and a modern drawing drawn on vellum, to Dupin, saying:

"I found this papyrus on the floor of the crypt where I was hiding. It's in hieratic and hieroglyphic writings, which I couldn't read at the time, nor, in fact, for over twenty more years, but with the work of Champollion..."

"Champollion discovered the hieroglyphic text was anything but '*sacred writing*', as the name implied, but rather prosaic," said Dupin. "Boasts and proclamations of Pharaoh and noblemen, smiting the enemies of Ra, doing the good works for the kingdom."

"*Oui, oui.* Nothing esoteric, no arcane knowledge. That, they left to undecorative hieratic text, like the papyrus in your hand." Then, the Comte pointed to the drawing. "I later returned to the crypt and drew this—what I'd seen on the wall there." He took in a deep breath, then let it out: "This is the secret of Isis... of the Great White Brotherhood... the Rosicrucians... the Illuminati... the Holy Grail... the Philosophers' Stone... the Golem... Paracelsus' homunculus... and all of the rest of the *occultum lapiden.* "

The papyrus showed a *djed* pillar—symbolic of Osiris' spine, and stability—which reminded Dupin of a chess rook with spikes erupting from its sides, like the insulators in the Comte's cellar. A lotus flower spawned a snake, and a human stood beside what appeared to be a over-sized Geissler tube with a sinuous snake inside, its pointed tail issuing from the lotus flower like an electrical socket. Adjacent to the two-human-armed pillars was a baboon demon holding two knives in his hands; which Dupin took to represent protective and defensive powers, or positive and negative. The Chevalier could easily see that it resembled the Comte's laboratory in his cellar.

"These are the instructions," Carignan added, indicating the papyrus. "I kept these and when I was able to translate it, I discovered that it contained the secret of electricity and... of resurrection! Then I learned another party was after this secret rite of life over death..." He took a sip from his brandy. "As I mentioned before, many call it the Holy Grail...the Philosopher's Stone... the Elixir of Life... but it is the Secret of Re-Animation... of raising the dead... of Necromancy..." Then, he looked directly at Dupin. "Have you heard of the *Habits Noirs?*"

"The Black Coats. Yes, of course, I have." Dupin didn't elaborate. He had ran across that nefarious group before, whom some believed were responsible for the French Revolution, not the Illuminati.

"I discovered that the rumors of Cagliostro being my father were just that—rumors," continued the Comte. "Because my *true* father is Colonel Bozzo-Corona, the leader of the High Council of the Black Coats, their All-Father. At least, I have plenty of reasons to believe so. After my return from Egypt, I was contacted by the Black Coats, which later arranged for my detachment with Lafayette, asking me to lay some groundwork in the New World..." He took a drink of brandy, then pointed at the papyrus. "But later, I had a falling out with my alleged father, when one of his cronies, Dr. Samuel, stole my secret. And it was *indeed* the secret of re-animation. The Colonel plans to use it to animate a mummy—a seven-foot tall monstrosity called *Pha-ho-tep*, which he will control with a golden ankh..."[5]

Dupin tapped his thumbs together. "You believe the Black Coats plan to use the secrets from your papyrus to re-animate a mummy?"

"*Oui.*"

"And you believe that you can use the same secrets to bring your mother to life after 60 years?"

"Mummies are over 2000 years old!" argued the Comte.

"But like the Golem and the *homunculi*, mindless husks."

"Frankenstein's monster was quite verbose, if I recall." When Dupin didn't reply, the Comte continued: "Damn it, it has... to work. I severed all my ties with the Black Coats, pursued the research began by Dr. Samuel, made several significant breakthroughs..."

Dupin knew that the Colonel had a long memory, and wondered if the Black Coats were truly done with Carignan.

"If you followed all the instructions correctly, then what went wrong?"

"The formula called for a conductive solution of virgin blood."

"And the girl, Juliette Saint-Fond, was not a virgin?" Dupin thought of the blood stained bed sheet, but said nothing.

"*Hélas oui,*" muttered the Comte. "I was assured of her purity, but..."

Before Dupin could respond, the Comte bolted to his feet, knocking over his chair, and, with a renewed burst of energy, rushed through his Egyptian room and into the cellar.

Dupin followed him and arrived just in time to witness the Comte grab a conductor with one hand and the creature—his mother—with the other, creating a loop as the lightning raged outside.

Carignan screamed: "Lord, help my poor soul..." Then he yelled an incantation, which Dupin didn't hear over the thunder booming through the cellar, and with that single magic word, the lightning rods outside captured the lightning and directed it to the laboratory's conductor, frying the Comte, and, through him, the creature. They burned, melting, congealing their flesh into an amorous mass of cellulose.

---

[5] See "The Death of a Dream" in our Vol. 9.

Then, the entire cellar caught fire!

Quickly, Dupin bounded up the stairs, collected Reginald Goodwin and Juliette, and escaped from the manor.

From their coach, they stopped and looked back.

It was over. Comte de Carignan's own personal reign of terror was over. He had tried to open Pandora's box, yet this time nothing had escaped—not even a drop of *espoir*. Yes, Hope was abandoned in this *inferno*, and the Comte was forever lost in the darkness.

After seeing Juliette Saint-Fond off on a train to Paris, Dupin and Reginald enjoyed a well-deserved vacation at Reichenbach Falls in Switzerland, where Dupin almost fell when his gout suddenly acted up, but fortunately Reginald was there to reel him in.

Later, back at their old *hotel particulier* in Paris, they settled into their study, nursed their drink, and discussed the recent events.

Dupin never believed in the praeter-natural, and rumors of re-animated mummies were just that—rumors!

"It's all superstitious nonsense... it's why people fear black cats, premature burial and spirits of the dead," he said, sipping his Amontillado. "From our recent adventure, what have you learned?"

"A fool and his mummy are soon parted?" Reginald saw the look Dupin gave him and added: "Ah...I don't know, you're the ratiocinator."

"Do I detect a note of sarcasm in your tone?"

"You detect? Now you're detecting? You're a what... a detective?"

"Hmm, detective... I like the sound of that."

"I have a name for our recent case."

"Do tell," Dupin sighed.

"I think the Comte was wrong. I believe that the 'Lifting of the Veil' has nothing to do with arcana but with the ultimate mystery: that of womanhood. Thus it should actually be the 'Piercing the Veil of Isis.' And this relates to our case."

"Do tell," Dupin said with a roll of his eyes.

"The Case of the Purloined Maidenhair."

Before Dupin could reply, his gout raged and he screamed:

"Quick, Goodwin—the laudanum!"

In the drug-induced haze, Dupin studied the bust of Pallas-Athena above his chamber door, his eyes seeming of a demon dreaming, and the light from the lamp threw his shadow on the floor, and out of that shadow on the floor, his soul shall be lifted... hopefully... once more...

Rick Lai returns to the character of Joséphine Balsamo, Countess Cagliostro, the devilish anti-heroine who graced the pages of his very first contribution to Tales of the Shadowmen *Volume 1, and whose life he extensively chronicled in his recent collection,* Sisters of the Shadows, *just released by Black Coat Press...*

Rick Lai: *The Mark of a Woman*

Madrid, 1806

The loud voice of Captain Cesar de Cabanil filled the auditorium:

"Ladies and gentlemen, the final bout to determine the winner of the Royal Competitive Trophy is about to begin. The two finalists, Ramon Castillo and Diego de la Vega, will assume their positions."

Two young men in dueling jackets faced each other. Each contestant gripped an *épée de cour*. The women among the spectators admired their handsome faces. While Ramon was clean-shaven, Diego had a small dapper moustache.

One young lady in particular was very appreciative of the two rivals this late afternoon. In 1806, Joséphine Balsamo was an 18-year old student at the Complutense University of Madrid. In 1785, this institution became one of the first universities to grant doctorates to women. This fact had convinced Joséphine to persuade her mother to arrange her enrollment at this most prestigious Spanish institution.

Joséphine was a remarkably independent woman. Spain had long been famous for its skilled swordsmen. She had sought to study under one of the famous local fencing masters, but none of them was willing to give lessons to a female. Therefore, she had had to embark on a clever stratagem to achieve her desires. She soon discovered that the two best members of the University fencing team were Ramon Castillo and Diego de la Vega. Joséphine had successfully charmed each of them into training her how to handle a sword. Neither Ramon nor Diego were aware of her involvement with the other. So far, Joséphine had merely flirted with them; but she had promised each of them a special reward if he won the Royal Competitive Trophy.

Captain de Cabanil had been chosen as referee for the match because he had won the Trophy years earlier when he was a student at the Complutense University. After graduation, he had secured a commission in the Spanish Army.

"At the count of three, the bout shall begin," he announced. "One... Two... *Three!*"

Ramon rushed Diego to launch a frenzied attack. For several minutes, Diego blocked his opponent's thrusts. With a strong flourish, Diego then knocked the sword out of Ramon's hand.

"Ramon Castillo has been disarmed," declared the Captain. "The winner is Diego de la Vega."

The crowd erupted in applause. Captain de Cabanil presented Diego with the large trophy cup. Joséphine ran up to him. The couple embraced and kissed. Ramon watched in utter shock.

Later, Joséphine rode with a triumphant Diego in a carriage back to the young man's apartment. Driving the vehicle was Bernardo, Diego's mute servant.

"I have unfortunate news, Diego," confessed Joséphine. "As you know, my godmother is my guardian. She wishes me to return to France."

"Did she give any reasons for this sudden decision?"

"Following the death of her first husband, my godmother remarried some years ago. Although her second husband had been indulgent towards her expenditures in the past, he has recently sought to sharply curtail her spending. He views the cost of providing a Spanish education for me as a needless expense."

"A short-sighted view," stated Diego.

The antecedents of Joséphine Balsamo had long been a mystery to the young aristocrat. Her surname was Italian, but she had spent her formative years in France. Diego had heard rumors of Joseph Balsamo, a confidence trickster known as Count Cagliostro. If the stories were to be believed, Cagliostro had engineered the collapse of the French monarchy. Cagliostro's coat of arms had been a golden ram, and Joséphine wore a ring bearing such an image.

Joséphine had always been circumspect regarding the identity of her French "godmother." It was claimed that Cagliostro had been a bit of a Lothario. Diego suspected that Cagliostro romanced a French noblewoman, who had then given birth to Joséphine. In order to avoid a scandal, Joséphine's mother could have raised her daughter under the facade of a benevolent godmother.

Ramon Castillo sought to drown his disappointment in wine at a local tavern. His despondency was immediately noticed by another patron, a clever thief about the same age. The young criminal decided it might be to his advantage to strike up a conversation. He advanced to the table where Ramon was seated.

"You seem quite despondent, Señor. My father always told me that no man should be left to drink alone in sorrow. May I join you?"

"You certainly may. My name is Ramon Castillo."

"And I am Marcos Estrada. What is the cause of your depression, my friend?"

"I've just lost the most prestigious dueling cup in Spain."

"Ah! You must be on the University fencing team. I heard the finals were today. Are you graduating this year?"

"No. I have one more year."

"What about the student who beat you? Is he graduating?"

"Like me, he's only in his third year."

"Then, what are you worrying about, *amigo*? You can defeat him for the trophy next year. That would be the perfect revenge!"

"Ah, revenge..." sighed Ramon. "There is an old saying: 'Revenge is a dish best served cold.' Yes, it will be very cold indeed when I have my revenge against *her*."

"Her? Who are you talking about?" asked Marcos, puzzled.

"A serpent, Marcos. A female serpent with luxuriant blonde hair and entrancing blue eyes. A serpent who beguiled me while she was secretly romancing my hated rival."

"If this woman is a serpent, then her head should be cut off."

"An excellent suggestion, *amigo*. I shall follow your advice at the proper time."

"Why wait? There's no time like the present!" exclaimed Marcos.

"You're quite right. I shall have my revenge tonight. Please excuse me, I must arrange a rendezvous with a certain lady."

As Ramon left, Marcos was quite content with himself. He had long sought a partner to assist him in his robberies. A skilled swordsman like Ramon would fulfill that role nicely. All that Marcos needed was a hold over him. Knowledge of his role in a murder would give the thief the necessary leverage. The young felon looked forward to hearing about the discovery of a woman's headless corpse in the morning.

In his apartment, Diego handed Joséphine an oblong box towards Joséphine.

"In anticipation of our little celebration, I commissioned a present to be made for you."

Joséphine opened the box and took out a cane whose handle was a golden ram.

"This is very lovely, Diego, but I can't see its practical use. I am quite agile. I have no need for a cane."

"This is no ordinary cane, my darling. Let me show you."

"One moment, Diego. Bernardo seems to have found something important."

While Diego had been entertaining Joséphine, the mute servant had been riffling through the mail that had been delivered while they were at the tournament. Bernardo gave his master an envelope.

Taking it, Diego read the postmark on the front.

"It's from California," he said.

Then, opening the letter, he read aloud:

My dear son,

It is with a heavy heart that I ask you to give up your studies and come home. Certain matters have arisen which I cannot face alone.

Father

"This quite disturbing," said Diego. "I must make arrangements to leave Spain at once."

Grabbing a sheet of paper, the young man wrote a few sentences.

"Bernardo will take this message to Captain de Cabanil. I must see him immediately."

"I don't understand," interjected Joséphine. "Why must you see the Captain?"

"My father wouldn't be writing me unless our *hacienda* was threatened. The British must be behind some new deviltry. Only recently did they try to invade the Spanish colonies in the Rio de la Plata. They must be stirring up the Indian tribes in order to drive us out of California. The Captain could advise me of the current military situation."

"You may totally be misinterpreting your father's message. Don Alejandro writes in veiled terms. Perhaps the crisis is not military but political?"

"Then the Captain will be able to provide equally valuable advice. In one of our conversations, he alluded to how a brave man should secretly combat political corruption. Unfortunately, Joséphine, you must leave."

"Why so soon? It will be at least an hour before Bernardo returns with the Captain…"

"What can we do in an hour?"

"Have you forgotten? I promised you a reward you for winning the championship…"

An hour later, Diego opened the door of his apartment.

"Are you sure you don't want me to escort you home, Joséphine?"

"There's no need, Diego. I only have to walk eight blocks. You should be here when Bernardo returns with the Captain."

Carrying her new cane, Joséphine walked into the night. It was a quarter after nine when she reached the building where she lived.

Walking up the stairs to the second floor, Joséphine reached into her purse and unlocked the door. She was just about to enter when she was shoved from behind. After being pushed through the door, she quickly turned around and saw a smiling man bolting the door with his left hand. His right hand held a sword.

"Ramon!" she exclaimed.

"You've betrayed me, Joséphine," said her jilted lover. "In your native France, traitors lose their heads. I may not own the dueling cup, but I soon shall have your head as an equally valuable trophy!"

Ramon slashed at Joséphine. Retreating backward, she grabbed the top of her cane and pulled out a blade of the finest steel.

Diego's gift had been a sword cane.

The blades of the two antagonists clashed. They parried back and forth.

"So you intend to prove yourself superior to your tutor?" sneered Ramon.

"You'll soon discover that I'm more than your equal!" spar back Joséphine.

"Did you really think I've taught you all my tricks?"

"You didn't have to. Diego taught me all of his!"

Delivering a vicious thrust, Joséphine stabbed Ramon in the forearm. He dropped his sword. Directing her blade towards his throat, Joséphine forced her former lover to retreat backward until his back touched the wall.

"Now, Ramon, you shall experience a gesture that Diego devised as a fitting farewell to an unworthy adversary…"

Swiftly removing her blade from Ramon's neck, Joséphine struck downward.

Ramon lowered his eyes. The letter "C" was now carved into the crotch of his pants.

"What does that stand for?" he asked.

"My family title," replied Joséphine. "You bear the mark of Cagliostro."

Unbolting the door, Joséphine opened it with her left hand.

"Now leave my abode and be thankful that I merely ruined your pants. I could have easily cut more deeply. If you ever cross my path again, I shall take a trophy to remember you. And it won't be your head!"

The Horla, the invisible entity created by Guy de Maupassant, is without a doubt one of the most terrifying concepts ever devised. It might have inspired Eric Frank Russell's classic SF novel Sinister Barrier, *and was the inspiration for the 1963 film* Diary of a Madman *starring Vincent Price. Has it finally met its match?...*

Olivier Legrand: *The Last Tale*

London, 1913

We had been without news of Carnacki for a little over a month when we received his traditional invitation to dinner. The dinner, as we knew well, was only the prelude to his telling us one of his amazing stories, as he had always done in the past, so we all waited with bated breath for him to begin.

When our host came to greet us at the door, I seemed to perceive a subtle alteration in his eyes; an inexplicable, momentary hesitation. At the time, that fleeting impression did not bother me over much, and I did not suspect that it was but the harbinger of the terrible revelation that would soon befall us all.

During the meal, Carnacki was unusually silent, despite repeated attempts by Jessop and I to engage him on the topic of the current cricket season. The atmosphere around the table was strangely heavy. Finally, after a while, all conversation seemed to expire, replaced with only an embarrassed silence. We saw our friend light his pipe and recognized the onset of what we called between us, his "storytelling mood."

"I have just returned from a four week trip to France," Carnacki began. "The Affair that kept me there is undoubtedly one of the most disturbing cases that I have ever had to deal with—and the threat which I discovered is far from defeated... if indeed it can ever be. When I say 'threat,' I mean one on scale that affects the whole of humanity—a psychic menace jeopardizing the very survival of our species on this world, of which we've so far believed ourselves to be the undisputed masters..."

We knew enough to know that our friend did not make this bombastic prologue for the mere purpose of creating the thrill of expectation, but that it was a carefully weighed statement. In his words as well as his actions, Carnacki was a measured man. Far from turning him into some kind of exalted visionary, his frequent forays into the unknown, his many confrontations with forces from beyond, had sharpened his rational judgment and hardened the strength of his will. After a few seconds, he continued:

"Towards the end of last month, I was contacted by one of my neighbors and colleagues, Sâr Dubnotal, a master of the occult who calls himself the

'Great Psychagogue.' He wanted to introduce me to one of his friends, a Frenchman named Leo Saint-Clair, whom he had described to me as an 'extraordinary gentleman and an explorer of the unknown,' but I rather felt that I was dealing with what I, myself, would dub a 'shadowman...'

"Saint-Clair knew my reputation and got straight to the heart of the matter:

" 'Mr. Carnacki,' he said, 'have you heard of the Horla?'

" 'Of course,' I replied. 'It's one of the most celebrated stories by your famous author, Guy de Maupassant... It tells the story of a man who believes himself to be persecuted by an invisible being—or maybe, he really is; the question is never solved. That psychic predator seeks to take control of his will and eventually tips him into dementia. The story is told in the form of a diary, which allows Monsieur Maupassant to gradually create a climate of unease and danger, while at the same time leaving the reader in a state of doubt as to the reality of the events and their outcome. If I recall correctly, the last lines suggest that the narrator's suicide is the only possible escape... a subterfuge which, incidentally, only reinforces the reader's terror: was the man driven to suicide by his own madness, or did the Horla drive him to it? I would say that, in addition to throwing a very astute light on certain psychic phenomena, this story is undoubtedly one of the finest French contributions to the field of fantastic literature... because it is, of course, fiction.'

" 'Your knowledge of our literature does you honor, Mr. Carnacki,' Saint-Clair observed with typical French surprise. 'But do you also know that Monsieur de Maupassant died insane, shortly after the publication of this story, twenty years ago... after trying to end his own days?"

" 'I see where you're coming from, Monsieur Saint-Clair. The search for truth in fiction—particularly that dealing with so-called supernatural events—is a particular hobby for some people, even an obsession for others. But it is always the result of excessive imagination, unable to conceive the essential differences between reality and fiction... I was talking recently to a Cambridge professor, probably more famous for his remarkable ghost stories than for all of his academic work taken together, and the poor chap seems doomed to explain to his friends—including noted academics—that writing ghost stories and believing in ghost stories are two very different things, and often mutually exclusive. The art of the writer requires a certain distance from its subject, something often incompatible with true conviction... Those who, like me, have some experience with the reality of these phenomena are well aware that their influence is generally much more subtle and insidious than the all too often melodramatic events we find in these kinds of stories.'

"Saint-Clair looked at me with his strange eyes. I think he expected my views on the subject to be quite different from what I had just told him. I thought it useful to drive the point further by adding:

" 'Some people describe me as a *ghost hunter*, but I consider myself a psychic investigator, which does not mean that I must give credence to all kinds of extravagant stories on the subject of ghosts, quite the contrary; to return to the subject of our conversation, we must never forget the clear line that separates fact from fiction. This discernment is, I believe, a *sine qua non* requirement of my job... and, from what I gather, yours as well, isn't it, Monsieur Saint-Clair?'

" 'You're absolutely right, Mr. Carnacki. We explorers into the unknown must learn to recognize hoaxes, superstitions and other tall tales; otherwise we'd spend all our time hunting shadows. And speaking of such, have you heard of the Seventh Bureau?'

" 'Yes. I believe it's a little known department of your Sûreté Nationale. It is sometimes known the *Brigade des Maléfices*, isn't it?'

" 'Yes,' replied Saint-Clair, lighting a French cigarette. 'This venerable institution was founded in 1830 by Vidocq himself... More than half a century before the general public read Maupassant's story, the Brigade's secret archives already contained a folder labeled *Horla*—a name that owes nothing to the imagination of that great writer. We find it first mentioned in the memoirs of a 16th century woman called Fausta...[6]

" 'I see. But none of this proves that the Horla is real. Maupassant could very well have had access to her writings and...'

" 'Maupassant died insane, the victim of psychological pressure exerted on him by the selfsame Horlas who chose him as their prey. I would add that these creatures are known by other names across the globe... The Arabs call them *Afrit*, the Slavs *Strigoi*... And you yourself, did you ever cross the path of the *Lloigor*?'

"As you may recall , I hadve in fact, already encountered this name several times during my investigations, especially during the sad affair that occurred in Wales last fall, but Saint Clair did not even give me time to respond.

" 'The truth,' he said with a dangerous smile, 'is that the Horlas are here, amongst us, and have been here since the dawn of time... Contrary to what Monsieur de Maupassant believed, these beings have not suddenly come from outer space to subjugate the human race and become its masters... No, they once were our masters, and aspire to become so again... Oh, no doubt they came from elsewhere, in the beginning, when our world was young... but they quickly settled here and became the dominant powers upon this planet, and we, humans, are but their cattle...'

" 'And upon what elements do you base such assertions?'

" 'I understand and appreciate your skepticism, Mr. Carnacki... I would just ask you two questions. Who were, according to you, the true masters of the lost empire of Mu? And why have all the recent discoveries concerning this forgotten age of humanity been systematically destroyed or ridiculed?'

"I was, I will admit, increasingly troubled by the course of our conversation. It was as if some obscure terror, long buried in my subconscious, had be-

---

[6] See "The Anti-Pope of Avignon" in our Vol. 4.

gun to rise to the surface of my mind. My voice seemed strangely distant when I finally replied:

" 'But if you are telling the truth... if humanity in ancient times was indeed subjected to the psychic influence of such entities... by what means, by what miracle, were we able to free ourselves?'

" 'This,' said Saint-Clair, crushing his cigarette, 'is what we need to discover; you, the Sâr and I... before it's too late. For all of us.'"

Having reached this stage in his narrative, Carnacki suddenly fell silent. We were used to his brief dramatic pauses, but, on that particular night, it became clear that something was seriously wrong.

Motionless, his eyes half-closed, Carnacki had acquired the look of a sleepwalker in a trance. When one of us said his name softly, trying to elicit a reaction, he jerked up with a strange, spasmodic movement and cast upon us a look that was not his.

"What does this mean?" he cried in a voice that was almost unrecognizable. "What are you doing here? Who gave you permission to enter my home?"

We became frozen with amazement. Then, we saw him, with a sweeping gesture, send the glass of brandy before him crashing to the floor.

"Milk!" Carnacki started screaming, jumping from his seat. "Bring me milk!"

It was Jessop, I believe, who first recovered his wits and exclaimed:

"Heavens, Dodgson! This is one of those damned things he was telling us about! It's taken him over!"

"*No!*" shouted Carnacki. "You don't understand! I've trapped him inside me! The Horla! I managed to trick him! It is he who is the prisoner, now!"

His voice became distorted, then turned into a sound that I can only describe as a mixture of two voices: the howl of a man being murdered mixed with a laugh entirely unrelated to humanity.

What happened next was a pandemonium. After a confused struggle that further strained our nerves, Taylor, Jessop and I succeeded in mastering a mad Carnacki, while Arkright called an alienist he knew, Dr. Seward, who was apparently accustomed to unusual cases.

At the time of this writing, two weeks after that fateful evening, Thomas Carnacki is still interned in Dr. Seward's private clinic. Despite various treatments, he remains subject to terrible fits of delirium, during which he speaks sometimes in French, sometimes in a language that nobody can either understand or recognize.

Dr. Seward, who has recorded several such episodes, told me that he succeeded in isolating several recurring words in that incomprehensible stream: *Horla*, *Mu* and something that sounds like *Lloigor*.

"The Event," as we have become accustomed to calling it, obviously took its toll on our nerves and our minds; it is still too early to fully comprehend its full effect on us.

Yesterday, I spoke at some length with Jessop. He is suffering from chronic insomnia and is getting worse, despite several hypnosis sessions with Dr. Seward. Frankly, the poor chap is but a shadow of his old self.

As for me, the last few nights, I've awoken with the sense that some invisible presence was lurking over my bed. This morning, I think I'm running a slight fever. Maybe I should get away from London for some time? The climate in our capital isn't doing me any good.

There is something in the air.

(translation by J.-M. & Randy Lofficier)

Most people are familiar with Edmond Rostand's play, which popularized and forever defined the character of Cyrano de Bergerac; fewer, however, know of L'Aiglon *(The Eaglet), his 1900 play in which the great Sarah Bernhardt played the tragic part of Franz, Duke of Reichstadt, Napoleon's son, kept prisoner in the Austrian Palace of Schönbrunn after the French Emperor's downfall. This story, like some of our previous tales, goes behind the curtain of History, and asks itself what might have been if only...*

Jean-Marc & Randy Lofficier: *Christmas at Schönbrunn*

Paris, 1860 / Schönbrunn, 1828

In a large canopy bed, sweating and groaning beneath the covers, lay Père Tabaret, the *bon vivant* of the Rue Saint-Lazare, better known as *Papa Tire-au-Clair* by the agents of the French Sûreté.

Seeing him, one could understand how his neighbors had never had the slightest suspicion about his amateur police work. No one with his looks would ever be credited with superior intelligence. With his receding hairline and his immense ears, his obnoxiously turned-up nose, his tiny eyes and big lips, Père Tabaret looked like an idiot—a rich idiot at that.

It was true that, if examined closely, his resemblance to a hunting dog, whose instincts and aptitudes he shared, was remarkable. When he went down the street, impudent urchins turned around to yell: "Fetch!" He laughed at this scorn, and even took pleasure in adding to his silly appearance, making even more striking the saying that "he is not truly intelligent he who does not appear to be so."

Seeing the young policeman, whom he knew well, enter his bedroom, Père Tabaret's eyes lit up.

"Good morning, Lecoq, my boy," he said. "I'm glad you still remember your poor old *Papa* from time to time!"

Lecoq was about 26, beardless, pale, with extremely red lips and an abundance of wavy black hair. He was short, but well-proportioned, and each of his movements showed unusual strength. There was nothing remarkable about his appearance, except for his eyes, which either sparkled brilliantly or grew extremely dull, according to his mood.

"I found something that I thought would be of interest to you, Papa," said Lecoq, "knowing your fondness for history, I mean."

"Ah! Ah!"

Lecoq pulled a notebook out of his pocket. The paper was yellow and the brown leather binding dirty. "This is something I recently found in a chest belonging to my father."

"You don't mean…?"

"No, not my adoptive parents," said the young policeman. "May they rest forever with the angels—my real father, he who was known as Lecoq de la Periere."

"I remember him well," said Tabaret. "I had to piece together the events surrounding his death in 1842 for those dim-witted folks at the Rue de Jesusalem. They are so easily confused… Certainly, anything chronicled by that fearsome rogue is bound to be of considerable interest."

"Indeed! There is one passage in particular, *Papa*, for which I would like your opinion. It takes place in 1828 in Schönbrunn …"

Lecoq's Diary:

Is it a coincidence that the Austrian Emperor chose to confine his 14-year old grand-son Franz to the same apartments that his father, Napoleon, occupied twice; once after Austerlitz and once before Wagram?

The castle has 1500 rooms. My master, the Colonel, does not believe in co-incidences, He thinks that Emperor Francis of Austria, or rather his *éminence grise*, the wily Prince Metternich, would never leave such a thing to chance. No, it is not a coincidence—they sought to humiliate the boy by making his father's quarters his prison—but it will serve us well in the days to come. Metternich will regret this final last slap to Napoleon's face!

Born Prince Imperial, King of Rome and Prince of Parma, the youth is now known simply as Duke of Reichstadt. He never sees his mother, his only company being that of his preceptors, all carefully hand-picked by Metternich himself: Count Districhstein, who teaches him the classics; Monsieur de Foresti, military tactics; Everard, English; von Prokesch-Osten, fencing; Nyberg, dancing… and Metternich himself, history.

What irony! Prince von Metternich teaching history to the son of Napoleon Bonaparte!

The Colonel and I arrived at the inn in Vienna in late November, giving ourselves a month to prepare. We posed as dry goods salesmen and, indeed, did good business while we were there. The Emperor's secret police were quickly reassured as to who we were and quickly stopped investigating us.

The first step in our mission was to reactivate some of the contacts Henri de Belcamp had set up in amongst the local *Rosenkreuz* in 1813. A few of them were servants at the Castle and it soon became natural for them to spend an evening drinking beer in the smoke-filled backroom of the inn.

As was the tradition, the Emperor's Court celebrated Christmas at Schönbrunn. Following the recent custom, a tall conifer tree was cut from the slopes of Schneeberg and set up in the Great Hall, decorated with bags of sweets, toys, oranges, stuffed birds, small sparkling bells of gold and silver, and multi-colored garlands.

The Emperor's intimate circle of friends and family, field-marshals in shiny uniforms, and ladies in munificent gowns, added to the joyous atmosphere of the season.

Emperor Francis made a point of including young Franz in the festivities; it was, after all, the one time in the year when the young recluse was authorized, nay, encouraged, to mingle with others. It was also a reward for his good results with his studies.

One of the Colonel's spies had reported to us that the Emperor had expressed concern about young Franz's interest in Cesar's *Gallic Wars*, fearing that the child would draw a connection between the Roman Emperor's military genius and his own father's. He instructed Districhstein to divert his studies to Horace and Tacitus instead.

As for history, as taught by Metternich, it focused on the high feats of Franz's ancestors—on his mother's side, of course: the Emperors of the Holy Germanic Roman Empire, not "the other Emperor!"

Franz was thus, in everyone's eyes, a perfect, young, loyal German.

The first time I laid eyes on the boy was the night of December 24. The Colonel and I had used a secret passage to gain entrance to the Prince's apartments.

When I saw him, he wore the standard white uniform of an Austrian cavalry commander. His skin was unusually pale and his lips lacked color His wavy blond hair, which he had inherited from his mother, fell to his shoulders Only the eyes seemed alive in that tragic face, even though it seemed as if he was trying hard to extinguish their flame.

He walked towards us at a serene pace, a figure of melancholy.

Did he remember the great radiant palace of the Tuileries, where he had spent his early years? The tricolored flag of his homeland? One could not tell, but I suspect that he did.

And what did he remember about his father, this fearsome man whose very name was never ever uttered in his presence? A man about whom no one dared ask any questions? These were heavy burdens for a child.

Earlier that day, the Colonel had bribed one of the servants to leave a present on Franz's nightstand.

It was a tiny Christmas tree, no more than a few inches tall, a mockery compared to the giant tree filling Schönbrunn's Great Hall. But that tiny tree— no more than a branch, in truth—was decorated with tiny blue, white and red *cocardes*, and a small roll of blue paper was tied to its "trunk."

Franz had surely unrolled the paper: it wasn't a letter, but a portrait, more akin to an *image d'Epinal* than a well-crafted masterpiece, with its bright colors and simple lines. It depicted a man wearing a black tricorn, a great grey coat over a military uniform. He stood at the head of a row of French soldiers bearing a French flag. In the sky flew an Eagle under a radiant sun.

There was only one word under the portrait: NAPOLEON.

And now, Franz had come to meet the man who had triumphed over the resources of one of the mightiest empires on Earth to deliver him that portrait: Colonel Bozzo-Corona.

"Do not fear, my child," said the Colonel. He took Franz's hand in his, and deposited a light kiss on it.

"Who are you?" asked the Prince. "Why have you come here?"

"I have come to tell you about your father, Monseigneur," said the Colonel. "And also to tell you of France, and the millions of people who have remained faithful to his memory."

"My father! France!"

"I have traveled 5000 leagues to bring you this branch taken from the Garden of the Tuileries, a piece of boxwood identical to millions kept in the hearths of those still faithful to the name Napoleon."

"The Tuileries... Napoleon..." repeated the youth, obviously trying to place an image over those names he remembered from his childhood.

"There are, Monseigneur, millions of men and women in France who think of you, believe in you, and would gladly give their lives for you. There is a tradition that, on Christmas' eve, the sky opens and the angels come down to Earth to bring joy and God's blessings to the children of men. I didn't want you to be the only one forgotten in this season. I'm not sent by God, of course!" Here, the Colonel allowed himself a small chuckle. "If my associate and I were able to come to you, it is only because of a secret passage set up by your father when he stayed in these very apartments. We seized the opportunity of tonight's festivities to reach you safely."

"You knew my father? What was he like?"

"I played merely a modest part in his ascension. Cesar, whom I'm told you admire, was but a dwarf compared to your father. He was the Emperor, a lord worshiped or feared by over 80 million people. Yet, he died alone, seven years ago, on a windswept rock lost in the middle of the Atlantic, just as trapped as you are here. One of my associates tried to rescue him, but in vain. Napoleon died after five years of painful agony, his eyes fixed on your portrait, and when his sun finally set, there were millions in France who screamed out their pain. Now, their faith has been transferred to you. Your name alone causes the powerful men of this world to quake in fear—ask your grandfather.

"But France is prideful. She wants someone who will seize her, conquer her despite all obstacles; she does not want to be courted politely by someone resigned to follow the edicts of Fate, without ambition or passion. Now, Monseigneur, the time has come for me to ask you what I came here to ask on behalf of those millions: Will you follow us? Will you take this secret passage that your father himself had built, leave this prison and come back with us?

"I have millions dedicated to your restoration, more money than God himself could count, resources that you can hardly suspect. If you come with me, your Empire will be even mightier than your father's. I have men in England that will destroy the perfidious Albion from within, conspirators in Russia that will pave the way for you... Your Empire will reach from Ireland to the Urals... The decision is yours."

"And...?"asked Pere Tabaret.

"Nothing," replied Lecoq. "The entry stops there. There is a brief note recording their return to France on December 27, but nothing at all about what happened that night in Schönbrunn. The only thing we know for certain is that Franz chose to not follow the Colonel and make a bid for a Second Empire."

"Hm-hm. And what do you think happened?"

"Myself, I think the will of the Imperial child had already been thoroughly broken by that bastard Metternich and his preceptors. He was scared by the brilliant, but dangerous future that the Colonel had laid out before him."

"Possible, possible, but I don't agree. What? You look as if you've fallen from the clouds, my boy," said Tabaret. "Do you think your *Papa* is trying to *tell you a salad*?" [lie]

"No, certainly not, but..."

"Be quiet! You're surprised because you don't know the first thing about history. You need to be educated on this point if you don't want to remain an idiot like Gévrol for the rest of your days. Now, would you please take down from my bookshelf, over there, on the right, the big folio edition by Mathieu Auguste Geffroy..."

Lecoq quickly obeyed and, as soon as Tabaret had the book, he began to flip through it rapidly, until:

"Ah! Here it is! Listen well, my boy! *'After 1828, the surveillance around the Duke of Reichstadt was tripled. No Frenchman was authorized to see him. Even poet Joseph Mery, who had traveled to Schönbrunn to present the Prince with a heroic poem written about Napoleon's Egyptian Campaign was denied admission and could only see the young man from the opposite end of the Imperial theater, sitting alone in a darkened loge. Some say the Duke was poisoned; others that he died of tuberculosis on July 22, 1832. The day he died, a thunderbolt destroyed one of the bronze eagles decorating the castle's gates. And Germany breathed a collective sigh of relief.'*

"Now, if fear or despair, as you believe, had motivated the Prince to refuse the Colonel's offer, why would the Austrian Emperor have tripled the security around him? The only answer is, far from being a broken man, the young Duke had, instead, inherited his father's iron will and determination. The Emperor realized this and became mortally afraid his captive would change his mind."

"I don't understand," said Lecoq.

"Clearly, there is another explanation for your father's account. Instead, Franz saw all to well what the Second Empire the Colonel offered him would bring. The wars, the devastation, the deaths and worse of all, the triumph, the iron heel of a French tyrant grinding the Old World beneath his boot. The Old World, I say? More, perhaps. With no England to challenge him, no Russia to crush his armies, with the power of the Black Coats behind him, perhaps a smarter and more flexible Napoleon might have easily become Master of the World. And that is what, in his considerable wisdom, the Duke rejected."

"But how could he know...? How could he be sure...? A mere boy of 14... Unless..."

"Ha-ha! Unless someone *showed* him, you mean?" said Tabaret, smiling.

"That's impossible..." whispered Lecoq.

"No. Merely *improbable*... You must learn to distinguish between the two, my boy. Tell me, what was the name of the Prince's English teacher?"

"Everard. I couldn't find much information about him."

"If what I suspect is true, you won't find any. I met a Manse Everard, once... A most charming English gentleman... Let me tell you a story about him..."

Memo: From Time Patrol Agent (Unattached) Manse Everard to Colonel Graigh.
Operation Caged Bird successful. Divergent Second Empire timeline eliminated. Colonel Bozzo-Corona will bear watching.

Jules Verne's Captain Nemo has rarely faced as wily an adversary as Ponson du Terrail's cunning Rocambole in this one-on-one confrontation orchestrated by our new contributor, French writer Patrick Lorin, also the author of a well-received sf novel, L'île Blanche. *But, in the end, who of the two champions emerges as the true winner?...*

Patrick Lorin: *Troubled Waters*

1864

Rocambole stripped, bound and gagged the man he had just knocked out. The first part of his mission had proved easier than he expected. He'd only needed to wait a few hours until the sentry dozed off so he could silently slip away. At the end of the first corridor, he had found a small room with the door ajar. Inside, a young man wearing a blue cap was folding laundry. One blow had been all it took to neutralize him. Rocambole saw that Lady Luck had smiled on him: his victim's size and appearance were similar to his. In addition, his broad-billed cap added to the effectiveness of the disguise. The only remaining problem was his hair color, but he solved this by donning one of the wigs he had brought, just in case. This done, he pulled on his victim's unusual clothes which were made of shiny, silky threads that were not plant fibers. Perhaps they were finely woven linen?

Rocambole carefully adjusted the cap so that it partially obscured his face, then he looked in the mirror, examining—not without pride—the results. His disguise was almost perfect, but he tempered his optimism. What came next was bound to be more difficult.

He left the room cautiously. No one was in the hallway. He closed the door and moved a few meters down the passage. An opening to his right overlooked a spacious living room whose ceiling was decorated with Moorish arches. Rocambole was struck by the richness of the decoration. Reproductions of ancient sculptures were mingled with suits of knightly armor, stacks of sheet music and a collection of exotic seashells. At the center of the room stood a fountain made from a giant clam. Most impressive were the dozens of paintings on the walls. Rocambole recognized works by Raphael, Delacroix and Ingres. How could the owner have accumulated so much wealth? And especially in this place? He resisted the temptation to steal anything. What he had come here looking for was worth more than all these paintings put together.

The living room was empty, but this was what he had expected. Right now, the staff was busy preparing a meal. Based on the information his sponsor had provided, Rocambole knew he had to pass by the kitchen to reach his objective. That was where that he would need be on his best game.

Rocambole pushed through another door and walked down a hallway. In the center, he discovered a library where thousands of books were stored on intricately decorated shelves. Once again, Rocambole fought down the urge to steal, even if some books—to judge by their age—were worth a fortune. His old demons struggled to assert themselves but, despite his history, he had decided to work on the side of the angels. This mission was a step in that direction.

The next corridor had two facing doorways. The delectable aromas of cooking tickled Rocambole's nostrils and he also perceived voices and a metallic clatter. At the end of the dimly lit hallway, he could see the heavy door of the room he wanted. If he could just reach it.

Rocambole stepped forward as naturally as he could, despite the stress that knotted his stomach. As he came near the kitchen door, a thin-faced man emerged with a dish in his hands and stared at him with large dark eyes. Rocambole was disconcerted and thought for a moment that he had been discovered.

"Where were you, Gustave?" the man growled. "We're running behind and the Captain is waiting to be served. Quick, take this dish to him!"

Rocambole had the feeling that a trap was closing in on him. However, there was no choice. He had to forge ahead, trusting that his subterfuge hadn't been discovered. He bowed his head as if apologizing and took the dish of scallops and aromatic seaweed the man handed him. The latter returned to the kitchen where Rocambole caught a quick glimpse of men busily tending the stoves. He felt reassured on two points: all wore caps and one that seemed to be the chef was no longer paying attention to him. Also, he saw someone in the dining room; a large bearded man with a dark, enigmatic countenance. Rocambole immediately guessed this was the Captain. Realizing that there was no escape, he decided to serve the man. Head down to hide his face, he walked up to the Captain who sat alone at the end of a large table. Rocambole was familiar with bourgeois culinary protocols and did his best to serve the man stepping to his right and carefully placing the food on his plate.

The Captain appeared both alert and absent. His brow furrowed, his eyes seemed lost as he gazed at the porcelain dishes sitting on the beautiful table before him. He didn't seem interested in the actions of the false server. Rocambole felt reassured and left the room with a polite nod of his head.

Back in the hallway, he saw he finally had a chance. The Captain was paying no more attention to him, while the cooks on the opposite side of the hall all had their backs turned. He moved to the front door at the end and gently opened it, then closed it behind him. The Captain's quarters were furnished with framed maps, antique furniture and a bed with an iron frame. Rocambole went straight to the trunk, knowing his time was limited. He pulled out his little stethoscope, put the end on the chest's lock and turned the dial. He surprised himself with how quickly he found the combination. Had the Captain felt himself so safe that he never changed it?

Rocambole smiled with satisfaction. Inside the box were a large number of documents. Rocambole flipped through them and quickly identified the sheet he was looking for: a plan of the engines complete with technical specifications showing how the Electricity Fairy powered the machine. Rocambole knew of several foreign powers willing to pay a high price for these. However, the purpose of this risky venture was a more selfless goal.

All that was left was his escape. He folded the papers and hid them in a secretcompartment in his belt and closed the trunk. He came out of the room and, seeing no one in the hallway, crossed. He had a moment of apprehension as he passed between the kitchen and dining room, but it passed. He saw only two cooks busy in the kitchen. As for the Captain, he was no longer seated at the table. Perhaps he had moved to the blind spot of the dining room?

Rocambole took the opportunity to navigate the corridors, quickly reaching the ladder that would take him outside. As he began to climb, several men came out of their cabins, rushed at him and wrestled him to the deck. He tried in vain to fight them off but there were too many and they were too determined.

Moments later, the Captain entered and cast a disdainful look at Rocambole.

"Gustave is left-handed," he said shortly, then turned on his heel.

Rocambole tried to reply but a solid punch from one of the sailors made him lose consciousness.

He awoke after a time, but he couldn't estimate how long. He was locked in a tiny room with metal walls. A throbbing pain filled his head and a deafening pounding rang in his ears, as if a gigantic machine was operating close by.

To his left and right stood two doors, each sealed by a large steel wheel. Rocambole stood up and rubbed his head. He cursed himself for being caught, but how could he have anticipated the mistake he had made? Was there still a way he could save his own life? He approached the window, which was placed high on the left hand door. Through the thick glass he could see an empty hallway. He pulled on the wheel with all his strength, but quickly realized it was locked. He tried the wheel on the other side and managed to rotate it a quarter turn. The door raised from the floor but Rocambole's flash of hope turned to terror when cold water gushed fiercely through the aperture, filling the chamber to his knees.

A narrow side window opened and the Captain's dark face appeared.

"You're in an airlock," he said in such an emotionless tone that Rocambole's heart sank. "The valve you just opened allows a diver to become accustomed gradually to the pressure of the water before exiting the ship. Your problem is that you aren't wearing a diving suit."

A dull panic seized the prisoner. The freezing water rushing in had already reached the level of his crotch.

"What do you want?" he asked.

"To begin with, your name."

"Rocambole."

"At one time, you were considered a criminal mastermind in your country. I've heard rumors that you had reformed. I see that that they were false."

This response unnerved Rocambole as much as the water, which had now risen to his abdomen. He tried to justify himself with an appeal to patriotism:

"Several nations are threatening to declare war on France. Your submarine technology would…"

Unspeakable anger contorted the Captain's face.

"The sea does not belong to the despots and their warring nations!" he stormed. "On the surface, they can kill and commit all manner of earthly horrors, but the ocean's depths remain a realm of peace and freedom."

The water reached Rocambole's shoulders as he realized that talking with the Captain was useless. He made a desperate effort to turn the wheel. If he could raise the airlock door—even if only enough to get his body into the gap—he might have a chance to escape. He managed to turn the wheel a third of a rotation, then the mechanism froze. Rocambole panicked; his action had increased the volume of water entering the room without giving him enough room to escape. He turned to the Captain, as angry as he was desperate.

"What is it you want?"

"If you manage to survive, deliver my message to those who sent you."

With these words, the Captain pulled a lever which seemed unlock the mechanism. Rocambole saw a strange expression on his face before he shut the window. He drew the conclusion that this man might be a great scientist, but he was also a madman who would never compromise his beliefs.

Rocambole dismissed his speculations. His survival would be decided in the next few seconds. He threw his weight against the wheel and turned with all his strength. This time, Rocambole managed to lift the airlock door. The water had risen to his neck now. He took a deep breath, plunged under the surface and slipped through the gap. Immediately, the pressure bruised his eardrums. The waters in which he found himself were black and chaotic. He saw a light far above him and kicked toward it, already running out of breath.

The submarine retreated, its dark and slender shape disappearing into the depths. The whirlpool of its passage failed to pull Rocambole down. Just when he had given up any hope of survival, he reached the surface. His lungs were ready to explode when he finally drank in fresh air. He could make out the outlines of the port, but it was so far away. How could he reach it?

Rocambole accepted his misfortune; he had no choice but to swim. All his movements were painful, but he was determined to regain the shore. He succeeded, exhausted, and as soon as he set foot on land, a gloved hand reached out to him. It belonged to the Admiral's aide, a cloaked man with a sinister reputation.

The last part of this adventure isn't necessarily going to be the best, Rocambole thought. The cloaked figure took him—still dripping water—to a carriage drawn by black horses. The Admiral was waiting in the darkened interior.

"It was far from easy to learn that he was making a stopover in one of our ports," the Admiral said. "I had to apply pressure to the Port Authority for the information. I hope that our venture has been successful. Did you manage to steal the plans?"

His tone sounded like a threat. Rocambole nodded wearily. He took off his belt and handed it to the Admiral's henchman.

"I was caught and had to risk my life in order to escape. Fortune favors the bold. I concealed the diagrams you wanted in the hidden pocket of my belt. They never noticed a thing.

The Admiral's sinister associate took the paper from the belt. He unrolled it, then whispered something in his master's ear.

"If this is a joke, you are courting disaster," the Admiral said, throwing the paper down with an agitated motion.

Rocambole, taken aback, picked up the paper. He saw that it was a white sheet, blank except for a pretty sketch of a scallop shell in the center.

"That damned Captain Nemo got me!" he exclaimed.

"Your failure is unfortunate, Rocambole," the Admiral said, his tone cold. "The success of this mission would have greatly pleased the government. You would have helped save French lives in war we are preparing for. And as agreed, I would have intervened with the Ministry of the Interior to have them forget the detestable actions of which you were guilty in the past."

"On the contrary, I think it is better that things happened this way," Rocambole retorted. "Nemo is right when he says the oceans must continue to be a realm of peace and freedom. He remains the sole master of his technologies, and no nation will be tempted to use them for military purposes."

The Admiral's only answer was an annoyed frown.

(translation by Matthew Baugh)

The notion that vampires may not represent the ultimate evil, especially when one considers the horrors of the Nazi regime, is not a new one. One of the best treatments on the theme may well be F. Paul Wilson's novel, The Keep. *Our Australian contributor, David McDonald, has chosen a more intimate, less cataclysmic setting than Wilson's to depict the cruel and merciless clash between these two dark powers...*

David McDonald: *The Lesser of Two Evils*

Poland, September 1942

Normally it would have savored the taste of their fear, it would have been the perfect seasoning for their flesh. But something was not right. Normally the humans would only venture into its woods when the hateful sun was high in the sky or, in times of great need, with flaming brands easy to hand. They would certainly not stay any longer than they needed to; as soon as they had found wood for their guttering fires or meat for their empty stomachs, they would scurry back to their hovels, throwing furtive glances over their shoulder all the way. The ones it didn't take for its meal, of course.

But, these humans—these humans were different. It had been following them for days and nights for it was old and cunning and wary of traps, and it had sensed something not quite right about them from the start. They were a ragtag group, old men and women, a few mothers and some sickly children, not an able bodied man amongst them. The old men wore their sideburns long and curled, and the women covered their hair with scarves. They seemed unaccustomed to the woods, each night they struggled to start a fire and often were reduced to huddling together for warmth in the dark.

It could have easily slaughtered them all, or taken them one at a time. But, it had lived so long that curiosity and a desire for novelty outweighed its hunger. Each night, it would creep close and listen to their conversation, trying to puzzle out the enigma of their presence in its forest. Sometimes, it would climb into the treetops and perch in overhanging branches, mere feet from the unsuspecting humans below. It was difficult to make out their conversation; they used a dialect that was far removed from the one it had spoken when it had walked beneath the Sun, long ago. But there was one thing that transcended any language barrier, and that was the sheer terror beneath which they constantly labored.

It began to pick out words that occurred with increasing frequency as they moved deeper into the forest. The first time it heard them say "*Leśny Dziadek*" it grinned, revealing snaggled yellow teeth with evil points. It was not without vanity, and it took pleasure in knowing that it was still remembered even by those who did not live on its doorstep. But, while they spoke its name with a vague dread, like the way a child speaks of the creature it only half believes lives beneath its bed, they saved their real fear for another word, a word which peppered their discussion: *Nazi.*

It puzzled over the word, turning it over in its convoluted mind. What could it mean? What could inspire such fear? What could inspire more fear than *it* did? There was only one way to answer its questions and it resolved to retrace the humans' trail and discover what it was they were fleeing from. It knew that it would easily find them again, for it knew this forest intimately.

It leapt from tree to tree, viciously clawed hands on the end of long, gnarled arms grasping at branches, digging into the wood and launching it to the next with a convulsive bunching of ropy muscle. Its yellowed eyes gleamed over a sharp pointed nose poking out from a stringy beard that was long enough to tuck into a plain black leather belt. Tattered grey robes flapped around its hunched and wizened body. It laughed an old man's cackle as it bounded from perch to perch; it hadn't had this much fun in decades! Every so often, it would drop to the ground and sniff the dirt, just to make sure it was still on their trail, but the stench of fear was better than a paved road. Finally, it came to the edge of its domain, and looked out over the local village.

The last time it had come close, after a smelling a particularly toothsome child, the village had been a sleepy little hamlet, a few horses and chickens the most traffic the one main street could boast. Now, it was a kicked hornet's nest of activity. Bright beams of light stabbed into the night sky, while columns of men tramped past. They were obviously soldiers; they were clad in identical grey uniforms and wore steel helmets. It didn't recognize the weapons they wore over their shoulders, but it could sense their latent menace. Massive wagons that needed no horse to draw them growled their way through the churned up mud, glowing eyes lighting their way.

Voices rang out through the still night air, and it snarled as it recognized their language: "*Niemiaszek!*"

It spat. For centuries, they had swarmed over the motherland, looting and plundering. They were powerful warriors, and preying on them had often brought great risk to the creature, despite the advantages it possessed over mere humans. And while it would take what meat it could, it preferred the young, and the warriors' raids would often drive the villagers away from its woods, leaving it only the tough, gamy meat of men in their prime. Oh, it had lots of reasons to hate the foreign invaders, even if it didn't... No! It would not think about the life it once had before it became what it now was, remembering was something that would cause it great pain.

It watched the soldiers come and go for the rest of the night, puzzling over their strange behavior. Over the years, it had seen enough armies to be able work out ranks and hierarchies, and this group was no different; in fact, they were strict when it came to formalities. However, no matter what the rank of the normal soldiers, there was one group that they all deferred to: these soldiers dressed in black, with silver lightning badges at their throats; they swaggered down the street as if they expected all to make way before them. They were not disappointed, the grey-clad soldiers avoided them whenever possible, and were appropriately submissive when it was not. Intrigued, it decided that it would follow the lightning soldiers and see what it was that made an object of fear. Maybe this was what the word *Nazi* referred to? No matter, it was confident that no mere man could rival its powers and offer it harm.

The next day, it carefully trailed a large group of the black-clad soldiers, almost a hundred of them. While it hated the daytime, and would only venture out under the greatest necessity, it could bear the Sun's light and the discomfort it brought. It flitted from shadow to shadow, so silently that not even the most alert of the men ahead of it had the slightest idea that something was stalking them. They marched for almost two hours before coming to another village, this one substantially bigger than the one at the edge of the forest. The risk of discovery meant that it could not follow them into the town, so it curled up in the fork of a tree and slept fitfully.

It was awoken by a commotion that grew rapidly louder and closer. The soldiers were back, and they had company. Using their fists and the butts of their weapons to keep order, they were herding a formation of villagers before them. The villagers had a similar look to those it had seen in the forest, from their clothes and facial hair to their expressions of fear. It wondered what the connection was, and whether this was what the others had been fleeing from. There were at least three or four hundred villagers all told, and the chaos that came with such a mass of confusion made it easy to follow them undetected.

They marched for another two hours, making substantially less progress despite the soldiers' best efforts to hurry the pace. Finally, they halted, and the soldiers divided the villagers, separating out the able-bodied men. It saw numerous blows dished out to protesting families, but the arguing came to an abrupt halt when one of the black-clad soldiers pulled out a small weapon and pointed it at a particularly belligerent villager. There was a sharp crack, and the villager collapsed to the ground. After that, there was no more debate; the villagers simply went where they were told, shoulders slumped in sullen resignation.

Once the healthy men had been separated, the soldiers took what looked like small folding shovels from their backpacks and distributed them to the men. There were some barked commands, and they began digging. The shadows lengthened as the day wore on, and it wondered what the point of their labors was, and whether it could be bothered waiting around to find out. Before its patience was tested any further, there was another series of orders; the men stopped digging and began to stack their tools in a jumbled pile. Once they were done, the soldiers poked and prodded them with the strange weapons he had seen slung over their shoulder until they lined up along the edge of the trench that they had dug, their backs to the soldiers.

The soldiers pointed their weapons at the villagers, and with a terse command, a wave of smoke and thunder erupted. The men fell like wheat under the scythe, toppling into the trench, and, in a matter of seconds, not a single one was left alive. There was a chorus of wails and moans from the villagers in the other group, but the soldiers on guard walked amongst them, using fists and boots to quieten any that got overexcited. They also began another winnowing, and it could see that those being culled from the herd were without exception young and lithesome women. A detachment of shoulders marched them off back towards the village, and once they were out of sight, the others were forced towards the trench. Already in a state of shock from the horror of what they had just witnessed, they put up little resistance.

The creature was still reeling itself, but not from any finer feelings or sympathies. It was trying to fathom what magic these soldiers possessed that they could slay without touching, and whether they might actually be a threat. Or, was it merely a newer type of crossbow? Another rippling wall of sound hit it as the remaining villagers were eliminated; those who didn't topple into the trench were rolled in unceremoniously by the laughing and joking soldiers. After a few minutes, the soldiers turned and began to march back to the village, leaving the creature to its thoughts.

It stood at the edge of the gouge in the earth, looking down on the piled corpses. There was little sentiment still burning in that withered chest, but, for the creature, death had always been something personal, something intimate. It killed to feed its hunger, both for flesh and for the chase, but it was never anything less than a sacred experience. This carnage was something else, seemingly indiscriminate and, above all, wasteful. It began to feel a strange emotion, one that had not stirred for centuries, that it eventually identified as anger. How dare these foreigners come into Holy Mother Poland and take what belonged to it? The anger opened other doors too, revealing memories pushed down and forgotten for so long they were only recalled in flashing images. It tore its long claw-like fingernails through the turf as images hammered into its eyes...

He felt the warm glow of pride fill him as the smiling woman held the baby up to him. He cradled it in strong, muscled arms, savoring the weight of his son. His son. Leaning forward, he brushed the damp hair from the child's forehead with a gentleness that belied his size, then kissed his wife softly on the lips.

"I love you, Zofia. Thank you for giving this farmer a strong son."

"I love you too, Ka..."

Her voice cut off and the smile fled her face as mailed fists hammered on the door. As he reached for the axe hanging above the lintel, there was the sound of splintering wood. Four men in chain mail, their surcoats emblazoned with

Maltese crosses, burst through the door and rushed across the room, their battle cry echoing from the low ceiling.

"*Gott Mit Uns!*"

As if responding in prayer, the first man fell to his knees, held up from the ground only by the axe blade buried deep in his skull. Before the new father could wrench it free one of the other assailants swung a viciously beaked mace, sending it crashing into the axeman's head. There was a flare of light and then only darkness.

He awoke to agony. His legs burned with a pain he would not have thought possible, and when he tried to move his head felt as if it had taken that blow of the axe. He gathered himself, and rose shakily, gasping as he saw the wreckage of his legs. The skin had melted and bubbled, cloth burnt away and charred into the flesh, as blackened and burnt as the ruins of the cottage that lay before him. Such was the devastation that it took a moment for the sight to register, and for him to recognize it as his own.

"Zofia!" His voice was hoarse, his throat raw with smoke. "Zofia!"

There was no answer, and he moved closer to the burning wreckage, shielding his eyes from the heat that still roiled from the coals. A strange scent wafted through the air, reminding him of the rare times they had pork on the table. Despite his pain, saliva filled his mouth and he swallowed nervously. He took another step forward and then froze. There in the heart of the flames were two shriveled, blackened figures, only barely human. One was much smaller than the other, cradled in the larger figure's arms.

"No! Zofia!"

He tried to move closer but, despite his best efforts, the heat would not allow him to approach. Sinking to his knees, his chest heaved as he was wracked with sobs, the outpouring of grief consuming him. How long he stayed that way, he could not have said but when he opened his eyes the red glow of the flames had died down, and had been replaced by an eerie green glow.

"You poor, poor man."

The farmer staggered to his feet, almost falling as he whirled around to face the direction from whence the voice had come.

"Be at peace, *mon ami*. I mean you no harm."

The man's Polish was fluent, but more like that of the *szlachta*, the nobles, than that of the villages. Still, the farmer could understand most of it, except for the strange foreign words. The accent, too, was like nothing he had ever heard. But all those oddities paled in comparison to the baleful green glow that shone from the stranger's eyes, washing across the clearing. As the farmer watched, it guttered out, leaving only the flickering flames to illuminate the stranger's nondescript features. The farmer crossed himself, but was too weak to run. All he could do was square his shoulders and pretend to be unafraid.

"Who are you? *What* are you?"

The stranger smiled, revealing sharp teeth that glimmered wickedly in the moonlight.

"You may call me Monsieur Goetzi. As to what I am?" The green light flickered again in his eyes. "I am merely someone like you, someone who has had what is his taken away from him by those who are more powerful than he."

"You are nothing like me!"

"You mean these strange qualities I possess?" Goetzi laughed. "They are nothing for you to be scared of, *mon ami*."

The famer spun to his right. The second sentence had been echoed by another voice, and its source was an exact duplicate of the stranger, green fire boiling from its eyes. As the farmer watched, it strode towards the original, and reached out its hand to meet Goetzi's outstretched hand. As they met, there was a flash of green light and the duplicate disappeared, absorbed into Goetzi's body.

"Demon!"

The farmer turned to run, but before he could take a step Goetzi was on him. Hands like iron pincers gripped him and bent him backwards, his spine screaming protest. The farmer struggled, muscles tempered by a lifetime of back breaking toil hewing wood and tilling the soil bunching as he pushed against the monster's grip, but for all his efforts, he might as well been a child in in its parents arms. Fingers wrapped in his hair, yanking his head back and baring the soft, vulnerable flesh of his throat.

There was a moment of pain as the creature's fangs pierced the skin, and then a blissful numbness spreading through his limbs. Strange visions filled his mind, a moonlit city, greater than all the tales the villagers had heard of Warszawa combined. The tall buildings were constructed from a striped, glistening stone that he would later learn was known as jasper, and their peaks capped by onion shaped domes. Vast amphitheaters were packed with baying crowds while strange beasts fought the death on ivory sands, and marble avenues shone under never ending twilight. Somehow he knew that the sun was a stranger here, and that the Moon, the silver queen of the night, ruled supreme.

"Ah, Selene," Goetzi whispered, his breath hot in the farmer's ear. "The Vampire City. One day, she will rule the world, and I will rule her."

The farmer whimpered as he felt the inexorable draining of his lifeblood ease slightly.

"You do not need to die, *mon ami*. Before I can take the throne of blessed Selene, I must build my own kingdom. Those fools who call themselves our Elders will never allow one they consider beneath them on the Council, and it is only from there that I can ascend to my rightful place. I must return as a conquering hero, or all my plans are as dust."

The peasant tried to speak, but all that he could muster was a low groan.

"Ah, so you wonder what this could possibly mean to you? I am but one man, and so I need loyal servants to do my will. From Dalmatia to Paris I am seeking out men, of—how shall we say?—suitable qualities to be my agents. While I put my plans into place, they will wait, their powers growing, until the day that I am ready and only then shall they rise up. Through them, all Europe shall be mine and the Council will not be able to deny me my rightful place."

Goetzi stroked the other man's face, almost tenderly.

"I can feel the anger burning within you. It permeates every drop of your blood. I can taste your rage, and I know that you would do anything for revenge. We are alike, you and me; I know what it is like to have what is yours taken away by those who are stronger. But I can give you the power to protect what is yours, and make you the one that other men fear. All you need to do is swear fealty to me."

The farmer thought of what he could have done with the stranger's strength, with his unearthly power. In his mind, the invaders fell beneath his blows, and his wife and son lived. No! They were gone, and nothing he could do would bring them back. But he could have revenge, if not on the men who had taken his family, then on the world that allowed such things to happen. Filled with a dark resolve, he nodded his assent.

"I thought as much." Goetzi drew a ragged thumbnail across his own throat, sending thick, black blood washing across the farmer's face. "Drink of my blood that I have given you, and call me Lord."

The villager fought his gorge as he lapped at the foul liquid, feeling it burn all the way down his throat, veins of fire spreading through his body. For a moment there was agony, then only darkness.

When he awoke the stranger was gone, and his wounds were healed. A burning thirst consumed him, a thirst that only grew as the days passed and could not be sated by any amount of water. In the end, he gave in to its demands, weeping as he drank the living blood from the throat of a poor washerwoman who made the mistake of straying from the safety of her village. Each kill was easier, until he began to glory in the hunt, savoring his strength and speed and the taste of blood and flesh beneath his fangs. Invaders came and went, his motherland groaning under the weight of their feet, but those who ventured into the woods he called home were never seen again.

Centuries passed and his powers grew, but Goetzi never called upon him. The dark magic of the woods filled him, changed him, and he became a legend. Whatever spark of humanity that remained flickered and died in the long lonely nights, but if it noticed it cared little. The woods, and everything within belonged to him, and no one would take them away from him. No one.

It screamed rage at the sky, feeding its anger in desperate desire to drown out the pain of the memories, letting its fury bring forgetfulness. It focused on what it had seen and resolved that it would keep its vow that no one would ever take what was rightfully its again. These strange soldiers might have weapons beyond anything it had ever seen, perhaps even magical ones, but it knew this land like the back of its twisted hand and how to make it a living hell for any invader. He would find out what the purpose of these soldiers was, and make sure they were thwarted. It chuckled deep in its throat, it was a long time it had thought beyond its next meal and it quite enjoyed the sensation.

Despite their head start, it arrived at the village well before the black-clad soldiers and settled into watch and wait. The first detachment arrived with their human treasures, and loaded the majority of them into trucks, which left immediately. The few who remained were escorted to a long low building, and swallowed up by its forbidding aspect. It dozed fitfully for a few hours, woken by the return of the remaining soldiers. This occasioned a mini-conference between a few men who carried themselves as if they were used to giving orders. Finally, there were more barked commands, and a group of about thirty men broke off from the mass and headed in the direction of the forest. It stiffened, and a green glow entered its eyes. They were obviously going after the group who had fled into the forest, and it was determined that they would not find the hunt to their liking.

The black-clad soldier walked as if there was nothing for him to fear in the forest. He had his strange weapon at the ready, and he was obviously well trained by the way he was constantly scanning his surroundings, and his bearing was of a man confident he could deal with any threat that presented itself. He was bringing up the rear of the column, and he was yanked up into the over hanging branches so quickly and neatly that none of his companions noticed.

It held the soldier at arm's length in front of, talons wrapped so tightly around the man's throat that he could not utter a sound, the air having no egress. It leered at him, enjoying the terror in his eyes, and the way its victim's fists hammered against its forearms in desperation. He may as well have been trying to strike an iron bar, and the soldier's face changed shades as he slowly suffocated. With a final twitch, and the reek of excrement as his bowels let go, it was over and it began to feed.

It fed well the next few nights. The soldiers were all seasoned men, but this forest had been its home for centuries, and it knew each twist in the path where it could lurk and snatch a man into the brambles, or the ravines where the only crossings were fallen logs where it could easily cling to the underside like some bloated spider, reaching up to clutch an ankle and send a man screaming into the jagged rocks below. There the victim would wait, dead or alive, for it to descend to consume the delicious flesh.

As the days wore on, it could see the well-oiled discipline that had distinguished these soldiers from others it had seen breaking down. The strain and tension was taking its toll, they began to talk back to their leader, and one man even tried to strike him. The haggard faced officer did not waste any time reasoning with the offender, but simply pulled out his smaller weapon and sent him crashing to the ground. He was a particularly tasty morsel, his meat well flavored with madness and with fear.

On the fifth day, it took the officer right from the center of the line, leaves shredding around it as their weapons popped and banged. They came after it, but they could not find it and its prey, despite the fact it teased them with the officer's screams, killing him slowly and savoring his torment. It ate his eyeballs first, scooping them out of the sockets while he still lived. Once it had stripped the most delectable morsels away from the corpse, it dropped the body into their hasty camp. As it had planned, this was the final blow to their discipline and, to a man, they turned and fled for the village, and for safety.

As they crashed through the undergrowth, it shadowed them in the branches above. In their panic, they were easy prey, far too simple to bring it any huge pleasure. There were too many of them for it to be able to taste them all; some it simply killed, snapping a neck with a twist of its powerful arms like a farmer's wife killing a chicken for the pot, or ripping out a throat with its claws like it was tearing off a hunk of the coarse bread the peasants lived on. Finally, there was only one soldier, sobbing with terror as he approached the edge of the forest. It could follow his progress easily by his labored breathing and the rank smell of terror sweat and it was waiting in the very last tree as the soldier ran beneath.

Its prehensile toes gripping a branch, it swung down and shrieked at the soldier, who back pedaled furiously trying to stop. He fell on his backside with a scream of his own, a dark stain spreading at his crotch, and waited for his end, but it was already gone. It wanted word of its hunt to spread through the soldier's camp as a warning not to trespass on its territory again, and to leave its property alone.

It was watching over its herd with a feeling of proprietary satisfaction when it sensed the intruders. It had been following the fugitives for about a week, leaving the odd deer in their path, or clusters of berries. It had not needed to feed on them, its larder was stocked with the slowly rotting bodies of the unfortunate soldiers, and for now it was simply happy to gloat over its victory. Their entire demeanor had changed, there was laughter and the occasional song as they wandered the forest, it seemed the oppressive shadow of fear had lifted from them. It was so in tune with the forest that it knew how many men had just entered its boundaries, and it felt no fear, only a malevolent joy, at the thought of slaughtering the half dozen men who even now were approaching.

Five of the soldiers were of the same kind as the ones it had feasted upon, but the sixth was somehow different. He, too, was in a black uniform, but of a more ornate style, with padded shoulders and a double breasted tunic. Even from where concealed itself, it could sense the power that burned in him. He was decked with amulets that prickled the air with their enchantments, and he was steeped in the stink of dark magic. The other soldiers treated him with the same mix of terror and subservience the grey-clad soldiers had afforded them. There was obviously no love lost; whenever they felt he was not watching, the other soldiers would discuss him in low voices, casting furtive glances in his direction. Even if they could not, it could see that he was aware of their speculation but the only sign he gave was the contemptuous half smile that seemed his constant companion.

Not for the first time, it cursed its ignorance of their barbarian tongue. It would have liked to have been able to discover more about its new foe, a man named Eckhart, who the soldiers constantly referred to as something called a *Thule*, but it would have to simply trust its powers and skills. It flexed its arms, listening to its knuckles crack and scratched its claws down the trunk, watching the sap bleed from the deep gouges. The creature grinned; no mere human would be able to challenge it, Monsieur Goetzi's gifts would see to that.

It found its harrying tactics a little more difficult this time around, as the soldiers made a point of keeping bunched together, except for Eckhart who strode arrogantly ahead of them. But when dark fell, it was easily able to creep in close to where the five normal soldiers slept and, without waking a single one before it was ready, dispose of them. It killed each one the same way, a calloused palm over their mouth pressing them into the ground, and a sharp nail drawn across their throat, leaving them to choke in their own blood. Once it had finished watching the light fade from the last man's eyes, it turned to take care of Eckhart, but froze. The Thule was gone! It scanned the ground for tracks, growled deep in its throat at the realization it had been tricked; the soldiers had been a diversion and Eckhart was headed straight for its herd.

It raced though the treetops, bounding from limb to limb. Thin lips were pulled back from a grimace that would have terrified any witness, such was its desperation to beat Eckhart. Why it felt such need, it didn't know, or wouldn't admit to itself that it might be born of any concern for its herd; instead, it tried to put it down to not allowing any one to take away what belonged to it. That would not happen, not this time. It knew to get to them, the Thule would have to cross a ravine; if it could just get there first, then it would have a considerable advantage. After all, this was its forest.

It stood just before the moss-covered log that bridged the ravine, panting with exertion that tested even its limits. Where was Eckhart? Something, perhaps one of the amulets or charms the Thule carried, was masking his exact location, but it knew that it had passed him on its way to ravine. Now all it could do was wait. There was no other way to get to the herd, unless the Thule spent days circling the edge of the woods. It sensed that Eckhart was not the sort of man to go around something if he could go through it. It turned to walk out on the log, where it could hide underneath and wait... Then, what felt like a boulder crashed into the side of its head and, after a flash of white light, everything went black.

When it awoke, Eckhart was casually leaning back against a tree staring at it. He realized it was awake and smirked at it, before addressing it in heavily accented Polish, with the occasional German word mixed in.

"So, you weren't just a devil made up by these Slav *untermensch* to frighten us, *ja*?" He spat on the ground. "*Gott in Himmel*, you are ugly."

It didn't reply, but merely stared back malevolently.

"It doesn't matter what you look like, anyway. You are going to earn me a promotion when I get you back to Germany." The Thule laughed; while it had little mirth, there was a cruel undercurrent. "The scientists will have a lot of fun finding out what you are. They are sick of working on filthy *Juden*; they will spend hours taking you apart piece by piece."

It rose unsteadily to its feet, still woozy from the blow. It hadn't felt anything like that since it had changed, and it didn't enjoy the sensation at all. It grinned and tilted its head from side to side, hearing the crack of bones settling back into place. It was going to enjoy ripping the flesh from this *Niemiaszek's* bones.

It came in low and fast, talons extended, aiming straight for his entrails. For a moment, it thought it had missed and run into the tree trunk behind the Thule, but, as it flew back, spitting blood, it realized the only thing it had run into was Eckhart's fist. Faster than even it could track, the *Niemiaszek* was upon it, fingers that felt like iron tongs wrapped around its throat. The Thule pivoted and hurled the creature, and, this time, it did hit a tree, sliding down and landing in a tangle of limbs.

How could this human be so strong and so fast? It shook its head trying to clear the cobwebs, and to fight down the rising fear. It was time for a different strategy.

This time when it came at the Thule, it waited until the last minute and feinted right before darting to the left. As it raked its claws across the human's upper thigh, it felt the wind of Eckhart's blow whistling over its head. It shuddered at the strength behind the Thule's limb; now that would have done some damage! As it was, its talons tingled with a dull ache where they had cut into the Thule's flesh, and, instead of the bright jets of arterial blood from a severed femoral artery, there was only a slow welling. His charms were potent indeed, but the wound was obviously hurting him; the human was now favoring the leg as he circled it, and there was a new caution in his eyes.

"I will take you back to the Fuhrer," Eckhart said. "Dead or alive, it is up to you, *ja*?"

It was too sore to bandy words with a human, even had it understood what he was referring to.

Eckhart continued, trying to distract it: "So, how long have you been skulking in this forest? The Slavs I tortured claimed you have been here for centuries." He paused, and spat. "Normally, I would just put that down to superstitious ignorance, but now that I have seen you for myself, I guess I owe them an apology. Not that it would do them much good right now."

It attempted to use the Thule's amusement against him, this time trying to go high and shred his throat to ribbons. Instead, the Thule's arm caught it across its chest, as solid as an iron bar, crashing it to the ground.

"The Fuhrer has commanded us to create a Reich that will last a thousand years. We will give him a master race that will live that long, and regain our rightful place in his favor." He smiled. "You look puzzled. We at the Thule Society use modern science to sift the truth from barbarian superstitions, unlike those credulous fools at the *Ahnenerbe*! We will discover what it is that gives you your powers and use it as it should be used, for the betterment of the Aryan race."

It knew the soldier was baiting him, trying to provoke it into another futile attack, and it resolved to bide its time, and wait for an opening. But what the Thule said next drove all thoughts of restraint from its mind:

"And as for the filthy *Juden* you are harboring in your woods, they will be my next order of business. They are trying to link up with the partisan bands to the east, but I think they would better serve as test subjects in my laboratory." His grin was as hungry as a wolf's. "At least, that way you will get to see them again!

It snarled, and flung itself at him as if trying to grapple with him, but, at the last moment, it rolled to the side and grabbed a fist-sized rock. Before the Thule could react, it threw it as hard as its unnatural muscles allowed and struck him in the face. His mouth exploded into spray of blood and pieces of teeth, and he reared back in agony. The soldier tried to say something, but all that emerged was a terrible guttural moaning, and then it was upon him. Its hands locked around his throat, and its jagged fangs latched onto Eckhart's face, and it began to chew, cartilage and skin and bone being no match for its fury. The Thule beat at the sides of its head with clenched fists, but the shock was telling on his strength, and it was able to shrug them off.

Trying to scream, the Thule staggered backwards until he felt the heels of his boots come down on the very edge of the ravine. His arms windmilled as he tried to regain his balance, dirt and rocks falling to the depths below. It shrieked its triumph as the warm salty blood gushed down its throat, clinging on even as they fell.

The last thought that went through its mind was that, this time, it had won, and that what belonged to it would not be taken away ever again.

The sounds of bird song cut off and the rustle of small animals stilled, as the forest fell silent. Nothing moved, as if the world held its breath in anticipation. A crooked hand rose above the edge of the ravine, before digging its claws into the soft, moist earth. The other appeared, and slowly, with pained and deliberate movements, it began to pull itself up and forward. It sobbed softly, wracked by the kind of pain it had forgotten was possible, yet propelled on by a compulsion that burned deep within.

As it staggered to its feet, it felt torn muscles sobbing in protest and broken bones grinding together. Its battle with the Thule, and the terrible fall, had left it battered and bloody and bruised, but it could feel Monsieur Goetzi's magic beginning to work through its body, repairing the damage. The healing was not gentle or soothing, merely concerned with restoring its body, and it shrieked as tendons writhed and bones popped back into position.

It held up its hand before its face and watched, mesmerized, as broken fingers straightened and cuts healed over. It could feel itself growing stronger and a terrible hunger rose up from within, its body crying out with the need to replace the energy expended on its restoration.

A feral green light shone from its eyes, and its nostrils flared as it caught the scent of more of the invaders entering the forest. The herd needed its protection still, and now it knew that until they were safe, the magic would not let it rest.

It threw back its head and shrieked exultantly, a terrible sound in the stillness. It was time to hunt once more.

In the following tale, Nigel Malcolm poses an interesting problem: faced with the discovery of a terrifying new weapon in the bloody aftermath of World War I, how would an English Detective, a French Detective, and a German spy react? Will patriotism trump sanity, or...?

Nigel Malcolm: *Von Bork's Priorities*

London, November 1919.

"Life is what happens while you're busy making other plans."
John Lennon.

Von Bork returned to Germany only to discover that his wife had divorced him and married someone more "respectable". Someone his children now called "Father." So, he returned to Britain to find the man who, in the lead-up to the Great War, had fooled, then destroyed, his intricate spy ring. The man who had captured him and taken away his family—Sherlock Holmes.

Holmes had mentioned in passing that he stayed in Claridge's Hotel when he was up in London. There was no reason to suppose he wouldn't stay there again. So, forging a new identity of "Jensen", Von Bork got a job at that hotel as a porter. Then he made his plans and bided his time, waiting for his nemesis to turn up...

The hotel's Breakfast Room was almost clear of guests by half-past eight. Von Bork and Cartwright were clearing the tables and putting the used plates, crockery and cutlery onto a trolley. They'd failed to notice the one remaining guest sitting alone at a table. He looked like he'd been working throughout the night, and had just returned to the hotel.

"I read in the paper that the *Annuncia* is moored in Docklands," said Cartwright, trying to be cheerful.

"Really?" replied Von Bork, trying to inject some politeness into his total lack of interest.

"They had to dock there. An emergency, apparently. They'll set sail again before sunset."

The two porters continued their work in silence. And the tired Chantecoq carried on drinking his coffee.

A few minutes later, the two porters were called into the manager's office.

"Our guest in room 109 was found dead this morning," said the man. "See to the removal of his body and assist the police with their inquiries. A Chief Inspector Teal is coming from Scotland Yard."

"Scotland Yard? So our guest is an important man?" said Von Bork, in a tone of voice suggesting surprise.

"Yes," replied the manager tersely. "You can both handle the body. You were both in the War, so you should be used to it."

A few moments later, the two porters were traveling up in an otherwise empty lift.

"Fancy saying it like that," said Von Bork bitterly, "What did he do during the War, I wonder?"

Cartwright shrugged: "Well, he's one of the lucky ones. Too old to find himself treading through mud at Ypres while shells never cease falling, wondering if he can smell mustard gas."

"You must have seen a lot of things out there."

"I'd rather not talk about it."

"Of course. I'm sorry."

They pulled open the lift door and walked down the corridor until they stood outside room 109. There were very few people staying the hotel at the moment. Just a sprinkling of guests on each floor. It was the low period between the summer and winter holidays.

They stood outside the room door and braced themselves. Suicides were not regular, but they did happen occasionally. It was a known phenomenon that a terminally ill person—or indeed anyone who wanted to end it all—would book into a five-star hotel, have a great last night, and then finish themselves somewhere where their loved ones didn't have to go through the distressing experience of seeing them after a suicide. Then it was up to the poor hotel staff to deal with the aftermath. As both Von Bork and Cartwright had been told when they each had joined the staff, the worst thing about the job was not dealing with the living guests, but the dead ones.

Although, as all the staff would find out sooner or later, it depended on the individual guest—there were some living ones that were just as difficult.

"Ready?"

"Ready."

They unlocked the door and walked in. It wasn't too bad. M. Legrand was just lying motionless with his eyes closed, his white face almost matching the bedsheets. There wasn't even any sign that he had taken his own life. Cartwright walked over to the window and drew the curtains open.

"We can't really do anything until the police get here. They'll want to examine the scene as it is.

"You sound like you've done this before," said Von Bork, intrigued.

"I once worked as a messenger boy for a private detective. A very long time ago."

This stirred something inside Von Bork's stomach. "Really? Anyone famous?" he asked, as casually as he could.

"It was a very long time ago. He's retired now, I expect."

Clearly, neither of them wanted to give away anything. Von Bork decided not to press Cartwright further. Instead, he looked around the room.

A suitcase of a pre-war design caught his eye. The design looked familiar. Very familiar. He walked over and examined it more closely.

"You'd better leave that for the police," said Cartwright.

"It looks suspicious," replied Von Bork.

He opened it. It was still mostly packed. Only a night shirt and some toiletries had been unpacked, probably. But Von Bork didn't rummage through it. He immediately felt for a secret pocket in the lid.

"It looks *very* suspicious," he added.

Von Bork felt a rush of excitement. His spymaster days returning, as though the last six years hadn't happened. He pulled out a large envelope. Cartwright looked at him disapprovingly.

The German pulled some papers out of the envelope. It was the design for a machine—an instantly recognizable machine that gave Von Bork a start.

"What are they?" asked Cartwright.

Von Bork took a moment to believe what he was seeing. "I saw these some time before the war," he said gravely. "They're plans for a deadly weapon."

Cartwright began to walk over to him.

"What kind of weapon?"

"The *Telephonic Assassin*," said Von Bork, "It is a monstrous invention. Basically, if the perpetrator wants to kill someone, he just needs to call his victim on the phone and send a fatal jolt of electricity. They've obviously refined the design. When I last saw this, it was at a crude phase. A killer could not assassinate his victim by telephone unless he was prepared to blow up several telephones in the area and risk killing others. In one district of Munich, the residents still wonder why they woke up one morning to find the receivers welded to their telephones…"

"How do you know all this?" asked Cartwright, suspiciously.

Von Bork paused to re-grasp his cover story. He'd given away far too much to his friend.

"I was involved in espionage before the war—but not after it broke out."

"The Swiss have a secret service?"

"Yes… But only to gather intelligence. They obviously want to stay neutral, but they still want to know what is happening in other parts of the world," Von Bork said as he began stuffing the envelope into his trousers and waistcoat.

He turned to Cartwright, who was still staring at him with intense suspicion.

"We must keep this to ourselves, Cartwright. It is imperative," he urged.

"But surely, this is exactly the sort of thing we should hand over to the police?"

"Which in turn will give it to the Government, who will adopt it as a new weapon against its rivals."

"Who are you loyal to, Jensen?" Cartwright asked.

"I don't think any country—any empire—should have this horrific device. Whether they are British, German or French. I'm neutral remember? Please Cartwright, trust me on this…"

"Trust you on what?" said a new voice coming from the door. It came from a man in a bowler hat, a moustache and a black winter coat. Obviously the man from Scotland Yard.

"Oh, nothing really, sir," said Von Bork in a sudden change of tone. "I spilt some cocoa on the carpet in one of the other rooms. We were discussing how to remove the stain."

"I see," said the man very slowly, before adding "I am Chief Inspector Teal of Scotland Yard. This is the body of Charles Legrand?" he asked, pronouncing the deceased's name the British way.

"That's right, sir. He checked in yesterday," added Cartwright.

"Who found him? You two?"

"One of the chambermaids, Agnes. She's downstairs with Mrs. Cornwall."

"What did she come in here for? To serve him his breakfast?"

"That's right, sir."

Teal paused for a moment, in deep thought.

"Was it a full English breakfast?"

"I wouldn't know for sure," answered Cartwright.

"I got called out here before I had time to have breakfast and I'm absolutely starving," said Teal. "What time do they stop serving breakfast here?"

"Nine o'clock, sir."

Teal looked at his watch and was disappointed.

"I don't think I'll be able to make it down to the Breakfast Room in time."

Von Bork was currently lost in his own thoughts. What should he do with the plans? Was it his patriotic duty to smuggle them to Germany? But Germany was a fractured mess—almost on the brink of civil war. The Telephonic Assassin could end up in the wrong hands. No, the best solution was to destroy these plans. A note on them showed that they were the only copy in circulation. That wasn't to say they didn't exist somewhere else, but at least there was only one copy. Maybe it was his duty to find any other copies and destroy them too.

He came out of his reverie.

"Do you serve any mid-morning snacks? Sandwiches, that sort of thing?"

"If you like sir, I could have coffee and biscuits brought to the room." Cartwright was hiding his bafflement well. Better than Von Bork, probably.

"Won't they charge that to Mr. Legrand's bill?" asked Teal, who thought for a moment and then said "Yes, alright then."

Another police constable approached Teal with a calling card. The Chief Inspector looked at it, and then at the door, where a well-dressed, self-possessed man was standing.

"Chief Inspector, rest assured that I, Chantecoq, have eaten a most hearty breakfast and I am ready and willing to aid Scotland Yard in this investigation."

Teal just stared at him for a moment.

"I'm sorry, who are you?"

The Frenchman was crestfallen. "Chantecoq" he said. "Often called the King of the Detectives! I have destroyed many German spy rings in France before and during the war. Now, I work as a private detective. I am currently staying here as a guest. I saw the presence of policemen outside in the corridor. I humbly offer my services."

Several other people in the room found themselves thinking that, whatever this man did, he almost certainly didn't do it humbly.

"What are you doing in this hotel?" asked Teal.

"I am staying here," said Chantecoq, blankly.

"I mean, what are you doing in London?"

"I am conducting an investigation on behalf of the French Government. It is a confidential matter, but the British Government are aware of it. I can say no more about it."

"Well, thanks for the offer, but this investigation is all in hand. And I have the assistance of that other 'King of the Detectives,' Sherlock Holmes."

At that, the normally calm Chantecoq lost his composure.

"Sherlock Holmes? But… I've heard he's retired! His book on beekeeping has pride of place in my library!"

Von Bork was equally shocked to hear the name. He felt like he'd just taken a call from the Telephonic Assassin. Feelings of overwhelming anger and hatred that had been festering underneath came to the top. He gasped and struggled to contain these emotions. He hoped no one else in the room had noticed.

A third police constable came into the room and said something discreetly to Teal, who nodded.

"I'll be downstairs," he announced to the rest of the room, before turning to go.

"Could I, at least, have a look round?" asked Chantecoq.

"Why not? The more the merrier," replied Teal. Then he left with the third constable.

"I must go with the Chief Inspector. Excuse me," said Cartwright, who followed him out of the room quickly before anyone else could object. Von Bork had too much else going on inside his head to wonder why Cartwright had to depart so quickly.

Chantecoq, meanwhile, had recovered his composure, and started to look around the room. He began by approaching the bed, pulling down the covers and examining the corpse.

"He looks like he just died in his sleep. This is not a murder at all. Nor is it a suicide. It looks like he had a heart attack…"

He then looked around the room more carefully, and noticed the suitcase.

"Now that sort of suitcase looks very familiar…"

He opened it and, like Von Bork before him, immediately searched for the secret compartment, much to the German's chagrin.

"Ah! Someone has beaten me to it!" said Chantecoq, "*Garçon*, who was the first person to discover Monsieur Legrand's body?"

It had been a very long time since anyone had called Von Bork, who was in his mid-thirties, *boy*. He almost didn't notice that Chantecoq knew the corpse's name. Instead, he recounted to the private investigator all the facts that Cartwright, Teal and he himself knew—omitting the discovery of the plans, of course.

Chantecoq listened patiently and attentively. When the porter finished explaining the situation, he paused for a moment and said:

"You're German, aren't you?"

Von Bork was taken aback by this. He reverted to his cover story.

"I'm Swiss, actually, sir."

"No, no, no—your accent is clearly German. Quite High Society German at that," said the French detective. He was clearly quite an expert in German society and culture.

"I come from a wealthy family in Basel on the north border of Switzerland. That is probably why my accent sounds German to you."

"Then how come you are a porter in a London hotel?"

"My family fell upon hard times. Anyway, I fail to see what my family history has to do with Monsieur Legrand's death." Von Bork was struggling to conceal his annoyance.

"You seem quite indignant for a bell boy." Chantecoq turned to the others and commanded: "Guards! Seize him and search him!"

The two constables just stood there, confused. This French lunatic, who they'd only met two minutes before, was giving them orders as though they worked for him. Addressing them as guards made them feel like soldiers. Later on, they would realize that Chantecoq was thinking quickly, but translating his words into the level of English he spoke.

But the thunderous command made Von Bork act on impulse. He immediately ran past Chantecoq and made a break for the door. Equally instinctively, the constables sprung onto him and wrestled him to the ground, as he shouted things in German they were probably glad they couldn't translate.

Chantecoq, who could understand the expletives, strolled over to him unfazed, and searched Von Bork's pockets and clothes. Eventually, he pulled out the envelope.

"Ah-ha! Now tell me, what is the Telephonic Assassin doing in your trousers?"

Teal, Cartwright and a constable went down into the hotel lobby, where they soon saw the familiar, tall, gaunt, figure of Sherlock Holmes.

"Chief Inspector Teal, I presume?"

"Yes… And you are Mr. Sherlock Holmes?" said Teal. "I am honored to meet you."

"You flatter me, Chief Inspector."

"There's something very odd about all this, Mr. Holmes," said Cartwright, discreetly.

"You know each other? Of course, you are a regular guest here," said Teal.

"A brilliant piece of deduction, Chief Inspector." Holmes led them all into a corner of the lobby away from prying ears. "Although my acquaintance with Mr. Cartwright goes back to the early days of my Baker Street years, when he was one of my Irregulars."

Teal stared at Cartwright, surprised.

"A lot of water has flown under the bridge since them days." said the porter.

"Indeed. Now, what news?" asked Holmes, with sudden impatience.

Teal told Holmes about Legrand's death. The detective listened, his head down, his eyebrows knitted and his hands, one of which was holding his hat, resting upon his cane.

"I see," he said finally. He looked up at Teal. "I'll come up and see the scene for myself, just before the body is taken away. You go on up, I'll just settle my bill from my last visit."

He smiled and patted his coat pocket.

Teal and the constable went back upstairs. Holmes knew by a subtle signal that Cartwright wanted to tell him something else. The former Irregular then told the detective about "Jensen" and the plans for the Telephonic Assassin.

They then joined the others upstairs.

Von Bork, along with Chantecoq and the policemen, was sitting in the nearby room 112. Some morgue attendants had come to remove the body. They had apparently been delayed by Holmes inspecting the room first, along with Cartwright answering his questions. This was not how the German had hoped to meet Holmes again. With his luck, he'd go back to prison. There'd probably be another war before he'd get out and have another chance. A war where the Telephonic Assassin would be used.

Teal was sitting there, chewing on some gum.

Finally, Holmes walked in, accompanied by Cartwright. The detective looked simultaneously older and younger to Von Bork. The last time they'd met, he'd had a chinstrap beard which made him look older. But that was five long years ago. He seemed uglier too.

Von Bork clenched his handcuffed wrists and slowly rose from his chair.

"Holmes," he growled.

"Herr Von Bork," greeted Holmes, cheerfully.

"You have the luck of the Devil."

"I make my own luck. I still have contacts in Scotland Yard, as well as other government agencies. They keep me informed of my old acquaintances' whereabouts. I knew that you were in London, in this hotel. I'll have to confess, though, I had thought you were here to get your revenge on me for destroying your spy network. But now that these plans for the Telephonic Assassin have emerged, I realize that you have returned to your old ways..."

Von Bork's fury erupted. He turned to Cartwright: "Did you tell him? You betrayed me!"

Cartwright looked guilty.

"My dear Von Bork," said Holmes, "Your quarrel is with me, not my colleague. Now, I deduce that you are working alone this time."

Von Bork was silent.

"He was going to take it back to Germany: To help them rebuild and become powerful again," said Chantecoq, who had just walked into the room.

The dramatic pause following that accusation was undermined by the sound of Teal chewing on his gum. Everyone else pretended to ignore it.

"You are wrong," replied Von Bork coldly. "I came across the plans and I made the decision to take them away and destroy them. No empire should have the Telephonic Assassin. Not the Germans, the French, and especially not the British!"

"You are a liar, sir!" said Chantecoq.

Von Bork looked at Cartwright. "Tell them!"

Cartwright, who was tired, repeated his account of what happened not half an hour ago. At the end, Holmes asked him a question:

"Did either you or Von Bork see Legrand before this morning?"

"We were both on early shifts, yesterday and today."

"The Concierge informed me that Legrand only checked in to the hotel yesterday afternoon, booking the room there and then. Would a porter know the names of booked-in guests?"

"Sometimes."

"Neither of us knew who he was, nor that he was carrying a secret document of that nature," said Von Bork.

"You are a liar, sir!" said Teal, unconsciously copying Chantecoq's intonation.

"I'm telling the truth!" roared Von Bork, standing up. Only to be pushed down again by a constable.

Cartwright stepped forward and picked up the envelope.

"Mr. Holmes, maybe the Concierge might have seen these documents? Perhaps he could shed some light on Monsieur Legrand's behavior?"

"I doubt it."

"But it's not improbable. It's worth asking him."

"Very well then," responded Holmes, irritably. He seemed lost in thought. Cartwright left the room with the documents.

"Monsieur Chantecoq, Chief Inspector, shall we step out into the corridor for a moment?" asked Holmes.

As the three detectives left the room, Teal took a cup of coffee—which he had ordered from room service—out with him.

Von Bork brooded. Everything was out of his control. He was suspicious of Cartwright's sudden departure. He had to regain control of events. Some of his now defunct revenge plan was still in place, and he could use it to get free and recover the plans.

The constable was now standing at the window, looking down at the street below.

Fortunately, while he was in a British prison, Von Bork had learnt from a convicted killer how to slip off handcuffs. He paused and focused for a moment, before applying what he remembered to his handcuffs and slipped them off, quickly and easily.

He then sprang to his feet and crept stealthily up to the policeman, striking him on the back of his head and rendering him unconscious. Laying the body down on the floor, he quietly eased the window open and scrambled onto the fire escape.

A floor down, he saw that the detectives were already giving chase clambering down the iron stairway. He climbed into the staff quarters and dashed towards the cloakroom area. He had to get to his coat—it contained money and a loaded revolver sewn carefully inside the lining.

He made it. Grabbing the coat and his cloth cap, he made to escape through the front entrance, gambling that his pursuers were making for the back entrance.

Von Bork left the hotel hurriedly.

Holmes and Chantecoq ran out of the back entrance, glanced around; and almost simultaneously shouted loud exclamations about how they'd been fools. They then hurried back inside and headed straight for the reception. Teal scurried after them.

Holmes asked the Concierge where Cartwright was. The Concierge informed them that Cartwright had just gone off duty.

Holmes was struck by a thought: "Did he show you an envelope by any chance?"

"No, sir."

Holmes looked very grave. Chantecoq broke the silence:

"Your informant, Holmes, has betrayed you. They were clearly working together."

"I wouldn't be so sure," said Holmes. "Indeed, Cartwright has double-crossed us, but I don't think he has the same agenda as Von Bork. Remember, Cartwright didn't know about our German friend's true identity. They were fellow porters, friends even, but there is no evidence to suggest that they both planned this together."

Teal put his empty coffee cup down on the desk, and asked the concierge for Cartwright's home address. The Concierge obliged.

Chantecoq thought hard, fiercely rummaging through his sleep-starved mind for an observation.

"I overheard Cartwright discuss a ship at the docklands. It is called the *Annuncia*," he said, almost surprising himself.

"Yes. He's fond of the docklands," said Holmes, thoughtfully. Then he added, "If the rest of you go to Cartwright's lodgings, I shall go to the docks."

Chantecoq looked at Holmes with bemusement. He clearly knew what Holmes knew, and Holmes knew it.

"Please indulge me, Monsieur. Allow me to resolve this."

Chantecoq thought for a moment. He had his own instructions from the French Government, but there were other factors to consider too, mainly ethical ones, and besides…

"How could I refuse *the* Great Detective?" he said.

Holmes smiled. "Thank you, Monsieur. You are truly a king amongst men."

Chantecoq bowed in acknowledgement. Teal and the other policemen had no idea what they were talking about.

The German ex-spy saw the ship, moored in the harbor. No one else was around, although he couldn't be certain because of the fog coming in from the sea. He saw Cartwright, hatless and still in his porter's uniform, walking briskly up to the gangplank. He'd caught him just in time.

"Stop right there!" Von Bork shouted out, pulling his gun out.

Cartwright stopped, and his head dipped, as though frustrated. He turned to face Von Bork as he approached. Cartwright's face was hard and tense. He didn't say anything. No acknowledgement of being caught. Anything.

"Now hand over the plans," said Von Bork, in a crisp tone of voice.

"For the Swiss Empire or the German Empire?" Cartwright replied, sarcastically.

"Actually, neither."

Cartwright quickly pulled out his own gun, a service revolver from the Great War. The two men were now pointing guns at each other.

Von Bork decided on a subtler approach.

"Think what you are doing, Billy…" he began.

But before he could talk further, the porter interrupted him:

"Oh, I've thought about it all right," Cartwright said bitterly. "You've never grown up on the city streets, have you? No, you *had* parents. And a home. And a good start in life. You never even had to fight in the war! You've never found yourself with the nearest you ever came to a family—your regiment—slaughtered on the battlefield."

Von Bork reflected that no, he had a comparatively easy war in some ways. He'd paid a heavy price, but not as heavy as some.

Cartwright was almost shouting by now: "Well, I'm sick of bowing and scraping to the rich. Groveling around and doing their dirty work while they just... *drift* through life healthy and happy, with all their arms and legs and eyes that haven't seen what I've seen."

He seemed to gag for a moment. Von Bork stayed silent. He didn't know quite what to say.

"My dear Cartwright, I had no idea," said Holmes, as he stepped out of the fog. He, too, had a revolver in his hand, but it was pointed at the ground.

"And you're supposed to be the *Great Detective*," Cartwright almost spat.

"I fear you may be right." said Holmes in a quieter, humbler voice. "But throughout my long career, I have seen many good men—and women—driven to perform the most desperate and dreadful acts. When I see what drove them to do so, I find I cannot condemn them."

Cartwright seemed to be quiet for a moment. Then, suddenly, as a thought occurred to him, he pointed his gun at Holmes, who flinched.

"Don't you try to sweet-talk me!"

Von Bork just stood watching this. He had a pang that Cartwright would kill Holmes before he got the chance to. His revenge would be denied. Yet, in flinching, Holmes seemed somehow more human. As though he could actually be killed.

Holmes regained his composure and continued to talk calmly:

"You still have a choice, Cartwright. You can get on that ship, sell those plans to whichever country or organization you are going to, and be hunted by every policeman and government agent in Europe. Alternatively, you can hand those plans over to Von Bork."

"Not you?"

"Not me."

"You'd rather the plans went to Germany?" Cartwright was incredulous.

Choosing his words carefully, Holmes replied: "Herr Von Bork has a choice too. You are taking a spur of the moment decision that will change your life forever—and not for the better. But you can still turn back from this."

Cartwright was still pointing a gun at Holmes. The porter's eyes showed desperation. As though he were about to burst into tears.

Holmes continued: "You have my word that I will vouch for you and your good character. You'll remain a free man. You can still have your job at the hotel—I'll see to that. And you can still work for me if you choose to do so."

Cartwright paused. Then with an air of defeat, he pulled out the plans and almost tossed them at Von Bork. Von Bork accepted them and backed away slowly, half expecting the other two to suddenly pounce on him.

He was distracted by Cartwright raising his gun again. He pointed it at Von Bork, then at Holmes, then finally at his own head.

"No, Cartwright, don't!" shouted Holmes in alarm.

Cartwright stood like that for a moment. Then he threw the gun away into the water between the ship and the harbor, and ran away crying.

Both Von Bork and Holmes were relieved by this. At least, the poor man had not killed himself. But the relief was only for a moment. The two long-time foes faced each other. Guns pointing at each other in stalemate.

"Strange that life never seems to turn out the way you expect, eh, Holmes?" said Von Bork, philosophically.

"Indeed," agreed Holmes. "Now I'm going to give you a box of matches." He slowly reached into his coat.

"No need. I have my own matches."

"Right."

Holmes moved backwards, still pointing his gun at Von Bork. The German knew he had a short time left. But his revenge plan had completely fallen apart. Eventually, the detective disappeared. Von Bork put away his revolver, and pulled out his matches. Maybe he would be shot through the fog before he'd had time to destroy the plans.

Taking the plans out of their envelope, the German lit a match and set fire to them. As they burned, he wondered why he had been given this chance. He was still alive. The plans were almost completely destroyed. Holmes had allowed him to do this.

As the last of the paper turned to ember and floated to the ground, Von Bork stood there, in the stillness, and wondered what he'd just done.

Normally, we don't publish "Elseworlds" stories in Tales of the Shadowmen, *but Xavier Mauméjean, whose extraordinary award-winning novel* The League of Heroes *(published by Black Coat Press) is certainly one of the best alternate worlds stories ever told, can be extremely persuasive. This brief, but twisted, retelling of the origins of the famous Caped Crusader is a gem certainly worthy of figuring amongst our pantheon of Shadowmen...*

Xavier Mauméjean: *The Wayne Memos*

From the Archives of the Glavnoïe Razvedïvatelnoïe Upravelnïe stored at 19 rue Znamensky. Original documents. No copies permitted.

From: Leon Trotsky
To: Semyon Ivanovich Aralov and misc. department heads.
Date: November 1918.
The creation of our division has been formally approved. Code: 44388. The GRU will not be referenced in any other secret services' charts. The Fourth Directorate of the General Staff of the Red Army will be tasked with collecting military intelligence and organizing subversive activities in the capitalist nations where the oppressed masses are not capable of launching an attack, even less defending themselves.

From: Leon Trotsky
To: Semyon Ivanovich Aralov and misc. department heads.
Date: January 1919.
We are ready to start the first of our five-year programs codenamed "People's Hero." As you have been informed previously, the concept is to program the conditioning of a pure product of the ruling class. In other words, a dialectical opposite which will turn an individual into a symbol of justice for the masses and popular revenge against the laws of the bourgeoisie. At first glance, his fight may appear to be selfishly motivated, but in reality, it will come to incarnate the universal struggle against capitalist order, which has reached the end of its life and is condemned to decline.

From: Leon Trotsky
To: Semyon Ivanovich Aralov and misc. department heads.
Date: May 1919.
We have identified our subject: Bruce Wayne, the son of Thomas Wayne, doctor and millionaire, and Martha Wayne, engaged in charitable activities. The couple has developed a real social conscience. Address: Wayne Manor, 1007 Mountain Drive, Gotham, New Jersey. As Karl Marx said, it is only the real man who

makes history, a man subjected to pre-set conditions, empirically determined. As part of our experience, we must gradually erase the alienating nature of his social class in the subject. Then we shall shape him into a well-defined worker, whose skills will be perfectly suited for the task ahead. It is understood that work is the expression of a man who tries to fill his available space and time with legitimate actions.

From: Leon Trotsky
To: Semyon Ivanovich Aralov and misc. department heads.
Date: October 1919.
We have succeeded in infiltrating Comrade Alfred Pennyworth into the Mansion. His socialist conscience developed during his studies at Cambridge. He was a military surgeon in the Scot Guards during the First World War. Amateur actor. The son of Jarvis Pennyworth, already butler to the older Waynes and committed to our cause since he joined the Fabian Society, a group co-founded by H.G. Wells, a writer too moderate in his beliefs, but humanist. Comrade Pennyworth will be both the political commissar and spiritual director of young Bruce.

From: Leon Trotsky
To: Semyon Ivanovich Aralov and misc. department heads.
Date: September 1920.
Traumatic impact action No.1. Proper ideology is acquired through a variety of means, spatial, temporal, visual and auditory. According to the plan of Professor Sponsz Petrovich Pavlov, Comrade Pennyworth arranged for young Bruce to fall into the "bat-cave." Much fear. Implementation of symbolic memory with delayed recovery.

From: Leon Trotsky
To: Semyon Ivanovich Aralov and misc. department heads.
Date: November 1923.
Traumatic impact action No. 2. Assassination of the Waynes in front of their son. 10:47 p.m., in Park Row, nicknamed "Crime Alley" by the residents of Gotham. Mission completed by Comrade Joe Chill. This action occurred after the boy saw the movie *The Mark of Zorro* chronicling the exploits of a hero of the Mexican people. Implementation of the second symbolic memory with delayed recovery.

From: Leon Trotsky
To: Semyon Ivanovich Aralov and misc. department heads.
Date: December 1923.

Bruce raised by his uncle Philip Wayne, a former member of Harvard's "Red Club." Medical supervision by Dr. Leslie Thompkins, feminist activist. As expected , Comrade Pennyworth has become the legal guardian of young Bruce .

From: Leon Trotsky
To: Semyon Ivanovich Aralov and misc. department heads.
Date: December 1931.
Diploma graduation with honors. Around the world tour for further education. Entered Trinity College, Cambridge, to study economics and history. Approached by the "Cambridge group" created by Comrades Philby, Burgess, Maclean, Blunt and Cairncross.

From: Leon Trotsky
To: Semyon Ivanovich Aralov and misc. department heads.
Date: December 1931.
Bruce now under the supervision of Maurice Herbert Dobb, professor at the University of Cambridge. Economist acquired to our cause since his stay in Moscow in the summer of 1925. Member of the Communist Party of Great Britain. Published *The Economic Development of Russia since the Revolution* (1928), a book that highlights the merits of the Soviet System's economic planning. Dobb acted as a recruiter, especially with Philby and his friends. Comrade Pennyworth will take over for a specific program designed especially for Bruce Wayne

From: Leon Trotsky
To: Semyon Ivanovich Aralov and misc. department heads.
Date: August 1934.
Bruce Wayne and Kim Philby embark on a grand tour of Europe. In Vienna, Bruce follows the clandestine teaching of psychoanalysis (admittedly Jewish bourgeois science, but its socially subversive nature has not escaped the Nazi censors); Philby met Alice Roeder-Kohlman (née Friedman) who works for the Comintern. He married her. At her request, Philby and Wayne transport secret funds to clandestine cells in Hitler's Germany and Great Britain. After that, Philby went to Republican Spain as *Times* correspondent, while Bruce went to Asia to study the doctrine of our brothers, the People's Ghouls.

From: Semyon Ivanovich Aralov
To: Misc. department heads.
Date: December 1936.
The duplicity of Leon Trotsky led him to an attempt to falsify the true values of Bolshevism for the criminal purpose of erasing the principles laid down by Marx, Engels and Lenin . They say he will find refuge in Mexico. Contact local peasant revolutionary cell "Sons of Zorro."

From: Semyon Ivanovich Aralov
To: Misc. department heads.
Date: April 1938.
Appearance of a "superman" over Metropolis. That could upset our plans. Physicists at the Lebedev Institute claim that he would be vulnerable to the light of a red sun. Coincidence or a sign of cosmic social order? Why did he not appear in Ukraine first?

From: Semyon Ivanovich Aralov
To: Misc. department heads.
Date: March 1939.
Traumatic impact action No. 2. Back to Gotham City, Bruce Wayne fight against various thugs. Severely injured. Assailants not arrested by the police. Comrade Pennyworth makes him understand that he must instill fear in the criminals' hearts. Enabling symbolic memories of "Bat" and "Zorro" to return; their psychological and moral effects are reincorporated into the subject's consciousness. Bruce Wayne has decided to adopt our symbol:

Final phase scheduled for May 1939.

From: Semyon Ivanovich Aralov
To: Misc. department heads.
Date: March 1939.
Launch of second phase of "People's Hero." Code name: "Robin Hood" after an English figure who resisted popular oppression. Subject selected: Dick Grayson.

Neither Michael Moorcock, nor his signature character Jerry Cornelius, need any introduction. And the arrival of a new Jerry Cornelius tale is certainly an excellent motive for rejoicing! In this story, there are pithy obervations, as well as some moving reflections about the course of events on Planet Earth. Tales of the Shadowmen *has always made a point to be about French characters, but this is a story that reaches beyond them to embrace France in this new century. The country was said to be behind the times by many technocrats, until those things they claimed were good began to fail, and now, much to their surprise, the French seem to be ahead... Yes, those are the kind of thoughts on which Michael Moorcock ponders...*

Michael Moorcock: *The Icon Crackdown*
A Jerry Cornelius Story

1.

After discovering he had less money than he needed at the checkout, Jeremiah placed the jar of spaghetti sauce on the supermarket counter and left. The packer murmured something to the assistant. He wasn't sure if the woman's expression was one of pity or contempt. He didn't care. Though humiliation had become familiar to him, he still found it hard not to blush. He left Safeway and walked slowly up Santa Monica Boulevard towards Barney's Beanery. How was he going to get back to Paris?

West Hollywood, gentrified, new-fashioned, gay, was no longer the funky neighborhood he remembered. He didn't belong here now, any more than he belonged in London. The funk had gone. Only Paris offered sanctuary. Shockingly, the Tropicana Motel and Duke's diner were replaced by anonymous cinderblock boutiques and offices. The last time he'd lived there both places had been cheap. There was nothing cheap in this neighborhood any more. Still trying to piece together what had happened to him, he turned left and headed up the hill flanked by poplars, cedars and low hedges towards Sunset. White miniature haciendas decorated both sides of the street. He heard the roar and screech of a lawnmower occasionally hitting the sidewalk.

When the noise stopped, he momentarily enjoyed the tranquility of the afternoon with its buzz of far-away traffic. Police and ambulance klaxons sounded as if from another plane. He looked for his old address on San Juan. Everything was so neat and clean now. That was where he and Judex had last met. His dark green Lagonda was still parked outside. Someone had taken the trouble to wash and wax his car. Los Angelinos loved automobiles the way the French loved movies. Taking the keys from his pocket, he unlocked the door, climbed in and started the engine, easing off the hand brake and turning the Lagonda into the street. At the window of his old duplex a curtain fell back into place.

Surely she didn't still live there? She might not have cleaned the car, but it was like her to pay someone to do it.

Their ghosts were everywhere. All a question of speed.

Soon he was climbing up into Beverley Hills, the palms casting long, blue shadows in the late afternoon light.

Time wasn't what it had been.

2.

Rally on TV. Texas had, at last, seceded from the Union. Resigning Gov. Ron was proud to announce the first Libertarian State in history. He would now be Cit One. In order to maintain the freedom of her citizens, Texas had granted the right of all Latinos to leave their camps for new homes and jobs in Mexico. Formal war between the two nations was rescinded when someone pointed out that the Texan army had been 94% Mexican now that Africanos had been repatriated to Mugabiland as part of the aid deal. Cit Ron had blushed when he told the second Libertarian Congress that Texas had taken the Christian option and was going to show those Catholics (by which he meant non-Baptists) the other cheek and forgive them for their high-handed demands.

Mexico was likely to have a very wealthy partner in her renewed ambitions to repatriate the South and West from Louisiana to California and get on an equal footing with the reduced US. He sat back and rolled himself a medicinal spliff. It was years since he'd had so much fun. The cards were still in the air. Mo was making a book on the first to fall.

In the motel room, Jerry thought through the psych factors. French hero-villains emerged, drenched in blood, from a Catholic culture. Torment and guilt. They who do not feel guilt are envied. Those who struggle within themselves are identified with Protestant Anglo-Saxons, like Sherlock Holmes or Sexton Blake: self-righteous, even smug, but admired.

Jerry was backing the Ace of Spades. All roads led to France. He trusted gravity far more than the human condition. He heard loud honking outside. A familiar noise. Mo had got hold of a massive old Nash from somewhere. He had dressed it up with Duisenberg fittings. The big engine was good as new and pumping.

Reluctantly, he left the TV running and stepped out of the motel into the burning Arizona heat. He wondered if he was still on the best road for New Orleans. And would Fantômas be there? His power could still be felt.

The Libertarian militias were taking a road tax every twenty five miles. On the other hand, the routes through Oklahoma and surrounding states were blocked solid. The toll roads were hardly any better.

Doc Didi Dee would be waiting near the border. She was supposed to flying her old Stokowski 10-2 modified gunship. Air was still free over Texas. And would be until the 13th Libertarian Congress met next year. The skies over all major cities were thick with competing aircraft. Last week, two massive zep cruise ships had collided by the main Austin mast at Port Sab' a few miles from Smithville. Kids were still trading shrapnel, seared human bones, bits of red, white and black silk. Tourists offered millions for skulls still in flying helmets and the region was doing a heavy trade in fakes which joined the jackalope and lamp-bleached long-horns on the shelves of the Sukey's and Shell convenience stores. Texas's income thrived on myth and legend almost as much as L.A.'s. Kennedy Plots alone brought millions to Dallas every year. Other cities had nothing like the same pulling power, but conspiracy theorists proliferated all over a country sensing the collapse of familiar currencies.

"So." Mo swung the great golden car on to Route 66. He could outrun any cop still around. Besides, local cities had long ago seen no profit to be made from a potholed two-lane blacktop going nowhere but Indian territory. On certain days you couldn't help loving reactionary feudalism.

"Ah, Utopia!" He let the wind get to his hair. "There's something about the past that always goes wrong." He took a deep breath and sighed. For a moment he enjoyed a frisson of melancholy. "We should be in Bordeaux by Tuesday. Of course, I can't say which Tuesday."

Then he was back on the road, driving into an impossible future.

3.

Holborn Viaduct, so far not greatly changed and the main route out of Brookgate to Tilbury and Le Havre, was bleak under the driving rain. Major Nye, lifting his collar against the wet, tipped his bowler hat, sending a stream of water down his neck. This civilian uniform identified him as an old-fashioned military man. An old colonial hand. Crossing above Farringdon Street, he heard the heavy thump of lorry tires below. Glancing over the railings, he saw a convoy moving steadily towards Blackfriars Bridge. They appeared to be civilian vehicles but he was unconvinced. He plodded on through the rain towards St Paul's. Not so long ago he had stood on firewatch with his Zeiss binoculars on his chest, listening for the approach of enemy bombers.

Jerry met him on the far side of the viaduct. Together they began to descend the filthy grey steps to Farringdon Street. Jerry handed Nye a thin file.

"That's all we have on the Parisian Opus Dei." Pausing at the first landing, he drew a silver cigarette case from the inside pocket of his black car coat. "Almost wholly after Collyn's control, of course." He offered Major Nye a tipped Sherman's. "Sorry. They're the best I could get. Rationing."

The major refused. "I still favor the old pipe, you know." He glanced through the damp red file. "So you found nothing on Tigris?"

"Not what you're looking for." Jerry waited for the wind to drop temporarily, then quickly lit his cigarette with an old silver Dunhill. "His main drugs of choice these days appear to be memory cakes and licorice allsorts. Both taste of nothing but sugar."

"Needs the energy, I suppose. Fat as he is."

"Oh, he's lost a pound or two since he retired."

"Dear me, is he unwell?"

A figure appeared in the grey light of the arch below. Even in silhouette, her slender skirt and form-fitting jacket identified her. Shaking her umbrella, Miss Brunner tapped up the stone stairs in her Jimmy Choos. "I knew I should have worn a mac."

"Your idea to meet here," Jerry reminded her.

"It's the only place we all *knew*, Mr. Cornelius." She directed a glare into his eyes which would have blinded anyone else. "It's all about geography, isn't it?"

"Or class," said Jerry.

"Pathetic. Little oik!"

"I say," murmured the major blushing.

Miss Brunner pursed her carmine lips and glanced back at the rain almost as if she expected it to be following her.

4.

In the middle of the rutted field smattered with heaps of muddy snow lay an injured ewe. The crows had pecked out her eyes and she bleated softly.

"Innocence under siege," said Miss Brunner sweetly. She licked her lips.

"Poor bugger." Loosening his Browning in its holster, Mo Collier started across the field.

Unseen in the distance, the West Oxfordshire bayed in pursuit of a rotten corpse dragged behind a Land Rover.

At the wheel of the Smartwagon, Major Nye did his best to keep the tiny engine running. He frowned over the map. "I think we should have turned off just before Doncaster. There's a ferry to France, but it involves a lot of Time. Apples and oranges," he murmured to himself. "Apples and oranges."

A moment later, he was lost in an hallucination of rising waters, of the fields outside Cheese Cottage swiftly flooding. He put the truck into reverse. This could not be an attack from the Left. Could it? He did not know what to make of this impossible illusion. He prayed he had misinterpreted the images.

Miss Brunner reached out from behind him and gave his shoulder a habitual shake. "Wake up, major. You were telling me about *In Which We Serve*. Shouldn't we be in Versailles by now?"

"Is everything all right?" Mo came back, reholstering the Browning. "I used to love Noel Coward."

Major Nye opened his eyes. "What happened to those anglers? What's the point in fishing water you can set fire to? What would you catch?"

"Precooked fish and chips?" suggested Mo.

Jerry shrugged. They were attacking the structure of Time itself. Was there still any point of warning them? Yet what could they do? There was no escape. Why was France locked off?

Miss Brunner continued to show disgust. "Martyrdom is no more than an elaborate form of human sacrifice. It's not so long ago that Anglo-Saxons were shocked to find Cornish Christians practicing those rites. Few of us are more than a step away from our primitive roots. We sent our young men to Iraq as a blood offering to our gods. Didn't we?"

Mo wasn't following her.

5.

Jerry sniffed the rich fauna of the Portobello Road. Summer. Slow moving Thursday afternoon. He leaned against Mrs. Bones's bookstall watching plump middle-aged women leaf through the latest batch of second-hand men's magazines. *Slave Blondes for De Gaulle's legionnaires! Nazi Brides wake up firing! Hell-hounds of the Waffen SS! French Vampires in Govt. Tell All.* Too warm for him. He loosened the stud of his stiff white collar. He lifted his head, whistling softly. Why on earth would they disguise themselves so thoroughly? Everyone knew they were dying to catch hold of him. The last hero of Kiev. He stroked the steel of his Khartron Tommy gun. Not the only good idea Kharkov got from the racketeers.

Was it really just about the narratives? What about the ideas the narrative carried? In the opposite gutter the two villains rolled about in the tricolor he had caught them in. Mrs. Bones pretended she couldn't see them. She continued to sort out her paperbacks, putting them into categories and then into alphabetical order. Her customers also showed no curiosity about Jerry's prisoners. On early closing day, there was almost no one about. They clearly did not want to get mixed up in anything unusual.

The spies cried out to him in harsh, accusatory sentences. Were they still talking about Dunkirk? Surely they didn't expect him to apologize?

The dark green Rolls Phantom was still parked across the narrow street. Major Nye woke up at the wheel. "Anything I can do, old boy?"

"You could let me have my car back. If you wouldn't mind, major?"

"That's the spirit. Off to France again, are we?" Major Nye picked up a bunch of red campions from the seat beside him. "Are these any good?"

Now, thought Jerry, there isn't time to go home. This was probably the best he could do. He opened his paper bag and lifted out the contents. He bit squarely into 170 g of Fortnum and Mason's pork pie. Not the best in London now that a second rate Melton Mowbray knock-off could be bought in any supermarket and Marks and Spencer's did a passable imitation of the best. But you couldn't get choosy these days. He'd been lucky to find his brother's stash. Not a sign of Branston, though.

His sister Cathy turned the corner from Blenheim Crescent and began running towards him.

6.

Back in Djemaa El Fnaa as the sun set, Jerry sipped another glass of Mecca Cola and wondered at the glory of the third millennium. The great square was crowded with the usual Moroccan water-sellers, food stalls, entertainers, almost drowning the sound of the last muezzin.

At the next table, a small boy begged his father to let him play in the ruins of a nearby mosque. He widened his large brown eyes appealingly. His father said: "Don't be ridiculous. The cuter you are, the quicker you die. Don't you remember your brother? Has Hollywood taught you nothing? Why do you think there is no music on the radio now?"

What was it about North African baguettes? They were almost as bad as the Spanish. He sighed. Imperialism didn't always improve the food. There was more to cooking than making things look the same. Another triumph of image over taste. The French understood that, surely?

Jerry left a few coins on the table and cut quickly across the square which had once been so peaceful. Now, despite the bustling crowd, the square began to live up to its name again. The architecture was over-familiar: Los Angeles, via Mexico, via Spain, via Marrakech. That's what he liked about the South. The crows chattered and quarreled in the remains of the Roman church some monks had tried to build in the wake of an unhappy victory. This time there had been no El Glaoui to maintain the balance of power. He heard a familiar puffing. Out of breath as usual, Professor Hira, the Brahmin physicist, fell in beside him.

"What a very extraordinary mind God must have." He turned his bright brown face to the sky as if to the deity. "To outlaw himself. How long can these wars of superstition continue, Mr. Cornelius? Another bloody century?"

Jerry raised an enquiring eyebrow.

"Of course, it's silly of me." Hira was suddenly embarrassed. "I know God isn't a person. But then they said the same about Fantômas."

"But do they know that? This is the century of the wars of superstition." Jerry caught his friend's arm. "Quickly. We need to duck into the Old Quarter. *N'est-ce-pas?*"

7.

Sometimes the ruins looked as if they had eroded naturally in a matter of hours. The great grey ragged landscape stretched to the horizon.

269

"Why should they be so sure of me?" Major Nye stroked his small, white-flecked military moustache. Was he crying? "Why did they tell me this was France when evidently—?"

"Because they trust you. Or, at least, they trust your class. They expect you to share their views."

The major puzzled over this. "Nice to know," he said vaguely, dragging from his pocket a map and a copy of *Film Fun*. On the front page, in beautiful black and white, Laurel and Hardy pursued a cartoon Adolf Hitler through English streets. For his capture in the final panel the pair were rewarded with a mighty plate of sausage and mash. "So what's the job?"

"Old school," said Jerry. "You'll love it. We're still looking for France."

Major Nye turned his wrinkled neck and regarded his old friend through elderly eyes. "It's a bit close to home."

"Isn't everything, these days?"

Miss Brunner considered this. "In an effort to accelerate the progress of history, Hitler's bombers had ultimately stopped Time altogether. But not in Alsatia. That's the situation in which we find ourselves now. Eh?"

The others regarded her with amiable concern.

8.

"Know what I mean?" Mo tipped back his pint and finished it. "Like the smell of a fresh girl the morning after you've pulled her." He replaced his glass in the hamper and sorted through the remains of their picnic, looking for some cheese.

"When was the last time you pulled a fresh girl?" Reminiscently 'Flash' Gordon played with the buttons of his long greasy mackintosh.

They sat as far from Flash as they could in the confines of the Rolls. "Ask me that question when you're sober and I'll punch you on the nose." Mo had the haunted look of a man who has left his Kalashnikov at home and only come out with a Walther PPK. He always avoided a fight when he couldn't calculate the odds. He was beginning to wish he had joined Karen von Krupp and the others on the Pathé Tour. His sense of nostalgia was almost unbearable. Everywhere he looked in Nice he saw signs of his Surrey childhood in the Spanish-style architecture, the tall poplars and cypresses. He clutched at his roiling stomach. If he was going to get this confused, he would rather be on moving water.

"I'm not sure what we should trust least." Miss Brunner fastidiously sipped her G&T. "Chinese caution or American recklessness?"

That was the last straw for Jerry. With an angry jerk he sent the Phantom V onto the motorway and pushed down on the accelerator, weaving erratically between the abandoned Porsches and BMWs. Sometimes there was nothing left to say.

"I say, is that the sea?" Major Nye was excited.

"Are we there yet?" Flash opened bleared eyes.

9

The Madeleine they had given him as part of the Set Tea smelled strongly of almond flavoring. Cautiously he replaced it in his pocket. Jerry was miserable. There was no doubt about it. Memory was eroding. The last time he had been here, London had been enjoying the last of her quiet summer afternoons. Now, dark grey smoke snaked through the streets below. Who had called this meeting? Ever since it had been transported stone by stone to the top of Bon Marché, Derry and Tom's Famous Roof Garden was beginning to show signs of wear. Parts of the brick wall in the Tudor Garden had collapsed and there was a green slime glowing on the flamingo pond. Was this the end of the end?

"I forget when my memory started to go." Major Nye narrowed his grey-blue eyes and pinched the bridge of his nose before replacing his spectacles. He washed down his own horrible little cake with the remains of his Darjeeling. "I'm a stereotype, these days, of course, but I can't rely on that." He sniffed. "Where was it I met my wife? In some Salon de Thé or other? You?"

Sexton Blake pulled down the peak of his oddly-shaped stalking cap. His job in Paris was almost over. All main transferences and exchanges were complete. He longed for the smell of heather and deer spoor in the breaking dawn. "Tell me about it," he said. "Even my stereotype is a stereotype. How does it feel? I wish I could say." His voice echoed self-consciously around the tall walls of the roof garden. "Oh, mugger!" He clenched his teeth tighter around the stem of his Meerschaum.

"Even though you don't love him, you still can't stop wanting to please him." Awkwardly, Catherine hefted her Purdy.

Una gave her friend a sideways glance. "Yes," she said.

"What?"

"Yes?"

"You know what it's like, don't you?" Jerry's sister heard an uncomfortable note in her friend's voice. "Oh, good heavens!" Why was she developing such a strong dislike of intimacy?

Blake tapped her shoulder. He had decided to leave. Business in Marseilles. He was still on the trail of Fantômas, Monsieur Zenith and A.J.Raffles, their new collaborator. His face was full of gentle concern. "I'll check the dry cleaners first. For evening dress."

"Come on, Missy. Here's your chance." He pressed the little Glock into her delicate hand.

10.

M. Pardon met Jerry by the statue of La Grisette at the point where Canal St Martin went underground and was roofed over by a long strip of leafy park in which drunks congregated for their early games of *boules*, their ragged figures staggering amiably back and forth from the abandoned bandstand, their dormitory.

"How was Giverny?" Jerry sat down carefully on a bench from which he could watch the proceedings. "Pretty?"

"You know it? You know Monet?" M. Pardon stared gloomily at his slender fingers. "I had a manicure in Faubourg du Temple while I was waiting. I didn't expect them to paint my nails."

"But it's very patriotic," Jerry murmured. "*N'est-ce-pas?*"

M. Pardon glared at him. "And how was Damascus?" he asked spitefully.

Jerry removed a card from his wallet and handed it to his unhappy colleague. "Does that tell you anything?"

M. Pardon appeared to grow still smaller.

"Best steel in the world," said Jerry.

11.

Jean-Claude Malpurgo saw that he couldn't impress Miss Brunner with his wall-to-wall displays of *The Thriller, Union Jack, Je Sais Tout* and *Harry Dickson*. "Rarer than rubies," he told her, running his skeletal hand over the clear plastic. "A kind of black museum, I suppose. All the cultural evidence is here. Virtually irreplaceable, most of them."

Miss Brunner raised a small handkerchief to her nose. "But who on earth would possibly *want* to replace them?"

Malpurgo was irritated. "Perhaps you would rather see my roses?"

"What? Do you have a garden up here in Pigalle?"

"A garden? Mademoiselle, we have a farm. Of course, much of it is underground, these days. But happily we have excellent drainage."

"Where do you find the labor?"

"My dear lady, this is Paris! The catacombs, naturally." Gently, his fingers encircled her wrist. "Do you waltz?"

She laughed spontaneously. "Naturally."

12.

The next time Jerry met M. Pardon was in Nice in the season of 19--. They were both playing 'blacks' and doing well.

"My luck doesn't usually run this long," said M. Pardon when they had cashed in their chips and stood on the casino's terrace smoking their Upmanns. Jerry was unusually comfortable in his evening dress, but M. Pardon seemed particularly ill-at-ease. He gave the impression of a butler impersonating his master.

They walked through near-deserted streets towards the harbor.

Pardon, edgy, perhaps a little shifty, was now one of the wealthiest publishers in the South and had recently bought *The Teddy Bear* from the estate of the infamous Arsène Lupin. The steam yacht had been in dry dock for a year, but was now thoroughly refurbished. She sat at her moorings, even more elegant than when she had served the mysterious gentleman-thief. Jerry knew her intimately. She had been part of his father's estate.

Pardon paused by the gangplank. "I suppose you don't want to look over the old girl again? We're off to Casa in the morning."

Jerry declined. He didn't much care where the yacht was going or what happened to her. She was a symbol of too much that he despised. He had his eye on an aerial schooner being built in the Zeppelin yards near Le Havre as part of France's war reparations. The future, he felt, was in the air.

Una Persson, in a wealth of Liberty silk, saw them on the quayside and came ashore. She held out a cigarette in a jade holder to be lit. M.Pardon obliged. "You had all the luck tonight," she said. "Sadly, I was roundly beaten."

Jerry wondered why she was making a play for the Frenchman. He bowed and stepped to the edge. The water was surprisingly clear. "Full moon tonight, by the look of it."

Saying goodnight to the pair, he left them beside the yacht and strolled back to the casino's smoking lounge. It was late. Only Major Nye occupied the room. Stiffly at ease, he was seated in a high-backed armchair placed near the open French window. He raised his snifter of Hine into the light by way of greeting.

"Hope I'm not disturbing you, major." Jerry signed to a waiter to bring him another cognac.

"Not at all, old boy. I thought I'd take a break and lick my wounds before I turned in. Didn't lose too much. A couple of colonies and a dominion. Yourself?"

"Absolutely ace, thanks, major."

"Top hole, thanks for asking! But between ourselves the games these days are a little warm for my taste. Should have taken my leave in Kent with the memsahib, what?"

Jerry knew Major Nye well and didn't suspect suicide. He was too honorable to put his wife and daughters at risk. "Care for another?"

"Thanks all the same, old boy." He peered suddenly into the night. There were now a number of figures standing on the terrace in the thick, velvet night. He frowned. "Mrs. Persson! Mr. Collier! Tremendous night, what?"

"Tremendous." Mrs. P stepped into the light.

Jerry heard music faint against the surf.

"I think that's coming off *The Panda*," he said.

"Is that what the bugger's calling the old *Teddy Bear*, these days?" Before he could offer further offence Major Nye lost interest in the subject.

Mrs Persson winked.

Jerry began to cheer up at last.

13.

In the thick of the shadows of Notre-Dame, Jacques Collin checked his heat. Why was Paris growing so cold? Maybe it was time for another change?

14.

The Luxor restored to her former sensational magnificence, though dwarfed by the overhead railway, stood splendid amongst the dowdy Haussmannesque apartments of Boulevard Magenta. *Les Enfants du Paradis* was playing on the late night classics season. Jerry could remember a time when it was much easier to hear the Wurlitzer. The Paris Luxor was swaggering Egyptianate, with all the confidence of that Depression era that didn't know it was depressed.

Jerry stepped out of his Duisenberg, shedding his panda skin coat. What had possessed him to revisit that appalling period of his life? Hadn't he realized what high heels did for your calves? With a certain reluctance, he walked into the cinema foyer where his mum was now in charge of tickets. "Two for tonight, please, mum. I'll owe you, all right?"

"All right, if yer like. Bleedin' littel pikey."

"Not me, mum. I was never the Egyptian's baby."

"Nar, I remember." She cackled over his tickets. "Yore the kikey's."

Jerry advanced through the doors into a cooling present. It was a relief just to have a few minutes here. The albino was already there. Jerry returned his bow. A quick shadow told them Fantômas had met Judex. Most of the Vampires were already seated. Jerry drew a deep breath. Sometimes danger was oddly comforting. "What's the time?" He checked his wrists. "My watch has stopped." He turned up the collar of his black car coat. Catherine was late as usual.

Elegant in her long, downton dress, she hurried up to him giving her Vpad the once-over. "You were going dead!" She kissed him with restrained passion. "Seen mum? She all right? I was in New Orleans. You get better reception from the cemetery. Isn't it supposed to be dangerous? Like Stalingrad?"

"Only if you don't know what you're doing. I had to come to Paris. The movie's better here. There's a sober respect for the past."

She gave her spent pad a final flip. "Oh, fuck. Now we're sunk."

"Would you rather be dead?"

She thought that one over.

Jean-Michel Nicollet: *Portfolio*

Jean-Michel Nicollet, who contributed the cover for this year's Tales of the Shadowmen, *is a renowned illustrator whose art has graced many French book imprints over the years.*

Nicollet was born in Lyon in 1944; he studied at the local branch of the Ecole des Beaux-Arts, where he met Jacques Tardi, who later created the popular comics heroine Adèle Blanc-Sec.

Nicollet's professional debut dates back to 1970, when he began contributing regular illustrations to the men's magazine Lui. *After a stint in advertising, he quickly made his name as a cover artist, working for publisher Gallimard's popular paperback imprint Folio. In 1977, he was amongst the first artists to contribute to the legendary sci-fi & fantasy comics magazine* Métal Hurlant, *which published a number of his stories, including the lengthy historical drama* Polonius, *written by Picaret.*

Nicollet has since become one of France's premier cover artists, working for too many publishers to be listed here; he has gained a special reputation amongst popular literature fans for his illustrations of Robert E. Howard, Arthur Conan Doyle, Jean Ray and other favorites.

Nicollet has had several major exhibitions of his paintings in Paris and also teaches at the Emile Cohl art school in Lyon.

We have selected here ten of his best covers illustrating some of the most popular "shadowmen" (and "shadowwomen"!) of all.

H. Rider Haggard: She

H. Rider Haggard: Allan Quatermain

Jean Ray: Harry Dickson

Robert E. Howard: Solomon Kane

Robert E. Howard: Red Sonja

Robert E. Howard: Conan

William Hope Hodgson: Carnacki

Arthur Conan Doyle: Professor Challenger

Robert E. Howard: Agnes de Chastillon

Robert E. Howard: El Borak

"What is the nature of beauty?" is the question asked by Christofer Nigro in his latest tale, which gathers together a remarkable trio of man-monsters: the Werewolf of Paris, Felifax the Tiger-Man (from Paul Féval fils' eponymous novel published by Black Coat Press) and a new Hunchback of Notre-Dame. Sparks fly when the three meet and discuss...

Christofer Nigro: *The Privilege of Adonis*

Paris, 1931

Early evening in the Luxembourg Gardens was generally a placid time for watchman Augustin Laurent to conduct his rounds. It was also the perfect time to simultaneously walk his loyal hound Fico. As was his routine, he sent Fico running ahead to do his usual business while he searched for homeless stragglers trying to use the grounds as a "flop house." Seeing no one around this evening as he walked past the imposing Medici Fountain towards the clearing that led to the Pantheon, he called for Fico. Much to his surprise, his dog didn't respond. When this continued after several calls, Augustin became concerned enough to search for the animal by backtracking into the last area where he had seen the dog.

This led Augustin past a few of the gargoyle statues, which suddenly took on an ominous connotation he had never experienced before. Finally, he noticed a commotion just behind a large bush, including a distinct growling indicative of a canine. Shaking his head, Augustin came to the relieved conclusion that Fico had cornered a rodent and was in the process of bullying it. But as he strode behind the foliage, the watchman was witness to a stomach-churning scene of horror that he would take with him to his grave.

Laying before him was the corpse of loyal Fico, being devoured by what appeared to be a naked young man down on all fours. The man was ravenously biting clear through the dog's furry hide, tearing out chunks of flesh. Petrified, Augustin could only stare gaping as the young man suddenly looked up. He had long, unkempt dark hair; his entire lean body was covered in filth, and the lower half of his face was smeared with blood. Most unsettling of all, however, were his excessively long incisors, which twisted his otherwise human mouth into a vile grin.

Pulling himself out of his state of shock, Augustin shouted, *"Au secours!"* at the top of his lungs. He then turn and ran from the nightmarish scene.

However, much to his dismay, the beastly man howled and gave pursuit. He ran with surprising speed on all fours for a (seeming) human being, and began overtaking Augustin despite the latter running faster than he ever did before.

286

After coming to within half a meter of the panic-stricken watchman, the beastly man leaped and struck Augustin on the back with his hands, knocking him down. Standing atop the fallen watchman, the beastly man snarled a few inches from his face; his blood-covered, sharp incisors dripped reddish saliva all over him, while his hands, with their dirt-encrusted, elongated fingernails, held him by the throat.

"*S'il vous plait!*" the watchman pleaded to his uncomprehending attacker. "Why are you doing this? Please, for the love of God, don't kill me…!"

Before the bestial man could carry through his threat, a determined shout was heard coming from the direction of the Pantheon:

"He's here! The feral man from the reports!"

Sensing that the newcomers were more worth his attention than the man he was holding down, the "feral man" stood on his normal two legs and snarled in their direction, sniffing the air to detect their exact location. But he was startled when four men leapt from different bushes nearby. Working in practiced unison, two of them splashed a container of water on the feral man, further startling him; the other two rushed towards him with rod-like implements that resembled flashlamps. They touched their water-doused target with the rods. There was a loud zapping sound accompanied by small arcs of electricity. The bestial man snarled in agony as his body was overcome by spasms; his eyes rolled back into his head, and he involuntarily emptied his bodily wastes. Then, he fell to the ground in a heap of filthy flesh.

"We got 'im!" one of the men yelled. "Marcus and Alain will carry him off to the carriage. Jules, you have the 'talk' with this unfortunate watchman."

"*Très bien*," Jules responded, and walked over to the still-stunned Augustin.

"*Bonsoir,* Monsieur," Jules greeted the trembling watchman.

"*Merci,*" Augustin said with sincere gratitude. "You saved my life! Did you see what that madman did to my dog? Why wasn't I made aware of that… thing? It's my job to know these things! It's my job!"

"Calm down and listen carefully," Jules said, covering Augustin's mouth to quell his blathering. "You did *not* see any of this. Your dog was slaughtered by a drunken, half-starved tramp with a long red beard, fully clothed in a greasy trench coat. You chased him away, and you saw him following a trail that led out of the Gardens. Do you understand, Monsieur?"

"But…"

Jules painfully tightened his hold on Augustin's face before repeating his interrogative with much greater emphasis. "*Do you understand?*"

"*Oui,*" the watchman nervously replied while frantically nodding his head.

"Good man," Jules said as he released his grip. "*Bonne nuit.*"

The darkly dressed gentleman then departed, eager to catch up to his compatriots. As he caught up with them, he saw them hauling the bestial man's heavily chained form into the barricaded back seat area of a large vehicle.

"It's a good thing the local constabulary hasn't been alerted," Jules told Louis, their leader. "And luckily for us, only that stupid watchman bore witness to this, er, chap's actions before we tracked him down."

"For sure," Alain replied. "I bet that circus owner who paid us a lot of money to retrieve this man for his show will appreciate our discretion."

"Hmph," Jules huffed. "I suppose the large audience he expects to show up at the Notre-Dame festival will make our fee more worthwhile. Clearly, they plan to make a killing at thre show..."

A week later, crowds were gathering around the Ile de la Cité in anticipation of a most unusual festival. Due to the enormous success of their recreation of the nine-day Hindu festival of *Durga puja* in London, the Rama Circus Menagerie had decided to hold it in another major European city—Paris. The head of the circus, Rama Tamerlane—also known by some as Felifax, the Tiger-Man—was walking down the esplanade of Notre-Dame checking on all the latest details. At his side were his 16-year-old surrogate sister, Djina, and his trusted valet, Baber.

The trio was impressed with the duplication of the awe-inspiring Temple of Kali, the feared but revered Hindu goddess of chaos, with her protruding tongue, six arms holding severed human heads, and a girdle comprised of human skulls. Other prominently displayed statues were devoted to other examples of the Hindu pantheon, such as Durga and Chandi—both of whom were avatars of Kali. Rama Tamerlane was believed by the Hindu of Benares to be the actual flesh and blood progeny of the goddess, so his presence was of great symbolic interest to the crowds. The esplanade was also filled with fetching *bayadere* conducting their exotic dances on raised platforms, to the accompaniment of festive religious *arias* sung in their native Bengali.

"Everything looks splendid, brother," was Djina's opinion.

"Agreed," said Rama. "I just wish we didn't have to wear these restrictive so-called 'civilized' garments."

"Well, you walking about in nothing but your *lamba*, and me in nothing but my animal skins, wouldn't do for the people of Paris," Djina reminded him.

Baber chuckled. "I suppose I'm fortunate for having been raised in Benares, so I'm used to wearing full-bodied attire."

"Fortunate indeed," Rama replied, followed by an exasperated sigh. "Well, now that I'm an international figure of note, I must learn to adapt to this new world outside the jungles of India that would embrace me. My goal of peace and diplomacy demands such compromise."

"As much as learning other languages and an appreciation for strange cuisines, I would say," Djina added with a smile.

The three shared a laugh together, unaware that a misshapen figure high atop the Notre-Dame bell tower stared down at them from the great height... with his glare focusing in particular upon the lovely Djina.

Later that evening, the day before the European-based Freon Side Show was to perform alongside the Rama Circus Menagerie, ringmaster Roland Frollo walked by the cages holding his notorious and profitable subjects to insure their readiness and well-being. He curtly asked his main assistant, a portly midget named Thibaut, if all was well.

"*Oui*, Monsieur Frollo," the servant nervously confirmed. "All is well in hand, the freaks are well aware of what is expected of them tomorrow."

"Very good," Frollo said as he walked around with his walking cane held out in an intimidating manner. "And how about our newest exhibit, the feral man? It cost me quite a lot to have him captured, and I expect him to be up to par."

"He's been consuming every live chicken or piglet we've fed him with all expected vigor, Monsieur. Perhaps you would like to see for yourself?"

Frollo followed his diminutive assistant through an isolated enclosure. All was quiet within, so the cruel ringmaster struck the bars of the cage with his cane. From under a pile of hay, designed to serve as a makeshift bed, the feral man jumped up, snarling and frothing at the mouth, his large incisors fearsomely displayed. He was now dressed in simple clothing out of deference to the public's sensibilities, but was otherwise as disheveled and uncivilized as ever. Stains of dried animal blood were smeared on the floor, as well as on his mouth and tattered clothing. Animal bones and chicken feathers lay all over the cage.

Though Frollo and his assistant didn't know it, they had captured Bertrand Calliet, the infamous "Werewolf of Paris," who had recently been revived under circumstances as yet unknown following a fatal shooting years earlier by the criminal scientist Doctor Cornelius Kramm.[7] Trapped in a psychotic state with the predatory animal persona that had shared space with his psyche now fully in control, Calliet was mostly in human form, but lacking any semblance of his former humanity. Unbeknownst to his captor, this was a situation destined to grow much worse the following night, as it would be a full Moon.

Frollo and Thibaut jumped back in unison as Calliet leapt against the bars, foam spewing from his mouth, howling in rage at the two of them. Thibaut screeched in terror, while Frollo moved forward and struck his captive's hand with the full force of his hardwood cane. Calliet yelped in pain, and drew away from the bars.

"Back, you animal!" Frollo demanded. "Remember who is the master here, and who is responsible for feeding and cleaning up after you! If not for me, you would still be running around the city hunting for every scrap you could find, and the gendarmes would probably have shot you like the filthy beast you are!"

Calliet snarled back without the slightest sign of comprehension, let alone gratitude.

---

[7] See "The Beast Within" in *The Shadow of Judex*, ISBN 9781612271781.

"Lucky for us, this horrid man will garner big money from the Parisian rubes, eh, Monsieur?" said Thibaut.

"Indeed," Frollo concurred. "My lineage has a history with adopting and caring for freakish creatures like this, including a man, a few centuries back, who was actually a pastor of Notre-Dame itself. Like my father before me, I have simply chosen to profit from that tradition, rather than be burdened by it. Now, see to it that tomorrow morning he is drugged and his cage thoroughly cleaned before we present him to the paying public."

The following day, the festival went quite well, and, as the evening came about, Rama and his entourage were pleased.

"This has been wonderful, brother," an enthused Djina proclaimed. "The Parisian people seem to be drawn to what our culture has to offer as much as the people of London."

"But, of course," Baber replied. "When what we have to offer them is scantily-clad girls dancing with their hips and cans undulating in such a manner, does this surprise you?"

"Baber!" Rama admonished while Djina giggled. "Let us show a modicum of respect to the people of this country who allowed us to enter their city and make so much money to benefit the needy in our native land. Do not forget that we are their guests."

"I know," Baber grumbled. "Just speaking my mind, sir. But despite the rules of decorum we must recognize here, why do we have to share our space with that other circus outfit?"

"Monsieur Frollo has generously agreed to share a fraction of his show's proceeds in exchange for the space," replied Rama. "Moreover, I believe it's a show of good faith that will attract more people if something from their own culture appears alongside ours."

"That, I understand," Baber said. "But I not only find that Frollo a most unpleasant character, but what his 'culture' passes off for entertainment leaves much to be desired. These 'side shows' of theirs exploit very unfortunate people for pure profiteering."

"I sympathize with your concerns," Rama noted. "But there may be two sides to that issue, my friend. Where else, in a culture so enamored with the concept of beauty, could these unfortunate individuals find gainful employment?"

"Granted," Baber replied. "But I believe Frollo is a poor example of such an employer. He treats these ill-fated people as mere property, with less consideration than we give to the sacred animals in our native temples…"

"I think you men need to stifle that debate for now," Djina said with her index finger over her pursed lips. "Because Monsieur Frollo is now moving his caravan in front of the Cathedral."

Shortly before dusk, Frollo had his show ready for the remaining crowd that still stood in front of Notre-Dame. Many people had returned home, but enough remained to make a decent profit.

"Behold, good citizens of Paris!" Frollo shouted, with a whip held dramatically in one hand, while his characteristic walking cane was used as a pointer for the other. "Before you in these cages are oddities of the human species who, to all appearances, may not seem quite human to the eyes of normal, civilized folks like ourselves! Such oddities are in my care, and I present them to you today for the gratification of your curiosity! May the fragile of mind and the meek of spirit not view what lies before you! But to those of you bold and curious enough to view some of God's worst mistakes, come forward with a meager *sou* in hand, for that will be sufficient to purchase a full viewing of every amazing and utterly revolting example of inhumanity in my caravan!"

An immaculately dressed Thibaut yelled, "Whoo whoo!" as further incitement.

The look on the countenances of Rama and his two companions were not of amusement or excitement, but rather sorrow. Yet, they were determined to honor their contract with the city, while being thankful that the Freon Side Show was the last activity of the evening.

After all the exhibits were described in explicit detail by Frollo, he finally reached his most recent acquisition, which he held for the grand finale of his show: the "Feral Man." Bertrand Calliet sat up in his cage as the attention of the public was now focused on him. His hunger and animalistic rage were barely held in check by the sedation he had been given an hour before the show.

"Here you have the ultimate expression of inhumanity, gentle folks!" Frollo flamboyantly declared. "A specimen of what was once a human being now reduced to only animal instincts! An example of what each of us would be like if we were forced to live a wild existence outside the boundaries of civilization! All behold: the Feral Man!"

The ringmaster banged on the metal bars several times with his cane, causing Calliet to stir and snarl before the awestruck crowd. Frollo then ordered Thibaut to fetch a chicken from their supply cart.

"Now, ladies and gentlemen, experience considerable revulsion as the 'Feral Man' feeds!" Frollo continued, with a rehearsed gesture of his cane.

Thibaut hurriedly moved forward and pushed the cackling chicken between the bars. As the hen ran about the enclosed space, Calliet's hunger caused him to push past the sedatives. He pounced upon the bird and began tearing it to shreds with his extended teeth. Blood and organs spattered about as the bestial man gluttonously feasted.

The crowd turned away with groans of disgust, some of them dry heaving, while others turned back; a few, however, began clapping and encouraging Calliet's savage behavior. Frollo bore a pleased expression on his visage, while

Rama and his companions shook their heads and turned around, refusing to be associated with this despicable tableau.

"Rama, this is abominable," Djina said.

"Did I not tell you this?" Baber added.

"I know, and I concede your point," Rama replied. "But this is the final show of a very successful evening, and the last of Frollo's exhibits. Let's allow it to end, and then after the show, we will approach him and let our disapproval be known."

However, several minutes later, the Moon began to rise—a full Moon—and it promptly made its eldritch effects known. Just as Frollo was about to bring his exhibition to a close, Calliet suddenly began howling louder than ever. The audience looked on with interest as the bestial man thrashed about in his cage, then fell on his back with his muscles contorting as if he were undergoing an epileptic fit.

"What's going on, Frollo?" one of the men in the audience asked. "Did you feed him a bad chicken, or something?"

"Rama, what is this?" Djina asked her brother with concern.

"I don't know, but I plan to find out, little sister," he answered.

Just then, to the abject horror of everyone present, the rays of the Moon took their full effect and Calliet began metamorphosing before their eyes. His muscles and skeletal structure reshaped themselves with a sickening cracking sound; his mouth grew into a slavering muzzle with rows of razor-sharp teeth sprouting out of his gums; his elongated fingernails became full talons; his ears sprouted into long, pointed organs; strands of reddish-brown fur sprang from the pores of his skin until he was covered in a fine coat… In less than a minute, Calliet stood up on lupine-jointed legs in full lycanthropic form. Howling like the savage beast he now was, the Werewolf of Paris was again unleashed upon the City of Lights!

As the crowd began to panic and disperse, the werewolf threw his massive and incredibly strong form against the door of the cage; it buckled, and the bars bent.

"Monsieur Frollo, do something!" Thibaut yelled. "That beast is going to get out!"

With a second, even more powerful, thrust, the door of the cage broke off its hinges and fell onto the street. The top part of it hit Thibaut on the shoulder, knocking him down. The werewolf then jumped out and lifted the screaming little man in his massive maw, twisting and turning his powerful neck and jaw muscles back and forth maniacally. He then released the midget, and Thibaut's body splattered on the ground, his belly ripped open and his bowels spilling out.

"God preserve me," Frollo said to himself.

Howling with fury, the werewolf faced the fleeing audience as three gendarmes rushed towards him. The first struck the lycanthrope with his billy club, which annoyed the creature more than anything else. The werewolf struck back

292

with a swing of his talons, eviscerating the officer on the spot. The other two pulled their firearms and shot at the beast. He bellowed in pain as the bullets found their mark, but mere lead projectiles were not sufficient to kill him. As the werewolf prepared to leap upon the two remaining officers, their lives were saved when, suddenly, Rama plunged into the creature with his full might. The force knocked the werewolf off his feet, and Rama used the creature's body as a springboard to effect a somersault into a fighting stance.

"Clear out the remaining crowd!" Rama shouted to the officers. "Baber, you help them! Let me handle this beast!"

A mere second later, the werewolf was back on his feet, ready to face the mighty Rama again. Rushing forward, he snapped at the jungle lord, whose reflexes proved up to the legend as he deftly evaded the attack. The Indian then struck the beast in the side of his muzzle, then followed it by a powerful haymaker to the sternum. Despite yowling in pain, the werewolf withstood these attacks, and swatted Rama back with incredible force. That single blow sent the Indian flying several yards through the air. His flight was ended by a collision with one of the nearby cages, and he lay upon the ground, stunned.

Djina knew she should flee as quickly as she could, but she found herself unable to leave the vicinity while her beloved brother was risking his life to save those of many others. While courageously thinking of a way to help, she failed to take into account another player who was determined to take advantage of the distraction caused by this melee.

The figure watching from atop the Cathedral had chosen this point to make his way down from the bell tower. Despite his misshapen form, the agility and climbing prowess he displayed was impressive. Within minutes, he had climbed down the many spires and statues making up the huge church to reach a dangling rope he knew was hanging near a spire, just a few meters above the street. Grasping the rope, the figure swung down with amazing speed and grabbed the contemplating Djina, taking her by surprise. She struggled valiantly but to no avail in the powerful grip of this interloper. He quickly carried her up to the top of the bell tower in which he resided.

Only Baber saw this, and while he shouted, he was too late to be of assistance.

Meanwhile, Rama came to his senses and jumped back to his feet as the werewolf approached him, his slavering maw determined to rip his attacker to shreds. The Indian knew at once that he needed to unleash his own formidable animal side to meet this creature on his own level. Tearing his white shirt from his body with a single move, he displayed the imposing physique beneath his bronzed skin. Summoning his full rapport with the spirit of the beast while praying to Kali for assistance, a series of brownish stripes appeared on his back and torso; he eyes took on a greenish hue with slit-like feline pupils; and his own incisors elongated. Snarling like a big cat with whom he was now in full spiritual connection, Rama Tamerlane truly became Felifax, the Tiger-Man.

Both opposing individuals growled with animal fury and charged each other. Ducking under another swipe of the werewolf's talons with his now increased speed, Felifax wrapped his powerful arms around the beast's waist and hurled him over his back. The lycanthrope crashed into the metal bars of one of the cages, terrifying the three-eyed man constrained within. Undaunted, the werewolf charged again, this time finding that Felifax had drawn his ritual blade from a sheath on his belt. He stabbed the werewolf in the chest as the beast pounced, and blood spurted out as the creature howled in pain.

The lycanthrope then struck Felifax, who went sprawling on the ground. The knife wound began closing itself before the jungle lord's eyes; a blade that wasn't composed of silver was not going to be able to deal a fatal blow to such an entity!

Realizing this due to his studies, Baber rushed to one of the cages holding two sacred tigers. Knowing they would instinctively rush to aid their master, the former animal-tamer opened their cages, hoping the tigers would prove sufficient aid for Felifax while he acquired a certain item from one of the temple reconstructions. Thankfully, he kept track of everything that was brought with them from India.

True to Baber's hopes, the twin tigers roared fiercely as they rushed towards the werewolf in defense of Felifax. The first one jumped an incredible distance, smashing into the werewolf with her full 300-pound weight. The lycanthrope was knocked off of his feet, and he and his great feline adversary rolled upon the ground, tearing into each other with their respective claws. Managing to get back onto his bipedal stance, the werewolf lifted the tiger by her haunches and tossed her several yards away.

But no sooner had he done this than the second tiger leapt on his back, knocking the werewolf down with his great weight and sinking his razor-sharp teeth into the beast's shoulders. The lycanthrope yelped in agony as he sought to extricate himself from his second feline attacker's hold.

Recovering thanks to the distraction of his sacred tiger brethren, Felifax jumped to his feet and rushed to aid the big cats. As the second tiger and the werewolf tore at each other with great ferocity, Felifax grabbed a one meter long steel chain from a nearby cage and wrapped it around the lycanthrope's throat from behind, trying to crush the creature's trachea. With all his incredible might, Felifax dragged the struggling werewolf several meters across the ground up to a huge stone statue of Kali the Black. He stood behind the statue with his foot braced against it for support, while entrapping the werewolf by the chain around his throat. The beast writhed with tremendous resistance, but Felifax pulled the chain harder, determined to do sufficient damage to the *loup-garou's* windpipe and larynx to at least make him lose consciousness.

Both tigers ran in front of the struggling werewolf, clawing and tearing at the beast's limbs to help prevent him from breaking Felifax's strangulation grip. Suddenly, after a particularly strong pull, Felifax felt the familiar rattling sensation that made it clear the creature's windpipe had broken. Blood dribbled from the beast's gullet as he began to go limp, yet instantly started to heal. This seeming impasse came to an end when Felifax saw Baber running towards him with a shiny object in his arms.

"Sir, this temple candelabra is pure *silver!*" his aide-de-camp said. "That substance is anathema to supernatural creatures like this!"

"Then let him have it!" Felifax ordered while maintaining his grip on the chain.

Complying with the order, Baber struck the beast on the skull several times, while each tiger held down one of the lycanthrope's limbs. After several such blows, the makeshift silver bludgeon had smashed open the werewolf's skull, and the beast suddenly reverted to the fallen human form of Bertrand Calliet, his life literally seeping out of him.

Felifax released the chain and, with a gentle order, escorted both tigers back to their cage. He made sure to embrace each of them affectionately before re-securing the lock.

Rama then approached Baber and thanked him, too. It was then that his assistant told him that another matter of great urgency was afoot.

"Sir, Miss Djina was captured by some hulking brute who swung on a rope from the Cathedral," he explained. "He then carried her up to what appeared to be the bell tower!"

"Then I must get up there immediately!" the jungle hero said.

It was then, however, that his intention was halted when a whip entwined around his throat from behind. Turning to see the cause, Baber noticed it was none other than the abhorrent ringmaster, Frollo.

"After what you just cost me, do you truly think I'd let you get away with it, you subhuman freak?" Frollo spat. "Now let's see how well *you* endure strangulation…"

As the irate Rama struggled to extricate himself from the whip, Baber unsheathed his own dagger and cut the entangling weapon, thus freeing his boss and friend.

"Sir, go and aid Miss Djina," Baber requested. "Leave this one to me!"

"May the Trimurti forever bless you," Rama told his friend as he ran towards the Cathedral and began climbing its many spires leading up to the bell tower.

Baber then turned to face the scowling Roland Frollo.

"You foolish ass!" Frollo yelled. He threw the remains of his broken whip aside and raised his walking cane, depressing a hidden switch that extended a long, sharpened blade. "Now I'll gut you like the lowly gutter fish you truly are!"

"By all means, please try," Baber goaded with an inviting finger gesture as he held his dagger at the ready.

Raising his cane blade, Frollo attacked first, slashing at Baber several times. The latter proved to have keen reflexes, however, and evaded most of the swipes. But one of them slashed his chest, sending droplets of blood pouring out of the laceration. Frollo laughed malevolently at the sight. Baber suppressed the pain and taunted his opponent anew with another finger gesture.

Overconfidently attacking again, the ringmaster fell for a forward movement by Baber that proved to be a feint. The former animal-tamer then moved in and slashed the back of Frollo's wrist, causing him to drop his cane.

Grasping his wound, Frollo looked up just in time to see Baber raise his clenched fist. The ringmaster then found himself laying on the ground with a broken jaw and two dislodged teeth after being struck by Baber's cuff.

"No more nonsense from you now," he said to his half-conscious foe.

A little earlier, just after Djina was brought to the bell tower, she was gently set down by her abductor. She looked up and forced herself not to shout in terror at the sight of the man who now stood before her.

His build reminded her of a tank from the Great War, with a disproportionately large frame compared to his lower contours; his legs being bulky but short compared to his long, massive arms. Most prominent among his features was a bony hump that protruded from his back, and looked as heavy as the rest of his torso alone. The man's facial features were terribly distorted, with long, straggly brown hair hanging from his skull; a mouthful of yellowed, crooked teeth adorning his twisted jawbone completed the grotesque package. He was dressed in a simple, old-fashioned, brown monk-like garment with matching sandals that all appeared specially tailored to fit his misconstrued form.

"Do not be afraid, *s'il vous plait*," the disfigured man said in a hoarse voice. "I mean you no harm."

Again forcing herself not to turn away in disgust, Djina pooled her natural courage and confronted her unwanted host. "Kidnapping me in such a fashion is not a good way to show a benign intent, Monsieur...?"

"You may call me Quasimodo," the hunchbacked man replied.

"But you can't be... *him*. An author named Victor Hugo wrote a book about such an entity, and though that... person was described in a way that resembles you, the story took place centuries ago."

"*Oui*," Quasimodo agreed. "But many do not know that Hugo's book was based on a factual account he uncovered, one dealing with a relative of mine from the 15th century. I come from a family that seems to produce the deformity I am cursed with every few hundred births, which is why I took the name and even the lonely vocation of my ancestor. After all, that has long been a tradition in this city for the freakish products of my clan!" The statement was followed by a hacking laugh that reviled Djina.

"Is there a reason why so many freakish mutations seem to appear in this city?"

"Most likely, and possibly connected to the alchemy and other such dark arts performed here to a heavy degree in the past, including from the priest who adopted my namesake ancestor. But that is not important!" The Hunchback's tone now became menacing as he moved closer to the girl. "What is important is the companionship I desire. That is why you are here."

"So it's your intention to force me to be your companion?"

"*Oui*, pretty *mademoiselle*, because for one such as me, there is no other way. Do you perceive a beautiful girl like yourself willingly choosing to give her love and affection to *me*?"

"So this justifies kidnapping and enforced slavery?" came a third voice from behind, this one strong and masculine.

The Hunchback turned to see Rama climbing through the window leading into the bell tower.

"How did you get up here?" Quasimodo queried incredulously.

"The same way you did, actually," the jungle lord replied.

"Impossible!" the Hunchback insisted.

"Not for me," Rama said. "Now it's time for you to answer for daring to abduct my sister to serve your vile desires!"

"You dare judge me!" Quasimodo stammered. "You who were clearly gifted with what the poets refer to as 'The Privilege of Adonis'? It's quite easy for one as lucky as you to cast stones on the actions of one like me. You cannot fathom what it's like to look like a monster and be denied all the beautiful things that you doubtless take for granted!"

"So you rationalize becoming a monster on the inside to match the outer shell?" Rama questioned. "By doing that, you accomplish nothing save appearing to justify the hatred and fear others have shown towards you. That also sets a bad precedent for those sharing your affliction, who will appear in years to come. Instead of inspiring them to prove the world wrong about them, you instead take actions that will incorrectly make them believe they have no recourse but to choose the dark path."

"Pfah!" the Hunchback scoffed. "The values of this society do not allow acceptance for those who deviate from the prevailing notions of beauty and normalcy. I was destined to be a monster the moment I was born, because the world will allow me to be nothing else. It's easy for the beauteous to preach moral platitudes to the hideous! But those naïve banalities collapse once we realize that we can never have what the world offers to those like you."

"So because of your misfortune, you justify revenge and hatred against the world?" Djina asked. "You believe you can't win love, so you feel the world should allow you to just take what you want? It's not your appearance that makes you truly horrible, Quasimodo, but the path you have chosen to deal with it."

"Don't condescend to me with your pious lectures!" the Hunchback decreed as he backhanded the girl on the side of her face.

Rama then roared in anger, his skin, eyes, and teeth taking on the bestial characteristics of the mighty Felifax. He effortlessly jumped off the five meter windowsill to land in the middle of the chamber, directly facing the Hunchback.

Djina looked up while wiping a stream of blood from her mouth, and said, "Now you have *really* gone and done it, Quasimodo."

Shouting in rage and defiance, the Hunchback raised his powerful arms and huge clenched fists as he ran towards his snarling opponent. Quasimodo took a swing at Felifax, only to have the Tiger-Man stop his fist with a raised palm. The jungle lord then dealt a blow to the Hunchback's chin, sending him reeling, though not quite knocking him off his feet. Impressed by Quasimodo's resilience, but determined to bring him down, Felifax rushed forward and delivered a powerful blow to the Hunchback's sternum. Releasing a strong exhalation of pain, the deformed man slid back several meters, banging up against a wall.

Roaring again, Felifax resolved to enact the *coup de grace* to this battle. He lunged towards his cornered foe. Much to his surprise, Quasimodo displayed incongruous flexibility, crouching down on one leg and pushing out with his other stubby limb, striking the Tiger-Man in his solar plexus. The Indian rolled on the floor, the wind unexpectedly knocked out of him due to the savage blow to his diaphragm.

Moving towards his fallen foe, Quasimodo effortlessly picked him up over his head and began the short walk over to the nearest window, intending to send Felifax on a multi-story fall to his death. This was a manner in which the original Quasimodo was fond of finishing off opponents, an M.O. the current iteration has mirrored.

However, the Hunchback had severely underestimated Felifax's recovery time, and the Tiger-Man smashed both of his ears with the palms of his hands. Despite lacking much of his hearing due to his frequent proximity to the enormous ringing bells of Notre-Dame, the sudden influx of wind served to completely pop Quasimodo's eardrums. Shouting in agony, he put his hands to his ears and enabled Felifax to flip back onto his feet. Roaring like a wild animal, his mouth slavering with froth, the jungle lord commenced payback by releasing a mighty blow to the Hunchback's own diaphragm.

Crouching over in further pain as his respiratory apparatus was paralyzed, Quasimodo was then subjected to a third blow from Felifax, this one directly on the bridge of his twisted nose. The cartilage shattered, and the deformed man found himself blinded by the stinging saltiness of his own blood being spattered in his eyes. Now unable to defend himself, the current Hunchback of Notre-Dame fell before a fourth and final haymaker to the chin by the enraged Felifax.

When it was clear his adversary wasn't going to get up again, the Tiger-Man allowed himself to calm sufficiently so that his human side fully regained control, and his animalistic features vanished. It was at this point that Djina ran over to see to his welfare.

"Well done, brother," she said. "Are you all right?"

"That's actually my question for you," he responded as he embraced his little sister. "You took quite a swat to the face by that brute. Let me see, is anything broken?"

"I've had worse, no need to fuss over me. My jaw isn't broken, and all my teeth seem intact. He just split my lip. It seems as awful as Quasimodo is, he restrained himself when striking me. Maybe some of what we both said to him reached him after all? We both know that everyone has the potential for good, even one as bitter and emotionally scarred as him."

Rama looked at the still unconscious form of the Hunchback, which was sprawled in a semi-sitting position against one of the walls.

"Perhaps, Djina. But only time will tell."

With their arms around each other, the two siblings departed the famed Notre-Dame Cathedral, as Rama regaled his sister with the story of how he survived his battle with the Werewolf of Paris just over an hour ago.

Tales of the Shadowmen *has, in the past, presented a few two-parters, as well as Brian Stableford's serialized novel,* Empire of the Necromancers. *John Peel, a regular contributor to* Tales of the Shadowmen *and* Doctor Who *writer extraordinaire, has crafted a unique serial that is a direct sequel to Jules Verne's ground-breaking (pardon the pun!)* Journey to the Center of the Earth. *We begin, of course, with the cast of the original novel, but many familiar faces will soon accompany us on a...*

John Peel: *Return to the Center of the Earth*
(Part One)

Germany, then Iceland, 1872

I. A Promise Broken

All men when they marry make promises to their wives that they fully intend at the time to keep. Yet, through no fault of their own, sometimes they are compelled to break one or more of those promises. To some men, of course, the abrogation of their word is a small matter and barely concerns them. To others, who truly love their wives and their own honesty, it is a momentous event that haunts their waking moments and disturbs even their sleep. I—whether through good fortune or evil—am of the latter. I had been married to my beloved Gretchen for a mere few years when I was forced to break the one promise she truly wished me to keep.

It was not a promise most men would have ever have had to consider making, but it was the only desire of her heart. Loving her as I did, I had little hesitation in making it. I vowed to her that I would not go away from her again adventuring—more specifically, that I would never again venture beneath the crust of our world. Gretchen extracted this promise from me because I had once engaged in such a journey.

This journey beneath the surface of our planet had been intended by my uncle, Professor Lidenbrock, as an attempt to penetrate to the center of our planet. We had not actually succeeded in this aim, but we had managed to venture to great depths, far below those that any human being had ever expected to accomplish, and we had returned to the surface again through the agency of an erupting volcano. We had then discovered that news of our quest had circumnavigated the globe with greater speed than we had managed to penetrate it, and we were famous by the time we arrived back home in Hamburg. The source of that news had proven to be my uncle's faithful, loose-tongued maid, Martha.

The journey—and my subsequent account of our explorations—had served to make us famous. This had barely impacted my uncle, who had immediately set to work examining and cataloguing the specimens we had managed to bring with us on our return to civilization. He was used to shutting out the world from his life and considerations, so he simply ignored what he did not wish to acknowledge and got on with his research.

For me, however, the results were more immediate and satisfying. I was given a teaching post at the University, and my salary allowed me to wed my beloved Gretchen—but not until after, as I have mentioned, she compelled me to promise not to go adventuring again. If truth be told, it was not a promise I had any qualms in making. I am by nature a rather quiet and private person, and my wife and my teaching position fulfilled all of my worldly desires. I should indeed have been more than happy if I could be certain that my footsteps from that point on would be limited to the world above the ground.

This was not, however, to be.

The relative calm did last for a few years. Gretchen and I welcomed a small daughter to share our happiness. Both my wife and Martha doted on the youngster—and I myself was far from innocent in that respect. To my uncle, a baby was merely another distraction to be shut out from his awareness as best as possible. Should my daughter cry, or laugh or burble in his presence he would simply snort and pass by as quickly as possible. Gretchen insisted that she could detect a twinkle in his eye as he did so, but I cannot myself confirm her gentle belief. Despite these distractions, my uncle was happy enough in his work.

I was aiding him in the analysis of one of his igneous specimens one day when there came a nervous rap at his laboratory door. I glanced at the door in puzzlement, but my uncle ignored the sound. He had issued strict orders that he was never to be disturbed whilst working in his laboratory under any circumstances. Martha, taken aback, had asked:

"But what if the house were on fire?"

"What of it?" he rejoined. "Let it burn!"

No amount of pleading had made him agree to change his order under any circumstance. So I was astonished to hear the rapping at the door. My uncle pretended not to hear anything—and, at least at the first, he may not have heard anything. When he concentrates on his work, he can close out the world at large.

Even he could not ignore the second knock. This was no longer nervous and diffident but strong, forceful and virile. "The Devil take it!" my uncle roared. "Go away!"

Instead of wisely obeying this imperious command, the person knocking threw open the door and strode into the room, Martha hovering nervously behind him. I glanced up, wondering who would be foolish enough to disobey Professor Lidenbrock in his own house and saw that the intruder was a soldier—a Captain, to be precise. He wore his full military regalia and if he were on parade before the Kaiser himself. There was not a speck of dust on his clothing, not a place on the metallic trim that didn't gleam, and his leather boots were polished to such a degree that they almost glittered even in the feeble light from the oil lamps.

None of this, of course, affected my uncle in any way. "Are you deaf?" he howled. "I told you to leave. Kindly do so—immediately!"

The Captain ignored his command. His heels clicked together formally and he stared at my irate relative without any visible emotion. "Professor Lidenbrock?" he asked, though he clearly already knew the answer. "I am Captain Manfred Gottfried von Mendeldorf und von Horst. I would ask that you accompany me, please."

"And I would ask that you go to the Devil!" my uncle snapped. "Without me."

"I am afraid that I must insist," the Captain said, not at all bothered by his reception. "Your presence has been requested by An Important Personage." I swear, you could hear the stress he placed on this quasi-title.

"Then have that Important Personage accompany you to the infernal regions," my uncle replied. He tried to turn back to his work, but the Captain took several steps across the room and gripped the Professor by the elbow. "What are you doing?" uncle demanded, though the answer was obvious. Without any apparent strain on his part, Von Horst was drawing the man of learning toward the door. "Let go of me at once!" the Professor cried. "I shall report you to your superior!"

"You may do so immediately," the soldier answered, unconcerned. "He awaits you in your dining room."

"My dining room?" This took my uncle by surprise. "Who on Earth would call on me uninvited?" I followed along as he was dragged through the house to discover the answer to his annoyed question.

"I couldn't help it, sir," Martha said, wringing her hands together as she trotted beside me. "They insisted on seeing the Herr Professor immediately. "There was nothing I could do about it."

"I am sure you did your best," I replied, knowing that would indeed have been true. But what could a maid avail against such brutes as this one?

There was a second soldier outside the door to the dining room and—I was later to learn—a small company of them stationed about our pleasant little domicile on Konigstrasse. The reason for such an escort became obvious when we entered the dining room—my uncle still being dragged, and Martha and myself of our own volition. Gretchen was there already, seated calmly and conversing with the man who had so imperiously summoned my uncle without due regard for the possible consequences.

Though I had never seen him before, I recognized him immediately. Accurate sketches of his face were in the pages of every newspaper in the country almost daily. The spreading moustache, the balding hair, the thick build, the elegant clothing—it was Chancellor Otto von Bismarck himself, and here, in our small house!

His eyes went at once to my uncle, and he stood, offering his hand. "Herr Professor Lidenbrock," he said. "I am most pleased to greet you."

"I'd be most pleased if you'd leave, now," my uncle snapped. "I have urgent work to finish." He glared at the Captain, who had finally released his arm. "And take your trained monkey with you!"

"Keep a civil tongue in your head!" the Captain snapped. "Do you not know who you are addressing?"

"Of course I know who I'm addressing," the Professor snapped. "Do you take me for an imbecile? It is Minister President von Bismarck."

"*Chancellor* von Bismarck," his eminence corrected. "As of last year."

"I cannot keep up with the vagaries of politics," my uncle replied. "It's all the same to me. Either way, would the *Chancellor* kindly leave me to my work?"

"My dear Professor," the Chancellor said apologetically, "I fully understand your desire to continue with such important work as you must perform –"

"Good," replied my uncle. "Then leave me to it."

"I am afraid that this I cannot do," Bismarck added in a kindly tone. "It is a matter of grave importance in this political world of ours that you hear me out."

"Politics?" the man of science snapped. "What have I to do with politics? I am a man of learning. I have important work to do. I am no mere politician." It did not seem to have occurred to him that he was insulting the most powerful man in Germany. Once started, however, my uncle resembled a volcanic eruption—one must endure the sound and fury and wait until it abates, and hope that no one is harmed in the meanwhile.

But Bismarck was used to dealing with angry politicians and temperamental monarchs; an annoyed scientist barely gave him pause. "Professor Lidenbrock, I would not be here bothering you if this were not a matter vital to the interests of your country."

"My country? Bah! I am a man of science, and therefore a citizen of the world."

"But, surely, not merely of the *surface* of this world?" Bismarck asked gently.

"What do you mean?" My uncle's interest had been captured, finally, and I could see that the volcano was starting to pass into a dormant phase.

"I mean that I know of your wonderful explorations, my dear Professor," the statesman continued. "Your journey to the center of our world has brought great glory upon Germany—and yourself."

"My journey had nothing to do with glory, either for myself or for this country," my uncle denied. "Which, incidentally, did not even exist when I began my journey."

"But it exists now, and you are a part of it." Bismarck smiled. "And, I believe, a very *important* part of it. I ask you to undertake a mission for the sake of this country—*your* country, now."

"A mission?" Uncle waved an airy hand. "I am not a donkey, to be sent on a journey at the whim of some master."

"It would involve returning to the world beneath our feet," Bismarck pressed on. "A world that only you and your nephew have ever experienced—so far."

"In that you are quite mistaken," my uncle replied. "We also had with us our invaluable guide—Hans Bjelke, an Icelandic citizen and not a *German*. And we followed the trail blazed by my esteemed colleague Arne Saknussemm, another Icelander."

"But it was *your* will and your determination that drove the expedition," the Chancellor insisted. "And it was thus a *German* expedition—that is the important thing."

"It does not matter," my uncle insisted. "Had someone else undertaken the journey, the results as far as science is concerned would have been the same."

"As far as science is concerned, perhaps," agreed Bismarck. "But it would not have been the same for *you*, would it? When you realized that the trip was possible, you rushed to ensure that it was *you* who made it. Being the first to set foot in such *terra incognito* mattered to you—and, I suspect, it still does."

Again, my uncle waved a dismissive hand." I have made the journey; I see no reason to repeat the experiment. Let others follow where Lidenbrock has led."

"But no other person could lead a return to the center of our world other than you with any true hope of success," Bismarck replied. "And this time you would be supplied with more resources—anything you might wish. You would have *my* backing for this undertaking, and that is not without importance in this country of ours."

"But I have already told you that I have no interest in returning where I have already been," the man of science explained, as if dealing with a dunce. "My work is now concentrated on studying what I have already discovered. I can see no point in further exploration."

"Can you not?" Bismarck shrugged his shoulders. "May I ask if you have heard of the Gun Club?"

"Why on Earth should I have heard of it?" my uncle demanded. "They are neither geologists nor mineralogists, else I should have heard of it."

For the first time since we had entered the room, my dear Gretchen stirred and spoke. "Uncle, you cannot possibly be so involved in your work that you have never heard of the Gun Club. They are those American adventurers who so recently sent three men on a journey to and around the Moon."

"Those charlatans?" my uncle cried. "Those fools? Those wasters of opportunities?"

I, too, had been silent to this point—I confess, I was rather awed by the presence of the great Chancellor—but at this terrible accusation, I could no longer be still. "Uncle! How can you say such terrible things about such brave men?"

"Because they were fools," he snapped back. "They went all that way to the Moon, and what did they bring back? Nothing! Not a rock, not a sample, not even a speck of dust! There are so many questions about our satellite that they could have helped answer with just a handful of rocks. But what did they bring back?"

"Themselves, alive," Gretchen said in her kind and gentle manner. "That is no mean achievement."

"It is an achievements accomplished by any couple who take the waters of a spa," my uncle said, dismissing their wonderful explorations. "There is no point in going and returning unless one brings back knowledge!"

"They did not land upon the Moon," I reminded my uncle. "How could they have brought back samples?"

"My point precisely," he said. "They were dunderheaded dolts who planned their explorations imperfectly. Why should I then know anything about them?"

"Because they have announced a further undertaking," Bismarck said. "They, like most of the world, have heard of your greater achievements and have announced that they will repeat your journey."

A cloud passed across the face of the volcano. "They do not possess the key," my uncle said, no longer untouched by the subject.

"They possess guns and other weapons," Bismarck answered. "They feel that they can effect a journey through brute force."

"Explosives?" The Professor was appalled. "The savages! The secrets of our planet are not to be ripped out by blasting powder! They require a gentle hand, a delicate hand, a trained hand..."

"*Your* hand?" suggested the Chancellor.

"Mine or one like it," uncle agreed. He no longer sounded as certain that this did not involve him. "But I don't understand—what do they expect to learn by such violent methods?"

"They expect to *learn* nothing," Bismarck said. "They expect to gain a country. It is their aim to take with them the American flag and plant it without our world and claim all of the lands they discover for their country. They are selling shares and have many rich investors who would gain a great deal from such an enterprise."

"They mean to *exploit* the lands beneath us?" The man of science could not understand the man of business. "This cannot be. It must not be allowed!"

"Precisely!" Having hooked his fish, the politician proceeded to play him in anticipation of landing a large catch. "What must be done is for *you* to lead a fresh expedition to reach those lands below us before they can accomplish this

305

foul enterprise of theirs. It must be the *German* flag that is planted within our world. We cannot allow Americans—and businessmen at that!—to beat us to this important work. If they reach and claim this world first, they will mine it and tear it apart. It is the way of the Yankee trader to exploit rather than to explore. We Germans are well-known as men of science and philosophy—it is *we* who should take command of the exploration of this subterranean world. And *you* must be in command of our party."

My uncle hesitated, clearly no longer as sure of his course of actions as before. "But I have so much work to do here," he finally said, weakly. "I cannot simply run off on an expedition."

"You must," Bismarck urged him. "It is either that or to cede the race to the Yankee traders. If you do not act, they will win. They will take their gun cotton and their weapons and they will blow holes through scientific research to seize their victory—and in so doing they will destroy much valuable information."

"There is much truth in what you say," my uncle agreed. "Very well: I accept that it is my fate to do battle with the forces of ignorance and greed. I *will* return to the center of our globe." Abruptly, he turned to me and clapped a hand upon my shoulder. "And you, my dear Axel, must accompany me."

I had not expected him to agree so readily to the Chancellor's proposal, so that had taken me by surprise. But it was with considerable shock that I received his latest statement. "Me? Uncle!" I protested. "I cannot go with you!" Memories of my previous trip crowded my mind—all of the dangers and terrors that we had faced. True, we had surmounted them—but in many cases this was due in part to luck and in a greater part to our wonderful, taciturn guide, Hans. Who could say whether either would accompany us again on any future endeavor?

"Cannot?" The Professor shook his head firmly. "Don't be absurd—you must be beside me again if I am to undertake this quest."

To face terrible thirst, or to be lost in the utter darkness underground, or to face such hardships or monsters as we had met with on the first trip… I am not a brave man; I confess it. I liked my quiet, peaceful life. I enjoyed the task of teaching up young minds, and of having Martha's wonderful meals, hot and plentiful before me. To exist on preserved foods, eaten cold, under adverse conditions… No, that was not the life for me. Besides, accompanying my uncle would mean that I would have to abandon my beloved Gretchen and our young daughter, and the thought of not seeing their sweet faces for several months was unbearable.

"You may recall, uncle," I informed him firmly, "that when I wed Gretchen, I gave her my solemn oath that I would never again venture beneath the surface of our world. You would not have me be an oath-breaker to my wife, now, would you?"

I could see the indecision written upon his face. The man of science was ready to pooh-pooh such matters, but the uncle and former guardian of Gretchen clearly favored me keeping my word. The two sides of his personality were at war with each other, but I allowed myself to be optimistic that the outcome would be the one I so desired.

But, as before, my darling, treacherous Gretchen did the unexpected. She rose to her feet and took my hands in her own delicate ones. "My dearest Axel," she said, calmly and lovingly. "I am overjoyed that you value the keeping of your word to me so strongly. It has been a great comfort to me these past few years, knowing that you are safe from danger and remain with those who love you." I was touched by her words, and even more resolved not to leave her on such a foolhardy quest. And then she sprang the trap! "But this is a matter that affects the futures both of Science and of our new country, Germany. How could I be so selfish as to insist that you place your word to me over your duties and responsibilities to them?" I began in shock to protest, but she placed her finger over my lips to silence me. "I freely release you from your vow, so you are now quite at liberty to do your duty to Science and Germany. Onwards!—to the center of the Earth!"

II. Our Voyage Begins

My stunned silence was taken, somehow, as overwhelmed gratitude and nothing more was spoken of the possibility of my not accompanying the expedition. I imagine that I did acquiesce to whatever was said following Gretchen's speech, but it was because I was in a state of shock and not one of agreement. By the time my senses had returned, matters had progressed too far for me to be able to back out. Whenever I attempted to broach the subject again in the following days my uncle invariably misunderstood me. He would clap me on my shoulder and say something along the lines of: "Don't fret yourself, Axel! You have not shamed yourself, and will not. We all know that you are a man of your word, but, more so, a man who faces his destiny with courage and conviction!"

Would that I had felt so much confidence in myself!

In his customary manner, the Chancellor of Germany had planned well, and had anticipated all but one problem in his scheme. That one problem, of course, was my uncle. To be fair to the great man, few people have ever anticipated my uncle's mind, and even fewer have ever gotten the better of him. His rank notwithstanding, Herr Bismarck fared no better than the fishmonger at the end of our street.

"No, no and again no!" my uncle cried in response to the Chancellor's suggestion that we find a good, patriotic German volcano as our means of entry to the world below our feet. "In the first place, there are no German volcanoes!"

"But, surely, in our great sphere of influence…" the Chancellor protested.

"And in the second," uncle continued, implacably, "we know that the route down certainly lies within Snaeffels. We do *not* know that any other such route lies within any other volcano. And in the *third* place," he continued, not allowing the great statesman a word, "we know that Snaeffels is dormant. It would be a very foolish act to chance a less somnolent entry point."

"But the volcano is in *Iceland*," Bismarck protested.

"I know that." My uncle folded his arms. "And it is to Iceland we must go."

Bismarck threw up his arms. "Very well, Iceland it is," he agreed. "We have a ship ready and waiting to transport you and the members of your party to the site in question. Any provisions you may need and such equipment you deem necessary should be listed and given to Captain Von Horst." He indicated the military man who had marched my uncle into the room, and who had been silent up to this point. At the mention of his name, he clicked his heels together sharply and gave a smart salute—whether to the Chancellor or my uncle, it was impossible to tell.

"That is simple," my uncle said. "We shall take along almost precisely the equipment we took last time, along with provisions for three men."

"Three?" The statesman shook his head. "You misunderstand the matter, my dear professor—the Captain and his men will be accompanying you on your journey."

"The devil you say!" Lidenbrock exploded. "I cannot be expected to be nursemaid to a group of clumsy soldiers."

"My men and I are *not* clumsy," the Captain protested. "We are highly trained professionals. It is our assignment to nursemaid *you*!"

My uncle glared at him. "In the matter of exploring the world below, there are only *three* experts," he said firmly. "Myself, my nephew and our companion Hans. That is the extent of our party, and on this matter I stand firm."

"You would take along an Icelander and leave behind a good German?" Von Horst cried.

"I know and trust this Icelander with my life," the professor replied. "I cannot say the same about you. I shall not budge on this issue." He crossed his arms again and glared at Bismarck, daring him to issue any fresh orders.

The politician was not so foolish; he was starting to get the measure of my uncle and saw that the only path to getting his way was to make my uncle think that it was the footpath he had himself chosen. "Quite right," Bismarck said, jovially. "You do not know the Captain or his men. I understand that. But you *will* know him by the time you reach Iceland, so there's an end to that problem. As to the Icelander…" He caught the warning flash of fire in my uncle's eyes. "Well, there's no saying whether he will be free to accompany you, is there? It may be that the good huntsman is busy. I understand he collects the feathers of the Eider duck for a living—it may be that he's off plucking feathers." He held up a hand to stave off a protest. "We shall, of course, in deference to your wishes, attempt to secure his services once again. But we must also be prepared in case that worthy is not available. That is only sensible, is it not?"

How could even my uncle argue with such logic?

"The men I have selected for this mission," Von Horst added, "are all experts in matters Alpine. I and they have extensive climbing experience—it barely matters that we climb *down* instead of *up*, does it?"

"If you think that, there is little I can teach you," my uncle replied, caustically. "No good will come of this," he snapped at Bismarck, and then sighed. "Very well, I shall agree to a compromise. The Captain and his men may accompany us for a week. If, after that time, I decide that they are an encumbrance and not an asset, they must agree to return and allow the three of us to proceed alone on our mission."

Von Horst was about to protest, but the Chancellor held up a hand to silence him. "Very well," he agreed, easily. "That sounds quite reasonable."

"But what is to stop him from simply declaring us a problem and rejecting us out of hand?" Von Horst growled.

"The good professor's reputation for honesty," Bismarck answered. "I have every faith that he is a man who is as good as his word—if he promises to judge fairly, then I believe that he will do so."

This considerably mollified my uncle, and planning could proceed without further altercations. My uncle was happy with getting his way, and the Chancellor was equally convinced that he was getting *his* way. Naturally, I was not considered by either man in their further discussions. Both men assumed I would concur with any decisions they made. And, indeed, what choice did I have? My darling Gretchen had assured them I would accompany the quest. I could not make her a liar, nor, to be honest, could I bring myself to disappoint her. She looked at me with such pride and affection in her eyes, and she had no clue that she had betrayed me. She believed me to be a brave man, and so I was forced to act the part, even with a heavy heart.

While the great men talked, I took the opportunity to examine our new traveling companion. Captain Von Horst was clearly career military, and probably from several generations of such men. He stood bolt-upright, as if instead of a spine he had a carbine, unable to deviate from the vertical. His movements were precise and considered, and he was extremely well groomed. I have had very little acquaintance with military men, thankfully, but he appeared to be a fine example of the breed. He interjected comments from time to time into the discussions, and they were always clear and to the point. Yet in all of this, I did not really know what kind of a man he was, not how he would react when faced with the realities of life underground. I full knew that it is one thing to *think* of traveling beneath the surface of our world, and quite another matter when actually *doing* it. In short, I thought the man had potential, but until we had been on our journey for that probationary week, I should not be able to tell whether he would be a good companion or not.

Eventually the talks wound down, and the politician rose to take his leave. He kissed my wife's hand and shook mine. As he grasped that of my uncle, he smiled.

"I have great confidence in you, Professor Lidenbrock," he announced. "The Captain will return in the morning, and then you shall be on your way."

"The morning?" I exclaimed. I had not been following the conversation closely, being preoccupied with my own thoughts. "But surely it cannot be?"

"Whyever not?" my uncle asked, puzzled. "The Captain has already arranged for many of the supplies and equipment we need, and he goes now to secure the rest. Our ship awaits, and we know the road ahead of us. And the members of that infernal Gun Club are well underway in their own preparations to race us on this path. No, indeed, tomorrow it shall be."

"But... but it is not midsummer," I stammered. "That is the time to descend the crater."

"Only when we did not know the right way to take," my uncle said, dismissively. "Now we already know the start of our journey there is no need to wait the change of seasons. Tomorrow it should be." He turned to Gretchen. "You and Martha must help us to pack our few personal items this evening, my dear."

My wife nodded, and then favored me with a radiant smile. "Is this not exciting, Axel?" she asked.

That was not the word I should have chosen.

As for the rest of that evening, I cannot say with any certainty what happened. I must have eaten, obviously, and I know I slept, for I was tormented by terrible dreams. These were partly rehashed memories of my previous trip and partially fears for what might happen on the impending trip. I recall monster teeth that turned into stalactites, both versions of which closed about my body, crushing the life from it. Somehow, though, I did not waken until the morning, and felt surprisingly ready to face the ordeal ahead of me.

My uncle was up and about, eager for the adventure to commence. Martha had laid on a hearty breakfast—"You'll be eating onboard ship next, and they don't have good, fresh eggs or newly-baked bread," she pointed out. "And, after that, only the good Lord knows what kind of food you'll have to endure under the ground." Thoughts of the dried rations we would be taking turned the taste of her good sausages and eggs ashen in my mouth. How would I endure months without good food?

Easier than I would the months without Gretchen, of course. I shall not tell you with what affections the two of us parted, nor of the numerous kisses bestowed upon our daughter. My uncle bore it as long as he could, but then demanded impatiently that our goodbyes cease so we might actually get started on our journey. After a final flurry of kisses, I left my dear Gretchen and daughter and settled into the coach that the Captain had sent to collect us. Our luggage was stowed, and we were off.

Iceland, our initial destination, is a colony of Denmark, and on our previous trip we had started by visiting the latter country and obtaining letters of introduction from colleagues of my uncle. This time, however, that would be unnecessary, as everything had been arranged by Chancellor Bismarck and his right-hand Captain. Hamburg is situated on the River Elbe and is one of the largest ports in Europe. The coach took us directly to the docks where our vessel awaited us. It was a smallish ship named the *Bremen*, but very modern and, as her proud Captain informed us, very fast. Certainly it was very efficient, for we were barely aboard before that worthy and proud gentleman gave orders for us to cast off. By the time my uncle and I were led to the cabin that we were to share, I could feel that we were already under way. I felt quite exhausted from all the activity going on about us and would have gladly taken the chance to rest—hopefully without further nightmares—but that would not be possible with my uncle about. As soon as we had placed our bags in the cabin, he seized my hand and virtually dragged me to the deck.

The buildings and people we lived amongst were already slipping behind us as the *Bremen* sliced its way toward the North Sea. The captain's pride in his ship's speed was not misplaced, it seemed. My old life was being shed as a snake slips its old skin. I was, however, far from eager to grasp my new. No such worries or regrets seized my uncle, of course. Like a prize stallion, he was champing at the bit and eager to be unleashed upon the world beneath us.

Captain Von Horst was drilling his men on the deck. There were six of them and I must confess that they looked very smart. They moved in unison, their faces blank of emotion, following whatever order their commander barked.

The Professor was less impressed. "That sort of thing won't do you much good under the ground," he remarked.

The Captain glared at him. "Efficiency and order are never wasted," he retorted. "My men act as one."

"Then they may also die as one," my uncle replied, off-handed.

"They will not die," the soldier responded. "They are an extension of my will and they are the most efficient of their kind in the German Army. You will find, Herr Professor, that they will be invaluable on our mission."

"Perhaps so," my uncle agreed, vaguely. "Meanwhile, before we leave German waters, I should like the chance to look over our supplies, so that if anything has been omitted, we may collect it on our way."

The Captain looked offended at the thought. "Nothing necessary has been left out."

"You may indeed be right," the Professor said. "But as leader of this expedition, it is my responsibility to be certain."

"Very well." Stiffly, the military man led the pair of us below decks. Behind us, his sergeant took over the drilling of the troops. They were not to be allowed to relax and simply enjoy the voyage, it appeared.

A portion of the main hold had been set aside for the supplies we would be taking along on our expedition. They had all been laid neatly out beside the packs that would contain them. There were, I could see, ten packs in all—one each for the soldiers, the Captain, my uncle, myself, and the final one for Hans. Each had a sign beside it, designating its bearer.

There were the concentrated food supplies I so disliked from the previous trip, but which would serve to keep us alive. There were water containers for each man, as well as small items of clothing such as socks that might need replacing. There was climbing gear and lengths of rope, spread between the packs the soldiers would carry. For them, also, was a supply of ammunition. The scientific supplies—compasses, barometers and so forth—were split between the packs of myself and my uncle. I noted with some satisfaction that there was even a supply of paper and drafting materials beside my pack. I was evidently to be the chronicler of whatever happened, as well as recorder of any lands we claimed. To aid in that there were several German flags to be planted. We and Hans were also assigned a revolver and a rifle each, along with a smaller supply of ammunition for the weapons.

Finally, there were six Ruhmkorf coils, along with the necessary supplies. These portable, strong lights had proven to be absolutely invaluable on our previous journey, and I was certain that they would do so again. Without the clear light they cast, we would hardly be able to move six feet below the ground.

"This appears to be quite adequate," my uncle finally said, after having examined every item carefully.

"More than adequate," the soldier replied. "As long as we are able to find water again on our journey, we have everything here we should need on our journey." Even my uncle was not able to dispute that, though I have no doubt he racked his brain for an excuse to do so.

And so we settled in for our sea voyage. It had taken us two weeks to reach Iceland on the previous attempt, but our Captain was certain that the *Bremen* could make the trip in seven. "This ship is the most up-to-date in the world," he said, proudly. "A masterpiece of German engineering."

"But we traverse the north Atlantic," my uncle pointed out. "This is not German weather, the seas are liable to be rough and there is always the possibility of icebergs in this season."

"Nevertheless," the good Captain vowed, "seven days!"

The soldiers drilled, my uncle studied the books he had brought along with him, and I worried. What was happening to my Gretchen and our daughter? Were they well? Did they miss me? And I worried about ourselves. What fresh dangers were in store for us below the crust of our world? How many of the dangers we had previously faced would we encounter again? Would we be able to endure this time? And what of Hans? Would his services be available to us again? Would he even be foolish enough to agree to go with us on another expedition? There were so many uncertainties and possibilities, and my mind kept playing them all out, again and again, fruitlessly, as the *Bremen* plowed on.

To my surprise and somewhat to my uncle's chagrin, on the seventh day we did indeed sight land. The lookout gave a cry and gestured. Using field glasses, my uncle confirmed the accuracy of the call.

"It would appear that our good Captain was correct in his faith in his ship," I could not resist observing.

"He was fortunate in the weather," was the scientific man's opinion. This was certainly true, to an extent—despite the lateness of the season we had encountered neither storms nor icebergs, which had helped. But a good deal of the credit must be laid, indeed, to the workmanship of those who had constructed and those who had sailed the *Bremen*. And now, dead ahead of us, lay the first rocky shores of Iceland.

The first and simplest part of our journey was now complete. The more difficult portion was about to commence.

III. A Dangerous Reunion

Iceland is a curious place. It was created from volcanic rock and there are many volcanoes still active on the island. The rock, once weathered, provides good soil for growing crops. When it is not weathered, it gives a landscape that is largely barren and gloomy, broken in places only by water bursting from the ground in what the natives call *geysers*—which are of volcanic origin and frequently hot enough to scald. There are few trees, mostly planted by the hand of man and not nature, so houses are mostly built of the ever-present stone and often fade into the surrounding landscape.

The inhabitants are descendants of ancient Viking explorers, and the island still belongs to Denmark, whose language is spoken here. Unlike their ancestors, the modern Icelanders are peaceful farmers, for the most part, though ancient passions and claims of blood-debt sometimes erupt like the geysers, hot and very active.

Our one-time guide, Hans Bjelke, followed a different profession: he was a hunter, though not with a gun or other weapon. Iceland's main export is the feather of the Eider duck, which makes exceptional filling for pillows and mattresses for the rest of the world. Hans' chosen work was the gathering of such feathers. As the ducks nest in out-of-the-way areas, this is not quite as placid a task as it may sound. Hans had to clamber among the rocks and on sheer cliff faces to reach his prey. As a result, he had become as adept at climbing these inhospitable outcrops as any mountain goat. This had made him invaluable to us as a guide on our last expedition, and my uncle was grimly determined to once again secure his services. This was one decision that I heartily concurred with— there is no man alive I trust as much as that quiet, unhurried man.

In the shadow of the extinct volcano Snaeffels itself, the *Bremen* anchored. I confess to a shudder or two as I looked up at the twin peaks of that once-mighty peak, knowing it to be the doorway into the underworld that we should shortly hazard. It seemed, though, that I was the only one stricken with any such feelings. My uncle was eager to be off, and the Captain and his men were quite prepared to follow. But first, there was the question of Hans. Could we find him, and would he again accompany us? The Captain was of the opinion that we really didn't need him; my uncle of the opinion that we could not do without him. I, of course, agreed with my uncle—that to proceed without Hans would be foolhardy and possibly deadly. However, I found myself wishing that the guide would be unavailable or else unwilling, and that we should then be forced to abandon our quest.

It was determined, in conference with the *Bremen*'s Captain that my uncle, myself and Captain Von Horst should proceed to search out Hans and that the soldiers and sailors would unload our gear and prepare it ready for our commencement. I am not affected by seasickness or other maladies, but I confess that it felt good to have the solid ground beneath my feet again when we reached Icelandic soil. Of course, the ground was not as solid as it felt—in a matter of days we should be venturing below the land on which we now stood.

The peninsula upon which Snaeffels stood was not close to any of the few small settlements in the area, so it took a little searching to locate a local. If this lonely man was surprised to see a troop of visitors to this quiet land, he gave little outward sign. Both my uncle and the Captain spoke sufficient Danish to be able to converse with this farmer, and he was able to answer their questions, at least in part. My uncle gave him a few coins for his help, and rubbed his hands in some satisfaction.

"Our old friend Hans is somewhere not too distant," he informed me. "It seems that he has become romantically attached to the daughter of a farmer." I was surprised to hear that Hans was prey to such a violent emotion as love, but pleased for him. "There are, however, complications. It seems that he has a rival for her affections, and this other man is noted for a violent temper."

"Then she is sure to pick Hans," I exclaimed. "Who would want to be wed to such a brute?"

My uncle shook his head. "But the brute, as you call him, is apparently quite a wealthy man, and offers the poor girl a very comfortable life. So she must chose temper and wealth or else calmness and more uncertain prospects with Hans. Still, what this little drama means is that Hans is in the habit of visiting the girl and her family on a fairly frequent basis, and so our best chance of intercepting him would seem to be to call on the farmer and simply wait."

"For how long?" Von Horst asked, impatiently. He turned to me. "Your uncle neglects to inform you that it seems that we are already behind in this race to the center of our world."

"I was about to tell him," the professor said coldly. "But my nephew is a man of emotion, and I felt that he would prefer news of our old friend first."

I glanced from one to the other. "Will *one* of you please tell me the news?"

314

"The Gun Club arrived here in Iceland a week ago," my uncle replied. "Being Americans, they made their presence known from one end of the island to the other. They have spent coin quite freely and were last seen three days ago heading on this very path toward..." He gestured dramatically at looming Snaeffels. "They have begun their journey ahead of us, it would seem."

"That is not good," I observed.

"It is not," agreed the Captain. "I think spending any time waiting for this local guide of yours is wasteful—we should head directly to the peak and begin our own descent."

"That would not be wise," my uncle informed him. "It hardly matters that they are ahead of us—they are traversing lands unknown to them, and may quite easily chose one or more of the many passages that lead nowhere. A few days here or there is meaningless. We know the correct path to take."

"Another reason why we do not need a guide!" Von Horst exclaimed.

"On the contrary," the professor said, refusing to change his opinion. "Hans is not to accompany us to lead the way—that is *my* task. He is to be with us to offer advice and insight, and to help us when things get rough. And, I assure you, they will get very rough indeed." He grinned widely at this hellish prospect. "Our chances of survival and success will probably depend highly upon this man, a man the Gun Club members do not have. Either we secure his services, or else I go no further."

The Captain could see when he was beaten. "Very well," he agreed. "Let us check that our camp here is being prepared, and then we can go on a search for this treasure of a man." He hurried to retrace our path back to the slight harbor where the *Bremen* was waiting.

"I am glad he has seen the sense in what we desire, Axel," my uncle commented. Sense? I could see no sense at all in any of this! But nobody, least of all Herr Professor Lidenbrock—was interested in *my* opinion.

Von Horst took the time to issue a few orders to his men back at the camp. This seemed unnecessary to me, as the men had the building of our temporary abode quite well in hand, but the Captain was one of those men who seems to feel that nothing will get done correctly unless he give detailed orders. And he complained of *us* wasting time! Eventually, convinced that affairs were well in hand, he joined us again and we made our way to the young lady's farm.

As I have mentioned, Iceland is for the most part a vast, rocky wilderness. Grass grows in abundance, and, with proper farming methods and diligence, other crops can be coaxed to do so. Many farmers keep sheep and goats, which provide them with milk and cheese as well as rare meat dishes. For transportation, most Icelanders rely upon their own legs, but there are quite a few small, shaggy ponies of an even temperament and good work ethic. Since there are few trees, most houses are built of the omnipresent volcanic rock. The domicile we reached proved to be quite typical of the island.

The farmer was a tall, muscular man, now a trifle past his prime. His wife was a sturdy matron, mother to a brood of children I was not quite able to number. Aside from their ebb and flow within the house, many had chores to accomplish and so were in a constant state of motion. There were at least six children, and perhaps as many as ten, apparently equally distributed between the two sexes. The object of Hans' affection proved to be a slender blonde girl some nineteen years of age with a ready smile and a polite manner. It was not difficult to see why she had two ardent admirers, and probably would have had more if she lived in even a small city instead of the backwaters of this island. Her name, I gathered, was Habby.

My uncle conversed with her and her mother—the father went about his work, using his mouth mostly to clench a pipe that he sometimes paused to light—and was able to ascertain that Hans was in the nearby hills and expected to show up as a guest for dinner later that day. We were graciously invited to partake of the meal also, which my uncle gratefully accepted for the three of us. When he passed along this information Von Horst was not happy.

"I prefer to eat with my men," he stated. "It is better for discipline that they see their Captain sharing their rations rather than eating in luxury."

"Hardly luxury," the professor said amiably, gesturing at our surroundings. "These are good folks, yes, but I would hardly term this *luxury*."

"My point is that I should be with them," the Captain snapped. "And I do not like the idea of waiting about for this Hans of yours. If he is in the hills, let us go and seek him out. The sooner we know if he will accompany us or not, the better."

My uncle glanced about at the turmoil around us. The father of the family might be taciturn, but the same could not be said of most of his offspring. My uncle disliked noise and confusion, so I was hardly surprised when he agreed with the Captain. He explained to our hosts that he and I would be back with Hans later, and that the Captain would not. We took our leave of the family then, though several of the children, curious and pleased with their unexpected and strange visitors, flocked about us like starlings as we left the farm house and started on our way. Thankfully for my uncle's temper, none of them strayed too far from the house and in a matter of minutes we were alone with our thoughts.

I was anticipating meeting our old friend again and hoping he would agree to accompany us once more. But having seen Habby, I doubted it—what man would want to abandon her to his rival simply to go on a possibly doomed adventure? Habby made me think of Gretchen again, and how much I missed her. If I could have my choice, I would never have left her; I should certainly not blame Hans if he turned us down. Thinking thoughts alternately gloomy and nostalgic, I hardly noticed the path we were taking into the hills. My uncle was leading the way with his usual conviction and I simply followed along silently. The Captain brought up the rear of our small group as silent as I.

I was jolted back to the present when my uncle gave a loud hail. I glanced up and saw a familiar figure a short distance above us in the rocks. It was our good Hans, making his way down the mountainous slopes toward us. I was so pleased to see him again that I was pulled from my reverie and my legs, unbidden, started forward quite swiftly. I found myself running to greet him.

Then, above the pathway to my right, I heard a loud cracking sound. I paused and looked upward. With a shock, I saw that a portion of the rock face several hundred feet above us had broken free of the hillside. Huge boulders crashed down the slope, and stones clattered through the air. Dust and noise abounded, and the entire mass began descending toward us. My uncle and the Captain, below us, we not in the pathway of this mass of volcanic material, but Hans and I were directly in its path. I heard faint cries from below, but my attention was almost entirely seized by the crashing, tumbling army of stone. For a moment I was paralyzed with indecision.

Hans had no such problems. He leaped forward, as agile and sure-footed as any goat, and he grabbed a hold of me, pushing me before him. I went willingly with his motions, but there was no chance we should be able to evade the lethal avalanche descending upon us.

Then I saw the escape was not Hans' plan. Instead, he propelled us underneath a slight overhang above the pathway, barely more than a bump in the rocky surface. He pushed me against the wall, and gestured for me to hold myself in as tightly as I could. I obeyed his unspoken command, and he, in turn, stood close beside me in a similar manner.

The rocks and boulders crashed down toward us and I was convinced that we would perish. An image of my dear Gretchen filled my mind as I thought I should never see her again, and then I gasped and choked as the dust accompanying the avalanche reached us, filling my nose and mouth. As the noisy rockfall crashed about us, I coughed and choked. I was struck several times, but thankfully only by smaller stones. The volcanic rock was sharp, though, and left streaks of blood on my skin. The overhang, slight as it was, proved to be sufficient, as it turned aside the larger boulders. Only the lesser stone and dust reached us. In moments, the terrible avalanche was over, and we could bend and move as we coughed to clear our throats and mouths.

After a few moments, I heard my uncle and the Captain crying out our names as they approached us. They had to tread carefully, as the pathway was strewn with rocks and scree. Hans and I started down toward them just as carefully. In a matter of moments, we were together, and my uncle grasped both of my arms.

"My boy, are you well?" he asked, anxiously.

"Merely minor cuts and scrapes," I assured him. "Hans, as ever, looked out for me."

"Ah! My good Hans!" my uncle cried, clasping the hand of our old friend. He spoke to him heartily in Danish, quite volubly. Hans, as was his manner, waited until my uncle had finished and then answered with a few calm words. "He says he is fine, and somewhat surprised to see us," my uncle reported. The pair of them spoke for a few minutes while I managed to return myself to some semblance of order.

"It seems quite a coincidence that there should be a landslide just as we meet up with Hans," I observed.

"Coincidence?" The Professor shook his head. "My boy, neither Hans nor I believe it to be a coincidence."

"I concur," Von Horst said. "The timing is highly suspicious, is it not?"

"Indeed." My uncle smiled. "Hans feels it is the work of his rival for the young lady's hand. He is noted for his temper and his dislike of obstacles to his plans."

"I'm not so sure," I said slowly. "It seems to me that it would be an awful coincidence that his rival decided to strike at precisely the time we come here to solicit Hans' aid."

To my surprise, the Captain announced: "I agree with Axel—it *would* be too much of a coincidence. I suspect that it is much more likely that the Gun Club has left an agent behind to ensure we cannot follow them."

"Would they go to such lengths as to try and kill us?" my uncle asked. "It seems a trifle extreme, even for Americans."

"They may not have intended to kill anyone," Von Horst replied. "They may only have intended injury to members of our party to slow us down. No, I feel that Axel's suspicions may well be correct."

The Professor dismissed the matter. "Well, it is of no consequence now— neither Axel nor Hans were injured, and our expedition can proceed."

"*If* Hans agrees to join us," I pointed out. "He has yet to be broached on the subject. He may not wish to leave his sweetheart to the mercies of his rival, especially if the man *was* the one attempting to kill Hans."

My uncle nodded and engaged in an earnest conversation with our guide. Hans, as ever, was calm and spoke little, and in the end my uncle beamed. "He has agreed to accompany us, on the same terms as before," he announced.

"And Habby?" I asked, curiously.

My uncle chuckled. "Hans has a definitely individualized approach to romance," he said. "He is of the opinion that the decision must be hers and hers alone. He aims to tell her of his plans and inform her that he wishes to marry her on his return. If, while he has gone, his rival's suit wins out, then he believes that clearly the young lady was not the woman he took her for, and he would be well rid of her. He did add that he does not expect this to happen."

I turned to Hans and shook his hand gratefully. If we were to undertake this madcap quest, I felt we had a much better chance of returning now that he had agreed to accompany us. Hans seemed to understand my mood and he nodded solemnly. I then realized that no obstacle now stood in our way.

We were on our way back to the center of the Earth...

IV. Our Party Is Complete

We returned with Hans to the farmhouse of his young lady. The chaos there had died down slightly with the approach of supper. As Habby's mother dished out the meal—consisting of a thick fish stew that was surprisingly tasty—Hans took Habby outside to speak with her. They were gone so long that they almost missed the meal entirely, but when they did reappear both of them looked very happy. It seemed that our guide's proposal had met a sympathetic response.

The decision had to be passed along to her parents, and met with their considerable approval. The father disappeared off and then emerged from an inner room with a bottle that appeared to have been stored for a while. He insisted on drinks all around to seal the engagement, and I managed to sip whatever the concoction was without gagging too much. Habby's younger brothers and sisters weren't allowed any of the alcoholic toast, but they seemed to have many comments of their own directed at the happy pair which—from the way my uncle raised his eyebrows—I assume were of light-hearted jokes in somewhat poor taste, much like that of any family anywhere.

It was arranged with my uncle that Hans would settle his affairs and join us at our camp in the morning. I assumed that he would also take a long and perhaps tender farewell of his bride-to-be and wanted as few witnesses to this as possible. Captain Von Horst was impatient with all of these matters, but he was wise enough to know that he could not hurry my uncle along. When we eventually left, shortly before sunset, he could barely conceal his impatience.

"There is still much to do," he snapped. He glanced back at the farmhouse. "Can we rely on your man to be with us at the appointed hour?"

"If Hans says he will do something," my uncle replied, "then no power on Earth can stop him from keeping his word. He will be with us at daybreak and we may be on our way." This answer mollified the soldier somewhat, but he still kept up a swift pace back to our camp.

Here we had two surprises to greet our arrival. One of the soldiers hurried up to the Captain, saluted briskly and informed him that one of the men had suffered an accident. It appeared he had been out on the volcanic rock and lost his footing. He had slipped and fallen, seriously injuring his leg. The Captain rushed to examine the man, and emerged from his tent a few minutes later looking angry and concerned.

"A foolish accident," he said. "The man disobeyed my orders and went off alone. He hasn't broken his leg, but it is severely sprained and he is quite unable to move it now after hobbling back to camp on it. We shall be one man short on our expedition tomorrow."

My uncle shrugged. "That hardly concerns me," he replied. "I have said all along that there are too many of us as it is. One less seems like a good move to me." Then, having clearly realized how callous he must sound, he added: "Nevertheless, I trust your soldier will recover."

The second surprise was even less likely than the first, and considerably more puzzling.

It seemed we had a visitor. An *American* visitor, waiting in our tent to speak with us.

"An American?" Von Horst asked, astonished. "Here? What could he want with us?"

My uncle snorted. "Let us go and ask him," he suggested.

We moved to the tent he and I were to share. Oil lamps had been lit since night had fallen, and as we entered, we saw our visitor in the light of one such lamp. He rose to his feet to greet us, and I was impressed by my first sight of him. He stood more than six feet tall, and was thick-bodied and muscular. He was dressed in a nautical jacket and cap, and there was a sailor's sack on the ground beside him. His eyes flickered back and forth over the three of us, and then he extended a large hand toward my uncle. "Professor Lidenbrock, I assume?"

"Indeed." My uncle shook his hand. "And you are...?"

"My name is Ned Land," he answered.

"And why is an American visiting us?" the Captain demanded. "Did you have something to do with the attack on our guide?"

"American?" Land was almost roaring. "I am not an *American*, I am *Canadian*."

"It is the same thing," Von Horst insisted.

"No, sir, it is not!" Land growled. He looked as though he might start a fight over the insult. "And I don't know what attack you speak of. I have not fought anyone today—yet."

"American or Canadian," my uncle said, hastily, before the Captain could make matters worse, "the question remains: what are you doing here?"

"I wish to join your expedition," Land said, folding his arms across his chest.

The Captain appeared about ready to explode with rage, but my uncle waved him to silence. "And what do you know of our expedition?"

"Why, that you're off to the center of the Earth," Land said. "I am a harpooner by trade, and my ship is docked at Reykjavik. I heard that you were here, and so I came along to offer my services."

"A harpooner?" The Captain seemed undecided whether to rage or laugh. "We have no need of such a man."

"Begging your pardon, but I suspect that you do." Land smiled grimly. "I read the account of your first expedition, and you spoke of a sea of monsters." His eyes lit up with passion. "I have been a sailor for more than twenty years and have crossed every ocean on the surface of this world. The call of a fresh ocean, one seen by few human beings, that stands ready to challenge and be challenged… How could I resist?" He glanced at me. "You, I take it, are the chronicler of that expedition. You spoke of giant sea beasts that almost killed you that time." He reached into the shadows of the tent and produced a large harpoon. "With me and this, you would have no need to fear a recurrence of the threat."

His simple statements and his air of confidence encouraged me. I found myself taking a liking to this seaman, wherever he was from. I could tell by the stiffness of his pose and the barely controlled anger on his face that the Captain did not agree with me. Still, neither of our opinions mattered, as my uncle had the only real vote on the matter, and it all depended upon what he thought of Ned Land. After a moment's contemplation, he spoke up.

"What you say might be true—and I say *might be* advisedly, since there is no way of knowing the hazards that we face. But the Captain is quite right in one respect—there *has* been an attack on one member of our party already; how do we know that you were not the man responsible?"

"Because I say so, and I do not lie," the sailor answered simply.

"For which statement we are expected to take your word?"

Land glared at the Captain. "I have sailed the seven seas all my adult life," he said slowly. "I have been from Cebu to Valparaiso, from pole to pole. In all the world there is not one man who knows me who would call me a liar. If you wish to be the first, I am willing to debate the matter." His fist clenched the harpoon and raised it slightly.

I could see that the Captain was unlikely to back down, and that blood might well be shed in the next few moments. I had to do something to prevent it, so I said, swiftly: "I am certain that the Captain did not mean to call you a liar, Mr. Land. But if you might happen to have some sort of credentials…"

"Credentials?" Land blinked, and I could see his grip loosening on his weapon. "Well, that's something easily arranged. Here, lad, hold this for me." He promptly tossed the harpoon in my direction—thankfully not point-first!— and didn't even bother to look to see if I had managed to snatch it from the air. Luckily, I managed this without fumbling or dropping the harpoon. Land picked up his sailor's kit bag and rummaged through it for a moment before producing a small bundle carefully wrapped in wax papers. He untied the bundle and passed a letter across to my uncle. "It's from Professor Aronnax—I don't know if you've ever heard of him?"

"Indeed we have," my uncle replied. "I have read his books on the subject of marine biology. There are one or two points he makes that I should like to debate him about, but on the whole he is a solid and reliable researcher."

I stared at the Professor, wondering if that was all he knew of the famous man. "And of his adventures with Nemo and the *Nautilus*," I prompted.

"Who? What?" My uncle glanced up a moment from the letter he was reading. "What are you babbling about, my boy?"

The mysterious submersible that was sinking ships in the world's oceans just a few years ago," I explained. "Professor Aronnax and his companions aided in ending the menace." I looked at Ned Land with fresh respect. "Were you one of them?"

"Aye," he agreed. "I was there—though *menace* is perhaps not the best word to describe Captain Nemo."

"I don't know what you two are talking about," my uncle declared, folding the letter and handing it back to Land. "But Aronnax speaks highly of your skills and loyalty in that missive, and I am inclined to accept his judgment of you, Mr. Land." He held out a hand. "Welcome to our expedition."

"I protest!" Von Horst rather predictably exclaimed.

"I rather thought you might," my uncle said. "But it is my place to decide these matters, and I say he accompanies us. His particular skills could prove invaluable."

"We have supplies for only ten men," the Captain argued.

"And one of your men can no longer accompany us," the Professor replied. "Therefore Mr. Land can take his place."

"I had planned on using a *German* in my man's place."

"I'm sure you were," my uncle answered. "But this is a scientific expedition, and science knows no national boundaries. My decision stands."

The Captain was furious, but he could see that there was little point in arguing further. Instead he turned to the sailor. "How is it that you did not accompany the American expedition, but waited for us?" he asked. "It seems rather suspicious to me."

Land shrugged. "I would have joined the American expedition if it were possible. But my ship did not dock until yesterday, and they had already set off. Then I waited for your party.""You see?" Von Horst pointed out to my uncle. "The man has no loyalty."

"The man *had* no loyalty," the sailor corrected. "But now I have been accepted as a member of your party, I *do* have loyalty. I assure you I will do my utmost to make this expedition a success."

"Capital!" the man of science exclaimed. "Well, now that is all settled, I suggest we have our evening meal and then settle down for the night—tomorrow is liable to prove a very busy day for us, gentlemen."

I looked from my uncle's calm face to Ned Land's smiling features, and then finally to the Captain. His visage was clouded with anger at being overridden in this matter. I had a strong suspicion that my uncle's heavy-handed manner of dealing with the issue might have serious repercussions once we were below the surface of the Earth. It was not merely my natural timidity that made me worry about what the future had in store for us all.

V. Descending

We were all up early—I because I had not slept well because of my worries, the others because of excitement (my uncle), duty (Hans) and discipline (Captain Von Horst and his soldiers). Ned Land rose early simply because of long years of doing so at sea. We had our last well-cooked breakfast thanks to the cook from the ship, and then our journey began. We shouldered our assigned packs, seized our rifles and walking sticks and set off along the coast road that led up the slopes of Snaeffels. The morning was cold but calm and the exercise kept us all warm. Once we descended into the volcano, we would find the temperature more amenable.

Conversation at this point was kept to a minimum and we all entertained our own thoughts. Mine were of Gretchen and our daughter and the possibility that I might never see them again. I should have been a very glum conversationalist if there were any to join in. Thankfully there were not.

That first day saw us climb to the waiting crater. This part of the journey was arduous but unremarkable. We were in the shadow of nearby Scartaris most of the time—the same mountain shadow that had pointed the way for us on our previous trip—and, though the views were spectacular, they were as nothing for those yet to come. It was evening by the time we reached the summit of Snaeffels, and so we prepared a camp for the evening looking down on the volcano's crater. As before, there were three deep shafts that would lead to the heart of the mountain.

Ned Land grinned cheerfully. "A strange sight for a sailor," he decided. "And there won't be an ocean for me to hazard for quite some time now." He pointed to the center shaft. "That is our path, I believe."

"Hardly," my uncle replied, with a slight smile.

Land scowled and glanced at me. "Your published account of your trip –"

"Said that the center descent was the correct one, yes," my uncle interrupted him. "That was *my* suggestion."

"It is not?"

"It is not," the Professor answered. "That learned man Arne Saknussemm went to great lengths to hide the correct entrance—and for good reasons. I persuaded my nephew to do the same. He named the *incorrect* start of our journey.[8] I believe it to be a wise choice."

Land's face was split by another of his huge grins. "Then if the Gun Club is relying on your manuscript to show them the way –"

"Then we need not fear that they have a few days head start on us, because they will have taken the wrong route," my uncle confirmed.

---

[8] I leave it to the reader to decide whether there is any greater truth in *this* account of our journey.

Ned Land laughed uproariously at this, and spent most of the evening chuckling as he thought upon the point. He was undoubtedly the happiest man in our camp that night, and I the glummest. But even the longest and most depressing night comes to an end, and in the morning we began our real journey.

The shaft below us was five thousand six hundred feet deep. Needless to say, we could not descend so far in one attempt. We therefore followed our former method of travel, lowering ourselves by rope some two hundred feet at a time down the left hand shaft. There were numerous small shelves and ledges on the way down the volcanic vent, but none large enough to hold all of our party at once. As a result, we made the descent in three separate groups. The Captain, my uncle, Hans and I led the way. Ned Land followed with two of the soldiers and then the final three military men made up the third party. Each group left at hour intervals so that there would be no chance of our bunching up on the way down.

Fortunately, we all had good heads for heights—or, more accurately, depths—as the climb down was for most of the journey a descent into an abyss without any view of the bottom. Had any of us slipped and fallen it would have been a horrible fate. Though every time I missed a firm grip or foothold I had visions of plunging to my death, I was always able to rectify my error and continue the descent.

We rested several times on that descent as it was extremely exhausting work. We were all in good shape, though, even my uncle who was at least ten years older than any other man in the party. Despite his age, he was as agile and excited as a young goat, stopping from time to time mostly to examine our surroundings. There was not, at this stage, much to see, because we were in a vent that had once contained lava, and the walls were coated with hardened igneous rock. Still, it all interested the man of learning, and he would make the occasional note in his pocket journal.

On we went, further into the depths, passing below the surface of the earth outside before our feet finally touched solid ground. Here there was a horizontal passageway that showed the way we were to go. A few feet inside the tunnel was absolute darkness, as sunlight could not penetrate it. My uncle led the way inside and lit his Ruhmkorf coil, which cast an electric glow over the rocks.

"Let us wait here," he said, cheerfully. It will be some two hours before the last of our party joins us." The Captain seemed impatient to press on, but understood the need and nodded curtly. Hans, phlegmatic as ever, simply sat with his back to the tunnel wall and fell into a swift sleep. I prowled back and forth until the next party reached us.

"An odd journey for a sailor," Ned Land commented, as his feet touched ground. "But I've been aloft often enough in the past for that trip to have seemed familiar enough." He peered into the gloom ahead of us. "But this next stage looks to be something else." He started forward, but my uncle held his arm.

"Do not go out of sight of the rest of us," he advised. "Distances and directions down here can be very confusing and it is far too easy to get lost." He gave me a sympathetic glance at that remark, knowing I had done precisely that on our former trip.

"I have a sailor's instinct for distance and direction," the whaler replied. "But as there is no sea in sight, I'll take your wise advice and promise to stay within view of your lamp. But I am intrigued, and would like to take a glance around." He grinned at me. "Maybe you'd be kind enough to accompany me, lad?"

I shrugged and acquiesced—looking around was better than sitting and waiting. Together we walked further into the tunnel ahead. Within twenty paces, the light from my uncle's lamp was all we had to see by. I could have lit my own coil, but it seemed better to save it for when it might be more urgently needed. The sailor had been examining the walls of the tunnel, and he called my attention to a short mark in the rock, perhaps six inches long and quite horizontal.

"This is really why I wanted to call you aside, lad," he said, softly, worried that his voice might carry. "It's clearly the mark of something striking the wall—a backpack, I imagine. I saw a few more of these back at the base of the shaft. It looks as if the members of the Gun Club might be ahead of us after all."

He was quite correct in his deduction as to the cause of the marks—they were made by something striking the wall at a height of about five feet from the ground. I could think of no natural cause for such marks. I could, however, dispute his conclusion. "It does not show that anyone is ahead of us," I replied. "Merely that someone has passed this way before, and we certainly know that— this is the route we ourselves took on our previous journey. Down here where there is neither wind nor rain to erode such marks, it is impossible to determine their age. They could simply be the marks we ourselves made on our last descent."

"Well, that's a relief then," he said. "I was worried about upsetting the Captain and the professor by saying anything about these scrapes around them. I'm glad to hear my fears aren't well-founded."

I touched his arm. "I do not say that the Gun Club is *not* ahead of us," I cautioned him. "Merely that these marks prove nothing either way. You will find that many things are very different down here than they might have been on the surface of our world."

In order to make Land's excuse plausible to the others, we looked about for a short while before returning to the main party. My uncle had been verbally sketching out the path ahead of us to the Captain, who was visibly restraining himself from plunging on ahead and letting his men follow behind as they arrived. My uncle, once again, cautioned that our party should not separate; well enough did I know the consequences of such an action. Though impatient to be off, Von Horst forced himself to wait until the last man joined us. At this point, we formed a single line, Hans in the lead, and we began the task of retracing our steps.

For the next several days, nothing of any great interest occurred. We experienced nothing out of the ordinary as we knew this portion of the journey well enough to take no wrong passages. The days were simply filled with walking, climbing, resting and eating our rations. We were frugal with our water supplies, mindful that this precious liquid might not be so simple to find down here.

Ned Land found everything fascinating, out of his native element as he was. He listened willingly to every lecture my uncle gave as we walked about the rocks and fossils we passed. The sailor was an intelligent man, and a quick study. Soon enough he was pointing out the shells of extinct marine life so well preserved in the tunnel walls, and mispronouncing their taxonomic names with great gusto. If the Captain or his men found any interest in the sights, none of them showed any evidence of it. They were men on a mission and devoted their attention and energy to that cause.

At the end of our first week's travel, we had made good progress. Having avoided errors we had made the first time around, we were much deeper and further along on our journey than the previous time, and it was now time for two things. First, as had become our habit on the previous adventure, Hans received his weekly pay for his services. He accepted the coins solemnly and stowed them in his pack.

Secondly, it was time for my uncle's promised decision about the Captain and his men. We were gathered together in a small cluster in a cavern some hundred or so feet long, thirty high and sixty deep. Each of us had managed to find a boulder to act as a seat, and two of the coils were lit to provide a faerie light that glinted off the rocks about us.

"When we began this trip," my uncle said, "I had my reservations, Captain, about the size of our party. However, I find myself in the position of having to admit that my worries have proven to be unfounded. You and your men have caused no delay in our progress, and you appear to have adapted to this strange life of ours down here rather well. If you are in agreement, then, I would propose that you remain members of our group for the rest of our journey."

"Naturally I agree," Von Horst replied. "We are here because of our duty, and that duty to Germany remains unchanged. We shall accompany you every step of the way."

To seal this agreement, the two men shook hands solemnly. Ned Land grinned, and I admit I was glad that we should have the company of the soldiers for the rest of the journey. Though they did not socialize with us at all, they were not a burden, and I was glad for the extra numbers. I could not then—nor indeed can I now—tell you the name of a single one of them, but that was how they wished it.

For myself, I was more than glad that we had Ned Land along. Hans was a good fellow, but he rarely spoke, and when he did it was in Danish, and only my uncle understood him. Land, on the other hand, spoke several languages pretty fluently, so he and I could converse without trouble. As the Captain stayed with his men in our rest times, and with my uncle the remainder of the time, I was sincerely glad for the sailor's company. We had become good friends by this point, and we had exchanged our tales. I filled him in on the events of my previous plunge into the Earth, and he responded by telling me of the adventures he had faced whilst captive of the strange Captain Nemo. When those tales had run out, he'd turned to speaking of his days on the high seas, and of hunting the great whales. Though his tales sometimes sounded a trifle fantastic, his quiet, earnest manner made me believe his every word.

He soon had evidence for one of my own tales. We were descending a sloping passageway when there was a faint murmuring ahead of us. The Captain signaled a halt and turned to my uncle.

"Could we have caught up with the Gun Club?" he asked, softly. He worried about sound being carried down these passageways, as sometimes the acoustics could make sounds from miles away sound as if they were right beside one.

"I don't know," the scientist admitted, just as softly, and just as disturbed. Despite everything, were we in second place after all in our mission?

Hans, however, was quite certain he knew the reason for the faint sound. "Vand," he said, in his normal voice.

"Vand?" my uncle echoed. Then he laughed. "Of course, Hans is quite correct, as usual."

"But what does he say it is?" Ned Land demanded. "You forget that we don't speak Danish."

"Oh, he means *water*."

The sailor frowned. "We have reached the underground sea already?"

"No, no," my uncle said, impatiently. "But I'm surprised that Axel hasn't recognized where we are. Come along." He led the way briskly forward, and we trailed behind. I racked my brain, trying to work out why I should know this passage of so many. It finally came to me as we reached the source of the murmuring sounds.

"The Hans-bach!" I exclaimed, and indeed it was that underground river, named for its discoverer, Hans. On our first trip we had been threatened by an acute shortage of water when Hans saved us by discovering a subterranean river flowing behind the rock wall of our tunnel. He had hacked a hole through to it, and water had gushed forth, saving our lives. And here, years later, we now faced the remains of that flow. It demonstrated how much underground water there must be that this river—now reduced to a gentle stream—had lasted so long.

And, as we quickly discovered, it was still extremely hot.

"There is a great deal of water associated with volcanoes," my uncle lectured. "In Iceland, these super-heated streams sometimes burst forth at the surface into powerful fountains known as *geysers*. They have also been reported in sections of the United States. I suspect there is now one less erupting on the surface of our planet, having been diverted down this passageway." He pointed onward. "And, as before, the faithful Hans-bach will lead our way for a while now."

We paused to refill our canteens, though we had to wait for a while until the water was cool enough to drink, and then continued on our way, descending once again.

Ned Land shook his head. "I had thought, lad, that I had seen almost all there was to be seen associated with water. But a stream miles beneath the Earth that runs hotter than a bath—now *that's* a new one for me." He chuckled. "I can see that this trip of ours in going to be very educational."

VI. The Shores of an Ancient Sea

On my previous journey I was able to provide exact dates and distances for our travels. This time, however, I am quite unable to do that for reasons that will shortly be made perfectly clear. Instead of being able to peruse my notes, I am forced this time around to rely upon my memory. Again, for reasons that will be made abundantly clear, those memories are not as accurate as I might have wished. So I am afraid that vagueness is all that I can offer. It is a poor excuse for a scientist, but cannot be helped.

We followed the path of the Hans-bach downward for the next few days. A trip to the center of our world might sound exciting, but day after day of walking, resting, eating and sleeping is far from enthralling, especially when much of it varied not at all. One tunnel through ancient rocks is much like any other tunnel. One rest-stop on convenient rocks varies not a whit from any other. The meals we ate were cold and monotonous and my sleeps—at the very least—were broken by the longing I felt to see my wife and child again. From time to time there might come some excitement if my uncle discovered a new vein of some igneous rock which he felt compelled to point out to everyone. From time to time Ned Land might laugh or marvel at some oddly-shaped rock. Other than that, the soldiers marched in grim silence and I was lost in my own thoughts, save for the times of conversation with the sailor, or with my uncle over matters scientific. Despite the potential perils and the urgency of our mission, boredom was our greatest foe.

And then we heard the sound of a great thunderclap from ahead of us. Even Hans appeared startled at this unexpected intrusion into our silent world. Save for the low murmur of the flowing Hans-bach, and the sound of our own footsteps, the world below ground is almost uniformly silent. With no native light, there are no plants, and without plants there is no animal life. There is no wind, for the air does not hurtle about, and so there is little enough to cause any noise. Hence our surprise and shock at this great roaring boom.

328

Captain Von Horst immediately signaled his soldiers. Dropping their packs, they immediately raised their rifles and set off at a trot. Hans fell in behind them, though without losing his pack. Ned Land was hot on his heels, and my uncle and I followed at the rear. We carried our own packs as at the time I had my coil lit and my uncle would not abandon his instruments for any strange noise. Down the passageway we plunged, following those ahead of us, and then into a large cavern. Here we halted, gathered with the others of our party.

The cavern was some fifty feet long, about twenty wide and over a hundred feet high. Stalactites and stalagmites abounded, and there was the faint sound of dripping that showed some subterranean waters were causing both to grow slowly over the millennia. At the far side of the cavern were two possible exits. I recalled that the left-hand one was the passageway we should take, and before that exit was a huge jumble of rocks, partially blocking access.

Hans said something in Danish to my uncle, who nodded and gestured at the pile. "That was not here the last time we passed this way," he said, confirming my own recollection. "It is partially blocking the road we must take."

Von Horst scowled. "The Americans must be ahead of us," he declared. "They must have caused this obstruction in the hopes of slowing us down or stopping us." The thought was alarming. Was the Gun Club willing to stop us at any cost?

"That is one explanation, to be sure," my uncle admitted. "There are, however, others."

"Such as?"

"If you examine these rock shards you will see evidence of recent growth of minerals on pieces. This shows that this debris once made up a stalactite, like so many above us." He gestured at the roof of the cavern. "It is possible that this one simply accumulated too much material and it was unable to stay suspended any longer."

"But we heard an explosion," Von Horst objected.

"No; we heard a noise that could be *interpreted* as an explosion. If the rock had merely fallen and shattered, these passageways could produce echoes and reverberations that would have made it sound similar to an explosion."

Von Horst clearly wasn't convinced. "And it just happened to fall as we approached?" he asked. "And it just happened to partially block the way we must take?"

"Coincidences do occur," my uncle replied calmly. "I do not say that is how it happened, merely that is it how it *may* have happened."

"Besides," Ned Land put in, "from everything I've heard of the Gun Club, they are very used to employing explosives. If they blew up this rock with the aim of blocking our way, I think they'd have managed a better job of it. We can clear the pathway is a few minutes, so it hardly holds us up at all." This seemed a valid point to me and to my uncle, but Von Horst remained skeptical. Still, proving Land's point, we had the pathway sufficiently cleared to allow us to proceed within fifteen minutes.

We were all quiet as we did so. Von Horst was probably listening for any signs that the Americans were ahead of us, but I was wondering whether the fallen stalactite had been a work of coincidence or of human agency. The idea that we might be following a party willing to take drastic action to slow us down or stop us was quite unsettling.

Was it possible that the Americans had realized that my uncle had tried to trick them when he convinced me to put the false entrance to the underworld in my manuscript? Had they taken advantage of their few days' lead on us to plunge ahead of us? Could we have been trailing them all of this time? There was no way to be certain, just as there was no way to discern whether the fall of the stalactite had been the work of Nature or the hand of man. As we all worked to clear our passage, we were all lost in such somber thoughts. After all of our efforts, we might still be in second place. To have gone through all that we had, and to see our efforts come to naught... It was too much to contemplate.

By early afternoon, we were able to continue on our way. Now, however, we were looking all about us not for whatever we could learn of the world about us, but to see if there was any evidence that we were on the Gun Club's trail.

There were marks from time to time on the walls and on the ground before us. The problem was, as I had explained to Ned Land at the start of our quest, that it was impossible to discern whether they were the marks we ourselves had left from our first trip or whether they were evidence of others before us.

We continued in this feeling of despair and uncertainty for several more days. Even Ned Land, normally talkative and cheerful, was uncommonly silent and withdrawn. As ever, only Hans seemed unaffected by our concerns. As long as he received his weekly pay when it came due, he was a happy man. If he was missing his young lady's company, or worried about her actions while he was gone, neither showed on his open, unworried face. He did his job as he always did, and left worries or cares to others more suited to suffering them.

Unlike Hans, I certainly suffered. Atop missing my little family and worrying for my life, I now had the terrible premonition that it might all be for nothing after all.

Finally, however, came the day we had been anticipating for so long. We came down a long tunnel, Hans in the lead, as usual, when the guide called back: "Vind!"

Wind! Even I understood that much Danish. *Wind!* Down here, far below the tumultuous weather on the surface of our planet, there could only be one source of wind. Excited again at last, we rushed forward and exited the tight passageway to stand within an immense cavern, almost unimaginably large. Our coils were no longer needed, as the place possessed a light source of its own. Far in the distance, near the roof of this great cavern, was the glow of an aurora, similar to those found in the polar regions of the surface world. Here, though, the glow was continuous and bathed the entire realm in a mockery of sunlight.

Ned Land whistled, and then grinned. "Now *this* is a sight!" he exclaimed. "Light and a stiff breeze—and I can hear the sound of waves, unless I am much mistaken."

"You are quite correct," my uncle said. "The Central Sea lies before us. Come, let us go and see it!"

The prospect of a break at last in the monotony of stone walls close about us had even the soldiers excited. We rushed together as a troop through the rocks and stalagmites, lit in strange and beautiful colors from the glow of the aurora, toward the waiting sea. The sounds of the waves and the whistling of the wind were wonderful to hear, and then we broke out onto the shore.

Ahead of us, fading into the distance, lay an immense body of water. Waves lapped or crashed upon the shore about our feet. It was impossible to calculate how large it must be, or how much water it held. Land, Von Horst and the soldiers stared at it in awe. It almost felt as though we had somehow been magically returned to the surface of our planet even though we all knew we were deep within the Earth. At our backs were the huge walls of rock that then rose over our heads and helped to contain this world within a world.

"Magnificent!" the Captain said, in an almost breathless tone. "This, *this*, is the start of New Germany." He signally one of his men who removed his pack and extracted from it a small flag bearing the emblem of our unified Germany. Von Horst took it carefully from the man and moved back about a dozen feet from the edge of the ocean before plunging it upright into the ground. "I claim this new land in the name of the Kaiser and the peoples of Germany!" he cried. The five soldiers gave a cry of acclaim. The Captain was almost glowing from patriotic fervor.

I confess that I had quite a different reaction to this statement. It seemed to me that any attempt to annex this inner ocean as part of Germany was both futile and a case of hubris. This world was its own master, without the need for the hand of man. Ned Land was as silent and inscrutable as Hans. My uncle, however, could not restrain his own emotions.

"You are claiming this land?" he asked, derisively. "What? Are you to move settlers down here? Do you envision starting up a factory on the shores of this sea? Or do you wish to sail a battleship or run a ferry here? My dear Captain, I can see no use for patriotism down here."

"You are mocking our Kaiser?" Von Horst asked, his face flushed.

"Not I!" my uncle assured him. "I rather think it is *you* who mock him by attempting to claim a land he cannot use. What will you do with this vast realm now that you have it?"

"But you agreed to lead an expedition here in order to claim it," the soldier protested.

"No," the man of science answered. "I could see that you were determined to come here on this mission of yours, and I knew you would not succeed without my help. But my aim was never to claim this land, but in the hopes of demonstrating the futility of your desire." He gestured about us. "There is nothing here for you or your superiors. This world exists on its own terms and is ruled by creatures you cannot conquer or understand. It is not a place for politicians to try and claim or squabble over. As we explore further, you will understand what I mean. All we can do here is pass through it and seek to understand as much as possible. It is not our land, and never will be."

"You are a traitor," Von Horst exclaimed, his face livid. "You mock Germany and our Kaiser!" He turned to his men. "Arrest him!"

"Arrest me?" My uncle laughed. "And then what will you do with me? Is there a jail nearby you can throw me into, or a dungeon where I can be chained up? Captain, you are being foolish."

"You will bow to my authority," Von Horst snapped. "If you resist, I can have you shot."

"Oh, that would be most sensible," the professor mocked. "Can you even retrace your steps to the surface of this world?" He held up his notebook. "The only route back is within this book—and it is written in a code of my own devising. If you have me shot, you may as well then shoot yourself and stave off a lingering death."

The captain was starting to feel less secure in his authority. He gestured at Hans. "He is your guide—I am sure he will know the way back."

"That may be so," my uncle replied, unworriedly crossing his arms. "But he speaks only Danish—and I am the only other member of this party who shares that tongue. So the only way you would ever know what he knows is through my assistance. My dear Captain, please stop posturing and use your mind for a change. Things must remain as they are, however you feel about matters." He gestured at the flag. "If it makes you happy to plant that here, then do so—but don't expect it to mean anything."

The Captain was livid, but I could see that he understood how things were. Confronting my uncle was a pointless exercise that would only serve to test his power. My uncle could be infuriating at times, but in this matter he was quite correct—there was little that Von Horst could do to him down here. What my uncle was forgetting was that we would, hopefully, not be down here forever. Once we regained the surface of our world, I had a strong suspicion that any resentments the military man felt now would be multiplied twentyfold, and that he would make my uncle pay dearly for his mockery. I resolved to have words with the Professor when we were alone and caution him against further challenges to Von Horst. I was by no means certain, of course, that my uncle would listen.

"So," the Captain said, finally, barely restraining his temper, "what would you have us do now?"

My uncle gestured at the expanse of the Central Sea. "That is our way forward," he explained. "It is time for us to build rafts to enable us to navigate it." He turned to Ned Land. "Do you think you could take the lead in the construction of a pair of rafts?"

Land grinned widely. I could see that he was eager to be out upon the waters of this unexplored ocean; this was why he had accompanied us. "I can do better than that," he vowed. "With the aid of these stout fellows –" He gestured at the soldiers, Hans and myself "—I am certain I can construct vessels that will serve us well." He inclined his head toward Von Horst. "With your permission, Captain, I should like to borrow your strong lads to collect the timber we shall need for the work."

The Captain looked puzzled. "I see no timber," he said. "Merely rocks."

"Farther down the coast is a veritable forest," I informed him. "Though not one such as we have on the surface of the world. It should supply us with all the materials we will need. It will take a few days to gather the materials and construct our craft, so this would be a good time to set up a base camp near the forest."

"Very well," the Captain agreed. "Let us take a look at the forest and we shall establish a camp there. And my men will aid in chopping down the trees."

I couldn't resist a grin of my own. "It's not trees, Captain—it's mushrooms."

"Mushrooms!"

"Indeed," my uncle said. "But mushrooms the like of which our world above has never seen."

We wound our way along the shoreline of the Central Sea. There was a strong breeze coming off the waters, and Ned Land laughed as he walked beside me. "The journey so far hasn't been one for a sailor," he commented. "But this! This was worth walking all that way to see. An unknown ocean, un-navigated and uncharted. This is what a sailor lives for, my lad."

"Our last trip on these waters was far from entertaining," I observed drily. "We suffered through an electrical storm and the clash of leviathans."

"But that time you didn't have Ned Land with you." He grinned again. "Things will be very different this time, I assure you."

I hoped that he was correct, but in these strange lands it is always best to expect the worst—far too frequently that is what arrives. But I had no idea how terrible things were about to become.

VII. Betrayal!

Walking along that shore, with the sea to our right and the strange electrical glow in the air, one might almost imagine oneself back upon the surface of our planet instead of miles beneath its surface. That is, until one looked up and saw the rocks curving up above our heads on the left until they were lost in the light. The stalactites thinned out and then we caught our first glimpse of the weird mushroom forest. On the surface of our world, often hidden from the rays of the sun, mushrooms achieve a height of but a few inches. Down here in the underworld, illuminated by an electrical glow that clearly possessed strange properties that normal light does not, mushrooms achieved a much greater height.

Ned Land gave a loud, clear whistle that echoed about us strangely. "I've seen sights from Zanzibar to Zebu," he murmured, "but never anything like this!"

Starting with a few scattered individuals of lesser height, the mushrooms spread before us, many of them topping forty feet tall. Large caps crowned stalks the size of trees, though possessing no branches. It was possible to discern different varieties of growths—most were tall and pale, like our earthly counterparts, but some had riots of odd color. Some were tall and thin, reaching toward the looming roof of rock, while others were shorter and fatter, more like the size of a small hut. The soldiers were all stunned by the vista before us, and even I—who had seen it before—found it profound and moving. Where there is water, light and heat, it appeared, life will find a way to exist.

My uncle, ever practical, gestured toward the forest. "The stalks of the gigantic mushrooms are as strong as wood," he commented. "There are many that have fallen in the electrical storms that ravage this world and we should be able to collect sufficient for our needs quite quickly."

Ned Land nodded. "I'll have to test the… well, I suppose calling it *wood* is incorrect, but it's what I'm used to saying… the wood, then, to make certain it's suitable, but I see nothing wrong with your basic plan."

At that moment, there was a strange howl in the distance that made everyone pause.

"What is that?" the Captain demanded.

"One of the inhabitants of this land, I should imagine," my uncle said lightly. "There are creatures within these forest that feast on the mushrooms, naturally—and other creatures that prey upon those beasts. We should have nothing to fear from them as long as we are careful."

"Animals down here?" asked Ned Land.

"Certainly," my uncle replied. "Life down here follows the same natural laws as it does upon the surface of our world. Where there is vegetable life, there is animal life to feed upon it. And where there is animal life, there are predators to snatch up what they can. Besides, you already knew that there are monsters in the waters—why are you then surprised to hear that there is life upon the land?"

"I simply never made the connection," the sailor admitted, a little ashamed. "This land is so austere and strange that I never imagined life upon it—but the sea is wild and beautiful and life there seems natural to me. The prejudices of a sailor!"

The Captain licked his lips. "Animals mean fresh meat," he said. "After so long on dried rations, that sounds delightful. I shall send two of my men off hunting—tonight we shall feast!"

"Perhaps it would be better for Hans to accompany them," my uncle suggested. "He is, after all, a hunter by profession."

"No!" the Captain said, sharply. "My men will go alone. Your guide is strong and will be of more use here helping to haul the wood that we require."

It did not surprise me that he did not want Hans to accompany his men—he had made it abundantly clear that he felt that the two non-German members of our party were somehow inferior creatures and not to be entrusted with any important tasks, and that they were more suited to menial labor. It was an attitude I did not care for, but there seemed to be little to be gained in remonstrating him for it.

Ned Land stepped forward. "Aye, he's a big boy," he agreed. "I'll take him along with me and Axel here and we'll scout about for fallen mushrooms and test their wood." He rummaged in his pack for a moment before straightening up, holding a large, heavy knife. "I have to be certain we can carve the wood." He turned to the professor. "Ask your man to bring his ax and to accompany us, if you would."

My uncle exchanged a few words with Hans, who nodded and pulled his ax from his pack. "I shall remain here with the Captain," my uncle decided. "This would seem to be as good a spot as any for our camp."

I shed my own pack, retaining only my own knife and a rifle. I doubted any of the local fauna would venture close to us, but I was comforted by its presence. Ned gave me one of his cheery grins and led the small party off into the mushroom woods. Two of the soldiers set off in a slightly different direction. In a few moments Ned, Hans and myself were alone in the strange growths. As we walked, Ned was occupied with something in his hand, and then I heard him give a sailor's picturesque curse. "What is the matter?" I asked him.

He held out his hand. In his large palm rested a bullet that he had pried open, spilling dark powder onto the skin. "When the Captain seemed so adamant that our friend Hans should not go hunting, I was seized by a sudden suspicion. I palmed one of the bullets I had been issued when I retrieved my knife."

"So?" I asked, puzzled.

"So," he said, grimly, "this bullet would not fire. It is filled with coarse black pepper, and not powder."

I was confused. "What does this mean?"

"It means that the Captain does not trust me—nor Hans, most likely—with live ammunition." He stared at the rifle I carried. "The question now is whether he trusts you and your uncle with it."

This thought was very disquieting. I opened up the breech of my rifle and extracted the bullet. As he had feared, when Ned Land opened the cartridge, pepper once again spilled out.

"So," he said, slowly, "you and most probably your uncle also have weapons that will not fire. Only the Captain and his men are armed."

"That's not good," I said. "We are unable to defend ourselves. He has placed our lives at risk."

"My lad, you are very naïve," the sailor said. "It is possible that he intends to do more than risk your life. If the three of us and your uncle were not to return from this expedition, who would ever think of blaming the Captain? He, after all, would be the one telling the story of our fate."

"You think he would do that?" I asked, aghast. "But *why*?"

He shrugged. "I do not *know* that this is his plan," he said. "Merely that it *may* be so. I think we should all prepare ourselves in case that is what he has in mind. You must take the opportunity to speak to your uncle alone and warn him of my suspicions. But we shall *all* take care and not let our suspicions slip. If he knew we were aware of his schemes, he might advance his timetable. For the moment I think we are safe because he needs us to construct our vessels. But after that?"

"But he needs my uncle for his map," I protested. "He knows he cannot decipher it without him."

"And what need does he have for the rest of us?" the sailor asked. "He might possibly require you as a hostage to ensure your uncle's compliance, but Hans and I are likely to be deemed superfluous. It all depends upon what his aim is and at the moment we do not know it. But we are aware that he *has* plans, and so we must make some of our own. It is essential, however, that he not know we are onto his schemes."

I glanced at Hans. "And what of him?" I asked. "How much of this does he understand?"

"He will understand all of it shortly," Land replied. "I can converse with Hans well enough with my little Danish. You learn a lot of languages living at sea, my lad."

"Then I will speak with my uncle at the earliest possible moment," I promised. "Who knows? Perhaps he can make some sense of this."

As it turned out, he could—but not the way I had expected. We had gathered quite a supply of fallen mushroom stems that the sailor thought looked promising, and returned with them to camp. While he and Hans set about turning these into usable planks and such, I managed to get my uncle aside and speak to him. When I told him of our discovery, he merely shrugged.

"I know all about that," he said. "And have since the expedition started."

"You *know*?" I cried. "And said nothing?"

"Keep your voice down low, my boy," my uncle admonished me. "I would prefer that the Captain not overhear this conversation. Yes, I knew—and I said nothing. Axel, my boy, you're a good man, but I don't know if you're a good actor. I was afraid that if I told you what I knew, you might blurt it out, honest

336

soul that you are, or eye the Captain and his men in ways that might arouse their suspicion."

"But you knew," I persisted.

"From the first day," he admitted. "I inspected our equipment while we were on the ship, you may recall. The Captain was wise enough to lay out live ammunition then, so that everything looked normal. But when we received our packed bags, I saw that the ammunition in it had been changed. The only reason for this I could think of was that blanks had been substituted. And I realized that if mine had been tampered with, then so had yours and that of Hans and Mr. Land. The only reason for this that came to mind was that the Captain wanted to be certain of having an advantage over us. I do not know why he should want that, but it was clear that he intended to control us in some way at some time."

"But what can we do about it?" I asked, appalled.

"I have already done something," he replied. "The real reason I wished to stay with the Captain and set up camp was because the soldiers had to leave their packs here while they hunted and worked. I was able to seize the opportunity to exchange all of mine and Hans' blank ammunition for live rounds. Now *we* have the advantage, for the Captain believes us powerless and his men to possess the only live ammunition. I am not yet certain how we make use of this, but any advantage must be to the good."

My uncle never ceased to amaze me. I was astonished and proud of his cleverness, but annoyed at being kept in the dark over it all. Still, though my pride was hurt, it was more important to plan for our future. "So what are we to do now?"

"Act as if nothing were wrong," he replied. "We build our two ships and continue our little expedition as planned until we discover what the Captain's intents are." His face clouded. "I fear they may be grave your our companions."

"You think he means them harm?" I asked.

"I think he has already attempted harm. The attack on Hans back in Iceland—I do not believe it was engineered either by the Gun Club or by his romantic rival. I suspect—but cannot prove—that the injured soldier we were forced to leave behind was the person who began the rock fall that was aimed at Hans, and that he himself was injured as he effected it."

"You think he means to kill Hans and Ned Land?"

My uncle held up an admonishing finger. "That is merely one interpretation of the facts," he cautioned me. "It may or may not be the correct one—but we should take the possibility quite seriously. Inform Mr. Land of my suspicions, but admonish him to take precautions but no precipitous actions yet. We must see how things are planned before we act."

My uncle appeared calm and in control of himself, but I did not find it as easy to keep in rein my own temper. That we should be so betrayed! I wished to face down the Captain and confront him with what we knew of his treachery— but my uncle was quite correct. That would avail us nothing. They were still six to our four, and they had twice as much ammunition as we had. Besides which, they were trained fighting men, and we… Well, I had no doubt that in a fight both Hans and Ned Land could more than hold their own. But my uncle and I were mere academics and completely unused to physical combat. It galled me to do nothing, but my uncle's advice had been good.

I hurried back to Ned Land. While I was supposedly helping him to work on the shaping of our vessels, I informed him quietly of the conversation I had just had with my uncle. The sailor thought about this for a few moments before replying.

"It seems to me that your uncle is right—at the moment the Captain has the advantages. But since we know he must be intending to act, we have an advantage there as he must assume we are still completely unaware of his actions. He is an egotist, and such men feel themselves superior to others. He is sure to believe he has us completely fooled. We must all act dumb in order to maintain his false state of belief. In the mean time, I shall endeavor to follow your uncle's example and exchange some of my bad ammunition for one soldier's good supply."

"I shall do the same," I vowed.

Land laughed and clapped my shoulder. "I think not, my friend," he said. "You're a fine fellow, and I'm glad to have you on my side, but your hands lack the required subtlety for the work of thievery. Leave that to me, and I shall slip you some good bullets as the time passes. Now, we have real work to do—shaping our boats!"

The two soldiers returned later, carrying two small, dead creatures my uncle and I readily identified as *eohippus*, a miniature ancestor of today's majestic horses. The men had sighted a small herd of the creatures grazing, and had brought down these two. When my uncle had named and described them, Ned Land expressed his wonder.

"Ancient horses supposedly dead these past few million years?" He shook his head. "This is a strange world we are in, indeed."

"Not at all," my uncle replied. "It is only logical. Some 13 years ago a British scientist, Charles Darwin, published his book *On The Origin Of Species*. In it, he proposed that creatures evolve over time to adapt to changes in their conditions." He spread his arms. "Down here, there *are* no changes in conditions. It is logical, therefore, that since there is no need for animals to evolve, they do not. So plesiosaurs in the seas here remain masters of their ocean and small ancestral horses still roam these strange forests. It is eminently sensible."

I licked my lips as the fresh meat roasted over a fire. "What is eminently sensible to me," I pointed out, "is that we are going to have fresh meat again for the first time in many weeks."

Ned Land laughed. "I think you have the best of this discussion, my lad."

Our "evening" meal—though there was neither night nor day down here, we allowed our pocket watches to rule our days—was a reasonably jovial affair.

We were all, soldiers included, glad for this change in our fare. Though the meat was a trifle on the tough side, I could not recall a time when I had eaten better. The only thing marring our enjoyment of the feast was the strong and certain knowledge that we were to soon be betrayed.

VIII. At Sea

The small vessels that Ned Land designed and supervised as we all helped to build them were a great improvement upon our previous attempt. The mushroom stalks proved to be remarkably wood-like in their qualities, enabling us to make planks from them and then to form them into the requited shapes to construct the boats. Naturally, we did not have metal for nails, but the sailor showed us how to use "wooden" pins and wedges to hold the planks together. Over the course of the next several days our two boats took shape. I refer to them as boats, but they were actually little more than elongated canoes, to which Ned Land added out-riggers, such as those he had seen in the South Seas, to make them far more stable.

All of this took time, of course—again, I cannot be sure of exactly how long, but it was certainly more than a week, but less than a month. Von Horst allowed us the use of three of the soldiers each day to aid with the construction, while he and the remaining two went hunting, to keep us supplied with fresh meat. At least, that is what he claimed, though later events make me now disbelieve that assertion. Tensions were quite high—partly because of the confrontation between my uncle and Captain Von Horst, but mostly because of the fact that we knew a betrayal was in the offing. While Ned Land kept us busy constructing the boats, my uncle and Hans managed to swap out more of our ammunition with that of the soldiers who helped us. I never did learn their names, as they had no interest in conversation and simply obeyed Mr. Land's orders as they were given.

The hunting parties proved to be very productive. We ate well, and were able to smoke and preserve a goodly store of meat in case it should be needed on the rest of our trip. On our previous voyage, the Central Sea was as close as we actually managed to approach the center of the Earth; shortly after we crossed it, we were hurtled back to the surface through the agency of an active volcano. We sincerely aimed to avoid the same route this time—we had been more than fortunate not to have been cooked on our last journey—and would seek a route leading us deeper into the Earth.

"It may be that our predecessor Arne Saknussemm managed to get no further than this, either," my uncle said over our supper one evening. "We discovered his initials carved on a rock beside the tunnel that took us back to the surface. There may be nothing more ahead of us than a return to the sunlit world above us. But I cannot accept that as inevitable, and am determined that we should press onward—and, hopefully, downward."

"That is my aim also," Von Horst agreed. "We are ordered to reach the center of the Earth, if at all possible." He glanced out across the waters of the Central Sea. Because our light was caused by electrical phenomenon, unlike on the surface there was no night here. Every hour of the day was as bright as any other. In the distance, churning the waters and lighting the sky, was a vast electrical storm. "Yet are you certain your boats will be able to withstand such weather, Mr. Land?"

The whaler laughed. "No sailor knowingly would engage a storm such as that," he observed. "Such forces of nature could swamp and sink much sturdier vessels than we are constructing. No, I do not propose crossing the ocean at all."

My uncle glanced at him sharply. "But we *must* cross it," he insisted. "If there is a way ahead, it is on the far side of the waters."

"Well now," the sailor said gently, "in the first place, we don't know that for a fact." He gestured about us. "There are many grottos around here, and any number of side passages, any of which might be the road downward for us."

"Far too many for us to explore in several lifetimes," the Professor objected. "And none with any certainty that it doesn't peter out pointlessly. We should look for more evidence that the esteemed Saknussemm has gone before us."

"But he, in turn, must have had a reason to select the passages that he did," Ned Land pointed out. "And there is no telling how many times he had to backtrack to advance. And what if your supposition is correct? That he got no closer to the center of the Earth than this sea here before us?" That thought shut off my uncle's objections for a moment. "In the second place," the sailor continued, "I have seen no evidence that this Icelander built a raft himself—the only indications of previous work at this site are those you and your companions left last time. This leads me to believe that your medieval explorer went on foot around the edge of the sea."

I had to confess that he made a good point there. "It's likely, uncle," I argued. Then, confused, I asked Ned Land: "But in that case, why the need for us to build boats?"

"Because of my third and final point. I suggest that we do not venture out too far at sea, but instead follow the coast and camp each night ashore. This way we shall be able to scout about and see if we can strike further evidence of the path our predecessor took and if he went deeper before returning here. And we shall be able to look for routes that he might not have taken that look likely. And, to cap it all, we shall be able to avoid the monsters of the deeps that almost killed you on your last trip. Such monsters need the depth to swim and feed, so they will not be able to venture close enough to the shore to imperil us."

For once, the Captain actually seemed enthused by Ned Land's ideas. "I agree whole-heartedly," he said. "It is a most sensible plan and gives us the greatest chance of success."

My uncle was still not convinced that we would not be better off striking across the sea, but even he was willing in the end to defer to the judgment of our only nautical member. If was thus decided that when we were able to launch our vessels we should stay close to land and scout the way as we went, camping each night upon the shore. I confess I was much relieved—I had no desire at all for another encounter with the pleisosaurs and ichthyosaurs we had narrowly escaped before. I had seen quite enough of the supposedly-extinct monsters to last me several lifetimes.

And so, with everything agreed upon, we embarked upon the sea-leg portion of our voyage. The Captain insisted on being in the lead vessel with Ned Land and two of the soldiers. I made up the final member of that crew. My uncle and Hans were to follow with the remaining three soldiers in the second boat. I didn't feel comfortable being confined with Von Horst in a small vessel, but there was little choice. I was, at least, glad of Mr. Land's company.

As he had promised us, the outrigger construction proved to be remarkably stable and a completely different experience from the raft we had previously employed. Each of the boats had a mast, to which we had rigged whatever canvas we had as sails, but the main motive power was our muscles driving oars. We were all, even my uncle, in good physical shape thanks to our continual exercise, and we soon learned to stroke in unison to power the boats faster. The rhythm we built up was quite effective, and sped us through the waters. We stayed in fairly shallow waters about a hundred yards from the shore line as we headed east around the sea.

There was little of any consequence for the first three days. We rowed, rested and allowed the wind to drive us, and scanned the shoreline. We saw animals from time to time that my uncle and I named from our studies, many of which were considered extinct thousands or even millions of years ago. Most were herbivorous, like the small herds of *eohippus* that seemed to infest the area. Twice we heard the sounds of some animal in pain and the cries of some ancient hunter, but we saw nothing. Evidently there were predators, but they did not venture to approach either the water's edge or our evening campsites.

There was an abundance of fish in the sea, and Ned Land rigged fishing lines for both boats. I cannot tell you with what pleasure we dined upon freshly roast fish when we camped for the "night". Neither the sailor nor my uncle was able to name the species we devoured, but most of them were quite delicious.

Gradually, as we sailed and rowed east, the landscape changed. The forests of giant mushrooms thinned out and were replaced by ones of gigantic ferns and trees common to more prehistoric eras of our planet. With this change came different creatures inhabiting the forests. I was able to recognize a family of *Brontotherium*—prehistoric relatives of the rhinoceros, but with twin horns on its huge snout, and a small herd of the immense *Megaloceros*, the fabled Irish elk, seven feet tall and with twelve foot antlers. Smaller creatures abounded, but stayed hidden from direct view. I could hear my uncle expounding upon these marvels in his own boat, and I could scarcely blame him—seeing these creatures finally in the flesh, perambulating and feasting was a dream unrealized by most paleontologists. His excitement was more than understandable, but I was also more than a trifle apprehensive. The final creatures that I saw and recognized were mastodons, those extinct relatives of the elephant, but of huge stature. These I had seen on our last trip to these regions and in the company of a nebulous figure that had terrified me more than any other we had encountered. This had been some twelve feet tall and shaped like a man. My uncle and I had fled from its presence before it could see us and we were never able to ascertain if what we had seen had indeed been some antediluvian species of *homo*. We were more than content to allow that mystery to remain unsolved.

Von Horst, however, seemed excited by the sight of these immense pachyderms and ordered the boats to make land immediately. Despite my protests and those of my uncle, the soldiers obeyed his command and we were forced to alight on the beach barely a mile beyond the great beasts.

"We shall set up our camp here," the soldier commanded. "I shall go with two of my men to explore the region."

"It is not safe," my uncle protested. "These mighty beasts we have been seeing are not used to mankind—there is no predicting their behavior. You may be courting your own deaths."

"That is none of your concern," Von Horst replied. "Do as you are told, and allow me to follow my orders."

"Your orders?" My uncle looked at him sharply. "And what orders might those be?"

"At this moment, no concern of yours," the soldier said. "Ready the camp and start the evening meal. When we return I shall explain further." True to his word, he wouldn't speak to us again before he and two of his men marched into the woods, their rifles at the ready.

Hans looked disturbed and asked my uncle a question. There was a short discussion carried on in Danish that left neither man happy. When it was concluded, Hans set about making a fire and I questioned my uncle about his conversation.

"Hmm?" He seemed very preoccupied. "Oh, my boy, don't bother me about that now. We have other things to concern ourselves over." And he refused to discuss the matter further.

I therefore turned to the only other man I trusted and asked Ned Land what he thought was going on. "The Captain clearly has instructions to do something he does not wish us to know about," he said. "This means he is fairly certain we shall not approve of those orders. Whatever he is up to, I'll wager it doesn't bode well for the four of us." He scowled. "It might be well to keep your rifle close at hand—you can always claim it's because these gigantic beasts are making you nervous. Heaven knows, their presence is affecting me." I rather felt that was because he was itching to hunt them, to be honest. Land was used to chasing monsters of the sea, and these were their closest terrestrial equivalents.

So we were a pretty quiet group as we set up our camp, each lost in his own thoughts. Mine were quite black. Whatever was happening, I felt that a confrontation was now inevitable. Unfortunately, I was quite correct.

The Captain and his soldiers returned as our evening meal—more fish and *eohippus* meat—was ready, and he refused to speak until after our meal was concluded. Then he finally gave in to my uncle's persistent and sharp questions.

"We merely explored the area," he insisted. "It would seem that we are in a region of monsters from the antediluvian past."

"And hence not a safe place for a camp," my uncle snapped. "So why, then, did you insist that we set up for the night here?"

"I have my reasons."

"Perhaps you would care to share them?"

"They are none of your concern," Von Horst replied.

"I am the leader of this expedition; *everything* that affects it in any way is of my concern." My uncle folded his arms stubbornly. "If you expect my further cooperation, then I must be fully informed as to what the objectives of this mission are, and what secret orders you have been given."

The Captain considered for a moment, and then nodded. "Very well. You would discover them soon enough anyway." He waved his hand about us. "I have been instructed to find the creature you referred to as *the Shepherd.*"

That comment made me shudder. He was referring to that peculiar hominid my uncle and I had witnessed who appeared to be treating a herd of mastodons as if they were domestic sheep. It had been a strange and terrifying figure, one we had both been glad to flee before it should have observed us.

"And why would you wish to do that?" my uncle asked. "Surely not simply to study the beast?"

"No, of course not." Von Horst dismissed the idea contemptuously. "But where there is one such creature, there are surely more of them. There must be at least a family unit and perhaps even a larger grouping."

"All the more reason to avoid even one of them," I said. "One is frightening enough—more of them would be abhorrent."

"You are a frightened chicken, not a man!" the Captain snapped. "Forever balking at shadows. Only a child is frightened by the unknown."

"And a wise man," Ned Land put in quietly. "Only a fool is not cautious when faced with a situation he has never dealt with before. I should take Herr Axel's concerns with a bit more respect—he has been here before—and you have not."

"Anyway, whatever the state of my nephew's nerves, why do you court death by seeking these shepherds?" The Professor in my uncle was curious. So was I, even though I was the subject of the Captain's insults and ridicule.

"I have been tasked with capturing and returning to Germany one of the youngsters of that species," Von Horst replied.

We were all quite astonished by that reply. Even my uncle could think of nothing to say for quite some time. It made no sense at all to me. Nothing I could think of could explain such bizarre orders. I glanced at the faces of my uncle and the sailor and saw that they were equally as confused as I. Finally, my uncle asked: "And why would you wish to attempt that?"

"Because Chancellor Bismarck himself has ordered it," the Captain said. "Can you not imagine the results of an army of such soldiers? Their appearance alone would terrify all opponents! Twelve foot soldiers fighting for the Motherland—a glorious sight!"

My uncle stared at him aghast. "You cannot be serious!"

"Never more so."

"This is madness," the Professor snapped. "These creatures, whatever they may be, belong *here*, among their own kind, not on the surface of our world! You cannot snatch them from their families and enslave them."

"They would not be slaves—they would be soldiers!" Von Horst said, enthusiastically.

"Soldiers you would have fight for a land and cause that is not their own," Ned Land growled. "They *would* be slaves, in all but name."

"They would be invincible!"

"*If* they can be taken to the surface of the world," I pointed out. "And if they were tractable enough to be trained. Has it not occurred to you that these conscripts of yours might not go along with your plan? That they may have a negative opinion of it?"

"Their opinion does not matter," the Captain said. "I have my orders, and I shall carry them out." He held up his rifle. "*We* have firearms, and they have only clubs. If there is protest, we can deal with it."

My uncle shook his head vehemently. "You are speaking of bringing war to this world," he exclaimed. "I cannot allow it! I *will* not allow it!"

"Then you have reached the limits of your use to me," Von Horst snapped. He nodded to the closest of his soldiers. "Kill him."

Before any of us could move, the soldier raised his rifle and fired point-blank at my uncle.

IX. Flight!

By good fortune, the bullet that should have ended my uncle's life turned out to be one of those he had switched earlier; instead of killing him, the soldier stared at my intact uncle in confusion.

"Now, my friends!" Ned Land roared. He lashed out at the closest of the soldiers, felling the surprised man with a single blow. He then scooped up his own rifle and pack. Hans clearly had been anticipating some such event, for he also jumped one of the startled warriors and sent him crashing to the ground before grabbing his own equipment. I had been unprepared, but seeing their actions I promptly followed suit, lowering my head and charging the closest soldier like a bull. I succeeded in knocking him down and snatched up my own pack and rifle. I followed hot on the heels of the sailor as he rushed into the ferns and trees close to the camp.

We ran as fast as we were able, dodging branches and following some trail created by the local fauna. I did not look back, but after a moment I heard the whine of bullets being fired behind us. Some of these were the blanks, but there were live rounds mixed in with them. Fortunately the forest at this point was quite thick, and none of the soldiers had a clear shot. I did not stop to plan or think, these events having taken me completely by surprise. Instead it was all I could do to keep up with the sailor I followed.

I realized that my uncle had been expecting some kind of confrontation with the Captain, and this must have been what he and Hans had been discussing earlier. I was more than a little hurt that he had not thought to confide his suspicions to me also, so that I might have been better prepared for what was happening. I realized, though, that it was not through any distrust of me but simply because he was too worried to even think of telling me.

On we plunged, getting further from the beach, our transportation and the fury of the Captain. We were, however, getting closer to potential trouble in the forests. There might be any number of the Shepherds about, along with local predators. I was about to call out to Ned Land and suggest we halt and gather our breaths for a while when the sailor himself called out for a halt.

Panting, exhausted and aching, I was glad to comply. I was bowed over, gasping for air, but still able to look around me. We were deep in the forest now, with ancient trees towering over us and swathes of ferns to hide us from pursuit. As I gasped for air, Hans emerged from the depths, still as impassive as ever, and—thankfully!—behind him came my uncle. He looked a trifle battered, but still in one piece. When he had regained his breath, he smiled at us and said: "Splendid. We are all still together."

"No thanks to you," I retorted, still angry over events. "You might have warned me that this was in store."

"Didn't I?" He looked puzzled. "No, I don't think I did, did I? I'm sorry, my boy, but I had a lot to think about and it simply passed from my mind. And I didn't exactly anticipate that the Captain would attempt to kill us. I had expected he would simply try and detain us. It really is very foolish of him—now he has driven us off, how does he expect to retrace his path to the surface?"

Ned Land gave a sharp bark of a laugh. "Do you think you are the only one capable of keeping a journal?" he asked. "One of the soldiers has done the same from the start. I'm sure the Captain believes he can find his way home again easily enough."

"And he aims to take along one of the ape-men from this world as a prototype soldier," I pointed out. "I'm sure none of us want that to happen. Warfare that involved these creatures would be too terrible to contemplate."

"We can hardly prevent him," Mr. Land said. "We surprised him with the substitution of fake bullets for real ones, but I am certain he will be sorting through his supplies right now and weeding out the blanks. We ourselves have some ammunition, but we are not soldiers and could not prevail in a pitched battle."

"No indeed," my uncle agreed. "Nor would I suggest that we risk our lives to attempt it. I think we shall have to rely on the natives of this land to defend themselves. The Captain's plan to steal one of the young of these ape-men might not be as simple as he thinks. He is making a very common mistake—he is assuming that modern man with his technology is of necessity smarter than ancient man. But to have survived all these millennia those ancient men must have been as intelligent as we are, merely lacking the technology. But this is *their* land. They grew up here, they live here, and they know it intimately. The Captain lacks those advantages."

"Perhaps so," I agreed. "Perhaps these locals need no aid from us. But you are forgetting, dear uncle, that *we* are still in trouble. The Captain wished to kill us in case we might interfere with his plans—I doubt he will have changed that aim simply because we fled."

"Axel is correct," Ned Land agreed. "The Captain will undoubtedly make hunting us down and killing us his first priority. We cannot stay here and talk for much longer—we must set off again and attempt to hide our path so that he cannot simply track us down. They are six to our four, and they have more training and experience at warfare. We are at a distinct disadvantage."

"Not entirely," my uncle said, a twinkle in his eye. "We have one weapon that he does not." He tapped his temple. "We have my scientific brain." He glanced at me. "Yours, too, Axel, though it is still forming. In any event, I believe we should be able to out-think him."

"Not unless we first out-run him," Ned Land replied. "Let us get moving once more."

We moved on, attempting to be as cautious as possible while still maintaining as much speed as possible. We did not want to make it easy to track us, but we had to balance that against the need to get away from the soldiers on our trail. From time to time we heard sounds of movement in the trees, but as no soldiers materialized, it was probably simply local wildlife that we had disturbed in our passage. We were fortunate that we did not stumble across the paths of any predators in our flight.

After a short while, though, we heard the distinct sound of a rifle. The great cavern we were within caused some echoes, and it was impossible to determine how far away the shot was. Nor did we know why it was fired. Ned Land speculated that it was a signal from one soldier that he had stumbled upon our path, but there was no way to decide whether this was true or not. We had to assume that they were indeed on our trail and keep on moving.

We were extremely fortunate in having Hans as our guide. He was uncanny in his ability to select the easiest paths for us to traverse, and he moved with barely a sound through the forest. Ned Land was surprisingly quiet for all of his size, but both my uncle and I appeared to stumble upon every stick that could break and every stone that could be dislodged. Probably these sounds didn't carry very far, but at the time I thought a blind man could track us with ease.

I cannot tell how long we fled. In that land where there is no change in the quality or quantity of the light time is very difficult to track. I recall glancing at my pocket watch and seeing that it was 7:15, but whether that was before or after noon, I couldn't say. Nor does it really matter. When there is no change from one hour to the next, one day to the next or even one month to the next, what is time but meaningless measurement? So we fled—whether for hours, days or weeks, I cannot say. I do recall stopping several times to eat and sleep—short, fitful naps rather than long, refreshing rests. We had no real idea where we were heading; we were simply following Hans, who, when asked his opinion simply stated: *"Fremad!"*—"Forward!"

As so we went. We did not dare hunt fresh meat, but we had amassed a good supply of smoked meat from our time beside the sea, so food was not a problem. There were plenty of brooks and streams within the forest so we had ample fresh water. We were suffering mostly mentally, from a fear of being caught, and physically, from the exertion to escape from that fate.

I did notice that, as we fled the sea, we were drawing closer to the walls of the great cavern we were in. After a while, the trees and ferns began to thin out and we could see immense rock walls parallel to our path. What we required was a passageway that might lead us out of this area and into fresh pathways that might take us deeper—or higher. Once we were on rocks, we should leave no clues for our pursuers, and we could duck into any passageway fairly certain that we would not be followed. Of course, we should have no way of knowing whether that tunnel would lead anywhere, as we had surely passed far beyond the travels of the famed Arne Saknussemm by now.

But the fact of the matter is that there was no tunnel to follow. The wall of rock was unbroken in either direction as far as we could see. I could only conclude—and here my uncle agreed with me—that we were in some fault zone, where slippage of the rocks in some ancient earthquake had caused a rift in the solid rock, and one area had fallen lower than the other. Until we reached the full extent of this rift, there would be no chance of finding a passageway we could follow. All that we could do was to press onward.

As so we did, constantly on the move, save for short periods of rest or sleep. It is all very hazy to me now, but at the time it was desperate and as swift as we could make it. We walked, we rested, we ate, we slept—over and over again. We had lost all purpose in our lives but this. To this day, I waken from nightmares of being lost in these prehistoric jungles, with some great evil on our trail.

Finally, though, it ended. One day Hans stopped and gestured for us to do the same. At first I couldn't imagine why he had called the halt as we had been only walking a couple of hours and it was not yet time for a break. But he called to my uncle and gestured ahead. The two of them spoke together urgently in Danish for a time, while Ned Land and I seized the opportunity to sit on a fallen log and rest. I was weary and discouraged, exhausted from the relentless trek, as were we all. But I looked up into my uncle's face when he came across to me and saw him grinning widely.

"There is a way down!" he exclaimed. "Hans has found a tunnel ahead of us."

A way down... Slowly the news permeated to my befuddled brain. I blinked and then started up from the log. "A tunnel?" I questioned.

"A tunnel," my uncle confirmed with another smile. "Come, see for yourself."

The four of us hurried ahead. Apparently Hans had been scouting—I had not even noticed he had been gone—when he had discovered our fresh path. After about ten minutes, the jungle thinned to nothingness. There was a stretch of rock about forty feet long, and there, in the wall of stone, was an entranceway to a tunnel. It stood some fifteen feet high and appeared to plunge downward at about a five degree angle. Light didn't penetrate more than about twenty feet, so there was no telling how deep it might go.

"It may be a dead end," the sailor cautioned, lest we get too excited.

"There is only one way to find out," my uncle replied. "We go on."

"Wait," I said. "There is only this one tunnel—no others."

"We need only one," my uncle said, "provided it is the right one."

"But Von Horst and his men will know we have taken it," I pointed out. "If they are still on our trail, we shall not lose them this way."

"True enough," my uncle agreed. "But what other choice do we have?" He gestured in both directions. "Solid rock as far as we can see. This is our only chance to leave this immense cavern. Once below, there should be further opinions for us to take, but here there is nothing. We must follow this pathway."

"Let us at least look and see if there are indications that this may lead down," I begged. "It may be that Arne Saknussemm still leads our way." No one objected to my suggestion, so we examined the area close to the tunnel entrance for any signs that someone had been here before us. Within moments, Ned Land gave a cry and called us to him.

There, upon the ground, was a knife. It was of good steel, with a bone handle. The edges were sharp and there was dried blood on it. The sailor looked at my uncle. "Could this belong to your explorer?" he asked.

"It could not," the professor said with certainty. "The knife is untarnished and the blood cannot be too old. Storms ravage this area from time to time, so if it were hundreds of years old, it would have washed clean and rusted by now. No, this weapon could not have been here longer than a few months."

"It cannot be from the Captain's men," I said. "We saw all of the equipment laid out in the ship before we began, and I do not recall any knife like this in the inventory."

"Quite right, my boy," my uncle agreed. "So there are only two possibilities left to us. The first is that the Gun Club expedition has passed this way before us and one of its members dropped this weapon."

"And the second possibility?" Ned Land asked.

"That it belongs to some native of these lands."

The sailor scowled. "Those prehistoric Shepherds you saw?"

"No," I answered. "That knife is made for a person with a hand near in size to our own—the Shepherds would need a weapon twice that size at least. Besides, it is made of steel, which requires manufacturing. We have seen no evidence yet of any mining or forging in these jungles."

My uncle beamed at me. "Quite right, Axel, quite right," he agreed. "You're using that brain of yours at last. Yes, if that belongs to some native, then it is a man we would recognize as a man of near our own kind. That it was dropped here suggests that there is probably a destination at the end of this tunnel in that case. Or, if it belonged to a member of the Gun Club, it means we may find allies ahead of us. Either way, it is clear that this is the way we must progress. Onward!"

So decided, we entered the passageway ahead of us. For the first time in many days, we had to fire up one of the Ruhmkorf coils for light. The eternal glow of the aurora was now behind us as we started back downward again. We had hopes once more to look forward to—and fresh fears. If it was the Gun Club ahead of us, would they actually prove to be friends or foes? And if it was some unknown native of these regions, how would they react upon seeing us? Ned Land told us stories of native people of the South Seas, encountering strangers for the first time. Some were warm and welcoming, others suspicious and murderous. There was no way to know how our hypothetical natives might behave, so we worried—or, at least, I did.

Downward we went, the light from our coil casting eerie shadows on the walls. Several times I mistook an oddly-formed shadow for movement and started with shock, but I seemed to be the sole member of our party inflicted with such nervousness. As always, nothing bothered Hans; Ned Land was used to venturing into fresh lands, so he was an old hand at this; as for my uncle—well, he had fresh rocks to examine, and this kept his mind from worrying about the unknown.

At one point my uncle gave a cry and we stopped. My heart was pounding, but it turned out that the professor had simply discovered the fossil of an unknown marine vertebrate in the wall. He was quite excited about it, and insisted on a short halt while he sketched it. I failed to see the reason for his excitement—yes, a fossil at this depth was certainly unusual, but we were close to an underground sea, so it was not particularly unlikely that we should discover a fossil here.

"My dear Axel," my uncle admonished, "this specimen proves that the Central Sea has been here for millions of years, and that it once extended to these depths, covering a much larger area than it does now. Don't you find that exciting?"

"When the Captain may be closing in on us while you scribble?" I asked, annoyed. "No, I do not. There is a time for science and there is a time for sanity."

He snapped his notebook shut. "Very well, then," he said with a sigh. "Let us continue. Axel, there are times when I despair of ever making a proper scientist of you."

"I should be happy if you do not make a corpse of me!" I replied.

And so we descended. The passageway had no side tunnels, so we were not tempted to stray from our course, and no indications that it would peter out. It gave every indication of being a true pathway. We found no other evidence of life within its confines, though. The floor was solid rock and could not carry footprints, and there were no other dropped or discarded items. We were back to our routine of walking, eating and sleeping. It lasted for at least a week without any indication of change until finally Hans—in the lead as always—called for a halt. He gestured to me to turn off the coil, and I did so at his bidding.

Our eyes adjusted to the sudden gloom—and then I realized that it was not entirely dark. In the distance was a faint spark of light. How Hans had managed to detect it, I shall never know, but he had somehow seen it and realized its significance.

We had reached the end of the passageway and ahead of us was a fresh source of light!

Even I forgot my fears momentarily as we were enthused and rushed ahead, almost galloping down the tunnel to its conclusion. None of us was at all prepared for what greeted us as we emerged from the passageway and into fresh air.

Stretching ahead of us as far as the eye could see was a fresh jungle—thicker, greener, more lush than the one we had left beside the Central Sea. We could hear the sounds of birds and beasts, and somewhere close by the tinkling of falling water. The air was warm and humid. And above us shone the Sun!

The Sun! We looked at each other in confusion. We had been descending constantly from the cavern that held the Central Sea! How, then, could we have possibly returned to the surface of our planet? Surely it could not be possible?

It was not.

My uncle gripped my arm. "Axel!" he exclaimed. "Look at the slope of the earth!"

At first I did not understand what he meant. But then it dawned upon me with a sudden shock. There was no horizon. Instead, as I looked at the ground in front of us, I could see that it *rose* in a gentle but consistent slope. Behind us, of course, lay the rock from which we had emerged, but in every other direction the earth rose away from us, fading into the distance. There was certainly nowhere on the surface of our world where any such effect had ever been noted.

"What does it mean?" I asked, confused and bewildered.

"Mean?" My uncle gave a great laugh. "My boy, it means that we have reached the center of the Earth at last! And it is not rock, nor molten lava, but a great spheroid inhabited by a central sun! We have discovered a world within our own world, a world on the *inside* of a gigantic sphere." He gestured upward, toward the strange sun in the sky. "There, my boy—there is the center of the Earth!"

We were witnessing our first views of the world that we should soon discover had a name—*Pellucidar!*

TO BE CONTINUED

It is tempting to wonder if, when he wrote his famous sequence of "Herbert West—Reanimator" stories in 1921 and 1922, H.P. Lovecraft had heard of Raymond Roussel's influential 1914 surrealist novel, Locus Solus, *even though it wasn't translated into English until the 1960s. Both contain a "reagent" capable of bringing the dead back to life. In the following story, Pete Rawlik cleverly brings together Roussel's and Lovecraft's characters in a chilly little yarn entitled...*

Pete Rawlik: *Revenge of the Reanimator*

Paris, 1919

5 May, 1919

My Dearest Hannah,

You must forgive me for dispensing with the usual pleasantries; I promise to send you a more formal letter at a later date, for now you must make do with this haphazardly written missive. Under the circumstances, it is the best that I can do. So much has happened in the last few hours, I have so much to tell you about, that I can hardly keep myself contained, and yet, at the same time, I am hesitant, for what I have seen defies the bounds of common decency, and borders on the absurd, and likely wanders into the realm of pure madness. It may all be simply too much for a simple boy from Arkham to take in. That, in itself, is amusing, for it was because of Arkham that I was drawn into the strange events that have so disturbed my mind, but I get ahead of myself.

Paris is a madhouse. I thought perhaps it was because of the end of the war, that the Peace Conference had drawn not only the great powers of the world to the city, but the madmen as well, but I think it is simply the nature of this place. As a member of the security detail attached to our mission, I must, on a daily basis, sift through the reports generated by the locals, constantly searching for evidence of some threat that might disrupt the conference or endanger the staff. Each day brings a new revelation, a new wonder, or a new horror. Last month, the authorities arrested a man they suspected of murdering dozens of women. Criminal geniuses joust with the police. Masked vigilantes armed with super-science haunt the streets, doing battle with infamous thieves, murderers, and nefarious organizations. It is not uncommon to see strange inventions roll down the streets or glide past amongst the clouds. Such things had become routine, so it was a surprise when my commander ordered me to the outskirts of the city to help the gendarmes. He wouldn't tell me much, but the words "Arkham" and "Miskatonic" had been uttered. He knew I was from Arkham, knew our family history, and decided I needed to be the one to take a more detailed look.

Montmartre is an odd little part of Paris. Before the war, it was home to a thriving artistic community, but now, it has slowly become home to a rather unsavory element that needn't be discussed here. Hidden within this labyrinth-like neighborhood are several small estates of several acres each, some of which have been turned into private sculpture gardens for the more well-to-do members of this community of eccentrics. One of these was named the *Locus Solus*, and was the playground of the prominent Dr. Martial Canterel, a scientist and inventor whose fame in Paris rivals that of Edison, but whose eccentricities rivaled those of Tesla. Although I have no direct knowledge, rumor has it that Canterel was responsible for the so-called "Miracle of the Marne," which used taxi cabs to transport reserve troops to the front lines: An absurd proposal to be sure, but one that worked, and changed the course of the battle. This, then, was the nature of Canterel's reputation and work: the adaptation of one invention to another use that seemed absurd or completely impractical, but in practice worked, and produced what could be thought of as scientific romances or engineering art.

As I left the street, the gateway to the estate was not unexpectedly bizarre, consisting of facsimiles of teeth from some titanic beast that curved into the air to form a kind of arch. Normally such a thing would be considered macabre, or perhaps *outré*, but the fact that each immense tooth had been painted in splashes of various pastel colors made the thing simply laughable. I may have been walking into the maw of an immense beast, but it was candy-colored, and that made it somehow acceptable.

The pavers upon which I trod were equally as whimsical, for each one was connected to a pneumatic system that responded to each step. In essence, as I walked from the street to the house, my gait provided its own processional beat, until I at last reached the door and was announced by a rich contralto bleating. The door, which was a thick steel thing colored purple, swung open to reveal a familiar face, one of my colleagues, a man who like me had served in the war, but was found to be to useful to ship home, at least just yet. Gatsby had a way with numbers, and with people, so the Brass had kept him on, though not for much longer. He had been accepted to one of the upper crust British universities, and was just days away from starting his life over as a student.

Gatsby ushered me inside and in a veritable whirlwind of activity moved down the corridor to the library. He sat me down in a chair shaped like an octopus looked at me oddly, and then smiled.

"In a few seconds a man, Dr. Martial Canterel, is going to come through that door," he said, pointing at a fragile looking panel of glass and lead. "When he does, he is going to talk to you as if he knows you. You need to play along, and follow him when he moves. Whatever you do, don't try to stop him. Do you understand?"

I nodded my affirmation as Gatsby backed away.

As soon as he was clear, the door swung wide and a suave man wearing a ridiculous green and purple paisley suit walked in. He was thin and well groomed, and walked with that odd way of carrying himself that told me he wasn't an American. He smiled as he approached and greeted me warmly taking my right hand in both of his.

"My dear Doctor, I am so glad you could come," he said as he vigorously shook my hand. "It has been so long since we last spoke, twenty years I suppose. Has it really been that long since I was in Arkham? I heard that you had some trouble with the faculty at Miskatonic?"

I was utterly confused. "I'm sorry, I'm not a doctor. I think perhaps you have mistaken me for Professor Nathaniel Peaslee, I'm his son Robert."

I looked around for help, but Gatsby had vanished.

Canterel let go of my hand. There was a smell, actually two odors. One of perfume, an attempt to mask the other, a stench that hinted at rotting food.

"Of course, still what do those old fools know?" he replied. "If it weren't for men like us, those milksops would still have us in the dark ages shaking bones and muttering incantations." He spun around and seemed to be listening to something. "Yes, but I assure you, my friend, there is no need. I have a demonstration set up in the garden, and I brought a suitable specimen, and a sample of my reagent." He paused once more. "Yes, it is derived from the one we worked on so long ago, but I've made a number of improvements since then. It may not produce the exact response we are looking for, but the results are consistent, reproducible between subjects."

He turned back toward me and leaned in to where I was sitting, so close that I had to slouch back into the chair. When he spoke again, it was in a sly, almost secretive whisper.

"Come into the garden, my dear Herbert, let me show you what my Resurrectine can do."

From his pocket he produced a small glass vial of fluid so green that it nearly glowed, and flecked with small grains of purple. Doing as I was told, I rose from my chair and followed Dr. Canterel into the garden. As we strolled down the hall, Gatsby was nowhere to be seen.

Outside in the garden, free from the bonds of architecture, Canterel's work was awash in the nonsense that has infused the art movement known as Dadaism. The whole landscape was surreal, and I was reminded of the worlds described by Lewis Carroll, and in some ways L. Frank Baum. There was a tree hung with lunch pails, which when Canterel touched would bark like schnauzers. There was a grove of books, chiseled out of marble, with the pages attached and moveable using great stone rings, themselves carved out of the stone.

He pointed to a goggled eye light fixture, "When I was a young man, I found that on the beach. I believe it to be part of Nemo's *Nautilus*. Some kind of death ray I suppose. For me, it is my favorite lamp, which I keep lit using a small jar of glow bugs." He paused suddenly. "You have no interest in such things do you, Dr. West?" He shook his head and went *tsk, tsk* through his teeth. He pointed at a large empty space. "Not even in my giant diamond aquarium? You see that cat? And the head?"

I looked, but there was nothing there. I could not understand why he could not see it. He paused and seemed to be listening.

"Yes, it is the head of the famed politician Danton. I reconstituted it and administered an early version of Resurrectine. The head still speaks, but it needs motivation. Thus the cat will occasionally stir the thing. Ignore the dancing girl, she was an afterthought, but now that the piece has been installed, I find it too difficult to alter it." It was as if he was seeing something that wasn't there, or had been once, but was no longer.

We wandered down the garden path a little ways before Canterel stopped once more.

"Indulge me for a moment my friend," he pointed to a bas relief map of Paris, upon which a small red light was slowly moving about. "Throughout the city I have placed a net of radio receivers tuned to capture the regular signal of a small transmitter which I attached to a feral dog. By using the signal strength from each of the receivers, I can estimate the location of the dog almost instantaneously on this map. By recording those locations, I can create a history of the dog's movements, a kind of travelogue if you will."

I looked at where he was gesturing, but again the space was empty.

"It is an amusing little project, but I cannot for the life of me find a practical use for it. It could be used to track people as they moved through the city, and perhaps direct police or reroute traffic as needed, but I find it hard to believe that we could convince the masses to wear my devices in support of such a cause." He paused and his face took on an annoyed expression. "Please, my friend, there is no need to be so angry. What you wish to see is just around the corner, come follow me, and you shall see what I have done with your reagent. It is truly a masterpiece."

Once more, he waddled down the path, and I dutifully followed, but, this time, as we came around a hedge, I was greeted by the most astounding of sights. There were eight enclosures; glass cubes each about ten feet on a side. Inside were people, one per cube, all different, and all doing different things. There was a woman rocking a child to sleep, though the child itself was a doll. She just sat there rocking the doll, singing to it, over and over again. She made no deviation from her pattern, made no attempt to acknowledge our presence.

More disturbing was the marrying man, a man dressed in a tuxedo in front of a dummy dressed as a priest. Beside him was an articulated mannequin on wheels dressed in a wedding dress. A speaker mounted on the side of the priest dummy would recite vows, which the man would acknowledge. There were pauses were the mannequin would supposedly speak as well. At the end of the ceremony, the man would kiss the bride and then run down an aisle. After about thirty feet, he would suddenly stop. A hidden cable would drag the mannequin back to the priest, and the groom would join them. The whole scenario took about eight minutes to play out, after which it would repeat. I thought it was a kind of performance art, but the precision with which it was repeated was disturbing. I might even say unnerving.

Canterel motioned me down the path in a way that made me think he was trying to be quiet, but as I approached he started giggling and then addressed me in a normal tone.

"I'm sorry, I tend to forget that they don't acknowledge our existence, so it doesn't matter how we speak or act. They are so life like, a magnificent *tableaux vivants*, all thanks to my reagent, my Resurrectine. It brings the dead back to life, and then they continuously reenact the most important event in their lives, at least from their perspective. It is not perfect mind you; there is still the matter of decay. They may the decomposition may have been slowed, but they do rot. And of course there is the matter of nutrition, but the less said about that the better."

He smiled, and I stared at the young man who was acting out fishing in the river and pulling up a rather large, but wholly unidentifiable fish. "Perhaps *tableaux vivants* is the wrong way to describe them, *tableaux morts* might be better."

He stepped away and then turned quickly. "My secret ingredient, of course it is the Vril energy. I infuse it into the reagent during formulation. It affects the mind, you see."

Suddenly Canterel spun around and looked at his arm. "Sir! just what do you think you are doing?" He reached for something that I could not see. Whatever it was, he found it. He twisted left and right, and then spun around. "I haven't corrupted anything," he yelled. "I haven't made a mockery of your work, I've turned it into an art!"

He suddenly spun around and screamed, "DOCTOR WEST!" His voice gurgled and his back arched. I saw the light in his eyes grow dim as he crumpled to the ground. He lay there for a moment, still as the grave, but only for a moment. Without warning, he was convulsing and screaming. Canterel's body was flopping around on the ground like a dying fish. He screamed again, and then went quickly silent. Without a word, he stood up and in silence he walked away, passing me and returning to the house.

I did not follow him, for as he stood, I saw what lay beneath him. I ran instead, ran from Canterel, ran from the estate called *Locus Solus*, ran through the streets of Paris, and took refuge in the American Consulate, where I could drown away what I had seen with French wine and Kentucky bourbon. I didn't need to follow Canterel back into his house to know what was going to happen next. I had seen enough, seen what had happened, and I knew I didn't need to see it again.

Canterel was going back inside, back to the library, where he would once again act out the last few minutes of his life, the moments during which he had met with the man who had invented the reagent, the basis for his own Resurrectine, and during which he could at last boast of his achievement to the one man whom he respected. It was an encounter that Canterel would consider the greatest of his life. One that would end with one man attacking the other, and Canterel being murdered.

If only he had stayed dead, but whoever had killed him, a man, a doctor by the name of Herbert West, had found it amusing to dose Canterel with his own creation, his own version of the reagent, his so called Resurrectine. Canterel was trapped, not alive, but not dead either, at least until he succumbed to starvation, or rotted away.

Until then, he was no longer Doctor Martial Canterel the artist; he had become what he cherished the most: a work of art.

Your dearest brother,

, Robert Peaslee

What kind of supernatural threat could possibly bring together such stalwart figures as Sâr Dubnotal, John Silence and Thomas Carnacki? Josh Reynolds' answer is to take a page from William Hope Hodgson's The House on the Borderland—*Hodgson, after all, being Carnacki's creator—and craft a terrifying tale entitled...*

Josh Reynolds: *The Swine of Gerasene*

October 31, 1911

The house hunched on the edge of a spur of rock that jutted out of a vast, circular chasm, downstream of a river that no one cared to name. The circular body of the house, now crumbling and overgrown, was covered in an encrustation of curved towers and pinnacles that, in the fast fading light of dusk, resembled leaping, snapping tongues of flame. Or so the two men who looked down at the house and its chasm from an overhanging bluff fancied.

"In Kraighten, they say that this house was built by the Devil," the taller of the two men rumbled in a voice akin to the crash of the rocks that occasionally fell from the cliffs into the chasm below. Beneath his overcoat, he was clad in a finely tailored hiking outfit, offset with a brightly colored sash about his waist, and on his head was a pure white turban. He held a walking stick in one hand, and the other rested on the Webley at his waist in its military style holster.

"Which one?" the other man said. He was dressed in black, and his clothes were of an archaic cut, like something from the days of gaslight and hansom cabs. His topcoat was from that era as well, and it was shiny in places with age and wear.

"Humor, John?" Sâr Dubnotal said, frowning.

He glanced at his companion, his aura and expression radiating disapproval. The other man smiled slightly. Unlike Dubnotal, he radiated a strange serenity that reached out through his eyes and voice to calm those whom he addressed.

"Laughter chases the Devil away, my friend," John Silence said. "And I fancy that there is more than one infernal presence in that decrepit structure. I can feel them, pressing against my mind and spirit." He touched his brow with two fingers. "I can taste them, in the back of my mouth, and I can smell them." He made a face. "I'm surprised that you can't."

"Some of us are not as psychically gifted as you," Dubnotal said. "Your mind's acuity puts my own to shame. And I am the greatest psychagogue my order has yet to produce."

"I fancy there're those who'd argue that point," Silence said softly. "There's a young girl in the Highlands—Crerar, I think her name is—who displays the first flickers of what I think will become a formidable psychical prowess when she reaches maturity. And, of course, there's that Vance fellow in London. His sensitivities easily rival my own. If he could learn to control his emotions, he would be an investigator second to none."

His pale, gentle eyes were locked on the house. A number of cars occupied the overgrown courtyard that sat before the crumbling ruin. He and Dubnotal had followed a trail that stretched from the shattered foyer of a certain house on Cheyne Walk to western Ireland. They had come close to their quarry in Cardiff, and then again in Dublin. Each time, the individual they pursued had slipped away, taking his captive with him.

"I cautioned him against involving himself in this affair. This Count Magnus is no Crowley or Karswell, to be taunted. He is more dangerous than either. Thomas was a fool to confront him so openly," Dubnotal said, following Silence's gaze.

"He saved that Baines fellow though," Silence said. "Surely that makes this misfortune worth it?"

"Yes, and because Baines was marked by the Brotherhood of Gerasene, Thomas, in saving him from his fate, took his place. We might have had time to prevent this, if he hadn't confronted Magnus at the Savoy like some hero from a two-bit penny dreadful. That is what his ill-considered heroics have gotten him." Dubnotal made a fist, and his dark eyes blazed. "I warned him, John. I warned him!"

There were a thousand and one esoteric societies, clubs, sects and orders in London. And among the most sinister was the enigmatic Brotherhood of Gerasene. Originally formed by a pig-farmer from Yorkshire, the Brotherhood had blossomed into something unpleasant. It attracted those inclined to greed, envy and brutality to its circle, and none more greedy, envious and brutal than the creature who called himself Count Magnus. His origins were a mystery—a medium in Berkshire claimed he was an antediluvian sorcerer-king; an Oxford don of Silence's acquaintance theorized that he was a 17th century Swedish mystic of ill-repute, come back to stalk the world; an elderly theatre owner in London swore that Magnus was the same trickster who had led the Tong of the Black Scorpion to its destruction in Queen Victoria's day. Magnus now controlled the Brotherhood, whatever his past.

And when the Brotherhood had set its sights on an unlucky fellow named Baines, it had attracted the attentions of Thomas Carnacki, the Ghost-Finder. Carnacki had extricated Baines from the Brotherhood's schemes, but at great cost. A few weeks after Baines had been safely delivered to a resort, to take the waters and recover from his horrific experiences, the front door of Carnacki's Cheyne Walk house had been kicked in, and his assistants clubbed and thrashed mid-meal. Carnacki himself had been kidnapped by the Brotherhood's hired thugs. That was why Sâr Dubnotal and John Silence had pursued Magnus from London to Dublin, and now to this remote outpost in the western wilds of Ireland. Both men were acquaintances of Carnacki, though in different ways—to Silence, Carnacki was something of a protégé, but to Dubnotal, he was merely a neighbor, an asset, a useful tool in Dubnotal's own war against the forces of darkness. Or so the Great Psychagogue insisted.

"So why are you here? Looking to tell poor Carnacki 'I told you so' to his face, then?" Silence said, smiling slightly.

Dubnotal frowned and glared at the older man, but only for a moment. He shook his head and turned away.

"I am here for the same reason you are," he said, after a moment.

Silence extracted a pocket-watch from his waistcoat and popped it open. "Then, I'd suggest haste. The evening shadows grow long, and it *is* Samhain, after all. Not an auspicious night to be confronting... whatever it is that's waiting for us."

"In Wales, they call the day after this night *Calan Gaeaf*," Dubnotal said. "They say that a tailless black pig roams the countryside, devouring all whom it encounters."

"Good thing it's the last of October, rather than the first of November, eh?" Silence said.

"One will be edging into the other by the time we get down there, I'm afraid," Dubnotal rumbled. "We must hurry."

They descended towards the chasm and the house carefully, moving along overgrown paths and through curtains of tangled greenery. They had come prepared for a hike, having come to their current location by boat, and then by train. The choked wilderness of vines, arthritic trees and moss-blanketed rocky outcroppings was all that remained of a once-great garden estate. It had not seen the attentions of a gardener in close to the century or more. Their coats snagged on briars and their shoes slipped in deep troughs of mud or soggy earth. They were forced to stop more than once, when they heard the sounds of movement, deep in the greenery, or above them, or below them.

Whether the sounds were caused by animals or sentries set by their quarry or something else entirely, neither man could say, nor did either give voice to an opinion. Both men had been in similar situations, and they knew enough to save their breath for the descent. When they at least reached the ruin, the Sun had long since disappeared and the only light was that provided by the Moon, and the electric torches both men carried. They turned off the latter as they reached the crumbled walls of the forecourt. There was a man on guard, strolling through the cars, with a halo of cigarette smoke above his head. He had the look of a dock worker, or professional pugilist, and he held a shotgun loosely in his hand.

Dubnotal shed his coat, handed Silence his walking stick, and drew his Webley. He pressed a finger to his lips and stepped through a hole in the wall. Silence frowned, but made no attempt to stop the other man. Dubnotal slithered through the cars, moving as silently as a cat. As Silence watched, the Great Psychagogue hefted a chunk of stone and tossed it. The guard turned, suddenly alert, as stone rattled against stone. Dubnotal shot forward, and slammed the butt of the Webley down on the back of the man's head. The guard fell and Dubnotal caught him, and rolled him beneath a car. He motioned for Silence to join him.

"I thought for sure you would kill him," Silence murmured as he gave Dubnotal back his coat. When he made to hand him his stick, Dubnotal waved it aside.

"You keep it," he said, "And I never kill, unless it's necessary. Every death weakens the great web of life." He hefted the pistol. "Besides which, this is mostly for show. Thomas is a better shot than I am."

"Thomas couldn't hit the broad side of a barn," Silence said.

Dubnotal grinned. "My point exactly," he said.

He nodded towards the entrance, and they continued on. There was no door, though there were signs that there had once been one. The entryway was covered in mildew and mould and it stank of wet stone and animals. There were great gaps in the roof, allowing in moonlight and the walls sagged abominably. There were a number of footprints in the carpet of fungus that covered the flagstones of the floor. They followed the footprints to the stairs that led down into the cellars of the ruin.

The cellar of the ruin was a huge, multi-room expanse, and like the ground floor, was encrusted with a century's worth of mould. The feathery bristles of the faintly phosphorescent patches that clung to the stones stirred in an unpleasant fashion as they descended. A strange smell hung on the air, like a pig sty or an animal lair. Strange sculptures of fantastic design crouched in niches and in corners, adding to the eerie air of the place.

A voice, deep and raspy, echoed through the cellar. It seemed to come from everywhere and nowhere at once. Silence pointed towards a faint glow that pierced the gloom. Dubnotal nodded and they crept through the brick and stone archways, moving swiftly, but carefully. Things moved in the darkness around them, things which grunted and clawed at the stone softly as they watched the two men pass by. Neither Silence nor Dubnotal paid any attention to the phantasms. They had seen too much in their respective careers to be shaken by unseen prowlers.

"This squalid ruin is but a tattered reflection of the glory upon the other side of the border, my friends," the voice intoned, each word echoing through the cellar like a gunshot. "It is a tombstone, marking wonder and mystery. The gate is shut, and the lock is rusted. But we will force it open and fling it wide, so that Our Father, the Hog, might enter this world to run riot upon it. He snuffles at the door even now, and his children wait in the shadows to be called to our celebration."

The speech continued in that vein for several minutes. Dubnotal and Silence reached the light even as a wave of applause greeted a pause in the recitation. They came to a large, domed chamber, where ribs of wood and brick held up a roof of stone. Water dripped from somewhere, creating tiny rivers of running wetness which curled between the stones of the floor. The swinish smell was stronger here, and it seemed to permeate everything.

A crowd of cowled and robed shapes stood in a semi-circle around an altar composed of a heavy flat stone set atop two others. Behind the altar, an immense circular trap door had been set into a hump of rock that rose at an angle from the floor and slumped against the wall. Several of the cowled figures held staves topped by flickering lanterns and before the altar stood the man whom Dubnotal and Silence had pursued from Kensington to Kraighten.

Count Magnus wore heavy robes, and a wide-brimmed curate's hat. His face was obscured by a steel mask and his hands were hidden by thick gloves. He gesticulated as he spoke, causing his robes to flap and flare.

"In this place, our master has set his hoof," he said. "And in this place, we shall call him forth from the roaring paddock!"

A small, dwarfish shape capered and bounced about Magnus with seemingly childish glee. Its all-concealing hood rippled with loud squeals as Magnus spoke.

"I have made the Black Pilgrimage, and in the ruins of one world, I beheld another and the Hog, that cunning Swine of Gerasene, came to me and spoke of the world to come, when he would show mankind new ways to shout and revel and *kill!*"

The hooded figures bellowed in appreciation, and as the noise rattled the stones, Dubnotal and Silence moved swiftly, striking and grabbing two of the Brotherhood from the back of the crowd. They dragged the unconscious cultists back through the archway and swiftly stripped them of their robes. Then, disguising themselves, they joined the crowd. No one had noticed the disappearance and sudden reappearance of two members.

Magnus continued to speak:

"Our chosen sacrifice was taken from us by the trickery of itinerant magus of little account, and thus, my servants have claimed him in recompense. In the dark places where man may not go, they have prepared him for what is to come. And now, they shall bring him to the stone of sacrifice."

As he spoke, he raised his hand and the lanterns sparked and crackled, as if some strange pulse had passed between them. The lanterns dimmed. All was silent for a moment. Then, with a grinding shriek, the trapdoor began to open.

Silence grabbed Dubnotal's arm. He staggered and the latter reached out to support him. "What is it?" he hissed.

He had his answer, even before Silence could form a reply. A wave of pure, unadulterated psychic foulness struck the defenses of his mind, tearing at his thoughts and soul for a moment before passing on. From within the yawning maw of the trapdoor, a fetid wind blew forth. It bore with it the stink of ages, of lightless caverns and spilled blood. Shapes moved within the darkness. Hunched, squat shapes that grunted and squealed abominably as they ascended from whatever noisome vaults lurked beneath the deep cellars of the house. On their backs, they bore a pale shape, clad in a tattered suit, smeared with phosphorescent muck. At a sweeping gesture from Magnus, they began to carry their burden towards the altar stone.

"Thomas," Silence murmured, "He's in one piece, at least; I—hsst!" He made a surreptitious gesture towards the front of the crowd, where Magnus' hunched familiar was slinking through the forest of robed legs, pausing only to occasionally snuffle at a hem or sleeve. Dubnotal frowned.

"Ready yourself," he said. "Get to him as quickly as you can. Time is as much our enemy here as Magnus."

"And you?" Silence asked, gripping the walking stick tightly. The creature was drawing closer. It seemed to be in no hurry. Then it stiffened and its cowled features turned in their direction. It gave a querulous snort and began to move directly for them.

"I? I will be making a bit of a scene," Dubnotal said, with a grim smile.

Carnacki's unconscious body was laid atop the altar and he was bound to the stone by thick ropes by the softly grunting creatures. In the semi-darkness, neither Silence nor Dubnotal could get a clear look at them.

"Now my brethren, we have only to wait. In a few moments, the Great Swine will rise from the depths and take his due, and give unto us his blessings," Magnus said, lifting his hands in benediction.

Whatever he was about to say next was interrupted by the sudden, loud squeal of his familiar as it pointed a stubby limb at Dubnotal and Silence. The crowd of cultists drew back with a communal gasp. Dubnotal reacted swiftly. He leveled the Webley and snapped off a shot. It struck the dwarfish creature dead in the centre of its mass, and the force of the bullet knocked it from its feet and sent it tumbling backwards.

The echoes of the shot had barely faded before Dubnotal roared out an incantation and the gloom was rent asunder by an explosion of light. Revealed by the flare of light, a horde of grotesque swine-things shrieked and squealed, cowering back. Taking his cue, Silence darted from the stunned crowd of celebrants and scrambled towards Carnacki's bound form.

A swine-thing gurgled and clawed at him, its tiny eyes still watering from the blaze of light that had swept the cavernous chamber. He pivoted and made the Voorish Sign inches from the creature's face. It squealed and jerked back hard enough to send it tumbling back into its fellows. As it fell, he caught the edge of the altar stone and vaulted over it, and Carnacki, putting the stone between him and the swine-things.

"Thomas," he hissed insistently. He slapped him. "Wake up!"

Carnacki's eyes fluttered. "Ugh—what—John," he mumbled, his bleary gaze fixing on her. "What's going on? What are you doing here?"

"Saving your hide," Silence barked.

He hefted Dubnotal's stick from within his borrowed cloak and swiftly drew the silver blade he knew to be concealed within its handle. Dubnotal had gotten the idea after a chance meeting with an American by the name of Pursuivant. The American had claimed that the sword-cane he carried had been forged by Saint Dunstan. He began slicing at the moldy ropes which held the occultist fast to the stone table.

"Is that Sâr Dubnotal?" Carnacki said, twisting around. "I say, is this a rescue?"

"Yes to both," Silence said, "Now stop squirming, this is difficult enough."

Dubnotal had stepped from the crowd of robed and hooded celebrants and dispensed with his disguise. He let the borrowed robes collapse to the damp stones as he stalked towards the gathered pack of swine-things. The squealing, snorting creatures glowed with the same faint phosphorescence that they had smeared on Carnacki's clothes and they gnashed cracked and yellowed tusks at the Great Psychagogue.

"Back," he roared, "Back, spawn of the lightless gulfs!"

"Stop him," Magnus rasped, flinging out a hand. "The sacrifice must not be interrupted!"

The small, cowled shape rolled to its feet and gave a squeal far out of proportion with its stature. Robes flaring, it scrambled towards Dubnotal on all fours, seeming no worse for wear for having been shot. Dubnotal spun about as the creature leapt for him and ducked aside. It crashed down where he'd been standing and whipped around with an ear-splitting screech. It drew a knife from within its robes and slashed wildly at the mystic.

"Oh no, my little friend," Dubnotal said as he backed away, out of its reach, "A fellow by the name of Doctor Omega warned me of letting you get too close, and you as well, Count Magnus. Or should I call you *Greel*?"

"Silence," Magnus thundered. He started towards Dubnotal. "Do not speak that name."

"Names have power, do they not?" Dubnotal said, "Even those names not yet assigned a soul, eh Magnus? Are you afraid that if I speak that name, the hounds of time will catch your putrid scent? Criminal, warlock, warlord, butcher and fugitive from all that is good and holy I call you, whatever your true name. You and your homunculus are damned thrice over, in this epoch and those yet to come."

Magnus snarled and clawed about in his robes for a pistol. Dubnotal shot a look towards Silence as he sliced through the last of Carnacki's bonds. The Great Psychagogue dove to the floor as Magnus drew his weapon and fired. It resembled an old fashioned flintlock, but it made a sound like a kettle boiling over, and the air stank of lightning as Magnus fired. The rock was scorched where Dubnotal had been standing. He sprang to his feet and Magnus turned, tracking him.

"You shall not stop me here, Rosicrucian, even as you failed to stop me in London," Magnus snarled. "The vessel has been prepared, and the great swine comes, even now!"

Odd, black puffs of something very much like smoke had begun to rise from between the flat stones which made up the floor around the altar. The cavernous cellar began to shake with a strange, oscillating rhythm, and an eerie ripple of ugly crimson light flashed through the cracks between the stones that made up the walls and floor. The swine-things began to grunt and squeal where they cowered and several struck the ground with hairy fists in time to the relentless, pounding rhythm. Slowly at first, and then more loudly, the members of the Brotherhood joined in, stomping their feet and making strange piggish calls.

"I bargained a life for a life," Magnus said, his voice carrying throughout the cellar, over the noise made by beast and man. "In that place of cold fire, where I had been condemned by treachery, I struck a deal—life for life! I shall tend the Hog, as a swineherd must, and in return—life! My veins thrum with the stuff of the outside, and I am eternal. I am Ouroboros, travelling from Reykjavik to Raback, from China to Chorazin and back again. I am a god, in the service of gods."

He took aim with his strange pistol and fired again. Silence grabbed Carnacki and jerked him off the altar just in time.

Magnus' familiar pounced onto the altar a moment later and squealed down at them. The sound was filled with equal parts triumph and promise. Silence shoved Carnacki aside, as the thing clawed for them with the blade it held. Carnacki scrambled aside. He caught hold of the loose knot of thick ropes that Silence had severed and snapped them at the hooded creature. It whirled with a brain-piercing squall, and lunged off of the altar after Carnacki. He dodged aside and flung a loop of rope about the creature's bulbous, cowled head.

Speedily, he crossed to the other side of the altar from it and yanked the ropes tight, dragging the creature back against the rough stone.

"I say old man, care to give me a hand?" he shouted, as the thing clawed helplessly at the improvised noose around its throat.

Silence saw at once what Carnacki had in mind. He circled the altar, his silver blade bared. The homunculus saw him coming and redoubled its struggles. It whined like a beast in a trap as he lifted the blade.

"Hurry John, the little blighter is stronger than he looks!" Carnacki shouted.

Silence steeled himself and made a single, smooth thrust. The creature shrilled once and went limp. Magnus howled out a curse in a language neither man recognized. He fired his weapon at Silence, but Dubnotal crashed into the latter, knocking him from the line of fire.

Magnus continued to fire, as all three occultists, and they sought cover behind the altar. He ranted and roared, and his weapon sizzled and snarled in accompaniment.

"He's mad," Carnacki said, "Utterly barmy. I mean, I knew he was bad when I bearded him at the Savoy, after that business with Baines, but this just ain't cricket."

"No, it isn't," Dubnotal said, glowering at Carnacki, who shrugged helplessly. "You were rash—no, worse, a fool!" the Great Psychagogue snarled.

"Enough, we have other concerns at the moment than Thomas' appalling lack of common sense," Silence said, peering around the altar. "He's trying to keep us trapped here."

On the other side of the altar, the swine-things were racing to and fro about the chamber, like confused pigs. Magnus was shouting. The cultists were milling about nervously, unsure as to whether they should interfere or not. No one seemed to want to get too close to the altar, or the black smoke which was billowing from beneath it.

"We're pinned down, chaps," Carnacki said. "I don't suppose you have such a thing as a Webley about your person, what? Or a set of brass knuckles?"

Dubnotal touched the floor and then jerked his hand away, as if he'd been scalded. "Weapons would be useless against what is coming," he said. Nonetheless, he handed his Webley to Carnacki, who clutched it as if it were a totem. Dubnotal reached into his coat, and began fumbling for something. "Luckily," he continued, "Some of us think before we act."

"Well think quickly," Carnacki said as he looked at the billowing black cloud that rose about them. "Last time I faced that monstrosity of Magnus' I almost lost my soul, not to mention my life. I'd rather not go through that again, if I don't have to."

The red glow seeping up from the cracks had grown brighter now, and the air felt close. The floor shivered, and something that might have been titan footsteps sounded, somewhere far below them.

"He is here!" Magnus cried, "The Hog has come!"

The black smoke had risen to thigh level, and the red hell-light had begun to flash faster and faster and the chamber suddenly shuddered as something vast and unseen unleashed a monstrous grunt. The swine-things squealed, as if in reply, and a second thunderous grunt followed the first.

"What about the Incantation of Raaaee, or the Saaamaaa Ritual?" Silence said.

He looked pale, in the eerie light. The smoke bulged and stirred, as if something were rising from beneath it. The stones of the cellar ground against one another, as if the ruin were changing shape, becoming something else. The chant of the cultists had reached a crescendo, as had the shrieks of the swine-things.

"No time," Dubnotal said. He finally retrieved the item he'd sought—a strangely angled sliver of ruby which flickered with an internal light. "Something climbs towards us, out of dark gulfs. We must knock it from the path, before it reaches our sphere." He licked his lips and held up the sliver. "Desperate times call for desperate measures."

"What the deuce is that?" Carnacki said, peering at the crystal.

Silence said, "Is that—?"

"It is," Dubnotal said grimly. "A sliver of the gem known as the Blood of Belshazzar, which was retrieved from the fire column of Kor before it found its way to the lands of men. Within its facets lurk the flames of the Faltine which are hot enough to burn the very stuff of reality. The reflection of those cosmic fires—the fires of creation itself—was captured in the gem, and a flicker of it yet lurks in this sliver." He looked at the others. "We must cauterize this wound in the body of our world. The holy spark of the Faltine will burn away the foulness that holds this place in its grip."

"And how do we do that?" Carnacki asked.

Dubnotal rose to his feet. "I hope your marksmanship has improved, since I last saw it demonstrated," he said, adding, "When I throw this, shoot it."

"And then?" Silence said.

"What is it you Englishmen say—ah, yes—leg it," Dubnotal said.

Then, without another word, he threw the sliver towards the greatest concentration of smoke. Carnacki rose to his feet and snapped off a shot.

The sliver exploded, and the cellar was abruptly awash in heat and light. The curling plumes of smoke caught fire, as did the swine-things, who screamed and began to stagger and stumble blindly towards the trapdoor. Magnus cursed, and threw up his hands. The unseen presence in the smoke yammered and squealed and the ruin shifted and shook, as if, thwarted in its desires, it intended to smash down the house and crush all within out of spite.

The cultists were screaming and running for the stairs. Unlike the swine-things, they weren't burning, but Carnacki had swiftly emptied the Webley at their feet to encourage them. Between the gunshots, the shaking of the ruin and the sudden, blinding light, the Brotherhood of Gerasene had had enough for one night. They began to push and shove as they fought their way up the stairs. Dubnotal, Carnacki and Silence followed more slowly. The three men paused at the top of the steps, allowing the cultists to scramble past and out.

The cleansing fires of the Faltine washed over the ancient brickwork of the cellar, searing away the mould and fungus. Crackling flames enveloped the altar, blackening the stone and causing it to crack and shift. The body of the homunculus burned and as they watched, it collapsed in on itself. Of Magnus, there was no sign. The heat and light pierced the gloom on the other side of the trapdoor, and they could see the writhing shadows of the swine-things, as they were consumed by the cosmic inferno. Flames crept across the roof of the cellar and the floor, devouring the mould and strange statuary alike.

As they left the cellar behind, the ruin shifted about them, with a momentous groan. Dust shifted down, and the roof began to slump. A wall collapsed behind them, showering them with dust as they reached the courtyard. All of the cars had gone. Even the man Dubnotal had knocked unconscious was gone.

"Looks like the only thing holding this pile together was the fungus," Carnacki said, glancing back as dust expelled by the house's slow collapse billowed around them. "I'd say it's about time, what?" he coughed.

Neither Dubnotal nor Silence replied. Carnacki fell silent, and the three men watched as the house slowly folded in on itself and then, noisily and with much complaint, sloughed into the yawning chasm. Smoke and dust rose from the heart of the collapse, and for a moment, the twin columns mingled to take the form of a great swine. Then, as the Sun crept over the horizon, it dissipated.

Carnacki handed Dubnotal back his Webley, butt-first.

"Many thanks, old thing," he said. "I thought I was a goner for sure." Dubnotal said nothing.

"Think nothing of it, Thomas," Silence said, brushing dust from his sleeve. "If we don't watch out for one another, who will?" he added.

"Still, it was dashed kind of you to come to my rescue like that, and after you'd told me not to get involved in the first place," Carnacki said, nudging Dubnotal's arm with the revolver.

Dubnotal took the weapon, holstered it and, ignoring Silence's smile and Carnacki's bewildered expression, simply said, "I told you so."

"Gouroull" is the mysterious name given to the Frankenstein Monster by screenwriter Jean-Claude Carrière, who penned six brilliant Frankenstein *pastiches in France for the "Angoisse" imprint of Editions Fleuve Noir in the 1950s. Unlike other versions of the character, Gouroull is a savage, cunning and thoroughly evil monster. Like in the Shelley novel, he endlessly seeks the means to create others like himself. In this story, Frank Schildiner pays homage to the Asian cinema (more specifically* Snake in Eagle's Shadow, Kid with the Golden Arm, One-Armed Swordsman, The 36th Chamber of Shaolin *and* Come Drink With Me*), pitting seven classic Chinese heroes (admittedly, from different eras) against seven golden vampires...*

Frank Schildiner: *The Blood of Frankenstein*

China, 1925

Gouroull knew he was in the location the coolies had mentioned—the land where the dead walked and ruled humanity. It was an engrossing tale, though he gave no hint of interest as they babbled on, frightened as all humanity were by the very sight of him—Victor Frankenstein's most terrifying creation. Gouroull cared neither about their fear or their gratitude; he merely wished their information.

It all began with the little man. That was how Gouroull thought of Dr. Herbert West, a small man with an agile mind. He'd been unafraid and fascinated by Frankenstein's most lethal creation, interested enough to speak to him and listen to why Gouroull was haunting the blood-spattered grounds of the trenches of France.

"You wish a mate, one like yourself. It can be done, there is a process I read about recently. I discovered the notes of a nobleman named de Musard. We will need the blood of a vampire lord," West explained, growing more excited as he spoke to the giant undead creature before his eyes.

"Dracula in Transylvania, Karnstein in Styria," Gouroull rasped and turned to leave.

"No!" West cried, "I was not finished. It must be a vampire who used an ancient process to create a copy of themselves. Only the oldest and most powerful can attempt this feat. It requires both ancient vampiric blood and certain alchemical processes that are unknown to all but their small fraternity."

"Where then?" Gouroull asked, studying the little man. Impressive in his own way, for a human, Herbert West was only moved by the creation of life from the dead. This was useful for Gouroull's plans for the future. Where Victor had once refused to create a mate for him, West would succeed—and his plans could then move forward at an even faster rate.

"I have information on Dracula, though what I have is sketchy at best. He is said to have created many of these copies. I have heard of ones in Mexico, the American Southwest, Africa, China..." West stopped speaking, seeing a reaction from Gouroull.

"China," Gouroull rasped, having visited the country in the past. He'd traveled to Tibet, having heard of monks that could raise the dead through the use of magic rather than science. That intrigued him enough to travel the distance, only to find their art was like that of the ancient alchemists—making clay golems, which was of no use to his plans. He'd left a short time later to investigate, finally finding of Ping Kwei and the connection to Dracula, Lord of the Vampires.

The journey was great, but the scent of death slowly grew stronger with each mile. The province of Szechwan was at the furthest end of the Earth compared to his more familiar grounds in Europe, but fatigue didn't affect him in the slightest. Though he resembled humanity, he never suffered from any of the human miseries that would have made such a long journey nearly impossible.

And this village, Ping Kwei, was remote, even for such a forsaken country. It was surrounded by barren hills and small deep caves. The scent of blood and death, a corrupt, horrific stench, amused Gouroull as he headed closer to its source. According to the coolies, the village was of no interest; the temple in the hills overlooking it was, supposedly, where the dead walked and feasted upon the living.

The tale told to Gouroull was of seven immortals made of gold, creatures called *Jiangshi*, who were stronger and faster than any man, and had returned from the dead time and time again. He grinned at the thought, his huge sharp teeth glinting in the darkness. That would be the test, whether they could return again after he had tested their mettle.

The temple was a many-storied building, a near ruin filled with many corpses. The coolies had been incorrect in one detail: instead of seven creatures of power, there were eight!

Gouroull soon realized that the eighth was by far the most powerful. The others were lesser beings, less important, and he would brush them aside if they got in his way when he dealt with their master.

Gouroull was about to step forward, but stopped when he spotted the torches approaching the temple. Seven humans were coming, their strides intent and war-like. This simplified his plan. Gouroull's interest in the lesser beings was minimal; he would deal with their master and test his power after the humans had disposed of the others.

"Sifu Lee, they are coming!" Chien Fu exclaimed, jumping about energetically.

He was a man of medium height, dark hair and a wide infectious grin that hid his true mastery at unique forms of fighting. His dark clothes were neglectfully tied and all knew he would remove his jacket the moment the battle began.

"Calm yourself," Sifu Lee intoned, his voice as relaxed as his tautly muscular form.

His every motion was precise, no action wasted in his every move. Everyone looked to him as the leader, sensing he could defeat any foe in the end.

"Bring them on! My fists will destroy them all!" Lo the Muscular roared.

He was a tall man with long hair held back in a topknot ponytail and a powerfully muscular physique that made him look taller than everyone present. He was even rasher than Chien Fu, but his kung fu was very dangerous.

"Men!" Lady Swallow said, rolling her eyes as she drew her golden sword.

She was a beautiful woman with hair in the same style as Lo's, but dressed in a loose brown jacket and pants. She was not quite beautiful, but she was striking and more than one of those present glanced at her delicate curves with interest.

"Sifu Lee is correct. Calm and control will be our way to victory," Sifu Wong stated, his umbrella swinging slowly as he walked with the others, looking more like a man out for a daytime stroll than one going into battle.

A tiny man with an intense face and a long queue that he occasionally tossed over his shoulder, there was an electrical air of power around him, one that belied his size and relaxed demeanor.

"They advance, prepare yourself," One-Armed Fang said, his voice just above a whisper. He held a shortened sword in his one hand and seemed to possess an air of melancholy that hung about his person like armor.

The final member of the team was a thin muscular bald man in the bright yellow robes of a Buddhist monk. His name was Liu and he possessed a mischievous air about him, as if he knew you were about to fall down and he intended to laugh as he stepped over fallen form with a gentle giggle.

"Buddha bless us. And remember to hit them, Chien Fu."

Chien Fun was about to answer when the seven vampires stepped into the torchlight. They were all tall, with green rotting skin, sharp incisors and faces hidden beneath their golden masks. They all wore large golden medallions in the shapes of bats around their necks and in their hands were huge Jian-styled swords.

The lead vampire, a twisted creature dressed in white robes, screamed a warbling unintelligible word and charged Sifu Lee. Lee stepped aside and tossed the vampire with a simple quick sweep. The vampire snarled and Lee adopted a deep fighting stance, his face impassive.

"Did that monster say 'destroy them,' or 'please wash my auntie'?" Chien Fu asked, tripping and causing the vampire's sword to miss him by mere inches. His fighting style was acrobatic and made him look as if he was perpetually falling down and causing nearby objects to hit his opponent.

"Pay attention to your opponent," Sifu Wong replied as he blocked the vampire's sword by knocking the attacker's arm aside with his umbrella. Just as before, he never appeared to waste his movements, moving in an off-handed manner.

"No opponent can defeat me!" Lo the Muscular screamed, just as a vampire stabbed him in the chest. He yelled loudly and waved his arms about before crashing to the ground and laying still.

"He was incorrect," Liu stated leapt over the vampire attacking him, landing on his feet, his hand before him in a pose of prayer. He tapped the vampire on the shoulder and ducked as it swung, kicking it aside and watching as the creature stumbled to the ground.

One-Armed Fang and Lady Swallow did not reply as they engaged their enemies, sword to sword. Their styles were vastly different, but fascinating to watch.

Fang's attacks were lightning strikes, his shortened sword moving too fast for the eye to see. Meanwhile, Lady Swallow sword snaked out like the tongue of a serpent, causing the vampire to leap about and block far more than it was able to attack.

Gouroull stood in the doorway of the main chamber of the temple, watching as the leader reentered the main chamber. The room was large, round and possessed multiple altars with chained dead women lying on the slabs. They were completely drained of blood and a large cauldron filled with blood rested nearby. The room stank of blood, rot and death, all perfectly incarnated by the tall, bald Chinese man who strode about, muttering curses.

Moving into the light, the man turned and stared at Gouroull. He seemed surprised but not too surprised to see the giant creature that was Frankenstein's masterpiece, a towering being with alabaster skin, a flat squared head and inhuman yellow yes. For a heartbeat, neither moved, their eyes locked and studying each other completely.

"I have met your kind before," the Vampire Lord stated in clear, lilting English. "You are one of the creatures of the accursed Frankenstein. Serve me and I shall reward you well."

Gouroull smiled, his sharp teeth glinting as he stepped closer.

"Who are you?" he rasped.

The vampire smiled and straightened, "I am Kah, High Priest of the..."

Gouroull snarled and shook his huge head: "You lie!"

The vampire's eyes widened, but he too smiled and nodded.

"So it is true! You are not a foolish wretch like your brothers. I am Count Dracula, Lord of the Undead! Again, I say: Serve me and I will reward you!"

Gouroull did not reply. Instead, he suddenly charged Dracula with a speed that belied his size. Grabbing the undead creature, he threw him across the room towards one of the altars. The stone shattered under the shock, and the dead girl who'd been lying on it flopped to the floor. But, in less than a second, Dracula rose and charged. Crashing to the floor, the Vampire Lord pinned Gouroull's arms to the ground and bit down, hard, with his stiletto-like incisors.

Gouroull's flesh was hard, stone-like, and completely alien, yet Dracula's powerful vampiric strength pierced the skin and he began to drink the monster's dark blood.

"Aaaahhhh!" Dracula shrieked as he reared back in agony.

Gouroull's blood was no blood! It was an ichor that resembled nothing human or animal; it was something so alien that it burned his lips and throat of Dracula like acid!

Gouroull pulled free of the Vampire Lord's grasp, grabbed the creature's neck and, in turn, bit down hard, ripping out most of his throat. Frankenstein's terrifying creation seemed to mimic the vampire's action, drinking deeply of the undead creature's blood. He shoved Dracula aside and pulled out a metal vial, spitting the lifeblood of his enemy into the container.

Sealing the vial, Gouroull rose and began to leave the temple, his goal accomplished.

"Hold," Dracula coughed, his body transforming into a large man dressed in black. He was coughing blood and aging, turning into dust as Gouroull turned to watch. "Know this, miserable unfinished thing... You have earned the eternal enmity of Dracula! I shall hunt you down and we shall meet again!"

Gouroull nodded once, smiled again and replied, "Good."

And he left.

Just as there are several fictional heroes named "Saintclair" (or variations thereof), there are a number of "Malones." Stuart Shiffman has taken great pleasure in bringing together Craig Rice's and Mark Phillips' Malones for this amusing supernatural yarn, where they're shadowed by none other than Sâr Dubnotal, out of self-imposed retirement, and a surprise guest-star whose name we won't reveal; here...

Stuart Shiffman: *True Believers*

Shangri-La, 1967

There was a large white room relieved by red and yellow terracotta tiles and a beneficial breeze from the lattice-framed window, the only sound being that of the birds singing outside.

"If Mr. Conway says that there is a guest for me, young Wang, then I must surely receive him."

The Sâr Dubnotal rose in a smooth movement from his seat on a thin mat. The acolyte nodded and gestured for a man in the shadows to come forward.

"This is the pilgrim Simon Ark, Sâr, who has come to the Shangri-La in search of you."

The stranger stepped into the bright Himalayan light. He was a large man with his head shaved bald, dressed in what looked like Scandinavian woolen and flannel skiing clothes and stout leather climbing boots. He was heavy-set and appeared vigorous and youthful, but, on closer study, his face was revealed to be covered in a crackle-finish of fine wrinkles. He might pass for an active man of 75. *But then*, Dubnotal thought, *I appear to be a man in his forties...*

The direction of the breeze changed and brought the scent of tuberose to him. When he had first come to Shangri-La, Dubnotal had been told by Father Perrault that in China it was called the "smell of moonlight."

"Welcome, Brother Simon."

Simon Ark came and took the hands that the Sâr held out to him in greeting.

"I have heard of you as the Coptic priest who intervenes in matters of possible occult peril," said Dubnotal. "Is it true what is said of you: Are you really almost two thousand years old, brother? I presume that you have a metaphysical puzzle that requires my aid."

He sent Wang off for tea and led his guest to lacquered table and chairs.

"Thank you, brother," replied the newcomer. "It is true that I am the one about whom such things are murmured; I make no such claims for myself. You know yourself how such legends accrue over time."

"You have obviously had plenty of time then. What do you wish of me?" asked Dubnotal.

"I have come to take you to the United States where the grand-daughter of your acolyte, the medium Annunciata Gianetti, is in great spiritual danger." Ark's eyes held a look of great age and expectation.

"Annunciata had a child...? So much for my Visualization of the All..."

"No doubt, you were contemplating in the other direction, worthy colleague. Yes, she married your assistant Rudolph Arcati after you left to retire to Shangri-la. Rudolph was captured by the Gestapo during the occupation of France and Annunciata, now Madame Arcati, escaped to England with their son to work for the Diogenes Club. Her son, Alphonse, joined the British Security Coordination and the Special Operations Executive training agents in Canada at Camp X, where his daughter Josette was born in 1948."

"If this young person, a descendent of my dear Annunciata, is in danger, I have an obligation to leave my Visualization of the Cosmic All. Tell me more, brother."

The acolyte returned with two rough ceramic cups of aromatic tea.

"Josette Arcati is currently a university student in Chicago in the United States," said Simon Ark. "She has been pulled into the orbit of a new cult there, led by a young and charismatic leader. Many young people in America have become seekers of new spiritual paths, disillusioned by the crass materialism and hypocrisy of their elders, but there are many snares for the unwary and this one is a path to darkness."

"Can't you help her, Master Simon? I have not left this sanctuary in a very long time."

"I would face this myself," said Simon Ark, "but I have a prior obligation of my own. It will take me to Collinwood Manor, which seems to be located over a Hellmouth... I must do something about it. Alas, I must leave the Josette Arcati affair to the Great Psychagogue himself to solve."

"My last visit to America was before I came to Shangri-La," said Dubnotal. "My former contacts there, like Prince Abduel Omar, known as Semi-Dual, are surely long gone. Can you make suggestions for new allies?"

"Ah, I remember Semi-Dual... There are some modern white magicians in New York's Greenwich Village that would be of immeasurable aid to you and might point you in the right direction in Chicago." Ark reached into his pocket and took out a white pasteboard business card, which he handed to Sâr Dubnotal. "You will probably need this too."

Sâr Dubnotal looked at the face of the card: *John J. Malone, Attorney at Law. Chicago, Illinois.* This did not sound like a master of white magic or psychic sciences.

The inside of Joe the Angel's City Hall bar was a mob scene, shoulder to shoulder from the narrow entrance back to the 1890s mahogany bar and the booths. The sounds of clinking glasses, beer taps, and laughing patrons filled the space. The fog of cigarette smoke made visibility near impossible, but the stranger in the white suit and turban managed to follow the traces of cigar fumes back to a booth occupied by two men, an attractive blonde and a brunette.

"I think that I finally got this figured out, Pop!" said the younger man, Kenneth J. Malone, a handsome brown-haired fellow in his early twenties. He wore a tweed sport coat over chinos and a button-down madras shirt. "There is always a perceived menace in every period: In 1914, it was the Boche; in the 1930, it was the Nazis. Now it's the Commies with an atomic sword of Damocles over all of us. No wonder a lot of my generation are looking for new answers anywhere they can!"

"Oh, Kenny, I think that you're still your father's boy, operating on hunches and instinct," said the brunette. Maggie Cassidy was his father's long-suffering secretary and his own surrogate mother. She wore a powder blue cocktail suit with a pillbox hat and white gloves, the Jackie Kennedy "tasteful lady" ensemble now a few years past its sell-by date. "We're just so proud of you, passing the Illinois Bar and getting accepted to the FBI Academy!"

"Yes, that's my boy!" agreed the short, dark-haired but graying man hoisting his whisky glass high. His red face was blazing with enthusiasm and alcohol. He was Chicago's legal eagle, John J. Malone, with the map of Ireland on his face, and the vest of his dark suit generously covered with cigar ash. He was ballyhooed as Chicago's noisiest and most noted criminal lawyer.

"If only my pal Danny von Flanagan were here!"

"He's off fighting crime," said Kenny, "that's what cops like Captain von Flanagan do, Dad. They stand between the darkness and the light."

Malone blessed that night that he had staggered to his door long after midnight to find one of his former chorus girl friends clutching the hand of a five-year-old. He'd looked into that boy's face and saw his own and that of his parents. The woman had disappeared with a clipped mutter of "He's yours now" and he'd never remembered which of his former intimate lights of love she had been, Dolly Dove (known as "the mouse who built a better man-trap") or Dawn O'Day, or some other statuesque blonde candidate. There had been many such fitting the profile over the years.

It hadn't mattered to Kenny or to Maggie Cassidy when she stepped in to help raise the child. In many ways, Maggie was Kenny's real mother. And that is only one of the many, many, fine reasons why John J. and she were going to be married after so many years.

"This is a wonderful night," yelled the blonde half-pint, Kenny's law school friend Lily Thrown. She was dressed up for the celebration with the

Malones since she had no family of her own in town. She wore an attractive black silk blazer over a red dress that was very flattering to her figure and set off her peaches and cream complexion.

"I am so proud, Kenneth! I could just eat you up!" she whispered in his ear.

She'd also passed the Illinois Bar and was going to work as counsel for a religious organization in Chicago. Lily hadn't mentioned which, but the Malones had jumped to the conclusion that it was the Catholic archdiocese.

They would find out later that their conclusion was not accurate.

The stranger was passing through the crush at the bar without effort, the rowdier clients reflexively opening a path before him. He was dressed all in white, like a pair of linen p.j.'s, with his feet in sandals, and a large pugaree-style turban on his head. He caught a barman's attention, Joe the Angel himself, and ordered a drink, a cranberry juice. His eyes watched the booth.

"Are you sure about that, mister? If you get jostled, it'll make a heck of a mess on your nice white clothes," asked Joe the Angel.

"That is not going to be a problem, Guiseppe de Angelo."

The black and white Motorola television over the barman's shoulder showed the face of UBS news anchorman Howard Beale in his coverage of to-day's space spectacular. Astronauts Anthony Nelson and Maurice Minnifield would in turn be conducting a "space walk," which Beale and veteran girl re-porter Jane Arden explained in NASA-speak as an "extra-vehicular activity," or EVA, from their Apollo space capsule.

No one in the joint seemed to be paying attention.

Sâr Dubnotal made his way to the Malone family's booth, his glass of cranberry juice held in his long ascetic fingers, with nary a drop spilled. He had a perfect bump of direction. A path opened effortlessly before him.

"To the law faculty of Compass University," called the senior Malone in salute, and all drank. Suddenly he noticed the man in white. "Oh, can I help you, mister? Are you lost?"

"No, Mr. Malone—you are the one found." The man squatted down on his heels beside the table and explained his problem and search for his "grand-daughter" Josette Arcati. "You may call me the Doctor, or El Tebib, or Sâr Dubnotal," he concluded.

"Czar? Does this mean that you are emperor of all the Russias?" said John J. Malone giggling; he had taken more than a few drinks.

"No, it is an ancient Sumerian title," replied Dubnotal.

The younger Malone muttered something into his glass about one swallow not making a Sumer.

"Gosh, you need a detective, not me, Mr. Doob-nottle. There's plenty of detective agencies in Chicago, like Continental or Nathan Heller's A-1, if you like a smaller organization."

Sâr Dubnotal corrected his name and title again for Malone's benefit. While he was explaining his need for just the type of legal assistance typified by Malone, Lily Thrown excused herself and frantically pleaded an incipient headache and an early morning at her new position.

"This is weird... Please don't go yet, Lil," pleaded the younger Malone. He looked stricken and reached for her hand to halt her progress. She avoided his clutching fingers but snatching her own back.

"No! I'll call you really soon, Ken, I promise you! Bye, folks, and thanks for everything!" was her reply as she blew him an airborne final kiss and disappeared into the crush.

Sâr Dubnotal looked back over his shoulder at her receding form. A lovely young woman, but there was something about her aura that he did not like. He'd seen auras like it before and it was seldom a good sign. That was how he and Judex had met at Notre-Dame in the course of the gargoyle adventure. The Malones exhibited strong bright auras from a lighter side of the spectrum, which greatly encouraged him.

He arranged with the attorney to meet the next day at his hotel, the classic Palmer House.

The Malones arrived early the next day with a black overcoat, red cardigan and penny-loafer moccasins for their client.

"You have to stop this pajama game, sir. You make us feel cold just looking at you."

The Sâr accepted them with appreciation for their feelings.

John J. Malone drove them away from the hotel in his late fifties Ford Fairlane (restrained in aquamarine and white, with modest chrome-edged fins) heading to Compass University in order to question Josette's roommate, Lacey Raintree. Kenny had the advantage of knowing all of these young people, had even dated Lacey at one point, and would serve as guide. On the way, John J. Malone discoursed on the subject of historic crime figures of Old Chicago.

"There's been a lot of change from the days of Mr. Dooley's Chicago and the 1893 World's Columbian Exposition. Over there is the old garage that was the site of the massacre by the goons of 'Spats'Colombo under the orders of Little Bonaparte," he proudly pointed out to his guest. "Two musicians accidentally witnessed the hit and lit off on the lam to Florida, even disguised themselves as women in an all-girl band."

"Oh, dad," said Kenny, "that's just musicians for you." He wore a red windbreaker over a black turtleneck and black pants.

"It's all different now from the old days when I was a kid, when the town was dominated by gang bosses like Little Caesar and Scarface during the corrupt administration of Big Bill Thompson. It was all wide-open back then, full of public enemies free to have their way in plenty of speakeasies. At least Robbo and his Robbo Foundation gave a lot of cash to orphanages and other needy institutions until Reform came in and suppressed them."

"I see," said the Great Psychagogue, without really understanding the attorney's references.

"As a kid, I wanted to be a defense attorney. And eventually, I did become one."

"You bet, dad."

"Then the Crash and the Depression came and the town was still wide-open with a different cast of characters and a thick odor of desperation among the populace. Crime was the only industry that was thriving. The Big Boy had it organized until he came up against detective Tracy's investigative team."

"It must have been harrowing to grow up in such an environment, Mr. Malone," said the Sâr.

"It's better now. Mayor Daley has things under control. That's why the Democrats are having their convention here next year..."

Compass University, Chicago

After parking in the guest parking, Kenneth J. Malone led the trio across Compass U's quad towards the dorms, which took them past the Student Union building. He sighted a friend manning one of the rows of tables outside the Student Union.

"Hey, there's my buddy, Jeff. He was a good friend of Lacey and Josette too. We need to talk to him."

The attractive young man with long fair hair, dark eyebrows and a nascent beard and mustache was seated behind a table with petitions on clipboards in front of him. The table bore a sign reading *Stop the War*. He wore an embroidered shirt of white Indian cotton, well-worn bell-bottom denims and Keds sneakers. He looked like a surfer washed up in the Windy City. A large poster was plastered behind him for the University Film Society, illustrated in the San Francisco psychedelic style. In front of the table was a pretty young woman with waist-length carrot-red hair, clutching a tattered copy of *Siddhartha*, wearing a white peasant's blouse with Kelly green macramé vest and a matching mini-skirt.

"...I remember when I helped write the Port Huron Statement..." Jeff leaned in close across the table, making deeply meaningful eye contact with his subject.

"Oh, come off it, dude, you were only 15-years-old in 1962." The younger Malone was laughing at his friend while the young woman stalked off.

"Kenneth J. Malone," replied Jeff, "your timing is execrable as usual. How do you do that?"

"A special talent that I have as master of time and space. Gents, this poor example of today's radicalized youth is Jeff Lebowski of the Compass campus

committee to stop the war. Jeff, this is my dad, and his client, the Sâr Dubnotal."
Hands were shaken enthusiastically. "We need some help. The Sâr's grand-daughter is Josette Arcati and she's gone missing."

"Ah," said the Great Psychagogue on taking Lebowski's hand, "don't worry about the carpet. Other things in your life will tie it all together." His Visualization was enhanced. This was obviously another case of coincidence and luck benefiting the Malones.

"What, what, that makes no sense at all! Oh no," replied Lebowski. "Look, I've been on this table all day and I'm starved. Let's go over to the deli and you can fill me up with hot dogs while I try to fill you in."

Malone led the foursome away into a storefront housing *Klaw's Best—Jewish Delicatessen*. Dubnotal was hit by a full sensory wave of steaming spiced meats, triggering a sense-memory of a visit to a charcuterie in Paris's *Pletzel*, the Yiddish name for the old 13th century Jewish quarter found in the Marais district.

Behind the register stood a darkly handsome teenage girl, with long black hair that was much curlier than she would have preferred, wearing a white bib apron over a man's white tuxedo shirt and a leotard, and a bored expression.

"Hi, Iris, where's the boss?" asked the lawyer.

"The sleeping prince is taking fifteen in the back. Can anyone else help you, counselor?"

"Always a good question. We'll see your father when he emerges. In the meantime, a round of kosher franks, Dr. Brown sodas and keep'em coming. And get a cool brew for me too, please."

"OK, remember you asked for him."

Iris turned away and yelled, "Dad! Get the celery tonic and get out here!"

A tall spare man in his forties came out, rolling out a flat of Dr. Brown's Cel-Ray soda cans on a hand-truck. He wore a black rayon skullcap on his graying hair, a white nylon short-sleeved shirt with a Black Watch clip-on bow-tie and gabardine trousers with wear at the knees.

He hauled the soda cans into a glass-fronted refrigerator and then turned to the senior Malone with a deep sigh.

"Oy, John J. Malone, I knew that you were coming but why do you have to afflict me today?"

"I wanted to introduce you to my friend here. Sâr, this is the occasional kabbalist, dream detective and master of cuisine, Maurice Klaw."

"A pleasure," said Dubnotal. "Did I hear correctly that Mr. Malone referred to you as a 'dream detective'?"

"Yes, I get it by way of my paternal grandfather, Moris Klaw, who according to family lore kept a musty curio shop near Wapping Old Stairs in London, filled with all sorts of broken statuary, old books, and assorted fauna, including an ancient parrot that guarded the door. It called out 'Moris Klaw! Moris Klaw! The Devil's come for you!' whenever a customer entered. Crazy stuff like that which can't have been good for his business. He was a bit eccentric and claimed to be a master of Odic photography."

"What's that when it's at home?" asked the lawyer.

"It's as obsolete terminology as mesmerism now, with Rhine's modern studies in hypnotism and telepathy, but the theory of Odic force—the name is derived from the Nordic deity Odin—was developed by Baron Karl von Reichenbach," replied the Great Psychagogue, "in the mid-19th century. According to this theory, every human being has an unknown source of power that produces rays. These not only inhabit the body, but also radiate from it, so that a person is surrounded by a virtual field of this Odic force, as von Reichenbach called it. Odic photography is like a snapshot of the phenomena by a psychically sensitive person giving insights into the inner problems, what we might better call *clairvoyance*."

"That supposedly was Grandpa Klaw's talent that he used to help his 'clients'," Klaw sighed. "My parents got fed up with his nonsense and came to America in the early 'teens and my brother Stephen and I grew up here. You'd like my brother Stephen, Kenny. He became an FBI man and a member of their special 'Suicide Squad' in the thirties and forties."

"I'm impressed, Mr. Klaw—that had a reputation as a rough and tough elite unit."

"Did you have a vision of anything besides Mr. Malone's advent, Mr. Klaw?" asked Dubnotal.

"Yes, beware of the winged cephalopod and the pretty priestess—she is not what you expect. Watch for the malefic influence of the *mazikim*. After midnight, the powers of evil are exalted."

"Oh, that's oracular," quipped Jeff Lebowski. "What's a *mazikim*—and whatever happened to those hot dogs? Can I get a black cherry soda too?"

"*Mazikim* are demons, I am afraid. I'm sorry, kid, but I'm not Edgar Cayce. I leave the interpretation to others."

"The Talmud says there are 7,405,926 demons, or *mazikim*, in the world," said Iris. "That seems to be more than a bit excessive to me."

"Now, Mr. Lebowski," began John J. Malone in his cross-examination mode, standing over the young man. "Do you know anything about the whereabouts of Josette Arcati, or can you point us to the whereabouts of her roommate Lacey?"

"I know what happened to Lacey; she's changed her name to Lakota Rainflower to embrace her Sioux ethnic heritage. She started working as a secretary for Dr. Spektor and who knows where they've gone off to now."

"Do you know where Josette is, Mr. Lebowski? Can you help us pull it all together?" asked Dubnotal. "She may be in danger both physical and spiritual."

"I remember that Josette was getting into a weird spiritual head space; somebody she met put her on to some old cult called the Ordo Templi Occidentalis," said Lebowski, scratching his nascent beard.

Dubnotal was distressed at his answer. He knew the name and history of the Ordo Templi Occidentalis from its original British roots in the Golden Dawn to its twisted destinies. It went back to the Arcane Order of the Black Sun, the creation of the man then known as Aloysius Trelawney, later Rowley Thorne, whose later Californian disciples raised the Temple of the Dark Truth in Pasadena and Berkeley in the 1940s. Even ignoring its embrace of the dark side, it was significant that it was used to funnel technical intelligence to the Axis.

"This is not good news, gentlemen," said the Sâr. "Mr. Malone, do you recall hearing about the Temple of the Dark Truth spy ring that was broken by the FBI during World War II?"

"My brother worked on that case," said Klaw. "Pretty dramatic case and high profile indictments."

"Sure I remember, they claimed an oath of fealty to the 'Lower Lord'," replied John J. Malone. "Just the usual run of California pop-diabolism. Before the G-men broke up the racket, they are supposed to have conjured up a wolf demon out of thin air. Later they traced the cult's links to Los Angeles and that big-time rocket experimenter Hugo Chantrelle at CalTech."

"I've got a hunch that temple is where we'll find Josette," said Kenny. "Dude, do you know where their sanctuary is?"

"I know it. It's in a part of Chicago undergoing major urban renewal," replied Lebowski, "and currently is an urban wasteland—used to be a local picture palace, the old Metropolis theater."

Lebowski guided them on a fairly quick trip to the blasted heath where the old Chicagoan Theater was located. It stood alone on the street except for a soda fountain and an isolated barbershop. On one exterior wall of the theater, one could still barely make out the partially effaced remains of a large 1940s Chicago *Times* tip-line ad that advertized *Call Northside 777*. A dozen hard-ridden Harley motorcycles were parked in the empty lot next door.

They entered beneath the marquee, modernized in 1963 with new neon and aluminum structure, past a closed box-office and through the brass door into the lobby. The Great Psychagogue noticed the bronze dedication plaque immediately, showing that the 1931 theater building had been designed by the architect Ivo Shandor. The design was like a modern rendition of the Alhambra. He remembered Shandor very well, whose buildings remained ticking time-bombs of eldritch purpose.

Dubnotal moved deeper into the lobby and the Central Asian patterns of the carpet, followed by the two Malones and Lebowski. Kenny Malone became to softly sing W. S. Gilbert lyrics under his breath:

"With cat-like tread,
Upon our prey we steal;
In silence dread,
Our cautious way we feel."

They were not alone in the lobby although the press of silence made them feel that they were. There were a half-dozen young men and women dressed in red boiler suits cleaning the lobby with broom and dustpan, brush, wash-cloths and carpet sweepers. They made no conversation and no eye contact.

"What the heck," whispered Lebowski, "these dudes have got to be stoned and they missed it."

"No," replied Dubnotal, "they are zombies. Not the undead, but sapped of their willpower."

"I don't like this," quipped John J. Malone. "For zombies, I should have had another beer and charge more per hour."

"Let's check the offices and perhaps we can find out some more there," advised Dubnotal.

They passed beyond the refreshments stand and found the old theater's management suite. The brass inlaid door held a signed reading *Private* below a roundel enclosing what looked like an Art Deco squid with cherub wings. The door was unlocked and they pushed in.

The outer office looked like a place of work, with a reception counter and old wooden desk. A couple of framed film posters decorated the walls. What struck Dubnotal was the obviously recently purchased new technology: Mandarin red IBM Selectric typewriters and Swingline staplers, a Varityper, Gestetner Stencil Duplicator and GesteFax Electronic Scanner. This equipment allowed cheap and readable copies to be made and distributed quickly. Virtually every school, office and union hall had a mimeograph in the back room, usually surrounded by reams of paper and the unmistakable odor of fresh solvent.

Dubnotal went immediately to see the large glass-fronted oak library cases and an antique text strapped down on a map table. His heart sank. It looked to be bound in an organic material of dubious origin.

"Look here, gentlemen," he said, "this is a private research library of iniquity." The others rushed over to him. "These are the magical prescriptions of Nephren-Ka, probably a later Gnostic creation. Here are the *Egyptian Secrets of Albertus Magnus* and *The Ruthvenian*, the so-called 'vampire's bible'; the horrid *Cultes des Goules*, attributed to the Comte d'Erlette. Only a handful of copies are in existence, one of which is locked and sealed in the restricted section of the Vatican library. I also see the more 'mundane' works of Montague Summers on magic, and Reverend Baring-Gould on werewolves, as well as the modern oeuvre by Sidney Redlitch, *Magic in Mexico* and *The Witches of New York*." He held up a smaller book with limp violet pages. "This slim, pale purple volume is the Psychical Society's report on the horrific 'Honeysuckle Cottage' and 'Bludleigh Court' manifestations. The presence alongside them of Dr. Rhine's studies is more surprising."

That was when they heard the Mighty Wurlitzer open up in the Auditorium and they all experienced a *frisson* of awful anticipation.

Dubnotal and the younger members of the party left via a doorway to the auditorium and viewed a stage set with memories of Nuremberg rallies in mind. Peeking through the curtains, they saw long black and red banners and an audience filled dressed in boiler suits. In the center of the stage stood initiates in crimson robes and pointed hoods covering their faces, like Klu Klux Klanners whose laundry whites would have been mixed with a red sweater. They wore the heavy hob-nailed boots of bikers and chanted a round in base voices which was heard as *Huggum squamish, nictzin dyalhis, squamish huggum.*

The initiates framed an altar bearing a nude female figure, sedated, with long brunette hair crowned with foxglove and nasturtium blossoms, behind which was a huge transparent column of space-age plastic, containing an alien creature whose form shifted, sometimes appearing to the human mind as related to the cephalopods and sometimes reptiles or humanoids.

"Oh, Godhead," whispered the Great Psychagogue, "It's an Arisian!" The alien was bounded in its prison by what he recognized as an electrical pentacle, whose distinctive blue glow suffused the contents. Its vacuum tubes had been updated to transistor and solid-state technology. "How foul—who would bind a beneficent being like an Arisian?"

Dubnotal knew from the ancient knowledge that he had studied that the Arisians were benevolent to human and other species fighting to build civilizations of law and peace. Their enemies had destroyed Atlantis and Lemuria, and here one was bound and being drained of psi power. Was this how the cultists had taken psychic control of their followers? Was this what was planned for Josette Arcati?

The focus was now on a shorter figure, the officiating adept in long crimson velvet robes and wearing a golden mask evoking the so-called Mask of Agamemnon found by Schliemann at Mycenae in 1876. However, this mask, instead of the bearded face of Agamemnon, showed the bullet-head and hatchet nose face of Rowley Thorne. Around its neck was an amulet of the Seal of Cagliostro, depicting a serpent with an apple in its mouth, impaled with an arrow. This officiant seemed to sense Sâr Dubnotal and companions, and turned violently to where they peeked through the curtain. It turned towards them and removed its mask.

"Lily, is that you?" said Kenny as he stepped through the curtain, with his father and Jeff Lebowski following. That was his last word. They were all frozen in place with a flick of her hand. It was all that the Great Psychagogue could do to slip mental shields around the minds of his associates and put their consciousnesses to sleep.

Lily Thrown stamped her feet, causing her floor-length scarlet robe to open in the front to reveal her more prosaic white tennis dress and PF Flyers training shoes on her feet.

"Kenny, what are you doing here? You interlopers dare intrude during my ritual? I am Lilia Destrue Pedibus Thorne, the Daughter of Rowley Thorne, the

Beast himself! This cult that my father founded in an odd moment is all mine now. My father wanted to obtain power by entering into compacts with outside entities, but I find that psionic power gives me all that I need..." Her purple aura blazed and obscured her figure temporarily. "What we are witnessing is a shift of total consciousness in America, the dawning of a new Age!"

"Miss Thorne, you obviously are an *esper* of startlingly high functionality," said Dubnotal. "Today, you intend to drain Josette Arcati of her psychic power, inherited from her grandmother Annunciata. I had already suspected that you were attracted to Kenny Malone's psychic potential as well, but I have shielded him from you. I cannot allow you to have further use of this psionic energy. I am reliably informed that a man named John Thunstone once defeated Rowley Thorne. What one man can do, another can emulate..."

"You should not be able to do this," cried Lily Thorne, seeing the Sâr free himself from her spell.

She extended her left arm out of her robe, displaying a gold identity bracelet with a sinister black lens.

"I have drained the psychic power of hundreds, as well as that of my alien captive. If that power cannot hold you, perhaps this will." She stamped her sneaker-clad foot in frustration and motioned her initiates to step forward.

"Ah, but I am the Napoleon of the Intangible, the Conqueror of the Invisible, my dear..." replied the Sâr, raising his hands.

"This is the Chicago Police Department," suddenly called an authoritative voice via megaphone, interrupting their exchange. "You are all under arrest for violations of statutes prohibiting witchcraft, devil worship, and involuntary psychic servitude. Please let yourselves be taken into custody and no one will be harmed."

Homicide cop Daniel von Flanagan strode down the center aisle, accompanied by several dozen of Chicago's Finest dressed in white helmets and riot gear. Several reached the stage and removed bicycle chains and switchblades from the initiates.

"The wheel turns, does it not, Miss Thorne? But who alerted the police?" asked Dubnotal

While two officers secured her wrists in the cold iron of handcuffs, after removing her power bracelet, John J. Malone picked himself off the floor and brushed himself off as much as possible.

"Sorry I hadn't mentioned it before, but I called before leaving the theater office. I thought that we would need backup."

Kenny and Lebowski freed Josette from the altar and wrapped the altar cloth around her.

"My dear," said Dubnotal to her, "your grandmother, Annunciata, was very dear to me. I would be proud if you regarded me as a grandparent."

Josette grabbed him and hugged him tightly and began to weep softly.

A husky senior plainclothes officer in a trench-coat over a black suit walked over and was introduced by Captain von Flanagan:

"This is Lieutenant Samms of the Chicago P.D. secret division, Special Unit 2, which handles all cases involving monsters, alien and domestic. He'll take custody of the, uh, extraterrestrial and make sure that it gets its one phone call."

Samms was a big man with red hair. On his right hand, Dubnotal saw a bright green malachite ring and a Navajo silver bracelet with a huge bright opalescent moonstone rather than the usual turquoise—items of power and protection. The aura was beneficial and his Visualization was able to perceive that matters were in good hands.

"Glad to meet you, Sâr. Looks like the Seventh Cavalry was in time."

Samms then faced the being in the Lucite cylinder.

"Sorry about any delay, sir or madam, but we do have procedure to observe before we can release you back to outer space. In the meanwhile, we do have a Dirac communicator if you'd like to send a message for a ride home."

Brian Stableford, who has so brilliantly translated over a hundred French pro-to-SF novels for Black Coat Press, has just finished adapting Gustave Le Rouge's marvelous The Mysterious Doctor Cornelius, which will be available as a trilogy of 300-page volumes in February. The fate of the eponymous mad sci-entist remains unclear at the end of the saga, one of the characters remarking that a recent issue of the Sydney Times *"contains a portrait of a certain Dr. Malbrough, who, in spite of his side-whiskers, bears an astonishing resemblance to Cornelius..." Brian provides here a pithy epilogue to the sprawling saga of the Sculptor of Human Flesh...*

Brian Stableford: *Malbrough s'en va-t-en guerre*

Kérity-sur-Mer, 1918

Oscar Tournesol had been on the Chemin des Dames ridge when the German bombardment began, but had somehow contrived to survive the initial shelling and the subsequent poison gas drop. When the *Sturmstruppen* divisions attacked, he was one of the few lucky enough to be able to join the retreat. His unit man-aged to reach the Aisne a matter of hours ahead of the Germans, and was initial-ly ordered to reinforce the allied lines there. When the Germans smashed through that position too, what was left of his unit fell back toward the Vesle, and it was there that he was finally caught, albeit obliquely, by the blast of a shell fired from a tank.

He recovered consciousness just long enough to be vaguely aware of being loaded on to a truck, and to feel both the wound in his head and the shrapnel in both legs, before the blood-loss left him unconscious, just giving himself time to convince himself that he was about to die. He only caught the merest glimpse of the other bodies laid beside him in the back of the lorry, but it was enough to tell him that most of them were not going to get past the triage officer, and that he was, in effect, riding in a death-cart.

After that, there was no real consciousness at all for a long time—but there must have been some kind of delirium, because much later, when he became partially self-aware again, in the limbo of numbness that morphine sometimes cradles when one dose begins to wear off but another is not yet urgently neces-sary, he returned to that awkward state of renewed being dragging memories of a kind. Most of them evaporated swiftly, in the fashion that dream-memories do, but two of them stuck, and continued to serve as bright anchors for his semicon-sciousness, which was as fugitive and flickering as a candle-flame.

One of the memories consisted of the opening lines of one of the songs that the British tommies making up the war-weary wreckage of the units assigned to "reinforce" the French along the Chemin des Dames had been singing in the trenches on the nights before the German push, which must have become fixed in his addled head like an earworm, repeating over and over again as his brain was maintained in muted activity by some kind of neural loop. Much of the song, he knew, was scabrous, but the two lines that had stuck fast in his head, taken in isolation, were simply plaintive: "Standing on the bridge at midnight/Throwing snowballs at the Moon."

Oscar continued to repeat those lines to himself, even when he was in a state closer to wakefulness, when the intermorphine limbo began to stretch and stabilize, and he was aware once again of who he was, and could, had he made the effort, have thought about something else. The two lines seemed somehow *safe*, all the safer because they were in a foreign language—albeit one that he knew well—and their incessant mental repetition seemed to be a valiant affirmation that he still existed, and of the continuity of time itself.

In principle, that existential anchor could have been the opening lines of any song—*Malbrough s'en va-t-en guerre/Mironton, mironton, mirontaine*, for example, which he had known since the earliest days of childhood, probably before emerging into self-awareness for the very first time, and which his fellow *poilus* had been singing valiantly since the Marne in '14—and it was probably just random chance that had given him that particular straw for his drowning mind to clutch. When a drowning and flickering mind has no choice, though, it clutches hard, and makes what brightness it can of what it finds.

The other memory that Oscar retained was that of Andrée Pagnot's face, which he had seen not once but continually—or so it seemed. The first time he became conscious of having seen it before, repeatedly, since the shell-burst and the death-cart he instantly and unthinkingly took it as evidence that he was in Heaven—evidence, indeed, that there was a Heaven, in which he had never been able previously to believe—because he assumed that it was the face of an angel.

He did not make that assumption because he thought Andrée was dead—indeed, she was one of the few of his pre-war acquaintances of whose death he had not had news—but because he assumed, even in the arcane convolutions of candlelit delirium, that because angels had no form of their own, those who saw them had to give them a face, and for him, *the* angelic face had always been that of Andrée Pagnanot...or Andrée de Maubreuil, as she had been when her face first acquired that iconic status in his mind. That association was not in any way a betrayal of Regina, or any diminution of his wife's importance in the chronicle of his life, but a matter of history, a matter of his initial salvation, the first time he had required salvation... and, for that matter, the second.

It was the eventual realization that the face he had seen—obviously not the only one he had seen, while he hovered in suspension between life and death, but the only one he contrived to remember as his delirium eased—was actually real, and actually did belong to Andrée Paganot, that informed him that he was somehow still alive, having been directly in need of salvation yet again, and gave him hope that salvation might still be possible.

Possible, but not likely; self-awareness also brought him a limited ability to explore his existential situation, to explore his injuries, not so much in the silver currency of pain, which was still being eroded by morphine, but in the small change of petty inabilities: the fact, for instance, that he could not move his legs at all, and could hardly activate his tongue when he was fed by straw and spoon.

When his feeble hands finally attempted to explore his face and the top of his head, they found dressings. His ribs, he judged, had only been bruised, and his spine was still straight—that, at least, seemed a release of sorts; one potential nightmare less—but his skull and his thighs had obviously taken a battering.

His skull had been cracked before, and he had been hit more than once by bullets before the war even started, but he knew that such past experience had left him physically weaker, not stronger, like a patched pitcher more vulnerable to further breakage in going to the well.

Somehow, he knew, from the very beginning of his return to semiconsciousness, that he "ought" to be dead, that his survival was one of those million-to-one flukes that only happen in fiction.

There was nothing wrong with his jaws and throat, though, and almost as soon as he could think in a manner that was vaguely akin to "straight," he could talk, at least in clichéd monosyllables. For a time, the return of true consciousness was straightforwardly proportional to the return of pain, but that deadly link soon broke, and he was eventually able to remain not merely awake but alert for as much as an hour at a time, when it became possible to string together authentic dialogues, provided that his own contribution was minimal.

By then, he was able to remember other faces: nurses other than Andrée, orderlies, and the individual he had thought of, from the very beginning of returning thought, as "the bloodstained man," even though he knew that he had to be a doctor, an officer, and presumably a gentleman.

The first question to which he was able to get an answer—not from Andrée, but there didn't seem to be any point in waiting, in the hope of making some mysterious esthetic point—was: "Where am I?" Unfortunately, the answer he got wasn't very helpful. He had already deduced, obviously, that he was in a field hospital, and it really didn't matter where, although he was slightly surprised to hear that he was nowhere near Paris but somewhere in the vicinity of Rouen. In any case, that answer inevitably became confused with what his own mind was still doing of its own accord, in the background of his consciousness, and he couldn't be entirely certain that the honest answer to his question wasn't that he was standing on a bridge at midnight, engaged in the essentially ludicrous pastime of throwing snowballs at the pallid moon.

To save him the trouble of talking, though—not because it was costing him too much effort but because it was interfering with their attempts to feed him broth with a spoon—the nurses and orderlies gave him more information, in dribs and drabs.

The German advance had eventually been stopped fifty kilometers short of the capital. The whole point of Ludendorff's dash, apparently, had been one last desperate attempt to get to Paris before the Americans had landed enough troops to stop him, but the Americans had arrived in time: fresh-faced, well-fed mid-Western farm-boys raring for a fight. The Boche offensive had been stopped, smashed and sunk. The war was as good as won. This time, it really would be over by Christmas… four Christmases late, alas, but even so...

Between spoonfuls of broth and not wanting to interrupt, it took Oscar quite a long time to form the questions he really wanted to ask, so he mostly let things drift, content, for a while longer—days, for sure, perhaps a week—to throw snowballs at the lunatic moon, and to try to salute the bloodstained man, and to try to smile at Andrée.

He didn't succeed in either of the more reasonable tasks, but the blood-stained man, in spite of being an officer, did seem to be a gentleman of sorts, and told him not to worry about protocol, or about anything. Only Andrée and the bloodstained man gave him injections, from which Oscar deduced that Andrée had the bloodstained man's full confidence—although that was only natural, since she was "Sister Paganot," not in the sense that she had taken Holy Orders, but in the sense that she was the senior nurse in the team, a veritable archangel: a seraph, perhaps, or at least a domination or a throne.

They all came and went, of course, just as his flickering candle-flame sense of self and reality came and went, and he was often alone—strangely in view of where he had to be and knew that he was—but it didn't matter, because he had his anchor to keep his mental ship in its protected haven; he was on that bridge, throwing those snowballs, knowing that when the bloodstained man and Andrée had finished their work, he would get to the second half of the verse, and even-tually to the chorus, and real life would begin again. *Mironton, mironton, mirontaine.*

His intervals of lucidity were lasting far longer, and he felt that he was on the very brink of recovering not merely consciousness of his being but coheren-cy and continuity: the true fabric of humanity.

At first, the question he asked most frequently was: "Andrée?" but when-ever he had to ask it, the answer was, inevitably, something along the lines of: "She's asleep right now, but she's been looking after you. Not breaking rules, mind—no playing favorites—but for you, she's shed tears, and I never thought I'd see that."

A time came, however, when he was sufficiently together to ask why he, a mere sergeant, had a room to himself instead of being in some makeshift equiva-lent of a ward.

"It was Dr. Malbrough who insisted you got the room instead of being on the ward," was the answer to that. "He's allowed to play favorites. Something to do with experiments. Very big with the General Staff, Dr. Malbrough—not just Duchêne but the *high* High Command. He's Australian."

"Malbrough?" Oscar contrived to query. He already knew that General Duchêne was in command of the Sixth Army, and had been responsible for packing the trenches in the futile attempt to hold the Chemin des Dames ridge; had he given it a moment's thought, he would have deduced that Malbrough was the bloodstained man, but he asked anyway.

"As in the song." that particular orderly remarked. "It really is *Mal*brough, it seems, not *Marl-burrow*. Australian, as I said. Really has gone off to war— been in it since the start, they say: came half way across the world in the first fortnight of August '14—just like you, Sarn't. Hasn't had a scratch, though." *Unlike you*, he didn't add, although the thought was readable.

Eventually, Oscar was able to hold himself together long enough to be told that he would soon be shipped out, no longer requiring to remain in the front trenches of the medical war. Ironically, it was only then that he was able to take stock of exactly where he had been for at least a week, maybe two: a tiny room, with no furniture except his own camp-bed, the stool on which the nurses or orderlies had sat to feed him and the bloodstained man—Dr. Malbrough—had sat to examine and inject him, and an empty ammunition-crate adapted into a table bearing a candle-tray, but a room nevertheless; the kind of privilege normally reserved for officers.

Oscar had worked his way up through the ranks, but not that far, and even that had been almost as much of a miracle as his being passed fit for combat in the first place. Standards were rumored to have fallen quite a way, cannon-fodder now beings in direly short supply, but in '14, people as puny as him had had difficulty getting passed fit, even if they were ex-members of the Gorilla Club, trained acrobats, and veterans of the storming of the Island of Hanged Men, who had come all the way from Florida because his homeland was in danger, and it was his duty.

Cynical as he was, he wouldn't have laughed or spat when he thought the word "duty," had he been capable of laughing or spitting.

The room also had a window, through which, on the eve of his being shipped out—or trucked out, now that he was capable of thinking pedantically— a slate-gray sky was visible; dusk was falling, very gently, behind a veil of cloud. There would be no visible moon that night—not that he had any snowballs to throw at it in any case.

He must have dazed off for a little, because it was dark when he received his next visitation from the angel—from *the* angel.

"No favorites," he said, trying to contrive a smile, but failing.

"To hell with the rules," she said, leaning forward on the stool. "Even on duty, let alone off. You've been my special project for a decade and a half; I'm not about to let it slide. I'd go with you if I could, but I'm under orders."

He felt able now to ask the question that he had never dared ask before: "How bad is it?" He knew that he didn't have to add that he wanted the truth.

"It *was* about as bad as it could be," his angel said. "The triage officer wanted to leave you untreated as a hopeless case. I couldn't have stopped him—but Malbrough could, and did. He had supplies of some kind of artificial blood-substitute, and other tricks that aren't in the standard kit. He took one look at you and selected you out as a subject. Since then... well, there isn't any five star treatment here, but you've certainly had his best attention, as you've doubtless noticed. Now...he's hopeful. Your head will heal, he says, and there's a good chance that you'll walk again. He won't put a percentage on it, but it's a good chance. Ask him yourself—he'll tell you. He can't go with you either, but I think he would if he could, and says that he'll come to see you when he can, in Kérity."

"Kérity? You fixed that?"

"Again, not me—Malbrough. You're one of his favorites, as I say, although he prefers to call them 'subjects.' His pride and his joy, anyway: his miracles. You're by no means the only one, but they're all precious to him. He's a saint."

"A saint as well as an angel," Oscar said, feeling a twinge of pain in his head that told him that he might soon need a booster shot of morphine. "I'm truly blessed."

He was, too; apparently, Andrée, with Dr. Malbrough's saintly help, had contrived to get him sent to Kérity-sur-Mer—to Frédérique Ravenel's home—instead of some crowded hospital in Paris or some recuperation facility in England. Eventually, no doubt, he would get back home to Regina, to Florida, but that might have to wait until the war really did end. In the meantime, Kérity was as close to Heaven as he could plausibly hope to get, even if Monsieur Bondonnat's Eden was running to rack and ruin again without him and Ravenel to tend it. That particular Tree of Knowledge was undoubtedly sick, and might not put forth leaves again for a long time.

"The saint's Australian?" Oscar remarked, repeating the only datum he knew about the bloodstained man whose experimental treatment had apparently save his life, and suddenly wanting to know more, now that he was to be sent away...at least until the bloodstained saint came to see him again, to check up on his "subject."

"Yes. He was with the Anzacs at Gallipoli, apparently; when they were disbanded in '16, he was redeployed to Flanders, and he's been up and down the Front ever since, performing emergency surgeries by the hundred, maybe the thousand by now. Obtained a reputation as a miracle-worker, not just because of his scalpel skills—initially for new anti-infection agents, more recently with this artificial blood-substitute he's developed. Supplies are direly limited, for now, but if it can eventually deployed on a large scale... after the war..."

"The war has been such a spur to new ways of killing," Oscar observed, faintly. "Only fair that it should provoke new methods of healing too..." His head was feeling a trifle ominous, but standing on the bridge and throwing snowballs was still able to drown out the pain and hold his train of thought steady.

His angel leaned a little closer, perhaps worried by the weakness of his voice. Whatever she saw in his face must have been welcome, though, because the expression of reassurance in her blue eyes was worth more than any forced smile.

She too gave the impression of no longer being able to smile, but that was understandable, given that four years of war had cost her not merely her husband, killed at the third battle of Ypres, but her daughter, who had died of pertussis. After that, Oscar knew, she had enlisted as a nurse. Frédérique had been slightly luckier, in that her son was still alive, although Ravenel had been killed too, during the initial German invasion.

In a sense, Oscar knew, he and Frédérique were all that Andrée had left, although she couldn't really lay claim to him any more, now that he was Regina's, or to Frédérique, who still had her own child to cherish. Even Pistolet was dead, simply having grown too old to keep on barking.

"I'm glad that Malbrough agreed to send you to Kérity," Andrée said. "For Frédérique's sake, as well as yours."

Oscar tried to nod his head, but it was beyond his present capacities. He was able to feel tears forming in the corners of his eyes, though, and he was glad that he was able to have these last few minutes with Andrée, before...

The door opened then, and the bloodstained man came in. He really was bloodstained, not having taken off the white smock he wore in the makeshift "operating theater." He rarely did, partly because he thought it unnecessary, given that it was impregnated with one of his own not-yet-patented anti-infection agents, and therefore posed no health-hazard, but mostly—or so Oscar suspected—because it was a badge of pride and status, his messy equivalent of the red cross of the Knights of St. John.

"It's all right, Sister Paganot," the bloodstained man said. "I'll sit with Sergeant Tournesol for a while. Get something to eat before you go back on duty. Don't worry—I'll make sure that he's all right."

Andrée didn't want to go. She had seen the tears in the corners of Oscar's eyes and she knew that it would be the last time that she would see him, until she too could get to Kérity. She wanted to be with him, for her own sake as well as his—but she got up, obediently. She made no protest. She had become used to taking orders, and the bloodstained man was an officer as well as a saint.

Everybody had become used to taking orders; the war had made automata of everyone, to some extent. It was a relief, in a way; taking full responsibility, in the present circumstances, was more than common souls could bear.

"I'll come back," Andrée promised, touching Oscar likely on the cheeks with angelic fingers. "If you're asleep, I'll make sure I'm there in the morning, to say goodbye when you leave." She left, closing the door quietly behind her.

Then Dr. Malbrough took her place, and inspected Oscar very carefully with his eyes.

The eyes in question were devoid of lashes, which made them seem reptilian, although there was also something raptorial about them. After the visual inspection, the bloodstained man reached out to check Oscar's dressings, and deploy his stethoscope in ritual fashion. Eventually, he nodded, in apparent satisfaction. He struck a match and lit the candle impaled on the spike of the tray on the ammunition-crate.

"How's the pain?" the bloodstained man asked, as the candlelight flickered in the eerie fashion that candlelight still retained, in a world from which electricity had not yet banished it completely. There was nothing particularly Australian about the doctor's voice. It seemed free of any particularly nationality, in fact: thoroughly cosmopolitan.

"Bearable, for now," Oscar answered, truthfully.

"I'll give you something to help you sleep," Malbrough said, although he didn't reach for the medical bag that he had set down beside the stool. For once, he didn't seem to be in a hurry. For once, he seemed to be hovering... waiting for something. Oscar knew how ungrateful it was for him to think "like a vulture," but just to make sure, he asked, aloud: "Am I going to recover?"

"I hope so. Your spine isn't damaged, so it's just a matter of letting your legs heal. You have every chance of being able to walk, although you'll probably never work as an acrobat again."

Oscar knew that he had never mentioned his days with the Gorilla Club to the doctor, but it was easy to suppose that Andrée might have done.

"Thank you," Oscar murmured, secretly throwing snowballs at the baleful moon of his increasing discomfort, but wanting to hold himself together, to prove to the saintly doctor that he was a good subject, a worthy favorite.

"Don't thank me," said Dr. Malbrough. "Thank science—and luck. Experimental treatments don't always work. My work has cost as many lives as it has saved. And thank yourself. Considering what you've been through, before as well as during the war, you've been surprisingly resilient, and exceedingly patient. You have every reason to be proud of yourself."

Oscar thought, vaguely, about the chaos of his past tribulations: starvation, tuberculosis, injuries sustained by violence, and the series of operations that had straightened his crooked spine. Obviously, he really had been surprisingly resilient Perhaps, he thought, he ought to have learned patience, but he was not at all sure that he had.

He was beginning to hurt now, and not just in his head, but in general. Dutifully, he reported that to Dr. Malbrough.

"I don't want to give you another injection immediately," the doctor said, surprisingly. "It would put you back to sleep, and I'd rather you were as fully conscious as you can be for a while. I need to talk to you."

"All right," said Oscar, assuming that what the doctor had to say was something to do with the experimental treatment to which he had been subjected. "I'll let you know if it gets to be unbearable."

The doctor nodded. He looked around at the door, as if to make sure that it was shut. Then he leaned close to Oscar, and stared at him again, with a strange attitude of expectation. The candlelight danced over his clean-shaven face and caused the black fuzz of his razor-cut hair to gleam like something newborn... or something artificial. That gleam was nothing, though, compared with the intensity of the raptorial eyes.

"Do you know who I am, Sergeant Tournesol?" the doctor asked, in a strangely affable fashion.

"Dr. Malbrough," Oscar said, thinking that it was a test. "Captain, I presume, or Major... sorry, I never asked."

The doctor uttered an imperceptible sigh of disappointment. "I suppose we've never been formally introduced," he said, "and until you turned up on my doorstep here, you'd only ever see me at a distance—but I knew you, instantly. My memory rarely lets me down. Madame Paganot hasn't recognized me either. I wish I could claim full credit for that, but I can't. As you can probably imagine, it's infinitely easier to change the faces of others by surgical means than it is to change one's own appearance."

Having said that, the enigmatic doctor waited, with evident expectation, for logic to take its course.

It did, but slowly—not so much because Oscar was intimidated by the incredible, but simply because the only thought that he seemed to be capable of holding in the forefront of his mind, for the moment, was that of standing on a bridge at midnight, throwing snowballs at an increasingly menacing moon.

Eventually, though, he responded to his cue. "Dr. Cornelius?" he said, trying to inject his tone with an appropriate degree of incredulity, for purely melodramatic purposes, although he wasn't sufficiently clear-headed, as yet, actually to feel astounded.

"The same," said Dr. Cornelius Kramm, alias Malbrough.

It suddenly occurred to Oscar that Dr. Cornelius must have chosen the name Malbrough as his pseudonym because of the popular song, and because he had imagined himself, in fleeing America for Australia after the catastrophic failure of his nefarious schemes, as yet again, stubbornly, "going off to war." And then the real war had come, and had brought him to France, where everyone who met him would see a completely different irony in his false name. *Mironton, mironton, mirontaine.*

Oscar would have laughed, had he been capable of it.

"I suppose you're wondering," said Dr. Cornelius, "why I saved your life?" He was still following the train of his own logical thought, unaware that the tracks in Oscar's brain had been scrambled.

"Yes," Oscar lied, obligingly. He was incapable of laughing, but he could still play ball. He was well aware of the fact that Dr. Cornelius Kramm had tried to kill him more than once—and Andrée too—most vilely and most recklessly by blowing up the Rochester railway bridge, but in actual fact, he didn't think it at least odd that in the present, very different, circumstances, the doctor had saved his life instead, by means of the science that he prized far more highly than anything as vulgarly human as a desire for revenge.

"First of all," said Cornelius Kramm, scrupulously, like a man who always demanded order and hierarchy in his arguments, "it was because I could. If you cast your mind back, you'll remember that I saved other lives too, even in the heat of our own little private war, because the challenge was there, and had to be met. If I'd killed Joe Dorgan, or allowed Fritz or Baruch to do it, I'd be one of the richest men in America now... but I needed him, as an experimental subject. Even if I hadn't... I saved Mademoiselle Bondonnat too, on the occasion when you and I saw one another for the first time in the flesh, simply because the challenge was there, and science had to meet it. If I had got to Burydan in time, on the Somme, I would have saved him, too... and if hazard presents me with further opportunities..."

"It won't," whispered Oscar, bleakly.

"Because all your friends are dead? Old Bondonnat, Burydan, Ravenel, Paganot, Noel Fless, even Kloum—but not quite all, Sergeant Tournesol. Pierre Gilkin is still guiding transatlantic convoys in the American merchant marine. Harry and Joe Dorgan are fit and well and disgustingly rich; Agénor Marmousier is in Paris; Bombridge is still breeding snails in Florida...and there are the ladies, of course: Andrée, Frédérique, Isidora, Dorypha...I kept careful track, you see, even when I was on the far side of the world, not because I was hoarding information for some future revenge, but simply because I'm a collector of data by nature and by habit. I still have agents in America, you know— dear old Leonello, the indestructible Slug, and a full dozen of my old hanged men. I always intended to go back, to start over."

"Pity about the war," whispered Oscar, wishing once again that he could laugh, if only to make it clear that he was being flippant, playing the gamin. The discomfort was increasing, and that always brought out the gamin in him, presumably in memory of the days when he really had been a street-urchin, living from hand to mouth, and leaving his mouth unsated more often than not.

"Do you think so?" said Cornelius, getting to his feet and going to the window to look out into the darkness, not because he wanted to see what was out there in the darkness, but because he was restless, unable to sit still for long. Officers were not immune to the automatism that claimed impotent souls like Oscar's and Andrée's, but they couldn't avoid their ration of responsibility, especially if they had to maintain steady hands for surgery. Officers developed all manner of neurotic symptoms, which made stillness difficult—even an officer like Dr. Malbrough, Oscar thought, whose mask of false identity hid the supposedly-imperturbable Dr. Cornelius Kramm, sculptor of human flesh and conscienceless master of the Red Hand. Or so it seemed. All this might, of course, be a nightmare.

"I suppose, in that," Dr. Cornelius continued, "you're in the majority. The war, almost everyone thinks, has shown us all how trivial everything else is—or was—by comparison. What were the few hundred people I killed in America by comparison with the tens of thousands slaughtered in a single day at Ypres or the Somme? What was the association of the Red Hand by comparison with the organized crime of the Boche war machine, of U-boats, mustard gas and zeppelin raids? What was the paltry scope of my insidious gathering of the experimental material of human flesh compared with the lavish provision of material laid on every day by bombardment and blast, flame-throwers and poisons, syphilis and staphylococcus?

"Flanders fields, you know, are among the most fertile in the world, enriched over centuries by animal and human manure—bacteria thrive there as nowhere else on Earth, and that's where the warriors of 1914 elected to dig their trenches, to bathe themselves in filth, to make absolutely certain that every wound they sustained, from barbed wire or machine-gun bullets, would become a crucible of infection... not merely a utopia of challenge for a man such as me but an ideal opportunity for an experimentalist like me to be hailed as a hero, or even a saint, and not condemned as a villain, or as a demon...

"Pity about the war? I don't think so, Sergeant Tournesol. If I were a lesser man, I'd say thank God for the war... but for all its wonderful advantages and opportunities, it's not what I want. Yes, all those mutilated bodies, all those men in the very jaws of death, almost beyond the reach of any possible snatching, are invaluable... and I certainly wouldn't want to be thought ungrateful... but it's not, at the end of the day, of any real significance. War is an inconvenience as well as a folly. The real challenge has to be fought on nature's battleground, against the everyday processes of aging and deterioration... and that's what I want, what I need, to get back to, in the fullness of time.

"Mending broken bodies and mangled flesh, like yours, is exhilarating, but at the end of the day, it's a distraction. I need to get back to experimenting on the healthy, not for the sake of repair but for the sake of improvement. I need to get past this stupid heroism, this repetitive fight to save lives that are hardly worth saving, to get back to the business of enhancement, the cultivation of the ultimate mutability of the flesh, the exploration of the further limits of possibility..."

Oscar wanted to tell the doctor that his need for a morphine booster was now becoming acute, but all he could contrive as a kind of strangled grasp. The metaphorical moon, unintimidated by snowballs, was beginning to glare at him

397

like a death's-head, for reasons that had nothing to do with Cornelius Kramm's compulsive confession.

In a way, the gasp worked. Realizing that his patient was in distress, Dr. Cornelius turned away from the window and came back to the candlelit bed. He sat down on the stool again, touched Oscar's forehead to test his temperature, and took his pulse—but he didn't want to be distracted, as yet, from what was on his own mind, from whatever crazy reasoning had led him to let Oscar in on a secret that he had surely not confided to anyone else.

"Don't worry," said the counterfeit Malbrough, "I won't leave you in distress much longer. I'm sorry—I've allowed myself to get carried away. But that's the point, you see. That's the second reason, the more important reason, why I saved your life. Because I need you, Sergeant Tournesol—may I call you Oscar? *I need you*, Oscar. Not so much now, while this stupid war is on, but afterwards, when I return to America, when I get back to work.

"The era of organized crime had only just begun, you see, before the war. Afterwards—and the German defeat can't be long delayed now; even setting propaganda and morale-boosting aside, this time, it really will be over by Christmas—afterwards, organized crime will really be able to take off, more so in America than anywhere else. It will be possible to make billions that way, and if billions are going to be made, it really will be far better that they're made by a man like me, who has a purpose in mind for them, rather than a decadent sensualist like my late brother Fritz, or a reckless hedonist like Baruch Jorgell, or a smug wallower in pathetic luxury like any common-or-garden billionaire.

"Organized crime will provide a context for field-experiments on a scale that might not be quite as vast as the Somme, but will be far more amenable to planning, to control, for strategy..."

Oscar had been trying valiantly to interrupt for some time, but it wasn't easy, not so much because of Cornelius' volubility as because of his own deteriorating condition. He felt now as if he were on a Medieval rack, as if he were under torture—as, in a sense, he was. Heroically, he managed to say "Me?" and make it sound like a question.

"What has it got to do with you?" Cornelius echoed, quick on the uptake, as befitted a genius of his stature. "I'm sorry, my dear Oscar, I know that I'm not going fast enough for you, but you have no idea what a relief it is, finally to be able to speak to someone who knows who I am, someone who's studied me, someone who knows what I'm capable of doing, someone who *knows my measure*. That's why I need you, you see—that, above all else, is why I had to save *your* life, more urgently than anyone else's.

"Nobody else will know, you see, once the war is over and I return to America, what's really going on. From everyone else, I'll need to hide, as I'm hiding now, because I'll have to, in order to be able to carry out the kind of experiments that I want to carry out, not merely on volunteers like my precious hanged men, but on the healthy, on the contented and self-satisfied: people who would never volunteer to put what they have at risk for the chance of helping me, in the long run, to develop something better.

"From the world, I'll have to hide—not merely in the sense of remaining unseen, but unimaginable, beyond belief. But alongside that, in addition to that, I need there to be someone who *knows*, not merely that I'm there, but what I'm about, and what I'm capable of doing. I need an audience, Oscar, and not just any audience, but a specialist audience: an opponent, an adversary. Burydan might have done, if he hadn't got himself killed, Paganot, probably... even Ravenel... but they're all gone. You have no idea, my dear Oscar—although I'm doing my level best now to give you one—what high hopes I have for you, what I expect of you in terms, not merely of the intellectual comprehension of my endeavor but the esthetic appreciation of it.

"You see, my dear Oscar, in order really to exist, we all need someone who *knows* that we exist, who knows who and what we are—and for that reason, you need me as much as I need you. You have Regina, of course, and the angelic Andrée, but they don't really know you, and never will, because you love them far too much ever to let them see you as you really are, just as I would love a wife, if I were ever to marry, far too much to let her see what I really am. It's because you and I have been adversaries, Oscar, and because we can be adversaries again, that we can dispense with our masks and look one another in the face. It's because we've hated one another, and might do so again—in spite of the gratitude you're bound to feel and the quasi-paternal affection that I shall have difficulty henceforth keeping at bay—that we can rip away the veils of illusion, and confront one another as our true selves..."

He broke off then, even though Oscar could no more contrive a scream than a laugh, and bent down to delve into his medical bag for a Pravaz syringe. With practiced efficiency the fake Malbrough filled the instrument, and plunged it into Oscar's flesh, near the hip.

Oscar felt the morphine rush almost instantly, but he knew—and knew that Cornelius Kramm knew it too—that he would still be capable of listening for a minute or two more, before the numbness overwhelmed his brain, and took him away, at least to dream and delirium, if not to darkness...

Standing on the bridge at midnight, Oscar thought, or, at least heard in his mind's ear, because he was incapable to real thought, *throwing snowballs at the Moon*...

"This is our secret, Oscar," said the bloodstained man, leaning forward yet again as if to soak up the frail, fleeting candlelight—and Oscar wondered, belatedly, whether he had begun to think of the man who had saved his life as "the bloodstained man" because somehow, deep below the surface of consciousness, he *had* recognized them man he had seen once before, at a funeral. "It's our secret, not because I'm forbidding you to tell anyone, but because I know that you can't, not so much to spare your reputation for sanity and to ward off the accusation that this is all a nightmare, but for Andrée's sake, and Regina's, because your instinct… your stupid, primitive, human instinct… is to protect them from the knowledge that the likes of Dr. Cornelius Kramm are haunting the world, and haunting *them*...

"But *you*'ll know, my dear Oscar. You'll know that this wasn't a mere fragment of delirium. You'll know, when the so-called war is over and the real war resumes—the war of all against all, the bloody war from whose agony true progress emerges, provided that there are men like me to make it—that I'm there, behind the scenes, immortal and unconquerable, doing my work. Perhaps you'll try to stop me—I hope you will, because nothing whets an appetite for progress like challenge and resistance—but whether you do or not, you'll know. You'll be on the lookout, ever-ready to read behind the lines of the news, ever-ready to say, of something anomalous and mysterious: 'That's Dr. Cornelius at work; that's one of his experiments, one of his sculptures, part of his quest to make human flesh malleable, and bring out the full potential, not merely of the clay of the body, but also of the clay of the mind.' And you'll..."

There was more. There was probably much more, in fact. Like all men who live in hiding, concealing their true selves—all men, in effect, and all women too—Dr. Cornelius Kramm, once having seized a rare opportunity to explain himself, wasn't easy to stop.

Oscar was no longer listening, however. Oscar was lost within himself, within the tide of chemical relief that was dulling his pain, dulling his consciousness, dulling his very being, his all-too-malleable clay. He could no longer hear Cornelius Kramm's passionate self-explanation and rebarbative boasting. He probably couldn't hear anything at all, in fact, but he thought, or dreamed, that he could. He thought, or dreamed, that he could hear a British tommy, on a ward somewhere down below, in some mysterious gulf, singing, no longer about hurling dirty snowballs at a sallow moon, but somehow having contrived, at last, to reach the plaintive and pain-racked chorus of his song: "It's the rich that get the pleasure/And the poor that get the blame/It's the same the whole world over/Ain't it all a bloody shame."

And Oscar thought, or dreamed, too, that he could hear an entire line of entrenched *poilus*, rising valiantly to that bizarre challenge, that crazy but stubborn resistance to the awful pressure of fate and circumstance, to counter anchoring gibberish with anchoring gibberish, by singing "*Malbrough s'en va-t-en guerre/Mironton, mironton, mirontaine…*"

Except that it wasn't gibberish, really, any more than the English song was really gibberish, because Malbrough really was going off to war, again...

Not that it mattered much, in the great scheme of things.

It didn't matter, because first thing in the morning, Oscar, conscious or unconscious, was trucking out. He would be on his way to Kérity-sur-Mer, to be cared for by Frédérique Ravenel: to the Earthly Paradise, doubtless damaged but not yet derelict, where he could rest and recuperate, if necessary until the war was over, when he could be shipped back to Florida, to Regina...

In the meantime, doubtless, he would see Dr. Malbrough again, having come to check up on his "subject," or the sharer of his secret. Now that he knew who Dr. Malbrough really was, it would no longer be a matter of saluting a saint, even mentally, but that didn't matter either—not so much because Cornelius Kramm now wanted him alive instead of dead, but because for him, Sergeant Oscar Tournesol, the war was over, and he was no longer on the bridge, but moving forward, into the future.

At the end of the day, and the beginning of the next, the future was all that really mattered, and all that ever would.

Mironton, mironton, mirontaine...

The death of King Kong was already revisited earlier in this volume by Nathan Cabaniss; this story by Michel Stéphan (who recently penned a new Madame Atomos *novel for the French market) could be read as a sequel of sorts, featuring Léo Malet's indomitable P.I. Nestor Burma (France's answer to Sam Spade and Lemmy Caution), and a truly, er, freakish supporting cast...*

Michel Stéphan: *Nestor Burma in New York*

New York, 1933

America! I don't go there often. It's too far away, too grand, too... whatever. Besides, my business is here. Yet, I've been just as fascinated by it as anyone else. Like any European, I'm curious to know what these people on the other side of the Atlantic are like.

My chance came years ago, before the war. It was 1933 and I hadn't become the dapper detective I am now. At the time, I was planning to drop out of my anarchist circles and try my hand at journalism, though I didn't have a degree, only a few contacts. More exactly, there was my friend Gouvieux who had done some freelance articles for the *Matin Illustré.*

Gouvieux was a real case. He seemed to draw assignments sending him to the most sordid places in the capital and I sometimes wondered if his editor didn't deliberately send him to very dangerous places only to see if he could make it back out alive. But Gouvieux *always* made it.

Gouvieux was my friend and, that morning, he showed up at my place with two round trip tickets from Paris to New York. His paper was sending him to cover the event of the century which was going to unfold in the United States in a few days. Initially, they'd told him that it was a one man job.

"I'll go," had said Gouvieux, "but only if I get another ticket so I can take an intern along."

He told me later that, for all his professionalism, he wasn't sober when he'd made that request, but that was how I found myself with a ticket to New York.

Aside from Lindbergh—who had demonstrated his skills a few years earlier—there weren't many folks who had crossed the Atlantic in a flying machine. *Air France* had just been founded, and the opening ceremony, which took place at Le Bourget, only seemed to add to the doubts that the airplane would ever replace the transatlantic liners.

The event we were going to cover was nothing less than the arrival of a gigantic ape in New York. King Kong—as this god among animals was called—was supposed to have been exhibited at a theater in that great city.Unfortubnately, the ape had found a way to escape, then had taken a dive ftom the Empire State Building, which put something of a crimp in my friend's article.

"I don't know what you think," I said, "but a monkey losing his balance and falling to his death? That sounds fishy to me."

"Let's hold off making any hasty judgments," he said. "We don't know the whole story."

When we got to New York, we heard the official explanation, which seemed to cover every angle. Everybody seemed to know the story, but only a few were eyewitnesses on the day the big gorilla fell. I've seen a lot of documentaries about the tragedy since. The Americans consider it chic to gloss over the blood and death with pretty clichés and mawkish poetry like "*It was beauty killed the beast.*"

That was the quote everybody remembered. It's fine to get sentimental over the big ape, but when I thought about the sidewalk vendors who opened their stalls never expecting several tons of monkey meat to fall on their heads… Well, that limits my desire to get all poetic about it.

Because of the extent of the carnage, the newsreels refrained from showing too much. The monster, King Kong, had burst open on impact and the blood spilled made an apocalyptic scene. Even Americans have a sense of restraint when it suits them.

Gouvieux and I arrived after the disaster. I spent a day watching the rain through the hotel window. I had decided to not get mixed up in the whole sordid, disgusting mess, when the door suddenly burst open. Gouvieux, smiling and bright-eyed, had arrived with fresh news.

"They've taken the body," he said. "And they're nearly finished cleaning up the streets." Seeing that I did not share his enthusiasm, he continued: "I asked around. They've been having problems disposing of the ape's body. The city was going to incinerate it, but there's a mountain of paperwork to be done first."

"That's strange for a country that prides itself on being at the forefront of progress," I said. "You'd think they'd have a standard form for giant apes falling from skyscrapers."

Gouvieux didn't miss a beat.

"The corpse was taken to the suburbs and dumped in a stadium. They covered the body with a tarp and are waiting for permission to destroy it. The problem is that decomposition has set in, and the air is getting more unbearable over there."

"And of course, you want to go for a ride?"

"Just to take pictures, Nestor. Just to take pictures!"

I expected to see—as I would have at home—a cordon of policemen holding back the crowds who had come to see the remains of King Kong, but there was nothing like that; just silence and the night.

The taxi had taken us several miles from the center of the city and dropped us off in a suburb with a name I couldn't pronounce. Behind us stood the dark mass of skyscrapers, silhouetted in the twilight, and before us, in stark contrast, nature rose up as if man had abruptly stopped building there. It was only after several minutes that I could make out the shacks and the tenements, all built low to the ground and teeming with life. Here were the souls who had the misfortune of being born on the wrong side of the tracks.

King Kong was there as well. We couldn't see him yet, but the smell of rotting flesh that filled the air left no doubt. The romantic old monkey had ended up in the garbage of the New World.

As we walked, shapes appeared on the horizon, human silhouettes that moved oddly. I was not sure what I saw, but Gouvieux clarified it for me.

"Look, Nestor," he said. "That must be the circus freaks heading our way."

After the first moment of surprise—to say these people were startling would have been an understatement—my shock gave way to a mild euphoria. We were surrounded by people of every size and shape, from dwarf to giant, to the physically deformed to the downright creepy, but the first words they exchanged with us were not in English. These people spoke in the language of Voltaire—maybe a Voltaire who was drunk—but still Voltaire.

By midnight, we had all gotten to know each other. Sitting for more than two hours at a huge makeshift table made of boards and sawhorses, we talked to all of the performers: the Siamese twins, the headless man, the woman with two brains... I'm embellishing a bit because I don't remember all of them, but everyone came to see us.

The one that impressed me the most was Frieda. She and her husband, Hans, were a couple of dwarfs. Since my arrival in New York; I hadn't met many people as distinguished or as fascinating as them. Hans was dressed to the nines, while Frieda wore a trapeze artist's outfit that accentuated her delicate, porcelain-doll beauty. However, the intensity of her gaze made me think that I'd better not risk making a joke about her, even if in good spirits.

Frieda spoke surprisingly good French and, like her husband, showed a willingness to shoot the breeze with two strangers like us.

And this little lady had a lot to say. She had an unusual need to spew venom at the decadent society that surrounded her. Gouvieux and I were captivated by the unexpected secrets of this little world and listened with open ears.

"Do not trust the air of euphoria that you see here," she said. "Our manager, Mrs. Tetrallini, brought us across the ocean because the atmosphere of the Continent had become too unhealthy for us. Too many stories, too many problems with the people who came to gaze at our differences without wanting to admit that we're still human beings. We expected to find a sanctuary in the New World, but none of us holds on to that illusion anymore. It's been weeks since we pitched camp in this cursed place. We're giving performances to make a living, but we still can't move about freely. Mrs. Tetrallini has gone into the city to try to regularize our situation, but we have no hope that life will be better here than in Europe. In addition, they have placed the body of that ape behind our quarters. The tarpaulin does not even completely cover the beast and the smell is unbearable!"

Hans had not spoken merely listened to his wife and taken an occasional swallow of booze from a bottle he carried in a paper bag. Now he began to wave his little arms frantically.

"We are the rejects of society," he said. "Wherever we go. We are worthless in the eyes of the good Americans, except to give them the thrill of a freak show, which they love. Tomorrow night is Sunday, and our performance will be for the kids. Do you think parents will bring their youngsters with that stench filling the grounds? The city promised they would remove the gorilla so that we can work in decent conditions, but that stiff is still here."

The dwarf dropped his gaze to the floor and I thought for a moment he was going to burst into tears. Then with an energetic gesture, he gulped a swig of his alcohol, a gesture that didn't seem to please the lady. Frieda opened her mouth but before she could say a word, Hans raised a finger and solemnly said to us:

"I want you to stay with us tonight, gentlemen. Frieda will prepare good beds for you. Please, consider this your home."

Gouvieux started to reply but the dwarf continued:

"I would like you to attend our performance tomorrow. As witnesses. As journalists. The circus may be ending, but we will show them, the good Americans, what the outcasts, the freaks, can do."

Our flight didn't leave until the following Monday. Before I could give Hans an answer to his proposal, Frieda took my hand and politely invited us to follow her.

The next morning, a bright sun pierced the scattered clouds. Unfortunately, it only underscored the desolation of the landscape around us. It felt like a huge landfill, dotted here and there, without any logic, with circus trailers. On the least rugged part of the field stood a worn-out tent. Behind it, a huge tarpaulin served as a reminder that the body of the fallen giant, King Kong, had not yet been disposed of.

Gouvieux entered the caravan we shared.

"I went to photograph the beast," he said. "It's not pretty. I had to take a few steps back in order to get it all in the frame."

"You weren't bothered by the smell?"

"No, not at all."

Gouvieux really was one of a kind."

On Sunday evening, the kids began to gather in front of the tent, bringing a little animation to this rotten landscape.

"The show will be starting soon," Gouvieux said, glancing at his watch. "I'll get some pictures and then we can get back to civilization."

We walked to the entrance of the tent, which seemed increasingly dirty as we approached. Inside, the stands were already half filled, mostly with heckling children under the eye of some sleepy adults.

Some people greeted us and inquired about how well we'd slept. One of these was Jane, a little bareback rider we had interviewed yesterday, who seemed quite normal to me. We exchanged a few polite phrases and Jane lingered there with us. Obviously, she enjoyed our company and wanted to talk. Gouvieux began to take some pictures of the public and the stage, which was still empty. It was a massive platform, topped with two huge wooden poles.

"What will happen?" I asked Jane. "Do you know what tonight's performance is all about?"

"I thought Hans told you. I saw you talking with him and his wife."

The lights suddenly dimmed, leaving only a section of the stage lit where a dozen extras disguised as Indians made their appearance to the beating of drums.

"What did Hans say to you, exactly?" Jane whispered in my ear as the faux Indians began their war dance.

"He asked us to be witnesses to your last show," I said. "That's what I understood, at least."

The sound of the drums became increasingly deafening. Then, suddenly, there was silence. Two small figures appeared: Hans and Frieda standing on the platform. The dwarf was dressed as a savage hunter and his wife was decked out in a grotesque platinum blonde wig. The costumes made a striking contrast with the lovely couple we had seen the day before. They seemed dismal in their Carnival get-up and their eyes shone with an eerie light.

"Hans should have warned you," Jane said. "We decided to do a final show for the Americans. I would advise you to get going as soon as it begins. This is something that's going to make the headlines."

Hans while smiling—or perhaps it was a grimace, for the dwarf did not look like his normal self—began, with great delicacy, to tie each of his wife's arms to one of the two poles on the platform. Just as gently, he repositioned the blonde wig, which had slipped slightly. Frieda wore such a foolish grin that I was convinced these two were drugged.

"What is this?" I asked Jane. "It looks like some kind of pathetic farce."

Laughter rang out from the audience. The kids weren't missing a beat of the show.

"You see, Mr. Burma," Jane said, "there's more to why our manager, Mrs. Tetrallini, brought us across the Atlantic. The dear lady met an American during one of our tours on the Continent. She fell in love with him, but he left to return to his country. I think she's still hoping to find him. This is the other reason for our presence in New York."

On the stage, Hans turned to the audience and showed that his wife was securely bound.

"Ladies and gentlemen, with us here tonight is the *real* Anne Darrow," he announced. "The girl who survived the savage jungles of Skull Island! The maiden who tamed the giant ape!"

The drums began again and the dancing resumed, more frantic than ever. Laughter rose from the audience.

"Dear members of the public, I have presented you the Beauty. Now I present the Beast!" Hans was now screaming to make himself heard over the drums and the children's excited shouting.

"This American was a kind of scientist," Jane continued. "When he told us what he had discovered, it was so incredible that we didn't believe him—scientists will say just anything—but when we found that it really worked, it filled us with terror. We never used his... invention until tonight. We all agreed to provide an appropriate spectacle for the people of the country that has welcomed us so grandly. That is why I advise you, one last time, to take off, Mr. Burma."

The noise of the rambunctious kids made my eardrums throb. They were out of control, and for good reason. Hans gesticulated on the stage as if he was in a trance. It was so ridiculous that the general hilarity was understandable.

Frieda rolled her bulging eyes. The dwarf couple must have taken illicit drugs before the performance. They created the illusion of savage pygmies so well that they would have put a director of horror films to shame.

Suddenly, there was silence, as if a camp counselor, invisible to the adults, had ordered the kids to be quiet.

Then came the noise; a sound emerging from beneath the tarp. Something moved, a huge shape that encroached on the circus tent. The smell of putrefaction became stronger. The stench of the Unspeakable. Still tied to the pillars with a mesmerized expression, Frieda waited.

"OK, Gouvieux, we're going," I said, grabbing the photographer's arm.

We started to hurry back through the crowd when we heard a roar. The sound didn't correspond to anything I had ever heard before, but I didn't want to investigate it. Something landed on the platform. I was too busy running away to look back, but I knew that, if I had been any slower, I would have seen the two pygmies crushed by an unknown force.

Gouvieux and I had barely managed to get out of the tent when the screams redoubled. It was dark outside and we ran for a while until we stopped and turned to look back. Actually, it was Gouvieux who slipped and fell in a mud puddle. Behind us, it was as if the gates of Hell had been flung open. There were no more lights coming from the circus, only frantic cries and an impossibly huge living thing, looming black against the dark horizon.

When we finally reached what we thought was a safe distance from that hellish place, I searched in vain for the lights of civilization. I recognized the gently sloping road where the taxi had dropped us off the day before, and the first houses. But everything was dark and deserted.

There, where the circus had stood, full of sound and fury, a gigantic shadow loomed in the dark. We could only see the silhouette, but it was undoubtedly that of an ape.

King Kong resurrected like Lazarus!

It couldn't be! Had the Barnum lunatics built a giant automaton? They couldn't possibly have done it so quickly. And what about the rotting stench that grew stronger... the grunting, or rather the complaint, born of gigantic, decomposing vocal cords? In all my life, I had never heard anything like it—a roar from beyond the grave.

From all sides, terrified adults and children ran past us, evidence that some had managed to escape the massacre. But the human cries we heard, mingled with the beast's groans, didn't allow us much hope for those who hadn't made it out.

I fancied I saw Hans and Frieda fleeing at full speed on my left, but I couldn't be certain. In any event, some of the freaks were bound to be among the survivors.

Sirens announced the firefighters and police long before the first vehicles arrived, blinding us with their lights and spreading panic among the fugitives.

Breathless, Gouvieux slowed and the little bareback rider caught up with us. She looked at me with amusement.

"A fantastic story for you Frenchmen! You're going to take back some truly sensational news!"

"But what have you done?"

"Come here," she said, taking my arm. "I'll tell you the truth so you can write it down and take it with you back to Europe, otherwise nobody will ever know. Tomorrow, the newspapers will only write twaddle."

The crowd became denser. More police and rescuers had arrived.

I felt the girl's hand lose its grip. The human tide would separate us soon. Gouvieux had disappeared, carried away by the flood of fugitives.

"But what should I write, dammit? This is clearly important, but if you don't tell me more..."

My voice was drowned by the noise of engines. Aircraft flying overhead at low altitude.

"Flee, Nestor. They will destroy everything. They will destroy Kong all over again. As they destroy all the unwanted within their own borders."

I tried to ask for more of an explanation, but I saw the little rider disappear, carried away by the crowd. I just had enough time to hear what she was yelling to me.

"Herbert West, Mr. Burma! Madame Tetrallini's fiancé was named Herbert West!"

Those were the last words she spoke to me. Then I lost sight of her forever.

Despite the reduced visibility, the aircraft opened fire on the thing. It ended, I suppose, when they killed it again. Honestly, I didn't care; it really wasn't my problem. My only concern was to find Gouvieux and get out of the country.

Back in France, I didn't read the newspapers for a while, and I never talked with Gouvieux about what we'd experienced. It seemed too unreal.

Later, I did some research, but it seems that there was no news of the event, either in the papers or on the radio. I took some comfort in the idea that it was wiser not to talk about it. After all, the Americans have their problems, and we have ours.

For my part, I would soon open my agency. I mind my own business and am content dealing with the likes of Riton le Nantais or Roger le Brestois and not monsters performing in circuses, or apes that aren't even alive.

I have nothing against Americans. I went, I saw, I triumphed, as they say. But I'll wait a bit before I go back there.

(Translation by Matthew Baugh)

It was ineluctable that the need for increased melodramatic tension would lead to heroes and villains with greater powers... The D'Artagnans of yesterday were eventually replaced by the likes of Rocambole, Lupin, Fantômas, the Nyctalope, Doc Savage, Judex and The Shadow, until the public's appetite for ever greater feats led to the creation of today's superheroes. David Vineyard's vignette-sized tale focuses on this transition...

David L. Vineyard: *Interview with a Nyctalope*

1938

"Leo Saint-Clair, also known as the Nyctalope," the soft-spoken reporter said, "you're a national hero in France and widely known throughout the world as the living embodiment of your nation. That must be a great burden, a great responsibility?"

Saint-Clair gave a very Gallic shrug. "One does what one can. I've been privileged to serve France on a few occasions."

Modesty was not normally the Nyctalope's greatest virtue, but this mission to the New World was as much diplomatic as adventurous, and, in this case, diplomacy, as they said, was the prerequisite for valor. These Americans were overly fond of humility, almost to the point of arrogance, but potentially too great a resource to ignore. And 1938 was a dangerous year for much of the world beyond these shores.

The reporter jotted down the Nyctalope's words at remarkable speed, even for someone adept at shorthand. Pushing his glasses up on his nose as he paused, his blue eyes seemed to look through Saint-Clair in their intensity.

"We're you surprised at your welcome here in the U.S.?"

"Honored. I had no idea my little exploits were known in this hemisphere. I don't believe my Boswell, Monsieur de La Hire, is even in print in English, much less available here." In many ways this bustling nation was still an unsophisticated backwater. Some embassies still considered its muggy capital a hardship post.

"We do get the world press," the reporter said a little defensively. "And we have heard of your exploits, though some of Monsieur de la Hire's accounts seem a bit fanciful."

Ah, my big friend, Saint-Clair thought, *not half so fanciful as my reason for being here.*

"Books must be sold," Saint-Clair replied. "I suppose some latitude must be given for the public taste. I've never thought of myself as a mystery, much less a mystery man, but it seems to go with my reputation."

The reporter removed his glasses to clean them with a corner of his red tie. A comma of black hair, almost a spit curl, fell over his right eye, and the transformation in his appearance was remarkable. He replaced the glasses, and pushed the spit curl back in place.

"There have been some rather remarkable accounts of your physical abilities as well. Fanciful seems a weak adjective for them."

This unassuming, even meek, reporter was more than he seemed. He certainly was no guileless rube.

"I was blessed with somewhat unusual vision," Saint-Clair admitted. Considering his remarkable eyes, he could say little else. "A gift—nothing more."

"Some might say superhuman," the reporter said casually, but Saint-Clair caught the inflection.

"Nietchzhe's *ubermensch*? An interesting proposition. Sad to say, unlike your Doctor Savage, I have no Arctic Fortress of Solitude."

"Perhaps not," the reporter said. Was he a little defensive now? "But according to records, you seem to be at least fifty, while you appear a youthful thirty ..."

"Really, Monsieur, do I look fifty?" He laughed, but it sounded hollow even to him. "And this business of an artificial heart? Come on, would that make me immortal? Perhaps I should try walking on water!" Good reporter or not, the fellow was fine detective.

"Perhaps, but rumors have it you're here to look into a certain wealthy man in this city, one with wide ranging interests, and a bit shadowy by all accounts."

"*Shadowmen*? There you have me, my friend. But not the wealthy kind. I'm far more interested in these fantastic flying men in your newspapers. I can't hope to equal the exploits of some of these chaps."

"I'm afraid some aspects of our more inventive press may have misled you. Fairy tales dreamed up by criminals with fervid imaginations. They are, by nature, a superstitious and cowardly lot. And not all my colleagues are above a bit of purple prose on behalf of their papers."

"*Je comprends*. My own country's press are no less imaginative about myself, Lupin, and that madman who murdered all those people before the Great War. I once met his nemesis, Inspector Juve, and was hardly impressed. Flying men? A great joke, *n'est-ce-pas*? To believe that, one would have to believe that absurd account about my traveling to Mars. Really, Mars?"

After a few more questions, Saint-Clair excused himself. He had an important reception he could not miss. Duty, and his beloved France, called.

The reporter rode the elevator to the lobby floor and quickly strode across it to the exit.

Parked in front of the main entrance stood a dark limousine, and beside it, a slender man in formal wear, including cutaway and striped trousers, and holding a brolly and bowler. He held the door for the reporter, then took the driver's seat and pulled into traffic.

In the rear of the car, the reporter quickly removed cheek pads designed to make his face fuller, and blue contact lenses, which reveled startling gray eyes that seemed to miss nothing.

"I take it we were a success, sir?"

"A bravura performance, Alfred. If I fare half as well at the reception to-night, I think we can eliminate any lingering suspicions regarding flying bats..."

From his suite, Saint-Clair watched as the reporter entered the big car and pulled away.

The fellow was good, but little escaped the Nyctalope's eyes.

The French Government had been concerned about these new "flying men," and they had dispatched him to investigate their activity. In today's world, these flamboyant and colorful American heroes could not be ignored.

His things were already packed for the next leg of his journey, after the reception at Wayne manor. His next destination: Metropolis.

The modern city had its own colorful mystery man. A figure whose exploits would even make La Hire's yarns look tame; stopping careening autos with his bare hands, outracing locomotives, leaping over buildings... Nonsense, of course; likely a bag of clever tricks, like those of this bat-themed vigilante—superior strength and training, great skill, a costume, and a few gadgets, but real superpowers?

He hoped to speak with the woman who wrote those fantastic stories for the *Planet*, but her editor had informed him that she was away on assignment. But, he was told, there was a new man, equally as good, available.

He spoke with the man on the phone. The fellow's dull name and manner didn't inspire much confidence, and he seemed none too bright or self assured.

Even worse, he sounded as if he had just come off the farm.

Jared Welch is a new contributor to Tales of the Shadowmen, *and a great admirer of Paul Féval's works. His idea was to bring together two very different characters, who nevertheless have in common the fact that they both have witnessed and/or caused much cruelty, ruin and devastation, and see what would come out of that interaction ...*

Jared Welch: *The Vampire of New Orleans*

New Orleans, 1941

It'd been three months since I had been transferred to New Orleans, and already I had a bizarre case on my hands. The bodies of five, previously reported missing young girls had turned up completely drained of blood, with their scalps removed. A week ago, the family of the first victim had hired me to look into it, because they'd become fed up with the complete failure of the police to find anything. A few days later, the relative of another victim had told me his theory that the girls had been the victims of some Satanic cult.

It was Monday morning, September 8, 1941. I was sitting at my desk, going over all my notes on the case again, when *she* walked in. Her height was a little taller than average for a dame; her eyes where hazel and her hair jet black. She was wearing a black felt fedora with a veil and feathers. She took off her coat and hung it on the rack. Her long black dress hugged her curves perfectly, leaving no doubt she had a figure like a statue. She walked across the office and then sat down in the chair in front of my desk and crossed her legs.

"I'm told you are the detective here looking in the *Scalp Murders*," she said.

That's what the newspapers had been calling these gruesome crimes.

"Yes, for a week now," I replied. "Do you have information on the case?"

"I saw the picture of the most recent victim in the paper this morning and I recognized her. I had seen her three night ago in my sister's apartment." She hesitated for a moment and then continued, "According to the article, this was after her family had last seen her alive."

I studied her face for a few minutes and detected no obvious signs of deception.

"How come you're bringing this information to me rather than the police?" I asked.

"My sister is a very rich and influential woman, a member of a number of secret societies. I'm certain the she has many important policemen in her pocket." She again seemed to hesitate for a moment and then added, "My name is Lillian, and my sister is the Countess Marcian Gregoryi."

I had heard of this Countess who had come to New Orleans last spring; she was the talk of the town in some circles, said to be incredibly beautiful, with the most radiant golden blond hair you've ever seen. If this was her sister, then it must run in the family, regardless of the different hair color. She was highly educated and intelligent for a dame, and mingled with many politicians and businessmen. However, I'd heard no indication before of her being suspected of anything criminal, although she was known to occasionally visit some classy mob-ran night clubs, but so did many other respected pillars of society.

"So, you suspect your sister is involved somehow?" I asked, not breaking eye contact for a second.

"The secret society my sister and her late husband belong to hold some rather unusual beliefs. I've managed to learn more than I was supposed to about them. Among these is a belief that human blood holds the secret of the Philosopher's stone." Twisted occult superstitions; I couldn't help being reminded of the Dain case. "Also," she went on, "to be honest, I suspected their so-called *Order* to be involved in this as soon as the bodies started turning up, but I didn't want to believe that my sister was personally implicated."

"Does your sister often have young women in her apartment?" I asked.

"Usually not when I'm there, so I can't say if she'd had any other known victims among them. But yes, she likes to, sort of, mentor young women of the lower social classes."

"Do you know what her whereabouts will be at all today?"

"I know she'll be visiting the Club de la Merci tonight. Before that, I'm afraid not"

"Well, I shall look into everything you've told me," I said.

"Good. It'll be a great ease to my conscience if I can prevent any more deaths."

She then stood up, took her coat, headed back towards the door and left.

"I'm a little suspicious of this lead, but it's the only one I got," I said to myself.

After talking one last time to the family of the latest victim, I headed to the *Club de la Merci,* a rather successful club known to be ran by a powerful Mafia Don named Franco Vitelli. It had become a very popular club lately, with their new attraction, a singer going by the name of Ziska.

The club seemed lively as I entered. There was a lot of gossiping in the background, as Ziska sang to piano music. Her ethnicity was very hard to place and was probably mixed. Being in New Orleans, I was inclined to suspect Caribbean ancestry, where interbreeding of African, Irish and American Indian slaves had been going on for centuries. But her name suggested something far more Eastern; it sounded like something out of *The Arabian Nights*, but that was probably just a stage name. She wore a purple dress, matching opera gloves, and a purple flower in her dark hair.

I asked around if Countess Marcian Gregoryi was present, and I was pointed the end of the bar. There, I saw a stunning blonde in a tight, shiny red dress, slit up the side, showing her long gorgeous gams.

As I walked closer to her, I saw that her resemblance to her sister was quite striking; if it hadn't been for the hair, I'd have assumes they were the same person. I'm pretty good at telling the difference between a wig and real hair, and fairly good as spotting dye jobs as well, and both dames' hair seemed natural to me. The spot next to her happened to be empty, so I took it and ordered myself a Scotch. She looked at me and said:

"I don't think I've ever seen someone as old as you here before."

"I don't usually come here," I replied.

After taking a large sip from my drink, I said:

"I'm surprised to see such a distinguished lady here, given the place's reputation."

"I see you're aware of who I am, detective."

I was a little taken aback by that comment. I didn't think I was that obvious. Maybe I was getting too old for this.

"I'm aware of who runs this place; it's his *competition* I'm interested in," she added.

"You mean Liam O'Breane?" I asked with genuine curiosity. O'Breane was a notorious Irish gangster, who'd moved his operation here from New York five years ago.

"Yes. He's supposed to be here tonight... hopefully soon."

"What interest do you have in him?"

"He may be a criminal, but he also has a political agenda. He very passionately wishes to free Ireland from British rule."

I was aware that O'Breane had been supposedly smuggling weapons to the Irish, but I was generally skeptical about any other motives other than financial ones.

"Why does an Eastern European Countess have an interest in Irish freedom fighters?" I asked.

"The Order of the Rosy-Cross has an interest in all who strive for liberty," she replied.

"You're a Rosicrucian?"

"Not strictly speaking. It's a fraternal order, after all, but my late husband was a very important Master."

I wondered is they were the *Order* Lillian had mentioned? But she had also implied the Countess was involved in more than one secret society.

"I don't think the British are the greatest enemy of freedom, presently," I said cynically.

"We also have people working on the German and Italian problems," she responded. "I serve Count Saint-Germain, and he sent me here."

It only hit me then that it was odd that she was revealing all this to me so willingly and casually.

"Why are you telling me all this?" I asked.

"You have a reputation too, detective, because of what took place in Poisonville."

"You would like to me help you somehow?" I asked.

"We might like to see Don Vitelli eliminated," she replied

"I don't do assassinations."

"Of course not, but you're good at bringing down gangsters"

"I don't take sides in gang wars, no matter what their politics are," I said.

"Why are you here then?" she suddenly asked.

I decide to get right to the point:

"I'm investigating the *Scalp Murders*, and I have reason to believe you were in contact with the most recent victim."

"I see. So my sister went to you," she said, with a slight smile. "Yes, she did see us together, but what she probably didn't tell you is that she also saw her leave perfectly alive."

"What reason would she have for deliberately leaving that out?"

"She hates me, out of jealously. She'd fallen in love with my husband before I'd met him, but as I am the older sister, the right to marry him fell to me."

"So you're older? I must say, I could never guess your age difference by just looking at you. Except for your hair, you could be twins." I made this comment just to gauge her reaction.

"Yes, we get that a lot," she responded without blinking, "But I'm older by a year and three months."

"Are there other witnesses who can verify your side of the story?" I said, returning to the topic of the murders.

"My bodyguard here. He escorted the young lady home, and can testify that she got home safely that night."

I spent about 20 minutes questioning the bodyguard. Then, I heard the Countess say: "He's here." I looked to the entrance and recognized Liam O'Breane.

"You've been amusing company, but now, I have some serious business to attend," she said.

She then walked over to the handsome Irishman. I observed the flirtatious manner of her interaction with him from a distance, but I was not able to hear their conversation. I let my eyes roam around the club some, and saw Ziska who had just finished her performance.

She caught my gaze and indicated subtly that she wanted me to head over to her. I did so.

"I see you're investigating the Countess?" she said immediately, with a sensual exotic voice.

"Yes, I am."

"I imagine she claimed to be a Rosicrucian?"

"Yes, she did," I answered. "Do you have reason to believe that's a lie?"

"She may have some connection to them, but her true loyalty is to the *Societas Draconistrarum*."

"And what is that?" I asked.

"A secret order of aristocratic Nosferatu."

"Vampires!" I said, with genuine shock.

"I noticed you didn't react to her mentioning Count Saint-Germain?"

"That's because I never heard of him."

"He is one of the oldest known living *Strigoi*. He only adopted that name when he was at the Royal Court of France before the Revolution."

"How do you know so much about vampires?" I asked.

"Because I'm a ghoul," she replied with a completely straight face. "You might say my people and vampires are the same species, but different tribes. My tribe is older, though I, personally, am young compared to Szandor..."

"Szandor?" I was surprising myself by what I chose to ask about.

"Szandor is a far older identity occasionally used by Saint-Germain. No one but him seems to know if it's his original name."

"I don't believe in undead bogeymen," I said.

"Perhaps, but you will be able to verify that there was a Countess Marcian Gregoryi in Paris in 1804 when a similar string of *Scalp murders* occurred."

"Checking old French Police records isn't as easy as you assume, but I suppose I can manage it..."

"What you'll also discover is that this Countess was blond, and that she posed as her own sister by changing the color of her hair."

I stood there taking all that in for a few minutes. Then I said, "Thank you for your help," and walked away.

Several days later, I had received the French documents I'd requested from a French P.I. I'd met who specialized in this type of business—Teddy Verano. The records confirmed everything Ziska had said about a string of *Scalp Murders* in 1804 Paris. Reading between the lines, I also noticed a reference to vampirism being suspected back then. None of this made me believe in the existence of vampires, but the possibility that someone was copying the M.O. of a conwoman murderer from a century ago was something I couldn't rule out.

The revelation about the Countess posing as her sister still confused me. I'm not arrogant enough to rule out that I'd overestimated my ability to spot a wig or a dye job, but what motive could she have had for putting me onto her in the first place? Also I hadn't failed for a second for recognize Elvira in Jeanne Delano, and that disguise involved far more than a change in hair color. Here, while I recognized their physical resemblance, their demeanor was quite different...

I interviewed Lillian again the following day. She denied seeing the girl leave alive, and laughed at the part about her having been in love with her sister's husband. On that matter, I had not located any evidence that a Count Marcian Gregoryi had ever existed, as a husband to either this Countess, or the one in 1804. I told Lillian about the woman from 1804, and she said she, too, was probably connected to the *Order*. She still didn't tell me anything about that "Order" of hers, so I chose not to mention vampires to her.

I was pondering all this while going over the files on the missing girls again when I noticed something. They were all either blond or dark haired, and all had their scalps removed. Is it possible it's not a normal wig or dye, but that this woman in cannibalizing the hair of her victims? A skilled actor could certainly make quite a disguise out of that.

That evening I went see an expert I'd heard about, a professor named Ruven Van Helsing, who lived in New Orleans and could tell me a little more about this vampire business. After explaining the entire case to him, he pondered for a few minutes and then said"

"I never heard of Count Szandor being identified with Count Saint-Germain before, or even that Saint-Germain was a vampire, though the stories around him suggest that he is indeed immortal. Count Szandor is notorious, he may be one of oldest vampires in the world, according to some legend. His origins are a mystery, but it was during the time of John Hunyadi and his son Matthias Corvinus that his documented trail begins. He was the true founder of the *Societas Draconistrarum*, the *Order of the Dragon*. When the House of Basarab was split, Szandor allied himself with the Danesti Boyars; some speculate that he might have been one of them. One day, a new bride of the Draculesti Voivode betrayed her husband and became his lover; she was known as Countess Addhema..."

I pondered over all this, and then asked:

"Do you believe in these legends?"

"I know there are still many mysteries not easily answered by science. It is possible that we're dealing here with a cult obsessed with the mystical power of blood, but it is interesting that Addhema's supposed M.O. of 1804 matches that of your *Scalp Murders*."

"What do you think of the possibility that this woman is also posing as her own sister?"

"Many vampires are reported to have shape-shifting abilities, able to turn into wolves, jackals, cats, reptiles, various types of birds, and even bats, especially since the discovery of vampire bats in the Americas."

"Thank you, Professor. You've been very insightful."

"You're very welcome. I hope you're able to put an end to these abominable killings"

"I do too," I said, and then left

Later that night, I decided to go to the Countess's residence and question her again. It had a very mid-Victorian design to it. I told her that I'd like to ask her a few more questions. She invited me in, offered me a drink and sat on a very comfortable chair.

"I've called a few people back in your home country, and I can't find any records about your late husband," I said, being quite frank about it.

"His family is very secretive, as is mine."

"How did your meeting with the Irishman go?"

"It wasn't our first; he seems to distrust me, and the people I represent. He says European secret societies claiming to be the Rosicrucians have screwed the Irish over before."

"Career criminals have a great need for caution."

"You're quite a judgmental person, aren't you?" she said, smiling.

"No more of others then I am of myself," I replied, philosophically.

"Have you heard of the great alchemist, Dr. Johann Georg Faust?"

"The name does sound familiar?"

"He lived in the first half of the 16th century. He studied day and night, seeking the secret of the Philosopher's Stone. One day, someone calling himself Mephistopheles offered him the secret, but warned him it would come with a Price."

"Was this 'Mephistopheles' Count Saint-Germain?"

"You catch on fast, don't you?"

"It was an easy guess."

"The secret would enable him to live forever, but the price was that he'd be cursed with an unquenchable thirst for Human Blood."

"You mean, he'd become a vampire."

"Indeed, he accepted the deal, and was very rapidly corrupted. He seduced the young virginal Countess Marguerite Karnstein and corrupted her as well."

"Does this story have a moral to it?"

"It's not a story, it's history," she affirmed.

"It sounds to me like a rewriting of *Faust*."

"It's the true history behind the legend that has been forgotten to all but the initiated."

"Sounds like a very ugly history your Order keeps," I said, shrugging.

"Once when I was traveling in Italy, I saw an interesting painting. It was of a great magnificent Golden Treasure. And in front of was a young man and a very old man, the old many had a bleeding gash on his neck, and the younger one was holding a blood-smeared stiletto. Clearly, the younger man had killed the older one in order to posses the Treasure, but what's interesting is that the blood of the murdered man seemed to be seeping into the treasure, as though it was feeding it."

"So the Gold itself was a Vampire?"

"Greed is the one, true vampire, is it not? The wealthy and rulers of the world leech off the labor of the proletariat. Sucking them dry to sustain their decadent lifestyles."

"You speak of the wealthy as if you were not one of them."

"I'm not—by birth. No one understands the lechery of the Oligarchs like those who have lived among them."

I took a sip from the scotch she's offered me, and my head began feeling a little woozy.

"Are you OK?" she asked, with a smile

I tried to stand up, but my legs wobbled.

"Did you drug me?" I asked.

"Yes, you could say that," she replied.

Suddenly, the door opened and a large man carrying a dark-haired young girl in a night gown with her hands tied behind her back and her mouth gagged entered. I jumped to my feet and grabbed my gun, but the large man quickly kicked it out of my hand.

I then recognized him as the bodyguard who'd supposedly escorted the last victim home.

The Countess grabbed the woman, holding her firmly in her arms, facing me. She removed her hair from her head and her skin suddenly appeared to rapidly age. As I tried to shake my head and to gather my senses, the Countess's canines suddenly grew into fangs and she bit the girl's neck. I tried to move to help the girl, but the bodyguard punched me in the face and I blacked out.

When I awakened, I was on the couch, in the same room. I could see the Sun rising through the windows, telling that several hours had passed. Everyone else was gone.

As I got up, Lillian entered.

"You're aware, finally, of what happened here last night?" she asked.

"I was drugged, so I could have hallucinated some of the details," I said, "but I'm pretty sure that your sister has claimed another victim."

"That's terrible."

The way she said it sounded fake to me for some reason.

"Do you know where she might be right now?" I inquired.

"No, she was already gone when I got here an hour ago."

I was reminded of my suspicion that the two sisters were one and the same, and I looked at her closely. I suddenly recalled that last night's victim had dark hair, just like hers...

"I would wait here until she returned, if I thought it likely she came back," I said.

"Do you trust anyone on the police force?" she asked.

"Possibly, but I don't have anything reliable to tell them."

I then I got an idea. I decided to pretend to leave, but stake out the residence from across the street.

At about 10 p.m. the following night, I saw the bodyguard return and enter the building; then, about a half an hour later, he and the Countess—not Lillian—came out and left.

I followed them for a while, keeping my distance, until they headed into a back alley. I turned into it carefully, but they seemed to have vanished. I looked around for any sign of them, but then, suddenly, I felt a sharp pain in my left leg.

Someone had thrown a dagger at my from behind. I turned around and saw the bodyguard holding a Tommy Gun. I lunged behind a dumpster for cover as the shots started spitting out. When he took a break, I jumped and fired my revolver. I was able to hit him in the stomach. He keeled over. I then instinctively turned and saw the Countess behind me.

I pointed my gun at her and yelled:

"Don't move!"

But, with surprising speed, she pulled out a revolver of her own and fired at me. I fired mine in response. I was hit in my right shoulder, but I thought I got her near the heart. She fell down and crawled behind another dumpster.

Suddenly, the bodyguard grabbed me from behind, trying to apply a choke hold, but I rammed my elbow hard into his ribs and broke at least a couple. I stepped back and turned around to fire at him again when he kicked my weapon out of my hand.

He now held another dagger, larger than the one he'd thrown at me before. He made a move as if to lunge at me when I heard a gunshot from somewhere behind me.

He fell down, having been shot in the heart. I turned and saw Liam O'Breane holder a smoking gun.

"I had a feeling she was crazy," he said.

I caught my breath for a few moments.

"You followed her, too?" I inquired.

"Yes. I suspected she was Draconian from the start. Ziska works for me."

"Well, thanks for saving my life. I would have handled this better when I was young, or even middle-aged."

"Age slows us all eventually," he said.

He then walked over to behind the dumpster where Countess Marcian Gregoryi had crawled and exclaimed: "She's gone!"

I headed over there and saw only a pool of blood on the ground. On the brick wall, a phrase was written in blood:

"*In vita mors, in morte vita.*"

Harry Dickson by J.-M. Nicollet

Credits

Quest of the Vourdalaki

Starring:	Created by:
Yvgeni	Matthew Baugh
Hella	Mikhail Bulgakov
Gorcha	based on Alexei Tolstoy
Ayub	Harold Lamb
Boris Liatoukine	Marie Nizet
Taras Bulba	Nicolai Gogol
Doroscha	Nicolai Gogol
Quentin Moretus Cassave	Jean Ray
The Magister (aka Woland)	Mikhail Bulgakov
Khlit	Harold Lamb
Menelitza	Harold Lamb
The Koshovoi Ataman	Harold Lamb
Ivan Sabalinka	Robert E. Howard
Zaroff	Richard Connell
Ivanushka	Richard Connell
Also Starring:	
Vseslav	
Chernobog	

Matthew BAUGH is an ordained minister who lives and works in the Chicago area. He is a longtime fan of pulp fiction, cliffhanger serials and old time radio. He has written a number of articles on characters like Zorro, Dr. Syn, Jules de Grandin and Sailor Steve Costigan. He has had stories published in *The Green Hornet Chronicles, More Tales of Zorro, Six Guns Straight From Hell, The Avenger Chronicles* and *The Phantom Chronicles*. He is a regular contributor to *Tales of the Shadowmen*.

The Green Eye

Starring:	Created by:
Phileas Fogg	Jules Verne
Rebecca Fogg	Gavin Scott
Rupert of Hentzau	Anthony Hope
Jean Passepartout	Jules Verne
Maboub Ali	Rudyard Kipling

A.J. Raffles	E.W. Hornung
Peachy Carnehan	Rudyard Kipling
Daniel Dravot	Rudyard Kipling
Amanda Darieux	Philip John Taylor
Mad Carew	J. Milton Hayes
Co-Starring:	
Joséphine Balsamo	Maurice Leblanc
Colonel William Creighton	Rudyard Kipling

Nicholas BOVING lives in Toronto. He was formerly a mining engineer and traveled the world widely. He also worked from time to time as a docker, fruit inspector and forester. His books and screenplays draw on these experiences to provide characters, backgrounds and scenes. He is the author and publisher of the *Maxim Gunn* series of action/adventure books. He has also written some fifteen other novels and screenplays which follow the central character to countries and places where the forces of nature as much as people provide the conflict. He is a regular contributor to *Tales of the Shadowmen*.

The Great Ape Caper

Starring:	**Created by:**
Arsène Lupin	Maurice Leblanc
King Kong	Merian C. Cooper & Edgar Wallace
Co-Starring:	
Carl Denham	Merian C. Cooper & Edgar Wallace
Doc Savage	Lester Dent
And:	
The Maltese Falcon	Dashiell Hammett

Nathan CABANISS lives and works in Atlanta, Georgia, where being crushed by his ever-growing stack of books and DVD's remains a constant threat. His passion for storytelling began at a very young age, where he routinely wrote and drew his own comic books and made his family suffer through recreations of various old TV skits. His musings on art and film can be found at his website, *Girls, Guns and Cigarettes*, where both Nicolas Roeg films and the finest of Italian exploitation sleaze are held in equally high esteem. Among other projects, he is currently at work on an interactive superhero novel entitled *Beyond Order and Chaos*, which will be self-published for free online and in blog-form. This is his first contribution to *Tales of the Shadowmen*.

So Much Loss

Starring:	Created by:
Dr. Jack Seward	Bram Stoker
Arthur Holmwood Lord Godalming	Bram Stoker
The Strattons	based on J. J. Abrams &
	Damon Lindelof
The Lyttons	Penny Vicenzi
Sâr Dubnotal	*Anonymous*
Co-Starring:	
Thomas Carnacki	William HopeHogdson
Count Dracula	Bram Stoker
Lucy Westenra	Bram Stoker
Quincey Morris	Bram Stoker
Jonathan Harker	Bram Stoker
Mina Harker	Bram Stoker
Abraham Van Helsing	Bram Stoker
Sherlock Holmes	Arthur Conan Doyle
Dr. John H. Watson	Arthur Conan Doyle
Also Starring:	
Bram Stoker	

Anthony R. CARDNO lives in northwest New Jersey when he's not traveling the country for his job as a corporate trainer. His short fiction has appeared in the anthologies *Space Battles*, *Beyond The Sun* and *Oomph: A Little Super Goes A Long Way*. He reviews books for Icarus, Chelsea Station and Strange Horizons, and regularly interviews authors, editors, musicians and other creative types on www.anthonycardno.com. This is his first contribution to *Tales of the Shadowmen*.

He Who Laughs Last

Starring:	Created by:
The Scarecrow (Dr. Syn)	Russell Thorndike
Colonel Bozzo-Corona	Paul Féval
Brotherhood of Mercy /	Paul Féval
Gentlemen of the Night	
Co-Starring:	
Mr. Mipps	Russell Thorndike
Jimmie Bones	Russell Thorndike
Charlotte Cobtree	Russell Thorndike

Matthew DENNION lives in South Jersey with his beautiful wife and daughters. He currently works as a teacher of students with autism at a Special Services School. Matt has been a huge fan of Edgar Rice Burroughs ever since he first picked up *A Princess of Mars*; he is also a big follower of Sherlock Holmes, Doc Savage, Spider-man, Batman and James Bond. In addition to being a regular contributor to *Tales of the Shadowmen*, he also writes stories involving giant monsters for *G-fan* magazine.

City of the Nosferatu

Starring:	Created by:
Boris Liatoukine	Marie Nizet
Count Dracula	Bram Stoker
Commander Sponsz	based on Hergé
Graf Von Orlok	Henrik Galeen & F.W. Murnau
Count Szandor	Paul Féval
Baron Iskariot	Paul Féval
Baroness Phryne	Paul Féval
Otto Goetzi	Paul Féval
Polly Bird	Paul Féval
Professor Van Helsing	Bram Stoker
Also Starring:	
Jure Grando	Historical/Mythical
Ann Radcliffe	Paul Féval
	based on the historical character
And:	
Selene/Sepulchre	Paul Féval

Brian GALLAGHER has a BA in Politics and Society and lives in London. He works in the media and for many years has written on the politics, economics and many other aspects of Croatia and has been quoted in Croatian and international media. In relation to that he has written extensively on Croatian-related cases at the International Criminal Tribunal for the Former Yugoslavia. He has always been interested in science fiction, classic horror, comics and is proud to be a lifelong *Doctor Who* fan. This is his first contribution to *Tales of the Shadowmen*.

Last of the Kaiju

Starring:	Created by:
Doctor Omega	Arnould Galopin
Barbarella	Jean-Claude Forest
Fred	Arnould Galopin

Tiziraou	Arnould Galopin
Godzilla	Ishiro Honda
King Kong	Paul Féval
President Dianthus	Jean-Claude Forest
Co Starring:	
Professor Ping	Jean-Claude Forest
Rodan	Takeshi Kimura, Ken Kuronuma & Takeo Murata
Angilas	Shigeaki Hidaka & Takeo Murata
Ebirah	Shinichi Sekizawa
Stella Starr	Luigi Cozzi
And:	
The Blinovitch Limitation Effect	Terrance Dicks & Barry Letts

John GALLAGHER is a freelance artist living in the North West of England . He divides his time between working on his own comic strip projects and painting fantasy subjects. Amongst other things, he has published, in collaboration with 'Archaic' Alan Hewetson, *The Complete Saga of the Victims*; a graphic novel compilation of the old Skywald *Horror-Mood* comic strip. He is a previous contributor to *Tales of the Shadowmen*.

Rouletabille vs. The Cat

Starring:	**Created by:**
Joseph Rouletabille	Gaston Leroux
Herbert Brown	Jules Verne
Cyrus Smith / Cyrus West	Jules Verne / John Willard
The Cat People	Algernon Blackwood
Roger Crosby	John Willard
Missy-Lou Pleasant	John Willard
Harry Blythe	John Willard
Annabelle West	John Willard
Charlie Wilder	John Willard
Cicily Young	John Willard
Susan Sillsby	John Willard
Hendricks	John Willard
Dr. Trifulgas	Jules Verne
Herbert West	H.P. Lovecraft
Co-Starring:	
Prince Dakkar	Jules Verne

427

Also Starring:
King John of Serbia/Jovan
Nenad
Basil Zaharoff
And:
Lyndhurst / Glen Cliff Manor   A.J. Davis

Martin GATELY is the author of the comics novella *Sherwood Jungle* in the *Phantom: Generations* series. He is a regular contributor to the UK's journal of strange phenomena *Fortean Times*, for which he also created the *Cryptid Kid Investigates* comic strip. His writing career began back in the 1980s when he wrote for D C Thomson's legendary *Starblazer* comic-book. He lives in a decaying mansion in Nottingham that has a view of a former insane asylum. He is a regular contributor to *Tales of the Shadowmen.*

The Brotherhood of Mercy

Starring:	**Created by:**
Marquis Henri-Jean de Sainte-Claire	based on Jean de La Hire
Henri de Ximes	based on Clark Ashton Smith
Chevalier de Villemonteix	Emmanuel Gorlier
Baron d'Ylourgne	based on Clark Ashton Smith
Charles d'Averoigne	based on Clark Ashton Smith
Roxane	Edmond Rostand
Also Starring:	
Comte d'Artagnan	
Savinien Cyrano de Bergerac	
Cardinal Mazarin	
J.-B. Colbert	
Nicolas Fouquet	

Emmanuel GORLIER lives in Puteaux, near Paris, with his wife and three children. He has been a fan of science fiction since the first grade and a devvoted player of *Dungeons & Dragons* for 30 years. That is probably why he became a tax accountant. He has contributed to *Enter the Nyctalope* and *Tales of the Shadowmen*, and is the author of *Nyctalope! L'Univers Extravagant de Jean de La Hire*, a Nyctalope companion book published in France.

The Frequency of Fear

Starring:	Created by:
Winnie Innsmouth	Micah Harris, Loston Wallace & Mark Schultz
Abby	Micah Harris
Teddy Verano	Maurice Limat
Jeb	Micah Harris
Michel Delassalle	Pierre Boileau & Thomas Narcejac
Diane Innes	based on Edgar Rice Burroughs
Doctor Karl Mantell	Jack Hill & Luis Enrique Vergara
Doctor Warren Chapin	Robb White & William Castle
Colonel Whiteshroud	Nick Cuti & Joe Staton
John-Walks-The-Wind	Micah Harris
Garland Briggs	David Lynch & Mark Frost
Professor Nolter	Edward Mann & Robert D. Weinbach
Professor Shiragami	Shinichiro Kobayashi & Kazuki Ohmori
Doctor Lorca	Reuben Canoy
Harrison Chase	Robert Banks Stewart
Ishakshar	Micah Harris
The Tinglers	Robb White & William Castle
Eric Cain	Micah Harris
Sally Hardesty	Tobe Hooper & Kim Henkel
Klan-Man	Micah Harris
Buzz	Micah Harris
The Lurk (Loulu)	Micah Harris
Co-Starring:	
Edwige Hossegor	Maurice Limat
Gilles Novak	Jimmy Guieu
Hareton Ironcastle	J.-H. Rosny Aîné
The Mineral-Vegetable King	Philip José Farmer
Dr. Duryea	William Pugsley & Samuel M. Sherman
Dracula	Bram Stoker
Mephista	Maurice Limat
And:	
Innsmouth	H.P. Lovecraft
The Black Lodge	David Lynch & Mark Frost
The Fear Chamber	Jack Hill & Luis Enrique Vergara
The Colour Out of	H.P. Lovecraft

Space	
The Daquapaw	Micah Harris
The Kingdom of the Plants	J.-H. Rosny Aîné
Scanners	David Cronenberg

Micah HARRIS is the author (with artist Michael Gaydos) of the graphic novel *Heaven's War*, a historical fantasy pitting authors Charles Williams, C.S. Lewis and J.R.R. Tolkien against occultist Aleister Crowley. His most recent publications are *Lorna, Relic Wrangler*, with illustrator Loston Wallace, the novella "On the Periphery of Legend" in Volume 2 of *Jim Anthony, Super Detective,* and "A Gathering of Peacocks" in the *Ghost Boy* anthology. He is a regular contributor to *Tales of the Shadowmen.*

The Next Omega

Starring:	Created by:
Doctor Omega	Arnould Galopin
Thea	based on Thea Von Harbou
Antoine Gerpré (Young Omega)	Alfred Driou
Madame Gerpré	Alfred Driou
Eugène Papillon	Emile Gaboriau
The Cult of Ubasti	Harry Earnshaw,
	R.R. Morgan & Vera Oldham
The Red Lectroids	Earl Mac Rauch
Baron Maupertuis / Ozer	Arthur Conan Doyle
	& Paul Féval
Professor Helvetius	Arnould Galopin
Co-Starring:	
The Lunian Immortals	Alfred Driou
Lecoq	Emile Gaboriau
Miss Marple	Agatha Christie
Dr. Watson	Arthur Conan Doyle
And:	
The *Cosmos*	Arnould Galopin
Metebelis-Three	Robert Sloman & Barry Letts

Travis HILTZ started making up stories at a young age. Years later, he began writing them down. In high school, he discovered that some writers actually got paid and decided to give it a try. He has since gathered a modest collection of rejection letters and had a one-act play produced. Travis lives in the wilds of New Hampshire with his very loving and tolerant wife, two above average children and a staggering amount of comic books and *Doctor Who* novels. He is a regular contributor to *Tales of the Shadowmen*.

Piercing the Veil of Isis

Starring:	Created by:
Chevalier Auguste Dupin	Edgar Allan Poe
Reginald Goodwin	based on Rex Stout
Juliette Saint-Fond	based on Marquis de Sade
Comte de Carignan	based on a Historical Character
Co-Starring:	
Dr Ponnonmer	William Dietrich
Capt Sabretash	William Dietrich
Giddon & Bickingham	William Dietrich
Allamistako	William Dietrich
Ethan Gage	William Dietrich
Colonel Bozzo-Corona	Paul Féval
Dr. Samuel	Paul Féval
Pha-Ho-Tep	Paul Naschy
Also Starring:	
Bérenger Saunière	
John Dee	
Edgar Allan Poe	
Benjamin Franklin	
Adam Weishaupt	
Christian Rosenkreuz	
Cagliostro	
Casanova	
Napoleon	
Edmé Francois Jomard	
Marie Thérèse Louise de Savoie-Carignan	

Paul HUGLI has a degree in Zoology, and has written for everything from *Cracked* magazine to general interest pamphlets, and for most of the first, second *and* third tier adult magazines. He is the author of three published "adult fantasy" novels, and the acclaimed *Traci Lords Companion*. He has also been employed as a science/math instructor, and as a "Floor Manager" at a local "Gentleman's Club." In addition, he once owned/managed Destiny Bookstore, which dealt in SciFi, comics and adult "fantasy" magazines, for 30 years. He now has three novels in the works. He is a regular contributor to *Tales of the Shadowmen*.

The Mark of a Woman

Starring:	Created by:
Joséphine Balsamo	Maurice Leblanc
Diego de la Vega (Zorro)	Johnston McCulley
Ramon Castillo	Bob Wehling
Marcos Estrada	Bob Wehling
Cesar de Cabanil (Captain Phantom)	Paul Féval
Bernardo	Johnston McCulley
Co-Starring:	
Alejandro de la Vega	Johnston McCulley

Rick LAI is an authority on pulp fiction and the Wold Newton Universe concepts of Philip José Farmer. His speculative articles have been collected in *Rick Lai's Secret Histories*: *Daring Adventurers, Rick Lai's Secret Histories*: *Criminal Masterminds, Chronology of Shadows: A Timeline of The Shadow's Exploits* and *The Revised Complete Chronology of Bronze*. Rick's fiction has been collected in *Shadows of the Opera, Shadows of the Opera: Retribution in Blood* and *Sisters of the Shadows: The Cagliostro Curse* (the last two titles are available from Black Coat Press). He has also translated Arthur Bernède's *Judex* and *The Return of Judex* into English for Black Coat Press. Rick resides in Bethpage, New York, with his wife and children. He is a regular contributor to *Tales of the Shadowmen*.

The Last Tale

Starring:	Created by:
Thomas Carnacki	William Hope Hodgson
Dodgson	William Hope Hodgson
Jessop	William Hope Hodgson
Taylor	William Hope Hodgson
Arkright	William Hope Hodgson
Leo Saint-Clair	Jean de La Hire
Co-Starring:	
The Horla	Guy de Maupassant
The *Brigade des Maléfices*	Claude Guillemot
	& Claude-Jean Philippe
Fausta	Michel Zevaco
The Lloigor	Colin Wilson
Dr. Seward	Bram Stoker

Olivier LEGRAND is a French literature teacher who lives in Caen, Normandy. He is a fan of RPGs, comics, and, in his spare time, the writer of the excellent Holmesian graphic novel series, *Les Quatre de Baker Street*. He has contributed stories to *Doctor Omega and the Shadowmen* and *Tales of the Shadowmen*.

Christmas at Schönbrunn

Starring:	Created by:
Père Tabaret	Emile Gaboriau
Lecoq	Emile Gaboriau
Lecoq de la Periere	Paul Féval
Colonel Bozzo-Corona	Paul Féval
Co-Starring:	
Manse Everard	Poul Anderson
Colonel Graigh	Henri Vernes
Also Starring:	
Franz, Duke of Reichstadt	
Emperor Francis of Austria	
Prince von Metternich	
Napoleon	

Jean-Marc & Randy LOFFICIER, the editors of *Tales of the Shadowmen*, have collaborated on five screenplays, a dozen books and numerous translations, including *Arsène Lupin*, *Doc Ardan*, *Doctor Omega*, *The Phantom of the Opera* and *Rouletabille*. Their latest novels include *Edgar Allan Poe on Mars*, *The Katrina Protocol* and *Return of the Nyctalope*. They have written a number of animation teleplays, including episodes of *Duck Tales* and *The Real Ghostbusters*, and in comics, such popular heroes as *Superman* and *Doctor Strange*. They created the Mayan detective series *Tongue*Lash*. Randy is a member of the Writers Guild of America, West and Mystery Writers of America.

Troubled Waters

Starring:	Created by:
Rocambole	P.-A. Ponson du Terrail
Captain Nemo	Jules Verne

Patrick LORIN is a longtime enthusiast of science fiction, superheroes and role playing. He has written two novels in France: *Les Seigneurs de la Terreur* and *L'île Blanche*, the latter published by Riviere Blanche in 2010. He regularly contributes stories to various anthologies. This is his first contribution to *Tales of the Shadowmen*.

The Lesser of Two Evils

Starring:	Created by:
It	David McDonald
Goetzi	Paul Féval
Eckhart	Eric Kripke & Ben Edlund
And:	
Selene	Paul Féval

David McDONALD is a professional geek from Melbourne, Australia, who works for an international welfare organisation. When not on a computer or reading a book, he divides his time between helping run a local cricket club and working on his upcoming novel. He is a member of the Melbourne-based writers group, SuperNOVA, and the Australian Horror Writers Association. He is a regular contributor to *Tales of the Shadowmen*.

Von Bork's Priorities

Starring:	Created by:
Von Bork	Arthur Conan Doyle
Cartwright	Arthur Conan Doyle
Chantecoq	Arthur Bernède
Inspector Teal	Leslie Charteris
Sherlock Holmes	Arthur Conan Doyle

Nigel MALCOLM lives in Kent, England. He works as a teacher of English as a Foreign Language. He is a long-term *Doctor Who*, *Star Trek* and *Prisoner* fan—long before all the new-fangled versions came along. He is currently working on a steampunk novel and an audio play. This is his second contribution to *Tales of the Shadowmen*.

The Wayne Memos

Starring:	Created by:
Bruce Wayne	Bob Kane
Alfred Pennyworth	Bob Kane & Jerry Robinson
Also Starring:	
Leon Trotsky	
Semyon Ivanovich Aralov	
Kim Philby	

Written by:

Xavier MAUMÉJEAN won the renowned Gerardmer Award in 2000 for his psychological thriller *The Memoirs of the Elephant Man*. His other works include *Gotham*, another thriller, *The League of Heroes*, which won the 2003 Imaginaire Award of the City of Brussels and was translated by Black Coat Press in 2005, and the recent *La Vénus Anatomique*, which won the 2005 Rosny Award. Xavier has a diploma in philosophy and the science of religions and works as a teacher in the North of France, where he resides, with his wife and his daughter, Zelda.

The Iron Crackdown

Starring:	Created by:
Jerry Cornelius	Michael Moorcock
Mo Collier	Michael Moorcock
Major Nye	Michael Moorcock
Miss Brunner	Michael Moorcock
Mrs. Bones	Michael Moorcock
Catherine Cornelius	Michael Moorcock
Professor Hira	Michael Moorcock
"Flash" Gordon Gavin	Michael Moorcock
Sexton Blake	Harry Blyth
Una Persson	Michael Moorcock
M. Pardon	Michael Moorcock
Jean-Claude Malpurgo	Michael Moorcock
Jacques Collin (Vautrin)	Honoré de Balzac
Mrs. Cornelius	Michael Moorcock
Co-Starring:	
Judex	Arthur Bernède & Louis Feuillade
Sherlock Holmes	Arthur Conan Doyle
The Ace of Spades	Hugo Pratt
Fantômas	Pierre Souvestre & Marcel Allain
Doc Didi Dee	Michael Moorcock
Tigris	Marcel Allain
Monsieur Zenith	Anthony Skene
A.J. Raffles	E.W. Hornung
Arsène Lupin	Maurice Leblanc
The Vampires	Louis Feuillade

Written by:

Michael MOORCOCK became editor of *Tarzan Adventures* in 1956, at the age of 16, and later moved on to edit *The Sexton Blake Library*. As editor of *New Worlds* from 1964 until 1971, he had a hand in the development of the New

Wave. Moorcock's best-known creation is the Eternal Champion saga in which various heroes, such as Elric, Hawkmoon, Corum, etc. are multiple identities of the same champion across many dimensions called the Multiverse. Moorcock's other literary accomplishments also include the Jerry Cornelius (himself an avatar of the Eternal Champion) series and the Colonel Pyat tetralogy which began in 1981 with *Byzantium Endures*.

The Privilege of Adonis

Starring:	Created by:
Bertrand Calliet (Werewolf of Paris)	Guy Endore
Rama Tamerlane (Felifax)	Paul Féval, *fils*
Djina Tamerlane	Paul Féval, *fils*
Baber	Paul Féval, *fils*
Roland Frollo	based on Victor Hugo
The New Hunchback	Sean Todd
	based on Victor Hugo
Co-Starring:	
Dr. Cornelius Kramm	Gustave Le Rouge
And:	
The Freon Side Show	Sean Todd

Christofer NIGRO is a writer of both fiction and non-fiction with a strong interest in pulps, comic books and fantastic cinema, and a regular contributor to *Tales of the Shadowmen*. He may be known to some by his extensive writings in cyberspace, including his websites *The Godzilla Saga* and *The Warrenverse*, as he is an authority on the subject of *dai kaiju eiga* (the sub-genre of cinema specializing in giant monsters), and the characters featured in the fondly remembered comic magazines published by Warren. He has recently revived and expanded Chuck Loridans' classic site MONSTAAH, and has since been published in the anthologies *Aliens Among Us* and *Carnage: After the Fall*. He is presently at work on a novel, and works as a website administrator and freelance editor.

Return to the Center of the Earth

Starring:	Created by:
Axel Lidenbrock	Jules Verne
Professor Otto Lidenbrock	Jules Verne
Captain Von Horst	based on Edgar Rice Burroughs
Hans Bjelke	Jules Verne
Ned Land	Jules Verne

Co-Starring:

The Gun Club	Jules Verne
Professor Aronnax	Jules Verne
Captain Nemo	Jules Verne

Also Starring:
Otto von Bismarck

John **PEEL** was born in Nottingham, England, and started writing stories at age 10. John moved to the U.S. in 1981 to marry his pen-pal. He, his wife ("Mrs. Peel") and their 13 dogs now live on Long Island, New York. John has written just over 100 books to date, mostly for young adults. He is the only author to have written novels based on both *Doctor Who* and *Star Trek*. His most popular work is *Diadem*, a fantasy series; he has written ten volumes to date. He is a regular contributor to *Tales of the Shadowmen*.

Revenge of the Reanimator

Starring:	**Created by:**
Robert Peaslee	H.P. Lovecraft
Martial Canterel	Raymond Roussel
Jay Gatsby	F. Scott Fitzgerald
Co-Starring:	
Hannah Peaslee	H.P. Lovecraft
Pr. Nathaniel Wingate Peaslee	H.P. Lovecraft
Captain Nemo	Jules Verne
Herbert West	H.P. Lovecraft
And:	
Arkham	H.P. Lovecraft
Miskatonic University	H.P. Lovecraft
Locus Solus	Raymond Roussel
Resurrectine	Raymond Roussel
The *Nautilus*	Jules Verne
The Vril	Edward Bulwer-Lytton

Pete **RAWLIK** holds a B.S. in Marine Biology and manages monitoring projects in the Florida Everglades. He has been a fan of the Lovecraftian fiction since his father sat him on his knee and read him Lovecraft's *The Rats in the Walls*. His fiction has appeared in *Talebones*, *IBID* and *Crypt of Cthulhu*. His literary criticism has appeared in *The New York Review of Science Fiction* and in *The Neil Gaiman Reader*. He is a regular contributor to *Tales of the Shadowmen*.

The Swine of Gerasene

Starring:	Created by:
Sâr Dubnotal	Anonymous
John Silence	Algernon Blackwood
Thomas Carnacki	William Hope Hodgson
Count Magnus	M.R. James
Magnus Greel	Robert Homes
The Hog	William Hope Hodgson
The Swine Things	William Hope Hodgson
Co-Starring:	
Sheila Crerar	Ella Scrymour
Aylmer Vance	Alice & Claude Askew
The Brotherhood of Gerasene	Josh Reynolds
The Tong of the Black Scorpion	Robert Holmes
Judge Pursuivant	Manly Wade Wellman
Dr. Omega	Arnould Galopin
And:	
The House on the Borderland	William Hope Hodgson
The Blood of Belshazzar	Robert E. Howard
Kor	H, Rider Haggard
The Faltine	Stan Lee & Steve Ditko

Joshua REYNOLDS is a freelance writer of modest ability and exceptional confidence. His sword & sorcery novel, *Knight of the Blazing Sun,* is due for publication by Black Library in 2012. Also to-be-released 2012 is *Out of Black Aeons*, the first book in *The Adventures of Charles St. Cyprian* from Pro Se Press. In other interesting facts, he was once bitten by a snake. It subsequently died. He is a regular contributor to *Tales of the Shadowmen*.

The Blood of Frankenstein

Starring:	Created by:
Gouroull	Jean-Claude Carrière
	based on Mary Shelley
Herbert West	H.P. Lovecraft
Seven Golden Vampires	Don Houghton
Kah/Dracula	Don Houghton
	based on Bram Stoker
Chien Fu	Ng See-yuen
Muscular Lo	Chang Cheh
Fang Keng	Chang Cheh
The Buddhist Monk	Lau Kar-Leung

Golden Swallow	King Hu
Co-Starring:	
Baron de Musard	based on Philip José Farmer
Karnstein	Sheridan Le Fanu
Also Starring:	
Sifu Lee aka Bruce Lee	

Frank SCHILDINER has been a pulp fan since a friend gave him a gift of Phillip Jose Farmer's *Tarzan Alive*. Since that time he has published articles on *Hellboy*, the Frankenstein films, *Dark Shadows* and the television show's links to the H.P. Lovecraft universe. He has had stories published in *Secret Agent X, Ravenwood, Stepson of Mystery, The Black Bat Mystery, The New Adventures of Thunder Jim, The New Adventures of Richard Knight* and *The Avenger: The Justice Files*. He is a Senior Probation Officer in New Jersey and a martial arts instructor at Amorosi's Mixed Martial Arts. Frank resides in New Jersey with his wife Gail who is his top supporter. He is a regular contributor to *Tales of the Shadowmen*.

True Believers

Starring:	**Created by:**
Sâr Dubnotal	Anonymous
Simon Ark	Edward D. Hoch
Joe the Angel	Craig Rice
John J. Malone	Craig Rice
Maggie Cassidy	Craig Rice
Kenneth J. Malone	Randall Garrett
	& Lawrence M. Janifer
Jeff Lebowski	Joel & Ethan Coen
Maurice Klaw	based on Sax Rohmer
Lily Thorne (aka Thrown)	based on Manly Wade Wellman
Josette Arcati	based on Noel Coward
Arisian	E.E. Smith
Captain Von Flanagan	Craig Rice
Lieutenant Samms	based on E.E. Smith
Special Unit 2	Evan Katz
Co-Starring:	
Robert Conway	James Hilton
Father Perrault	James Hilton
Annunciata Gianetti	Anonymous
Rudolph	Anonymous
Madame Arcati	Noel Coward
Prince Abduel Omar	J. U. Giesy & J. B. Smith

Dolly Dove	Craig Rice
Howard Beale	Paddy Chayefsky
Major Anthony Nelson	Sidney Sheldon
Colonel Maurice Minnifield	Joshua Brand & John Falsey
Jane Arden	Monte Barrett & Frank Ellis
Continental Op	Dashiell Hammett
Nate Heller	Max Allan Collins
Judex	Arthur Bernède
	& Louis Feuillade
"Spats" Colombo	Billy Wilder & I.A.L. Diamond
Little Bonaparte	Billy Wilder & I.A.L. Diamond
Little Caesar	W. R. Burnett
Scarface	Armitage Trail (Maurice Coons)
Robbo Foundation	David R. Schwartz
Dick Tracy	Chester Gould
Big Boy	Chester Gould
Lacey Raintree (Lakota Rainflower)	Donald F. Glut
Doctor Spektor	Donald F. Glut
Aloysius Trelawney	R. A. LaFevers
Rowley Thorne	Manly Wade Wellman
Hugo Chantrelle	Anthony Boucher
John Thunstone	Manly Wade Wellman
Ivo Shandor	Dan Ackroyd & Harold Ramis
Sidney Redlitch	John Van Druten
Comte d'Erlette	Robert Bloch
And:	
Shangri-la	James Hilton
Visualization of the Cosmic All	E.E. Smith
Diogenes Club	Sir Arthur Conan Doyle
Collinwood, Collinsport	Dan Curtis & Art Wallace
Hellmouth	Joss Whedon
The Ruthvenian	Donald F. Glut
Le Cultes des Goules	Robert Bloch
Honeysuckle Cottage / Bludleigh Court	P. G. Wodehouse
Call Northside 777	Jerome Cady
Dirac communicator	James Blish

Stuart SHIFFMAN is a native New Yorker long resident in Seattle, where he attempts to say dry and uncovered in moss. He regrets having to give up the Manhattan apartment on the 101st Floor of the Empire State Building and his autogyro. He is a long-time science fiction fan, winner of the Trans-Atlantic Fan Fund in 1981 and the 1990 Hugo Award for Best Fan Artist, Sherlockian and Wodehousian and has contributed cartoons, illustrations and articles to *The Baker Street Journal* and *Plum Lines and Wooster Sauce*. Stu has written on alternate history and is a member of the judging panel for the Sidewise Award for Alternate History. He lives with Andi Shechter, book reviewer and past chair of Left Coast Crime, in a hobbit hole with too many books. He is a regular contributor to *Tales of the Shadowmen*.

Marlbrough s'en va-t-en-guerre

Starring:	Created by:
Oscar Tournesol	Gustave Le Rouge
Andrée Paganot *née* de Maubreuil	Gustave Le Rouge
Dr. Marlbrough aka Dr. Cornelius Kramm	Gustave Le Rouge

Brian M. STABLEFORD has been a professional writer since 1965. He has published more than 50 novels and 200 short stories, as well as several non-fiction books, thousands of articles for periodicals and reference books and a number of anthologies. He is also a part-time Lecturer in Creative Writing at King Alfred's College Winchester. Brian's novels include *The Empire of Fear* (1988), *Young Blood* (1992), *The Wayward Muse* (2005), *The Stones of Camelot* (2006), and *The New Faust at the Tragicomique* (2007). His non-fiction includes *Scientific Romance in Britain* (1985), *Yesterday's Bestsellers* (1998) and *Glorious Perversity: The Decline and Fall of Literary Decadence* (1998). Brian's translations for Black Coat Press include numerous Paul Féval titles, Jean de La Hire's *The Nyctalope vs. Lucifer* and *The Nyctalope on Mars*; and many others. He is a regular contributor to *Tales of the Shadowmen*.

Nestor Burma in New York

Starring:	Created by:
Nestor Burma	Léo Malet
Gouvieux	Léo Malet
The Freaks	Tod Robins & Tod Browning
King Kong	Edgar Wallace & Merian C. Cooper
Herbert West	H.P. Lovecraft

Michel STEPHAN was born and lives in Brittany with his wife and two children. He has been a fan of science fiction, fantasy and horror since age 10. He loves Universal monster movies (especially the *Frankenstein* series), sci-fi serials and collects Aurora model kits. He has recently written a new *Madame Atomos* novel for Black Coat Press's French sister imprint, Rivière Blanche, and is a regular contributor to *Tales of the Shadowmen.*

Interview with a Nyctalope

Starring:	Created by:
Leo Saint-Clair (The Nyctalope)	Jean de La Hire
Bruce Wayne	Bob Kane
Alfred Pennyworth	Bob Kane
	& Jerry Robinson
Co-Starring:	
Doc Savage	Lester Dent
Arsène Lupin	Maurice Leblanc
Fantômas	P. Souvestre & M. Allain
Juve	P. Souvestre & M. Allain
Perry White	J. Siegel & J. Shuster
Lois Lane	J. Siegel & J. Shuster
Clark Kent	J. Siegel & J. Shuster
Also Starring:	
Jean de La Hire	

Written by:
David L. VINEYARD is a fifth generation Texan (named for his gunfighter/Texas Ranger great grand-father) currently living in Oklahoma City, OK, where the tornadoes come sweeping down the plains. He has useless degrees in history, politics, and economics, and is the author of several tales about Buenos Aires private eye Johnny Sleep, two (nearly published) novels, several short stories, some journalism, and various non-fiction. He is currently working on several ideas while battling with a three month old kitten for household dominance and the keyboard of his PC. He is a regular contributor to *Tales of the Shadowmen.*

The Vampire of New Orleans

Starring:	Created by:
The Continental Op	Dashiell Hammett
Countess Marcian Gregoryi / Countess Addhema / Lillian	Paul Féval
Ziska	Alexandre Dumas
Liam O'Breane	based on Paul Féval
Riven Van Helsing	Jean-Marc Lofficier
	based on Bram Stoker

Co-Starring:

Don Franco Vitelli — Mario Puzo
Count Szandor — Paul Féval
Count Saint-Germain — Chelsea Quinn Yarbro
Teddy Verano — Maurice Limat
Jeanne Delano — Dashiell Hammett
Countess Marguerite Karnstein — Jeff Patrick based on Sheridan Le Fanu

Also Starring:

John Hunyadi
Matthias Corvinus
Johann Georg Faust

Jared WELCH lives in Racine, WI. He is a long-time fan of Batman, J.R.R. Tolkien, C.S. Lewis, Nintendo, Buffy, Pretty Little Liars and the Star Wars Prequels, and has now become a very big fan of Paul Feval. He is currently working on a few plays, novels and essays about Bible Interpretation. This is his first contribution to *Tales of the Shadowmen*.

IN THE SAME COLLECTION

Volume 1: The Modern Babylon (2004)

Matthew Baugh, Bill Cunningham, Terrance Dicks, Win Scott Eckert, Viviane Etrivert, G.L. Gick, Rick Lai, Alain le Bussy, J.-M. & Randy Lofficier, Samuel T. Payne, John Peel, Chris Roberson, Robert Sheckley, Brian Stableford.

Volume 2: Gentlemen of the Night (2005)

Matthew Baugh, Bill Cunningham, Win Scott Eckert, G.L. Gick, Rick Lai, Serge Lehman, Jean-Marc Lofficier, Xavier Mauméjean, Sylvie Miller, Jess Nevins, Kim Newman, John Peel, Chris Roberson, Brian Stableford, Jean-Louis Trudel, Philippe Ward.

Volume 3: Danse Macabre (2006)

Joseph Altairac, Matthew Baugh, Alfredo Castelli, Bill Cunningham, François Darnaudet, Paul DiFilippo, Win Scott Eckert, G.L. Gick, Micah Harris, Travis Hiltz, Rick Lai, Jean-Marc Lofficier, Xavier Mauméjean, David A. McIntee, Brad Mengel, Michael Moorcock, John Peel, Jean-Luc Rivera, Chris Roberson, Robert L. Robinson, Jr., Brian Stableford.

Volume 4: Lords of Terror (2007)

Matthew Baugh, Bill Cunningham, Win Scott Eckert, Micah Harris, Travis Hiltz, Rick Lai, Roman Leary, Jean-Marc Lofficier, Randy Lofficier, Xavier Mauméjean, Jess Nevins, Kim Newman, John Peel, Steven A. Roman, John Shirley, Brian Stableford.

Volume 5: The Vampires of Paris (2008)

Matthew Baugh, Michelle Bigot, Christopher Paul Carey, Win Scott Eckert, G.L. Gick, Micah Harris, Tom Kane, Lovern Kindzierski, Rick Lai, Roman Leary, Alain le Bussy, Jean-Marc Lofficier, Randy Lofficier, Xavier Mauméjean, Jess Nevins, John Peel, Frank Schildiner, Stuart Shiffman, Brian Stableford, David L. Vineyard.

Volume 6: Grand Guignol (2009)

Matthew Baugh, Christopher Paul Carey, Win Scott Eckert, Emmanuel Gorlier, Micah Harris, Travis Hiltz, Rick Lai, Roman Leary, Jean-Marc Lofficier, Randy Lofficier, Xavier Mauméjean, William P. Maynard, John Peel, Neil Penswick, Dennis E. Power, Frank Schildiner, Bradley H. Sinor, Brian Stableford, Michel Stéphan, David L. Vineyard.

Volume 7: Femmes Fatales (2010)

Roberto Lionel Barreiro, Matthew Baugh, Thom Brannan, Matthew Dennion, Win Scott Eckert, Emmanuel Gorlier, Micah Harris, Travis Hiltz, Paul Hugli,

Rick Lai, Jean-Marc Lofficier, David McDonnell, Brad Mengel, Sharan Newman, Neil Penswick, Pete Rawlik, Frank Schildiner, Stuart Shiffman, Bradley H. Sinor, Brian Stableford, Michel Stéphan, David L. Vineyard.

Doctor Omega and the Shadowmen (2011)
Matthew Baugh, Thom Brannan, G.L. Gick, Travis Hiltz, Olivier Legrand, Serge Lehman, Jean-Marc & Randy Lofficier, Samuel T. Payne, John Peel, Neil Penswick, Dennis E. Power, Chris Roberson, Stuart Shiffman.

The Nyctalope Steps In (2011)
Matthew Dennion, Emmanuel Gorlier, Julien Heylbroeck, Paul Hugli, Jean de La Hire, Roman Leary, Randy Lofficier, Stuart Shiffman, David L. Vineyard.

Volume 8: Agents Provocateurs (2011)
Matthew Baugh, Nicholas Boving, Matthew Dennion, Win Scott Eckert, Martin Gately, Micah Harris, Travis Hiltz, Paul Hugli, Rick Lai, Joseph Lamere, Olivier Legrand, Jean-Marc & Randy Lofficier, DavidMcDonald, Chris Nigro, John Peel, Dennis E. Power, Pete Rawlik, Joshua Reynolds, Frank Schildiner, Michel Stéphan, Michel Vannereux.

The Many Faces of Arsène Lupin (2012)
Matthew Baugh, Anthony Boucher, Francis de Croisset, Matthew Dennion, Viviane Etrivert, Matthew Ilseman, Maurice Leblanc, Alain le Bussy, Jean-Marc & Randy Lofficier, Xavier Mauméjean, André Mouëzy-Eon, Thomas Narcejac, Jess Nevins, Bradley H. Sinor, Jean-Louis Trudel, David L. Vineyard

Night of the Nyctalope (2012)
Matthew Dennion, Martin Gately, Emmanuel Gorlier, Julien Heylbroeck, Travis Hiltz, Jean de La Hire, Roman Leary, Jean-Marc Lofficier, David McDonald, Chris Nigro, Philippe Ward.

Volume 9: La Vie en Noir (2012)
Matthew Baugh, Nicholas Boving, Robert Darvel, Matthew Dennion, Win Scott Eckert, Martin Gately, Travis Hiltz, Paul Hugli, Rick Lai, Jean-Marc Lofficier, Nigel Malcolm, DavidMcDonald, Christofer Nigro, John Peel, Neil Penswick, Pete Rawlik, Josh Reynolds, Frank Schildiner, Bradley H. Sinor, Michel Stéphan.

The Shadow of Judex (2013)
Matthew Baugh, Nicholas Boving, Thom Brannan,Matthew Dennion, Emmanuel Gorlier, Travis HiltzRomain d'Huissier, Vincent Jounieaux, Rick Lai, Jean-Marc & Randy Lofficier, David McDonald, Christofer Nigro, Dennis E. Power, Chris Roberson, Robert L. Robinson, Jr.

WATCH OUT FOR

TALES OF THE
SHADOWMEN

VOLUME 11: FORCE MAJEURE
TO BE RELEASED DECEMBER 2014